NIGHT RAID ON CAT ISLAND

"*Q-qui va là?*" The voice seemed surprised and shaken—no wonder, when there were two columns of armed men dashing for the ramparts where previously there had only been sand, marsh grass, and alligators. The sentry did not wait for an answer but began to scream a high-pitched alarm. Favian, across the open ground at last, slid into the ditch in a cloud of sand.

"Give me a back!" he gasped, and one of his boat's crew obligingly bent down at the base of the rampart. Favian planted a boot on the man's backside and sprang, clawing for a handhold, bringing a shower of sand down on the men below. He found a hold and rolled over the top onto the firing step.

Above him was a glowing red eye; for a moment Favian thought the sentry was still clenching his cigar in his teeth, but then he recognized it for what it was—*a slow match about to be applied to a six-pounder cannon!*

PRIVATEERS AND GENTLEMEN

CAT ISLAND

Jon Williams

A DELL BOOK

Published by
Dell Publishing Co., Inc.
1 Dag Hammarskjold Plaza
New York, New York 10017

ISBN: 0-440-11109-9

Printed in the United States of America
First printing—April 1984

Thanks to
C. J. Cherryh for her Napoleon stick,
Melinda Snodgrass for her dance,
Julie Beiser for her song

ONE

The crew of the frigate *Macedonian* didn't know Captain Favian Markham well; he had been aboard less than a month. Appearances didn't tell them much: he was a tall man, four inches or so over six feet, and rail-thin. He spoke a fussy, precise sort of English that didn't match his New Hampshire background. He dressed well and fashionably in civilian rig, except when he wore an old pea jacket and battered trousers to supervise a gang of men working aloft; he was always careful to wear doeskin gloves—to hide an injury, some of the men said. They knew he had a furious, lightning temper, for they'd heard him roar in anger against both officers and men when he'd thought they were being careless or stupid; and they knew he wouldn't stand for any nonsense. There'd been two floggings aboard, both cases of bad, roughneck types among the seamen testing their new captain to find out how far they could press him: he'd conducted a miniature court, accepted evidence for and against, gave the orders for the floggings, and furthermore explained his reasons why in a little speech—unusual procedure, for most shipboard discipline, even from the quarterdeck, was of the rough-and-ready sort.

They knew he had a regard for science and scientific practices. He had painted a "naval square" just aft of the mainmast, to aid the watch officer in tacking. He was a demon for good gunnery and had demonstrated on one occasion since he'd come aboard that he practiced what he preached in that regard, for during a running fight with a British frigate he'd gone below to lay the guns of the middle gundeck section himself and blew the mainmast of the *Tenedos* into the water. He had added much to the practice of gunnery aboard *Macedonian* since he'd come aboard: rotating the gun crews with the sun, so each knew the other's job; adding Broke's aiming slats behind the guns; introducing fire by section as well as by full broadside and firing at will; making the sections compete against one another at drill . . . at first the men grumbled, but not after they'd seen *Tenedos*'s mainmast go by the board.

There were other examples of Captain Markham's science: they'd seen Markham's Recording Log, a mechanical gadget trailed astern every half hour to gauge the ship's speed; they'd laughed as they overheard through the skylight his famous French dinners, in which he'd invite one or more of *Macedonian*'s hapless midshipmen for a dinner in which all the conversation was supposed to be conducted in French. They'd seen him aloft—it was rare enough for any captain to leave the privilege of the quarterdeck and spend time in the rigging, where the aristocracy of the foretop was determined by agility and skill, not by rank; the crew admitted he knew his business there.

This left an impression of a lean, fussy, scholarly man—but they knew his record, too, and the record spoke in another direction. They knew he came from a family of New Hampshire privateers, that his father and uncles had waged war against the British during the Revolution. One of his uncles, in fact, was the great Malachi Markham, who had captured the battleship *Bristol* back in '78, a stunning feat still celebrated in broadside ballads.

They knew he was widely regarded as a protégé of Stephen Decatur ever since he'd served, as a midshipman, on Decatur's reckless raid into Tripoli harbor to burn the *Philadelphia*. That spoke well for him—the seamen almost worshipped Decatur—but Decatur had a reputation for heedless risk-taking and devil-may-care adventure, and a good many of the *Macedonian*'s crew were uncertain as to whether they wanted to be included in any rash undertakings—particularly by someone who wasn't Decatur and might not be good at it. They knew Favian Markham's record had been full of mad scrapes: he'd commanded a gunboat off Tripoli and captured a couple of corsairs at the point of a cutlass; he'd been Decatur's first lieutenant aboard *United States* when they'd captured *Macedonian* from the British in the first year of the war; afterwards, rewarded in 1813 with the command of a slow, crotchety old tub of a brig, *Experiment*, he'd taken his command on an insane circumnavigation of the British Isles, burning forty-odd merchant ships, at the end of the journey sinking the brig *Teaser* in a yardarm-to-yardarm engagement: the whole exploit was known as Markham's Raid. Later that same year he'd driven ashore a Canadian privateer, *Loyalist*, in the teeth of a raging gale, and then clubhauled *Experiment* off a lee shore—it would have succeeded, too, said a couple of the brig's survivors, had the wind not headed them and smashed *Experiment* into a mudbank. There'd been a fuss over that, a court-martial on John Rodgers's flagship in New York harbor, but Favian Markham had come through with flying colors and the commendations of the court.

Was Captain Markham reckless, or was he cunning enough, as some of the hands maintained, to imitate recklessness when the occasion called for it? No one knew enough to say.

It hadn't been intended that he should command *Macedonian*. She'd been given to Jacob Jones, a genial, chinless lion of a man; but he'd been blockaded by the British in New London for almost the whole of 1814, and then been transferred to Lake Ontario just as it looked as if he might finally make his escape to the open sea. Favian Markham had been in New London at the time, watching his new command, the sloop of war *Shark*, abuilding and in his spare time, it seemed, had located a gang of British spies, shot their ringleader, and arrested the others. Stephen Decatur had been involved in that escapade, but even Decatur conceded it had all been Captain Markham's idea.

Whose idea it had been to steal *Macedonian* was not known, but it was acknowledged that Favian Markham had certainly stolen it. The frigate had been fully provisioned and ready for the sea when the orders came for Captain Jones to go to the Lakes, and Jones had not been happy about it but in the end had obeyed. *Macedonian*'s officers, thwarted for their chance at the British, had been in a towering rage—but suddenly Favian Markham had come aboard, assumed command, and taken *Macedonian* to sea through the teeth of a tearing October gale, neatly avoiding the enemy blockade. The old salts noticed, as he read himself in, performing the little ceremony that acknowledged he was taking command of the frigate legally, that his orders came from Decatur, not from the Secretary of the Navy. Another mad adventure, they concluded: Favian Markham was stealing *Macedonian* without the knowledge of the Navy Department. Just a few days later the frigate had the bad luck to run into a British squadron, and then had followed the mad running fight with *Tenedos* and two other enemy frigates, from which they'd escaped by virtue of good luck and Captain Markham's good gunnery.

There were those who claimed the voyage was doomed from

the start, of course. Lazarus the fiddler for one, a strange, half-cracked old man who had followed Captain Markham for two years or so and who claimed to have sold his soul to Old Nick in 1682. Not everyone was willing to concede Lazarus's age or sanity, but most acknowledged his authority in things supernatural. There was a chaplain aboard that Captain Jones had brought with him from Princeton, and sky pilots were universally acknowledged to be bad luck on a ship, right? And there was a Finnish seaman aboard, right? And Finns were witches to a man, deny it though the man would, true? And a witch aboard would bring bad luck, right? And no warship, alone in a sea full of enemies, could possibly survive with so much bad luck aboard, correct? So why should anyone object when the Finnish witch had his hammock cut one dark night and his ribs stove in by a few choice kicks? But object Captain Markham had, and even promoted the damned Finnish witch—whose unpronounceable name was Kuusikoski but who was called Koozey Koskey by all aboard—to coxswain to keep an eye on him. This perverse defiance of the gods of the sea had earned Favian Markham enmity in the eyes of many of the crew, but the enmity had gradually declined.

For no disaster had occurred: in fact the voyage had been a lucky one. There had been several raids in the British West Indies resulting in the destruction of much enemy commerce, and one dark night southwest of Antigua the *Macedonian* had crept up on the enemy corvette *Carnation* and taken it by surprise attack with scarcely a single American casualty.

It was then that the character of the voyage had changed. Rumor had it that *Macedonian*'s eventual destination was the Indian Ocean to lay waste to the British East India fleet and gain a fortune in gold and prize money. All that changed with *Carnation*'s capture: suddenly the captain was cracking on sail to the westward, for the Gulf of Mexico and the Mississippi, and suddenly the crewmen were looking aloft at the madly overcanvassed yards with apprehension.

The captain worked his crew like a man possessed. The frigate's upper masts had been so recklessly overcanvassed, not just with topgallants and royals, studding sails, staysails and all the jibs, the inner and outer and flying and the one that no one could think of a name for so it was called the jib jib, not simply the standard suit of sails but all the little sails above the royals, sails not much bigger than a handkerchief and so rarely used they were simply called skyscrapers or moonrakers or hope-in-heavens or trust-in-gods, the last two names in particular striking the seamen, apprehensive with all this canvas aloft, as appropriate.

Captain Markham had worked as hard as any man on the crew. He had been on deck every moment except when plain exhaustion drove him below. He'd drunk coffee by the gallon and driven the crew half-mad with his demands, forever sending them to the sheets or braces to make a trifling adjustment, manning the weather main and lee crossjack braces, fussing with the studding sail guys and the squilgees, watching intently as the upper masts groaned with every gust, a sound to make every seaman aboard shudder as they envisioned the sticks tearing right out of her in a ruin of splinters and canvas. Markham listened as the chesstrees moaned and the hull worked, letting in seawater through the straining seams that had to be pumped out daily—and then when the hairs on the back of the sailors' necks were erect, anticipating the topgallants all going by the board, the captain would call up the watch and calmly order them to lay aloft, put on the lift-jiggers, and stand by the booms to rig the starboard topgallant studding sails. The watch would go aloft half convinced that they were doomed, that their very silhouettes on the yards might catch enough wind to bring the whole complex system of sticks and rigging down.

Presumably some of the *Carnation*'s crew had given the captain some news that had caused him to make this mad dash, and there were new rumors every day concerning the character of that news. None of this helped the seamen in their estimation of their captain. He seemed an exacting, fidgety, overnice man, hardly a daredevil; but on the other hand he had a service reputation for recklessness and mad bravery, and this crowding on of canvas seemed deranged. Unlike Stephen Decatur, whose character was apparent at a glance, whose charm and chivalrous nature were obvious to all, Favian Markham was a private man and a solitary one, keeping his counsel and watching the crew, and the canvas, with an eagle eye.

Perhaps a clue was given by another piece of Favian's history: he had fought three duels. This was not unusual; Navy officers were always fighting duels for one reason or another. What was unusual was the excuse for two of the fights: though one appeared to have been fought over a woman—the record seemed unclear on this—two had been fought to uphold the honor of the United States Navy.

Captain Markham was a Navy man through and through, that much was clear. Perhaps he had no life other than the Navy, for if he had a private existence no one had been able to discover it. There was a rumor that he'd kept a woman in Poquetanuck during his time in New London, and that he'd earlier been engaged to a society belle in New Hampshire, but it was clear where his chief loyalties lay. He had fought for the Navy and the Navy's honor; he was surrounded by Navy men and Navy ritual; perhaps there was nothing in him but the Navy, first, last, and always. As far as the men on *Macedonian* knew, the Navy was their captain's entire life.

Uninterested in the hands' speculations, Favian Markham watched the groaning masts and yards and hoped his calculations were correct. In the end he was proven right: no damage was done, and no crewman hurt; two studding sails were carried away, but there were replacements; two studding-sail booms were cracked, but another pair were shifted over from the lee side. The driving paid off: during every day of its nine-day journey Markham's Recording Log proclaimed over two hundred nautical miles left astern. *Macedonian*, though a slug heading to weather, showed itself a demon driving downwind.

Finally, when the frigate lay for four hours off the Southeast Pass of the Mississippi waiting for the tide, Favian was gratified to see the crew standing by the rail fidgeting, as impatient as he to get the Father of Waters under the keel. Even the tide didn't add enough to the fourteen foot over the bar: *Macedonian* was kedged over the bar only after pumping out most of her water and shifting some supplies into the boats, and then had to work its way up the long river—a frustrating and difficult job, for by then it was night and there was no pilot available. In the morning the frigate anchored under the guns of Fort St. Philip on the Plaquemines Bend seventy-five miles below New Orleans, and Favian, his boat's crew, Lieutenant Eastlake and Midshipmen Lovette and Stanhope, impatient with the slow journey in the frigate, took swifter passage on the pilot boat *Beaux Jours*, hailed just after dawn as it was heading downriver to the Head of the Passes.

Favian, happy to let another captain do the work, spent the journey in his bunk asleep, using as a pillow his satchel of British documents taken from the *Carnation*. The sleep was dreamless, obliterating, and totally free of interruption. He was oblivious to the stamping of the crew, the movements of the other passengers, the sound of the mainsheet block being shifted over his head, the final splash of the anchor and the roaring of the cable—oblivious of everything until the hand of Lieutenant Eastlake came mercilessly on his shoulder and shook him awake.

"Captain Markham," came the calm, Virginian voice. "We've arrived. We're becalmed just under the city—Captain Poquelin says we'll have a wind shortly. There's coffee and a cold breakfast in the saloon."

"Thank you, Mr. Eastlake."

Favian drew on trousers and a coat and stepped up on deck. The crew were crowded forward, eating breakfast from a common pot with Kuusikoski and the crew of Favian's boat. It was not yet dawn; the sky was a deep blue, spotted with fading stars; the banks on either side were pitch black, devoid of detail. The river, a moving darkness grander than anything Favian had ever seen, tugged insistently at the pilot boat. Without a wind the air seemed thick, and it carried scents that were alien to Favian, the aromas of a strange land that he did not know but was bound to defend. Far off, on the left bank, a rooster crowed and was answered by another rooster on the right bank. There was no sign of the roosters' owners or their habitations.

The naval commander in New Orleans was Master-Commandant Daniel Todd Patterson, who had fought in Tripoli and been captured with the *Philadelphia*. Favian did not know him, but he knew that a great deal would depend on him and on his readiness—Patterson's readiness, not only in the military sense but his readiness to cooperate as well. Favian outranked Patterson by a full grade, and that was easy enough, but then Patterson, as the commander of the entire New Orleans squadron—a couple of schooners, Favian remembered, and perhaps a dozen little dandy-rigged gunboats—was entitled to call himself *commodore* and to wear the silver stars of that honorary rank upon his shoulder straps next to his epaulets—or epaulet, rather, since a master-commandant had only the one.

Patterson had been his own master for years, Favian knew. He had been freed from the interference of Washington by his distance from the capital and his federal authority had freed him from interference by the recently formed State of Louisiana. The

New Orleans station had in essence been Patterson's private fief. And now there arrived in New Orleans Captain Favian Markham, a more senior officer who could alter any of Patterson's arrangements, redispose his forces, and strip the silver star from Patterson's shoulder. And Favian was an officer who, because of the documents he'd taken from the *Carnation*, *would* do all those things if he thought them necessary.

Master-Commandant Patterson could prove as dangerous to the American cause as the British, Favian knew—or, if he saw the danger, knew his job, and showed himself ready to cooperate, he could prove as valuable as a ship of the line. Whichever he was, a risk or a blessing, Favian would have to know soon; and so he had determined that, before he did anything else in New Orleans, he would call upon Commodore Daniel Patterson.

The sky had lightened to a pearly gray in the east; the stars were fading, and details of the low landscape were becoming visible. The Mississippi River had created all the land here, carrying the soil from the interior; Favian could see the levees raised to keep off the flood, a long plain to the north, cut by canals, with a blackness of an unknown swamp behind. An alien land, he knew. He would need allies here, and he hoped Patterson would prove to be one.

"The plains of Chalmette," said a voice. Favian turned to find Captain Poquelin, a thin, short, unshaven man with a big voice, his hands in his pockets. "The city is just ahead, 'round that big bend." Poquelin removed a hand from a pocket and made a sweeping gesture, indicating the curve of the river. "The wind will come up soon—I can see the cat's-paws on the water. We should arrive at the city in an hour."

"Thank you, sir," Favian said.

"Have you been to New Orleans before?" Poquelin asked, with difficulty wrapping his tongue around a name that he was probably more used to pronouncing as *Nouvelle Orléans*.

"No," Favian said politely, in French. "I have not had that pleasure."

Poquelin grinned, replying in the same language. "It is very unusual for a Kaintuck to speak French—even the governor does not, and the people used to call him *ce bête* to his face. Not any more—M. Claiborne was elected by a handsome majority after Louisiana became a state."

"All my officers speak French," Favian said, trusting that

Captain Poquelin would never encounter Tolbert and a few of the other midshipmen. "But what was that name you gave me? Canuck—that is a Canadian, is it not?"

"Kaintuck." Poquelin shrugged. "It is the local name for American flatboat men because the first we saw all came down the river from Kentucky. It's often used as an insult, of course. *Allô*—the wind comes, Captain. I must get you to the city."

The hands were called to the windlass, topping lifts, and halliards; Favian, aware that the *Beaux Jours* was not his own ship, and that here he was only in the way of the trampling crew, went below to the saloon and had his breakfast of coffee, cold beef, and pickles.

After the pilot boat was under way and the addition of passengers to the deck would not crowd the crew, Favian went on deck again to watch as the boat, tacking laboriously against the current, passed the plantations of Chalmette, Macarty, Languille, Sigur, Pierhas, Dupré, and Montreuil, each pointed out by the captain who stood by the rail and spat tobacco into the great river. New Orleans appeared ahead as the schooner zigzagged across the water. The day had lightened, though flambeaux were still burning on the New Orleans wharves, indicating that work had been going on through the night. Through his pocket telescope Favian could see gangs of black workmen rolling barrels up the gangplank of a steamboat, the *New Orleans*, one of Robert Fulton's boats that had been built in Pittsburgh and had sailed down the Ohio and Mississippi a few years before.

The waterfront consisted chiefly of great brick warehouses, showing the region's Gallic influence in their shingled mansard roofs. The few private homes Favian could see over the long levee reminded Favian of the homes he had seen in Toulon and Marseilles. They were stacked close to one another between wide streets, had a wide balcony out front shading a pillared veranda, and many were painted in pleasant pastel shades. These graceful riverfront homes were flat-roofed like the houses of Tripoli, allowing visitors to walk from one roof to the next: the effect was graceful though alien, confirming Favian's intuition that this was not a typical American frontier town but a hybrid city, half-American, half-European, with well-established traditions of its own that he would have to tread warily around. He shifted his spyglass to the vessels flying the American commission pendant.

These were two schooners, the *Louisiana* and *Carolina*, both anchored in the river some distance from the wharves. They both appeared in good order, their rigging well maintained, the white trim glistening on their billetheads and taffrails. Favian could see a commodore's forked pendant flying from the main truck of the smaller, marking the flagship. He did not know if Patterson slept aboard his flagship or had apartments in town, but he'd pay his respects to the flagship first.

There were three dandy-rigged gunboats anchored near the schooners, and they did not present as fine an appearance. Though one seemed in trim condition, the others were not: their sloop-topmasts and running rigging had been sent down; they were not flying commission pendants; the air of disuse and neglect was obvious. Favian had himself spent five hated years as a gunboat commander; he thoroughly detested the offspring of Thomas Jefferson's attempt to purchase national defense on the cheap with these absurd, unseaworthy craft, and it was not unusual, he knew, for half a dozen of the incompetently designed boats to be laid up in any port of the Union, abandoned by the Navy as unsafe or useless. But he also knew that if New Orleans was to be defended from what he knew was coming, such gunboats as were present would form an important part of the city's naval defense. Their neglect here seemed alarming.

More of the city came into view as the *Beaux Jours* rounded the bend; Favian focused his glass on the waterfront and saw, much to his surprise, a black vessel he recognized. He had last seen her in Portsmouth over a year and a half ago, just before he'd taken *Experiment* out on its raid to England; she'd been unfinished then, lying on the ways at Stanhope's shipyard, but there was no possibility of a mistake—her lines were unforgettable. They had been drawn by Joshua Stanhope, the grandfather of the midshipman Phillip Stanhope now finishing his breakfast in the saloon of the *Beaux Jours*. Old Joshua had designed ships for the Markham family since before the Revolution, and this was clearly a work of something like genius.

She was a tern schooner of radical design, designed for one thing only: to be the fastest Yankee privateer on the high seas, overtaking any prey, even the swift Post Office packets, and able to outrun any pursuit. The rake of her masts was prodigious, particularly the mizzenmast that leaned aft like a drunken sailor in a three-reef gale, actually overhanging the projecting stern; the yards were as long as those on a frigate and could raise aloft a cloud of canvas so awesome that her fine-lined hull could drive through the waves as fast as a dolphin. She would be dangerous, Favian knew, and require constant watching. In a wind the oversparred schooner could be rolled right over on her beam-ends, but to any American seaman that possibility represented a challenge rather than a threat. Favian remembered the jealousy he had felt seeing the radical schooner on the Portsmouth yards and knowing that it would be at sea gathering to its owner a fortune in prize money while Favian himself captained the slow, cranky *Experiment,* which would be lucky if it were not captured by a fast British cruiser the minute it stuck its jib out of port. Even now that he commanded a thirty-eight-gun frigate, Favian felt a touch of that jealousy.

Favian knew the tern schooner had done well since: on her very first cruise she'd not only captured every single vessel in a British convoy but sunk one of the escorts. Since then she'd brought back laden prize ships on every cruise. He knew of her success because he knew her owner and commander: Captain Gideon Markham of Portsmouth, New Hampshire, Favian's privateering cousin. Favian had not seen Gideon since before the war: Gideon had been at sea constantly, first in his *General Sullivan* schooner and then, after the *Sullivan* was lost to the enemy, in the new tern schooner. He knew Gideon for a thorough seaman of an old-fashioned, pious type, the sort of Congregational deacon known for the way he mixed privateering with preaching and served his hands coffee instead of grog. Gideon had lost his wife and son tragically during the Embargoes—while Gideon had been pressed aboard a French man-of-war they had died in Savannah of a combination of consumption and starvation, much to the disgrace of the rest of the family, who had never approved of Gideon's wife and seemed to care little whether she lived or died once she was safely out of sight in Georgia—and after their death Gideon had turned bitter, living exclusively aboard his schooner and rarely setting foot ashore except to attend church. Favian had heard that Gideon had married a Spanish lady in Mobile over a year before, and he wondered if marriage had softened him.

With sudden surprise Favian realized that he carried bad news for Gideon. Gideon's father, Josiah, had died in September; he wondered if Gideon knew. The mail might well take a long time getting down the Ohio and Mississippi from Pittsburgh, and

Josiah Markham had died only ten weeks before. . . . Favian feared that it would be he who would bring the sad report to his cousin.

"Mr. Stanhope," Favian said, seeing the midshipman coming out of the scuttle with his friend Lovette. They were both exceptionally promising apprentice officers, intelligent and standing fair to make their mark in the Navy; Stanhope had been with Favian in the *Experiment* and Irwin Lovette had been given high marks by all *Macedonian*'s officers. Stanhope gave the low, lush, leveed land a glance, then approached and saluted: a dark-haired, lithe, serious young man in a battered, much-mended uniform. Favian handed him the pocket telescope. "There is one of your grandfather's designs—that schooner yonder."

"Is it? Thank you, sir," Stanhope said. He focused the glass on the tern schooner and whistled. "I remember her, sir," he said. "My grandfather was particularly proud of her—said he was the finest thing he'd ever done."

"She's been very successful," Favian said. "Your grandfather had reason to be proud. Perhaps we can arrange for you to visit her."

"I'd like that, sir," Stanhope said, returning the pocket glass. "Thank you."

The pilot boat, under the practiced direction of Captain Poquelin, came sweeping up to the Custom House wharf, the crewmen scampering to put out the fenders in time for the bulwark to brush against the timbers.

"Mr. Stanhope," Favian said, "pass the word for Kuusi—for my cox'n."

"Aye aye, sir." Stanhope ran forward, nimbly dodging among the busy sailors. The Finn, Kuusikoski, known as Koozey Koskey even to Favian, who found the double vowels of his surname baffling, was a tall, burly blond man with a strange history, first exiled from his homeland by the Russian invaders, then persecuted because *Macedonian*'s superstitious sailors insisted he was a witch. The Finn had shown himself a regular jack, though, and most of the sailors had decided that if the Finn was a witch, he was a benevolent one. There were still a few diehards among the crew, Favian knew, and Koskey would have to step warily, but the majority of the hands had become Koskey's allies.

The Finn, who had been helping with the furling of the headsails, bustled back and saluted; Favian ordered him to get his men into his pinnace, which the *Beaux Jours* had been towing astern, and prepare to receive the officers' baggage. Kuusikoski saluted again, then ran forward to collect his crew. They were all turned out smartly in embroidered jackets, white duck trousers, red sashes, and the knit cap *Macedonian*'s crewmen preferred to the more usual glazed hat, all provided at Favian's expense in order to support the dignity of his captain's rank. Favian remembered, when he first took command of the *Experiment*, how he had counted the pennies to outfit his boat's crew with even the most rudimentary uniforms and was now thankful for the proceeds of Markham's Raid in his purse.

Favian went below to take his number one coat and hat out of his sea chest; he dressed carefully, knotting a black silk cravat over his white linen neckcloth, combing carefully the fashionable spit curls on his cheeks and temples, brushing the long side-whiskers, struggling into tight white breeches. He would present himself in full uniform to Commodore Patterson; he would not insult the dignity of the New Orleans commander by appearing in travel-stained clothes. His uniforms fit him superbly, he knew, thanks to his father's tailor, Tracey, in Portsmouth; he attached the heavy bullion epaulets to his coat and slipped the coat on; he stamped on a pair of jackboots, hesitated for a moment, and then clipped to his belt the gaudy-hilted smallsword given him in New York for his part in the original capture of the *Macedonian* a little over two years ago, in 1812. He collected the briefcase of captured documents, went on deck to supervise as the officers' chests were brought up and put down in the pinnace, then said a French farewell to Captain Poquelin and stepped down into the stern sheets of his boat.

"Let go painters and stern fasts," Kuusikoski said in his accented English, aware that this was his first official occasion as coxswain of the captain's pinnace and quick with the proper orders. "Fend off forrard. Out oars! Give way smartly. Where to, sir?"

"Take us to the flagship yonder, cox'n. The small schooner."

"Aye aye, sir."

The steamboat *New Orleans* vented steam with a hissing white cloud as they passed nearby, drowning the chanty of the black workmen as they rolled her cargo over the levee and onto the wharf. The pinnace skimmed over the brown water, her oars moving in perfect unison, Kuusikoski grinning with obvious pride as he held the tiller. Their destination was obvious to the quartermasters on the schooner, and they were hailed when they'd gone halfway across the intervening water.

"Boat ahoy!"

"*Macedonian*!" Kuusikoski shouted, half rising from his seat in the stern of the pinnace. Answering with the name of Favian's ship instead of "aye aye" (for other officers) or "nay nay" (for a boat without officers aboard) would alert the schooner to the fact of a frigate captain's arrival, allowing them to make the appropriate welcome. Favian could imagine the surprise created by the unexpected answer, the sudden dashing for telescopes to confirm the fact of a man in the boat with *two* coveted epaulets, the sign of a post-captain outranking even the commodore, and sudden panic on the part of the watch officer as he tried to remember the required size of the welcoming party and the proper number of sideboys—if there had ever been a full captain in New Orleans, he had come purely on private business, Favian knew, for the station had always been held by a master-commandant.

There was the sudden shrilling of bosuns' whistles as the astonishing sight was confirmed, the trampling of feet in the hatches, the sudden explosion of the schooner's crew on deck. Favian watched as the sideboys dashed to the entry port, pulling on their white gloves as a squad of marines appeared on deck with a rattle of muskets. The schooner was making a creditable performance in response to a completely unprecedented circumstance. The pinnace swept under the bow of the schooner, and Favian glanced up to see the name: *Carolina*.

"Toss oars," Kuusikoski shouted. "Hook on there, forrard."

"Pipe the side, bosun," came a firm voice from the schooner, and Favian made his jump for the battens that served as a ladder, the sideboys reaching down to hand him in as he scrambled up the *Carolina*'s side. Before him there were the rows of sideboys forming a lane that led him to the schooner's officers, with drawn swords at the salute, backed by the row of marines.

He took off his hat to the quarterdeck and then to the officer standing before him. "Captain Favian Markham of the *Macedonian* frigate, at your service, sir. I bring urgent dispatches for Captain Patterson." The "captain" had been chosen by Favian as a compromise between "master-commandant" and "commodore"—Patterson could legitimately be called by any of the three, at least according to the dizzying world of naval etiquette. As the senior officer present, Favian had arguably usurped the role of "commodore," and so he had tried to compliment Patterson by giving him the highest title still available; he wondered what apprehensions Patterson might discover in Favian's choice of words.

"I am Patterson," said the officer, returning his hat to his head. He was a compact, well-formed man a little below middle height. Though it was not quite seven in the morning, he was dressed in full uniform: a splendidly cut coat with rather more gold lace than was usual in a mere master-commandant, the single epaulet with the silver star of the commodore, neckcloth and two cravats, dandyish Hessian boots, and a full-dress cocked hat. Favian was glad he had chosen to dress formally on this occasion: Patterson obviously ran a taut ship. The deck was spotless; the officers standing on the quarterdeck were rigged out in full undress uniform, with blue trousers and round hat; the marines' uniforms seemed complete and well tended. Favian could see at first glance that the attention was not given entirely to appearances, either: the *Carolina*'s rigging was well set up and tended; the carronades were ready to be cleared for action at a moment's notice, even here in a safe harbor; the crew seemed understrength but in good health and were all well clothed from the slops chests. Windsails were set up over all the hatches and carefully trimmed to the morning breeze in order to ventilate the berth deck for the health of the men.

"Captain Markham, may I introduce Lieutenant John Henley, Acting Lieutenant Coleman, and Ensign Carados of the Marines," Patterson said. Favian received the salutes of the officers and introduced his own officers in turn.

"I was eating breakfast when the lookouts sighted your boat, Captain Markham," Patterson said. "Would you care to join me? I'm sure Lieutenant Henley will be happy to offer the hospitality of the gunroom to your officers."

"Of course, sir," said Henley smoothly, knowing a command when he heard one, however courteously it might be phrased.

"I am honored, sir," Favian said, realizing this was no time to mention he'd eaten on the pilot boat. He knew that Patterson's eating this early bespoke an active officer, whatever his other talents might be: there were far too many captains in the service who slept until nine thirty, ate breakfast at ten, dinner at four or five, and supper at nine in the evening, regardless of the more severe hours allotted to the people for their meals.

Favian followed Patterson down the aft scuttle to his cabin and took the seat offered. Patterson offered Favian coffee, sent for his steward, and called for another breakfast; Favian urged the commodore of the New Orleans station not to wait for the new meal to arrive but to finish the breakfast Favian had, by his arrival, interrupted. Patterson thanked him, tucked his napkin into his neckcloth, and began to finish his shrimp omelet, chop, and cheese.

The formal exchange of courtesies, Favian knew, had been a testing of the waters, opening salutes in the gentlemanly game of commodores, in which officers in the same service quietly battled for power and precedence; Patterson had been watching carefully for any clue as to the meaning of Favian's presence with a clear weather eye out for sign he was to be superseded, while Favian had been observing the routine of the *Carolina* schooner, making his judgments, and reflecting on the business of supersession himself. He decided to relieve Patterson of at least some of his suspense.

"We escaped New London over three weeks ago," he said.

"A fast passage, sir," Patterson said. "You must have been cracking it on to get here."

"Aye, a fast passage," Favian said. "The more so because we did not set out bound for New Orleans. I intended to head for the Indian Ocean, but off Montserrat we captured a British corvette, the *Carnation* of twenty-four guns."

"My heartiest congratulations, sir," Patterson said, a smile breaking out over his face. Favian wondered how much of the man's cheerfulness was occasioned by the sudden revelation that Favian had not come to New Orleans bearing orders from the Secretary of the Navy to take charge of the station.

"Give you joy of the prize money, sir, give you joy," Patterson said, beaming.

"Thank you, Captain," Favian said. "It happened that we took the *Carnation* in a fast boarding action after sunset, and so surprised her that we captured her secret papers and dispatches for the British commanders in Jamaica."

Commodore Patterson's fork paused halfway between his chin and the plate, his eyes suddenly intent. The fork returned to the plate with a clink.

"Did you?" he asked quietly. He took the napkin from his neckcloth and dropped it on the table. "I take it you've discovered British intentions?"

"We did, Captain Patterson," Favian said, picking up the briefcase he'd brought with him, surprised to discover his hands were trembling. He lowered his voice, delivering the news as calmly as he could. "They've pulled their fleet and army out of the Chesapeake. It's waiting under Admiral Cochrane at Negril Bay in Jamaica. Once they're reinforced from the British armies in France to the number of five thousand, they'll head for New Orleans. Wellington's veterans from the Peninsula, mostly, under one of his generals, Sir Edward Pakenham. There are another eight thousand waiting in Europe, ready to form an army of occupation once the city's taken. The details are here, sir."

Patterson took the sheets handed him, looking at Favian keenly as he did so. "You are certain these papers were not meant to fall into our hands?" he asked.

"Not unless the British were able to predict *Macedonian*'s movements even before I knew them," Favian said, surprised and a little pleased that Patterson was able to think of the possibility of planted papers so soon after being informed of their existence. "They couldn't have known we would have been cruising that stretch of water—the British in the Caribbean couldn't have known *Macedonian* had got out of port."

"I see." Patterson leaned back in his chair and, after examining the broken seals, read through the documents without a word, his breakfast forgotten. Favian's own meal came, a beautifully cooked omelet which he would at any other time have devoured gladly; he picked at it politely but kept his attention on Patterson. He had himself read the documents over and over; he knew they contained an exact list of the British forces, every regiment and battery, every ship of the line and transport.

The papers fell to Patterson's desk with a soft rustle. "I thank you for bringing the news with such dispatch, Captain," he said. "This will turn a good many heads, sir. I only hope we can respond to the threat in time."

"Amen to that, sir."

Patterson rang for his clerk, glanced again through the captured papers, and looked up at Favian. "This is not the first indication we've had of British intentions in the Gulf," he said. "In July a British squadron took possession of Pensacola, in

Spanish Florida, with the connivance of the Spanish governor. Following this illegal usurpation, in September they and some of their Creek Indian allies launched an attack on the fort guarding the entrance to Mobile Bay."

This was far worse than Favian had suspected; the merest glance at a map of the Gulf of Mexico showed that Mobile, which had been taken from the Spanish only two years before, was a perfect base for an attack aimed at New Orleans. The British orders taken by the *Macedonian* would have been written before the capture of Mobile had become known in Europe and wouldn't have taken Mobile or Pensacola into account. With Mobile gone, the British could march across country and take Natchez, cutting New Orleans off from reinforcements from Kentucky and Tennessee. It was a terrifying picture.

"How many men do the enemy have in Mobile?" Favian asked, his mind working madly on a plan. *Macedonian* might be able to take on board some of the army, retaking Mobile before major British reinforcements appeared in the Gulf. . . .

"You mistake me, sir," Patterson said. "The British attacked Fort Bowyer, but failed to take it. Thanks to Major William Lawrence and his garrison of regulars, Lieutenant Blake of Gunboat Number 163 and his battery of naval guns, and Captain Gideon Markham, your brother. Gideon captured a sloop of war and a schooner in a fight in the Mississippi Sound, and the British were forced to abandon their flagship under the fort's battery and set it afire. It was a complete repulse, sir."

Favian felt relief swim into him. The situation was not so desperate after all. "I'm happy to hear it!" he said, breathing easier. "By the by, Captain Gideon Markham is my cousin, not my brother," he said.

"Pardon my mistake," Patterson said. "It was a natural one to make—you are brothers in gallantry, after all." Favian accepted the flattery without comment, pleased that his cousin had made a name for himself.

"He has performed brilliantly here and has shown what American sailors can do," Patterson said, then scowled. "I wish other privateersmen in the Gulf would profit by his example," he said darkly. "Most are mere pirates. Because they make such tempting profits, in part because they are allowed by the civil administration to dispose of their goods without paying the duty, they lure the sailors away from more honest trade—I have nearly a full crew for *Carolina* here, but *Louisiana*, my heaviest boat, is virtually unmanned, and I've had to lay up six of my eleven gunboats for lack of men to put in them."

"Perhaps the news of the British moves will spur enlistments," Favian offered, understanding now why Patterson had his flag on the smaller, more easily manned *Carolina* instead of the more powerful *Louisiana*, and why the forlorn, abandoned gunboats were rotting at their anchors.

"Thus far it has not," Patterson said. "As a good Navy man I hate to grant the Army a great deal of credit, but I must give them their due in General Jackson. He is in charge here in the Gulf, and he's performed wonders—earlier this month he stormed Pensacola, Spanish flag or no Spanish flag, and ended the Creek Indian menace for once and all. I'm embarrassed to say he had precious little help from me in his endeavors; the Navy sat on its anchors waiting for the patriotic citizens of New Orleans to enlist. We're still waiting."

He drummed his fingers on the table, then went on. "Jackson's returned his army to Mobile for the present, after leaving a garrison—he expects the British to attack him there and has called up troops from Tennessee and Kentucky to meet him. He can march his present forces to the city in a few weeks. So New Orleans may not be entirely unprepared, sir—but I am much afraid the Navy shall be."

"Captain Patterson," Favian said, drawing himself up formally, "the city of New Orleans may consider that *Macedonian* has enlisted in its service, and I think we should tell them so. I had to send some of our complement off with the *Carnation*, but we also obtained some recruits, Americans pressed into British service, and the result is that we have nearly three hundred eighty men aboard, as well as the power of a thirty-eight-gun frigate. It isn't much compared with the fleet the British will send against us, but the British will not be expecting to find *Macedonian* waiting for them, and we may count surprise as being on our side."

Patterson leaned back in his chair, a smile of grim pleasure playing over his face. "Aye," he said, "it might raise the spirits of the town. Though I must inform you, Captain Markham," he said, speaking flatly, "that a big frigate may prove less use here than you might think. The waters are shallow here; many of the approaches to New Orleans are suitable for nothing larger than barges. Here, at least, Mr. Jefferson's gunboats can be used to good effect, and mere schooners like *Carolina* and *Louisiana* can serve better than a ship of the line."

"I am glad to hear it," said Favian.

Patterson smiled a satisfied smile, having made his point in the gentlemanly little skirmish being fought between the two American captains over ultimate command of naval forces in the Gulf. His words devalued *Macedonian* by showing it might not prove as important as Favian seemed to think, implied that only Patterson and Patterson's men knew the waters and channels of the Mississippi Delta, and suggested to any astute listener that Favian could not be expected to command in shoal waters he did not know. Favian expected Patterson's next play to be the suggestion that *Macedonian* transfer some of its crew to *Louisiana* and the gunboats, in other words from Favian's sphere to Patterson's, but Patterson refrained; perhaps he expected Favian, sooner or later, to suggest the idea himself.

"I think we may have some recruits from the, ah, the gentlemen of the coast," Patterson said, using a phrase that meant *pirate*. He folded his hands in front of him. "Not tars of the best quality, to be sure, but men-of-war's men of a sort, who know how to lay a cannon. I have recently put many of them out of business," he said with satisfaction. "Many of their captains are in irons in the *calabozo,* where we may expect them to rot."

Favian had been expecting this sooner or later: a demonstration from Patterson of his own effectiveness. Patterson was a good player, but Favian had seen the game played by more expert hands: Stephen Decatur had been a master at seizing control of a situation, even from captains more senior than he, and Favian had served under Decatur for seven straight years and had learned all the tricks. At this point he could look at the game with fair objectivity, first because he had no intention, as yet anyway, of superseding Patterson in command of the Gulf squadron, and second because if supersession proved necessary Favian had the ultimate card to play, his own superior rank.

"The banditti have been an embarrassment for years," Patterson said. "They operated from an island called Grand Terre, in the Barataria Gulf, carrying privateering commissions from the Cartagenian Republic that allow them to prey on Spanish ships. They unloaded the cargoes at Grand Terre, moved them by bateaux north to New Orleans or to The Temple, an old Indian mound, where they've been sold by auction. Until this year they've been impossible to suppress—half the state legislature has been doing regular business with them."

Patterson signaled for more coffee. Overhead Favian heard the schooner's bell strike eight, followed by the drum of feet as the watches were given their breakfast. Patterson looked at Favian with a frown.

"The blackguards killed some customs officers in skirmishes, and that proved their undoing," he said. "Last year we were able to put a price on the head of one of their leaders—a man named Jean Laffite—and this year we arrested his brother Pierre, although the confounded man escaped later. In September I took my squadron to Grand Terre and seized their base. Burned their huts, captured their ships. The pirates didn't resist, and there will be half a million in prize money!"

An unfeigned grin rose on Patterson's face at the thought of the prize money, and Favian understood it well. Patterson, with his captain's share, would get three twentieths of the money, an ample reward, certainly, for spending the years in command of this frustrating, neglected, provincial station, without enough strength to enforce the laws and without any chance of acquiring, in the war with the British, the glory, money, and promotion unashamedly desired by every officer worth his epaulet.

"My congratulations," Favian said. His words seemed to bring Patterson back into an awareness of the present, and he frowned, playing with the silverware on his plate.

"Thank'ee," he said reflectively. "It's odd, you know, but Jean Laffite, the pirate I just mentioned, brought the first warnings of a British attack on New Orleans back in early September. We had his brother in prison, you see, and we were assembling and equipping the squadron for the attack on Grand Terre—he couldn't have been unaware that I was moving against him. And suddenly his attorney showed up with some letters purporting to be from Captain Percy of the *Hermes*, the British sloop of war that was lost at Mobile a few weeks later. The letter offered Laffite and his brigands gold, land, and a pardon if they would join the British forces attacking New Orleans. The governor was near panic, was ready to swear the Laffites and their crew into the service of the state and apologize for ever putting the damn bandit Pierre into prison in the first place."

Patterson's face hardened. "I thought the letters were a forgery, and I said so. Laffite had reason to ingratiate himself with the authorities—he knew that I was going to put him out of business, and it seemed a last desperate attempt to convince Governor Claiborne that he could be of service." He gave a short laugh. "It seems the documents were genuine after all." He rubbed his chin uneasily. "All for the best, I suppose," he said. "Good military strategy to clear your rear before engaging the enemy to the front. And the pirates who fled—there were five hundred or more that got away, though we got all the leaders except the blasted Laffites—may yet enlist in the Navy, now there's no other prospect of employment."

"I daresay," Favian said, leaning forward. He knew a great deal about Patterson now: he had seen the frustration that must have gripped the man over the years, confronted with the impossible task of enforcing the laws of the United States, without any cooperation from Washington and in the face of the will of the State of Louisiana, who preferred to deal with pirate-smugglers. He had seen Patterson's pride in his accomplishments and in the Navy; he understood why Patterson was to be found, at six in the morning, in full dress uniform and cocked hat aboard the *Carolina*—it was the only way to maintain his dignity, his sense of self, in the face of intolerable disappointment. He had to run a taut ship here simply to keep his command from disintegrating; and before he could do that he had, by a prodigious act of will, to keep from disintegrating himself. The dress uniform was a means to that end; he was driving himself harder than he drove his men.

Favian put any idea of supersession out of his mind. Patterson was a man he could work with. He and Patterson might never be friends—they were both too reserved, too private for that—but Favian thought they could work together.

"Captain Patterson," Favian said, "shouldn't we inform the authorities? The governor, the legislature, the military?"

Patterson nodded tersely. "Aye. I'll call a meeting of the Committee of Defense for this evening—that will be the governor, General Villeré of the militia, Colonel Ross of the 44th Regulars, the collector of customs, and ourselves. I'll try to persuade them to declare martial law. That will give us the authority to deal with the situation without the blasted mayor or th' legislature interfering." He looked up, his eyes meeting Favian's. "I thank you, Captain Markham, for this windfall," he said, pushing his plate aside and standing from the table. "It may bring to the State of Louisiana what it has long needed. A sense of urgency."

TWO

Favian's boat, the current behind it, sped down the brown waters, the crew stroking easily at the oars even as they turned their heads to look at the city built up beyond the levee. Kuusikoski, the tiller clasped easily in his hand, craned his neck as he peered over the heads of the rowers at the black New-Hampshire-built privateer schooner, the boat's destination. Now that his audience with Patterson was over, and he and his party were now quartered in the roomier cabins of the virtually crewless *Louisiana*, Favian was bringing to his cousin Gideon the news of the death of Josiah Markham, Gideon's father.

The privateer's lookouts were sharp-eyed; there was a hail from the privateer while the boat was still two hundred yards off, and Kuusikoski's answering shout of "*Macedonian!*" while probably not understood since no one but Patterson knew the frigate was in Louisiana, created a stir about the entry port. Gideon's men seemed to know their business and to be performing it smartly.

The pinnace swept under the towering jibboom, and Favian looked up in surprise at the figurehead, the rudely carven, brightly painted visage of a Russian Cossack, a fierce green-eyed young man with a red beard, a gold ring in one ear, waving a saber. It had originally been the figurehead of the Revolutionary privateer *Cossack*, commanded by Malachi Markham, uncle to both Favian and Gideon. Malachi's career had been a spectacular one, filled with violence and danger—perhaps more danger than had been strictly necessary. Favian had often wondered if perhaps Malachi had been addicted to risk-taking, because each successful act of daring seemed to drive him to the next. It started with his first victory over a British frigate off Puerto Rico and culminated in his spectacular mid-ocean capture of the fifty-gun liner *Bristol*, the largest enemy ship taken by any American during the entire war. Whatever the reason, Malachi had been unable to rest on his laurels or his riches and had spent his life careening from one mad adventure to the next.

The Cossack figurehead was said to resemble him and had been taken down from the privateer after the war and put in a place of honor in the home of Josiah Markham. Josiah had always said the icon was for use in war and would not be happy gracing a ship in peacetime. Now it seemed that Josiah had given the figurehead to his son, in essence giving the privateer its coat of war paint, a talisman of success. Favian looked up to see the schooner's name carved into the bulwark near the cathead: *Malachi's Revenge*. Appropriate, Favian thought, this invocation of the family war god. He had himself flown the Markham viper banner, designed by Malachi, from the *Experiment*'s main truck during his successful cruise to the Narrow Seas and back, and for much the same sort of reason: a little of Malachi's luck could make any war cruise easier.

The bowman hooked on forward, and Favian came up the schooner's side to the twitter of pipes, sideboys in white gloves reaching down to help him in: some privateers disdained naval practice, but others, apparently including this *Malachi's Revenge*, seemed determined to outdo the Navy at their own game. Favian uncovered to the American ensign flying from the peak and walked forward through the lane formed by the sideboys, the schooner's officers with drawn swords, and the "gentleman volunteers," who served as marines and who wore uniforms of a sort, green coats and red caps. Favian recognized the faces of the officers, New Hampshiremen for the most part: Francis Allen, a dashing devil-may-care young man, perfectly suited for his apparent role in command of the gentleman volunteers; Michael Clowes, a veteran New Hampshireman, who had probably been aloft overhauling the rigging, since he had a marlinespike on a thong around his neck and was spotted with tar, a thorough sailor whose own merchant schooner had been unlucky enough to have been captured by the British during the first month of the war; George Willard, a black-eyed Gay Head Indian from Martha's Vineyard who had served Gideon for years; and finally Gideon himself, successful privateer and congregational deacon.

"Favian, by Jerusalem!" Gideon said, a broad smile on his face. "My heart rejoiceth; I'm glad to see ye here! I thought it was Commodore Patterson, come to celebrate his new step!"

That, Favian knew, might well have been the first report: if anyone in New Orleans saw a naval officer with two epaulets from a distance, he might well assume it was Patterson with a promotion. His memories of Gideon flooded him: the strong New Hampshire speech laced with biblical tags, the sunbrowned sailor's face under the round beaver hat.

"Ye know my officers, I suspect," Gideon said. "Mr. Willard, Mr. Clowes, Mr. Allen, Mr. M'Coy the second bosun—the rest are ashore. Ye're lucky I wasn't ashore myself; I and my wife are staying at a hotel."

"I came with dispatches," Favian said. "My ship is at Fort St. Philip. I was surprised to see you here." He clasped each officer's hand and offered his greetings and offered news of their families where he knew it, wondering all the while how he could get Gideon apart to give him the news of his father. Gideon was not in mourning, nor was he wearing a mourning band, and was therefore ignorant of Josiah's death. Gideon had worn full mourning for his wife for at least two years and would almost certainly show some sign of mourning for his father.

"Captain Markham, I've brought news of our family as well as dispatches," Favian said. "Perhaps we could speak privately?"

"Aye," Gideon said, with a careful look. "Mr. M'Coy, pipe the hands to their dinner. Captain Markham, will you join me below?"

"Certainly, sir."

They went down the aft scuttle to Gideon's cabin. It was a handsome, well-lit place, with its arched deckhead beams and graceful stern windows, but its looks were marred by battered, secondhand cabin furniture, relics of Gideon's earlier poverty. Favian accepted the place at the table Gideon offered him and sat down with a careful look at his cousin.

Gideon Markham was in his middle thirties with no gray in his brown hair; but his hard life—he'd been at sea constantly since the age of fifteen—had aged him and lined his face. Favian remembered a spare, lithe man of average height, reserved in the New England way and often grim. The Gideon he saw before him had thickened slightly about the waist and was older, which was to be expected, but the grimness seemed to have gone. Remarriage had changed him for the better, that was clear, and Favian's curiosity about his wife increased. Gideon dressed plainly in a coat of brown broadcloth, a round beaver hat, gray trousers, half boots that were polished but had obviously seen a lot of wear, and a jewel-hilted sword. This last seemed out of place on such an unassuming man. The hilt was beautifully crafted, and Favian thought the jewels were diamonds.

Gideon perceived the direction of Favian's eyes. "A trophy," he said. "Captured from the captain of the British sloop *Alastor* that I sank last year. It was the maiden voyage of *Malachi's Revenge*."

"It's a worthy memento, I'm sure. I've heard something of that fight," Favian said. "Captain Patterson was most complimentary, earlier this morning, concerning your conduct at Mobile in September."

"The Lord was with us," Gideon said simply. "We took a schooner and a sloop of war, *Musquetobite*. That's why we're in New Orleans; we're trying to get a privateering commission for the sloop."

"I hope it will give you joy, Gideon," Favian said. He looked at his cousin and took a breath. How many times had he told men of other men's deaths? he wondered. Off Tripoli, after storms and accidents, in this war with the British? He had written to the survivors of all the *Experiment*'s dead, informing them of the loss of the men he had grown to know well aboard the little eighty-foot brig, all men who had trusted him until their little man-of-war had gone on the sands. He should be good at it by now, he thought; the words should be learned by rote, the consolation automatic. Somehow they were not; each time was a repetition of the same agony.

"Gideon, there is bad news," he said. "I can see you haven't heard it; I'm sorry to be the one to bear it. Your father passed away in September."

Favian saw Gideon's eyes turn away, his face hardening into a stern mask, the look Favian remembered from years ago. So the grim scowl was a way of hiding hurt, Favian thought; now it would no longer be Gideon speaking, but the Congregational deacon.

"The Almighty give him peace," Gideon said. His fingers absently stroked a pewter coffee mug that had been resting on the table.

"He was a good man, Gideon," Favian said. "Hundreds came out for the funeral, every public official, John Maddox, Andrew Keith, every privateer in the state. Daniel Webster spoke the oration. I wish I had kept the newspaper clipping I was sent, but I mailed it back to New Hampshire when we sailed."

Gideon looked up at him; despite the rigorous mask, there was a surprising amount of sorrow in the brown eyes. "When did it happen?" he asked.

"He passed away in his sleep while visiting my father," Favian said. "The night of September eleventh. He went very quietly." He considered adding what he knew about the old man's will, about Gideon inheriting Josiah's Portsmouth house, but decided to let the official letter inform him. It wasn't what Gideon needed to know.

"September eleventh. While I was dawdling here in the Gulf. First David, then Father. I should never have left New England," Gideon said.

David Markham was Gideon's brother, a charming rogue who, the year before, had got himself hanged for conducting a communication with the British, one of the few casualties produced by the lax New England habit of seeing nothing wrong with trading with the enemy providing enough profit was made.

"Don't reproach yourself," Favian said. "You've done well here. My father and mother were with him. Your brothers represented you at the funeral and did very well. And as for David, you know there was nothing either of us could have done to stop him."

"I wish the Lord had spared him until I could have seen him again," Gideon murmured.

"He was proud of you, Gideon. You carried on his labors; you went to sea and fought the British. I'm sure he felt your work was here."

Gideon gave no reply, just looked down at his hands as he absently rubbed the old pewter mug. Favian sat through a long silence, then saw a shiver run through Gideon's body as he snapped out of his fit of abstraction.

"I'm sorry, Favian," he said. "I thank ye with all my heart for bringing the news. But I think I would like to be alone."

Favian stood. "Of course, Gideon. Captain Patterson has given me quarters aboard the *Louisiana*. I hope you will send for me if you want company."

"Come to my hotel tomorrow for luncheon. Hotel Esplanade, noon. You can meet my wife." His eyes flickered from Favian to the table and back, making an obvious effort to be civil.

"I would be honored," Favian said. "Please don't get up. I wish I had brought happier news."

He returned to the deck, blinking in the strong light. He saw some of his boat's crew on the deck inspecting the privateer with critical man-of-war eyes and motioned them into the boat. Michael Clowes came politely forward, the marlinespike swinging on its thong around his neck.

"Leaving so soon, sir?" he inquired.

Favian nodded. "Aye," he said. He leaned toward Clowes and lowered his voice. "I've just informed Captain Markham of the death of his father," he said privately. "Perhaps you might tell the other officers and arrange so that Captain Markham is not disturbed today."

Michael Clowes's eyes were grave. "Certainly, sir. Do you think the wardroom mess might send Captain Markham our condolences, sir?"

"That would be appropriate, yes. I'm sure Captain Markham would appreciate it."

"Thank'ee, sir, for your advice. Mr. M'Coy, pipe the side for the captain."

Favian swung down into the boat to the twitter of the privateer's pipes, settling into the stern sheets. It was barely noon and already he felt exhausted; he tugged at his cravat and neckcloth and opened his collar, feeling the weight of the epaulets burdening his shoulders.

All day he had carried bad tidings, first to the city and then to his cousin. One public tragedy, soon to be the cause of the blowing of bugles and the tramp of marching feet, and another private one, an old man dying alone in a bed in New Hampshire. Received by a man who shut himself in his cabin alone with his reproaches.

He had brought enough bad news for one day, Favian thought cynically; he could be excused the rest of it until the Defense Committee met that night. He looked forward to his cabin on the *Louisiana*, where he could tear off the dress coat of Captain Favian Markham, U.S.N., the naval *beau sabreur*, and spend the afternoon alone, like his cousin, away from the prying eyes of men.

THREE

The Defense Committee, once presented with the captured documents, moved swiftly. Express dispatches, including copies of the British orders, were sent to General Jackson in Mobile, urging him to march for New Orleans without delay and with all the forces he could muster. In the meantime General Villeré's Louisiana militia regiments, who had been drilling only twice each week, were to be called to full-time duty; General Philemon Thomas was to bring his brigade of militia from Baton Rouge; the nuns of the Ursuline Convent were to be requested to make bandages; the forts around the city were to be put in order; a Committee for Public Safety, encompassing the prominent men of the city, would be formed in order to expedite matters. Martial law, despite the urging of Patterson, Favian, and Colonel Ross of the 44th Infantry, would not be declared, lest the legislature and judiciary unite in opposition. Also, needless to say, everyone concerned would be printing up a great many proclamations meeting the emergency with suitably florid rhetoric.

The Defense Committee were properly grateful, Favian was told, for the offer of a thirty-eight-gun frigate, but seemed to have no suggestions concerning how *Macedonian* might best be employed. Having heard a report concerning the state of the forts, Favian himself made a suggestion: Fort St. Philip on the Plaquemines Bend, where *Macedonian* was riding at anchor, was reported to have its full complement of guns and men, but most of the guns were not mounted, and there were few gun platforms; the parapets and glacis were decaying, and the barracks were old and would be set afire by any enemy cannonade. Favian offered to send word to the officers of the frigate to assist in readying the fort, siting its water battery and building the gun platforms: there were no better judges of how to place a water battery than Navy men, who knew all too well what damage a properly sited fort's guns could inflict on warships. Colonel Ross accepted the offer with thanks, but seemed less than pleased when Favian also mentioned that his officers could instruct the fort's men in gunnery.

Most of the meeting was spent in a long and profitless wrangle over whether a second battalion of Free Men of Color, a black militia unit, should be formed; it appeared there were many volunteers. Ross and Patterson, who said that any offer of help should be accepted, were fully in favor of the idea; Claiborne was equivocal; Villeré, who thought that arming the colored population—even the freemen, many of whom owned slaves themselves—would result in a black insurrection, was outspoken in his opposition. In the end the decision was put off.

"What hypocrisy!" Patterson snorted afterwards, as they were walking to where Favian's pinnace waited by the levee. "Villeré and the other plantation aristocrats are afraid to give muskets to free men—to free colored American citizens, whose contribution to the life of this city is considerable—but they see nothing wrong with selling guns to pirates like the Laffites! The Free Men of Color want to protect their liberties here, because they at least know how much worse it would be for them under British rule, and they've volunteered to fight, but Villeré would deny it! And all along the *real* question of the defense of New Orleans has been whether the Creoles will fight!"

"Is that in doubt?" Favian asked, surprised. Villeré had seemed a martial enough individual; many of his suggestions had been sensible enough, though he'd been dressed, like many a part-time soldier, in a fantastical uniform, all epaulets and braid.

"Aye," Patterson said sourly. "I suppose they can't be blamed entirely—they've only been Americans for ten years, and they resent having to obey laws laid down in Washington and being forced to stop importing slaves. Under Spanish rule the Creoles were, for the most part, allowed to run New Orleans to suit themselves, but when Claiborne was made territorial governor ten years ago, and given a free hand, it was greatly resented. And of course they've had to put up with a lot of Americans from the north—'Kaintucks,' we're called—who don't speak their language, don't know the local ways, and don't respect their religion. The Creoles consider themselves superior in all things, and their vanity has even affected the slaves, what with 'Creole niggers' believing their station higher than 'Kaintuck niggers'!"

Patterson paused to scrape muck from his Hessian boots—the

streets were not paved here, and the ground was low and swampy; no wonder the houses had been built so that the occupants could travel across the roofs from one to the other without soiling their feet. Favian shrugged deeper into his boat cloak: he'd thought New Orleans would be tropical even in November, but it was remarkably cold here at night. Patterson looked at him with a cynical twist to his lips. "Now that Louisiana has achieved statehood," he said, "and the Creoles have a larger say in the state's affairs, the resentment has died down, but the question remains: Will the Creoles fight for the United States of America, or will they wait to see what offer the British will make them?" He shook his head. "Even if they fight, they may be paralyzed by their own damnably complicated politics. This Defense Committee that met tonight is not the only Defense Committee. The legislature has their own Committee of Defense, three of the local Creole leaders, and they try to run the city's affairs without consulting the governor or the mayor." He straightened his shoulders and began to walk to the levee. "It may work out, somehow. Come along, Captain—my steward will have some hot punch ready."

Favian looked up at the graceful low buildings fronting Chartres Street as he walked. Many of them, built on the soft, half-sunken ground, leaned at odd, erratic angles. How alien was this Latin, Catholic, slave-owning society, he wondered, and how might they be safely integrated into the rest of American society—Anglo-Saxon, Protestant, industrious, and for the most part free? Commerce would do it eventually, he knew, for the "Kaintucks" were moving into New Orleans at ever-increasing rates and would eventually submerge the native population. But would the Creoles see that as a threat and a reason to make their peace with the British, who could protect them from the thousands of Americans moving downriver?

Favian knew himself ignorant: he had never lived in a slave state, never traveled, within the boundaries of the United States, any farther south than Norfolk. Yet here he was cast into a situation in which he would have to make decisions, decisions on which the fate of Louisiana could depend, with no real understanding of the vast majority of the inhabitants.

His cousin Gideon, who had married a Spanish lady from Mobile, might be able to give him aid. Gideon owned several plantations north of Mobile together with his wife, Anna-Maria—or was it Maria-Anna? Something typically Spanish, with paired saints' names; Favian could not remember.

Gideon had apparently made a life for himself here, and Favian would hope for good advice. Strange that it had happened to Gideon, Favian thought, the family puritan—such a rigid and unbending Protestant character would not, one would think, make a success out of living with the Creoles. Perhaps Ann Marie—whatever—had more charms than he had formerly suspected.

"Speaking of Creoles and fighting," Patterson said, clearing his throat. "I should like to advise you and your men to be careful when visiting the town. The Creoles, taken as a whole, are touchy on the subject of honor, and it's easy for a Kaintuck to offer them insult without meaning to. When the young men of the city are called to their militia companies tomorrow the spirits of the town will be excited—there will probably be a dozen duels within the Creole battalion alone, and since the Laffite gang of smugglers has been broken up, the Navy is not at all a popular thing." Patterson touched Favian's arm. "Just be wary, Captain Markham. Enjoy the town, by all means, but take a little care."

"Thank you, sir," Favian said.

The whistle of the *New Orleans* steamer shrilled from the docks, echoing from the houses; it was followed by the threshing sound of its paddle wheels, clearly audible on a still night. They turned the corner and caught a glimpse of the steamboat, its stack flinging sparks to the sky, putting on speed as it turned northward. Favian knew the boat's owner and designer, the inventor Robert Fulton—in fact Fulton, in his other capacity as portrait artist, had made some pastel sketches of Favian, studies for a portrait. Favian had seen *Demologos,* Fulton's steam battery built for the defense of New York Harbor and the destruction of the British blockade off Sandy Hook, a weapon of terrible potential. Fulton also had plans for iron-plated steam warships, an even more frightening idea, but one that would end the blockade that was strangling American commerce. In the cold air, still scented with the smell of stale blossoms, Favian sensed the vastness of the change that would come. Steamboats like *New Orleans* would be bringing the Kaintucks downriver to the Creole city, and much of its native culture would be lost; steam batteries would soon be dominating the harbors of the world and perhaps eventually the deep seas as well. It was in the American spirit to bring about such change, whether for good or ill; and it was the British who were standing for the Old World, the old order, the old way of doing things. More than two nations would be clashing soon on the Mississippi Delta, Favian thought; it would be two epochs, changeless eighteenth century Britain with its aristocratic privilege, its rigid social classes, battling nineteenth century America—democratic, turbulent, and inventive.

The Louisiana Creoles, Favian knew, would play a critical part, yet from all that he had seen and heard the Creoles were much closer to the eighteenth century; their formal, stylized way of life, based on slavery and rigidly maintained social classes, seemed closer to the British ideal. Somehow, Favian knew, the Kaintucks and the Creoles were going to have to be brought closer together, to be made to work together against the British, but yet he could not see how.

Kuusikoski and the crew of Favian's pinnace leaped to attention as he and Patterson walked over the levee, ready to transport them to the *Carolina*, then deliver Favian to the *Louisiana*. He would save his meditations for the morrow, Favian thought; the last weeks had been too tiring for coherent thought. Perhaps the Defense Committee knew best how to handle the British; Favian, to be sure, did not.

"Captain Markham?" The lady was a soft-spoken Creole of about thirty, with dancing black eyes and a white, somehow suggestive smile; Favian hastened to rise from his seat in the hotel lobby where he'd been reading an old copy of *Salmagundi Magazine*. She was small, he noticed as he bowed, not rising even to his chin; there was a mourning band on her arm.

"I am Captain Markham, miss." He was dressed in civilian rig, a gray coat with a black velvet collar, a round hat, and yellow nankeen trousers; but he was wearing the New York presentation sword and that, presumably, marked him as a military man. He had arrived at the hotel for his luncheon appointment with his cousin Gideon and had sent up his card; no word had yet come down.

"I am Mrs. Desplein, Mrs. Markham's housekeeper," the Creole said. Of course, Favian thought, the servants would be in mourning as well. "Captain and Mrs. Markham left this morning to conduct some business, and they've not returned. There's only a girl servant and myself—even Mr. Grimes is gone, the steward—

but I'm sure Captain Markham would wish you to have the hospitality of his rooms."

"I'm most obliged, Mrs. Desplein." Favian bowed, and followed her to his cousin's room.

He had spent the morning in the city watching the militia companies assembling at the Place d'Armes in response to Governor Claiborne's proclamation. Each company was dressed in a wildly romantic uniform of a different color and the women of the city had been out in force to see them off. The officers were, almost without exception, riding thoroughbred horses and had made the most out of the occasion, attempting daring feats of horsemanship in the crowded square—levades, caprioles, the whole routine of chivalric horseback warriors. For the most part they had succeeded, except when a few horses grew upset at the crowding and threw their less-than-expert riders, a sight the crowd had seemed to enjoy even more than the more successful acrobatics.

In the end Governor Claiborne arrived in a fanciful uniform of his own, blue with a very high, stiff collar, heavy braided epaulets, a blue ribbon of watered silk across his chest with the badge of a pelican on it, and a ruffled neckpiece like something out of the sixteenth century. He saluted General Villeré, in his red coat with epaulets and gold brocade, and Major Plauché of the New Orleans Battalion, who was also dressed in an epauletted coat buttoned down the side instead of the front with bold V-shaped velvet lapels pinned back on his shoulders. After a suitable number of bombastic speeches the parade got under way, and the Hulans, the Louisiana Blues (who seemed to be Irishmen), the Carabiniers, the Chasseurs, a small company of Choctaws and the Free Men of Color under their white officers, formed up and marched through the streets of the town to their bivouac, decked with the flowers and kisses of the ladies of the town. This was only the city militia. More companies would be assembling in the countryside and marching into the town as soon as word of the mobilization was carried to them. And, of course, General Thomas's Baton Rouge brigade would be marching south within a few days. There would be another meeting of the Defense Committee tonight, Favian knew, to decide where to post everyone once they were mobilized. In the meantime it was possible to enjoy a carnival atmosphere.

Favian watched the militia with only half his attention; they were not his department, after all, and however gorgeous their plumage they failed utterly to outshine the ladies of New Orleans. On his walk to the Place d'Armes he had passed through districts other than those government and warehouse areas he had visited, and it had not escaped Favian's attention that New Orleans was a delightfully sinful city.

Saloons and gambling houses were doing a mighty business, even early in the morning, full of uniformed men anxious to have a last fling before marching off to the restricted bivouac outside of town. The brothels seemed to be doing landmark business among the officers and men of the New Orleans Battalion. They operated quite openly, with touts standing outside describing, in half a dozen dialects, the pleasures available. This surprised Favian, who was used to the more discreet palaces elsewhere in the United States.

Nor were illicit pleasures the only ones available. It was possible to walk the streets and stand among the crowds at the Place d'Armes, and feast his eyes, without disturbing propriety in the least, on the extraordinary number of beautiful women. The Creole ladies were out in large numbers, dressed in their finest, and Favian concluded that whatever mix of nationalities and races had come to make up Louisiana, each seemed to be composed of surprisingly handsome stock. The women carried themselves proudly, head high, in a way that the New England women would have thought immodest. Each race and mixture of race provided its own striking examples of loveliness and grace: the whites standing in their gowns, flashing dark eyes glancing boldly from beneath their bonnets; the blacks carrying themselves proudly, their handsome faces, which seemed somehow physically different from the blacks Favian had seen in the East—long-jawed, long-nosed, perhaps with a Choctaw influence—flashing gracious smiles. Those of mixed blood, quadroons and octoroons, contributed their exotic appeal and seemed the most beautiful of all, tall, erect, with languid Egyptian eyes. All the women showed wild enthusiasm at the parade, hurling bouquets and running out amid the troops to kiss unblushingly their husbands, brothers, lovers, and, for all Favian knew, complete strangers. As he stood enviously by in his fashionable city rig, it was one of the few times in his life Favian had ever wished himself in uniform.

The ear, as well as the eye, found much to delight in. The languages and dialects heard in the streets teased Favian's polyglot mind: three tongues seemed most common, with French of one variety or another being the dominant speech of the city, with Spanish heard often and English least. Other languages spoke for the unassimilated minorities: Favian saw two Indians conversing in what he supposed was Choctaw, a few Portuguese fishermen haggling among themselves, a number of people speaking in German, and two reverend physicians discussing a patient in Latin.

Even though French was the most common language, most of it was uncommon French: Favian, who had learned French from his father's manservant St. Croix and had a good ear for dialects, heard purest Parisian, Norman-French, a strange dialect he thought might be Alsatian, and unadulterated Gascon. These were only heard from recent immigrants; most French speakers spoke a Creole tongue, but hardly ever the same Creole. New Orleans Creole predominated, but there was also Acadian Creole, and since Louisiana had been the refuge for many colonists driven by the wars from Haiti, the Lesser Antilles, and the Indian Ocean, Favian heard Martinique Creole, Saint-Domingue Creole, and Mauritius Creole. Most of the black inhabitants spoke Creole languages formed from a mixture of the Creole spoken by their masters with their own African additions; in effect, a Creole Creole.

Favian thought it possible that he was falling in love with this gloriously polyglot city. Despite the grandiloquent silliness expressed by the New Orleans bravos, their absurd comic-opera uniforms and horseback caprioles, Favian knew there was something in New Orleans, besides the economic necessity of controlling the mouth of the Mississippi, worth fighting for. There was something here that the United States needed, an easy, sunny tolerance, antidote to the chilly Calvinism of New England, a window on languages and cultures that the Americans would find needful as their territory, wealth, and outlook expanded. It was with reluctance that Favian heard the church carillons ringing the hour of noon and remembered his luncheon appointment with his puritan cousin Gideon, who would by now be in mourning, in solemn opposition to the festive atmosphere of the city.

Following Mrs. Desplein into Gideon's suite at the hotel, he saw a girl of about fifteen sitting on a chair reading a book; she jumped up at Favian's entrance and curtsied.

"This is Campaspe, Mrs. Markham's maid," Mrs. Desplein

said offhandedly. She pursed her lips. "You shouldn't be here, girl."

"I wanted to fetch this copy of Wordsworth, *gouvernante*," the maidservant said. She spoke with a slight Spanish accent and watched Favian with lively dark eyes; she, too, wore a mourning band on her arm. "I started reading and forgot where I was."

"Campaspe," Favian repeated. "That's Greek, isn't it? An unusual name.

> "Cupid and my Campaspe played
> At cards for kisses. Cupid paid,"

he quoted, and saw the girl flash a dazzling smile—a truly remarkable smile—in answer.

"You know the poem!" she said. "Don Carlos used to quote it when he saw me."

"Don Carlos," said Mrs. Desplein, "gave Campaspe her name, since her father had been killed. Don Carlos was Mrs. Markham's first husband."

"He must have been very well educated to know John Lyly," Favian said, surprised. He had been made to read *Euphues, or the Anatomy of Wit* when young and found it precious stuff and hard going. His resistance had increased with each page and in the end he'd mutinied and been given the plays instead, but his resistance to Lyly's affectations had been fully formed.

"Don Carlos spent a lot of his time with English poetry," Campaspe said. "He was writing a book about Shakespeare and Jonson and Vega and Cervantes when he died."

"Very comprehensive," Favian said, bemused that a Spaniard of knightly rank would spend his declining years tracking down similarities between the leading playwrights of the two warring late-Renaissance societies—he doubted that Shakespeare and Lope de Vega would even have heard of one another.

"He used to give names to all his servants," Campaspe said, rapid-fire. "We had Lightborn and Mosca and Dromio and Touchstone and Dido and Mephisto—"

"Campaspe," Mrs. Desplein said firmly, "that is enough. Go about your duties."

"And Bottom," said Campaspe. "I don't have any duties, Madame Desplein, the hotel maids did everything." Her eyes shifted from Mrs. Desplein to Favian. "You captured the *Teaser*, didn't you? Last year?" She spoke with her head cocked to one side, her eyes seeming, for a reason he could not guess, to challenge him.

"Yes. No. Not captured; I sunk her," Favian said, baffled by the girl's sudden change of tacks, agile as a pilot boat.

"I've been to sea," Campaspe said. "I've been in a mutiny and a stern chase where I was a quartermaster, and I ran away once to a privateer where I fought a British schooner. She shot away our foremast, but Captain Markham, that is *our* Captain Markham, saved us. I was also in a revolt in Mexico, where my parents were killed, but I was too young to remember."

"Campaspe, go read your book," Mrs. Desplein said in exasperation.

"Yes, ma'am," Campaspe said, apparently a fine judge of just how far she could press her luck. She curtsied again, then left the room, pausing with her hand on the door to flash an impudent, dazzling, all-encompassing over-the-shoulder smile, and to recite:

> "O Love! Has she done this to thee?
> What shall (alas!) become of me?"

She leaned back in a stage swoon, the back of her hand to her forehead, and then vanished. Favian recognized the final two lines of the John Lyly poem.

"Two years ago she couldn't speak any English at all, except for that poem," Mrs. Desplein said. "It must have been very peaceful. Please have a seat, Captain Markham. Shall I ring for coffee? Or perhaps some rum punch?"

"Rum punch, thank you. Or should I? Gideon, I mean Captain Markham, the other Captain Markham, is a temperance man, is he not? Would I offend him?"

"He does not object to spirits when ashore," Mrs. Desplein said, tugging the bellpull. "But aboard *Malachi's Revenge* he and his crewmen drink only coffee, with cocoa on Sundays. Perhaps, with your permission, we could agree to call you Captain Favian, and the other Captain Gideon?" She pronounced the "Favian" as a French-speaker would, with two broad *a*'s. Favian smiled; he had always thought that pronunciation preferable to the usual New England way of giving the first syllable a long *a*.

"Thank you. It would suit me perfectly," Favian said, hitching his sword around to permit him to sit down without disemboweling the furniture. Mrs. Desplein released the bellpull and turned toward Favian.

"Did Campaspe really run away to sea?" Favian asked. A frown crossed Mrs. Desplein's face.

"Yes, she did, on the *Franklin* privateer with Captain Fontenoy. She was dressed as a boy, of course. If you give her half a chance, she will be giving you a description of the rigging of the *Franklin* and comparing it with the bumpkins and jibbooms and lower studding masts, or whatever they're called, of the *Malachi's Revenge*."

It must have been some time ago, Favian thought. Campaspe was clearly a young woman in the making; no one would possibly mistake her for a boy. "Please sit down, Mrs. Desplein," Favian said. "I realize it's not supposed to be your place to sit down among company, but speaking like this, ah—" He was about to say, "makes me nervous," but amended it at the last minute to "must be uncomfortable for you."

"Thank you, Captain," she said, smoothly seating herself on a settee.

"My uncle Malachi—the one the schooner is named after—spent part of the war in New Orleans," Favian said. "He was a privateer under Governor Bernardo de Galvez, fighting the British on Lake Pontchartrain and on the river."

"*Captain Boston* and his brother!" she cried suddenly. "That was what the city called him—I didn't realize that Captain Gideon was of the same family. The name *Markham* is really not known, just the name the city gave him, but I will wager it was the same man."

Favian smiled; he had heard from his father that the French thought all Yankees were from Boston, and recited the song his father had taught him:

> "Bon, bon, les matelots de Boston,
> Ont rompez les anglaix aux canons."

Mrs. Desplein laughed and clapped her hands. "I have heard that song! Your accent is quite Parisian—we shall have to add a little Creole to your speech."

There was a respectful knock on the servant's door in an alcove set off from the parlor where servants would wait while their employers were entertaining in the parlor. Mrs. Desplein rose from her seat and walked to the alcove, where she spoke to one of the hotel servants in French, ordering coffee and rum punch. She returned to her seat and was about to sit down when the main door opened behind her, and she artfully adjusted her position so that it would not appear that she was sitting in the presence of a guest. Favian stood and bowed as Captain and Mrs. Gideon Markham entered the room, followed by a middle-aged, graying black man. Each wore tokens of mourning, though even Gideon had not dressed entirely in black; Gideon seemed less withdrawn, less the scowling puritan he had been the day before. Obviously the company of his wife improved him.

Gideon crossed the room and clasped Favian's hand, a solemn smile on his brown face. "I'm glad to see ye here, Favian," he said. "This is my wife, Maria-Anna. And Grimes, my steward."

"Gideon. Ma'am. Grimes. I'm happy to meet you here, but I wish I were here with better news," Favian said as Maria-Anna offered her hand. Favian bowed to kiss it.

Favian looked with polite curiosity at Gideon's wife, who had somehow snatched the reclusive, pious Gideon from his self-imposed exile and turned him into a prosperous planter. It was a mystery to Favian how Maria-Anna had so much as dragged the reclusive Gideon off his schooner long enough to propose marriage to him, since after the death of his first wife Gideon had become something of a nautical hermit.

She was short, her hair pulled back *à la Chinoise* to show her ears and temples, with a slight, small-breasted figure that fit to perfection her white, high-waisted gown. It was clear, on the evidence of the gentle rounding beneath the gown, that Maria-Anna was with child. Her face seemed almost as sunbrowned as Gideon's, and bore the signs of a life in the outdoors; at first he thought her plain, but on second glance he doubted his first impression—there was a vitality animating her features that made them very much worth a second look. She did not look a Creole; there did not seem to be the exotic grace, the unique carriage, that Favian had seen in the street, and this surprised him.

"I'm glad to see you under any circumstances, Captain Markham," she said in an accent perfectly American, though southern. "I'm just sorry we weren't here to greet you. One of Gideon's investments just sailed into port, the privateer *Franklin*, and we had to interview the captain." She smiled slyly as Favian straightened over her hand. "I see you have been in New Orleans long enough to learn how to kiss a hand, sir. Gideon has never learned."

"The Navy, ma'am, runs a school of gallantry along with its schools of seamanship," Favian said. "We learn hand-kissing and flattery along with gunnery and spherical trigonometry."

"Goodness. I can see you were an apt pupil." She took off her bonnet and handed it to Grimes, who also carried Gideon's hat and stick. "Have you sent for refreshment, Mrs. Desplein?"

"Yes, ma'am. I ordered coffee and rum punch just now."

"I thought I saw the girl leaving. Will you run down and tell them to bring up our luncheon?"

"Yes, ma'am." Mrs. Desplein curtsied and left the room. Grimes disposed of the bonnet, hat, and stick, bowed, and disappeared down the hallway; he came back carrying a birthing stool. It was an old-fashioned piece of furniture—the current mode was for women to give birth lying down—but Favian had seen many standing in New England houses. It was a large, comfortable apparatus, quite obviously specially made for Maria-Anna by a local master carpenter, and well pillowed to support her back. Practical wives used them as ordinary furniture before and after giving birth: it struck Favian that Maria-Anna was nothing if not practical. Gideon helped her to sit, then took a place near her on the settee.

"Favian, sit down, please," Maria-Anna said. "I hope Mrs. Desplein has been looking after you."

"She and the girl Campaspe were quite hospitable."

"So you've met our Campaspe, eh?" she asked. "I thought she'd find an excuse to see you—she was quite excited when she heard you were coming. She is a partisan of sailors; the gallants of the New Orleans Carabiniers hold no charms for her." She reached out for Gideon's hand and took it. "She shows good taste in that, I think." She smiled.

"She said that she once ran away to sea," Favian said.

"In the *Franklin*, aye," Gideon said; there was something of the old frown on his face. "The same snow Maria-Anna and I just visited on the river. She's an impetuous girl; that was only the most dangerous of her pranks."

Maria-Anna leaned toward Favian, a confiding gleam in her eye. She spoke in a low voice. "I think I should take advantage of Mrs. Desplein's absence to, ah, mention something. Her husband was killed last year in a duel with one of the Mississippi

Dragoons—they're famous for calling out people on the most ludicrous pretexts—and she was left in a bad way."

"Desplein was a blasted fool," Gideon said, his frown deeper still. "He had lost everything in the Creek War—his house was burned, his slaves run off, only the land left and his wife to help him make a new start. He was penniless, and he got called out and shot by some horseback bravo. If Maria-Anna hadn't bought the land sight unseen and employed Mrs. Desplein as a housekeeper, she would have starved."

Maria-Anna nodded. "True, but not to the point," she said. "The point is that she is a widow, is very attractive, and would have no objection to marrying again. Unless you intend to acquire attachments in New Orleans, I would advise caution with our Mrs. Desplein."

"Ma'am, I'm sure nothing occurred between us," Favian said, surprised. "Campaspe was here for most of the time, and—"

Maria-Anna dismissed his protestations with a wave of her hand. "I had no intention of implying anything of the sort," she said. "I just wished to drop a word of warning. Mrs. Desplein has her nets out, that's all. She's a good woman, I know, but I suspect a little unscrupulous."

Good but unscrupulous, whatever that meant, a strangely ambiguous warning. "Thank you, ma'am," Favian said, uncertain how else to respond.

"I hope you will stop *ma'am*ing me," Maria-Anna said. "We are kin, after all."

"Certainly, Maria-Anna," Favian said. "I was surprised to find you speaking southern American; I had thought you were a Spanish Creole."

She smiled. "I was born and raised in Charleston," she said. "My first husband was a Spaniard with estates in Mexico. When he died I was left with a house in Mobile, where I met Gideon."

Favian suspected there was more to the story than that, but there was a knock on the servants' door at that point, a brief murmured conversation in the servants' alcove, and then Grimes entered with a tray, coffee, and punch.

"Thankee, Grimes," Gideon said as he was served with a cup of punch and turned to Favian. "Is the news we heard this morning correct?" he asked. "Are the British moving on New Orleans?"

"Aye," Favian said. "British regular troops and a large squadron of the line, as well as frigates and small craft. It isn't a secret; so long as the information is likely to produce readiness rather than panic, you may feel free to spread the word."

Gideon nodded. "How long do we have?" he asked.

"A month at the outside," said Favian. "Probably less."

Gideon looked at Maria-Anna, then set down his cup of punch. "We'll take the schooner to New England before that," he said. "We meant to leave Mobile last September, but the British attacked and prevented us."

"I told Gideon yesterday that Captain Patterson praised highly his conduct at Mobile," Favian said.

Maria-Anna smiled with pleasure, looking proudly at her husband. Gideon only answered with a few short words. "We thank the Lord for our success," he said, "but the captures have been nothing but trouble. We had to take them before the prize court here, which is damnably slow, and that was one delay. Since we wanted to keep one of the captures to use as a privateer, after the schooner and the sloop were declared lawful prize, we kept the sloop and sold the schooner to pay off the prize money owed to our crew for both ships—that meant a double payment to the hands for a single sale, which meant that we haven't made a penny yet. But because most of the privateers around here are pirates, the authorities are taking their time about granting us the commission."

"As if Gideon were not a well-known captain who hasn't been sailing from New Orleans and Mobile for two years," Maria-Anna said indignantly. "As if he weren't the only lawful privateer in the entire Gulf of Mexico! The Laffites were allowed to operate for years with nothing more than a few worthless certificates from Cartagena, but when a law-abiding citizen wishes to earn a legal profit from his bravery, the law steps in to prevent him. It's enough to make me sympathize with the Laffites."

The servants' door opened quietly, and Mrs. Desplein glided into the room and announced that their luncheon would be sent up shortly. When it came, Grimes served them; Favian discovered, to his delight, the wonder of Creole cooking, the soup with its rice and peppers, the fried fish with its delicate dusting of spices, the duck lying brown beneath its glaze of sauce. Over coffee, Favian asked Gideon about the British attack on Mobile, and Gideon bent over, seizing table implements as aids to his description of the battle, the knife indicating the direction of the wind, the sauceboat Dauphin Island, bones representing the ships . . . for the first time Gideon grew animated, his color rising, his words stumbling over one another in their eagerness to describe the action. The professional side of Favian found himself admiring Gideon's tactics: the British had launched a clever two-pronged assault, intending to bring the American fort and its defenders between two fires, but Gideon had been still more clever: while the fort had fought off the frontal assault, destroying a sloop of war and driving the rest off with losses, repelling a land attack at the same time, Gideon had dealt imaginatively with the other prong of the assault. He kept the British *Musquetobite* at long range until it was too late to do otherwise, then closed to board, the privateer's superior numbers assuring success.

It had been a well-played game, the boarding maneuver, normally a desperate tactic against any enemy that had a hope of resisting, only made possible by the careful preparation of the long-range fight. Favian found himself looking with increased respect at his cousin: he had known Gideon was a good seaman and a fighter, but he had never been aware of this latent tactical ability.

Then Gideon's flow of words slowed abruptly; his look grew abstract. "The battle was fought on the thirteenth of September; the British appeared off Fort Bowyer on the twelfth," he said slowly. "You say that my father died on the night of the eleventh, or in the early morning of the twelfth?"

"That's right, aye," Favian said.

"The morning of the twelfth," Gideon said, his face troubled, "I woke early, with a premonition of death. That day I thought nothing of it, but when the British appeared later in the day I was certain the premonition would come true, that it had been sent by the Lord that I might make my peace with him before I died. I went into the battle knowing that I would die, but I lived—I was not even injured. Until now I thought the premonition was false."

Gideon turned to Favian. There was anguish in his eyes. "D'ye think, Favian, that it was my father? That the Almighty allowed him to bid me farewell, and that I did not recognize him, but thought him Death?" He lowered his head into his hand. "I'm sure it was my father," he said. "And I did not know him when he came."

Favian looked in alarm at Maria-Anna and saw her watching

Gideon with tight-lipped concern. He had seen many such premonitions in his wars—suddenly a man would see his death, write a will, distribute his valued possessions to his friends—and within days, hours perhaps, he would find the death he had seen in combat with an enemy.

But Favian had never heard of this kind of presentiment, the ghost of a man's father flying across two thousand miles of ether to bid him farewell—yet Gideon clearly believed it and felt incomparable loss that he had not recognized Josiah's spirit, if Josiah's spirit it was. Favian felt an odd wish that Lazarus, *Macedonian*'s chanteyman, a madman who claimed to have sold his soul to the devil in 1682 in return for unnatural skill with the fiddle and various other mysterious powers, were here. He would have an explanation even if it was a crackpot one. But that was nonsense, and Gideon would never have countenanced a devil-worshipper in his house. Favian would have to deal with this himself.

"If the Lord . . ." Favian began. He hesitated, choosing his words carefully, and spoke again; he had no religion himself, and wasn't used to this. "If the Lord allowed your father to cross all the distance from New Hampshire to Mobile, he would certainly have allowed him to make himself known to you without question."

Gideon looked up. "Think'ee so?" he asked.

"I am certain of it," Favian said, attempting to put as much false sincerity into his voice as possible.

"But the coincidence," Gideon said. "That same morning, the twelfth of September. How could it be anything other than my father?"

"There are mysteries, Gideon, whose answers we cannot comprehend," Favian said. It was strange to speak in this way; no doubt his acquaintance with Lazarus helped him. "You can't blame yourself for something you can never know."

"It would be a sin, Gideon," Maria-Anna said earnestly.

"Aye," Gideon said slowly. "Reproach may be self-indulgent, I know. I will meditate on it, and pray."

Maria-Anna turned to Favian. "How are your father and mother?" she asked. "They gave us a lovely wedding present, a beautifully carven pair of tables sent down from Pittsburgh on a flatboat. I don't know if our thanks have yet reached them."

"They are well," Favian said, leaping on the chance to change the topic. "My father has reentered political life to speak against the Hartford Convention, along with my brother Lafayette and Congressman Webster. They succeeded in preventing New Hampshire from sending official delegates, though some local busybodies are going as observers."

"When does the convention meet?" Gideon asked. He seemed to have come slowly out of his disturbing meditations, making an obvious effort to join the conversation.

"Next month. The middle of December," Favian said.

"More madness," Gideon said, frowning. "Madness to declare the war in the first place, madness to break up the Union over it rather than see it through. The Lord wants both the British and ourselves humbled, I think, and he has chosen the war as a means of doing it, letting our madness run loose and showing it to ourselves."

The last was said with fire, and Favian saw Maria-Anna's eyes glowing: Gideon was himself again. They spoke of politics as Grimes served cordials and cigars, Gideon venting his intemperate opinions mixed with biblical quotations and intimate knowledge of the inner workings of New England's soul. The afternoon waned, and Favian, recollecting that he would have to go to the *Louisiana* to change into his dress uniform for the Defense Committee meeting, stood to take his congé.

"Can you not stay for supper?" Maria-Anna asked. "We are having some acquaintances over and will be playing a little cards. We would have liked, considering the news about Gideon's father, to have called it off; but there was no way of letting everyone know."

"There is a meeting of the Defense Committee. I must attend," Favian said, surprised that Gideon would allow card-playing in his rooms, a habit denounced by every New England parson as a certain route to Hell—Maria-Anna had very obviously made a change in him.

"Perhaps you can come afterwards. We shall be going quite late, I think," she said. Favian bowed.

"I will do my best," he said.

"Favian, I notice that ye wear a sword," Gideon said, standing, walking with Favian to the door. "I would like to caution ye—if ye wear a sword in this city, and not a uniform with it, it signals ye're ready for a fight."

"Does it?" Favian wondered, looking down at the presentation sword.

"It's so," Gideon said. "If ye don't wish to be called out, do not wear a blade. I know you are a stranger here and ye might be afraid to walk without protection, so carry a pocket pistol or a swordstick, like me." He reached for his stick in its stand by the door and pulled out a wicked two-foot blade.

"I'll take your advice. Thank you," Favian said. The thought he had been wearing a challenge at his side all day was alarming; he had fought enough duels in his life to be wary of blundering into an unnecessary one.

"I'll walk Favian to the lobby," Maria-Anna announced, taking his arm. Favian took his hat and bade farewell to his cousin, then turned into the corridor.

"I want to thank you for diverting Gideon so expertly just now," she said. "Black moods can fall on him so easily—though it's not so common as once it was," she added with self-satisfaction.

"It's a family trait, I'm afraid," Favian said, and then wondered at himself for this sudden confession.

"Is it?" she asked. Her arm felt warm at his side. Favian was suddenly aware that it had been weeks since he'd touched a woman. "I wonder if Grimes has them."

"Grimes? Your butler?"

"He's not a butler; he's Gideon's cabin steward. We have a house nigger as butler back home," Maria-Anna said, relinquishing his arm as they entered the lobby. She looked up at him. "Grimes is your uncle Malachi's bastard. One of many, I gather."

"Good heavens!" Malachi's cheerful leaps from one bed to another were a family legend; it had long been a worry that some offspring would appear to claim an inheritance.

"He's a good servant, though," she continued. "I hope I will see you tonight."

"I'll do my best," he said and took her hand to kiss.

"I'm glad you're here," she said. "Gideon has been fretting over his family; he can't stand not being in New England."

She turned away. Favian watched her disappear in the corridor, then turned away and walked out into the street. It was a hot day, the streets still full of laughing people in a holiday mood. He watched the Creole ladies as he walked, seeing their proud bearing, appreciating the way they cultivated their own immodest beauty; but strangely he could not get Maria-Anna out of his mind. Odd, he thought, that she should seem much more alive in his memory than the Creole women were in his present—she was not beautiful; her face bore traces of a hard life; she was with child; but still there was something in her that Favian could not forget.

He bought some fruit punch from a vendor to quench his sudden thirst, then walked to the levee to find his boat.

FOUR

"Interesting that you should have resurrected Porter's old game," said Master-Commandant Daniel Todd Patterson, walking beside Favian on the precariously narrow single sidewalk beside the muddy quagmire of Chartres Street. "I hadn't thought about it in years."

"It wasn't I who resurrected it," Favian said. "That was Jacob Jones; and Lieutenant Stone did most of the work. I just watch; the midshipmen learned it faster than I could, and their suggestions have been quite valuable."

"I suppose they find it preferable to conic sections and French irregular verbs," said Patterson.

"Truly, sir, they do. During our cruise we let them play, as a voluntary thing, on the wardroom floor on Sundays, if they weren't on watch. The attendance was quite good; even the chaplain became an enthusiast."

They were speaking of a sailing game, played with little ship models on a floor or table, that Favian had approved for the purpose of teaching midshipmen fleet maneuvers and tactics. The original had been designed by David Porter, the same Porter whose famous cruise in the Pacific had come to such a tragic end the year before, when Porter was a mere lieutenant and held prisoner with the rest of the *Philadelphia*'s crew in Tripoli. The purpose had been to continue the education of the prisoner-midshipmen during their confinement, and the game had been forgotten after the prisoners were released. Jacob Jones, *Macedo-*

nian's first American captain and a midshipman who had learned the game in the Moorish prison, had been blockaded by the British for over a year, and had been confronted by a gunroom full of untrained midshipmen to whom, because of the blockade, he'd been unable to teach their tasks. He'd remembered the game, and his excellent first officer, Adrian Stone, had created a much more elaborate version under Jones's direction; *Macedonian*'s mids had for the most part become enthusiasts and were continuing the games even now that the frigate had broken the blockade.

And, as Favian had stated, even the chaplain was a player. Dr. Talthibius Solomon had been, like the frigate's other officers, picked by Jones; Favian had initially found him pleasant, but a little ineffectual and more than a little foolish: the man's sermons had been strange rambling discourses on academic subjects best left in the academies. But a strange metamorphosis had taken place—Dr. Solomon had proved a surprisingly martial preacher. During the capture of the *Carnation,* Solomon had been the first aboard the enemy corvette, slicing at the British with his cutlass. Since then he'd begun taking an active, growing interest in elements of the midshipman's curriculum. At noon he had been found on the quarterdeck with a sextant, doing the noon sight along with the mids; he had stripped off his coat and collar and gone aloft to learn the lines, shrouds, and sails; he had learned to operate Markham's Recording Log. Lieutenant Hourigan, acting as first officer now that Stone was off with the *Carnation,* had informed Favian that the preacher had begun borrowing books on seamanship and tactics.

Favian, during the mad dash from the Leeward Islands to New Orleans, had been far too busy to spare any thought for the chaplain. Most chaplains knew nothing about the sea, and cared to know nothing. In most elements of a warship's life, save that of drinking port in the wardroom, they were useless, and the crews treated them with the half contempt they reserved for all landsmen, and in general thought them unlucky Jonahs. Dr. Solomon, at least, stood fair to earn some respect from the hands by becoming something of a sailor, and Favian could hardly do anything but approve. It was odd, though, to look up aloft to check the trim of the sails and see an ordained priest of the Episcopalian Church, with a doctorate from the College of New Jersey, skylarking in the rigging like a fifteen-year-old midshipman.

Even his sermons had improved. Though they still bore a

lamentable tendency to wander into odd philosophical and etymological culs-de-sac, Dr. Solomon had made a laudable attempt to stick to the point, and his "double-shotted" sermon on the subject of intolerance, delivered after the reputed witch Kuusikoski had been beaten, had included some fine ranting passages, complete with nautical jargon supplied, Favian thought, by the wardroom officers, which had greatly impressed the hands.

"I would be honored, sir," said Patterson, "if you would present me with a copy of Porter's rules. With only one manned schooner and six gunboats on station, our junior officers here get no opportunity for learning the tasks involved in maneuvering larger ships, let alone fleets. The game might prove useful."

"I shall send to *Macedonian* on the next pilot boat," Favian said. "It will probably take them some time to write a copy; the rules are not well codified and keep changing with each game."

"No hurry, sir, no hurry," said Patterson. "With the present emergency, I think it is best to keep the boys' minds on their current tasks." He shrugged deeper into his gold-laced coat. "It will be cold tonight," he said.

"I'm surprised at the extremes of temperature, sir," said Favian. "It was a hot afternoon."

"The British invaders will be surprised as well, let us hope," Patterson said. "Sweltering in the daylight hours, befogged in the morning, freezing at night . . . half the British force may die of sickness before we fight them. Certainly the West Indian regiments, used to the climate of Jamaica, will be greatly handicapped here."

"I hope so, sir." They entered Governor Claiborne's residence and handed their hats to the black butler; they were shown into Claiborne's study, where the Defense Committee was meeting.

It had been much enlarged since the previous night's meeting and contained so many dazzling uniforms that the two in Navy blue stood out simply by their plainness. Villeré had brought his two sons as aides-de-camp, Plauché had brought aides of his own, and also present was General Jean-Joseph Humbert, a French immigrant, who, as Patterson informed Favian, had led an invasion of Ireland in 1798, and with a motley army of French regulars and Irish rebels had inflicted several defeats on the British before the "Republic of Connaught" was smashed at Ballinamuck by Cornwallis—the same Cornwallis who had surrendered Yorktown and ended the American Revolution. Humbert, a French republican, had subsequently opposed the Empire and been exiled by Napoleon; he was a plump, gray-haired man, wearing the uniform of the Louisiana Blues, the Irish regiment who had adopted him, but Favian saw that his unmartial appearance was belied by the cynical, knowing eyes of the professional officer. The speaker of the Louisiana House, Magloire Guichard, had made an appearance, along with Philip Louallier, a prominent legislator. The legislature's Committee of Defense was present in the person of Bernard de Marigny, the wealthiest planter in Louisiana, and a haughty leader of the Creole faction—evidently the governor had invited him in an effort to compose the differences between one Defense Committee and the other. Edward Livingston was present, a local attorney and man of affairs, brother of the chancellor Robert Livingston who had been partners with Robert Fulton back in New York, and there were a number of other people, uniformed and in mufti, who had, Favian thought, no conceivable business there at all.

The meeting was disorderly and accomplished little. The original few members of the Defense Committee had been far from united; expanding it to a Committee for Public Safety did little but encourage chaos. Ostensibly the purpose of the meeting was to decide where to station the available forces, and everyone seemed to have their own ideas, most of which were spoken at the top of their lungs. Governor Claiborne, Favian thought, seemed to consider himself a master strategist, an opinion which most of the others seemed inclined to dispute. The arguments were bewildering: Favian heard reference to Lake Borgne and Bay St. Louis, the English Turn, the Gentilly Road, Bayou Terre aux Boeufs, and Bayou Lafourche, none of which he had ever heard of. He sat by Patterson and watched the other officer's frown deepen, his face growing scarlet and his eyes hard; in the end Patterson stood up, whispered "let us withdraw" to Favian, took a map from the table under Claiborne's nose while the governor was arguing a point with Livingston, and walked with Favian into the next room.

"Blasted Creole ballroom dancing!" he snarled. "That's all it is. Change partners and dance! Everyone wants to have his say in the saving of Louisiana and doesn't want anyone else to get the credit! What a farce!" He spread out the map on a desk, took a cigar from one of Claiborne's brass-bound leather cigar cases, and used it as a pointer.

"Here's our problem, Captain Markham. I knew you couldn't understand more than half of what they were saying—not your fault, o' course, you just don't know the conditions here—and I thought I'd take you apart and show you what the Navy can accomplish. If we can make up our minds what the Navy will do—we're not under their jurisdiction, so we can do what we want—perhaps it might show them how to conduct a united strategy."

"Very well," Favian said. He wondered if Patterson was playing the old Navy game, trying to get Favian to waive his superior rank and leave the station in Patterson's hands; but he thought not. Patterson seemed too angry, too earnest in his tone, too vigorous in his gestures. He was clearly a man who wanted things done, and he was prepared to make a positive example of the Navy even if he had to forego his commodore's privileges.

"As you can see, the defense of New Orleans presents a devilish problem from start to finish," Patterson said, pointing at the map with his cigar. "There are far too many ways to attack it. We would prefer that the British simply come straight up the river; it's a ninety-mile journey, against the current the entire way, and with bars over the mouths of the river that are too shallow for many of their largest ships. Fort St. Philip, planted right on a bend that is tricky navigation even without worrying about a masked battery suddenly opening fire, could hold them off for weeks, with or without the *Macedonian,* and quite possibly sink large numbers of their ships right in the bend, forming obstructions. Ships have been known to hang in the Plaquemines Bend for weeks, waiting for a wind to get them upriver—the fort's in a good place."

Favian knew the truth of Patterson's observation. When *Macedonian* had sailed, with painful slowness, to the bend in the river, his first glimpse of the fort, in bad repair though it was, had made him thankful it wasn't in enemy hands.

"There's another fort farther up, Fort St. Leon, but it's in very poor condition and wouldn't stop them for long. Then there's the possibility that the British might take Mobile and march overland to the Mississippi, cutting New Orleans off from the north," Patterson said. "That was obviously the enemy's preferred method, but the battle of Fort Bowyer in September stopped them, at least for the moment."

Favian looked down at the map, a maddening confusion of

waterways, lakes, and islands, each with a neatly scribed name in French, Spanish, or English, sometimes all three. "New Orleans is almost surrounded by water," Patterson went on, "and there are dozens of water routes can be used to get to the city, outflanking the forts. The most important of these are the two lakes, Borgne and Pontchartrain. If the enemy take Borgne, there is a waterway—they call them *bayous* around here—from Borgne almost to the walls of the city, called Bayou Bienvenue. Bienvenue has a number of tributaries that feed into the Mississippi downriver from the city, Bayou Jumonville, and Bayou Mazant that feeds into some old canals that lead straight into the river. That's six easy water routes to the city just from Lake Borgne, and there's a land route as well, the Chef Menteur Road that leads from just north of the city to the lake. If the British take Borgne, all we can do is hope they don't find any of these routes, the land route in particular.

"If the British get through Les Rigolets from Lake Borgne, then they'll have broken into Lake Pontchartrain. Fortunately the chief water route from Pontchartrain to the city, the Bayou St. John, is guarded by Fort St. John, which can easily be put into repair. The land route is undefended entirely. The British could land on the Gentilly Peninsula here, a rocky ridge—firm ground in the midst of all this swamp, a good place for a military encampment—and then they could take the Gentilly Road straight to New Orleans."

Patterson straightened, looking at the map with a tactical eye. He pointed at a little bay north of the Mississippi Sound marked Bay St. Louis. "That's where I've put the gunboats," he said. "Five gunboats and a pair of tenders under Lieutenant Thomas Ap Catesby Jones—Tac Jones, he's called. D'ye know him?"

"No, I do not."

"A thorough sailor, and a fighter," Patterson said. "There's a little fort in Bay St. Louis, and a magazine; Jones can supply himself from the magazine, even if he's cut off from the city. From Bay St. Louis he can move along the Mississippi Sound to Mobile Bay if Mobile is threatened again, and if the British appear to be moving through Lake Borgne he can move to block them. If he can't hold Borgne, he can retreat to Pontchartrain. Borgne and Pontchartrain are shallow lakes; the deepest soundings are three fathoms, and the entrances to Borgne are no deeper than two. The gunboats will be at their best there, since no

British vessels larger than a barge will get at 'em. The two tenders can be used to carry messages to the city."

There was a satisfied, grim little smile on Patterson's lips; Favian understood it, knowing Patterson had made the best use out of his cranky Jefferson gunboats, putting the normally useless little craft where anything that came at them would be of their own size or smaller.

"There are dozens of other waterways," Patterson said. "Some of them are large enough to get a sizeable force through. I know, for I've done it myself."

He pointed with his unlit cigar. "There's the reason we had to clear the Baratarian pirates out of our rear," he said. "From Barataria Bay the Bayou Pierrot leads into Little Barataria Lake, and from there to Lake Ouatchas, and from there to the right bank of the Mississippi near New Orleans. The Laffites have been running their contraband through there for years; they could just as easily put a British army into their pirogues.

"And then there's Bayou Lafourche. It runs from the Gulf west of Barataria to a point on the Mississippi halfway between New Orleans and Baton Rouge. I brought the *Carolina* and the gunboats through there earlier this year when we burned the Baratarian commune; if it's big enough for the *Carolina,* the British could get their schooners and all their armies through on barges. I can only hope the British don't know of these routes; they're unfortified and there would be no warning of their approach until redcoats started forming up on the levee.

"There are other bayous as well. Bayou Terre aux Boeufs runs from the Gulf south of Lake Borgne straight to the English Turn below New Orleans, bypassing both Fort St. Philip and Fort St. Leon."

"Can the bayous be blocked?" Favian asked. "There can't be a current to speak of; perhaps they could just be dammed up."

Patterson looked up from the map, his eyes narrowing. "Could be," he said. "Most of them, anyway. Lafourche is big, but it could be blocked with timber."

"I think," said Favian, "we should bring that motion before the committee."

"Aye, sir, we should," Patterson said. "As soon as possible."

"Your plans for the gunboats strike me as sound," Favian said. "But there are other ships present: *Carolina* and your gunboat; *Macedonian*, and *Louisiana*."

They turned as a door opened behind them. It was General Humbert, the French exile; he gave them a sly look and closed the door behind him.

"*Vouz parlez français?*" he asked.

"*Mais oui, mon général,*" Favian said. In the same language, he continued. "May I be of service?"

"You can divert me from those fools out there," Humbert said, strolling up to the table, glancing at the map thrown over the table. "It was the same in Ireland. Talk, talk; the Irish are good at talking." He helped himself to another of Claiborne's cigars, cut the end, and lit it. "In Ireland I was able to maintain order; I had my Frenchmen to keep the Irish in line, and I gave the orders. At least until Crauford's dragoons cut my men to pieces." He gestured with the cigar toward the door he'd just passed through. "Many hounds without a master, that is all," he said. "They are many small men: Claiborne is the best, but he thinks he is a genius and is not, and he has been in New Orleans long enough to have taken sides in most of the city feuds; his political opponents will not trust him.

"The city needs a strong man," Humbert continued. "A strong man from outside, not poisoned by the quarrels of the city and leader enough to bring these hounds to heel."

"Yourself, sir?" Favian asked with polite cynicism; he had seen enough would-be Napoleons putting themselves forward, intending to save the republic with one absurd plan or another, and incidentally make their reputations at the same time—the Army was full of such amateurs, and far too many had managed to make themselves general officers; for the most part they simply got in the way of those competent professionals who knew what needed doing and how to do it.

"Not I, sir, not I," Humbert said, shaking his head. "I, too, have been here for too many years. And I can't speak English—until now there seemed no reason to learn, and now it's too late. I was speaking in general terms only; I had no one person in mind. Perhaps Governor Claiborne will yet rise to the occasion; his brother Ferdinand became an adequate general with no training and defeated the Creeks at the Holy Ground."

Favian sensed a certain condescension in that *adequate* and understood Humbert's implied criticism. *Adequacy* was sufficient, perhaps, to beat the disorganized Creeks, but to fight Major

General Sir Edward Pakenham and his Peninsular legions *adequacy* would clearly not be enough.

"We were speaking of deploying the squadron," Patterson said. His French was not as fluent as Favian's and had the New Orleans accent, a sign he had learned most of it here. His tone was curt; he clearly intended to dismiss Humbert with the remark.

Humbert just as clearly declined to be dismissed. He waved his cigar vaguely, sat in a stiff-backed chair, and said, "By all means, gentlemen, continue."

Patterson watched Humbert with clear distrust, then turned to Favian, speaking deliberately in English. "I had planned to use *Carolina* as our reserve. When the British strike the river, they can only move comfortably along the banks of the river, along the ground of the plantations—their forces would have no hope of getting through the swamp farther away from the river. *Carolina*, and *Louisiana* if we could ever find crew for her, could be invaluable in breaking up any columns of march or in harassing encampments."

Favian nodded. "Very sound," he said.

"I think," Patterson said, "our problem now is what to do with *Macedonian*." He rubbed his jaw. "If you had arrived with a schooner like your cousin Gideon's, I'd have a notion of what to suggest—but a thirty-eight-gun frigate! That's like praying for a meal and being granted a banquet for fifty. It's just never been in my considerations."

Favian looked at the map, at the soundings with their shallow depths, the bars over the mouths of the Mississippi. The area was clearly unsuited for large warships; shallow-draft vessels, like those Patterson already had, were ideal. Patterson's little gun-boats and schooners would not only be able to navigate in the shallow waters but would be able to have a certain amount of freedom on the great river itself. *Macedonian*, as its experience in sailing the Mississippi as far as the Plaquemines Bend indicated, could only sail upriver if weather conditions were ideal, and could scarcely maneuver at all. If she were deployed against the enemy, she could never be retrieved once she was committed; once set to bombarding an enemy shore, she would remain there until the winds were suitable to get her out, a sitting duck for any enemy artillery. Perhaps he should simply take her crew off her, Favian thought, and use the Macedonians to crew Patterson's unmanned boats. Or perhaps, he thought, now that he had delivered his message, he would be of more value to the United States should he simply head back to sea and continue his journey to the East Indies.

But no; *Macedonian*'s duty was here, at the mouths of the Mississippi. A British force, better equipped, better officered than any that had landed on America's shores since the war had begun, was about to strike at New Orleans. Even if the waters were unsuitable, *Macedonian* was the largest American naval presence, and Favian the senior naval officer. He would have to stay.

"*Macedonian*, I think, must wait," Favian said. "I cannot hope to fight the large fleet Cochrane will bring with him; there will probably be half a dozen ships with twice *Macedonian*'s number of guns. What *Macedonian* can do is delay the enemy for longer than they can afford. I can keep at the enemy's heels; I can cut out their transports; I can force them to divert ships to hunt me down, as Porter did in the Pacific. They will be expecting nothing larger than your schooners; I can give them something they will not expect. As long as *Macedonian* is free, the British will never be able to move on New Orleans without looking over their shoulders. I can make them *uneasy*, Captain Patterson."

Patterson looked at him, his eyes blazing; Humbert, not understanding, shifted uneasily in his seat. "By Jerusalem, sir!" Patterson said. "That's well said!"

Favian smiled; it was a professionally cultivated smile, the sort he had allowed himself on board the *United States*, standing on the horse block watching his guns hammer the *Macedonian* at her capture, encouraging the hands. It took so little to inspire these martial men, really; a speech, a far-off victory, news of an enemy coming closer, but not yet too close. Favian had said little concrete, for there was nothing too concrete to say: any real planning would have to be done after word was brought that the British had appeared.

"Thank you, Captain Patterson," he said. He looked down at the map. It was time to clarify the command situation here; after seeing the Committee for Public Safety baying and howling at one another, it was more important than ever that the Navy had a united command. "I think your squadron is well deployed; I have no intention of altering your dispositions. I intend only to act here as the service and the situation may require, and as the captain of the *Macedonian*. To alter the chain of command, at a time like this, would be to invite chaos. Captain Patterson, I put my trust in you."

And so, seeing Patterson's heightened color, the war-horse fire in his eyes, Favian knew he had, more than if he had simply and brusquely stepped into command, made Patterson his subordinate; by confirming Patterson in a job he already possessed, and by all appearances was doing well, he had made a friend bound to him by a debt of gratitude, to whom a suggestion would have as great an effect as a command. Favian had not served those years under Decatur for nothing; for all his resentment of the Navy's strictures, he knew how to play the Navy game as well as anyone.

"I am honored by your confidence, Captain Markham," Patterson said, trapped—Favian wondered if he realized it—by honor and confidence, by the shameless manipulation of his own better qualities.

Favian saw General Humbert's cynical look, and only by the purest effort of will managed to keep from answering it by one of his own. The old French republican, Favian was certain, knew well the contradictions of the service and how to manipulate them: he knew the massive paradox implied by the existence of an autocratic, privileged officer class, dependent on rank and seniority but sworn to the service of a republic where all men were equal in the eyes of the law. The officers commanded a class of private soldiers and sailors who were enslaved to the Roman tyranny of the Articles of War, living a subterranean existence under a system of martial law that recognized no Bill of Rights or Declaration of the Rights of Man. They were contradictions that the republic required for its survival—even now martial law might save New Orleans, while the freedoms granted by the Bill of Rights, as currently represented by the bickering inanity of the Committee for Public Safety, might lose it—but Favian knew they were contradictions that one day would have to be faced squarely.

The Navy having finished its discussion of deployments, and having concluded on various resolutions to be passed before the committee, Patterson and Favian lit Claiborne's cigars and sat down comfortably to speak with the general. Humbert was a born raconteur; his tales of France during the Revolution and the Directory, and of the short-lived Republic of Connaught, were told in a coarse, colorful soldier-French that made clear his contempt for *aristos*, incompetents, politicians, bureaucrats, and the entire Bonaparte family, whom he blamed for the destruction of the ideals of the Revolution and its replacement with a tyranny far more efficient and encompassing than that of the ancien régime.

Humbert, after his capture at Ballinamuck, had grown to know his adversary Cornwallis quite well, and Favian listened with considerable interest to Humbert's anecdotes about the able British general who had rampaged so effectively through the southern colonies during the American Revolution, and whose eventual surrender secured American independence. Humbert hadn't known of Cornwallis's adventures in America, and Favian and Patterson had known nothing of Cornwallis's subsequent career in India—where he had apparently become known for his liberal reforms, concerning which he had told Humbert in detail, apparently in an attempt to demonstrate the superiority of enlightened liberalism over revolution by guillotine—and in Ireland, where he had put down the Republic of Connaught, treating his French captives well while exercising a well-bred restraint on the number of atrocities visited on the rebel Irish. "The very best sort of Englishman," Humbert concluded. "Far superior to that barbarian Crauford who unleashed his dragoons on the Irish who had already laid down their arms. I quite liked Cornwallis, but you must agree with me, gentlemen, that a decent man in service to a poisonous system only makes the poison taste sweeter without altering the nature of the poison, no?"

Favian agreed, but privately wondered at Humbert's assessment of Cornwallis's character. When hearing of how Cornwallis's vicious subordinate Crauford had butchered the Irish militia after their surrender, Favian was reminded of how, in the Revolution, Banastre Tarleton's Legion had been unleashed on the population of the Carolinas, a cruel spree of murder, plunder, and atrocity—perhaps it had been Cornwallis's policy to unleash brutal men to chastise a rebellious population, while keeping his own hands clean in the event the cruelty miscarried. If that was his policy, it had certainly succeeded; during the Yorktown surrender no one had cried for Cornwallis's execution as they had cried for Tarleton's.

Stubbing out their cigars, Favian, Patterson, and Humbert rejoined the meeting of the Committee for Public Safety. It appeared that nothing had gone forward since they'd left; if anything, matters had degenerated. Calling for the floor, Favian quickly introduced motions to block the bayous (accepted; word would be spread to the planters to get their slaves to do it, an irregular, inefficient procedure but the best anyone could hope for), to provision, garrison, and repair the forts (accepted, though no mechanism existed for carrying out the resolution), to provide a bounty for sailors enlisting in the Navy (taken under advisement for consideration by the legislature), and for the declaration of martial law (rejected after an indignant speech by the Speaker of the House).

This sudden burst of activity concluded, the Committee for Public Safety found itself a bit breathless and adjourned. Favian said a formal farewell to all present, resolving to pay a private call on Governor Claiborne the following day in order to present a few suggestions. Claiborne was, after all, the commander in chief of the Louisiana militia and was constitutionally permitted to issue them orders without the necessity of going through these turbulent meetings. Favian hoped he could convince Claiborne that the occasional use of a few arbitrary military powers might not shake the foundations of New Orleans society.

Turning down invitations from both Patterson and Claiborne, Favian headed for Gideon's hotel, wondering if Gideon and Maria-Anna were still receiving guests. The night was chill; Favian's breath frosted before him as he walked, and he saw thin skins of ice forming on the surface of street puddles. Despite the cold the life of the city continued unabated; saloon doors stood open to the raucous throngs while dandified men and elegant women promenaded on the narrow sidewalks or rode slowly past in open carriages. Even the brothels' touts were still busy soliciting business. Favian bought a hot toddy from a sidewalk vendor, warming himself with hot tafia—the local rum—while watching the evening throngs, and then walked briskly to Gideon's hotel and sent up his card.

Mrs. Desplein came down to welcome him; at the sight of her pretty face Maria-Anna's phrase came to mind, *good but unscrupulous,* and he smiled privately as he followed her to Gideon's rooms. The phrase seemed symbolic of New Orleans itself: tropical days and cold nights, expanding but decaying, slave but riotously free, decadent but vigorous. This city, this woman, were both far more interesting than the martial contradictions by which Favian himself lived—the iron code of the serving officer.

Gideon met him at the door, clasping hands, ushering him into a room full of chattering guests, almost exclusively male with the exception of a pair of beautifully groomed Creole ladies surrounded by a swarm of peacock admirers. "I'm glad to see thee, Favian," he said. "I would like to introduce Mr. Edward Livingston, my agent here, who was curious about the Hartford Convention. Ye're fresh from New England; perhaps ye can enlighten him."

"We have met," Favian said, surprised to encounter a member of the Committee for Public Safety in Gideon's suite so soon after the first meeting had ended.

Livingston murmured polite greetings. "It so happens, Mr. Livingston," Favian said, "that I'm acquainted with your late brother's partner, Mr. Fulton. I had occasion to visit the *Demologos* last summer and was quite convinced of its inevitable success."

"Then I must monopolize you, sir," Livingston said. "I have not met previously with an eyewitness to Mr. Fulton's steam battery—and I am still curious about the Hartford Convention."

Favian was willing to answer questions concerning the *Demologos*; he was professionally qualified to render judgments on its design and prospects for success. Tempted though he was to denounce the Hartford Convention as a treasonous assembly best dealt with at the point of Marine bayonets, he held his tongue. Livingston might be a supporter of the convention, or at any rate an opponent of Madison, and Favian did not want to politically alienate this obviously important man. Instead he delivered impartially what news he had, and before his opinions were solicited, excused himself on the grounds that he had not yet paid his respects to his hostess.

Maria-Anna was in the suite's withdrawing room; she was half reclining on her birthing stool, playing cards on a table of red baize. She called his name with a smile; he approached and kissed her hand and was introduced to the players: Denis de la Ronde, owner of the "Versailles" plantation; another Creole named Declouet; Captain Fontenoy of the *Franklin* privateer, the extraordinarily handsome man whose unexpected arrival that morning had resulted in Captain and Mrs. Markham being late for their luncheon appointment; and a smiling, lean Kentuckian named

Hardy, who rose and excused himself from the table as Favian entered.

"I regret I must take my leave, Mrs. Markham," Hardy said.

"Must you, sir?" Maria-Anna asked with a smile. "Favian, will you take Mr. Hardy's place? We are playing *poque*."

"Gladly, ma'am, but I don't know the game," Favian said, happy for an opportunity to get away from military affairs and politics.

"*Poque* is easy to learn," Maria-Anna said, sweeping up the cards from the table. "Grimes will give you tokens. I suggest you start with a hundred dollars."

Favian was surprised at the size of the stakes; it must have shown, for Hardy bent over his shoulder and grinned. "Easy to learn, she tells'ee, but hard to master," he said. "Take care, Captain Markham; I'm skinned."

Favian gave Grimes a marker for a hundred dollars and received a neat pile of tokens. Maria-Anna explained the game in a few practiced words and dealt the cards.

Made cautious by the size of the stakes, Favian played at first with great care; he only plunged on a full hand or better and strove not to increase his capital but to keep from losing it. Gradually he began to acquire an idea of the odds and, what was perhaps more important, a notion of opponents' characters: de la Ronde staked large sums when he had a good hand, driving his opponents out of the betting when a better strategy might have been to have kept the play moving, gradually increasing the stakes so as to win larger sums—but then de la Ronde seemed more interested in impressing the others with his wealth than with winning. Declouet was strictly a plunger, throwing his money into the play without any notion of strategy, losing heavily. Fontenoy's strategy seemed to be similar to Favian's, to avoid losing rather than to win. It was by watching Maria-Anna play that Favian learned the game.

She played hostess and cards at the same time, calling for Grimes to bring drinks—she drank only tea herself—greeting from her half-reclining position the procession of people moving in and out of the drawing room; but Favian saw the way the smile hesitated, her eyes narrowing, as she examined the cards, as her gaze flickered from one player to another, gauging Declouet's desperation, de la Ronde's gallant play, Favian's careful impassivity. Her play was precise, mathematical; when she folded she would speak with someone outside the game, playing hostess, but Favian saw the way her eyes rarely left the table, how she would still be sizing up her opponents even though she had left the game. Favian suspected Maria-Anna Markham was giving a masterful performance, knowing the game and her opponents far better than her smiling, flirting exterior could ever have indicated, and wondered if anyone less adept at dissimulation than himself would ever have seen it.

At the end of the evening she had won hundreds of dollars, Declouet had lost a small fortune, de la Ronde, who had rallied toward the end of the evening, was down a few hundred, Fontenoy, having reached his limit for the evening, had been driven out of the game, and Favian was thankful to have lost only twenty dollars. Favian, though not by nature a gambler, knew enough about gambling to know that when a single person in a card game wins heavily while everyone else loses, for that person gambling is not a pastime, but a profession. Maria-Anna played *poque* as well as Stephen Decatur, for example, played hero, and with the same ruthless, intelligent dedication.

Declouet and de la Ronde kissed her hand as they left the table, offering gallantries, Declouet mopping his brow. Maria-Anna turned to Favian while Grimes, acting as banker, swept up her tokens. "You play well, Favian," she said.

"All that I know of *poque* I learned from watching you," Favian said—a pleasantry, but the truth.

She smiled—was there in her smile that same cynicism he had seen in Humbert's speech, and in his own heart? The ability to counterfeit the appearance that society demands while remaining her own disbelieving self? Favian suddenly felt himself at a loss; he had never known a woman to play this deceptive game; he had known it only as the province of men. Favian felt the earth falling away beneath him; it was fortunate that she accidentally moved him to firm ground by her next question.

"Is the city of New Orleans safer now, following the meeting of the Defense Committee?"

"I think not," Favian said. "Some small matters were concluded, but there were simply too many people involved—a warship can only have one captain."

"That is Louisiana in small: far too many captains," Maria-Anna said. "I am beginning to agree with Gideon, that it is time to be away. Though I hate to leave these games of *poque* behind; I gather the Yankees do not permit their women to gamble."

"It would be a very liberal Yankee house that had so much as a pack of cards," Favian said. "They are, in the popular phrase, 'the devil's tickets to Hell.' I'm surprised you have found Gideon so willing to countenance gambling in his establishment."

Her eyes flickered wryly. "Gideon and I have achieved a certain éclaircissement in regard to our hobbyhorses. We are both strong people, and we found it necessary to grant one another certain liberties. And now," she said, seeing Grimes had finished counting out her winnings, "if you'll excuse me, I must play hostess a little."

Favian rose, kissed her hand, and relinquished her to her guests. He returned to the salon, saw that Livingston had departed and he was safe from delivering political opinions, and found Gideon at his elbow.

"I hope ye did not lose more than ye could afford, Favian," Gideon said.

"I was lucky in that regard," Favian said.

"Declouet and de la Ronde are the heads of wealthy, established Creole families," Gideon said. "They can afford to play at Maria-Anna's table." He lowered his voice to make certain no one overheard. "It is a wicked habit, I know, but she acquired it before she met me, from her first husband. I don't know what the man was thinking of. These Creoles are confounded lax where their women are concerned. My conscience will be much relieved when we return to New England and Maria-Anna will be forced to discontinue the practice."

"At least she adds to your income instead of draining it," Favian said.

"Aye," Gideon said. "But what to do with the winnings? I do not wish to have such money in my house." He lowered his voice again. "I have Grimes keep a total of the winnings and privately give the exact amount to charity," he said. Favian looked at him in dawning surprise, realizing that he was observing a marriage in which, despite Gideon's puritan conviction and Maria-Anna's predatory ferocity, the husband and wife understood each other very well indeed.

"I was happy to see ye getting on with Livingston," Gideon went on. "Ye will accomplish little here without him; he is the most important man in the state, more important, I think, than Claiborne."

"Is he? I was not aware of that."

"He was the mayor of New York, I believe," Gideon said. "One of his clerks stole a lot of money, and Livingston was legally responsible for it. He honorably made good the debt, but the affair left him bankrupt; he came to New Orleans to start over and soon became a wealthy man. The governor resents him, and not without reason; Livingston can accomplish much more than Claiborne can, and with less effort. That is why I have made him my agent here; he is honest enough, as these Louisiana men go, but sees no reason why he should not make a profit with his inside knowledge."

Livingston, the governor, Kaintucks, Creoles—Favian felt a burst of impatience against these disunited factions. "But will these parties ever form ranks?" Favian asked. "There is genuine danger here, and all I have seen is squabbling."

"They will unite behind a strong man who knows his business," Gideon said. "Otherwise they will bicker until the British are in the Place d'Armes, and once the city is lost, they will bicker over whose fault it was that New Orleans fell."

"You are not the first who has expressed that opinion," Favian said. "General Humbert privately gave me a similar view."

"Humbert? I've heard the name, but I don't know him." Gideon reached in his pocket for chewing tobacco; he cut himself a chaw and spoke on. "Commodore Patterson is Livingston's man; ye'd do well to remember that."

"Is he?" Favian asked in surprise. "I saw no indication of that."

"Patterson's father married into Livingston's family," Gideon said. "It was the Livingstons who secured Patterson his appointment here and got him his lieutenant's commission when the Secretary of the Navy would have turned him down; Patterson owes him for that favor."

A naval commodore owned by a Louisiana attorney. Favian's training resisted the idea; he knew there were politics in the service, that many officers—himself included, truth to tell—had friendly congressmen who looked out for their interests, that sometimes harsh court-martial verdicts had been overturned due to political influence in Washington. But still he could feel his

Navy side closing ranks against the idea: even if such a thing were true, no Navy man should admit it. "I thought he owed his appointment to Captain David Porter, the last commodore here," Favian said. "I know they are friends."

"Whether the story is true or not, the city believes it," Gideon said. "Governor Claiborne certainly believes it, and until now it has prejudiced him against the Navy. Ye will find that New Orleans will believe any wild tale of intrigue, true or not."

Madness, Favian thought, to play at factional strife on the eve of an invasion. Hadn't the example of Washington, its public buildings burned by the British just a few short months ago, made clear the peril of making speeches and indulging in private vendettas when the enemy were marching on the gates?

Denis de la Ronde approached and bowed; Favian returned the greeting. "The invitation will reach you presently, Captain Markham," de la Ronde said, "but I would like to invite you personally to a ball held at my town house, in the Faubourg Marigny, next Wednesday night. I hope you will be able to attend."

"I am honored, sir, by the invitation. If my duty permits me to be in New Orleans, I will be present without fail."

"Your servant, sir."

"Your servant."

De la Ronde took his leave, and Favian found Gideon looking at him with a wondering eye. "For an American to be invited to one of the Creole balls is quite an honor, Favian," Gideon said. "Maria-Anna and I have never been invited, and de la Ronde is a frequent guest at Maria-Anna's card table."

Favian watched the Creole making his way across the room. "No doubt I am a novelty, Gideon," Favian said. "I've become accustomed to it." He was a victorious military leader, Favian knew; and that meant others attempted to use him, to use his reputation to further their own designs, from his hometown Federalists to the Society of Saint Something-or-other in New London. It was an inevitable consequence of celebrity, and one he loathed.

Gideon saw some friends leaving and went to bid his adieus; Favian walked back through the drawing room and went in search of a jakes. The convenience was through a short passage; after concluding his visit, he discovered Maria-Anna's maidservant Campaspe waiting in the corridor.

"Campaspe!" he said as she bobbed him a curtsy. "I thought you'd be long abed."

"I should be, Captain Favian," she said. "But I crept in through the servant's door to stay up and see some of the guests through the curtain. And now I've been given this message for Captain Fontenoy." She held up a small letter sealed with red wax. "I can't go in and give it to him or Mrs. Markham will know I've been here. Will you deliver it?"

"What the devil is it?" Favian asked, taking the letter and peering at the inscription, simply "Captain Fontenoy, snow *Franklin.*"

"It's from one of his lady friends," she said. "She wanted me to give it to him."

Favian looked at the letter, a kernel of suspicion growing in his mind. "Are you certain this letter isn't from *you*?" he asked.

"Captain Favian! Of course not!" Campaspe said, blushing. He looked at her closely—there was a certain sense of mischief in her, but that could be explained simply by her being entrusted to carry a billet-doux, and the blush seemed to belie guilt.

"Very well," Favian decided.

"Thank you, Captain Favian," she said, bobbed him another curtsy, and fled.

When he returned most of the party had left, but Fontenoy was speaking to some of the Creoles in the parlor. Fontenoy was a few years younger than Favian, and the life of the sea had only just begun to cut into his looks; he was still very handsome, and dressed with style. Favian recognized his French as an East Indian Creole, probably from Mauritius or Réunion. Favian waited for a pause in the conversation, then spoke quietly to Fontenoy.

"A word with you, sir, I beg."

"Honored, sir."

"I have been given a message for you by a servant," he said. "I do not vouch for it, but I am told it was given the servant by a lady."

Fontenoy looked down at the message in surprise, took it from Favian's gloved hand, and opened it. An expression of relief and contentment gradually spread over his features. "It is genuine, Captain," he said with a smile. "It is a message I have waited for for a long while. Forgive me, sir, but I must take my leave. Your servant."

"I'm happy to have been of some service, sir," Favian said,

bemused by the unusual message and Fontenoy's instant dash to meet the woman who presumably would, if she wasn't already, soon become his mistress. The privateer took his leave of Gideon and Maria-Anna and left the suite.

It was clearly approaching time to leave himself, and he hunted up Maria-Anna in the withdrawing room. She was speaking privately to Grimes, presumably concerning the *poque* receipts; Favian, not wishing to interrupt, waited for them to finish their business.

Grimes, Favian remembered, was a cousin, Malachi Markham's natural son. There seemed to be no family resemblance in those distinguished, middle-aged mulatto features, but Favian knew that for Gideon to accept the claim Grimes must have presented solid evidence.

Maria-Anna concluded her business and turned to him with a smile. It seemed strange to Favian how he had ever thought her plain; her sunbrowned face was animated by a liveliness unequaled by the pale, carefully groomed Creole women he had seen that day, and even with her advanced pregnancy she moved with grace as she walked toward Favian. He kissed her hand.

"I should return to the *Louisiana*," he said. "My boat's crew must be freezing on the wharves, if they aren't drunk in half the saloons on Custom House Street."

"You should take rooms in town, Favian," she said, putting her arm through his as she walked him back to the parlor. "Your boat's crew will thank you for it, and you will be able to attend the balls and social events of the season."

"I will take your advice, but not tonight," he said. "I still must think of my poor boat's crew."

He said his farewells, collected his hat and cloak from Mrs. Desplein, and left the hotel. The weather was freezing; there was ice on the sidewalk, but the brothels and saloons still seemed to be busy. For a moment he paused before the door of a sporting palace and considered the resumption of an old habit, but decided against it: the women would be tired after all their customers, and the boat's crew was still waiting. Perhaps after he was lodged in town he'd go in search of an elegant place.

His boat's crew were huddled under a tarpaulin as they rested on the thwarts; they gave off a collective reek of tafia, but he couldn't blame them for seeking consolation from the cold. None of them seemed outright drunk; Favian was uncertain whether to credit Kuusikoski for imposing a successful discipline or the likelihood they hadn't been able to afford more rum.

"Give 'em a 'nay nay,' Koskey," Favian said as *Louisiana* challenged the boat. He would decline the honors due a captain on his arrival; there was no point in getting the whole crew out of their hammocks.

He spent a restless night, his periods of wakefulness mixed with odd dreams in which Maria-Anna was delivered of her child on the red baize *poque* table, a child that was discovered to be General Sir Edward Pakenham, complete with red coat. The unnerving arrival brought Favian bolt awake, and he was able to resume a fitful sleep only hours later. Tafia punch, he decided, and Creole food; a deadly combination. That morning, drinking a potful of coffee to keep himself awake, he was not in the best frame of mind to receive a visit from Midshipman Lovette, who, it seemed, was about to fight a duel with one of the Mississippi Dragoons.

FIVE

"I don't understand it, sir," said Midshipman Irwin Lovette. A short, burly youth of seventeen whose broadening shoulders had clearly outgrown his best coat, he stood with Phillip Stanhope in Favian's cabin, ill at ease under Favian's baleful gaze. "I went to a restaurant yesterday for supper with Mr. Stanhope, here. The bill of fare was in French, and I didn't understand it all, so I pointed to the next table and told the waiter, 'I'll have what that man is eating.' The next thing I knew the man from the next table was standing up shouting challenges. Saying I'd insulted him. So now Mr. Stanhope has an appointment to meet the man's second this afternoon at five o'clock at the Place d'Armes at Chartres Street to arrange for the duel."

Favian's eyes turned to Stanhope. "That's *all*?" he asked.

"Mr. Lovette ordered the same meal, and this man challenged him?"

"Aye, sir," Stanhope said. "I have never heard of ordering a similar meal as being a cause for calling anyone out, and so I thought—" He hesitated for a moment, choosing his words carefully, then spoke. "I thought, sir, that as you had, ah, more experience in these matters than we, that we should apply to you for guidance."

"Sir, I am perfectly willing to be called out if the situation requires it," Lovette said. He reddened, searching for words, and Favian understood: Lovette would not want to be thought afraid to fight. "I consider my honor as precious as any man's," he blurted. "But for such a cause as this—! The man must be mad!"

Favian took a long draft of coffee to clear his head. This sounded like a French farce from the time of Louis Treize. "What did you say the man's name was?" he asked.

"Levesque, sir," Stanhope said, producing a card from his pocket. "Theseus Armand Levesque, lieutenant in the Mississippi Dragoons. His second is M. le Chevalier Jean Noel Gabriel de la Tour d'Aurillac."

La-di-da, Favian almost said, but restrained himself. He had heard neither of Levesque nor de la Tour d'Aurillac during his trips to town; but Gideon, in connection with the late Mr. Desplein, had mentioned the Mississippi Dragoons and their reputation for duelling. "Mr. Stanhope, I trust you will try to make up this quarrel when you meet M. de la Tour d'Aurillac—blast it, does the man actually use all those names? Just call him M. le Chevalier." Favian hated to grant knightly rank to a presumed American citizen, but it seemed to make the mouthful of a name easier to swallow.

"I will do my best to compose the quarrel," Stanhope said. "But if they insist on regarding Mr. Lovette's action as a mortal insult, I do not understand how I can avoid the encounter."

"I will not," Lovette said, turning red, "give an apology. There is nothing to apologize for."

Do you have a favorite biblical verse you wish read at your funeral? Favian almost asked. Any dragoon confident enough to call people out for such trivial reasons would be deadly, that stood to reason. Lovette's refusal to apologize would probably end any hope of reconciliation, Favian knew; if proper apology were not received for an insult, a duel would usually go forward.

"My hope, Captain Markham, is that Lieutenant Levesque might be known in town as a, er, madman," Stanhope said. "One cannot fight the insane."

"I doubt the Mississippi Dragoons would carry a lunatic on the rolls, Mr. Stanhope," Favian said. "But he might, I suppose, claim a rank that is not his. I will inquire in the town."

"Thank you, sir."

For a moment Favian considered forbidding the duel entirely; that would give Lovette a reason for refusing the engagement. During the *Experiment*'s cruise the year before, Midshipman Tolbert had wished to fight Midshipman Dudley, and Favian had forbidden it on the grounds that the brig was in enemy waters and could not afford to have two of its officers disabled.

But he had known that once the brig reached the United States, there was nothing he could do to prevent two midshipmen from going out if they were determined to do it; he had merely assured Midshipman Tolbert—the principal instigator—of his own personal opposition to the duel, and the fact that if the encounter went forward he could consider Favian an enemy. That approach would probably not work here. The earlier duel had been a fight between two Navy men, both of them subordinate to Favian, and Levesque was not under Favian's orders. Besides, Favian thought Lovette objected not so much to fighting a duel as to fighting one for such a ridiculous reason; he seemed in a belligerent mood otherwise. Lovette might well conclude that a duel with a man ashore was none of Favian's business, and fight it anyway.

On the other hand, if it weren't any of Favian's business, why had they come to Favian's cabin for advice?

"Gentlemen," he said, "I will give the matter some thought. I shall go into town and inquire as to local custom. Report to me this afternoon before meeting M. le Chevalier. Dismissed."

The two midshipmen saluted and left Favian's cabin. He poured himself more coffee and ordered breakfast. He would need as much fortification as the food would provide, he knew, to withstand the pressures of the day.

That afternoon, taking Gideon's advice to heart, he stopped by a little shop in the Rue de Camp to purchase a sword cane. The shop sold cutlery of all sorts: cleavers and kitchen knives fanned in the windows alongside racks of elegant smallswords and sturdy cutlasses. The master was not present, but the apprentice, a boy of about fourteen, showed what he had.

Sword canes, perhaps more than any other weapon, needed to be made well. The blades were necessarily slender; any with less than first-rate steel would snap at the first parry, or break off between the target's ribs. Favian had decided on an extremely well-made model, keen-edged as well as pointed, with a groove down the blade that would give it spring—it made an attractive cane even without its martial qualities, with its curiously patterned head, a succession of lathe-fashioned roundnesses, presumably to improve the grip, surrounding the central length of the tang and its surrounding hilt. No guard or quillons, of course, Favian thought as he lifted the blade; in use it would be difficult to avoid getting one's fingers cut.

And then the proprietor entered, a large graying Frenchman with a sapper's square-cut beard. He looked at Favian in surprise and horror, then addressed his apprentice in a hushed, angry voice, speaking in Gascon French. "Do you not listen? Do you never listen? That cane is not for an American, but for the members of the Guard!" He slapped the boy hastily, striking him on a shoulder raised to ward the blow, then turned to Favian and assumed a smile meant to be servile, but in the event appearing grotesque.

"I am sorry, sir," he said in painful English. "This cane has already been purchased by another gentleman. I will be happy to sell you another, please."

"I prefer this one."

"I have tried to explain, sir. Another gentleman has purchased this one. You may have any other."

"*Un gentilhomme,*" said Favian, "*de la Garde?*"

The man's eyes widened at the revelation of a Kaintuck speaking French with a better accent than his own, and then his brows came together in a scowl. "*Pardon, m'sieur*. As I said, this cane has already been purchased. Please take another—with my compliments. No payment necessary."

Bemused by this haste and mystery, Favian made his second choice, an ivory-handled straight cane with tarnished silver fittings and a fine, blackened old blade. There was little to choose between them as swords; Favian had chosen the other because it was a more attractive walking stick.

His new, deadly acquisition clicking on the narrow flagged sidewalk, Favian made his way to the levee. A newly arrived militia company, covered in mud from boot to shako, marched jauntily past, the crowd applauding, women throwing kisses. It had been a busy, discouraging morning. He had found a room in a hotel and moved his chest into it, sending his boat's crew back to the *Louisiana*—they would not have to spend any more evenings shivering on the levee. Afterwards he had paid a call on Claiborne, urging martial law without success but at least getting the governor to issue orders to establish outposts on the various approaches to New Orleans as well as sending men to garrison Fort St. John on Lake Pontchartrain. At luncheon with the governor and his spectacularly beautiful Creole wife, Sophronie, Favian asked him if he knew of Lieutenant Levesque or one Mr. de la Tour d'Aurillac.

Indeed the governor had. It appeared that Levesque was infamous.

Claiborne, without appearing to try his memory, came up with at least a dozen affairs in which Levesque had participated. He had won them all, killing at least seven men and wounding the rest. He was expert with both pistol and sword, having killed with both. A professional bully from the time of Richelieu, Favian thought, transplanted to the enlightened nineteenth century and the mouth of the Mississippi. As for de la Tour d'Aurillac, he was a recent arrival: the heir of an émigré aristocratic family returned under the amnesties of the Empire, he had been a colonel of Napoleon's hussars and had been made a Chevalier of the Legion of Honor for bravery. Apparently he was a duellist as well, though he had fought all of his encounters abroad.

"There is nothing I can do to stop it," Claiborne had said. Favian was growing tired of the number of things Claiborne could not do. "The practice is accepted here. I have fought a duel myself—not something I'm partic'larly proud of, but it was made necessary by the, ah, the mores of this place. Besides, I remember that you yourself, Captain Markham, had a little trouble once—in New Jersey, was it? Captain, ah, Brewer or something?"

"Brewster," Favian said, aware of the curiosity in Sophronie Claiborne's languid eyes. There was still a warrant out in that New Jersey county; it had come too soon after the Burr business. A drunken bully of a merchant captain run through both lungs, the consequence of some intemperate speech in a New York tavern, speech made with the intention of provoking a fight from that new-made lieutenant, swaggering perhaps in his new uniform, cadging drinks off his *Philadelphia* medal. "You have a good memory, sir," Favian said.

"There was a speech made in Congress about it, something about the Tripolitan war making Turks out of our Navy men."

"I have never," said Favian sternly, "provoked a fight. I have never sought one out." A direct lie, of course; there had been that duel in Norway the year before. There had been a deliberate, nasty joy in the way he'd provoked Count Gram, much though the man deserved it.

"Of course not," Claiborne said. His eyes did not seem convinced. "I remember it because I met your father at about the same time—I think it was your father. Shorter than you, dressed very well, spoke with a kind of English *zézaiement*? Come to buy ponies in Virginia, I think."

That sounded like Jehu Markham all right: a well-dressed, cultured Revolutionary privateer, a friend of Franklin and Lafayette, buying horses for his legendary stables, the breeding program that had lost half his fortune for him. "He made several buying trips south. He's always enjoyed travel."

"I hope he is well . . . ?"

"Oh. Yes. Very well."

"Did you hear," asked Madame Claiborne, clearly tired of news of people she hadn't ever met, "the latest news about that Captain Fontenoy? You know, the privateer from Mauritius? It seems he was off in the Faubourg Marigny last night, knocking on the side door of the Listeau mansion, whispering *'Marie, it is your loving slave. How happy you have made me!'* " Madame gave a delighted laugh and clapped her hands. "Listeau, of course, answered the door himself. Carrying a horsewhip. It is common knowledge that Fontenoy is one of Madame Listeau's admirers. Fontenoy had to pretend he was drunk. Of course the servants heard everything—by now the entire town knows."

Favian remembered the little note Campaspe had asked him to carry to Fontenoy and decided to keep silent about it. Did the little wench play these sort of tricks often? "The poor man," Favian said.

"Which one?" she asked gaily. "Fontenoy, or M. Listeau?

Madame Listeau is the one you should pity, rather; the town gossips will devour her.''

The interview ended with a number of gossipy anecdotes, more or less in the same style as the first. Midshipman Lovette, it appeared, was going to have his hands full. Favian concluded he would have to intervene directly in the business by offering himself as another of Lovette's seconds: He would attempt to get Lovette off the hook, and if he failed would try to get Claiborne to order the Dragoons' colonel to send Levesque off to command an outpost on the Bayou Terre aux Boeufs or someplace equally dismal.

On the levee he hired a boatman to take him to *Louisiana,* then sent for Lovette and Stanhope. ''It appears the man you have offended is something of a professional duellist,'' Lovette was told; Favian watched him try to conceal his dismay with a deliberately careless shrug. ''If you will accept me as another second, I will attempt to pry you out of this difficulty.''

A touch of hope crossed Lovette's face. ''I'd be very grateful, sir,'' he said.

''Very well. I realize this fight is none of your making, and I will do my best on your behalf, but I hope you understand that it may not be possible to convince M. le Chevalier that no offense has taken place. In that event, as challenged party you have your choice of pistols or swords. Which will you prefer?''

Lovette swallowed hard. ''Either. No. Pistols, I suppose,'' he said without hope. It was the choice Favian would have urged, unless Lovette suddenly proclaimed himself an expert with the sword. With pistols there was the chance Levesque would miss, or that the wound would be minor; in the case of swords an expert like Levesque would probably run Lovette through at the first exchange.

''I'll try to do my best for you,'' Favian said. ''I've acquired a few tricks over the years. Mr. Stanhope, I shall expect you to present yourself at my hotel at four thirty this afternoon. Wear your number one uniform and your dirk; we'll want to look our best. Gentlemen, you are dismissed.''

There was, Favian thought, a way to handle it if all else failed; in these matters, as in so much else, his lengthy apprenticeship to Stephen Decatur helped. In the year '02, the Tripolitan war sputtering on inconclusively in the Mediterranean, the American fleet under Morris had been based at Malta. A man named

Cochran, secretary to Governor Sir Alexander Ball and something of a professional duellist, had jostled Midshipman Joseph Bainbridge, U.S.N., four times in the opera lobby, on the last occasion making a sneering remark about Americans never standing the smell of powder. Bainbridge had knocked the man down, of course, and duly received his challenge. Decatur had acted as second and insisted on pistols at four paces. The British second had been aghast, but Decatur had insisted; Bainbridge was inexperienced, and the range had to be short in order to make the combat fair. Both men were so nervous that the first fire amazingly missed, but Cochran was so angry he insisted on a second round; Decatur told his man to hold low; and Bainbridge shot the man dead. Governor Ball made a fuss and the American fleet moved its base to Palermo; Joseph Bainbridge was promoted lieutenant by a Congress grateful for his defense of the American uniform. If Favian could not work out a way for Lovette to slide out of the duel with honor, he was perfectly prepared to insist on pistols at four paces: let Levesque stand *that*, if he could.

That afternoon another muddy militia company was marching to its bivouac, detouring through the Place d'Armes to receive its share of adulation. The crowds still applauded, but there was sign that the novelty was wearing off. The full-dress naval uniforms of Favian and Stanhope attracted little attention; New Orleans was reserving its adulation for the native battalions.

M. le Chevalier Jean Noel Gabriel de la Tour d'Aurillac was not difficult to distinguish; he was a short man, dressed well, carrying a walking stick, with waxed hussar mustachios and a bandy-legged cavalryman gait. The cross of the Legion of Honor was pinned to his coat. Seeing the two naval officers, he bowed and introduced himself, the names rolling off his tongue. "At your service," he said in English. "I am acting for Lieutenant Levesque."

"This is Mr. Midshipman Stanhope," Favian said, returning the bow. "I am Captain Markham. We are acting for Mr. Midshipman Lovette." There was a formal rhythm to these proceedings, to the artificial deadly ritual that would match one blade against another. Formal speech, dress coats, silk stockings, all leading to foul and stupid death. Favian could play the game, moving through the motions: in this the Navy had taught him well. He felt a seething hate for the whole business.

"Does your principal choose swords or pistols?" asked My

Lord the Knight Jean Noel Gabriel of the Tower of Aurillac—the name seemed so much more elegant in French.

"We would not," said Favian, "be doing our duty as seconds if we did not first explore the possibility of a reconciliation."

De la Tour d'Aurillac shrugged. He touched his mustache with a finger, making certain it was in place, his cane dangling from his raised fingers. "My principal," he said, "is willing to forget the insult if Mr. Lovette will offer a public apology in the same restaurant in which it was given." In front of a crowd of jeering Creole duellists, no doubt.

"I am by no means satisfied that there was an insult given," Favian said. "As I understand it, Mr. Lovette's offense, if such it may be termed, consisted of entering the restaurant and ordering the same meal as Lieutenant Levesque. I fail to understand how this can be considered an insult."

"The meal was ordered in a loud voice, with much bad French and by offensive gestures. No gentleman enjoys being pointed at in such a graceless fashion."

"Mr. Lovette and Lieutenant Levesque are both serving their country," Favian said, trying another tack. "They are fighting the same enemy. Mr. Lovette has participated in several battles at sea, and Lieutenant Levesque has no doubt distinguished himself in the Mississippi Dragoons. It would be a great shame, would it not, if New Orleans lost two promising officers on the occasion of such an emergency? Surely a duel at such a time, for such a reason, will not reflect well on the *combattants*. There is a higher duty involved; we are comrades in arms who must fight the common enemy."

De la Tour d'Aurillac's cane was tapping impatiently on the pavement. Favian had seen the cane somewhere before; he wondered where. "Sir," the Frenchman said, "I do not understand your reasoning. A man who will not fight for his own honor cannot fight for his country's."

"Perhaps in any case the combat can be postponed until after the British are dealt with," Favian said. And Levesque done in by some British rifleman, he hoped.

The Frenchman frowned. "All the more reason to do it quickly, sir," he said. "We do not wish the British to interrupt our *affaires d'honneur*. There must be an apology or a fight, sir, one or the other. Does your man want swords or pistols?"

Favian felt his temper rising, but fought it down. Another few minutes of this bullying, insistent stupidity and he would end up crossing swords with this swaggering Frenchman himself. He was about to bark out, "Pistols! Four paces! If we're to do murder let us do it right!" when he heard Stanhope speak at his elbow.

"Neither, sir. We choose topmauls at the main yardarm."

Favian looked at Stanhope in amazement. The midshipman was glaring at de la Tour d'Aurillac, his mouth pressed into a grim line, and suddenly Favian saw Stanhope's inspiration.

"Captain!" the Frenchman was saying. "I protest! We must obey the forms!"

"The forms will be obeyed," Favian said, trying to keep his amusement hidden. "Topmauls at the main yardarm: it is a way we have in the Navy of settling our differences." Topmauls were light sledges used to drive a fid home when topmasts were swayed aloft atop the lower mast of a ship. Lovette with his burly figure and broad shoulders would wield a topmaul quite effectively, Favian thought—more effectively than a sword, certainly—and of course he would be at home on a yardarm. If any landsman even *got* out on the yardarm, hanging a hundred feet or so above the water with his feet on the swaying footrope, he would be doing very well; anyone who could swing a twelve-pound sledge in such circumstances would have to be a perfect acrobat.

"I have never heard of this kind of fight!" de la Tour d'Aurillac snapped. He ground his cane into the pavement, and Favian realized where he'd seen it before—that rounded, lathed head was the same he'd seen in the shop that morning. "This is irregular, and very unfair!"

"I have told you it is not," Favian said, pressing his advantage. "We have the choice of weapons. Lieutenant Levesque is a master of sword and pistol, and our man is not; it would be no more unfair if we chose pistols. Of course, if your principal would agree to withdraw his challenge, no meeting need take place. We do not insist it be done publicly; a written note will suffice."

The Frenchman glared at Favian, red-faced. Favian felt an urge to step back out of range of that swordstick but refrained; instead he shifted his grip on his own cane in case he needed to block a sudden thrust. "There will be no withdrawal," de la Tour d'Aurillac snapped finally. "If Lieutenant Levesque withdraws, I will fight him myself for putting me in this absurd situation."

"As you wish, sir," said Favian, grimly triumphant.

"Where can this encounter take place?"

"I think the main yardarm of the *Louisiana* is of sufficient height," Favian said. He was the senior officer in New Orleans, he reflected; he could use the schooner for purposes of a duel if he wanted. "Would noon tomorrow suffice?"

"It shall have to," said the Frenchman. His mouth twitched as if he were swallowing something distasteful. "I will bring Lieutenant Levesque to the *Louisiana* at the appointed time. Your servant, sir."

"Servant," Favian said and bowed. The Knight Jean strutted furiously down Chartres Street; it was only after he had disappeared in the crowd that Favian dared turn to Stanhope and burst out in laughter.

"Whatever inspired you to step in like that?" Favian asked. "Topmauls at the main yardarm! Perfect, Mr. Stanhope—it couldn't have been arranged better!"

Stanhope, a serious young man, allowed himself a brief smile. "I don't know, sir. M. le Chevalier was being such a stubborn pig about it, demanding swords or pistols, and I had a recollection of Mr. Lovette last summer, when the *Macedonian*'s masts were being swayed up, using the topmaul to bang the fid in, and I thought it was a shame that Lovette's shoulders couldn't be put to better use. The next thing I knew I was blurting out that we chose topmauls. I hope you did not resent my interruption, sir."

"Of course not," Favian said. "If you have any more such inspirations, blurt them as you will. For the present, I think we should return to the *Louisiana* and relieve Mr. Lovette's anxiety. Perhaps he'll want to practice with his topmaul."

"Yes, sir. I'm sure he will." Favian glanced at Stanhope as they walked: Stanhope's first cruise had been with Favian on *Experiment*, the journey to the North Sea and back now famous as Markham's Raid. Favian had thought Stanhope an exceptionally promising officer, and this was more evidence in his favor. Most midshipmen were so eager for action they would cheerfully have gone duelling with battle-axes and morning stars; here Stanhope had acted not only to prevent Lovette from being butchered by a professional duellist, but in such a way that the entire system of the *code duello* was being mocked. How could anyone witnessing Lovette and Levesque hanging on the foot-ropes swinging at each other with sledgehammers possibly take a duel seriously afterward? The encounter would prove another nail in the coffin of the formal duel; and good riddance, Favian thought. He'd had two duels forced on him in his life and knew that every moment he wore the uniform of the United States he might be forced into another one—private individuals could ignore insults if they chose, but an American uniform could not.

As they walked across the Place d'Armes, Favian saw another cane similar to M. le Chevalier's—a Guard cane, as he was beginning to think of it. It was in the hands of a very tall man, a man very nearly topping Favian's six feet four inches. The man was graying, broad-shouldered, and wore a grizzled mustache; his bearing was so erect that Favian could not help but think of him as a soldier even though he was dressed in a plain broadcloth coat. A shorter, younger man watched as the veteran held the cane out like a baton, holding it by the middle as if inviting the other man to admire it in the sun. A strange tableau, Favian thought; they were like freemasons with their secret handshakes and passwords. He wondered what the cane signified: a veterans' organization, perhaps. He would ask Claiborne when time permitted.

For the present, of course, he'd have to work out the details of the duel, preferably in such a way that no one got hurt. Though, he admitted, he had conceived enough of a dislike against the unknown Lieutenant Levesque that if anyone was to go tumbling off the yardarm to the waters below, he would try to make certain it was the Creole.

SIX

The morning had been bitterly cold, a fog blanketing the river and the town; Lovette, as he'd gone aloft into the mist for his morning's practice with the topmaul, had puffed frost into the air like a steam engine. The midshipman was in good spirits, enjoying his reprieve from the inevitable bullet; Favian had cautioned him about tiring himself with excessive practice.

The mist faded early in the morning, and as noon approached, the river began to fill up with small boats, each filled with a battered local waterman and a collection of the well-dressed gentry. The news had spread like wildfire, and it seemed that half the city's population was on the levee. Favian and his officers were dressed formally, waiting for the boat that would bring Levesque and his party to the schooner. A boat had already set off from Carolina, carrying Patterson and his officers, ready to witness the Navy's proud defense of its honor. Another boat was being filled alongside *Malachi's Revenge*. Fontenoy had been invited, but had declined; apparently he was not yet ready to appear in public after his humiliation two nights before, and then there had been sightings of M. Listeau walking the streets carrying his horsewhip. Yet winks of lights were flashing from *Franklin*'s quarterdeck: there were men with long glasses trained on *Louisiana*'s main yardarm. The duel between Lovette and Levesque would be a public spectacle spoken of for years, both by the Kaintucks and the Creoles.

There was a challenge and response from *Louisiana*'s quartermaster, followed by the assembly of the welcome party at the entry port. Patterson came aboard to the whistling of pipes and the rattling of officers' swords from their scabbards, Favian returning his salute as Patterson uncovered. "Damned bad business, Captain Markham," Patterson said.

"I am confident the outcome will be favorable, Captain," Favian said.

"That's not what I mean," Patterson said. "I'm not certain how the town will take it—if the Creoles think we're mocking them by perverting their sacred traditions of honor, this may outrage them. The Navy is held in little enough repute as it is, sir."

"I'm sure the Navy is capable of defending its honor," Favian said. "But in the case of this little dandified bravo, the more mockery the better. Levesque deserves whatever humiliation we give him."

Patterson scowled and said nothing. Perhaps he did not agree.

There was another sharp whistle at the entry port, and Gideon Markham appeared on the quarterdeck. Favian and Patterson returned his bow. Favian wondered if he should tell Gideon of Campaspe's little plot; he decided to wait until later.

"Allow me to introduce my officers, gentlemen," Gideon said. "Mr. Martin, my first officer. Mr. Willard, my second; Mr. Clowes, the third; Mr. Allen of the gentleman volunteers."

"Happy to meet'ee, Captain Favian," said Finch Martin cheerfully. "Sorry I didn't get to see ye t'other day—it's been five years or more, ain't it? I was ashore on business—had to find some clapped-up whore who had spiced one of the men of his prize money an' given him a dose at th' same time. I got the money back, minus ten percent for my services." He leered, scratching his gray hair, as Patterson stared in amazement.

Favian had known Finch Martin all his life; Martin was a Portsmouth character of long standing. Dwarfish, grizzled, his face weathered like an old post and fixed in a constant insinuant leer, Martin was at least seventy, a dissipated Revolutionary remnant who had once served as Malachi Markham's sailing master. He was a superb sailor and a masterful vulgarian; he made no secret of the fact that the considerable fortune he'd made privateering in the Revolution had been spent in a decade-long spree of gambling, drink, and whoring, after which he'd had to return to the sea to earn his bread. Favian had no idea how Martin and the puritanical Gideon managed to exist on the same ship; there must have been some interesting compromises.

"Mr. Martin, it's good to see you again," he said. "I trust you are well?"

"Well enough to visit Corinth from time to time and play buttock ball with Miss Laycock." He grinned, after first looking over his shoulder to make certain Gideon was out of earshot. Patterson stared at the man in shock.

"I am glad to hear it," Favian said. There was little else to say. It was clear that Gideon, at least once out of hearing, had little control over Martin's language.

"Beg pardon, sir." It was Phillip Stanhope, his hat raised at the salute. "Lieutenant Levesque and M. le Chevalier are putting out from shore."

"Thank you, Mr. Stanhope. Please go aloft with Mr. Lovette. He may want to exercise a little in the fighting top to warm his limbs."

"I will pass on that suggestion. Thank you, sir."

The two midshipmen mounted to the rigging. Favian walked to

the entry port to watch the other party approach. M. le Chevalier Jean was unmistakable, his slight figure overdressed in a green jacket with embroidered collar, scarlet sash, a pair of silk cravats, and the Legion of Honor pinned to his breast. Next to him was a gray-haired, black-garbed individual who could only be a surgeon; so the other must be Levesque. The duellist was dressed in a green uniform coat and helmet, presumably that of the Mississippi Dragoons. His trousers were fashionably tight. Favian's eyes flicked to the welcome party, the appropriate number of sideboys and officers to receive a militia lieutenant.

"Duelling," said the grim voice of Gideon Markham, standing beside him. "Such a waste. Such an outrage against God." Favian, his eyes on the approaching boat, could picture his cousin's scowl. "The Lord trieth the righteous," Gideon said, "but the wicked and him that loveth violence his soul hateth."

"I think today might serve as a lesson to the bullies ashore," Favian said, unable to think of a biblical tag in reply.

"I pray you are right," said Gideon.

The pipes blew, and the first through the entry port was de la Tour d'Aurillac, his narrow-set eyes flicking over the deck. He returned Favian's bow stiffly. Favian noticed he was carrying his distinctive sword cane.

The dragoon lieutenant then came through the entry port; Favian, during the terse introduction and bow, had an impression of fierce black eyes, high color, and restless intensity. Levesque was no taller than de la Tour d'Aurillac; he carried his body well, with an athlete's assurance. No sword cane, though he carried his dragoon saber. "Perhaps your surgeon would care to remain in the boat," Favian said. "We already have two boats, one with a surgeon, standing by in the water, in case anyone falls from aloft." De la Tour d'Aurillac nodded, leaned over the rail, and spoke in French to his surgeon.

"Shall we go to the maintop, gentlemen?" Favian asked. He preceded them up the main shrouds, then swung out inverted on the futtock shrouds, hanging upside down until he hauled himself to the top. "You will not need to follow my example, gentlemen," he said. "You can work your way through the futtock shrouds and come up through the lubber's hole, if you like." The lubber's hole was an easier way, but, as its name implied, was disdained by those with pretensions of being true seamen.

De la Tour d'Aurillac followed Favian's advice, squeezing

through the futtock shrouds at the cost of one of his coat buttons, but Levesque in following came up the futtock shrouds, moving slowly but with determination, his dragoon saber dangling down into space. No fear of heights, Favian thought, good balance. He may be dangerous yet.

On the big platform Favian performed the introductions; Lovette and Levesque bowed stiffly. "We have here a selection of topmauls," Favian said. "Lieutenant Levesque may choose his weapon." The topmauls were in pairs, six-pound sledges ranked alongside nine-pounders, twelve-pounders, and the heavy, short-handled, twenty-four-pound mauls. Levesque, as expected, chose one of the lightest six-pound topmauls—a six-pound head was enough to do whatever damage had to be done and minimized the possibility of momentum sending one flying clean off the foot-rope at the first swing. Lovette, expressionless, chose the other six-pounder.

This part, Favian knew, had to be scrupulously fair, or at any rate to have the appearance of utter fairness. Duels were marked by their formality, their rigidity, the only things that distinguished them from brawls. Any deviation from the rigid requirements of the *code duello* would be remarked by the other party, and could result in more challenges, an endless round of bad feeling and spilled blood.

"You will observe that the larboard main yard has been marked in two places by colored line," Favian went on. "One line is near the yardarm, the other halfway out. Both are over the water; anyone falling will strike the water and not the *Louisiana*. One of the combatants will stand at the yardarm, behind the place marked by the line. The other will advance from the maintop to stand behind the other line. At a signal, both may advance toward the other. The combat will continue until honor is satisfied. In the event of one combatant wounding the other, the combat will cease until the extent of the injury has been determined and until it can be decided whether honor is satisfied. Do you understand?"

Levesque and M. le Chevalier nodded.

"M. le Chevalier and I shall spin a coin to determine who has choice of position. Is that agreed?" Two more nods.

Favian fished in his pocket for a five-dollar piece, flipped it spinning into the air, and let it fall to the fighting top as de la Tour d'Aurillac said, "Heads, sir." Favian peered down at the coin. Tails. He looked at Lovette.

"I will wait at the yardarm, sir," he said. Favian nodded.

Lovette stripped off his uniform coat, his boots, stockings, and hat; carrying his topmaul, he walked effortlessly and barefoot out on the footrope, one hand lightly touching the heavy yard for balance. Past the marker he turned and faced the maintop, his hip resting against the main yard, the topmaul held in both hands. His pose seemed casual, but Favian could see his high color, the dancing light in his eyes. He was ready and confident of victory; Favian had seen the look before.

"Lieutenant Levesque, you may take your position." Levesque unclipped his saber, dropped it to the maintop, and then took off his coat and hat. Stooping, he pulled off his half boots, and then reached into his sabretache for a pair of soft leather moccasins. He laced these tightly on his feet and stood up, flexing his knees, testing the moccasins. They would grip the footrope quite well, Favian knew; the man was prepared. Favian looked at Lovette and saw doubt cross the boy's features. Perhaps this would not be easy.

Levesque, his face absolutely vacant of expression, stepped out onto the footrope, moving carefully, one hand resting along the main yard. He moved back and forth, testing his balance. The footrope trembled under his feet. He looked over his shoulder at his second and nodded.

"M. le Chevalier, you may give the orders to commence if you wish," Favian said with a nod toward the Frenchman. "May I suggest *ready, advance*? And *hold* if a wound is struck?"

De la Tour d'Aurillac bowed. "Honored, sir," he said. He looked toward the two figures balanced precariously on the footrope. "Gentlemen, I shall call *Ready, advance!*" he said, raising his voice. "This shall be the signal for you to commence the combat. If I or Captain Markham cry *hold*, the combat shall cease instantly. Do you understand?"

A pair of terse nods. De la Tour d'Aurillac looked at Favian and bowed again.

"Ready!" he shouted. He raised his cane high; Favian saw its silhouette, strangely reminiscent of something he had seen before, cast on the planking of the maintop. The cane dropped, cutting air. "*Advance!*"

Lovette, his topmaul held two-handed, advanced a confident two paces, then halted. Levesque hesitated, then stepped forward, inching his way along the footrope. He was right-handed, and his left side was turned toward Lovette; his topmaul was held two-handed over his right shoulder; his abdomen pressed against the main yard for balance. Lovette raised his topmaul to a guard position. Levesque, the footrope trembling under him, came to a stop six feet away.

For a moment motion ended; the two combatants were suspended a hundred feet or more above the muddy river, balanced between the sky and silver-threaded water, the object of a hundred flashing spyglasses on shore and on the nearby vessels. Favian felt his heart beat thrice, marking the motionless instant, and then the balance ended and Levesque was moving, springing forward, his hammer coming down. "*Cochon*!" he roared; Favian could imagine the bared teeth, the sudden ferocity calculated to stun Lovette into a second of helplessness. Lovette stepped back, his motion effortless, and the topmaul swished through empty air. Lovesque was off-balance, facing the gulf, his left arm windmilling as the maul tried to drag him into space; and then Lovette stepped forward, a satisfied smile on his face; he touched Levesque's ribs with the handle of the topmaul and exerted steady pressure. Levesque went over, arms flailing, legs kicking, the maul arching away from him as man and weapon plummeted into the Father of Waters. From the height of the maintop the splash seemed very small.

The boats arrowed in on the splash, but before they arrived a tiny head broke surface; arms thrashed out. The dragoon was brought back to *Louisiana*. Lovette, a relieved, exhilarated smile blazing from his flushed face, received Favian's congratulatory handshake and began to put on his uniform coat. Favian looked down through the lubber's hole and saw Lieutenant Levesque, his teeth clenched with pain, coming up the shrouds again.

"It is not over!" the lieutenant shouted. "It is not over! I demand we continue!"

"It *is* over, sir," Favian insisted firmly. Levesque stood defiantly, dripping on the maintop. He was white-faced, in pain. His left arm clutched at his side; perhaps there were ribs broken.

"Blows were not exchanged," Levesque gritted. "I missed. He did not strike me. It is not over. Honor was not satisfied."

"Sir, it is over," Favian said. "Mr. Lovette gallantly chose to spare your life. I cannot think that you would be so ungracious as to insist we continue. You are hurt. I urge that you see a surgeon."

"Blows were not exchanged!" Levesque raved. "I insist on continuing the combat!"

Favian looked at de la Tour d'Aurillac. The Frenchman was watching the antics of his principal with an expression of distaste; he turned and said, "Sir, I'm afraid my principal insists. Technically he is correct."

Rage tore at Favian's composure as he pictured himself hurling Levesque bodily off the platform, but he throttled the impulse. "I wish to speak privately to my principal," he said.

The others crowded to the other side of the fighting top, giving a minimal amount of privacy, while Favian leaned close to Lovette and spoke in a low voice. "Mr. Lovette, I'm afraid we shall have to go another round."

Lovette took a breath. "Yes, sir," he said.

"Kill him," Favian said. Lovette's eyes flickered to Favian's. It was a deliberate decision on Favian's part; this farce had gone on long enough. Lovette, he knew, had been in the boarding party that had taken *Carnation*, but had he crossed swords with an enemy in that fight? The British corvette had only resisted for a few seconds before their crew ran for the hatches. Favian hoped the midshipman was blooded; it would be easier if he'd had experience. "Kill him if you wish to live," Favian repeated deliberately. "Or cripple him. Otherwise he'll keep on fighting until he kills you. Can you do that?"

Lovette glanced at Levesque, seeing the dragoon boiling with rage and dripping Mississippi water, and then looked back at Favian. "I'll try, sir," he said.

"Let's get it over with," Favian said. "Take your position."

Lovette took off his uniform coat and folded it neatly, then picked up the six-pound topmaul and stepped out onto the footrope. Favian turned to the other party.

"Lieutenant Levesque, you may continue the fight if you insist," he said. "But I would like you to know my opinion. It cannot be continued in honor."

Levesque's lips curled with contempt. "I do not need lessons in honor from you," he said.

"Perhaps, sir, you do," Favian said, the words slipping out before he could stop them. He remembered his blade going between Count Gram's ribs in Norway, the surprise in the rufous bully's eyes.

The sneer left Levesque's face. "I will remember that," he

said. He picked up a nine-pound topmaul, wincing with the pain. He held the weapon close to his chest, protectively, and inched out onto the footrope.

He did not stop at the marks, did not wait for M. le Chevalier to give the proper commands. The Frenchman, startled, took an involuntary step forward, as if to intervene. "Hold!" he shouted. "Hold! *Attention!*" Levesque ignored him.

The man simply wants to kill, Favian thought. This is no longer a duel, no longer protected by the code. I'll have him hanged for murder if he wins. "Lovette!" he roared. "Defend yourself!"

Lovette was slow to realize Levesque's intent; he hesitated before stepping out past the mark, his topmaul raised. "*Salaud!*" shrieked the Knight Jean. He cleared his sword cane from the scabbard and stepped out onto the footrope, balancing precariously, his teeth bared, ready to run Levesque through if he didn't obey: too late.

Both men swung; there was a crack as the sledge-hafts came together. There was a second devoted to balance, the footrope shaking wildly, then the topmauls blurred through the air. A pair of squelching thuds: the two combatants hung for a second suspended in air, and then the knight Jean was standing alone on the footrope, looking wide-eyed down at the tumbling figures falling through space, at the inevitable pair of silver splashes. Favian had already launched himself through the air, limbs spread to catch a backstay; he would scrape half the skin from his palms in his hurry to reach the deck.

By that time a head had broken water, pale-faced, blood dripping from the ears and nose: Lovette. Of the other there was no sign. The Mississippi had taken Levesque and with him his mad and brutal code of honor.

SEVEN

"Broken ribs, a broken collarbone, fracture of the humerus," Favian said. "Perhaps a concussion. But he'll live." He sipped his coffee, a certain satisfaction coming into his voice. "Mr. Lovette will live. A story to tell his grandchildren, if he has any."

"Praise God," said Gideon. "His countenance doth behold the upright."

They sat in Gideon's parlor, the remains of their dinner spread before them, Gideon's steward Grimes—Favian was slowly getting used to the idea of Grimes as a cousin—standing by attentively with the coffeepot.

"I hope it will make the Creoles less likely to challenge sailors," Maria-Anna said. Her dish of coffee was propped elegantly on three fingers; she blew to cool it. Gideon and Favian drank their coffee from mugs, a habit encouraged by life on shipboard where in a rolling sea drinks stayed better in tall containers. She sighed. "It's a touchy thing. A man is shunned by the entire community if he declines a fight, even on the most frivolous of pretexts. If a man won't go out, he has no alternative but to sell out and move. Captain Fontenoy is hiding on the *Franklin* now, not wanting to fight Listeau. Though from what I've heard," she said, a mischievous smile on her face, "he deserves at least the horsewhipping Listeau wants to give him." Favian remembered he had not yet spoken to Campaspe and vowed to catch her alone before the evening was over.

"It is a wicked thing," Gideon said. "The papists permit their flock to live alongside sin, their priests allow it. Madame Dufour's, er, establishment," he said, with a careful, sidelong glance at Maria-Anna, "is right next to that little chapel on St. Philippe Street—and it's a blatant place, very fancy; all the Creole planters go there. But that is only the sins of the flesh, not murder. In

Portsmouth it would be a man like Levesque who is shunned and exiled, not his victims."

"There have been duels in New Hampshire," Favian said.

"Aye," Gideon said. "But the men who won them did not stay—they ran one step ahead of a murder charge."

Favian nodded: true enough, no one had fought a duel in New Hampshire in recent memory and been able to escape without inconvenience, though some of them were able to return later. It was difficult to convince the public to prosecute because their sympathies were easily engaged by the survivor of a duel, who had, after all, faced his enemy's weapon in a fair fight. The victor of an encounter, so long as he was able to present a fair and modest face to the public, would almost always go free. Luckily, Favian thought, remembering Captain Brewster. New York had declined to extradite, Brewster having a bad reputation. Unpleasant memories crawled up Favian's spine. Time to change the subject.

"I've taken your advice, Gideon, and bought a sword cane, a nice little weapon," he said, "but there was an interesting disagreement in the shop beforehand. Over a curious cane, with a lathed head, so." He sketched the handle on the tablecloth with the blunt end of his knife and told the story of the shopkeeper refusing to sell the first cane, and of seeing others in the hands of de la Tour d'Aurillac and of the gray soldierlike man in the Place d'Armes.

"I've never noticed anything like it," Gideon said, shaking his head.

"A secret society, I suppose," Maria-Anna said. There was a faint abstraction to her eyes; her hands were linked over her belly as she sat on her birthing stool, the unborn child kicking. "The Creoles are riddled with them. Conspiracy is in their blood."

"A society of Napoleon's veterans?" Favian asked. "De la Tour d'Aurillac was a colonel of hussars, and that man in the Place d'Armes had a military bearing—he looked so military he could have been one of the *Chasseurs à Pied de la Garde Impériale*. In fact," he said, growing enthusiastic, "that would explain the storekeeper saying it was reserved for the Guard. Was de la Tour d'Aurillac a member of the Guard Hussars?"

"Were there Guard Hussars? I don't know," Gideon said. "But I think if de la Tour d'Aurillac were a guardsman he would have let the city know."

Favian shrugged. "Perhaps it's just a coincidence. I suppose it doesn't matter." Grimes filled his coffee mug, and Favian thanked him. How to get to Campaspe? he wondered. He hadn't seen the girl all day.

He left early that evening without seeing her, declining Maria-Anna's offer of some instructions in *poque*; he had other plans for the evening. His thoughts lingered on Maria-Anna as he stepped down to the hotel lobby, and he realized he had been outside the company of women for too long.

His mistress Caroline had been left behind in New London when *Macedonian* had broken the blockade in October, and he would probably not see her again. She had loved him, he suspected, and not loved wisely. He had enjoyed her zestful company, her warmth, her playfulness, but the Navy demanded its officers live its code on land as well as on sea, and to marry a professional courtesan would have been to put his career at risk. Knowing this, he had treated Caroline well, and as fairly as he could; he'd left her with enough money to live honestly for years, to marry well if she wished, or to fulfill her dream of going to Europe and pursuing a stage career. She had understood: marriage had never been mentioned.

If only, he thought, Emma Greenhow had married him. He had been New Hampshire–born Emma all his life, and she had been so perfectly suitable. For years, when Favian had been a lieutenant living in poverty between the wars, he and Emma had an informal sort of understanding—not an engagement precisely, knowing old Greenhow would never have approved, but a commitment of a sort. But something had gone wrong after Favian had returned from the Narrow Seas of England. Emma, in the end, had refused him, marrying instead Benjamin Stanhope, the widowed father of Midshipman Phillip Stanhope, a leader of the Peace Federalist faction to which the entire Markham family—and for that matter his son—was bitterly opposed. Now, Favian supposed, Emma was in transit with her husband to Hartford, where the peace faction would try to bring New England out of the war, presumably under the protection of the British, undoing all the work of the War of Independence. From undeclared fiancée to political enemy; Favian would never understand why. After all his calculations . . .

He left the hotel and saw, as he stepped into the street, another figure entering the hotel through the women's entrance. Mrs.

Desplein, he thought, and there, some distance behind, was Campaspe, following with a shopping basket full of material: someone, Maria-Anna probably, was getting a new gown. He called her name.

She came, but he saw wariness in her eyes, and her body was tense as if ready to bolt. "I saw the duel from the levee today," she said, giving her head a careless shake meant to throw him off the scent. "Mrs. Desplein told me I couldn't, but she was upset all day and I managed to get away from her. Her husband died in a duel, you know. I'm glad the Navy won."

"I'm sure the Navy is grateful for your support," Favian said. "Tell me, have you seen M. Listeau today? With or without his whip?"

Campaspe covered her alarm well; there was only the merest flash of guilty knowledge behind her smile. "I don't know any Listeau," she said.

"But you know Madame Listeau, do you not? Two nights ago you asked me to give her message to Captain Fontenoy. And that was very curious, because your mistress told me that Madame Listeau was not at the party."

"She sent a messenger. Do you think there will be a horsewhipping?" Campaspe asked, trying to turn aside the direction of the inquiry.

"I don't know whether there will be or not," he said. He narrowed his eyes and scowled, assuming what an old shellback would call his *quarterdeck face;* she took a step backward. "But I know what will happen if there *is* a horsewhipping. Captain Fontenoy can't allow himself to be horsewhipped in public, not without either challenging Listeau or leaving the country. Either he loses all he's built here, or he's in a fight for his life. In a duel anything can happen: both men could be killed. And all over a misunderstanding. Do you think you would enjoy knowing, for the rest of your life, that two men died because you wanted to play a prank?"

Her eyes widened; she took another step back. "No," she said quickly. "No, I didn't think of—I thought it would be amusing to make Captain Fontenoy think—everyone knew he was following Madame Listeau around Madame de la Ronde's party! I didn't think anyone would be killed." The thought seemed to terrify her.

"Perhaps there won't be a duel," Favian said. "But if there is word of any more trouble between Captain Fontenoy and Listeau, I want you to give me your word on something. I want you to promise you will send M. Listeau and Captain Fontenoy a letter telling them what you have done. Will you give me that promise?"

Campaspe stared at him for a long moment, and then swallowed hard. She nodded dumbly. Favian unshipped his quarter-deck face and permitted himself a thin smile. "Very well," he said. "You may not have to write that letter. But it will be better if you have to face a little embarrassment if we can spare some lives."

"Yes, Captain Favian," she said. She looked up in sudden alarm. "Have you told Captain Gideon or Madame Markham?"

"Nay. I did not."

She brightened, her smile flashing out. "Thank you, Captain!" Campaspe cried and threw her arms around him. She stood, jumped up to kiss his cheek, then ran into the hotel, dragging her bundle. Favian looked up in alarm to see if any passersby were looking; he caught an indulgent look from a strolling Creole gentleman, perhaps a father of daughters himself, used to similar scenes.

Favian walked toward his hotel, but was halted on the sidewalk for a few moments by a religious procession, worshippers parading the statue of a saint. The priest led the procession gravely, ignoring the fact his parishioners were parading past a bordello. The papists permit their flock to live alongside sin, Gideon had said: true enough. The Roman religion, old and cynically wise in its fashion, understood the needs of the body as the New England faith did not; Favian had been in enough papist countries to know that.

The parade passed, and Favian stepped on the way to his hotel. He would change his clothes, dressing a little less conspicuously, and then go to his appointment. At the vaulting academy.

EIGHT

Favian was drinking amontillado with his chaplain when the package was brought up by the hotel porter, who called him *Mr. Markham* because he had avoided giving his rank at the desk. "One moment, Doctor," he said, tipped the porter, and cut open the package with his pocketknife. There was an overwhelming scent of eau de cologne springing from the package, and then Favian saw three embroidered handkerchiefs, monogrammed *FM*, with a neat little fouled anchor stitched in each corner. There was also a card.

> Dearest Captain Markham:
> A gift from your devoted servant. Thanks for saving my life!
> A thousand kisses,
> Campaspe.
>
> XXXXXXXXXXXXXXXXXXXXXXXXXXXXXXXXXX
> PS: O Love! Has he done this to thee? What shall (alas!) become of me?
> C.

The Lyly couplet again, one word altered. Favian read the card with an indulgent smile and put the package away.

"I had some linen made," he said. "There is a good tradition here—French lace and so forth."

"Is there?" said Dr. Talthibius Solomon. He was a youngish man, still under thirty, enthusiastic, ingenuous, and a late convert to martial virtues. He had led the boarding party during the *Carnation* fight; Lieutenant Stone had said he couldn't hold the chaplain back. "I shall have to investigate, sir. It is a various city, to be sure."

"To be sure," Favian said.

"I hope you are not displeased by my unexpected arrival," said Solomon. "My flock seemed to need little tending; I had always wanted to see this Creole city—when I joined the *Macedonian,* Captain Jones promised me exotic sights, you know—and there was a pilot boat headed upriver. I can be back at the *Macedonian* for my next service, if need be. And I discovered pastoral work here, comforting the afflicted Mr. Lovette."

"Enjoy the city while you can, Doctor. I think we shall be at sea soon. As soon as I can speak with General Jackson." If Solomon had been a line officer Favian would have bitten his head off for leaving the frigate in that fashion, but staff officers were most often supernumerary anyway, and best indulged. Favian had neither served on a ship with a chaplain before nor wanted to—and if Solomon decided to fall in love with New Orleans and remain here preaching to the papists, Favian would cheerfully bid him farewell.

"General Jackson!" Solomon said. "Would that be the same Jackson who was connected with the Burr Conspiracy?"

"I don't know, sir."

"Burr. Such an interesting man. A Princeton man, you know, like myself." Solomon launched himself into a long discourse in which an analysis of the character of Aaron Burr was oddly mixed with a description of the history and curriculum of the College of New Jersey. Favian's attention waned rapidly, and the scent of eau de cologne brought his mind back to his appointment, two nights before, in the elegantly appointed sporting palace of Madame Dufour.

Dressed as discreetly as his six-foot four-inch frame would allow, Favian had gone to the place and picked out a slender, auburn-haired girl named Marie, with the intention of staying the night. She reminded him slightly of Caroline in the way she moved, in the way her auburn hair was pulled up to reveal the curve of her ears and nape. Marie was delighted to have only the one customer for the entire evening, and eagerly led him upstairs by the hand. Her room was filled with heavy, ornate furniture, a carved teak bedstead, a mahogany wardrobe; it was scented and lit by a pair of discreet rose-colored lamps.

It was not until he faced her on the bed that he realized she was not well; she turned away from his kiss to cough, and he saw the pink tinge around her nostrils. "Just a cold, *mon cher,*" she said. "It's almost gone now." She slid onto his lap, her hands playing with his shirt buttons. There was a narcotic taste on her tongue: laudanum, he thought, cough medicine.

Somehow the night had been off-key, not entirely satisfactory. Her moans of pleasure were professional enough, but had a rehearsed quality that he found a little disturbing—not unexpected, of course, just somehow not right. The whiskey she offered had been watered. During a critical moment of the second engagement she reached for a handkerchief on the bedside table and blew her nose. This demonstration of her lack of attention to the task at hand led Favian to call an early end to the evening. Afterwards, while she was dosing herself with more laudanum, he began to dress; she stopped him with a hand on his thigh.

"*Chéri,*" she said. "You will go now? Are you unhappy with your Marie?"

"Not at all." He kissed her shoulder. "I just don't want to catch your cold."

"Too late for that, I think," she said. There was a silence; perhaps she sensed his lack of enchantment. He left her a moderate tip on the bureau and stepped out of the room, shrugging into his overcoat, and saw for a startled second a blue Navy undress coat coming up the stairs, single epaulet on the left shoulder, the badge of a junior lieutenant. Instantly he turned and reentered the room, amazed at that lieutenant's lack of discretion—the Navy permitted their junior officers to sin in secret, and so Favian had always done, but flaunting one's carnal habits before the population was more than the Navy would tolerate. Was this the usual practice on the New Orleans station?

Even if it was, Favian thought, he would be damned if he'd let some whoring lieutenant catch him at Madame Dufour's. He was not about to be the subject of gossip at the *Carolina*'s wardroom table.

Marie, reclining on the bed, one leg drawn up as she scratched her calf, looked at him incuriously. "Did you forget something, *chéri*?" she asked.

"I changed my mind," he said, slipping out of his overcoat. She summoned a smile and lay back on the pillow, one arm over her head, showing him her body, flexing the muscles of her belly as she pointed her raised leg at the ceiling, a lascivious danseuse. "I'm so glad you want me again," she said.

He managed to summon the desire for a third complex embrace; it was better this time, more prolonged; Marie paid attention and perhaps enjoyed it. Afterwards he felt drowsy; Marie swallowed more laudanum as a sleeping-draught and slept like a stone until morning. There was an early morning encounter, Marie a little groggy but smiling; her tip was increased and Favian was off to his hotel, making certain there were no epaulets on the stair.

Since then he had been awaiting the first sign of Marie's cold. It had not yet appeared, but Favian realized he might have a need for Campaspe's embroidered handkerchiefs some time in the next few days.

Dr. Solomon was winding up his analysis of Burr and Princeton, apparently concluding that Burr was an atypical product of the college and no real blot on its escutcheon: no other graduate, to the doctor's knowledge, had ever been convicted of treason.

"Aye," Favian said. "Nor was Burr, remember. He was acquitted."

"An extraordinary man," said Solomon. "This amontillado is quite good. You know, the midshipmen have been playing Captain Porter's game every day, now the frigate is anchored. Mr. Stanhope is missed; he was a very good player."

Porter's game, the wardroom full of model ships every day. The lieutenants must be annoyed. "I think," said Favian, "they should practice engaging an entire British fleet with the *Macedonian* alone. That, unfortunately, is likely to be our task."

The chaplain looked up at Favian with curiosity. "You have been in a great many battles for so young a man. Thirty, are you not?"

"I am."

"And you helped to burn the *Philadelphia* in Tripoli harbor. Participated in the bombardments. Served as Decatur's lieutenant when the *Macedonian* was taken from the British. And then there was Markham's Raid."

Plus three duels, numerous skirmishes, and a small battle with spies on Groton Long Point near New London, Favian thought. That should be enough blood for one lifetime. But more will be spilled, he knew; spilling blood was his profession.

"Aye," he said.

"That fight between *United States* and *Macedonian* must have been exciting," Solomon said, enthusiastic. "*United States* was hardly hurt at all, and *Macedonian* suffered such a great many casualties. I remember the papers at the time: prodigious casualties. I wonder, sir, if you could tell me the details. I only know the fights we have had on this voyage, the running fight with the blockading squadron, the capture of the *Carnation*. Lieutenant Hourigan told me the *Carnation* fight was quite unusual. Was it really the case?"

"It was a surprise attack at night, and they weren't keeping proper lookout. Didn't see us till we were on them. And then we had twice their weight in guns—I had to take care not to fire too many broadsides and sink them by accident, when all we wanted to do was take them. I won't testify as to typical—no sea fight is *typical*, in my opinion—but it was certainly not a fair one."

Solomon frowned slightly; perhaps he was disappointed. "There are very few sea fights that are ever fair," Favian explained. "Matched fights are rare. Perhaps it is better thus: the inferior ship will have a better knowledge of when to surrender."

"Like the *Macedonian* when you took her?" Solomon asked.

Favian frowned. "Carden was a fool," he said. "The man played his hand badly. Didn't understand Captain Decatur's tactics at all. Hung off at long range and took a pounding from our superior ordnance, then decided to charge in close and carry us by boarding—but by then it was too late. We tore him to shreds. He didn't have much of a chance at the beginning, you understand, we overmatched him considerably with a bigger ship and more guns. But he could have played his hand better."

"Such a cost," Solomon said. "All those honest sailors paying for their captain's errors."

A picture of the beaten *Macedonian* flickered through Favian's mind. He had been the first American officer aboard and had expected a beaten ship—he'd seen those before—but nothing like what had confronted him. All masts gone, the frigate was rolling its gunports under with each wave, bringing the sea in to create a lake in the well deck, a lake in which bodies and parts of bodies sloshed to and fro, staining the water red. The wounded had been stacked like cordwood in the dripping cockpit; their moans filled the ship like a flock of mad spirits. The survivors had broken into the spirit locker and drank to end their own pain and guilt; they staggered singing over the ship or danced insane hornpipes. Defeat. Horrible. He had never spoken of it to anyone but his father, who had seen beaten ships in his own war; he had never told Emma Greenhow, though she had wanted to know. He had wanted to spare her the knowledge, the burden.

"Those lives are on Carden's conscience, if he has one,"

Favian said. He knew he was speaking too vehemently, too bitterly; Solomon was looking at him in surprise. "You have seen a little combat at sea; you know what roundshot and grape can do. You have seen nothing compared to what you will see if we are in a major fight with another frigate our size or larger. Neither we nor the British are used to defeat; we fight till one side is finished. There have been a lot of ships sunk in this war, and that is unusual. Warships are hardly ever sunk; usually they fight till it is obvious that they have lost and then surrender. But we Americans and the British are different. *Diamond cut diamond:* that is what Dacres of the *Guerrière* said. True enough. It is the honest sailors that will suffer if the officers guess wrong, but the honest officers are capable of suffering as well."

"I don't doubt it, sir," Solomon said. His voice was unusually solemn. "It is a great burden, to have so many lives in one's keeping. But our church teaches us that no soul belongs to another man—it may not be our own fault if we meet our death, but it is entirely each man's responsibility to meet it as a Christian."

"Just so," Favian said, not believing it. He had no religion and did not believe in Dr. Solomon's comforts. In a few weeks, perhaps days, he would be bringing *Macedonian* out against an entire fleet, and the lives in his keeping would answer for any wrong decision. He had been court-martialed once already for the loss of a ship, his *Experiment* brig that had gone on the mud of North Massachusetts, and did not want to go through it again. *Experiment* had been lost in a capricious storm, and he did not believe it had been through his fault. If *Macedonian* was taken by the enemy, it would be a different matter. Another picture of the beaten frigate passed through his mind, the blood dripping from the scuppers, the wounded howling in the red-splashed cockpit, but this time it was Favian standing beaten on the quarterdeck, not Carden, handing his sword to a triumphant British captain. The court-martial would go easier if there were a lot of casualties; the bloodier the battle, the more it would show the captain had done his best. Better still if the captain could arrange to die, like James Lawrence of the *Chesapeake*, gasping out some immortal last words like "Don't give up the ship!" It avoided the bitter court-martial altogether. The Navy would prefer lots of blood, the captain's included, and a ship so battered it would be useless to the enemy. The Navy was in business to gather glory, not to save lives. Well, Favian would do his best to give the Navy what it wanted, as he had all along.

"I wonder, Doctor, if I might ask your advice," Favian said. "It is a matter concerning an officer here, on the New Orleans station."

"Of course, sir. That is why I am here," Solomon said. His eyes were dancing; he always enjoyed moments of this sort.

"Two evenings ago, while I was admiring a little papish chapel on St. Philippe Street, I saw an officer leaving the house next door," Favian said. "The Corinthian establishment, if you take my meaning, of one Madame Dufour. I am not," he said hastily, as Solomon tried to speak, "concerned about the act itself. The officer was a lieutenant and a gentleman by act of Congress; there is no possibility of ordering him to keep chaste. Especially considering the, ah, the licentious atmosphere here in New Orleans. What concerned me was the fact that the officer in question wore his uniform, and therefore his behavior reflected on the Navy. I wonder, sir, if you might know some tactful way in which to make the officer concerned aware of his, ah, indiscretion."

Solomon smiled indulgently. "I think, sir, you might leave it to me. Was it one of the *Carolina*'s lieutenants? I need not know the officer's name, sir, just his ship."

"I do not recall the man's name, Doctor, so that's just as well," Favian said. "But I believe he is one of the *Carolina*'s lieutenants, aye."

"Then, sir," said Solomon with a grin of impish glee, "I know precisely how to handle the matter. I am invited to dine with the *Carolina*'s wardroom tomorrow, and I shall mention the incident. Two nights ago, I shall say, I was walking on St. Philippe Street when I saw an officer leaving a disreputable house. The officer belonged to one of the local militia companies, as I could see plainly by his uniform. Whether a man patronizes such a place, I shall say, is surely between himself and God; but how could a man reflect dishonor upon his uniform and his regiment? I shall catch one of them in a blush, Captain! Then I shall know I've struck home!"

Favian looked at the enthusiastic chaplain with indulgent regard. Perhaps the man had his uses after all.

"Splendid, sir," he said. "I think that will serve."

They chatted for a time about the city, its attractions and

polyglot inhabitants, and then Dr. Solomon rose to take his leave. They bowed farewell; Favian poured himself another glass of amontillado and went to stand by the window, considering what he was going to do for the rest of the day. He had paid his morning visit to Claiborne, urging as usual the declaration of martial law, that men be sent to see to the obstruction of the bayous, that the Navy be given powers to find crewmen for its vessels—he was careful not to use the word impress. Claiborne, as usual, had deferred all decisions to the next meeting of the Committee for Public Safety, or the arrival of General Jackson, but he had at least wavered on the impressment business. Favian and Patterson had decided between them to take it in shifts; each would visit Claiborne once per day, making the same pleas. Perhaps the governor would eventually say yes just to avoid the nuisance.

His only other duty, that of visiting Lovette in *Louisiana*'s sick bay, had also been performed that morning. Perhaps he would take a stroll through the city streets, a pleasure at any hour. He had made up his mind to change his clothes and leave when there was a knock on the door.

"A lady visitor, Mr. Markham." It was the same lackey as before. "A Madame Desplein. She wishes to bring you a message."

"I know the lady," Favian said. "Tell her I will be down to see her directly."

"Not necessary, m'sieur. She will come to your room." The porter, expressionless, bowed and closed the door. Favian wondered if other New Orleans hotels permitted women to visit single men in their rooms; certainly it was permitted nowhere else in America, where most hotels, to avoid even the appearance of scandal, had separate entrances for men and women. But of course Campaspe, he thought, might be with her as chaperon.

She was, he discovered, alone; she bobbed a curtsy in return to his bow. The porter closed the door behind them. "You seem a little out of breath," Favian said. "Please sit down. Can I order you some tea or coffee? Or perhaps offer you a glass of wine?"

"The wine, thank you, Captain," she said, glancing out his window at the rooftops. "Most New Orleans buildings, you know, don't have a third storey; until recently they've been afraid to build high on this soft ground. I suppose I'm unused to the climb. Nice view you've got." He handed her a crystal glass; she tasted the wine delicately and smiled. "Madame Markham sent me," she said. "She requests the honor of your presence at dinner tonight, seven o'clock."

"Of course. I shall be happy to come."

"Good. There will be *poque* afterward." She smiled and sat down on the bed, smoothing the coverlet with an inviting hand; Favian felt a taut, cynical grin tugging at the corners of his mouth and repressed it.

"Do they expect you back," he asked carefully, "anytime soon?"

She shook her head slowly, the smile still on her face. "Would you mind," he asked, "if I sat beside you?" Another shake of the head, impatient this time.

"You're so damned polite," she said as he joined her on the bed. "A Latin would have raped me the second I stepped into the room. That's what the porter thought; I tipped him for his silence." She alternated the flavor of his kisses with that of amontillado.

"You understand," he said, remembering that *good but unscrupulous,* "that this is not an offer of permanence? *Proposition d'une affaire,* not *demánde en mariage*?"

"I understand," she affirmed, her lips tightening for a moment, a fierce little V appearing between her eyebrows; Favian was suddenly glad to have made the distinction. Then she threw her head back and laughed. "Are you so cautious in combat with the British? What dull battles you must fight!" Teasingly, but a little forced.

"Good intelligence," said Favian, "is a necessity to any successful engagement." He kissed the hollow of her throat. She exclaimed as she removed his doeskin gloves, revealing the mutilated fingertips, mementos of the *Experiment* wreck, when he'd kept Midshipman Stanhope from being swept overboard at the cost of most of his fingernails. Some had never grown back; the others were black and horny. She kissed the hands, the scars, the ridged horn, and in an instant of swelling compassion Favian forgave her entirely the display of thwarted ambition.

Her modest gown and shift were disposed of; his own complicated layers of clothing took a little more effort. Her breasts were large in relation to her small body, entirely out of fashion; but when he cupped her breast with his torn hand, feeling the engorged nipple under his palm, her lively eyes half closed with delight, and he fancied he could almost hear her purr.

Madame Desplein's small, white body was a joy: Favian found he could cover her entirely with his tall, lean frame, or pluck her easily from the bed, her limbs winding around him, her sex still gripping his priming iron as he whirled her about the room in a laughing venereal waltz. So much better than Marie with her sniffles, opiate-tasting tongue, and bored eyes. Favian and the amontillado were both near exhaustion before he realized that he didn't know her forename, still thought of her as *Mrs. Desplein.* She smiled at his question.

"Eugénie," she said. She rolled over, resting her chin on his pectoral. "I will have to drink some lemonade with mint. Otherwise Mrs. Markham will think I've been at the wine."

"I can have some lemonade sent up."

"No. We'd have to dress." Eugénie kissed his chest, licking his little nipples. "I still have some time. I hope we can put it to use." Fingers pursued his quiescent manhood, detecting a hesitant response. Her kisses tracked down his chest and belly, then began to warm and encourage his growing tumescence. Favian gazed down at her bobbing head, at his hands possessing her dark, scented hair, and thanked the goddess Fortune for the appearance of this lusty Creole woman, the current personification of New Orleans and its happy carnal nature. M. Desplein must have been mad to trade her for a bullet from the pistol of some dragoon bullyboy.

Satisfied with the product of her endeavors, Eugénie rose to straddle his bone-thin body, her pelvis proudly outthrust: guess what I've got here! He sat up to kiss her breasts, her throat; she sighed as she slipped down on his lap, fitting herself to him. There was a long and energetic coupling, ending with Eugénie beneath him on the bed, her hands clutching him to her as they spasmed to completion amid a bed littered with their clothing, the blankets and sheets and pillows scattered as if by a hurricane, and somewhere two crystal wineglasses that rang against each other with each bounding movement of the mattress.

Refreshed, Eugénie jumped to her feet, a laugh on her lips. "Late. Must go. Let 'em think I was drinking, a more permittable offense than this. Ooh." She bent over suddenly, arrested in her movement toward where her shift was draped over the brass headrailing. "Handkerchief." She snatched at the embroidered linen on the table, and Campaspe's gift was baptized, Eugénie dabbing clinically, peering at herself while Favian watched; there was a little frown on her face, but no trace of modesty.

"Can you come tonight?" Favian asked. She shook her head, crushed the handkerchief into a ball, tossed it on the bed.

"Best not, my love," she said. "I'll be working late with guests tonight, and I'll be expected to be up when Madame rings at dawn. But tomorrow afternoon . . ." She flashed him a smile of purest lechery. "Tomorrow afternoon I shall be free."

"I will wait," he said. "I'll have them bring up luncheon." She slipped the shift over her head, her movements brisk and energetic. "Can you help me with my hair? I'll have to put it up."

"Of course." He assisted with the braiding of her sweet-smelling hair, the coiling of the braids about the crown of her head; he kissed her nape. She jumped up, took her bag, and stood on tiptoe to peck him lightly. After her departure, Favian assembled his clothing, straightened the bed, and considered ordering a bath. Her scent was heavy in the room. The sun seemed very low; there was probably no time for a bath as long or luxurious as the one he wished for. A sponge bath would have to do. He went to the heavy porcelain basin, picked up the pitcher, and splashed water into the basin. New Orleans, he reflected, was beginning to fulfill its promise.

NINE

"I hope," Maria-Anna said, "that you know the waltz and the cotillion. The Creoles won't dance American dances—it's a matter of pride. There were riots, you know, when the Americans tried to substitute the reel and the jig—almost an insurrection, in fact. There won't be a fandango at de la Ronde's."

"I'm familiar with the European dances," Favian said. "M. St. Croix was a good teacher."

"Ah. I forgot your father's body servant was a former dancing master." Her hands shuffled the cards expertly on the red baize table. They had just finished dinner, and Maria-Anna had moved with her birthing stool to the drawing room, waiting for the other guests to arrive so that the gambling could start. "We can't play *poque* with only two," she said. "Perhaps piquet?"

"Why not with two?"

She smiled thinly. "Because the opponent's hand would be clear. No mystery." Favian remembered, cursing his stupidity, that *poque* was played with only a partial deck, five cards for each player.

"Why not play with a full deck?" Favian asked.

"I've tried it—it's desirable, really, because with the full deck the odds of being dealt a given hand would not change every time someone left the table." She signaled to Eugénie to bring her a cup of coffee. "But the play is dull with a full deck; the odds of getting a worthwhile hand are very much reduced."

Favian considered the problem. *Poque* was played with five cards per player, the size of the deck increasing with the number of participants. After an ante, the cards were shuffled and dealt, after which betting commenced. After any number of rounds of betting those players remaining showed their hands and the winner took his money. Scoring was simple: two pair beat one pair, three of a kind beat two pair, and so on . . . in the event of a bluff, which was not unknown, the hand with the highest card would take the stakes. The very simplicity of the game was its strong point; the scoring was elementary and did not require a sophisticated knowledge of odds and play as did whist, and with play being swift, a great many hands could be played in an evening. The relative swiftness of the play resulted in the potentiality of a very large amount of money changing hands in one night, and in addition the large number of hands played would eventually even out the luck involved. Someone with a string of bad hands early in the evening would probably find a proportionate amount of good luck later in the play. This meant that a plunger, hoping for a string of luck, would lose to the persistent player who knew the odds and who bet wisely with each hand. Favian considered that as long as the two attractions to the game, the simple scoring and swiftness of play, were continued, then any tampering should be justified.

Eugénie brought Maria-Anna's cup of coffee, her eyes modestly downcast so as not to cross accidentally with Favian's. Maria-Anna, they both knew, was an acute woman; it would be hard to keep any relationship concealed from her. And concealed it must be, to keep Gideon out of it: there were certain things it was best for Favian's cousin not to know.

"Where's the nigger?" Maria-Anna asked, glancing up at Eugénie. "He's supposed to be serving in here."

"Captain Gideon asked him to go for a newspaper."

"Mph." She waved a hand, dismissing Grimes, dismissing Eugénie, then looked up at Favian. "Did you say yes to piquet?"

"That's my cousin you're speaking of," Favian pointed out.

"Your nigger cousin."

Favian shrugged: not worth the fight. "Let's try playing *poque* with the full deck," he suggested. "Perhaps we can work out an improvement."

With the first few hands, played by betting only counters, not real money, it became obvious why the game had most often been played with a reduced deck: play was simply dull. Favian won the first hand with a pair of treys against Maria-Anna's empty hand; Maria-Anna won the second with an empty hand queen-high against Favian's ten-high, and then won the third with a full hand against Favian's pair of fives. Favian, facing Maria-Anna's steadily increasing bets, found himself wondering how he could improve that pair. If only there were some way to get a new deal. He laid down his hand and watched Maria-Anna rake in the counters.

On the next hand he was blessed with a pair of deuces and resigned himself to watching his bet join Maria-Anna's accumulated wealth. In sheer annoyance he reached across the table and seized the cards. "Pardon me." He slammed the deck down in the middle of the table, making the counters leap; he discarded his three worthless cards and took three new cards from the deck, pleased to find a pair of jacks among them. Maria-Anna looked at him with shock. "New rule," he said. "Discard and take new cards."

"It alters the odds."

"Try it."

She grimaced, discarded her whole hand—Favian was surprised to realize she'd not had as much as a pair—and drew five more, slip-slap, from the deck. Favian plunged a ten-dollar counter; Maria-Anna raised another ten, and then triumphantly displayed three queens in her hand. Favian found he didn't care about the loss.

"It works," he said, enthusiastic. "Another round of betting added; that'll make for higher stakes and more interesting play. And another element of skill added—you knew I had a pair because I kept two cards. I knew you had nothing because you discarded your whole hand."

Maria-Anna was clearly reserving judgment. "Let's try again and see if it works," she said.

It did. Favian managed, with a wild gamble, to give himself a flux in hearts on the second draw, beating Maria-Anna's two pair, the second of which she acquired on the draw. In the next hand Maria-Anna's three of a kind beat Favian's two pair. By the time guests began to arrive, Favian's innovation had been smoothed into a successful game.

The guests were familiar: Denis de la Ronde; a smiling Declouet, ready to drop another fortune; the lawyer Edward Livingston, Claiborne's political enemy and perhaps Patterson's patron. There were also a number of sea captains who, Favian gathered, were to provide company for Gideon, but who were not part of the gambling set. Before any playing began, they stood chatting in the parlor, eating the excellent shrimp remoulade and oysters en brochette sent up by the hotel kitchens. "I am happy to see you, Captain." Livingston smiled. "I have been speaking with Commodore Patterson about the current emergency, and he assures me that the Navy is ready to do its part."

"As ready as the Navy can be, considering that the New Orleans station's largest ship, the *Louisiana*, has no crew," Favian said. "If we were able to acquire sailors for our ships, I should be more sanguine about the Navy's part."

"That would require martial law, dictatorial power," Livingston said.

"If the current emergency is not excuse enough to declare martial law, I don't know what would be," said Favian.

"So much power in the hands of one man. Dangerous," Livingston said. Meaning dangerous in the hands of Claiborne.

"Dangerous. So are the British. If the British catch us unprepared, everyone loses."

"Ah. Very true. Have you tried this shrimp? Excellent, I thought." General Jackson, Favian thought despairingly, had better arrive soon. Claiborne could not hold these people together.

If Jackson were not a leader behind whom all these factions could rally, Louisiana would continue blundering onward to disaster. Somewhere in his spine Favian could feel the British keels slicing through the water, cutting away the time Favian's capture of the British documents had given the city. "And now *poque*, Captain?" Of course; why not? There was nothing else to do, nothing except to throw up his hands and take *Macedonian* on its interrupted journey to the Indian Ocean.

No, he would wait for Jackson. If Jackson could not somehow retrieve the situation, Favian would do what little damage a single frigate could to the British and then run for it. He'd do his best, then hope an expedition to the Bay of Bengal would weaken the British enough to make them concede Louisiana at the peace talks.

Then Campaspe entered with a tray of pastry, and Favian excused himself from the *poque* party to thank her for the handkerchiefs. "They were put to use right away," he said truthfully. "Perhaps I am getting a cold."

"Try one of these—I ate one bringing the tray up, and it was quite good," Campaspe said. She looked up at him, eyes shining. "I hope you will not be sick for M. de la Ronde's ball!"

"I don't think so," he said, taking Campaspe's advice in the choice of his pastry.

"M. de la Ronde's balls are all quite famous. Even in Mobile they speak of them. Do you have an escort yet, Captain?"

He should have been warned by the sudden trace of eagerness in her tone, but instead he bit into his pastry and shook his head. "Will you take me, Captain?" she asked, seeing her opening. Favian looked at her in utter surprise.

"I've never been to a ball, not really—a little servants' ball, once, downstairs in the Mobile house," she said quickly. "I've never had a chance to, to go to a real Creole ball—and Captain Gideon and Madame will never be invited, not after she betrayed the Mobile Creoles by marrying an American. Perhaps I'll never get the chance again, not with Captain Gideon taking us to New England as soon as he gets the captured schooner free!"

Favian considered the situation as Campaspe spoke. He hadn't an escort to the ball; he had, in fact, intended to ask Maria-Anna to introduce him to a suitable local girl, preferably a Creole so that he could demonstrate Creole-Kaintuck solidarity in the face of the crisis. He couldn't take Eugénie Desplein: that would be to publicly legitimize a relationship he far preferred to keep clandestine. But Campaspe was safe—she was too young to be taken seriously as a romantic prospect; Favian would be considered to be chivalrously escorting her to her debut, as if presenting a cousin. He wouldn't mind; he'd done that sort of thing before, escorting the sisters of brother officers to one event or another, a ball or concert.

"I will speak to Madame Markham," Favian said. "If she has no objections, I will be honored."

The delight that crossed Campaspe's face was so extreme that Favian was afraid she'd drop the pastry and kiss him on the spot, but instead she blushed crimson and dropped him a low curtsy. He bowed in return and excused himself to the card game.

The new version of *poque* was an immediate success, despite the fact that the new players lost heavily, not yet having acquired knowledge of the new strategies: Favian and Maria-Anna each won several hundred dollars apiece. Favian was beginning to admire her style of play, the way she kept her opponents off-balance, thinking that she was playing conservatively by plunging only on pat hands, then surprising everyone with a full-blown bluff. Even though Favian had invented the new version, Maria-Anna had absorbed its principles more quickly, and Favian found himself imitating Maria-Anna's style and profiting thereby. It wasn't until after the game came to its conclusion that Favian could address Maria-Anna on the subject of Campaspe. She gave him a startled look, and then an intelligent, amused light entered her eyes. "You're safe enough, I suppose," she said. "I can guess whose idea this was."

"I don't mind. I had no plans to take anyone else."

Maria-Anna tilted her head, smiling wryly. "You realize," she said, "that this will turn my household upside down for the next week."

"It won't be anything unusual, then." She laughed and linked her arm in his as they walked to the parlor, where Campaspe was standing by the buffet, dispensing food, tea, and coffee while Eugénie Desplein handled the punch, rum, and whiskey, which the assembled sailors were swilling down with their accustomed sangfroid. As Campaspe saw them approaching, her face went through a series of remarkable transformations: delight, apprehension, fear, hope, anxiety—Favian found himself grinning at her swift metamorphoses, and the girl took his grin as a hopeful sign;

her final transformation was to her blinding, remarkable smile, projecting her radiant joy through the dense, tobacco-fogged atmosphere of the room.

"Miss Campaspe," Favian said, bowing low before her. "May I have the honor of your company at M. de la Ronde's ball Wednesday next?"

This time she *did* rush up and kiss him; as he grinned and uncoiled her arms from around his neck, he caught Eugénie giving him a cynical look from behind her punch bowl.

"Back to the pastry tray, my dear," Maria-Anna said, steering the girl back to her station. "You may be the envy of the Creole girls on Wednesday night, but tonight you're still serving our guests."

"Thank you, Captain Markham!" Campaspe said breathlessly. "I won't embarrass you, I promise!"

"You'll be enchanting, I'm sure," Favian said, trying to keep the grin from breaking out again. Maria-Anna patted his arm and went to speak to a guest, and Favian cut one of Gideon's cigars with his pocketknife and held it to a candle.

"Captain Markham," said a voice at his side. He straightened to see a short, dapper man at his side, a Creole whose hair was twirled into carefully fashioned lovelocks on his forehead. "I am Captain Grailly."

"Honored, sir."

"*À votre disposition,*" the man said perfunctorily, inclining his body forward in a civil bow. He took another cigar and cut it with an elaborately decorated clasp knife. Favian wondered whether this dandy was actually a seaman, or whether he had a commission in the militia.

"I, Captain Markham, am the representative of a group of merchants," Grailly said. "We have been wondering how long you intend to stay in our city."

"That," said Favian, who knew when he was being pumped and when he wasn't, "will depend on the situation."

"But you are senior, I believe, to Commodore Patterson?" Probing. "You will supersede him?"

"I am the senior officer on station, yes," Favian said. "But he is assigned to this station, and I am not. I am perfectly satisfied," he said, fixing his eye on Grailly, making certain he was understood, "perfectly satisfied with Commodore Patterson's dispositions."

"You are senior," Grailly mused. "Do we not call you *commodore*?"

"I do not claim the title," Favian said.

"I do not understand. *Commodore* is the highest rank, is it not? Patterson is a commodore. You outrank Patterson by a full grade, do you not? But you are not a commodore?"

Favian blew smoke and explained the complications inherent in any honorary title. "It's like all the militia colonels they have in Tennessee," he concluded. "If one of those 'colonels' came to New Orleans and tried to take command of a company of regulars from its captain, there would be trouble. Commodore is an honorary rank, but real rank is what counts in determining seniority. I'm a post-captain, and Patterson is a master-commandant. I outrank him."

"But you do not claim commodore," Grailly observed, cocking an eyebrow. "That is strange."

"The Navy has too many commodores as it is," Favian said truthfully. And too much squabbling over who was entitled to the rank, with appeals reaching to the Secretary of the Navy and the President, who presumably had better things to do than deal with such inane bickering.

"I believe I understand," Grailly said. "You outrank Commodore Patterson, but you are only here temporarily, and so you do not wish to supersede him. That is good sense. I wonder, however, if you can help but bring a breath of change into the naval affairs here."

"I'm sure," said Favian, "I do not know what you mean."

Captain Grailly shrugged. He glanced about the room, then leaned in closer. "My friends and I would very much like to know," he said, "what we can do to assist New Orleans in this time of trouble."

"Offer every assistance and cooperation to the forces of the government," Favian replied promptly, not liking this atmosphere of melodramatic conspiracy that Grailly seemed intent on injecting into the proceedings, these probing questions that seemed intended to reveal lord-knew-what. "If you are really the friend of the merchants, perhaps you can persuade some of them to convince some of their men to join the Navy as volunteers. *Louisiana* needs crew."

"Slaves?"

Favian frowned. Some masters had sent their slaves on board

Navy ships for the purposes of collecting their pay, the slaves themselves working entirely for their masters' benefit. It was an odious system; Favian would never have permitted the practice on any ship in his command. Yet in the present emergency, he reflected, anyone who could pull a rope would be used.

"If they are slaves that can sail," Favian said. "Able-bodied, intelligent, able to follow orders. But what the Navy needs most are real sailors, black or white. A few hundred of those men I see loitering about the Hôtel de la Marine every day, drinking and getting into trouble. What supports those men, I wonder? There hasn't been any work for them here since the war started."

Captain Grailly gave a thin smile, and Favian realized at once the answer to his question: privateering, or rather the piracy that operated here under the name of privateering. "So it is men you need," he said, as if confirming to himself something he already knew.

"Preferably experienced men," Favian said. As long as they were dreaming aloud, he might as well give Grailly the complete fantasy. "Men who can hand, reef, and steer, and also know how to point a cannon."

Grailly nodded again. "Do you think, Captain Markham," he asked, "the government would express its appreciation to any who so volunteered?"

"I'm sure it would," Favian said, wondering what the man was getting at. Enlistment bonuses, medals, the handshake of the governor?

"To anyone at all?" Grailly asked. Favian heard a careful emphasis on each word, as if Grailly was making a point too obscure for Favian to fully grasp. Favian took particular care with his answer.

"I should think," he said, "the authorities would be grateful for any offer of help." He was just stating official policy, he assumed; anyone applying to Claiborne would, he thought, get the same answer. But Captain Grailly seemed to hear the words with special absorption, his cigar held by his ear as if it were some kind of witching-wand to help him comprehend the implications of Favian's words. He nodded gravely.

"Thank you, Captain Markham, for this illuminating conversation," he said. He looked at his watch with an elaborate gesture and bowed. "I regret I must take my leave. Your servant, sir."

"Servant," Favian said. Captain Grailly took his hat and stick from the hotel maid who was on station by the door, kissed Maria-Anna's hand, and left.

"Who the hell *is* that man?" Favian asked Gideon as Grailly's form vanished behind the door.

"I think he said his name was Grailly," said Gideon, frowning at Favian's language. "I don't know him. He came with Captain Turner there."

But Turner, startled by Favian's question, said he was not acquainted with any Captain Grailly, though he said he'd seen the man before, probably around the wharves; Grailly had simply entered the hotel at the same time and walked up the stairs with him. He'd assumed Grailly was a friend of Gideon's.

"Why do you ask?"

"The man just asked me some damn odd questions, that's all," Favian said. He wondered if Captain Grailly was a spy for the British, but that didn't make any sense: his questions didn't seem calculated to reveal any military secrets, or dispositions. That *Louisiana* had only a skeleton crew was obvious to anyone with a telescope, and the fact that Favian was senior officer on station was no secret, nor was the notion that the government would be grateful for volunteers. What the devil had the man been driving at?

Perhaps, Favian thought, he was one of those who simply enjoyed creating mysteries about themselves. Whatever Grailly was, he didn't seem worth bothering about. He spent the rest of the evening talking of Portsmouth society to Maria-Anna, who felt she had to be prepared for whatever New England had in store for her; then he kissed her hand, clasped Gideon's, waved to Campaspe, and took his hat, cloak, and stick from Eugénie at the door.

"Tomorrow, my dear," she said, bobbing a curtsy. Her eyes were sparkling, lascivious. "About two o'clock, I think."

"I'll be counting the hours," Favian said gallantly and made his way out. When he reached his hotel, he found her scent still perfuming the sheets. It was odd, considering the romp that afternoon and the promise of another tomorrow, that before sleep came the face conjured in his fantasies was not that of Eugénie Desplein, but rather the features of Maria-Anna Markham.

TEN

"You're doing *what*?" Favian demanded, springing from his chair.

The Reverend Doctor Solomon's reply was cheerful. "I'm going out with Lieutenant Glimph. Sometime this week. Pistols, I think. Lieutenant Cunningham of Gunboat 65 is acting as my second, so you have no need to involve yourself—I just thought that as my commanding officer you would like to be informed."

Favian stared at the chaplain in blank amazement. "Doctor, you must be mad. You are a chaplain, sir—think of your position. Will you not disgrace your collar?"

Solomon's answer was delivered calmly; clearly he had thought this out beforehand. "I will not be going out as a priest, sir. Were the church insulted it would be my duty to turn the other cheek. But I was challenged as an officer of the Navy, and the Navy's honor must be defended to the last."

"Good God." Favian's first impulse had been to tell the chaplain that the Navy's honor would be defended quite well by the line officers without the need for the staff, but that would probably not sit well with his martial doctor. Realizing that he was pacing up and down the room, he forced himself to sit down and face the chaplain once more.

The situation was incredible. Solomon and Lieutenant Cunningham had been visiting a restaurant the night before, the night a company of militia had come marching in from the German Coast upriver. A few of the militia officers, having obtained leave from their encampment, had been visiting the saloon attached to the restaurant and had been talking loudly about the topmaul duel between Levesque and Lovette; one Lieutenant Glimph, it appeared, had been particularly in his cups and had denounced the Navy's perceived cowardice. Dr. Solomon, who was not wearing his collar at the time, had chosen to resent

Lieutenant Glimph's remarks, Glimph had chosen to repeat them, Solomon had called Glimph a liar, and Glimph had challenged.

"I am perfectly well prepared," Solomon said. "Since the *Carnation* fight I have been practicing with sword and pistol. Lieutenant Glimph is a fat, blustering bully, not by any means a professional duellist like Levesque, and I am not a half-grown boy like Lovette. There is no need for any trickery such as the topmaul fight; I'm perfectly capable of using a pistol in this matter."

"Doctor," Favian said, "I cannot help but think that this will subvert your position in the ship. You are the chaplain, not a—forgive me—not a line officer; your job is not to fight."

"Sir," Solomon said. His color was high; his eyes sparkled; clearly he was enjoying himself. "The Navy is a martial service; I am perfectly prepared to do my bit."

"You are aware, I assume, of the evils of duelling, so I won't bore you with a lecture," Favian said. He'd try another tack, he thought, acting the fellow sophisticate—if only Solomon weren't such a boy! A precocious, intelligent, enthusiastic boy, more suitable for the midshipmen's berth than the dog collar he so rarely wore. "If a *man*, a grown man, chooses to risk his life in such affairs, then I'm certain he is perfectly capable of apprehending the consequences. But it is not the grown man I'm concerned about.

"You've known my concern for the midshipmen, for their education," Favian said. "They are eager, untried, and desperate for action. They are naturally aggressive. Out of this difficult material officers must be made—officers mature, responsible, cultivated, sophisticated. That is our job—yours in particular." Talthibius Solomon was beginning to perceive the direction of this argument and didn't like it; he was beginning to look sullen, resentful. His lower lip was actually outthrust, like that of a sulking child.

"Once the gunroom becomes infected with the duelling fever, there is no getting rid of it," Favian said. "The young gentlemen can go mad with it, challenging everything that moves, much to their discredit. Perhaps you know the story of Richard Somers, fighting six of his fellow midshipmen in one afternoon? I'm not saying Somers was wrong—I think he may have been right in challenging them all—but it was an inflated, unnatural, peevish sense of honor that created that situation, and that fostered the fight. And you've heard of Joseph Bainbridge and the duel he fought in Malta, and that he was promoted for it—but how did that promotion affect the other midshipmen? Suddenly all one had to do to receive a step-up was to call someone out—how much mischief did that cause?"

"You've been out," Solomon said, his tone resentful. "You've fought that Captain Brewster, and all over his insulting the Navy. And that fight in Spain, with all the mids of the *Vixen* fighting the mids of that Spanish ship . . ."

"That fight," said Favian, "was none of my doing—*I* did not challenge anyone; that was our lieutenant, who challenged on behalf of every American officer in port. And as for Captain Brewster, I was on half pay, ashore without hope of a command, and I had no responsibilities to anyone—not to subordinates, not to superiors. I was free to act. I was not in your position; I was not responsible for the moral tone of an entire ship. I had no need to set an example for four hundred of my flock." He was not being candid about that Brewster fight, where he had taken a grim delight in running the bully through, but the object was to prevent Solomon's duel, not teach a history lesson.

"I don't understand," Solomon said. "I fail to comprehend how I am setting a bad example in defending the Navy's honor."

"If you fail to understand how many young gentlemen are going to find themselves facing pistols because of this, your powers of comprehension are surely very limited, sir!" Favian snapped, leaping to his feet again, his temper finally giving way. "Blast it, man, the Navy's honor is perfectly capable of fending for itself—it won't stand or fall by your action, I assure you!" The entire body of Navy private sailors had learned to beware that temper; now Solomon was facing the full force of it. But Talthibius Solomon refused to be overawed by Favian's roaring; before many seconds had passed, he was on his feet shouting red-faced, high-flown phrases on the subject of honor—personal honor, the honor of the Navy, and the honor of the College of New Jersey, all of which Favian, it seemed, was in danger of slandering. Suddenly Favian realized that in another few seconds there would be challenges flung and another fight begun; he clamped his mouth shut and sat down. Dr. Solomon shouted into empty air for a few minutes, and then looked down in surprise, gasping for air like a fish.

"Fight and be damned, sir," Favian said. "Good afternoon."

Solomon goggled at him, then turned abruptly and tore the door open. "Blasted huge boy," Favian said a few hours later with Eugénie Desplein in his arms. "Perhaps if he loses an arm or a leg, he will show himself the example the midshipmen need."

"So many sailors are boys, I think," she said. "Have you ever seen a bigger fifteen-year-old than Finch Martin, Gideon's first officer? Like a boy just learned to swear and liking the sound of it. And Gideon, like a boy gone mad about religion—not a grown man's sort of religion at all. Perhaps there is something in the sea that keeps men in their teens."

"Perhaps you're right," Favian said. He thought of some of the Navy men he knew: Decatur, the son of Mars; Favian's particular friend William Burrows, the unhappy, eccentric intellectual who died clasping his defeated enemy's sword; James Lawrence, killed aboard the *Chesapeake;* Isaac Hull, the happy warrior; David Porter of the hair-trigger temper and pugnacious manner; Richard Somers, who had died trying to equal Decatur in glory. Yes, all could be thought of as adolescent types—but there were grownups too in the Navy, like Charles Stewart, Thomas Macdonough, Johnston Blakely: seeming almost preternaturally wise even when Favian had first met them, when they were all boys together off Tripoli. The Navy had all sorts, the foolish and the wise, the daring, the cautious, the corrupt: each sipped from the wisdom of the sea as he saw fit, or listened to the clanging trumpets of vainglory.

"There is a lot of truth in that," Favian said. "Some are boys enough."

Eugénie touched his chin, turning his head into the light to view his profile: long nose, tousled dark hair, sculptured side-whiskers. "Not you, my Favian. You are not a boy," she said. "A very careful old man, very cautious. I could listen to you all day and not learn a thing about you."

Favian felt the muscles in his cheek twitch. He clasped the hand beneath his chin, brought it up, and kissed it. "New Orleans," he said, "has far more boys than the Navy. All those militia companies in their bright uniforms, all to impress the girls on parade. The Creoles strutting, quarreling, challenging one another; the governor with his fancy general's coat and ribbon of watered silk. It makes the Navy seem old."

"You have changed the subject very artfully, my Favian. We

were talking about you,'' Eugénie said, smiling. ''But that is forgiven. If you don't want me to know about your girl friend back in Portsmouth, I will not press it.''

Favian felt an ironic laugh bubbling up. If she wanted to think he had a girl in Portsmouth, he would let her. It would make the parting easier.

''I will have to return to Madame Markham's soon,'' she said, leaning forward to kiss his ear. ''Campaspe must have her gown, and that means more work for us all. Your fault, my dear, but I understand why you could not take me.'' She spoke close to his ear. Her tone was one of purest lechery. ''Let us make the most of the time remaining,'' she said, riding her bare foot up and down his inner thigh. ''There is no sense in letting our last moments go to waste. Agreed?''

''Agreed,'' Favian said. That was one motto the Navy had taught him: Never lose a moment. He could be grateful for that, at least.

The next evening Favian presented himself at Gideon's hotel. There had been difficulty acquiring a carriage until he'd thought that there might be one on permanent hire to the Navy, which proved to be the case. He had dressed carefully in his number one rig, the gold tape on his cuffs and collar brushed until it shone, his small, elaborate presentation sword from the City of New York clipped to his belt. Eugénie Desplein, as usual, came to conduct him to the upstairs rooms after he'd sent up his card.

''You must swoon over her gown,'' she instructed. ''I've spent the entire day making adjustments.''

''I'll do my best,'' he said, and sneezed. Marie's cold, he thought. Blast it.

On the landing Eugénie turned to him and pressed her mouth to his. He returned the sudden, fierce kiss, feeling her arms go around him, and then Eugénie stepped back, a thin smile on her face. She reached out and half-playfully pinched his arm. ''Just so you don't forget who your New Orleans girl is, hey?'' she said, and led him up the stairs.

Gideon rose from his chair as he entered the parlor and clasped Favian's hand. Eugénie bustled behind the screen that hid the passageway to the living quarters. ''Campaspe will be out presently,'' Gideon said. ''Can I have Grimes get you a drink?''

"I think not," Favian said. "There will be drinks enough at the party, I think."

Gideon nodded gravely. "I've heard a story," he said, "that one of your crew will be fighting another duel. A Lieutenant Solomon?"

"Doctor Solomon," Favian said. "The Reverend Doctor Solomon, in fact—my chaplain." He watched Gideon's face as he absorbed the shocking news. "The blasted glory-struck fool. This afternoon I received a note from Lieutenant Cunningham that the fight would be with pistols and take place tomorrow morning."

"Your chaplain? Fighting a duel? Madness!" Gideon breathed. "Look at what this war has done! Next it will be the women fighting each other."

Favian grimaced. "It's utter lunacy," he said. "Solomon and I almost came to blows yesterday over the matter. Perhaps he'll come to his senses once he faces that Glimph's pistol. Of course, by then it will be too late."

"A chaplain!" Gideon said, awe winning over disapproval in his face. "Nothing good will come of it. God judgeth the righteous, and is angry with the wicked every day." Psalms, Favian thought, the Seventh; for once he'd recognized the source.

They were interrupted by the appearance of Maria-Anna and Eugénie coming from behind the screen. "I would like to present, Captain Markham," Maria-Anna said with a smile, "Doña Campaspe María Luisa Rodríguez y Sandovál."

Campaspe appeared, trying to act the lady with downcast eyes, but her natural enthusiasm got the better of her, and she looked up, eyes sparkling, her brilliant smile radiating through the room. Her ball gown was the universal white muslin gown of Josephine and the Directory; there was a lace Betsy ruff around her throat. She was wearing a spencer over her gown, and it was colored an astonishing scarlet, as bright as a British lobsterback—and what was more surprising was that the color complemented her dark coloring perfectly. She was wearing a veil over her hair, which was braided up intricately; the veil was tied off on the left side and flowed dashingly over her left shoulder. Campaspe was, in fact, a lovely young girl who showed promise of growing even more lovely in the coming few years; Favian found himself rejoicing in his choice of a partner.

"Miss Campaspe," he said, bowing to kiss her hand, "I am ravished. The Creole women will be mad with envy."

Campaspe blushed scarlet and did not reply. "Shall we be off, miss?" Favian asked. "I know you won't wish to miss any of the dances." She gave him her arm.

Favian bowed to Maria-Anna and Eugénie, then took Campaspe's hand and put it on his arm. "Don't forget," Maria-Anna lectured. "You may have one glass of champagne or wine, but no more. No tafia or brandy. Understood?"

"Yes, madame."

Favian put his cocked hat on his head as he left the hotel, then handed Campaspe into his carriage, which he had filled with flowers. She bent forward to smell them, then spoke to him for the first time since her appearance. "Thank you, Captain Markham! The flowers are wonderful!"

"You're most welcome," Favian said. "You must save the first cotillion and the first waltz for me—you can give the rest to whomever you like."

"You can have them all, if you wish," she said seriously.

Favian smiled. "No, Campaspe. Give the beaux of New Orleans a chance to see your smile." She gave him the smile then, the brilliant, remarkable smile that seemed to brighten the room. Basking in it, Favian told the carriage driver to head for the Faubourg Marigny.

There was a line of carriages in the street before the ballroom, but most of the attendees seemed to be coming on foot, the women with heavy, muddy boots peering out from beneath their gowns, one slave in the lead lighting the way with a lantern, another bringing up the rear, carrying the ladies' dancing shoes. Campaspe leaned close to Favian, peering out at the glittering men and women to name the families as they appeared. "There are the Villerés! That's Major Gabriel and General and Madame—and that's Celestin! There's Abbé Dubourg. And that's Dr. Shields."

At the door Favian handed Campaspe out of the carriage, then handed his invitation to the majordomo. "*Capitaine* Mark'am!" the man boomed in French. "Mademoiselle Rodríguez y Sandovál!" the man boomed, Favian checking his hat and Campaspe her spencer as they entered the Creole hall.

The orchestra was beginning to tune, and the ballroom was almost full: there were at least two hundred people in the room, those who had come to dance, to conduct business, to see friends, get drunk, make love, to gossip, or merely to be seen in their expensive finery. Favian spoke briefly to a few individuals he'd met at the meeting of the Committee for Public Safety; he introduced Campaspe and was introduced to their wives, sons, and daughters. The majordomo bawled out the announcement for the first cotillion: Major Gabriel Villeré, the son of the general, and his escort were to lead. Favian and Campaspe took their places, bowed to the couples on either side—General Jean-Joseph Humbert, still in his battered French uniform, was on the left, dancing with a formidable-looking Spanish woman, introduced as Señora Castillo.

"That's a pretty young thing you've got there, Captain," Humbert said, cocking an eye at Campaspe. "I bet she's a juicy little peach, eh?" Favian, stiffly surprised, recalled that Humbert had been a dealer in rabbit skins before the Revolution and that his language was not the sort usually heard in a ballroom. He was thankful Campaspe did not know French.

"Thank you, sir," he replied coldly. Humbert beamed at him, unabashed. The orchestra began to play.

Gabriel Villeré and his partner set a vigorous example, and Favian was thankful that his father's body servant St. Croix had trained him well in the art of the dance, and trained him also in such borderline military arts as dancing with a sword while avoiding the lashing of his neighbors with the scabbard, a problem that seemed to be occurring with considerable regularity among the amateur militia officers. Campaspe glanced at her feet and neighbors as she learned the patterns, then danced with enthusiasm and, as she gained confidence, growing grace. She was a natural dancer, lithe and dexterous; soon she was improvising on the patterns, and when the moment came for Favian to exchange partners with General Humbert, he cast a glance at the general and saw a pleased smile break out on the old revolutionary's face as he saw his new partner's skill.

The dances were long, twenty or thirty minutes, with extended pauses between them for the dancers to regain their wind, to indulge their appetites for wine and rum punch, and to nibble at the buffet. Etiquette insisted on the partners spending the dance gazing into one another's eyes: the result could be either extreme boredom or smouldering sensuality, and in any case one would learn a great deal about one's partner—with Favian and Campaspe neither extreme occurred; Campaspe was so excited that her eyes were darting everywhere, taking in the spectacle, learning the patterns from other dancers, watching the orchestra. Favian watched her enjoying herself and smiled: if nothing else came out of his New Orleans expedition, he could at least point to this. He saw Campaspe attracting the attention of a number of the New Orleans bravos, and as the ball went on, saw her card for the next cotillions add the names of two dashing militia officers, among them Celestin Villeré.

"Who is your lovely companion?" he was asked more than once. "Why has she never been seen at the balls before?"

"She is the ward of Captain Gideon Markham, my cousin," Favian said, thinking *ward* sounded better than *maidservant*—and in fact Campaspe seemed to fill a position somewhere between the two. He danced himself with a tall, willowy blond girl from the German Coast, who was probably thankful to have a partner taller than she. At the announcement of the first waltz Favian found Campaspe among the throng and took her in his arms. The older Creoles sat out the scandalous new dance, watching while the young people enjoyed themselves, murmuring to themselves if the youngsters seemed to be enjoying themselves to excess. Campaspe had clearly never waltzed before, but learned quickly, and was soon smiling up at him bravely. The waltz as practiced here was quite formal, with several changes of partners written into the program, and by the time it was over, and Campaspe had been retrieved from her latest partner, Favian felt the clear need for restoration.

"Would you like your glass of champagne?" Favian asked. Campaspe nodded eagerly. He escorted her to the buffet and produced champagne for her and tafia punch for himself. The servants piled a plate high with stuffed crab, and he and Campaspe shared it. He caught jealousy in the eyes of a few of the young men as they looked at him and smiled inwardly. It was a pity, for Campaspe's sake, that Gideon and Maria-Anna were leaving New Orleans: it was clear that Campaspe would not be forgotten here. Though it was probably better to spare her the inevitable disappointment: once her position was clear, and the fact of her having no fortune, these planters' sons would evaporate.

The next waltz was announced: a cornet of the Hulans asked for the honor of Campaspe's company, and with a sideways, somewhat regretful look at Favian, she accepted. Favian looked for his tall German and saw she was dancing with a chasseur half a head shorter than herself and decided it was time to thank M. de la Ronde for the invitation to his ball. He acquired another cup of punch and went in search of his host.

Denis de la Ronde accepted Favian's thanks with a smile and nodded toward Campaspe, whirling in the arms of her hulan. "I'm glad you brought Maria-Anna's little maid," he said. "It's time society saw her without an apron."

"I'm honored to have her," said Favian. "It's good, every so often, to see things all new, through a young person's eyes."

He talked briefly with Madame de la Ronde, complimenting her on her arrangements, and was introduced once again to the leader of the legislature's Creole faction, the creator of the Marigny suburb, and probably the wealthiest planter in Louisiana, Bernard de Marigny, and his stunningly beautiful wife, the former Anna Mathilde Morales, over whom, Favian had been told, he had once challenged six men to duels. Favian chatted in French with the couple, complimenting Madame on her gown, and then bowed his farewell. Returning to the buffet, he found General Humbert and nodded his greetings.

"Greetings, Captain," the general said heartily. "Have you a moment? There's someone I think you should speak to." He craned his neck over the heads of the crowd, then waved with a chicken leg to attract someone's attention. "Captain Markham," he said, "this is Captain Grailly."

"We've met, sir," Favian said, bowing to the dandy. Grailly had outdone himself for the ball: he was wearing green-and-yellow-striped trousers, Souvaroff boots with tassels, a dark brown coat with a splendid red-and-gold-quilted piqué waistcoat, in all an extravagance of color that suited him not at all.

"Captain Markham, I would regret to take you from your charming companion," Grailly said, "but she seems to be happily occupied with young Lacarrière. I think there is someone you should meet. Would you mind leaving the ball for a short while, for just a few moments?"

"It would," said General Humbert, just as a nettled Favian was about to decline, "be very much to your advantage."

Favian glanced at the general, who was regarding him soberly, with compelling urgency, and then looked at Campaspe happily dancing with the hulan Lacarrière. What the devil was this about? Humbert seemed to be taking this very seriously indeed, and

Grailly's odd behavior two nights before had surely had some purpose behind it. "Very well," he said shortly. "If my young friend comes looking for me, please tell her I will be back shortly."

He followed Grailly out of the ballroom, then down the street filled with ranked carriages. Grailly halted by a closed carriage and opened its door. "Captain, if you please," he said. "Please seat yourself, sir."

Favian, wondering what piece of intrigue Grailly was presenting him, climbed into the carriage and sat on the unoccupied seat, hitching his sword around so as not to stab the polished leather. The carriage was lit by a small oil lamp set on the starboard side of the interior. Two men faced him. Directly opposite was an olive-skinned man a few years past thirty, probably once slim but now growing a little stout; his features were regular, his dress somber black. Next to him sat a portly man of about forty, his face cheerless; there was enough of a resemblance between them to suggest kinship, but the second man seemed afflicted: the left corner of his mouth drooped, as did his left eye; the eye also wandered independently, refusing to focus, a strabismus.

"Captain Markham, I am honored by your presence," said the younger man. His English was excellent, though there was a slight, undefinable accent. "Allow me to introduce myself: I am Jean Laffite, and this is my brother Pierre."

Favian told himself he was not surprised: the appearance of the two infamous pirates, he reflected, seemed entirely consistent with everything else that had happened to him since he'd arrived in Louisiana. He leaned back in the carriage, studying them.

"Gentlemen," he said. "To what do I owe this singular honor?"

Jean Laffite smiled pleasantly; there was something in his eyes that suggested that Favian's laconic answer had confirmed some inner judgment. His elder brother, however, continued to look balefully at Favian, his roving left eye twitching unnervingly.

"You are now the senior naval officer on station," Jean Laffite said plainly. "It is possible you and I may come to some sort of éclaircissement—such a thing was impossible under Commodore Patterson."

"Captain Patterson," Favian said, "is a most worthy officer."

"Indeed he is," Laffite said quickly. "But he is a most

uncompromising partisan of the, ah, the vices in the current laws—the vicious laws, it seems, that I have transgressed."

Favian felt a cynical smile touch his lips. The laws against piracy, it seemed, were "vices." Laffite was very eloquent in English, but not eloquent enough to completely blur the boundary between piracy and legitimate commerce.

"Let us be frank, Captain," Laffite said, apparently encouraged by Favian's accepting silence. "Master-Commandant Patterson, Colonel Ross, and the others who have oppressed me—they have seized twenty-six of my vessels and arrested eighty of my men, including many of my captains. I and my brother are wanted men. I have reason, do I not, to feel ire toward the city of New Orleans, and to the national government?"

"If you desire a pardon," said Favian, "you will have to apply to the governor, not to me. And if you desire your ships, you must go to the courts."

Pierre Laffite turned away with a snort of impatience. His brother shook his head vigorously. "No, Captain, that is not what I ask," he said. He leaned forward, lowering his voice to increase the intimacy.

"The city is in great peril," he said. "The British will come within a few weeks. It will not be forgotten, I hope, that it was I who provided the first warning of their movements."

"The British threaten your livelihood as well as ours," Favian said. "I do not imagine they will allow you to continue your private war against their ally Spain. And of course your brother was in prison at the time. I am sure the government was grateful for your timely warning, though I am certain they were also aware that the warning may well have been in your interest."

Jean Laffite paused, his brow wrinkling as he chose his course. One eyelid dropped in a lazy wink.

"Your ships," he said, "lie idle for want of crews. My ships are fully crewed; they have excellent gunners, many trained in the wars in Europe, most with years of experience on my privateers. I have hundreds of muskets, as well as powder, shot, and flints. And do not think Master-Commandant Patterson's raid on Grande Terre captured all my men—I still have three thousand men willing to follow me. And all—every one—is willing to fight for the United States against any British attack on Louisiana.

"Do not think," he said solemnly, his eyes holding Favian's, "that I am boasting. I am quite willing, given the opportunity, to prove all that I say. But how can I prove it if I am subject to arrest every time I set foot in the city? How can I aid the defense of the city if the city insists upon my persecution? I am certain, Commodore Markham, that your voice can make itself heard in the matter."

"You wish a pardon?" Favian asked.

Laffite frowned, composing his answer. His elder brother turned to Favian and spoke one word.

"How?"

"Maybe you ought to tell me what you wish to offer," said Favian.

"Our assistance," Pierre said. His accent was more noticeable than Jean's, and he had some slight difficulty with articulation, but his emphatic speech left no doubt where he stood. "Our knowledge of the land. Our men, our guns, our ships."

"If the offer is sincere, I'm sure the government will be grateful," Favian said.

"But how can we prove our sincerity?" asked Jean Laffite. He had become eager, speaking rapidly, making swift gestures. "You see our dilemma. The government will not offer us forgiveness unless we prove ourselves first. But we cannot prove ourselves unless we have the freedom to move without fear of arrest."

"Perhaps," Favian said, "a conditional pardon might be arranged. Or a safe-conduct. In any case, might I suggest that the best way to demonstrate your good faith would be to turn yourselves over to the authorities?"

"*No!*" bellowed Pierre Laffite. Favian felt flying spittle touch his cheek. "Never!"

Jean put his hand on his brother's arm, restraining him. "I am afraid," he said, turning to Favian, "that is impossible. My brother's health is not good; he had a stroke some years ago, and he has not recovered. His treatment in the *calabozo* was brutal—he was in irons for weeks and not allowed sufficient exercise. I would fear for his life if he were to return. And," he said with a smile, "with my best captains currently in prison, I am afraid that we will have to remain with our men. Otherwise incidents may result. I am sorry."

Incidents, Favian thought. Pirate chieftains had uncertain control over their men at best, he knew; if the Laffites and all their chief supporters were confined for any length of time in the *calabozo*, their less trustworthy associates might seize control of the Baratarian colony. "Then," said Favian, "we are at an impasse."

Jean Laffite, smiling again, shook his head. One eyelid dropped in a wink: Favian was beginning to realize it was a habitual gesture. "I am willing to offer you certain information," he said. "I do not ask that you give anything in return for this, simply that you remember who gave it." He leaned forward again, touching Favian's knee. "I think this information may show the world how much I am to be trusted.

"Are you," he asked, "familiar with a place called Cat Island?" Favian shook his head.

"There are two islands of that name," Laffite said. "One is north of here, in the Mississippi Sound. We are not speaking of that island, but rather of the Cat Island west of Barataria, a little place situated in Terre Bonne Bay, a very nice anchorage. From Terre Bonne Bay many waterways lead north to Bayou Lafourche, which leads to the Mississippi above the city. From Cat Island a British force could take boats north to the Mississippi and cut New Orleans off from the north—do you understand?"

"Yes," Favian said.

"I have used Cat Island from time to time—it's a nice anchorage, as I've said," Jean Laffite said. "There is a little town there, and communication with New Orleans is swift and easy. At the moment," he said, "none of my men reside there. Please accept that, Commodore."

"Very well," Favian said. It was the second time he'd been addressed as *commodore,* and he considered correcting the pirate. Laffite probably thought the term flattering, but Favian found himself feeling annoyed at the title.

"There are, however, a number of privateers who do make their residence there," Laffite went on. "They are chiefly Frenchmen who have moved to Louisiana following the defeat of General Bonaparte, although some of them are older residents." He spoke with distaste: apparently Jean Laffite was not an admirer of the former French emperor. "They came to Barataria earlier this year. These men and I were not able, you understand, to come to an agreement." Laffite grinned cynically, then shrugged. "They elected their own captains and moved to Cat Island. I have nothing to do with them, and I refuse to be responsible for their actions. I have been unable to make the authorities here understand that the Cat Island people and the Baratarians are not in association."

No doubt one pirate looked much the same as another, Favian thought. Was Laffite offering the Cat Island privateers to the Navy in return for a pardon? "Go on," he said.

"You know," Laffite said earnestly, "that Captain Lockyer of the Royal Navy, in September, offered me a captain's commission, thirty thousand dollars, and grants of land if I should assist them in their project. This offer, of course, I refused."

Favian could only barely keep the smile from his face. "You did not refuse, I believe," he said. "You merely neglected to reply." There had been no chance for the offer to be refused or accepted, he knew: Patterson and Ross had eliminated the Barataria colony long before the British could ever have returned for their answer. And Laffite would have been foolish to accept in any case, since the thirty thousand was a pittance to him—he was probably worth millions—the captain's commission would have given him little more than a pension on half pay, since the British would almost certainly have refused to employ him actively. The grants of land would have only been worth anything if the British had managed to take enough of Louisiana to give away to their friends.

"But these Cat Island people know of the offer," Laffite said. "And I am not entirely certain they will not accept it. They have their reasons—they are fanatic on certain subjects. They have a project in mind much grander than privateering."

"Indeed." That seemed extremely unlikely. Laffite clearly saw Favian's skepticism. He turned to the oil lamp on the side of the carriage and adjusted the flame, increasing the brightness. He turned to his brother. "Pierre, the stick."

Pierre Laffite reached behind him to where a walking stick was leaning between the seat cushion and the side of the carriage. He handed the stick to his brother. Favian, recognizing the lathed head of the sword stick carried by de la Tour d'Aurillac and the military-looking gentleman in the Place d'Armes, watched with growing interest as Jean held the stick up in the air, between the lamp and the larboard side of the coach.

"I told you that most of the Cat Island people came to Louisiana following Bonaparte's abdication," Laffite said. "I told you they have certain loyalties. Keep what I have told you in mind and look at the shadow of this stick—see, my Captain Markham, if you recognize anything.''

Favian glanced at the shadow and felt his heart leap. There was an instantaneous recognition of the sort that made his mind cry, *But of course! Why hadn't I seen it before!* He realized he had seen it clearly once, when M. le Chevalier gave his secret away in *Louisiana*'s maintop, but Lovette and Levesque were just beginning their duel and he had been distracted.

He should have wondered, he thought, why the curious round lathework on the grip should have been so exact, so eccentric. He had even seen it used, when that tall, broad-shouldered, iron-gray individual had been holding his cane out to the noonday sun, casting its shadow on the surface of the Place d'Armes. But if he had expressed an interest, would the Cat Island people have let him live? There was a reason for the sword hidden in the walking stick—it would be used to execute those who guessed the secret.

The shadow cast by the sword stick was a perfect silhouette of Napoleon the First, late Emperor of the French, currently sulking in Mediterranean exile on the island of Elba.

''These people, these Cat Island people,'' said Laffite, confident in Favian's recognition. ''They are devoted to their emperor. There are many here—over two hundred members of the *Chasseurs à Pied*, the Middle Guard. *Three* hundred members of the *Grenadiers à Pied*, the Old Guard. And others—members of the Légion d'honneur, heroes, courtiers, men who remember the bridge of Arcola, the sun of Austerlitz—men whose noses were frozen beside their emperor's on the road from Moscow. They are devoted to their memories; they are very well organized, and they are hardened to killing—they have their master's ruthlessness and will happily murder in service to his cause. These people have taken their old uniforms with them to America; they have their battle flags stored carefully in trunks, their decorations, their Imperial Eagles. They have every intention of wearing their old uniforms again, of serving honorably under their old flags. And they are perfectly willing, for reasons that seem adequate to them, to sell Louisiana to the British.''

Favian felt himself being reined in by some interior, cautionary self—good: he had almost been carried away by the sheer romanticism of it all. Jean Laffite, he realized, was quite good at casting spells, but he was used to the romantic, fiery temperament of New Orleans—he shouldn't have tried this approach on a phlegmatic Yankee from New Hampshire.

"Why," he found himself asking, "would these imperial devotees want to sell Louisiana to Napoleon's enemies—to Perfidious Albion, no less? The greatest enemy Bonaparte ever faced?"

Laffite gave a brief smile. "You must understand that these people are in very close contact with their friends in France. A year ago France was weary of Bonaparte, weary of war—weary enough, even, to welcome the Bourbons back. But now, after a few months of Louis the Eighteenth and his unpleasant little brother Monsieur, months in which the emperor's old war-horse generals, his new nobility, found themselves snubbed by the old, titled friends of Bourbon who spent the wars lazing in cozy exile, France is growing restless again. The Bourbons have learned nothing; they are not—it is not possible to *like* them, Captain Markham, understand?" Laffite looked intently into Favian's eyes, eager Favian should comprehend his meaning. "Maybe the people are growing nostalgic for the old Eagle, maybe they are forgetting the police and the conscriptions. Perhaps they would be willing to welcome their emperor back."

"That is an interesting picture, Mr. Laffite," Favian said. "It has very little to do with Louisiana."

"But you see, Captain Markham, it does," Laffite said confidently. "These Cat Island people want to bring Bonaparte back to France. They have many ships, fast ones with expert crews. If they agree to the British proposals, they will have thirty thousand dollars, which will buy a great many military supplies. If they can snatch Bonaparte from Elba, they will be able to present him with a well-equipped force with which to make his initial strike at France.

"Further," Laffite said, "they know that in the event of the British capturing New Orleans, the American government will stop at nothing to prevent them from keeping it. The United States would send large forces down the Mississippi. The British have much of Wellington's army here in America, both in Canada and aimed at New Orleans, and with an American force bound to retake Louisiana they would have to reinforce their garrison here. Several British armies would be tied down fighting the Americans—the British would not be able to contribute a force to the Continent to fight Bonaparte."

Laffite held up a finger. "One," he said. "A naval force,

freed from British interference, with which to liberate Bonaparte from Elba. Two." Another finger went up. "A large sum of money with which to equip an army. Three." Another finger. "British forces, land and sea, tied down fighting an endless war in America, unable to interfere with the Eagle returning to his nest in Paris." He paused, then gave his easy smile, and shrugged, pretending to dismiss his story now that he knew—he knew very well—that Favian was hooked. He leaned back on his coach seat. "A fantasy, maybe, eh? Certainly a gamble. Maybe it couldn't work: maybe the French would not want their Eagle back, and maybe the British wouldn't be so cooperative. But I assure you, Captain, that these people believe this fantasy, and that if you give them the chance they will put their beliefs into practice."

"Who are their people?" Favian asked. "Their people in the city? Besides de la Tour d'Aurillac and that shopkeeper in the Rue de Camp."

Another smile, a nod complimenting Favian on his sources of intelligence. Laffite's eyelid dropped again; he looked a sly, quick bird of a man, peering at Favian with one glittering eye. "De la Tour d'Aurillac is one of their leaders, yes. And the Rue de Camp shop, run by a man named Serurier, is their headquarters in the city, the only place where one can purchase their little walking stick. Do not think, by the way, you can worm your way into their bosom simply with the use of one of these little swordsticks—they have passwords and such, masonic stuff. You would find the sword in your heart."

"We were speaking of their leaders," said Favian.

"I beg your pardon. Cat Island is run by a privateer captain named Mortier. That is a nom de guerre, we assume; many of our associates use them. He has been in the Gulf for years, in my ship the *Bolivar,* but I had to dismiss him for, ah, breaches of the regulations. Now he has worked his way into the association of the Cat Island people—I believe he calls himself their admiral." A condescending smile aimed at Mortier's pretensions. "There is another privateer named Guieu. An attorney in New Orleans, Dallemagne, their agent. Some captains, Santos, Gardanne, Pijon. Their association, by the way, is called—"

"The Guard. Yes. We know," said Favian. Pierre Laffite looked troubled: were they treating with information the Navy already possessed? He had not bargained often with Yankees, Favian thought, beginning to enjoy this.

Jean Laffite, however, was unruffled. "*La Société de la Garde de l'Aigle,* in full," he said. The Society of the Guard of the Eagle, another one of those titles that sounded so much better in French. "The name is not a great secret; their organization is too large to be entirely unknown. But most people believe it is an organization of veterans, and the Guard is happy to have them believe this.

"I urge you to take your forces to Cat Island," Laffite said. "Crush this society, take their ships. If you find old guardsmen's uniforms and battle flags packed away, you may begin to believe me."

"It will be difficult," said Favian, "to do as you suggest. The gunboats that were at Barataria last September are guarding Lake Borgne and cannot be spared. Neither can the *Carolina*. And Colonel Ross's regulars must be held here to defend the city."

"You have a large frigate," said Jean Laffite. "Though your frigate could not enter Cat Island Pass—there is not enough water—you have a number of ships that you took at Barataria. You have my permission," he said rather loftily, "to use them. You can put your frigate's men in them and take Mortier and Guieu by surprise. End this menace to New Orleans."

And this menace to Laffite's authority over the pirate colony, Favian thought. It was nice of Laffite to make a gift of what he had already lost, both his captured ships and his rebellious former allies. There were wheels within wheels, he knew. Perhaps the Guard was a threat to New Orleans, perhaps only to Laffite—difficult to tell. Laffite may have made the whole thing up: the Guard might truly be little more than a secretive organization of Napoleon's veterans, the Cat Island people might be little more than pirates who had rebelled against the Laffites' authority, and there might be no real connection between the two. But now that the information—oddly plausible information—had been dropped in his lap, could Favian afford to ignore it?

"What is their force?"

"Perhaps fifteen ships, none very large. Not all will be present at once, you understand. Two hundred cannon. Two thousand men."

"I will have to consider it," Favian said.

Laffite nodded happily. "We give you this information, remember," he said. "We give it to prove we can be trusted to help the city against its enemies. Do what you can, but be very careful—and trust no one who carries one of these!" He brandished the swordstick. "I shall be in touch; perhaps Captain Grailly will be able to carry messages to you, or General Humbert. If you wish, I can send you a pilot who knows Cat Island well." He fell silent for a moment, then added an afterthought. "The general, you know, is not one of our association—he just hates Bonaparte; we are allies strictly on that account."

"I understand," Favian said.

"These causes," Laffite said with a sigh. "Everyone must have their cause, their obsession, to give their life meaning. Mere pleasure is not enough; it is not virtuous, I suppose." He looked up at Favian, his eyes twinkling. "I am not virtuous; I want only a comfortable life. Not fame, not glory, not Bourbon, not Bonaparte. Pleasure only, and a little security for my family, my brothers and daughter. It is not so much, eh?"

"Forgive me, sir," said Favian, "but if you wanted only pleasure and a little security, you could have become a corn merchant in Marseilles." Jean Laffite laughed; his brother Pierre turned away, looking uncomfortable.

"Maybe you're right, Commodore Markham," Laffite said, dropping his eyelid once again in his sly wink. "There are more secure businesses than mine."

"I must repeat that your case would look better if you turned yourselves over to the authorities," Favian repeated. "Perhaps a parole could be arranged so that you would have your freedom within the city."

"For God's sake, Jean, let us leave," growled Pierre Laffite, his patience gone.

Jean looked at Favian, his face holding a touch of regret, and then shook his head. "Impossible, sir," he said. "I think, in any case, that the authorities would find us an embarrassment. It was Governor Claiborne, after all, who allowed Pierre to escape. It was his thanks for my sending him Captain Lockyer's documents."

Favian stared at Laffite in astonishment. It had not occurred to him to wonder how Pierre Laffite, still partially paralyzed from his stroke and ironed hand and foot, had managed to escape the New Orleans jail—it was obvious, now, that there had to have been arrangements made on high. *That cunning dog,* Favian thought, meaning Claiborne. The governor had disassociated himself from the Laffites' enemies, Patterson and Ross, and put the Laffites in his debt—and Patterson and Ross had still descended on Barataria and put it out of business, ending that particular nuisance. But if the blow proved less than mortal, and Claiborne needed them, the Laffites owed him a large favor. Though he might be an indecisive military leader, Governor William C. C. Claiborne of Louisiana was assuredly a master of his own political element.

"And now, perhaps I should let you return to the ball," Laffite said.

"Indeed. It was, ah, interesting, gentlemen," Favian said. "You have given me much to think about." He reached for the carriage door and opened it.

"If you wish a meeting, contact Captain Grailly," said Laffite. Favian stepped from the carriage.

"I will not forget. Good evening, gentlemen."

"Good evening, Commodore."

" 'Evening," grunted Pierre Laffite. His brother tapped twice with the Napoleon stick on the roof of the carriage, the driver shook the reins, and the carriage pulled slowly away. Favian looked up and down the street: Grailly had disappeared.

As he entered the ballroom, he looked at his watch: perhaps half an hour had passed. The orchestra had just begun another tune; Favian craned his head and saw that Campaspe had exchanged the hulan for a Feliciana dragoon. He smiled and went to the buffet for a glass of champagne. He was going to have to tell someone of this extraordinary meeting, he knew, but who? He could imagine Patterson's emphatic reaction: "Lies, treacherous pirate lies." Claiborne would turn nervous, finger his neckcloth, and say a great deal without actually saying anything. He did not know any of the others well enough.

But he knew someone who knew most of the prominent Louisianians, he realized. Maria-Anna was discreet and knowledgeable. He would call upon her the next day—she was experienced enough in the ways of the Gulf Creoles to be able to offer sound counsel.

General Humbert was at his elbow before he realized it. "*Capitaine* Mark'am," the old revolutionary nodded. "I hope you found the meeting interesting."

"Interesting, yes. I thank you for your part in it, whatever it was."

"I hope," Humbert said, looking at him carefully, "you will take the knowledge to heart."

Favian made no reply, but sipped his champagne. He would create an empty space which Humbert might find uncomfortable enough to fill with information, he thought, enjoying this intrigue. But Humbert gave nothing away; he merely raised his own glass of champagne.

"Captain Laffite was once my good friend," Humbert said, a bit sadly. Favian realized that Humbert was in his cups. "But on my birthday two years ago I got a little drunk at the Hôtel de la Marine and called him a pirate—his men wanted to kill me. He prevented my murder, but he has not joined me at my table since." Humbert shook his head. "I am a little too fond of brandy," he said. "And he is a true gentleman; he never forgets. I regret my words, but I cannot call them back."

"I'm sorry," Favian said. "Perhaps you and he will have the chance to serve together now, against the British."

"Perhaps." Humbert shrugged sadly and drifted away. Favian chatted with the citizens in French and in his halting Spanish, the latter badly learned years ago in the Mediterranean and since forgotten; his attempt to fill in his vocabulary by using French words with Spanish articles and suffixes resulted in some amusing embarrassment. Grinning, he claimed Campaspe at the end of the dance and whirled her into the next waltz. He was growing very pleased with New Orleans.

The ball, like most balls, went on until five in the morning; Favian and Campaspe, who, for different reasons perhaps, had thoroughly enjoyed themselves, were among the last to leave. She was flushed and glowing with excitement and almost skipped into the carriage while he paused to light a cigar from a lamp at the door of the ballroom. "It was wonderful, Favian," she said, taking his hand as he seated himself next to her. That *Captain Favian* had not lasted the night. "Thank you so much. Ah! It's cold tonight." She placed his arm around her shoulders and leaned her head on his shoulder. He blew smoke and told the driver to return to the hotel.

"You were enchanting," he said. "Quite the accomplished dancer—the sensation of the evening, in fact." It was her first and last Creole ball: let her carry the memory of being the principal attraction.

"Was I? Oh, thank you, my darling!" Campaspe turned his face toward her and kissed him full on the mouth.

There was passion in that kiss, and a naïve eroticism that

startled him. He detached her hastily. "Don't be so much in a hurry, my dear," he said. "You're lucky I'm not the sort of man who—never mind. You have a few years yet."

"I'll be sixteen in a week. Most girls here are already married by sixteen."

Younger than she are happy mothers made, Favian thought, but look what came of that: Juliet lying dead in Capulet's tomb. "Campaspe," he said with a glance at the expressionless, unsurprisable neck of the driver. Why the devil hadn't the Navy hired a closed carriage? "I don't want to disappoint you. But my life is not my own, and—don't cry, please. It was a beautiful evening; don't let it end like—here, take my handkerchief."

It was one of the handkerchiefs she had embroidered; she looked at the anchors stitched on the corners and broke down entirely. "Damn!" Favian said, temper eroding.

"I love you," Campaspe gulped.

"Damn!"

She tried to control the weeping and failed; seeing nothing else to do, he got rid of his cigar and took her in his arms until her trembling ceased. "I understand," she whispered. "I'm all right now. I suppose you won't want ever to see me again."

"Don't be silly. You're a lovely young lady, and you will make a fine partner for some lucky man. When the time comes, mind. In a few years." Why, he thought, had his life been so cursed with the antics of adolescents? Midshipmen who kept fighting duels, preachers who acted half their age, love-struck maidservants. It was his particular curse, it seemed.

The carriage stopped at the hotel, and he handed her out. "I hope you are not too disappointed," he said. "You were a wonderful partner, and a beautiful one. I'm not in the least sorry."

Campaspe managed a brave, dry-eyed smile. "It was splendid," she said. "Thank you so much, for everything. I'll never forget it." He gave her a fraternal kiss and saw her through the women's entrance. Through the glass panes in the door he saw her giving him a last, forlorn little wave. He waved back and returned to the carriage.

The carriage was alone on the streets, the hooves of the horse ringing in the narrow lanes. Weariness began to flood his limbs; through his mind came images of the evening, the swirling gowns of the Creole ladies, Jean Laffite's careless laugh, General

Humbert's careful intrigues, Campaspe's surprising kiss. He would see Maria-Anna on the morrow; he wondered what she would say when she heard about the Laffites' revelations. An organization of Napoleonic veterans happily selling Louisiana to the British: so very contradictory, but also in an odd way logical.

But it was time for rest now, he thought. And tomorrow, the pleasure of Maria-Anna's company.

ELEVEN

"You must speak to the governor, Favian," Maria-Anna said. "He has information you do not; he'd be able to evaluate Laffite's intelligence better than you."

"I think certain members of the Committee for Public Safety might be informed as well," Gideon said. "But ye'll not wish to inform all of them—the news would be all over town in hours, and then this Guard of the Eagle would be aware of yer interest."

"Which of the committee do you suggest?" Favian asked. He swiped at his nose with a handkerchief. He had seemingly caught a mild version of Marie's cold.

"Edward Livingston—he's a friend of the Laffites anyway, one of their attorneys," Gideon said. "Patterson, of course. General Morgan, maybe, or George Ogden."

"Possibly Augustin Macarty," Maria-Anna added.

"He may be Irish in ancestry, Maria-Anna, but he's a French Creole at heart; his ancestors all fought for the papist French," Gideon objected. "The Creoles may be sympathetic to the Guard's purposes. Born Americans only, I think."

"Claiborne, anyway," Favian said. "I thank you."

It was late afternoon, the afternoon following the ball. Favian, sleeping in his hotel, had been awakened just after twelve by Lieutenant Thomas Cunningham of Gunboat Number 5, who had acted as Dr. Solomon's second. Cunningham politely reported that the duel had been fought that morning, as arranged, at "The

Oaks" duelling ground: both had missed at the first fire, and at the second Solomon had wounded Lieutenant Glimph in the knee. It was not yet known whether Glimph would lose his leg. "Dr. Solomon conducted himself bravely, as a gentleman," Cunningham reported.

"Very well," Favian had told him, noncommittal, a sour taste in his mouth. He wondered if, to avoid further duels, he would have to confine every Navy man in New Orleans to his ship.

"I thought you would wish to know, sir. I won't take up any more of your time." Cunningham had saluted and left.

News of the duel had passed rapidly through the city. Solomon had become something of a popular hero, the idea of a fighting priest appealing to the popular romantic imagination, while Glimph was being disparaged as a man who had apparently felt himself free to insult the clergy until brought up short by Solomon's challenge. None of the stories Favian heard in several versions in the café in which he'd eaten his midday meal seemed to bear any resemblance to the truth as he understood it—Glimph had almost certainly fought the duel unaware he was shooting at a priest—but at least the Navy seemed to have come off with some credit, and Favian did not bother to correct his informers.

Eugénie Desplein had not come that afternoon, but Favian had not expected her: no doubt she was performing Campaspe's duties as well as her own. He had waited, though, for her appearance; later he'd paid his daily visit to Claiborne to make his usual speech in favor of a declaration of martial law. The newspapers had mentioned a meeting of the Defense Committee that evening—the Defense Committee, chaired by Bernard de Marigny, that was created by the legislature in rivalry to Livingston's Committee for Public Safety.

"I will speak to Claiborne early this evening," Favian said. "Before he meets with the Defense Committee."

"De Marigny is chairing that committee, isn't he?" Maria-Anna asked, her bright eyes bespeaking a lively interest. "I would very much like to get Marigny to my *poque* sessions; he's a high-rolling gambler. Been known to lose thirty thousand in a night, rolling dice. In the Faubourg Marigny there's even a lane known as the Rue de Craps, named after his favorite game. I would like to convert him to cards. Do you think you could arrange to bring us together?"

Favian, amused, saw Gideon's expression of woe: if Marigny

dropped thirty thousand dollars in Maria-Anna's *poque* parlor, it would be difficult to give a like sum to charity without his wife finding out—and even Gideon, Favian assumed, would have a long, exhausting battle with his conscience before giving away that kind of money. Thirty thousand would make any American a wealthy man for life. But then Gideon was already wealthy: his successful privateering had probably brought him a fortune.

"I've met the man—he gives himself regal airs, and I suppose he's the nearest New Orleans has to royalty," Favian said. "I doubt he'd accept any invitation to a Yankee privateer's parlor." He saw the relief in Gideon Markham's eyes, and then added, "But certainly he will be at any number of public receptions in the next few weeks. I will introduce you if I can." Dismay flooded Gideon's face. Favian controlled his smile with ease.

"Gideon," he said, "you know the naval forc[illegible] the New Orleans station, with the exception of the *Macedon*[illegible] are committed to their stations. We can't spare any force to deal with the Cat Island menace except for the frigate, and the frigate's unsuitable for those shallow waters around Cat Island."

"Aye," Gideon said. " 'Tis a shame that our government has not recognized the menace to the Mississippi and given us the force we need."

Favian recognized the uncompromising tone: Gideon's hatred for Thomas Jefferson, James Madison, and the others of the Democratic-Republican government was bitter, and of long standing. Given Gideon's history, Favian knew, he would probably have hated as relentlessly as Gideon: a wife and child who had died of starvation due to the Embargo were reason enough for hate.

Favian had met Madison two years before and rather liked him, sympathizing with the position of this retiring intellectual who had found himself the head of a country at war with the greatest power of old Europe. But he had thought Madison unsuitable: a man of greater force might have withstood the demands of Congress for war long enough to have made certain the country was actually prepared to fight a war and to pay for it, rather than simply wander into the fight and affect surprise when every army sent against the enemy collapsed or surrendered. If the Navy had not held firm on the lakes the British would have taken everything north of the Ohio. The United States was bankrupt now, Favian knew; the armies were being equipped on credit, and the Navy as well—a little greater expense earlier on could have ended the war sooner, and saved money in the long run.

"Yes," Favian said. "We're sadly underequipped. But the country itself is strong; our little force can be used for defense with some good effect. But striking out, acting offensively, we are weak. If I could get *Macedonian* to Cat Island, we could smash the Guard there, but the frigate draws too much water—I barely got it into the Mississippi.

"We need small vessels with good crews, Gideon," Favian said. "And you have them. *Malachi's Revenge* is ideal; you're part owner of Fontenoy's *Franklin;* and you'll have the captured schooner once the prize court rules. If you can contract your vessels to the government, we can arrange to split the prize money between the government forces and your own, and—"

"On what basis?" Maria-Anna asked quickly. Favian looked at her calculating expression and smiled.

"Fifty percent is what I would suggest," Favian said, "but that depends on the precise terms you can get out of the authorities here."

"Fifty percent," Maria-Anna mused. "It will be our privateers, it seems, who will be doing most of the work."

"Under Navy command," Favian said. "And your vessels will have Navy men and officers aboard, plus *Macedonian*'s marine complement."

"Who pays for the powder and shot?"

"The government, I suppose," Favian said. He glanced from Maria-Anna to Gideon, who was slowly cutting himself a plug of tobacco with his pocketknife.

"I opposed the annexation of Louisiana," he said. "America was big enough, I thought; if we took so much territory, we would be involving ourselves in European disputes. And I was right. Why should a New Hampshireman fight for New Orleans?"

"I thought you were a Federalist," Favian said. "We—the Navy anyway—swear allegiance to the United States of America, not to our state of origin. The obligation is to defend all citizens, not just those of our region. New Hampshire would have no objection to Louisianians marching to its aid were New Hampshire invaded."

"The Louisianians would not come to New Hampshire," Gideon said. His tone was contemptuous. "During the Creek War these grand gentlemen would not even march to help Baton Rouge or Mobile. Said it was none of their affair." He snorted contemptuously and popped the chewing tobacco into his mouth. "What the frogs meant was that they would find it inconvenient to be absent for a few weeks from their brothels, saloons, and gambling hells! Even now that their city is in direct danger of attack, they can raise only five hundred men from a population of twenty thousand! They expect Jackson's men from Tennessee and Kentucky to do their fighting for them."

"Use of your ships for a few days, Gideon," Favian said. "That's all I need. A few days to take Cat Island and drive off the Guard. You'll have half the prize money, at least half. The prize money from fifteen ships and whatever we find on the island, and all for a few days' labor."

"How many months will it take to get the prize money?" Gideon asked. "Sitting here in this doomed city, waiting for the prize court to rule—it was bad enough with *Musquetobite* and the schooner."

"You don't have to stay here for that. The money can be sent to New Hampshire."

Gideon frowned. "Specie payments have been suspended from all local banks," he said. "There's a financial crisis here because there's been no export since the war began. No, the money won't be transferred until the war is over, and the war will probably end with the British in possession of Louisiana."

Favian looked at Maria-Anna and saw that he would have no help there: Gideon's arguments made sense, at least from the self-interested perspective of a privateer. "Gideon," Favian said, "I want to stop the British. Our enemies, Gideon—we've both spent years fighting them, as did our fathers before us. The *British*, Gideon. They've kept their forts in our land, they've burned and plundered from Falmouth in the last war to Hampton in this one, they've given the Indians the guns and tomahawks to kill our people, they've pressed our sailors into their wars, and even made them fight their countrymen—and now they're sending an army and fleet to this city.

"I want to stop them, Gideon. And I want you to help me."

He saw Gideon's face harden, his eyes grow fierce. There was a lot of his father Josiah in him, Favian saw, Josiah the pious, uncompromising hater of the British, but would the father win out over the businessman? Gideon was a privateer—he could sail for New Hampshire tomorrow and there was no way short of piracy to stop him.

"Very well," Gideon said. "I will help you if the business arrangements are satisfactory."

"Thank you," Favian said, his mind chattering relief. "I will—it's a generous thing you've done, Gideon, and I will make certain the world does not forget it."

"Do not thank me," Gideon said, his eyes aflame. "It is the will of the Almighty that we are here together—and he is bringing the British here as well. We will have a reckoning, we and the British, God's will be done."

Maria-Anna looked at Gideon with resignation: no point in contradicting him in these moods. Favian felt exultation in his heart. Gideon's strength and determination were qualities New Orleans needed, and he was truly grateful—to God, Gideon, or merest Chance, whatever force applied.

With Gideon's assurance in his pocket, Favian approached Claiborne that night, before the scheduled meeting with the Defense Committee, and told him of his encounter with the Laffites. Claiborne turned pale, muttering "My God!" as Favian told him of the Guard's reason for helping the British, and then turned thoughtful as Favian related his plan for the suppression of Cat Island.

"It's a convincing story," Claiborne said in the end. "We can't discount it." He was dressed in his immaculate self-designed uniform, pelican ribbon and all; his collar was so high he couldn't turn his head, and during Favian's entire speech his face had been fixed straight forward, immobile. "Even if the people on Cat Island are not allied with the British, we can't take the chance."

"But our expedition must be a secret one," Favian said. "The Defense Committee can't know, nor can the Committee for Public Safety or the legislature. We can't trust the Creoles in this matter."

"Commodore Markham, one cannot *ever* trust the Creoles," Claiborne said flatly. "And I am speaking as one who has married into the Creoles here. They are a frivolous, disunited people, and they blow hot and cold as the mood takes them. New Orleans was a colony for too many years, I suppose, dependent on decisions made in Europe—these people are not used to thinking and acting for themselves. No, we can't tell them. We can't tell anyone."

"Gideon's volunteering his squadron makes it easier," Favian said. "He won't have any trouble getting crew for the schooner once it's ready, and he can keep a secret better than most."

"General Jackson will have to be told, of course," Claiborne said. "I've received word that he's spending this evening at John Kilty Smith's plantation, upriver. He'll arrive there tonight. My wife is making arrangements for a formal reception—the orders will be going out later tonight, under my signature. Apparently he'll be staying at de Marigny's." He leaned back in his chair, looking uncomfortable, plump, and unmartial in his stiff uniform, and smiled. "I'll be thankful to have someone else dealing with the Committee for Defense."

So the long-awaited Major General Andrew Jackson would finally appear tomorrow, Favian thought. There would, he supposed, be a grand review of the New Orleans battalion, all five hundred of them; there would be speeches, banquets, illuminations, balls—and in return for these entertainments, Jackson would be saddled with the heartbreaking problems of mobilizing the reluctant citizens to fight a British attack that could come from any one of a half dozen different directions. He hoped Jackson was up to it—outside of a number of duels, the man had only fought Indians, and although he had fought them well, Favian would personally have preferred a man more accustomed to combat against a regular army: General Harrison, for instance, or Jacob Brown. Well, no doubt the city would be happy to have Jackson—or at any rate the thousands of veteran soldiers from Kentucky and Tennessee that would be following him.

Favian made his farewells to the governor, satisfied with his visit, and made his escape before the Committee of Defense could embroil him in their tedious business.

The next morning he stood on the speaker's platform at the Place d'Armes with Patterson, Edward Livingston, Mayor Girod, and Claiborne, waiting with half the city for the appearance of General Jackson. Patterson had been told of the Cat Island situation early that morning, over breakfast in Favian's hotel, and after his initial surprise had faded, Patterson had pronounced himself in agreement with Favian's plan. No wonder, Favian thought; it would leave Patterson in command in New Orleans again.

At ten o'clock the minute guns began booming from Fort St. Charles announcing the approach of the general, heralding as well a drizzling rain that began to patter down on the heads and shoulders of the citizens; soon there were cheers from distant crowds, the cheers nearing the square as the general's party approached. The party on the reviewing stand rose; the Chasseur band began to play "Hail, the Conquering Hero Comes." Jackson and his party appeared across the square.

What, Favian wondered afterward, had the crowd been expecting? A military dandy like Claiborne, a stern, plainspoken soldier like Ross, a polished, distant, formal disciplinarian like Patterson? Whatever New Orleans was expecting, surely this scarecrow apparition was not it. Jackson rode, wearily, out of the rain astride a horse wearier than he, his face a long, pale smudge against the dark horsemen behind him. There was a battered old leather cap on his head, a mud-stained short blue Spanish cloak around his shoulders. The worn leather of his dragoon boots showed through cracked polish. The wild hair that stuck out from beneath the leather cap was gray, and the face was long and yellow. The deep-set eyes were sunken, and there was a disturbing apparition of pain in them. It was clear that General Jackson was very ill.

Favian gave an inward smile. Ill though he might be, Andrew Jackson knew how to cause a sensation. Favian remembered, two years before, Stephen Decatur stepping onto the bloodstained deck of the *Macedonian* dressed in a plan black homespun coat and battered old hat, looking like a plain Yankee farmer amid all the glitter and gold of the other American and British officers. He had stood out all the more because of the triumph he wore: he had come to take possession of the frigate his guns had pounded into submission. Decatur had always known how to stand out in a crowd; and it was clear that Jackson did as well. The stained old travel dress plainly told the crowd that here was something they had never seen before.

Jackson and his staff dismounted, and the general climbed painfully to the reviewing platform. "Are you ill, General?" Claiborne asked as he clasped the general's hand. "Shall we cancel the reception?"

"Keep it short, for the love of God," Jackson said. Claiborne introduced the others on the platform. Favian saw a flicker of interest in Jackson's eyes as he shook the general's hand: there would be a little maneuvering between us later, Favian thought, as we try to feel one another out. Jackson had met Patterson before, but Favian was someone new; there would be a delicate little military minuet between the two, probably at the scheduled council meeting that afternoon.

"This is Mr. Edward Livingston," Claiborne said. "He will translate into French any remarks you may care to make."

"Very well." Jackson took a breath and straightened: he was built like Favian, tall and thin, and like Favian he bore the scars of his campaigns. There was an old saber cut, Favian saw, on Jackson's cheek.

The Chasseur band wheezed to a halt with a flurry of drums and an extended chord that fell flat in the moist air. Through a gust of wind that rattled the papers of his written speech, Claiborne gave a shortened version of his flowery address, extemporizing to the extent of remarking, as the rain pattered down, that "the sun is never shining more brilliantly than when you are among us." Mayor Girod also gave a short welcoming speech, and then Claiborne stepped in to introduce Major General Jackson.

"Citizens!" Jackson barked as he brought out a written address, Livingston's echo of "*Citoyens!*" coming on the heels of his opening. Jackson looked at the address, hesitated a moment, and then stuffed the speech back into his pocket. "I want to say only a few words," he said. "I am a fighter, not a writer." There were scattered cheers as this was translated, but the general held up a hand to quiet them. "I wish simply to say that I have come to your city," he said, "to drive your enemies into the sea, or to perish in the attempt!" Favian saw the sudden burning light in the deep-sunk eyes, and thought: *My God, this man is a hater!* There was a bitter passion in Jackson, it seemed, akin to that in Gideon—the two, Favian thought, were much alike.

Jackson abruptly stepped back from the platform, pulled his speech out again, and handed it to Claiborne. "Please see that the full text is printed in the papers," he said. "I'd be much obliged." His words were buried in sudden cheering as the crowd realized the speeches were at an end. The startled band began to blunder its way into "Hail, Columbia." There was a swift consultation on the platform: Claiborne wondered if the general would like to postpone his meeting with the authorities until he was more recovered; the general looked at the military figures sharing the platform and said he would see them all in an hour's time at his headquarters. Rain began to come down in buckets, and by the time the band finished its tune, the Place d'Armes was nearly deserted.

Jackson and his party left on horseback, splashing through the muck; Favian and Patterson huddled into their boat cloaks and followed on foot, arriving at Jackson's headquarters nearly as streaked with mud as the general. As they approached Jackson's assigned headquarters at 106 Rue Royale, Favian saw Major Bernard de Marigny stepping into his carriage, his face crimson and his eyes hard. There was a curt command to the driver, and de Marigny's carriage sped off through the streets, arrogantly flinging clumps of mud at the passersby.

"What set Marigny off?" Favian wondered. "Jackson was supposed to be his houseguest."

"No longer, I suspect," Patterson said. "I suppose it has to do with de Marigny's father-in-law."

"Someone named Morales, isn't it?" asked Favian. "What's he got to do with— Good day, Major," he said, addressing the young officer guarding Jackson's door. "Captains Markham and Patterson present their compliments to the general and request some of his time when convenient."

"It's convenient now," came a voice from the interior: Jackson's. In the gray light of the windows Jackson looked jaundiced and emaciated; the lanky body moved as if with considerable pain. "Come in. This is Major Tatum, my chief engineer."

"Pleased to meet you, Major," Favian said. "Wasn't that Major de Marigny I just saw leaving?"

"Oh, yes," Tatum said carelessly. "I sent him packing."

Good God, why? Favian almost shouted. Insulting the most powerful Creole in the city was not a good way to begin Jackson's stay in New Orleans. Jackson, watching pensively as a silent black servant took the naval officers' hats and coats, answered the unspoken question.

"I won't be staying at the house of a damned spy," he growled. "He's the son-in-law of Juan Morales, who used to be the Spanish consul—knee-deep in plots to return West Florida to Spain."

"Major de Marigny," said Patterson, "is an important man. I'm sure he's not a spy."

"Mm," Jackson growled. "Maybe not. But I'm not taking any chances. This way, gentlemen."

In Jackson's study Favian was introduced to Colonel McRae and Colonel Hayne, aides-de-camp; Colonel Ross of the 44th was already waiting. Jackson lowered himself wearily into a padded leather chair. Favian noticed Jackson had been leaving muddy footprints on the carpet. "There's a banquet being prepared," Jackson said. "You gentlemen have all you want, but I won't be joining you." He gave a skeletal smile. "I've got the old soldiers' disease. Dysentery. Come from riding eleven days through the swamps on my way here—I wanted to see the ground. Couldn't get any maps. I hope Claiborne will be bringing some."

"About Major de Marigny," Favian said. "Perhaps you should, ah, give him a good appointment. He's a capable man, though perhaps a little young."

Jackson sniffed. "I'll think about it," he said offhandedly. He looked up at Favian. "I was pleased to hear of your arrival. Without orders, wasn't it? I like a man who can use his initiative."

"It was imperative that the news be brought," Favian said. "I brought it as quickly as I could."

"Some of the generals I've met could learn a little from the junior service," Jackson said with a thin smile. "Would you gentlemen like a warm drink? And then perhaps you can tell me what you've been doing with your little boats." Well, Favian thought. That's put us in our place.

The servants brought hot tafia punch. Before Patterson could begin to explain his dispositions, a carriage drove up outside, and Claiborne, walking stiffly in his uniform, entered the house, followed by a man in civilian dress with a bundle of maps. Jackson rose to greet him.

"Gentlemen," Claiborne said, "this is Arsène Lacarrière Latour, a civil engineer. He is the gentleman who had drawn all the maps we'll be using, and he knows the ground very well. He is happy to volunteer his services."

"The Spanish used my maps," Latour said, cheerful. "They'll probably have given them to the British. I think, General, you may wish to see what the British see."

For some hours they went over the situation. Jackson sat nodding as the others explained the deployment of their forces; occasionally he would turn and ask a pointed question. His aides took notes. Latour was useful: he had surveyed most of the land himself. "I'll have to see the ground," Jackson kept saying. "I've been over the ground north of here—now I'll have to go over it downstream. Fort St. Leon. Fort St. Philip. Maybe even Barataria."

Go over the ground. A sound notion, Favian thought; knowledge of the terrain was one of the few advantages the defenders possessed. At the moment, until the reinforcements from Jackson's army of Tennesseans arrived, and until the Kentuckians came down on their flatboats and the Baton Rouge militia brigade marched south past the German Coast, there was very little Jackson could do except go over the ground: there were fewer than a thousand armed men in the city, and this included the Free Men of Color, whom the others distrusted. Jackson, it seemed, did not look at Fortier's colored troops with the same suspicion as the majority of the white planters—early in the meeting he accepted, without comment or hesitation, the written proposal of a Santo Domingan named Savary to raise another black battalion, this one to include black officers, a decision Claiborne, fearful of the consequences, had been deferring for weeks. Clearly a man had arrived who knew how to make decisions and stand by them—even if some of the decisions, such as the deliberate snubbing of Bernard de Marigny, were less than wise.

Favian and Patterson discussed the deployment of their "little boats," and Jackson nodded, asking intelligent questions about the strength of the current at Les Rigolets, the depth of the water on Pontchartrain, the size and number of guns on the boats and the frigate, the number of marines *Macedonian* had available, perhaps to add to his own ground forces. The questions seemed to lead naturally to the more ominous question of Cat Island; Favian glanced at Patterson and saw in the man's face a reflection of his own query. Favian nodded; they both turned to Jackson.

"Sir," Favian said, "Captain Patterson and I have received some interesting intelligence. Governor Claiborne has been informed, and he agrees it's serious. We would like to share it with you, General, but—" He looked at the others in the room: Latour, McRae, Hayne, Tatum, a quiet black servant who had been bringing them food and tafia punch. "We would like to brief you privately, if we may. There is a problem, a delicate problem, connected with this, and I think the fewer who know it the better. You see," he lied, "our informant is close to the British. If too many people knew of his existence, it would put his life at hazard."

Jackson looked at Favian somberly, then glanced up at the others. "Gentlemen, if you will excuse us," he said. Favian's lie had come plausibly—he didn't want any of those present even to *think* of the Cartagenian privateers, or that the problem might be right here in Louisiana. The others filed out, only the civilian Latour looking surprised: Jackson's staff, it seemed, was used enough to these little moments of intrigue.

Jackson looked at his three guests remaining: Favian, Patterson, Claiborne. "I am at your service, sirs," he said.

"General Jackson," Favian said quietly, "there is a place near here called Cat Island. Let me show it to you on Mr. Latour's map. We don't mean the Cat Island in the Mississippi Sound, but the other one, here on Terre Bonne Bay . . ."

Jackson listened in silence. At times he seemed almost asleep, leaning back wearily in his chair, his eyes half-closed. At the end of Favian's presentation, he closed his eyes entirely and frowned. "The source," he said. "How can we trust the source?"

"You mean Laffite?" Patterson growled. "We can't trust him at all."

"Laffite and his banditti, yes. These men on Cat Island may not be a menace to us," Jackson said. He looked half-dead, a skeleton with parchment skin, dressed in clothing stained with graveyard mud. Favian wondered if he could possibly last the winter. "They may only be a challenge to Laffite's authority, not British collaborators."

"We can't afford to take the chance they aren't a menace," Favian said.

"And even if they have no designs against us," added Patterson, "we must deal with them for the same reasons we dealt with the Baratarians. We have to clear our rear before we can fight the British."

"The source," Jackson said again. "It troubles me."

"I've seen the Laffites, sir," Favian said. "This may strike you as an odd thing for me to say, but—" He struggled with his impressions of Jean Laffite, the dramatic, black-clad, vigorous buccaneer he'd seen across from him in the carriage seat. "I think, sir, he's an honorable man," Favian said. Jackson opened one eye and looked at him; for a moment Favian was reminded of Laffite's own strange wink. "Not honorable as we understand it, perhaps," Favian said. "But as honorable as a pirate can be. I think his offer of help is genuine—it may be a self-serving gesture, but it's no less truthful."

Jackson opened both eyes and straightened in his chair. "It's Navy Department business, gentlemen, whether you go or not," he said. "Keep me informed of your decisions, and tell me if you need my assistance."

I like a man who can use his initiative, the general had said earlier. The Cat Island expedition had been given Jackson's indirect blessing, but the responsibility would be Favian's. *Navy Department business*—if only it were. The Navy Department was far off, in Washington, and had no idea of Favian's location within ten thousand miles; he had taken *Macedonian* to sea on his own initiative, when he was not her assigned captain, a situation that would have destroyed him had he lost the frigate to the blockading ships—the court-martial would have crucified him. Only success could have justified his action. A measure of success had been won with the capture of the *Carnation*, but not much. He was still trapped.

He was like a gambler in one of Maria-Anna's *poque* games, caught in a round of betting. He had already bet more than he could afford when he had stolen the *Macedonian* from the Navy Department's control—his reputation, his career, his future—and he had no choice but to keep on calling as the British raised the bet. Now it was not only Favian and the frigate that were lying on the table, but New Orleans, Louisiana, and British control of the Mississippi. Well, he thought. The British don't know our cards, either; they don't know I'm here; they don't know we know about Cat Island and the Guard of the Eagle. I don't just have to call.

Favian would raise the stakes.

"We'll go, sir," he said.

There was an approving smile on General Jackson's scarred, sickly face. Suddenly the deep-sunk eyes came alive with a feral, unsettling light. "We have a saying in Tennessee, gentlemen," he said. "I didn't repeat it for any of these Louisianians—I knew they wouldn't like it. The saying comes from the Indians, I believe, and we learned it fighting them: *War to the knife, and knife to the hilt*. I intend to stop the British in front of New Orleans, and the only way I know to do it is to kill them. *War to the knife*. But if I can't kill enough of them to keep them from taking the city, I'll burn the city to the ground before I let them have it—Admiral Cochrane will lose his millions in prize money. These Louisiana men won't stop me; I'll have my Tennessee people here ere long, and they've burned towns before, Creek towns. And if I have the time, I'll open the levees and let the river take the ashes. By the Eternal, I'll make all Louisiana a desert before I give it to the enemy."

Knife to the hilt. Jackson did not have to say it; those feral, glowing, deep-sunk eyes said it for him. *A hater:* Favian remembered his intuition on the reviewing platform. *A few centuries ago they would have thought him a werewolf if they could have seen him like this.* A few moments ago he'd been wondering if Jackson would last the winter, but now he knew that unforgiving, steely will would keep the sickly body going for years, unless the body was burnt to a husk by the intensity of that hatred.

I hope my decision is a wise one, Favian thought suddenly. If it isn't, the alternative may be a city in flames.

"In that case we had better stop the British before they get to the city," Favian said. Jackson looked at the door, then asked Patterson to ask the others to return. The general leaned back in his chair, his eyes hooded once more.

"Please have some more of this excellent food, sirs," he said. "As for myself, I believe I will have a bowl of hominy."

Later that afternoon Favian sent Midshipman Stanhope to the Hôtel de la Marine with messages for General Humbert and Captain Grailly. The messages were identical: "Please tell our friend to send me his pilot. Enclosed is a safe-conduct signed by General Jackson and Governor Claiborne. Your servant, Captain Favian Markham, U.S.N."

TWELVE

Favian, after writing his instructions to Midshipman Stanhope, returned to Jackson's company, automatically receiving another cup of tafia punch from the servant as he entered. "There is a ball planned in your honor this evening," Claiborne was saying. "Do you think you are well enough to attend?"

"I will be there for a time, at least," Jackson answered. The werewolf look was gone; he leaned back in his chair, a weary gray man once more. "Tomorrow I think I will visit Fort St. Leon—the reports concerning its readiness seem a little contradictory. I would like, as well, to see your boats, Captain Patterson. Would seven o'clock tomorrow morning be suitable?"

Patterson seemed a little surprised at this show of energy—Favian wondered if Patterson had ever received a visit from Claiborne during the man's entire tenure as governor—but he rose to the occasion. "Of course, General," he said.

"If General Villeré and Major Plauché," Jackson said, "would like to accompany me on my tour of the fort, they are most welcome."

"I shall extend an invitation, General," said Claiborne.

"Thank you, Governor. I would like to review the New Orleans troops, by the way, sometime soon. Would the day after tomorrow be convenient, Governor?"

"Certainly, General."

"Gentlemen, I hope you will excuse me. I would like to dictate a few orders and then retire for some hours before the, ah, the occasion this evening."

Jackson rose to bid them farewell. He clasped the hand of each of his visitors, a polite Tennessee planter saying his adieus. "I hope for all our sakes, Commodore Markham," he said as he shook Favian's hand, his eyes flashing into Favian's, "you are good at judging buccaneers."

"I hope so, too, General," Favian said and made his exit.

Patterson was rushing toward the levee, ready to set his crews to preparing *Carolina* and *Louisiana* for Jackson's visit. Favian put on his cocked hat and boat cloak and made his way through the muddy streets to Gideon's hotel; he cleaned his boots on the scraper by the door and sent up his card. "Will I see you tomorrow?" Favian asked as Eugénie Desplein led him to Gideon's room on the second floor.

Eugénie gave him a wry look from under one arched eyebrow. There was a little redness around her nostrils, Favian saw; he should be thankful, he reflected, that a cold was the worst infection Marie had spread. "The way Campaspe's been talking, I'm not sure I want to take you away from her."

"What," Favian asked carefully, "has she been saying?"

She gave a short laugh and took his arm. "Nothing alarming, my dear. You're just her *beau sabreur*, that's all, everything grand and chivalrous. She is writing a poem expressing her devotion."

Harmless enough, apparently. Favian breathed a little easier. "I hope you will be free," he said.

"I hope so, too, my Favian." Outside Gideon's door she stood on tiptoe to kiss his cheek, then opened the door to let him in.

Grimes had just opened a bottle of wine, and with it Favian, Gideon, and Maria-Anna toasted the success of the Cat Island expedition. Favian was beginning to feel a little light-headed—years of attending public banquets had accustomed him to round after round of drinks, but the tafia punch and wine on a nearly empty stomach were having their effect. There was supper afterward, fortunately, but with supper came another bottle of wine; and then there was brandy following.

"Do you realize we have had two of the local beaux here, sending up their cards for Campaspe?" Maria-Anna asked as they ate. "I turned them away saying she was much fatigued and could not receive anyone—but what can I do, Favian? I can't have planters' sons coming to call on my maidservant. Next Mrs. Desplein and the other servants will be receiving their callers, and then where will the household be?"

"No doubt it would be a much more cheerful place," Favian said.

"Hah!" she sniffed. She rearranged the pillows set behind her back on the birthing stool. "What do you know—you've never had to run a house."

"Just a ship," Favian reminded her.

"And how efficient would your ship be," Maria-Anna asked, "if all the sailors could receive their jills on board?"

"It would be," said Favian, "more cheerful." He was feeling quite cheerful himself; it was a fine thing to be indoors out of the mud and rain, with wine warming his stomach and Maria-Anna for company. "I said nothing about efficiency or tautness," he said. Gideon looked at him, frowning: there was nothing frivolous about ship's discipline.

After brandy the entire household marched to the public ballroom for Jackson's reception; the occasion was sufficiently extraordinary for Eugénie and Campaspe to be allowed to accompany their master and mistress. Maria-Anna was wearing the dramatic lace veil that Campaspe had worn the night of the ball, but Campaspe, on Favian's right arm, still wore her gown and red spencer and had borrowed another piece of headgear, an elaborate pleated turban of gray, scarlet, and golden spangles—old-fashioned, the Orient having gone out of vogue, but suiting her very well. On Favian's left arm Eugénie was dressed much more conventionally in a white gown, blue cloak, and an embroidered veil over a wickerwork bonnet. Grimes followed behind, carrying the ladies' slippers.

The ballroom was packed with a cross section of New Orleans humanity, white and colored both: a delegation of Choctaws, standing stiffly in their uniforms from the Creek War, stood aloof in one corner. Campaspe craned her neck, eagerly looking for her beaux of the other night, then, seeing them, suddenly turned demure, hiding behind her fan. Favian smiled at this coquetry, then saw the unmistakable figure of General Jean-Joseph Humbert across the room. "I'm afraid I must leave you for a short while, ladies," he said, bowing to Campaspe and Eugénie. "There's someone I have to speak to."

He shouldered his way through the crowd. "General Humbert," he said. "I should have realized you would be here. I—"

"Here." Gruffly, thrusting a cup into Favian's hands. "Have some of this *petite gouave*."

"Thank you, sir. I sent you a message earlier, to the Hôtel de la Marine—"

"I received it and sent it on its way. Grailly received his message also."

"I am grateful, sir," Favian said. He sipped the drink Humbert had handed him and received a shock. "Good heavens! What's in this stuff?"

"A mixture. Everything poisonous to mankind," Humbert said placidly. "I hear that the British will be commanded by Sir Edward Pakenham, is that not so?"

"That's what our reports indicated," Favian said, cautious. The story that he'd captured dispatches with the *Carnation* was probably in wide public circulation, but there was no point in confirming it.

"I've met Pakenham, did I tell you that? He was with the Ulster Dragoons in '98, a major I think, one of Crauford's young men. They called him Ned." Humbert gazed into his cup, no doubt seeing pictures of his old captors, his old prison. "A pleasant man, cheerful. Everyone liked him."

"You've met him? You should tell General Jackson—I think the general would very much like to know about young Ned Pakenham." Favian remembered Jackson's wolfish eyes, his readiness to devour the enemy. *A pleasant man*, Ned Pakenham. Jackson would be happy to chew on Humbert's old bones for a few hours, Favian thought.

"I will call on him tomorrow," Humbert said. He drained his *petite gouave* and held out his cup for the servant to refill it.

"I hope you will. I've mentioned you to him, in connection with—with certain matters," Favian said. "He will be inspecting Patterson's squadron tomorrow morning, then join General Villeré and Major Plauché for a trip to Fort St. Leon."

"I'll remember," Humbert said. "I will—" The room suddenly stilled as a drum rattled. A single trumpet gave a call, and General Jackson walked into the room, followed by Governor and Madame Claiborne.

Jackson had known just how far to push those battered traveling clothes, Favian thought as the crowd went mad with cheers: now he was dressed formally in a blue uniform coat with fire-gilt buttons, buff facings, and heavy bullion epaulets; he carried a cocked hat in his white-gloved hand, and his jackboots were lovingly polished. "Such a distinguished carriage," Favian overheard from an iron-spined Creole matron. "And this morning I thought he looked like an ugly old Kaintuck flatboatman!"

There were a number of speeches and toasts; Favian emptied his cup of *petite gouave* in salute to the distinguished guests, and was given another by Humbert, who was tossing them down as if they were fruit juice. The majordomo announced the Virginia reel, and Jackson offered his arm to Sophronie Claiborne. Favian quickly drained his cup and set off in search of Eugénie Desplein.

"Honored, sir," she said; they jostled for their places among the throng, and only Favian's relative prestige—signified in this case by his twin epaulets, presentation sword, and the ferocious glare with which he fixed a cornet in the Francs trying to worm his way into line—secured them a place in the dance.

The orchestra commenced—Haydn, Favian thought—and Eugénie fixed Favian's eyes with her own in a way that made Favian acutely aware that it had been two full days since he had possessed her last. The dance went on, thirty minutes at least, without a word spoken between them; but certainly communication was there—the Virginia reel, outwardly a lively, old-fashioned dance, had become intensely erotic. Much of Favian's burden, the worries about the British, about the Cat Island expedition, the danger to Louisiana, vanished in the body-flame lit suddenly by Eugénie's proud, triumphant stare. The *petite gouave,* the wine and brandy and tafia punch, had all concentrated Favian's attention entirely on the woman he partnered—with whom he coupled, really, through the medium of the dance. Behind Eugénie's flaming eyes he saw flashes of movement: the flashing fan and brilliant smile of a black dancer, the green jacket of a dragoon, a swirling line of white gowns, the brightly colored waistcoats of the male onlookers. By the end of the dance he was dizzy, intoxicated in more ways than one; he tottered as Eugénie took his arm.

The smile she directed up at him was one of knowing, intimate lechery. "I don't know whether I will be free tomorrow or not," she said. "But I know I am free tonight, following the ball."

"Where is your room?" Favian asked.

"The servants' stair is at the end of the hall. Ground floor, second door on your right as you come down the stairs. Or larboard, as you sailors say."

"Starboard."

"Larboard, starboard, all the same," she said lightly. "Madame won't be wanting me tonight, so I hope you will." Shouldering a way through the throng, he lurched against a Creole woman and apologized. Eugénie looked up at him critically. "How much have you drunk tonight? Love is better without rum, I think."

"It's Humbert's fault, blast him. He kept feeding me *petite gouave* and reminiscing about his damned campaign in Ireland."

Gideon and Maria-Anna had come in from the dance floor at the same time, Maria-Anna looking resentfully at a bootprint on her white gown. "Knocked me down and stepped on me," she said. "Some little ruffian in a green coat!"

"He apologized, my love," Gideon said.

"The oaf." She made a face as another swarm of locals pushed into the room.

"It's getting too crowded," Gideon said, looking up at Favian. "There's nothing more to see—Jackson has already disappeared into a back room to confer with the Choctaws, and that's the last we'll see of him. Shall we leave, Favian?"

"That suits me." Favian's body exulted.

"There's Campaspe," Eugénie said. "I'll fetch her."

Campaspe came under protest, but Maria-Anna ended her objections by promising to take her to one of the public balls later that week—the threat of British invasion, it seemed, was providing endless excuses for social events. Favian collected his hat and cloak and bought a cup of coffee from a vendor outside the ballroom, then was annoyed to find that the coffee had been spiked with tafia. He walked with the party to Gideon's hotel, Campaspe on one arm and Eugénie on the other. The strange mixture of drinks and the torrid nature of the dance had the world whirling about Favian's head, his body in a state of erotic madness—strange, he thought, drink in these quantities usually quelled desire. Not tonight, it seemed.

Once in Gideon's rooms Eugénie and Campaspe were dismissed. Eugénie left the room, her eyes demurely downcast, not daring to hint at a collusion with Favian—she was intelligent, Favian thought, and lovely; perhaps she would make a wife after all. No fortune would come with her, but then he was rich with prize money and had no need to marry an heiress. A Louisiana Creole, dark and lively; he could see her charming the eyes out of Portsmouth and the old men in Washington who ran the Navy. But would she make a good sailor's wife? Favian wondered. Her physical urges were strong, he knew; could she subordinate them during the long, inevitable absences, when Favian might be two years away from home on convoy duty to China? A cuckolded man had two choices, Favian knew; suffer in silent humiliation or issue a public challenge. Either way a Navy career could be ended. The matter would take some thought, he decided; and he'd think about it when he was less aflame with lust and drink.

Gideon ordered coffee and wanted to talk about the Cat Island expedition, but Favian, after two cups of coffee, made his excuses early. "Please come to the *Louisiana* tomorrow morning—I can have my own Lieutenant Eastlake and Midshipman Stanhope act as secretaries, and General Jackson may be present as well. And the pilot may have arrived by then." The world spun on its heel as he stood; he gripped the back of his chair and waited until it stopped. Maria-Anna was looking at him with an indulgent smile, Gideon with a slight frown. "Beg pardon," he said. "All General Humbert's fault; he fed me all this *petite gouave* without telling me what was in it. Tomorrow, Gideon. Maria-Anna." He bowed to kiss her hand and straightened without losing his balance, then stepped into the hall as Grimes expressionlessly opened the door.

Once he heard the door close behind him, he turned in the direction of the servants' stair, undoing his cravat and neckcloth. The stair had been illuminated only with a candle, and that candle had gone out; he moved cautiously, the stairway illuminated only by the glow from the hallway below. Once on the ground floor he walked two doors down and hesitated. "Larboard, starboard," he muttered to himself and slipped quietly through the door on the left.

The little room was black, but there was a reassuring female presence—a pleasant scent in the room, a little sound as Eugénie turned over in her sleep—on the narrow bed. She'd fallen asleep waiting for him; he hoped he hadn't been too long. Favian unclipped his sword and laid it in the corner, then got out of his heavy uniform coat and shirt; there seemed to be a little table of some sort behind him, and he laid his clothing on that. He knelt to take off his boots, then moved to the bed, reaching out, touching braided hair. Eugénie woke up with a start and a shocked intake of breath.

"I'm sorry I frightened you," he murmured. "It's your Favian, my darling." He leaned forward to kiss her, feeling her lips unresponsive, and stroked her cheek. "I'm sorry I'm so late. I was delayed. I should have brought you flowers." He kissed her again and felt a flutter of response, and that was enough to set off the tiger in him. If her hesitance, her naïveté, penetrated his whirling perceptions, he discarded them; perhaps it was nearing her time of the month, and she was uncomfortable. It was not until it was far too late that he realized, when at last she spoke to him, that the woman in his arms was not Eugénie Desplein, but Campaspe.

THIRTEEN

"You *what*?" Gideon demanded, thunderstruck.

Favian replied quietly, his voice matter-of-fact; but he wondered if his face betrayed the harrowed desperation he felt within. "I respectfully request the hand of your ward, Campaspe Rodríguez y Sandovál, in marriage. As soon as possible. Before we leave for Cat Island, if it can be arranged."

Gideon could do nothing but stare; Maria-Anna, her hand frozen on her morning dish of coffee, looked in astonishment from Favian to Gideon and back again. Even the unflappable Grimes seemed startled.

"Does Campaspe know about this?" Maria-Anna asked.

"Yes. She agrees we want it to be as soon as possible."

"Campaspe," said Gideon, "is a foolish girl. I would have expected more sense from you." He looked at Favian, unblinking. "Who knoweth whether he shall be a wise man or a fool?"

Maria-Anna looked down at her hand, then raised the coffee to her lips; she appeared not to taste it. The coffee returned to the table. "I think," she said, "that Gideon and I should talk. You will excuse us, Favian."

"Certainly." Favian stood, wincing at the appalling pain the movement brought to his skull. He heard the murmur of voices in the corridor; there was the phrase "conspiracy under my roof!" from Gideon. Favian sat down again. Grimes looked at him with a forced, if kindly, smile.

"Would you like, sir," he asked, "for me to bring you a little brandy for your coffee?"

"Yes. Please." Grimes silently left the room, and Favian pressed his fingers to his temples. His brain was awash with pain and guilt; there was a sick feeling in his stomach as he remembered the previous night. *Ravishment*. My God. What kind of madman had he become? Killer, man of honor, despoiler of virgins. The iron, uncompromising tones of the Articles of War echoed in his mind, repeated every Sunday to every man aboard the United States vessels of war: The commanders of all ships and vessels of war belonging to the Navy are strictly enjoined and required to show in themselves a good example of virtue, honor, patriotism, and subordination; and be vigilant in inspecting the conduct of all such as are placed under their command . . . Any officer or other person guilty of oppression, cruelty, fraud, profane swearing, drunkenness, or any other scandalous conduct tending to the destruction of good morals, shall, if an officer, be cashiered . . .

He was, he had thought, a man of honor; he had upheld the code strictly, living by it even when it had cost him dearly—perhaps Emma Greenhow had refused him because she could not live with a man whose life was wrapped so completely by strictures of the Navy. He had lived the rules laid down for him, he had duelled and killed, he had kept his honor. Until last night. And then, in the reeling, sickening confusion, as he had lit the candle and seen Campaspe looking up at him with flushed cheeks, her eyes astonished and strange, he had blurted out the words that might retrieve for him his lost and fleeting honor; he had proposed marriage; he would wed the girl he had ruined. She had dissolved at his proposal, throwing her arms around his neck and weeping—there would be love on one side, at least. He would have to be very careful to prevent her from knowing that his own was feigned.

He heard a door open behind him and turned his head—even that movement brought a knifelike pain rocketing through his skull—he saw Eugénie Desplein, grim-mouthed, entering the room. He rose, overhasty, feeling awkward as a boy.

"Is it true what I hear? What Campaspe tells me?" He had seen that ferocity once before, that first day they had lain on his hotel bed while he spoke of *proposition d'une affaire;* there was a little V between her brows and her dark eyes flashed dragon-fire.

"Yes. Whatever it is, it's true." Hopelessly.

"You simpleton. Desplein was worth ten of you." Her scorn was withering. Favian sank back into his chair. What was the point of explanation? He had not meant to betray her with Campaspe, but he had. Nothing he said could alter that.

"So cautious. So superior," she hissed. "You'll have your hands full now!"

"Be thankful," he said, fixing her with his own glare, "that you're rid of me." She paused for a second, chewing that over; Grimes entered with a bottle of brandy he'd bought downstairs, and the appalling moment was over. Favian blankly held out his coffee cup and Grimes, his eyes avoiding them both, poured. There were voices coming from the next room.

"She can't marry Favian! It's madness!" That was Gideon.

Maria-Anna's voice was tolerant, perhaps even a little amused. "I think it's obvious by now she had damn well better marry *somebody*." Gideon snorted. Maria-Anna's voice went on. "Send for Campaspe," she said. "We should ask her what the devil has been happening behind our backs."

Oh no, Favian thought. If she told them . . .

He should have eloped with her, he thought fiercely, taken her from her narrow little bed and gone to the nearest preacher.

Eugénie was sent to bring Campaspe up to her mistress's rooms. Campaspe came through the parlor with Eugénie a fierce little shadow behind; she was a little pale, a little frightened, and Favian took out his handkerchief, one of the monogrammed ones she had made him, and touched it to the corner of his mouth; she saw it and gave him a brave, slight smile. Perhaps it would work out all right.

Favian could hear the tone, if not the words, of the united attack Gideon and Maria-Anna launched, but he also heard Campaspe's short answers—it was clear she was digging in her heels. *Brave girl*, he thought, admiring her bravery even though he knew it doomed him. When they came out of the parlor, Campaspe's eyes were shining triumph.

He stood, a condemned man facing the stern visage of the law. "We'll arrange it," Maria-Anna said. "You can be married tomorrow. That will give you headstrong fools twenty-four hours to change your minds."

Gideon's cheek bulged with a chaw of tobacco. "The great God that formed all things rewardeth the fool, and rewardeth transgressors," he said. Proverbs, Favian thought. Or maybe Ecclesiastes. Typical Gideon, anyway. His blessing.

Campaspe moved over near him and took his hand, holding it through the doeskin glove. He squeezed her hand encouragingly; she gave him a ghostly smile. Eugénie stood by the door, her anger smouldering.

"Thank you," Favian said. "Maria-Anna. Gideon. I know we'll be very happy." And he turned to kiss her, tilting her chin up to face him; Campaspe regarded him gravely with her dark eyes, then stood up on tiptoe to press her lips chastely to his. He could, he decided, carry this off fairly well; the Navy had taught him civility and polite subterfuge, and this wouldn't be much different. He heard Gideon clear his throat, and ended the kiss. There was probably not, he thought later, a snort of contempt from Eugénie; but somehow he fancied at the time that he heard one.

The next twenty-four hours passed swiftly. Favian later remembered Patterson's stiff face turn startled, then his hearty congratulations followed by those of his staff; he also remembered the knowing leer from Finch Martin, Gideon's first officer, who nudged Favian's side with an elbow and muttered, "Like 'em young, eh? I've had my eye on that Campaspe myself!" Favian had muttered something darkly, and Martin had taken a step back, looking puzzled.

He remembered also the moment when he and Maria-Anna had found themselves alone in her *poque* parlor, and the sudden ferocity in her tone as she looked at Favian and said, "I don't know what's been going on here, Favian—but if you hurt that girl I'll cut your ears off." There was no question, Favian knew, that she was capable of just that; and for a long moment of regret he wished he'd had the luck to meet Maria-Anna long ago, before she had tied herself to Gideon. But there was no point in foolish, wistful thinking; he put it out of his mind and gave her a reassuring speech.

Even more memorable was a talk with Campaspe, late that evening when some unusually tactful maneuvering on the part of Gideon had resulted in their being left alone for a few moments in the drawing room. Favian reached out over the red baize table, and she gave him her hand. She looked at him solemnly—odd, he thought, that she had been so thoughtful, so subdued since she had been given permission to marry.

"You don't have to, you know," she said. She dropped her eyes, looking at the clasped hands on the table. "Not if you don't want. I won't insist."

Favian looked at her with growing astonishment. "Of course I want to marry you!" he said. "Whatever makes you think I don't?"

"You seem so—I don't know," she said. She shook her head. "It's not what I thought."

"Things scarcely ever are," Favian said. She shot a look at him, and he was sorry he had chosen to be glib. "Campaspe," he said, "I wish things weren't in such a rush. I wish we had been given more time with each other. I wish last night hadn't been so, so sudden." There were tears falling down her face. "Things will be better," he said. "We'll have more time later."

Her shoulders were trembling. There was only one thing to do, so he did it; he folded her in his long arms and stroked her until the tempest ended. Afterward she kissed him and smiled up at him bravely—it wasn't the flashing, encompassing smile he remembered, but that the smile existed at all was encouraging. He would have to be very careful, he thought. Very careful indeed.

FOURTEEN

At noon the next day Favian and Campaspe stood in front of the Presbyterian pastor and were married.

Gideon gave Campaspe away; Eugénie Desplein was a very stiff matron of honor; outside the church an enthusiastic Coxswain Kuusikoski shouted, "Attention! Present! Salute!" and the bride and groom walked under the arch of cutlasses formed by the crew of Favian's pinnace. General Jackson, in muddy boots, found time to stop by the reception and drink a glass to the couple's health; he then spent the next forty minutes conferring with Patterson, Gideon, and Favian concerning the Cat Island expedition before kissing a blushing Campaspe farewell and dashing off to inspect the New Orleans Volunteers, who were parading that afternoon. Finch Martin, in his cups, launched into an address, lewd even for him, that had all of the ladies present blushing crimson, along with most of the men. At the end of the afternoon, the crew of Favian's boat by then roaring drunk, detached the horse from his rented carriage, put themselves cheerfully in harness, and dragged the carriage through muddy streets to Favian's hotel while singing a lengthy ballad about the whores of Pearl Street, a song Favian hoped Campaspe did not understand.

He had shifted his quarters to a larger suite and filled his rooms with flowers; Campaspe gasped as he carried her through the door, then hugged him fiercely. Favian kicked the door shut, and they were alone. Carefully, he set her on her feet.

There was a moment of silence, broken only by the distant, fortunately indistinct song of Kuusikoski's crew, still bellowing out their ballad in front of the hotel. Campaspe slowly lifted her gaze to Favian, and he took her hands. "My darling," he said. The words seemed awkward to him. Her arms went around him, and she pressed her cheek to the front of his uniform coat.

"It's wonderful," she said, and Favian felt relief flood him. He had carried it off thus far. She stepped back and turned slowly, taking in the room, the flowers, the table set for two, the cold buffet, the bottles of champagne standing on the sideboard, ready to be drunk at room temperature: there was no way to chill them. Favian put his cocked hat on the rack and unclipped his sword from its belt. Campaspe walked to the window and gazed out; there was a burst of cheering from the crew of the gig, and she giggled and waved down to them before backing away out of sight. Gratefully she took off her veil.

"Would you like something to eat?" Favian asked as he lit a lamp: in December the days were short. She shook her head.

A virgin, Favian thought. In all but the most technical sense, anyway. He was used to women of far more experience. And the other night had been appalling: there could be no repetition of that sort of scene. Carefully, he thought, carefully.

"Your clothes have been moved to the bedroom," he said. "Would you like to see they're all hung properly?"

Campaspe nodded eagerly, brightening. He followed her to the other room. She examined the contents of the drawers and closets; everything had been done to her satisfaction. Favian untied his cravats, loosened his neckcloth, lit a lamp. "It's very nice," Campaspe said.

"Perhaps," said Favian, "you would like to change?" She turned awkwardly to face him, nodded hurriedly. "I'll give you some privacy, then," he said. He brought his dressing gown out from the closet, then bent to kiss her cheek as she stood motionless in the intimacy of the tiny room.

Back in the parlor he shrugged out of the uniform coat, then laid it carefully on the settee, detaching the heavy epaulets and laying them neatly aside. Outside the singing had stopped; no doubt the patrol had put an end to it. He hoped he would not have to bail his boat's crew out of Cabildo tomorrow. The sky was darkening; there would be sunset in a few minutes. He undressed, laying his clothes out neatly on the settee to be packed in the morning for the Cat Island trip. He looked down at the clothing spread out on the settee. There, he thought, was the Favian that had stood at the altar, the public Favian in his blue coat and epaulets, the chivalrous hero of the Navy. In a few moments a different Favian would be facing Campaspe on their marriage bed, a Favian bereft of the authority and burden of the post-captain. All his life Favian had privately grudged the Navy its authority over his life, its demands that he assume in public the cloak of virtuous, stainless hero—demands that had forced him into an artificial, affected style of behavior, both when he lived by the code and when, in careful secrecy, he violated it.

Now, astonishingly, the code was irrelevant: there was nothing in the situation but a thin, thirtyish, dyspeptic man and a young girl waiting for him in another room. There had been nothing in his life to prepare him for this, not all the battles and adventures, not the women in his life, the various Maries in the various bordellos, Emma Greenhow, Eugénie Desplein, his former mistress Caroline Huxley. The facts were simple and human; the situation would have to be addressed in its own terms, terms entirely outside Favian's experience. Favian put on his dressing gown and waited a decent interval, then he poured two brandies, put the tiny glasses on a tray, and knocked on the bedroom door.

Campaspe seemed pale in the light of the lamp; she was lying stiffly in the bed, dressed in her lace nightgown, the covers up to her armpits. Favian tried to smile. "You're beautiful, my dear," he said. "Would you like some brandy?"

"Thank you."

He gave her a glass, took one himself, and made a toast. "To our future." Expressionless, she touched her glass to his and drank. Favian blew out the lamp, took off his doeskin gloves, and slipped into the bed. He reached over to take Campaspe's hand; it was cold as ice.

"My dear Campaspe," he said, "the last days must have been very tiring. If you wish simply to go to sleep—well, I'd understand."

There was answering pressure on his hand; he could see the faint light glimmering on her eyes as they slid toward him: no speech. She raised his hand and kissed it, then finished her brandy and leaned across him to put the glass on the bedside table. She kissed his cheek. "I think I would like to sleep," she said.

Favian touched her brow with his scarred fingers. "I don't want you to be afraid of me," he said. "The other night—it isn't all like that. It can be wonderful." He could see her dark eyes watching him; he took a breath and went on. "I think the other night I must have been a little mad. But please don't think I don't love you, or care for your feelings. I'm very happy just being here with you."

Campaspe kissed him again, impulsively; her arms went around him, and she rested her head on his shoulder. He put an arm around her, drank his brandy, and contemplated his falsehoods; they seemed successful enough. The nearness of Campaspe's body, her obvious femaleness, had brought, despite his attempts to control it, an aggravating arousal; the night might well be a long one. Campaspe spoke only once in the next few minutes, before she fell asleep. "It's very strange," she said. Favian, silently agreeing, sipped his brandy till it was gone.

Shortly after three the next morning Campaspe came into the parlor to find Favian working by lamplight at his desk. He turned at the sound of her footfalls, seeing her walking in hesitantly, looking lonely and very young in her long nightgown, her hair down, shrouding her face. He reached out his left hand, and she came across the room and took it.

"What are you doing?" she asked.

"I'm making an inventory of my property," Favian said. "I want you to have it. In case anything happens to me."

She pressed his left hand as he wrote with the right. He signed the paper, dated it, and put the pen aside.

"I haven't seen your hands before," she said.

"They're not pretty, are they? I hurt them in the wreck of the *Experiment*. They don't give me any pain, though."

"I'm glad."

"I'll make a will tomorrow, when there are witnesses," Favian said. "The house in Maine is probably under British occupation, and if the peace lets them keep what they've conquered, then it will probably be confiscated. The rest, the property in New Hampshire and New York, can come to you free and clear. I'd suggest you follow the advice of my father and brothers when it comes to investments—they're intelligent men."

"Let's not talk about it," Campaspe said suddenly. "It's bad luck."

"Very well." If he were killed at Cat Island or afterward, he thought, his will would have to be very explicit on the subject of who was to have charge of the money and property during Campaspe's minority. His father, he thought; but then his father was over seventy and might find it a burden, and in any case might not have enough years left to him. His brother Lafayette, then: a brilliant man, if a cold one; he and Campaspe would not like each other, but he would make her money. He looked up at Campaspe and wondered how New England would see her. Latin, impulsive, and suspect, no doubt; they would offer her little charity. Emma Greenhow, he thought, would be as appalled by his choice as he was by hers. New York was less narrow, he thought; Campaspe would probably be happier dwelling in his property on Manhattan.

He realized with surprise that all his thoughts had been based on the likelihood of his own death—not a good sign, he thought. Was he really, secretly hoping for death in the upcoming campaign, some glorious end that would enable him to avoid the responsibility he had just undertaken? Not good; fighting men who had anticipated their own death all too often found it—he had seen such deaths many times during his violent career. Yet it was clear that his Navy career might well be over. He had stolen a United States frigate and compounded his disobedience by sailing it into a situation in which it might well be taken by an entire British fleet. . . . There was no way he could survive the court-martial that would result from that. And even if all worked out for the best as far as *Macedonian* was concerned, he knew that his marriage would not help his career. Campaspe was not, he judged, the best material for an officer's wife; somehow he could not see her alongside the staid, proper wives of the other captains. Perhaps it would be best for all concerned if some sharpshooter's ball found him, and he was able to make his quiet exit and leave Campaspe a wealthy widow. . . .

No. Damnation, no. He had seen enough death at sea to know how appalling it could be, and he knew he did not want it. With an act of will he banished the thought from his mind.

"You may keep this place if you like," Favian said, indicating the hotel room, "but it's probably too large for you, alone. You may want to take rooms at the Esplanade so you can be near Maria-Anna. I'll leave you some money to buy new clothes to fit your station—I hope you'll take Maria-Anna's advice; she has good taste in such matters."

Campaspe nodded. "The British may come, you know, while Gideon and I are away," Favian went on. "In that case I want you to follow Maria-Anna's advice. She'll know when to leave—you can make your way to Mobile or Baton Rouge, maybe farther upriver. General Jackson will burn the city if he has to retreat, and I don't want you caught up in it—I don't want you telling that to anyone else, by the way, just to Maria-Anna. No sense in spreading panic."

"Please," Campaspe said insistently. "Let's not talk about it."

He fell silent, then remembered something he had intended to do before he left. "I want you to have something," he said. "Here." He stood and went to the sea chest that had been readied for the morning's departure; he opened it and took out a locket on a chain. Campaspe took the locket and opened it.

"It was painted by Robert Fulton, the steamboat man," Favian said. "It's a miniature of a larger portrait he wanted to do—it was very nice of him to send me the miniature, I think. . . ." It was a somewhat idealized portrait, a dashing, stern-eyed Favian in full-dress uniform standing before a background of billowing cannon smoke, looking in every line like a mature, commanding hero.

"Thank you," Campaspe said. She stood awkwardly for a few moments, uncertain whether to put the locket around her neck or not; and then she ducked and slipped the chain over her head.

She pulled her hair out from beneath the chain, the gold glowing on the whiteness of her gown. "I'd like a lock of hair, too, please," she said.

"Of course. Do you have some scissors with your things?"

"Oh, yes." Campaspe returned to the other room and came out with a pair of scissors. Favian returned to his chair and let her choose a lock of his dark hair and snip it off. As she bound the lock with a little ribbon and placed it in the locket, he saw she was shivering, standing barefoot on the cold floor.

"You're cold," Favian said. "You should go to bed. Let me stoke the fire in the bedroom." She stood quietly by while he crouched by the bedroom stove and added to the wood, then reached out to take his hand as he rose.

"Please don't do any more work tonight," she said. Favian put his arm around her, and she hugged him closely, her weight shifting slowly from one leg to the other. He looked down at her for several long moments, one hand stroking her back slowly. Campaspe tipped her head back, and then reached down to take his hand and place it firmly over her breast. "I'm not afraid, you know," she said. *A gallant liar,* he thought; he could feel her panicked heart. There was nothing else to do but kiss her.

It went, he thought later, rather well. For the most part she was passive and let him do most of the work; he was slow and careful, trying his best to show her the possibilities of pleasure without alarming her with her own body's reactions, or for that matter with his. She tried her best to act as if she were relaxed, but he knew she wasn't—by the end he thought her tension was much lower, her capacity for pleasure increased. Next time, when Campaspe had a better idea of what to expect, things would go better.

She wept quietly, next morning, when his luggage was carried out by his boat's crew; he could see their sympathetic glances as they saluted him and carried his chests past the door. He kissed her farewell and hoped Maria-Anna would come soon, as soon as she said her own good-bye to Gideon. The room smelled of stale flowers; he opened the window and said, "I'll be back." Campaspe smiled bravely; he kissed her again and left, feeling an unusual mixture of regrets and responsibilities.

The weight of the epaulets on his shoulders and the swinging sword by his side—the weighty fighting sword, not the little wasplike decorative smallsword—reminded him that he was going to war. Any future meeting with Campaspe might come after New Orleans had been leveled, leaving the British in control of the mouths of the Mississippi, *Macedonian* taken or sent to the bottom, and Favian cashiered after a long court-martial. He looked up at the window of the hotel, seeing a handkerchief fluttering out of the window. He turned and waved, hoping Campaspe would do all right. There was nothing more he could do for her, he knew, except survive the coming campaign—or perhaps not to survive.

He turned and walked toward the wharf and the enemy.

FIFTEEN

Favian came aboard *Malachi's Revenge* to the twitter of bosun's pipes and the clatter of swords and muskets raised to the salute: Gideon was still intent on outdoing the Navy at its own spit and polish. Favian uncovered gravely to the salutes, seeing Gideon standing by the helm. His face was grimmer than usual; clearly something unfortunate had occurred.

"Lieutenant Cunningham and Gunboat Number 5 are ready to weigh on our signal," Gideon said as they exchanged salutes. Patterson had agreed he could spare his one uncommitted gunboat for the Cat Island expedition. "Fontenoy and the *Franklin* are ready as well. Mr. Clowes is trying to recruit crew for the *Musquetobite* and will join us if he can."

"Very well." It had been settled that Gideon's ex-British sloop of war *Musquetobite*, when fully crewed, would go to Finch Martin with Clowes as his lieutenant, but Martin had insisted on remaining with Gideon's tern schooner as long as action was in the offing. Martin, acknowledged a brilliant sailor, had been allowed to remain.

"The pilot is aboard," Gideon said, his mouth tightened into a grim line. "I think you'd better see him."

"Very well." Favian followed Gideon down the aft scuttle and down the short passage to the captain's cabin. He opened the door and stepped inside; the pilot, who had been waiting within, stood and bowed.

"Captain Laffite," said Favian, "you surprise me."

Jean Laffite, dressed again in solemn black, grinned pleasantly. "The safe-conduct is good for anyone, no?" he asked. "Don't worry, I was discreet. I came downriver in a pirogue just at dawn; I was not seen."

"General Jackson," said Favian, "will be aboard shortly. I cannot guarantee his reaction will be favorable."

"I should think," Laffite said, "that you and he would be pleased to have me along. I stand ready to back up my words with my life. If I am deceiving you about Cat Island, you may inflict whatever penalty you wish."

"The United States Navy," said Favian stiffly, "does not take hostages. We are not Turks, sir."

"I most humbly beg your pardon," Laffite said, bowing again. "I was merely trying to point out that my presence is meant to be reassuring."

Plus, Favian thought, his being with the government forces moving on Cat Island would not go unnoticed by the rebel pirates. Rebel against the Laffites' authority, the gesture would say, and you not only face their vengeance but that of the legitimate authorities as well. But he only said, "Your apology is accepted, sir."

"I heard this morning of your marriage, Captain Markham," Laffite said. "May I offer my most sincere congratulations? The bride is a lovely girl; I'm sure you will be well suited to one another."

"Thank you, Captain Laffite," Favian said, wondering if he detected a hint of irony behind Laffite's black-eyed smile. No, he thought, he was seeing his own misgivings in the pirate's face; the man was being sincere.

There was a shout on deck that echoed down the skylight, and Favian turned to his cousin. "More guests, Gideon."

Gideon's eyes glanced disapprovingly from Favian to Laffite, then back. "Aye," he said, and led the way from his cabin.

"I don't want that pirate on my *Revenge*!" Gideon burst out as they made their way up the companionway to the deck. "It may destroy my reputation as an honest privateer—I don't want my name associated with Laffite's. His grapes are grapes of gall, their clusters are bitter."

Deuteronomy, Favian thought, though he wasn't positive. "Can you not bear with him for a day?" he asked. "I can put him aboard *Macedonian* tonight. In the meantime he can be kept in the cabin. If you insist we can move him to the gunboat, but that might insult him."

"Party from the *Louisiana*, Cap'n," Finch Martin reported as they came on deck.

"Stand by to render the salute, Mr. Martin," Gideon said. "Reeve a whip through the yardarm so Mr. Midshipman Lovette can use a bosun's chair." He stood pensively on the deck, his hands automatically cutting himself a plug of tobacco.

"Blast that Laffite!" he finally said. "The man's clever. Half the crew saw him come aboard, and many will recognize him. The damage is done." He put the tobacco into his mouth. "Very well," he said. "He may stay until we reach the *Macedonian*. Then I'll hand him over to you."

"I'm sure that's wise," Favian said.

"Mph," Gideon replied, not in the least convinced.

There was a shout from Kuusikoski alongside, followed by the thud of a boat against the tern schooner's hull; the bosun's pipes rendered a salute as Favian's courtly Virginian third lieutenant, Eastlake, came aboard, followed by Lovette (who disdained the bosun's chair and came up one-handed), Stanhope, Dr. Solomon, and the rest of the Macedonians that Favian had brought with him to New Orleans. They saluted the two captains; Favian and Gideon uncovered in reply.

"Mr. Willard will show you where you can store your dunnage," Gideon said.

"Thank you, sir," said Eastlake, glancing over *Malachi's Revenge* with professional appreciation. Schooners like this were the envy of the Navy, not to mention the rest of the world.

"The hospitality of the wardroom is open to ye," said George Willard, Gideon's second officer. He was a Gay Head Indian from Martha's Vineyard, a black-eyed, silent man, a devout Calvinist brought up, like the rest of his sea-bounded tribe, to spend his days on the broad ocean.

Favian watched as his boat's crew went forward to mix with Gideon's foredeck men, as his officers filed down the aft scuttle. Solomon, he thought, was strutting a little, like a victorious fighting cock; Favian thought sourly about the airs that successful duellists insisted on giving themselves, and once again silently damned the whole practice.

"General Jackson's setting off from the levee, Cap'n," reported a quartermaster, and Finch Martin recalled the welcoming party. Favian considered popping down the aft scuttle to bring up the Navy men, but Eastlake was alert and came up with his party, ranking them with Gideon's people.

Jackson was back in his stained traveling clothes once more; he looked aged and frail, and his hawklike eyes were hooded with exhaustion. McRae, the engineer Tatum, and the civilian mapmaker Latour, his staff for this journey, looked after him with obvious concern. Jackson nodded, apparently without interest, at Allen's green-coated sharpshooters ranked on the quarterdeck, then saluted Gideon. "Gentlemen," he said. "I hope you were not delaying on my account?"

"The pilot is aboard, General," Gideon said, evading Jackson's question. "He is below in my cabin."

"Very good," Jackson said. He gave a tired smile. "I should probably go below myself and get my lubberly bones out of your way."

"The pilot, General," Gideon said. Jackson looked up at him.

"Yes, Captain Markham?"

"The pilot, General Jackson," Favian said, interrupting, "is Jean Laffite himself. We thought you ought to be warned."

"Laffite. Indeed," said Jackson. His voice was very quiet; there was a hint of menace in the tone. He shook his head, clearly considering the possible consequences of this meeting, and then looked up. "Very well," he said. "I shall meet this celebrated bandit."

Gideon spat his tobacco overboard and then led the party below. "Captain Laffite, General Jackson," he said by way of introduction. Lafitte bowed elaborately; the general inclined his torso civilly forward, then back. Neither offered to shake hands.

"Honored, sir," Laffite said, "to be of service."

"I have heard a great deal about you, Captain Laffite," Jackson said, a noncommittal opening.

"Most of it lies, sir," Laffite said. "It is my misfortune to be a man about whom false rumors gather."

"That," said Jackson, "is not necessarily a misfortune in your line of business, I believe."

"Indeed, sir, it is not." Laffite smiled.

"General Jackson," Gideon said, his disapproving tone indicating his attitude toward the whole business, "may I offer you and your staff some coffee, or hot chocolate? I regret we do not carry alcoholic spirits aboard; this is a temperance vessel."

"Very kind of you, Captain Markham." Jackson smiled. "Coffee, if you please."

"Please sit yerselves," Gideon said. He rang for Grimes and told him to bring coffee.

Gideon offered Jackson the place of honor at the head of the table, then asked everyone to make themselves comfortable while he saw about getting the vessels under way. The party sat itself on Gideon's old, worn furniture. Favian seated himself on Jackson's left; Laffite kept the chair, in the center of the table, he had used before.

"I hope, General, to be of service," Laffite said. "My men stand ready to help defend the Republic."

"Very commendable," said Jackson. "I shall look forward to seeing them enrolled in the militia, or on Captain Patterson's ships."

Neatly parried, Favian thought. Laffite seemed a bit taken aback. He heard the tramp of bare feet on the deck as the privateers manned the forward capstan, ready to heave the anchor short.

"Perhaps the general," Laffite said, "would care to see a map I have drawn of Terre Bonne Bay."

"Very well. I hope Mr. Latour may copy it."

"Certainly, sir." Laffite produced a map from one of the two carpetbags he had brought with him. Favian half stood to view the map.

"Here, General, is Cat Island," Laffite said, pointing to a little crescent-shaped island in the middle of the bay. "It is very small, but it is sheltered and solid ground. Here the Guard of the Eagle will live when not at sea. At last report there were no works on Cat Island itself—there is a magazine there, with small arms and powder, and some rude barracks, but no fortifications or great guns. These have been placed elsewhere.

"This, gentlemen, is Timbalier Island," Laffite said, indicating a long, thin island stretching across the mouth of the bay. "It is a low, sandy island, much of it marshy, and it is exposed to the autumn hurricanes, so there are no living quarters on the island. But because it controls the entrance to Cat Island Pass, here to the west of the island, there is a battery here, and a little fort. The ramparts are of cypress logs covered by sand and are quite well made. A garrison will be kept there at all times, perhaps thirty or forty men. The garrison is small, but no doubt they can be reinforced from Cat Island in the event of an alarm."

"What sort of guns?" Favian asked. From the skylight came the sound of the schooner's chanteyman, accompanied by the clatter of capstan pawls and the roar of the seamen bending to the bars. The *Revenge* lurched as the anchor cable began to be drawn in.

"Eighteen-pounders, six of them, in the water battery," Laffite said. "A half dozen six- or four-pounders facing east, so the fort cannot be stormed from the rear without risk."

Eighteen-pounders, Favian thought. Equal in size to *Macedonian*'s main deck guns, and also emplaced. Presumably the Napoleonic veterans in the garrison knew how to use them, too. The battery could smash up *Malachi's Revenge* if it tried to run through the pass, although *Macedonian* could probably survive. But could *Macedonian* even get into these restricted waters?

"How deep is the water in Cat Island Pass?" Favian asked. Laffite frowned.

"Fifteen feet or so. Less water inside the bay itself."

That was definite, then. As Favian had long assumed, *Macedonian* had no hope of getting near enough to the battery to hurt it.

"And to the east of Timbalier Island? Is that passage any deeper?" Favian asked.

"Petite Passe Timbalier draws only two feet at high tide," Laffite said. "Even your gunboat might have difficulty getting over the bar."

"I see," Favian said.

"There is another battery to the west of Cat Island Pass, here on the Isles Dernieres. A small battery, two eighteen-pounders. Here, in the water between Timbalier and Cat Island, the Guard's ships will be anchored here in the sheltered water." Laffite pointed to an expanse of water that included two small islands, Terrebonne and Caillou. "If we achieve surprise, the ships will have only the anchor watch aboard—we can take them without a fight, and then the Guard will be stranded on Cat Island with no way off. It is the batteries that offer us the most difficulty."

"I am confident, sir, they can be dealt with," Favian said, straightening. He was by no means sure, but he knew full well how he was going to try it. Laffite looked at him without expression. Jackson cocked an eye at him.

"Can you force the batteries' surrender with your frigate?" he asked.

"That would be the orthodox way, General," Favian said. "But I think *Macedonian* draws too much water to get within effective range, and in any case a prolonged bombardment would lose our advantage of surprise. No, we'll have to storm the forts from their landward side—as your men did, General, at Horseshoe Bend."

There: Favian had made a point of studying Jackson's campaigns in the last weeks, hoping to better understand the man—and incidentally have ready ammunition for flattery. A faint smile appeared on Jackson's jaundiced face. "I wish you a like success, Captain Markham," he said.

"Thank you, sir. And now, gentlemen, I must take my leave. I'll have to be on deck to signal to the other vessels."

Favian bowed and withdrew. Once on deck he passed the word for Stanhope, his signals midshipman, and walked over to where Gideon was standing by the wheel, watching his men as they strained at the capstan.

"Is the general enjoying the pirate's company?" Gideon asked.

"Laffite has been showing us the enemy's dispositions," Favian said. "He has a map."

Gideon frowned and said nothing. Stanhope appeared with his signal books. "Throw out the signal to weigh anchor, Mr. Stanhope," Favian said.

"Aye aye, sir."

The signal rose up the halliards, streaming in the wind; duplicate signals went up on Gunboat Number 5 and, after some hesitation because of the privateer's lack of familiarity with the Navy signal book, on Fontenoy's *Franklin*. The repeating of the signals was an acknowledgment only: the signal would not be obeyed until the original flags were hauled down.

Favian peered at the *Franklin*, already at short stay and ready for weighing, and then at the gunboat, which was sending men to its windlass. It was a curious, exhilarating feeling, unlike anything he'd ever experienced—he was responsible, under the agreement, for the whole of the force that was to be sent against

Cat Island, but his own ship *Macedonian* was not present. *Malachi's Revenge, Franklin,* and the gunboat each had their own captains; Favian's role was simply to throw out signals to the other two craft so that they could conform to the schooner's movements. This was what being a commodore was like, he thought, responsible for an entire squadron, but not the individual ships. Makeshift and irregular as the squadron was, Favian found the feeling a heady one.

The men at the capstan gave one last heave, then rested on their bars. "Short stay, Cap'n!" Finch Martin's voice echoed from forward.

"Very well, Mr. Martin," Gideon said. He cut himself a plug of tobacco and turned to Favian.

"Yer gunboat seems a mite tardy," he said. The clanking of the gunboat's windlass was clearly heard in the still morning.

"No doubt they're on New Orleans time, Gideon." Favian smiled. "We'll set them on New England time presently."

Gideon nodded. "Aye," he said. The windlass ceased its noise.

"Haul down the signal, Mr. Stanhope," Favian said. He nodded at Gideon. "Whenever you're ready, Captain."

Gideon picked up a speaking trumpet. "Hands to set spanker and heads'ls! Capstan there, heave 'round!"

Favian, uninvolved in the action, stood quietly by the binnacle and watched admiringly as the tern schooner got under way. *Malachi's Revenge* was a brilliant example of the clipper schooner, long, narrow, and low in the water, its masts raked precipitately backward; and Gideon had clearly trained its crew to a standard many Navy men would envy. The sails billowed out, crackling, tugging at the schooner as it stood over its anchor; when the anchor finally broke free of the Mississippi mud, the schooner fell swiftly off the wind, spinning on its heel, and ran downstream fast as quicksilver. It was breathtaking. Favian found himself, not for the first time, envying Gideon: had Favian not tied himself to the Navy at the foolish and impressionable age of sixteen, he might be carrying on the family privateering tradition, like Gideon, in a fast and beautiful vessel such as this. Free of Navy orders and responsibility, free of the unforgiving code of the professional officer, on a vessel able to defeat any enemy it could not effortlessly run from.

But he was tied to the Navy, and to everything the Navy stood for—its aggressive, combative traditions, its fierce, enforced comformity to iron regulation, its insistence on an uncompromising code of honor . . . the decision had been made years ago, and there was no turning back. He could envy Gideon his freedom and his ship, and he could envy Gideon his choice of Maria-Anna, but the envy was hopeless: he would try not to let it turn bitter. The Navy and Campaspe were his lot, and that would not change.

"Mr. Stanhope, throw out the signal to follow the flag," he said, seeing topsails appearing on the *Franklin*, seeing the gunboat sheet home its main and turn into the wake of the *Revenge*. He turned to face forward, seeing the *Carolina* on the *Revenge*'s starboard bow. He took up a long glass and trained it on the Navy schooner's quarterdeck, seeing the unmistakable, formally dressed figure of Patterson stalking stiffly on the planking. They had agreed that there would be no booming guns, no dipping of martial ensigns, nothing to indicate that a military expedition had just set forth, but as the privateer swept closer to the *Carolina*, Favian saw Patterson turn and raise his hat in salute. Favian let the long glass fall by his side and raised his own hat. They passed between twenty yards of one another: one Navy man charged with the nigh-impossible defense of a city in the face of overwhelming strength, and another setting out on a dubious expedition on the word of a pirate. Neither man, Favian suspected, envied the other; both knew full well that the chances of ultimate success were almost nil. But the code by which they both lived did not contemplate defeat; both had no choice but to do what they could and hope for the best. They raised their hats in salute to a quixotic and probably futile endeavor and did not need to speak.

"*Franklin* and the gunboat acknowledge the signal, sir," Stanhope reported.

"Haul it down, Mr. Stanhope."

"Aye aye, sir."

Favian settled his undress round hat back on his head and listened to the chuckle of water passing beneath the schooner's keel. Gideon was setting his foresail and mainsail, the schooner responding, surging ahead. Favian hoped the other vessels in the squadron would be able to keep up, particularly the clumsy, beamy little gunboat. It didn't matter, he supposed; they would all reach Fort St. Philip and the *Macedonian* before nightfall no matter how fast they sailed, but Favian found himself wanting to keep his little force in sight awhile longer, even such a heterogeneous and strange squadron as this. The sight was splendid: New Orleans on one bank, the flat roofs of the pastel buildings huddling behind their levee; on the other side the white sails of the squadron in sharp contrast to the dark mass of the far bank. He watched until the city vanished from sight, thinking about its muddy boulevards, its lively, quarrelsome inhabitants, its bold and lovely women. He wondered if this was his last glimpse of the city before Jackson turned it into the charred ruin he had promised to leave to the enemy.

Enough. His thoughts were turning morbid. He turned to the scuttle and went below to the cabin.

The council of war had ended: Jackson was resting, feet up and eyes closed, on the thwartship settee; Jean Laffite was engaged in a murmured conversation with McRae and Latour. Favian seated himself facing the stern windows so that he could keep an eye on his squadron and nodded to the others as Grimes poured him a cup of coffee. Latour produced a pack of cards.

"We were considering, Captain Markham, a game of whist," he said. "Would you honor us by making up a fourth?"

A game of cards: good. Something unrelated to the war, to his responsibilities; it would take his mind off his gloomy meditations.

"Happily, sir," Favian said. "Though, if you're not absolutely set on whist, I know an interesting version of *poque* that you might never have encountered."

"*Poque?*" Latour asked. "Very well, if you like. Gentlemen?"

The others agreed. Favian, smiling to himself, shuffled the cards, explained how the new version differed from the old, and dealt. He put the deck facedown in the middle of the table so each player could draw new cards, and then turned to Laffite to commence the betting. General Jackson, on the settee, began to snore.

Favian possessed one advantage already, that of having created this version of the game in the first place, but his knowledge of the game was rendered almost unnecessary by the cards. He began turning up full hands, fluxes, and fours of a kind with astonishing regularity; the stakes began to pile up in front of him. His opponents were intelligent men and caught on quickly to the principles of the game, but their cause was hopeless; Favian simply blew them from the water with the strength of his cards.

By the time Grimes announced dinner at noon, Favian possessed markers for over three hundred dollars.

Jackson sat up at the announcement of dinner and quickly scanned the table. "Captain Markham, I hope you're as lucky in battle as you are at cards," he said. "The British won't stand a chance."

"The British play their cards very well, General," Favian said. "I'll be needing some aces."

"Preparation, aggression, surprise," Jackson said. He stood, buttoned up his battered coat, and sat at the table. "Those are three aces we can deal ourselves. The fourth is luck; and maybe we can make a little of that if we try hard enough." He seemed alert after his rest, his deep-set eyes darting from one face to another. "We must make the British play the game our way," he said. "We must never let them control the play. That coffee smells mighty fine, gentlemen. Will you pass me a cup?"

Gideon joined them for dinner, reciting a stiff grace as the stuffed crab, glazed duck, and roast venison were placed on the table. Jackson confined himself to a single slice of venison and a bowl of hominy, washed down with strong coffee; he steered the conversation toward the Tripolitan War, asking about the burning of the captured *Philadelphia*, the bombardments of the harbor.

"It was Preble, of course, that made the difference," Favian said. "He was lucky enough to have a large enough squadron to do the work, of course, but another commander had the force before him and had done nothing with it. If he hadn't been superseded, we might have forced their surrender entirely and got the *Philadelphia*'s crew released without having to pay ransom. As it was, the peace has lasted, and we haven't had to pay further tributes—though we may have to send another squadron to the Mediterranean in the next few years; the corsairs have been growing a little arrogant with all the major powers fighting their own wars."

"But did Preble pass on his skills?" Jackson asked. "That's always the question—can one generation of leadership pass on its success to the next? Or will each generation have to relive the previous generation's mistakes?"

"The Navy is a young service, General," Favian said. "Commodore Rodgers is forty-four, and he's considered old. I'm only thirty, and I've already been promoted to the highest rank the Navy possesses. Preble sought out young men, young enough so that he could press his methods on them." He smiled. "We've been called 'Preble's Boys,' you know—but we consider it a compliment. Every successful action in this war, all except the Lake Erie battle, was fought by one of Preble's Boys. I think that shows how we've learned our lessons."

"And the lessons?" Jackson asked. "Can you tell us what they were?"

"Build the finest fighting ships on the globe," Favian said. "Fill them with the best men available—no pressed men, all volunteers. Treat the men with respect, as the free citizens of a republic deserve. Look after their health, listen respectfully to their grievances, but discipline them tautly. Know your job—know *everyone's* job and how to do it—that way you can gain the men's respect. Never forget, even in times of peace, that a warship may have to fight, and keep the guns ready and the shot scaled and trimmed. And if fighting is needed, always strike the first blow. If the enemy is too busy counting his wounds, he won't be able to wound us." He grinned uneasily, realizing that Jackson had drawn him out and probably done so deliberately, wanting to find out what he was made of. "There's more," he said, "but I'd sound like a preacher. I think I've covered the essentials."

Jackson seemed pleased with his success in bringing Favian out. "Is Captain Patterson one of Preble's Boys?" he asked. "I'm not familiar with his career."

"He was on the *Philadelphia*, sir. He was under Preble for a time—enough, I'm sure, to learn his method—but missed most of the fighting."

"Your Preble sounds like a remarkable man," Jackson said. "I think, seeing two of his disciples here on the Mississippi, I feel that much more secure about the fate of New Orleans."

"Thank you, sir. I'm flattered."

"Flattery was not my intention." For a moment there was the glint of steel in Jackson's eyes. "I was pleased to see a pair of fighters, that's all. If you mistook my remark for flattery, I must have failed to make myself clear."

Well. The lion had come from his den at last. "I must have misunderstood, sir," Favian said.

"Very well." Gruffly. Jackson set down his knife and fork.

"We'll be having our gun drill shortly," Gideon said. "General Jackson, Favian, ye're welcome to observe."

"I will, thank you," Favian said. He wanted to see the caliber of the men he would be leading against the Guard of the Eagle.

"I will be happy to see your men at their drill, sir," Jackson said. "Perhaps they can teach our militia a thing or two."

"Please God they will," said Gideon.

Favian stood by the binnacle near Gideon during the drill, with Jackson and his staff standing just behind, near the wheel where they would be out of everyone's way. Finch Martin actually conducted the drill, Gideon observing merely: starboard and larboard gun crews were set against one another, competing to see which crew could sponge, mock-load, and run out their guns. "I do not expect a perfect drill," Gideon said. "They've been too long within scent of the fleshpots of New Orleans and grown slack. But we'll have a live-powder exercise later—they've been too long without the smell of powder."

"Very good," Favian said. "I try to conduct live-powder exercises whenever I can spare the powder."

"If my men can learn to hit what they aim at," Gideon growled, " 'tis worth the expense, certainly."

"Load and run out!" Finch Martin roared, his voice remarkably loud for such a small man. The privateers bent to their work, Martin running along the row of guns, his gray old-fashioned pigtail swinging, as he harassed and chivvied the men as they labored. "That's a cartridge ladle, not a pig's tit," Favian heard him say, "put yer shoulder into it." He smiled at Gideon's frown.

"I have urged Mr. Martin to control his language," Gideon said. "Sometimes, though, he forgets."

Favian saw Phillip Stanhope come up through the scuttle, Dr. Solomon following. "I've heard the *Revenge* called a tern schooner," Solomon's voice coming clear as the last gun truck rumbled to a halt. "Is it from some fancied resemblance to the water fowl?"

"No, sir," Stanhope said. "But because it has three masts."

"Indeed," said the chaplain. "Perhaps from the Latin *terni*, signifying three of a kind. Would you agree?"

"That seems very likely, sir," said Stanhope.

Favian smiled inwardly: he remembered very clearly, eighteen months ago, Stanhope undergoing similar instruction aboard the *Experiment*, when he had just acquired his midshipman's warrant. Stanhope and Solomon saluted Favian as they passed him, Stanhope with a cheerful grin, and Solomon stiffly—clearly he had not forgiven Favian for trying to forbid him his duel.

"The helm," Solomon said as they passed the wheel, "the attentive timoneer applies. Bringing us unerringly to our destination."

Timoneer, Favian thought, picturing the helmsmen's amusement at the label. The sort of romantic fool who called a helmsman a "timoneer" was just the sort to get involved in idiotic duels. Next he'd be referring to the sailors as "matelots."

Favian looked aloft as the canvas suddenly began to roar; Gideon turned to snap some orders to the helm, and *Malachi's Revenge* swung to a new tack, the sails filling once more. The wind had shifted to head the schooner, and Gideon had corrected effortlessly. *Macedonian,* in the same situation, might still be gaining sternway, with the crew running madly trying to set the headsails flat aback—the tern schooner was a beautifully responsive vessel; Favian felt the taste of envy, and then conscientiously fought it down.

The gun drill wore on into the boiling afternoon. Melting tar began to drip from the rigging; Favian loosened his collar. Gideon's men, despite their relaxed discipline during their time in New Orleans, were competent and efficient at their drill and improved with each round of practice. Just possibly they were better than *Macedonian*'s men, who were new to the ship and each other, having been aboard only a few months. Eventually Gideon decreed a live-powder exercise; the schooner's boys ran below for their cartridges, and the crewmen began to tie their bandannas over their ears, protecting themselves from being accidentally deafened. "Tate, pick yer own targets!" Gideon ordered the tall black man who captained the privateer's pivot gun, a long eighteen-pounder just forward of the mainmast, able to fire on either broadside. Gideon turned to Favian.

"That's Thomas Tate," he said. "A prodigy of a gunner—we're lucky to have him. The sailors call him 'Long Tom,' of course."

"Of course." A thought struck Favian, and he turned and called out to Stanhope. "Cut along below and bring us your signal book. Throw out a signal that the flagship is conducting gunnery exercises. We don't want them thinking we've found the British hiding here in the swamps!"

"Aye aye, sir," Stanhope said with a grin, and ran for the scuttle.

The signal flags went up the halliards, and the cannon boomed. Gideon picked out landmarks to use as targets: a bluff, a tall pine, a piece of flotsam drifting in the wide river. The privateers' accuracy was excellent; they seemed to know quite well how to anticipate the motion of their vessel and put the iron shot where it was wanted, just the sort of first-rate gunnery that only long practice with live ammunition could produce. Gideon, as well as his superb schooner, had a finely drilled, disciplined crew—Favian's confidence in the Cat Island expedition had increased by a vast amount.

After five rounds apiece Gideon ordered the guns secured, and the weary crewmen thankfully put away their gear. Gideon turned to Favian. "I hear that ye rotated the gun crews on *Experiment*," he said.

"Aye. So that each man knew the duties of all the others and could replace their mates if they fell."

"But did it not take a long time to learn their tasks, with each man's load more than doubled?"

"That's true," Favian said. "But our efficiency was greater once the tasks were learned. It's a balancing act—I thought the risk was worthwhile, since I had no intention of taking *Experiment* against an enemy until the men knew their duties. We were lucky—got all the way across the Atlantic before we had to run out the guns against a real enemy."

"It's different with a privateer," Gideon said. "We have to pay off our backers' investments as soon as possible—and that means getting to sea and finding prizes quickly."

Aye, Favian thought. Privateers were not as free as, in his moment of wishful thinking, he had thought. The privateers' owners and backers demanded early returns on their investment, and only captains like Gideon, who was also the principal owner of his own vessel, could afford to make the extended cruises that had made *Malachi's Revenge* one of the most successful privateers in American history.

"That was quite an exercise, Captain Markham," said Andrew Jackson. Now that the drill was over, he had stepped forward to join them. "Most of my battles have been fought in the woods—there was no getting heavy guns into the fight. I got a few batteries of light guns to Horseshoe Bend, and we bombarded the

Creek lines for hours, but the enemy just laughed at us. If we'd had some of your twelve-pounders, or that long eighteen, and some of these naval gunners to man 'em, it might have been a different story."

"Thank'ee, General."

"Trained nautical gunners are used to hitting a target from a platform that's bounding up and down with every wave," Favian said. "Land gunnery becomes child's play after that. If you could get some gunners like these men," he nodded to the privateers securing their guns forward, "New Orleans would be all the safer."

Jackson frowned. "You can't even get gunners for your own Navy boats," he said. "New Orleans has plenty of cannon in the armories, but no one to shoot them."

"General," Favian said, "this may be out of my department . . ." He hesitated, forming his words, and then spoke on. "General, there are hundreds of men available. Some of them are hiding in the swamps, some are loitering around the docks, some have been placed in irons in the jail. Laffite's men."

Jackson's frown deepened; he looked at Favian with glittering eyes. "I do not wish to strike bargains with these banditti," he said. "This Cat Island attack is bad enough, doing Laffite's dirty work for him—but it's a necessity."

"It may be a necessity to find men for those guns," Favian said. "Coerce them, promise them pardon, or press them—you're going to need them in the end. Laffite has powder and ammunition as well, and small arms, too. His smugglers know every bend in the bayous—if the British come through there, they'll know it; they might even be able to prevent it."

Jackson turned away, watching the low, dark land passing, the endless tracts of delta known only to alligators and water moccasins. "That is what Governor Claiborne said," he murmured. "Livingston said the same thing—urged me to meet with Laffite."

"If Claiborne and Livingston agree on something, then it must be something very obvious," Favian said. "I think you and Laffite should speak privately—that way no one else will be able to give reports of any agreement you might reach. It would be a private agreement between the ruler of Barataria and the general in charge of New Orleans' defenses—of course the agreement would have more force if it were enforced by the martial law commander of the city."

Jackson turned back to Favian, an amused smile tugging at the corners of his mouth. "You are impudent, sir," he said. "How many dangerous moves d'you want me to make in the same day? A deal with pirates is bad enough, but a declaration of martial law at the same time might be more than the Creoles will take." Favian opened his mouth to speak, but Jackson silenced him with a wave of his hand. "I have moved very carefully since my arrival, sir. I have handed compliments to everyone I've met, I've attended a number of balls to let the people look at me, I've reviewed troops and tried to put the forts in order, but I've only made two minor decisions in the way of controversy—I've agreed to create a company of Choctaw scouts under Pierre Jugeat, and I've ordered the creation of a second battalion of the Free Men of Color under Savary. Claiborne and the legislature were hysterical enough about that. And now you want me to declare martial law, giving myself dictatorial powers, usurping the governor and the legislature, and all this before the British even appear?" He gave a short, dry laugh. "You are audacious, Captain Markham—I suppose from a man with your record I could expect little else."

"Toujours l'audace," Favian said helplessly. Despite the brevity of their acquaintance, Jackson knew him too well to fall a captive to Favian's showmanship. He would have to present his ideas coherently and in succession; simple appeals to duty, camaraderie, and the flag wouldn't work here. But there was something else working in Favian's favor, and he knew it: Andrew Jackson was himself an audacious man; his campaigns against the Creeks had shown it. "Danton said it," Favian went on, "but our Navy lives by it. Perhaps it's not always wise, but in the current situation there's nothing else to do. We're badly outnumbered by the finest army and navy in the world; we can't hope to beat them in any conventional way—we have to use desperate methods. We have to be audacious. If we can make use of anyone—colored troops, Choctaws, pirates—we'll have to do it. There's simply no choice, General."

Jackson listened to him with his head cocked to one side, his eyes still twinkling, amused. "Very well, Captain," he said. "I'll meet with Laffite, if you can arrange something private. Not here—too many witnesses. That's why I took a nap this morning; I didn't want to hold a long conversation with the man in front of the others."

"You can use my cabin on board *Macedonian,*" Favian said quickly. "I'll make it available for as long as necessary."

"I'll have to ponder a mite longer on this martial law business," Jackson continued. His gaze hardened; for a moment Favian caught a glimpse of the feral Jackson he had seen before during that private moment in the general's headquarters. "But I can promise you this, Captain Markham. If I see the necessity for martial law, I'll declare it, by the Eternal I will—and damnation to the consequences."

Favian felt triumph glow in him, but he resolutely tried to keep it from his face; instead he nodded. "I'm sure that's best, sir," he said.

Jackson seemed further amused by Favian's cautious answer. "You're a deep one, Markham," he said. "I wouldn't care to play against you in *poque*. Gentlemen, I hope you will excuse us—I feel in need of another little rest." He turned to Gideon. "Thank you again for an enlightening demonstration. .he smell of powder always helps to clear the head." Jackson and his staff made their way to the aft scuttle.

Gideon looked balefully at Favian. "I hope ye know what ye're doing," he said. "Bringing together that pirate and an adventurer like Jackson—that's like playing with fire in a powder magazine."

"What choice do we have, Gideon?" Favian asked. Gideon scowled.

"None I know," he said. "We can only trust that the Lord's will shall be done."

"Amen," said Favian.

An hour later the squadron sailed into the sight of the two vessels anchored off Fort St. Philip, the frigate *Macedonian,* dominating the low vista of the delta, and Captain Poquelin's little pilot boat *Beaux Jours,* which would take Jackson and his staff back to the city once their inspection of the fort was completed. Favian found himself looking with relief at *Macedonian,* its sleek lines, raked masts, and gilded figurehead of Alexander the Great—it would be a pleasure to be on board, free from the confusions and distractions of New Orleans, of marriage, standing on the decks of the frigate with its single, deadly purpose.

The transfer was accomplished quickly; Kuusikoski's boat's crew were happy to stretch their muscles. Jackson, as a major general far senior to Favian as a Navy captain, went through the entry port first, the bosun's pipes and rattle of arms bidding him welcome, and Favian followed, returning the salutes of the assembled officers. Laffite followed last of all, a black-coated civilian pilot carrying his own baggage.

"May I be the first aboard, sir, to congratulate you on your recent marriage," said Lieutenant Hourigan, the senior lieutenant—a spare, serious man who played expert wardroom concerts on the German flute. Favian looked at the spare, bushy-browed man in surprise. "I thank you," he said, "but I can't think how you could possibly have heard."

"Captain Poquelin of the *Beaux Jours* brought the news of your engagement two days ago. He said that the marriage should have taken place yesterday. I hope you are soon blessed with many little sailors to carry on the family tradition."

"I thank you again," Favian said. "I would like to introduce you, gentlemen, to General Andrew Jackson, commanding the Seventh Military District. This is Mr. Hourigan, my acting first officer; Mr. Eastlake you've met; Mr. Chapelle, Mr. Ford, Mr. Swink; Mr. Seward, our sailing master; Lieutenant Byrne of the Marines; our bosun Mr. Tucker; and all the young gentlemen, our midshipmen."

"Pleased to meet'ee, gentlemen," Jackson said.

"Honored, sir."

"Gentlemen, this is Colonel McRae, Major Tatum, and Mr. Latour; and this is our pilot, Captain Laffite. I hope the wardroom will offer these gentlemen their hospitality. General Jackson will have the commodore's cabin for tonight. You may dismiss the hands."

"Aye aye, sir. Mr. Tucker, pipe 'em down. Please come this way, gentlemen."

The sun was touching the cypress in the west; soon it would be dark. Favian went up the poop ladder to cast his eyes over the frigate before it grew entirely dark. He had informed Eastlake, as they'd approached *Macedonian*, that he hoped for an invitation from the wardroom that night. The officers' mess, theoretically, did not have to invite their captain to dine unless they wished it; but in practice the lieutenants and master ignored their captain's wishes at their peril, and Favian had every confidence that Hourigan would shortly approach him asking him to supper. Wardroom meals generally went on forever if there were guests, and in the meantime Favian's cabin would be clear for a meeting between Laffite and General Jackson.

The boat's crew disappeared belowdecks, carrying the officers' luggage in their horny hands. "Thou hast been married," came a voice from the shadow of the mizzenmast. "The girl is very young. Thee are uncertain about the outcome."

"Hello, Lazarus," Favian said. "Gossip travels fast on a ship, doesn't it?" He watched as the mad fiddler stepped from the shadow of the mast, seeing the lunatic glint in the man's strange, pale eyes.

"I listen to the tongues of spirits," said Lazarus. "Not the tongues of men. Your bride loves thee very much. Her love may save thee. So say the powers."

"Your spirits are unusually optimistic."

"It is the voyage that is cursed. Not thy bride."

Favian looked at the madman for a moment in silence. He had first met Lazarus almost two years before at a sailors' tavern near the Navy Yard in Washington. Favian, on a celebratory debauch with his friend William Burrows—both of them had just been ordered to their first commands—had been dressed as a common seaman, an impersonation Burrows had always enjoyed, but which Favian had never tried before. Lazarus and his fiddle had entertained at the tavern that night; he had seen through Favian's disguise instantly, an insight he'd promptly ascribed to the spirits with which—according to Lazarus at any rate—he held daily converse. Lazarus also claimed to have sold his soul to the devil in 1682, in return for an unnaturally long life and his skill with the fiddle-bow.

Favian had never believed him, but Lazarus had kept appearing in Favian's life. A year ago in Maine he'd appeared from a boat to rescue *Experiment*'s survivors. Since then Favian had more or less adopted him, letting the lunatic travel with him, paying him for running errands. He had brought Lazarus aboard *Macedonian* with the intention of using him as a sort of informal bridge between the lower deck and the captain, keeping him informed of what was going on among the men. But Lazarus had turned strange when he heard of Kuusikoski, the Finnish seaman; in Lazarus's peculiar view Finns were all witches, and the spirits of the deep resented their powers and tried to do them harm: hence any ship in which they traveled was cursed. *Macedonian* also carried Dr. Solomon, a chaplain, and according to long-standing seamen's tradition chaplains were also bad luck.

Lazarus's prophecies had turned bleak and strange: *Macedonian* was doomed unless one of the two Jonahs could be got off. Favian was fairly certain that he had laid plots among credulous or evil seamen for Kuusikoski's murder. The situation had remained dangerous until *Macedonian* had outrun a blockading British squadron and then captured the *Carnation* off Montserrat, after which it was clear to most that, if anything, Kuusikoski and the chaplain had brought luck. Lazarus was still preaching doom and destruction, but so far as Favian could tell, scarcely anyone was listening.

"Remember what I told thee," Lazarus said. With the long evening shadows crossing his lined face, he looked ancient, a corrupt and evil spirit himself. "A roundshot at my head. Remember."

"Yes," Favian said. "I remember." The madman had also predicted his own death, but like most of his recent prophecies it had failed, or at least proved premature. A man who had sold his soul, he had asked for a non-Christian burial, the roundshot at his head instead of his feet as he was committed to the deep.

"Remember what I told thee," Lazarus repeated. "Remember *all* I have told thee." He tugged at his leather cap in a sketchy salute and walked to the poop ladder, disappearing into the shadows in the ship's waist. Favian looked up at the sky; the first star had just appeared. He took a deep breath. Lazarus and his spirits were often unsettling, and there was enough on his mind without them. Tonight, at the wardroom mess, he would inform his lieutenants of the expedition to Cat Island.

SIXTEEN

Four days later *Macedonian* got over the bar at the Southeast Pass; collision mats were hung over the side, and Gunboat Number 5 and *Malachi's Revenge* were warped alongside. The gunboat and schooner had taken off many of the frigate's guns and just about all its water, lightening her so she could approach the bar; the rest of the afternoon would be spent transferring them back.

Favian had wanted to leave two days earlier, but he had been held back by General Jackson. While Favian was in the city, *Macedonian*'s men under Lieutenant Hourigan had been working with the garrison of Fort St. Philip to put the fort in order: the parapet had been rebuilt, flammable buildings torn down, and the water battery, all heavy twenty-four-pounders, now rested on a strengthened platform. Jackson had wanted to add to the defenses of the Plaquemines Bend by sending men across the river to the old, ruined Fort Bourbon, a relic of the Spanish occupation, and by building another battery, as yet unnamed, half a mile upriver. Jackson had considered that, as Navy men, they knew best where to site guns that would repel any British fleet trying to ascend the river; Favian had chafed a little at the delay, but in the end agreed. *Macedonian*'s men had helped to clear growth from the overgrown Spanish ruin and thrown up earthworks where necessary, the officers giving advice concerning where to plant the guns. Jackson had been everywhere, amazing the observers with a phenomenal display of energy for a man so ill and haggard; he had nearly worn out both his staff and the crew of the boat Favian had loaned him.

Just that morning Jackson had said farewell to Favian, the grizzled old Indian fighter clasping hands with him on *Macedonian*'s quarterdeck. "You've given me food for thought, Captain," he said. "I'll be sending some reinforcements downriver. Major

Overton, some men from the 7th Infantry, and some of the Free Men of Color. If I've made up my mind by then, I'll send a message with them."

"Toujours l'audace," Favian said. The general smiled, waved his cap to the other officers, and walked for the entry port, Tucker saluting him with his pipe as the marines presented arms. Jean Laffite, dressed as always in black, stood behind the officers on the quarterdeck. He and Jackson gave no sign they were acquainted.

Whatever had transpired that night in *Macedonian*'s cabin, neither Jackson nor Laffite had ever spoken of it. Jackson merely said they would have to meet again in New Orleans, and Laffite had said nothing at all.

Most of Laffite's time had been taken up with the preparations for the Cat Island expedition. Favian intended to take the enemy batteries by storm from the landward side, but that would entail landing, at night, on low, swampy islands, and marching over terrain that none in the parties had ever seen. Laffite had been asked in detail about the terrain features of the Isles Dernieres, Timbalier Island, and Cat Island, at least insofar as he could remember them; on the last day Captain Poquelin of the *Beaux Jours,* without being told why, had been asked the same questions, and his information had confirmed Laffite's. Favian was fairly certain of his ground and that the practice exercises he'd been holding would bear some resemblance to reality.

The exercises were being conducted with David Porter's old nautical war game, the one he had used in prison in Tripoli to teach the midshipmen their seamanship and subsequently improved by Jacob Jones and *Macedonian*'s first lieutenant, Adrian Stone, now off with the captured *Carnation*. The wardroom furniture had been moved, and the checkered canvas carpet rolled up; Terre Bonne Bay had been drawn with chalk on the deck planking, and little model ships maneuvered over the surface. Gideon, Fontenoy, Cunningham of Gunboat Number 5, and Laffite had all been surprised by the model maneuvers, participating with varying degrees of enthusiasm: Cunningham had been taken with the idea; Gideon thought it was tedious, if useful; Fontenoy clearly thought the game silly. "I would prefer to depend on my strong right arm and this," he said, brandishing a weapon. The man carried a strange one, a fighting iron antique even in the

Revolution: a flail made of three linked steel bars, deadly but requiring expert handling.

"Even your strong right arm requires practice before you can handle that iron, Captain," Favian said. "A little practice at storming those forts won't hurt us."

Favian had tried to use the game to show all possible variations of the upcoming attack. What if there was a British warship present? What if the pirates had strengthened their batteries on the islands? What if they had stationed ships in the Cat Island Pass to help repel assault? What if the assaults on the batteries failed and the earthworks had to be reduced by gunfire? All these eventualities, and more, had been covered by the exercises; Favian had strained his imagination trying to think of things to go wrong. In the end he was fairly confident that his men were as familiar with the topography as they were ever likely to get without actually seeing it.

In an old black frock coat and his undress round hat, Favian stood on the quarterdeck as the guns were hoisted inboard, their trunnions being bolted down on their carriages as another party of seamen ran the canvas hoses of the channel pump down into the water butts of the *Malachi's Revenge*. The privateer, like the city of New Orleans, drank Mississippi water with the mud filtered out of it; having lost most of its water trying to get over the bar, *Macedonian*'s water casks needed replenishing.

"Pump away!" roared the bosun's mates, and the crewmen heaved at the pump handles. Lazarus, the chanteyman, pressed his fiddles against his chest and struck up a tune. It was perhaps the fastest capstan chanty in the repertoire, which was presumably why he chose to use it—the pump handles could be driven faster than the capstan—but the song itself was inappropriate. It should have been clear even to the ordinary sailors that *Macedonian* was not going home.

"Well, have ye heard the news, my Johnny?
  One more day!
We're homeward bound tomorrow,
  One more day!

Only one more day, me Johnny,
  One more day!
Well, rock and row me over,
  One more day!"

Favian watched as a party of privateersmen from the *Revenge* stepped aboard to offer their help in heaving the heavy guns onto their carriages, then bolting them down. He saw their officer, George Willard, the Gay Head Indian from Martha's Vineyard, look at the work party on the pumps, then stand for a few seconds with amazement written on his face. He glanced fore and aft, saw Favian standing by the poop barricade, and then took a step toward the quarterdeck; he hesitated, turned back to his party, gave them some swift orders, and then hastened up the quarterdeck ladder.

"Beg pardon, sir, but d'ye know that chanteyman?" Willard asked as soon as Favian returned his salute.

"That man? Lazarus? I know he's mad," Favian said.

"I could swear he's a man I used to know," Willard said, his dark eyes troubled. He turned to Lazarus and looked at the madman for a long time, then turned back to Favian. "Aye," he said. "I know him. Joshua Mandrell, from Nantucket. He used to preach at the Congregational church there, when I was a boy. My mother used to take me whenever we visited our kin on Nantucket."

"Lazarus? A preacher?" Favian looked down at the snaggle-toothed fiddler who claimed he had sold his soul to Satan. "Are you certain?"

"Aye." His eyes cast back to Lazarus to make certain, then returned to Favian. "He played the fiddle even then—a lot of the congregation thought there was something wrong in it, but he laughed at them and said it was his way of lifting his voice in praise to the Lord. He had a wife and a lot of children. Four or five, I think. His wife was a good woman. She used to give me gingerbread."

"What happened?"

"I don't rightly know, sir. It happened while I was at sea. But I heard his wife and children died of yellow fever in the New York epidemic—that would be the Year One. I heard the Rev'rend Mandrell resigned his post just afterward. No one knew where he went."

Just took his fiddle and ran for the sea, Favian thought. On Nantucket Island there would have been plenty of ships to choose from, many of them with crews who would never have heard any of his sermons. The deaths of his loved ones had driven him mad, and he'd run—and then somewhere, gazing on the emptiness of some distant ocean, he had decided to curse his former life. Working for his God had brought him nothing but anguish; instead he would work for the devil. He had substituted one religion for another. It explained a lot.

"I remember that he once talked about Nantucket. Something about Virgin Hill." It had been that first acquaintance in Washington. Lazarus had terrified a saloon girl named Dulcey with his tale of meeting his cloven-hoofed Master amid tombstones, the ghosts of witches dancing as he played his fiddle.

"Virgin Hill. That's the Quaker graveyard," Willard said. "He was a scholar. Wrote about the Quaker persecutions in colonial times. The Quakers were thought to be in league with the devil."

"Oh can't you hear the Captain growling?
 One more day!
Can't you hear the master howling?
 One more day!"

Lazarus sawed at his fiddle, the dark water gushing into the freshwater butt. The crewmen stamped and sang on the chorus. "I think," said Favian, "you'd better keep this mum. It's been thirteen years, and he's made a new life for himself. He obviously doesn't want anyone to know. Perhaps digging up old memories would only give him pain." He would have to look up the head of some madhouse, Favian thought. Perhaps the man could be cured.

Lazarus, as if sensing their words, glanced up at them. His face contorted by the strength of his singing, he roared out a final verse.

Can't you hear the cannons crying?
 One more day!
Can't you hear our sailors dying?
 One more day!

One more day, my Johnny,
 One more day!
Well, shot and shell me over,
 One more day!

With a defiant squawk Lazarus brought his fiddle-playing to an end. One more day to Cat Island, Favian thought. He realized the verse had been meant to anger him, but the anger had not come, only thoughtfulness. Many times chanties were used to express anger or resentment at the ship's officers—that was why Navy ships almost always worked to the bosun's pipes and not to the voices of chanteymen—and though Favian caught nervous glances among the hands directed toward the quarterdeck, he could not detect the smug self-righteousness of someone exulting in putting something over on the captain. The hands were startled or annoyed, but not triumphant.

Lazarus, he realized, was losing his congregation. He wondered how that would affect the man.

"That," said George Willard, "was not meant as a joke."

"No. He wants to frighten them, but he won't succeed. I think his madness is getting worse. I'll speak to the doctor about him."

"I think that's a good idea, sir."

Willard's party finished their tasks, and the last of the great water butts were sealed and stored below. The mooring lines were cast off, and the Macedonians ran up the shrouds to loose the great sails. The canvas boomed as it filled, and the frigate heeled over to the warm ocean breeze. "Squadron to follow flagship in prescribed order," Favian said, and Stanhope dashed to his signal halliards. Favian looked back as his squadron slipped into the frigate's wake: *Malachi's Revenge*, its sails well reefed so as to slow its swift hull to the speed of the relatively sluggish frigate, the *Franklin* just behind, and then the gunboat; each vessel flew the bright gridiron flag, its red and white stripes in stark contrast to the darkness of the bank. A fine sight, a prideful one. It would take them all of the night, and most of the next day, before they would be in sight of their objective.

"Permission to speak, sir." Favian turned to discover his chaplain. As soon as he saw the set of the man's jaw, he knew what the man wanted to say.

"Go ahead, Dr. Solomon."

"I would like to request permission to accompany one of the landing parties. In any capacity whatever, sir."

The man hadn't yet got his fill of shooting people, Favian thought. It would be a shame to disappoint him.

"Very well, Dr. Solomon. You may join Mr. Eastlake as a messenger."

Solomon's eyes blazed with pride and anticipated glory. "Thank you, Captain. I shall endeavor to conduct myself in keeping with the highest—"

"I'm certain you shall, Dr. Solomon." The man was nothing but an eager middy after all. "I'm sure," Favian said finally, "that any wounded and dying will be consoled by your presence."

There was a hesitation in the chaplain's smile. "Ah, yes, sir," he said. "Of course."

Favian was tempted to add that his place on board *Macedonian* would be taken by the Reverend Joshua Mandrell of Nantucket, but he kept silent. He and the chaplain exchanged salutes again, and Solomon left the quarterdeck. Favian turned to look into the frigate's wake, seeing the sails of the little squadron glow orange in the light of the setting sun. One more day, he thought. He wondered if Campaspe would be made a widow in the next forty-eight hours, and whether it would be for the best.

One more day.

Macedonian's big thirty-six-foot pinnace pitched on the heavy seas. The frigate, black and silent, towered over them. Favian could see two whaleboats rocking heavily on the waves, their bulwarks crammed with dark-coated figures: sailors and marines. Starlight glinted softly on cutlass hilts, the tips of boarding pikes, and on the white rags tied around each upper arm for identification in the dark. The party were all wearing their boarding helmets, and their faces were in deep shadow. Ahead was the sound of surf. There was the smell of spindrift, salt marsh, and fear.

Macedonian lay hove to about two miles from Timbalier Island, drifting slowly out to seaward with the land breeze. It would tack up again toward morning and be ready off Cat Island Pass once the battle began, ready to take off her children in case of disaster. Stroking toward land, the boat party were heading for the center of the six-mile-long island; they would then row parallel to the beach until they were nearer their objective, then disembark and march for the pirate fort on foot. They had fifty sailors and thirty marines in three boats, which should be enough to overwhelm the defenders—assuming, of course, the Guard of the Eagle were caught by surprise.

Somewhere in the dark—ten miles to the west, or thereabouts, there were more of *Macedonian*'s boats under the command of

Hourigan, the senior lieutenant. The boats would be astern of *Malachi's Revenge*, being towed toward their dropping-off point; they would then ghost eastward along the marshy coast of the Isles Derniere to take the smaller battery from the rear. Thirty seamen and ten marines seemed adequate to that task, but their problem would be to get ashore at all. According to Laffite, most of the Isles Dernieres were swamp and unsuitable for landing; the swamp gave way to sand within a mile or so of the battery, but it appeared the sands were also guarded by breakers. Favian did not like the idea of his men going ashore so close to the battery, where they might be spotted before they even got out of their boats; but there seemed little choice if the battery were to be taken at all.

Another worrying aspect was that Hourigan, in command of that particular party, had never, before this voyage, actually been in combat. Since the frigate had left New London, there had been the running fight with the blockading squadron and the swift capture of the *Carnation*, and in neither of those incidents had there been any reason to complain of Hourigan's conduct. But still the man had never participated in anything like the storming of a fort, or the terrifying demands of hand-to-hand combat, with its prospects of being hacked down and cut to pieces by some berserk enemy's cutlass. Since Hourigan was the senior lieutenant after Mr. Stone had left with the *Carnation*, there had been no choice but to give him his chance for glory—to leave him behind would have been to insult him gravely. Favian had no particular doubts about the man: he seemed steady and sober, but still he was an unknown factor. Favian had tried to give him help—if he was wise enough to take advantage of it—by assigning Lieutenant Eastlake to his party. Eastlake had been with Charles Morris in the *Adams* corvette and had participated in the defense of that ship when it had been attacked last August by an overwhelming ground force. Several British attacks had been beaten off, but eventually the *Adams* had to be burned to prevent capture: Eastlake, the dashing, wealthy son of a Virginia planter, had gained Morris's praise by his conduct in that action, and Morris was an old Tripoli hand, a veteran of the burning of the *Philadelphia*, whose judgments Favian was inclined to trust. He hoped Hourigan would lean heavily on Eastlake in the upcoming action.

The uncertainties of taking the smaller fort fretted him; he wished he could somehow command the other party as well as his own. But he had made his decision; the fort on Timbalier was much larger and more important, and he had made it his responsibility.

The sound of surf was much closer. The waves were long ocean rollers off the Gulf; the fact that locally the wind was blowing out to sea from the land seemed to suppress the waves but little, instead creating foam on the wave-tops that blew into Favian's face as he craned his neck to observe the island. The smell of tropical vegetation was heavy; they were probably coming up onto the swamp. "Turn us to larboard, Koskey," he said.

"Aye aye, Captain." The pinnace commenced a slow turn to larboard; Favian twisted around in the stern sheets to make certain the other boats were following. Bobbing on the swell, the boats began to parallel the shore.

How close to the fort should he disembark? He would prefer to keep the march to the fort as short as possible: if the sand wasn't hard-packed, it would be hard on the party to slog through more than a mile of it; rowing in the boats was much easier on them. He decided he'd press his luck and try to get as close as possible.

Sand gleamed softly on their starboard side. Favian asked Stanhope for his night glass and peered ahead: the inverted image showed only more sand, nothing resembling fortifications. But the fortifications were made of sand, weren't they? At night they'd look just like a dune. Favian cursed softly under his breath.

He kept his glass fixed on the farthest extremity of beach, hoping to pick up the end of the island, but the sand just seemed to curve away from him endlessly. He wished there was something to take bearings on; but there was no significant landmark within miles. He stood up, his glass still trained on the island: far distant, he thought he could see breakers gleaming in starlight. That would be the breakers on the eastern end of the Isles Dernieres. If he could see them, he had to be near his objective. He ordered the boats to turn inland.

The pinnace threatened to swing broadside to the surf, but Kuusikoski fought the tiller and brought the boat in on an even keel. Favian thought he saw Jean Laffite, a black shadow, leading the crewmen out of the boat forward; they steadied it in the waves, hauling it onto the sand. Favian slung the glass over his shoulder, whispered to Stanhope to be certain to bring up all his gear, and moved forward in the boat. One hand holding his sword-hilt to keep it from flailing around or tripping him, he jumped lightly to the ground. The keels of the other boats grated on the beach; there was splashing as the men disembarked.

Favian set Stanhope to counting heads as the empty boats were drawn farther up on the sand, as their anchors were hauled well up above the high-tide mark. Laffite, a delicate smallsword hanging from his waist, materialized near his left elbow. Stanhope reported the entire party present: Favian's six-man pinnace crew, reinforced to the gunwales by the ship's boarders. Lazarus had been left behind, and not only because of his quarrel with Favian's coxswain. There was worry at the back of Favian's mind that Lazarus was so bound and determined to produce a disaster he might somehow arrange one. Favian didn't quite believe it, but he didn't dare take the chance the intuition might not be right.

A portly figure, his round face enveloped by his boarding helmet, came up and saluted. "My party's all present, sir."

"Very well, Mr. Chapelle." Chapelle was the fourth lieutenant and a gunnery expert, a pleasant man. At his elbow Favian saw his assistant, Mr. Midshipman Tolbert, one of *Experiment*'s survivors and a headstrong, impulsive, brave, and basically stupid young man—Tolbert was in himself everything Favian saw wrong with the system of bringing raw adolescents aboard ships to become apprentice officers: the midshipman was courageous, quarrelsome, eager for combat, and totally heedless of consequences; he had failed his exams for lieutenant and, unless he got ashore and had some private coaching, would never pass on the second try. But Favian knew that Tolbert could be trusted to lead his party into the enemy works, and that was what was needed here: dash and bravery, not a tactical mind.

"The marines are all present and accounted for, sir," reported Lieutenant Byrne.

"Very well. I'll want each officer to check his men's weapons once again to make certain they're unloaded. I don't want any guns going off accidentally and alerting the enemy. It'll be cold steel only. Once that's done, I'll lead off with my party. Mr. Byrne, your marines will follow, then Mr. Chapelle with his sailors. If we come suddenly on the enemy's works, and an alarm is given, I'll try to storm straight ahead with my party along the beach. Mr. Byrne, your men will strike off to the right and try to get into their works farther inland. Mr. Chapelle, you're our reserve. Hold your men ready, and I'll send a messenger back to tell you when to bring them up. But Mr. Chapelle—if you see an opportunity the rest of us have missed, run for it. Just be damn certain the opportunity is real. Clear, gentlemen?"

Nods, muttered "aye ayes."

"Very well. Mr. Laffite, stay with me, if you please."

Favian waited as the officers ranked their men on the beach and went down the line, gunlocks clacking, the sound faintly heard over the boom of surf and the whistle of the cold wind as each was checked to make certain it was unloaded. Midshipmen came pelting through the foam to report each division ready. Favian turned and led the long line forward, setting a brisk pace through the harder-packed sand below the tide line. His breath steamed in front of him, and he cursed the chill wind, then remembered that the alternative to the cold would have been a plague of insects; in the end he was thankful it was December.

It was still difficult going, even on the hard, the sand crumbling away beneath every step; Favian soon found himself out of breath. The party disturbed a flock of resting geese, who boomed out of cover like a crack of thunder, uttering their harsh, protesting cries; Favian took a deliberate breath to calm his trip-hammer heart and waved the column on. The beach kept curving away from him; he had no idea where he was in relation to the fort. He called a halt to the column, the sailors gratefully throwing themselves down on the sand, and craned up on tiptoe. All he could see was more sand. He turned to Laffite.

"Mr. Laffite, d'you know where we are? I can't see any landmarks."

Laffite shook his head. "I think we should be less than a mile from the place, Commodore Markham," he said. "But I've never been on this island at night. I can't be certain."

Favian turned to Stanhope, unlacing the chin strap of his boarding helmet, pushing the heavy, plumed iron and leather contraption back on his head to relieve his aching skull. "Give the column a rest," he said. "Mr. Laffite and I are going ahead for reconnaissance. Pass the word to Mr. Byrne; tell him he's in charge till I return."

"Aye aye, sir."

"Mr. Laffite?" The pirate nodded, and they set out into the dark. Favian huddled into his pea jacket, one hand holding his scabbard so his sword didn't rattle, his eyes aching as they searched the dark. He paused again to use the night glass. Ahead, across a dark gulf of water, he barely made out a white line: surf crashing onto the eastern point of the Isles Dernieres. He had to be close to the fort. He signaled to Laffite and moved forward again, crouching. The beach curved away to the right, then seemed to straighten; Laffite touched his arm and pointed ahead. "That mound," Laffite said. "It may be the fort."

Or a dune, Favian thought. There was a log half-buried in the sand ahead: a piece of driftwood. He readied his glass and stepped up onto the log to gain an elevated view. He heard Laffite's sudden intake of breath, and then his heart lurched as the log moved out from under him. His arms windmilled as he tried to regain his balance and failed; the fall to the sand knocked the wind out of him. Favian heard an angry growl and saw the opening jaws of the alligator; terror seized him and he rolled frantically, the boarding helmet spilling from his head; he heard the rasp of Laffite's sword being drawn from the scabbard. There was a terrible chopping sound as the alligator's jaws clamped shut on air, and then the animal turned and lumbered slowly into the water. Favian sat up, sand dripping from his pea jacket, watching in relief and amazement as an entire pack of alligators, moving out of the concealing darkness and grumbling among themselves, followed the leader into their element. Laffite, standing guard with his ineffectual-looking little smallsword, breathed heavily in relief. He put his sword away and helped Favian to his feet.

"We were lucky, my friend," he said. "My sword wouldn't have been much use against that monster."

"Thank you," Favian breathed. He picked up his boarding helmet, emptied the sand from it, and returned it to his head. "All I could see were those teeth. It must have been twenty feet long."

Favian waited until he caught his breath and then moved up the beach to the shadow of the trees and vegetation, Laffite following. Keeping under cover as much as possible, they moved forward, approaching the suspicious-looking mound. A hundred yards from the mound, the vegetation suddenly ended, obviously cleared away by human hands, and the dune suddenly became, very obviously, a rampart running clean across the narrow neck of the island. Favian dropped to one knee and put the night glass to one eye. The sand gleamed softly in the starlight, revealing the fort's outlines: he could see embrasures for guns, the ditch in front of the rampart, the rampart itself, loose sand piled up on a foundation of logs. Once he could get his men across the ditch, he thought, the rampart itself should be no great obstacle. He waited another few moments for sign of a sentry, detecting none, but was then rewarded by the sight of a glowing, moving dot moving from one embrasure to the next. The sentry was enjoying a cigar. Enough.

He turned to Laffite, seeing the pirate gazing at the fort with a practiced eye. "You see the sentry?" Favian asked. Laffite nodded. "D'you think he's the only one?"

"Very likely," Laffite said. "They have no warning of an attack." He shrugged. "It is always difficult," he said, "getting these people to keep an adequate watch."

"I've seen enough. Let's go." They slid away through the high grass, carefully passing the area where the tribe of alligators was once again setting claim to its part of the beach, and hurried to where the party waited at the water's edge. Stanhope and Byrne stood up to salute. Favian spoke quickly.

"We've located the fort. Mr. Byrne, bring your party up with mine. My party will still go straight in. Yours, Mr. Byrne, will angle off to the right. We could only find one sentry, so we'll go in at the run—we should catch 'em by surprise if we move quickly enough. Any questions?"

There were no questions. Byrne's marines were brought forward, their bayonet-tips winking starlight. "Mr. Laffite," Favian said, "you'll attach yourself to Mr. Byrne as his guide. Ready, gentlemen?"

Nods from Byrne and Laffite. Favian turned and led the united parties forward, two lines of men in Indian file followed by Chapelle and his reserve. Favian heard his heart hammering, his breath rasping in his throat—not fear, he thought, but all this marching on soft ground. The fear was under control. But still the thought of running into those mute cannon made his hand clench on his scabbard.

The alligators, grunting, gave way as the Macedonians came up the beach; Favian saw the white rampart of the fort in the distance. Still breathing heavily, he led the column into the shade of the trees, then closer to the enemy. When he knew the cleared area was just ahead, he signaled the column to halt; they squatted invisibly in the shadow of the trees. "Mr. Byrne," he said. The marine came forward. "The fort's just ahead. They've cleared all the brush away to give themselves a field of fire," Favian said. "Take my night glass. Crawl forward and take a look at the fort. Take Mr. Laffite with you—report back when you've seen all you need."

Glad for the chance for a rest, Favian sank gratefully on the ground as Byrne and Laffite slipped forward. His pounding heart slowed; his breathing became more normal. It was perhaps ten minutes before Laffite and the marine returned; when he heard them crawling back, he tied the strap of his boarding helmet and got to his feet.

"We only saw one sentry, sir," Byrne reported. He offered the night glass to Favian.

"Give it to Stanhope," Favian said. "Pass the word to get ready." He felt his heart pounding again, fought angrily to control it. "Cold steel," he said, raising the volume of his whisper so that all should hear. "Take special care to make certain none of 'em get off the island. Remember the passwords: 'Macedonian,' the challenge; 'Hornet,' the countersign."

"Aye aye, sir." The passwords had been chosen carefully, the first because it was familiar to everyone in the party, the second because it would be difficult for a native-born Frenchman to pronounce properly. Anyone answering the challenge with " 'Ornet!" was likely to find himself run through with a pike.

There was a rustling behind Favian as the column got to its feet with a subdued rattle of equipment and weapons. Favian thought for an instant about those cannon behind the embrasures, then took a firm grip on his sword and drew it from the scabbard. He swallowed, then turned to the column. "My men follow me. Marines follow Mr. Byrne to the right. At the run now, boys, and quietly—let's go."

And then he had turned and dashed for the ramparts, his sword clutched in his gloved hand; within seconds he was out of the cover of the trees, and running over the cleared area. He stumbled over a tree stump, recovered his balance, ran on. Behind he could hear the clatter as his column raced up behind him. The sand slid under his boot, and he went down on one knee, pain shooting through him as he scraped his flesh on the sand. Stanhope pelted up behind, helping him rise; he brushed the midshipman off and kept running. He chanced a look to his right and saw the column of marines bearing off at an oblique angle, heading for another part of the rampart.

"*Q-qui va là?*" The voice seemed surprised and shaken—no wonder, when there were two columns of armed men dashing for the ramparts, armed men where previously there had been only sand, marsh grass, and alligators. The sentry did not wait for an answer but began to scream a high-pitched alarm. Favian, across the open ground at last, slid into the ditch in a cloud of sand.

"Give me a back!" he gasped, and one of his boat's crew obligingly bent down at the base of the rampart. Favian planted a boot on the man's backside and sprang for the rampart, clawing for a handhold, bringing a shower of sand down on the men below; he found a hold and rolled over the top of the rampart, falling with a jar and a clatter onto the firing step.

Above him was a glowing red eye; for a moment Favian thought that the sentry was still clenching his cigar in his teeth, but then he recognized it for what it was, a slow match about to be applied to a six-pounder cannon. With a shout he lunged to his feet, his hanger slicing at the shadowy figure of the sentry; he felt the impact all the way to his shoulder as the blade went home. Blood spurted onto Favian's hand as the sentry folded, the slow match falling from his hand. There was the scrabbling of another man coming over the rampart and babble of chaotic French from inside the fort. Favian wrenched at his sword to clear it from the sentry and stamped on the glowing slow match, extinguishing it. Stanhope rolled over the rampart in a hiss of falling sand and rose to his feet, his cutlass in his hand.

"We have them," Favian said in triumph. Three seamen came lunging up the rampart, falling to the firing step. A few figures came running toward the rampart from some half-seen buildings in the distance, shouting incoherent questions. Favian waited until half a dozen more of his men had cleared the rampart.

"Stay here," Favian told Stanhope. "Gather the others, then follow. The rest of you, with me!" There were nods from the boy, from the sailors—most of them his boat's crew, he realized, Kuusikoski standing tall and burly among them, cutlass waving as he gathered his crew around him.

Favian led them pounding over the sand, cutlasses and pikes leveled at the gaping pirates standing in shock at the sight. The enemy broke as soon as they gathered their wits enough to realize their fort was being stormed; they scattered into the darkness, calling warnings. Figures were running antlike among the buildings; Favian and his men ran for them. Somewhere there was a flashing pistol shot. *No more of those,* Favian thought angrily. His men were screaming now, half-Indian war whoops, and through the darkness Favian saw the gleam of weapons in the hands of his foes.

Favian's men smashed into the pirates with an impact that drove the enemy back a few shuddering paces; Favian himself saw a man standing with a clubbed musket, bellowing French curses, and flung himself at him. Favian, even in motion, was perfectly balanced, his hanger ready to absorb the shock of an enemy blow—he had been fencing since his childhood, had fought two duels with the sword, and his body fell without thinking into a poised position. The man grunted, a little involuntary exhalation of breath, as he swung the musket-butt at Favian's head, his face screwed in fierce concentration. Favian ducked, his hanger throwing the blow off over his head; he came up from below while his enemy was off-balance, his sword cutting upwards through the pirate's bowels, and then, without conscious thought directing it, the sword came chopping at the man's neck to finish him off. Before the man had fallen, Favian was balanced again, the sword ready to probe into the darkness, looking for new enemies. Blood surged through Favian's body in direct counterpoint to the suspiration of his breath, all his senses alert.

To his right one of his boat's crew was fencing, pike against bayonet, with a pirate: Favian darted toward the combat and, as the enemy raised his bayonet to parry a blow, slipped his sword into the pirate's armpit even before the man was aware of him. The man froze, astonished, and was promptly impaled on the pike. He fell, and at the same time the pirates broke.

Favian, suddenly, was almost alone; the Macedonians, bloodmad, had run shouting after the broken enemy. "Macedonians! Here! Don't run off, damn you!" Favian roared desperately; a few obeyed—Favian recognized Kuusikoski's bare, blond head, his boarding helmet gone—but the rest had vanished. It was not the broken enemy that concerned Favian, but rather the tall shadows that were ranking themselves just beyond the line of huts. Tall men, some in taller caps, broad-shouldered and moving with the deliberation of veterans. Favian felt his blood chill. These, he knew, were not pirates; they were *La Garde de l'Aigle,* Napoleon's finest, undefeated on the battlefields of Europe.

There was the rasp of ramrods down musket barrels coming clearly across the suddenly silent night. If that corps of phlegmatic veterans could get a volley off and follow it up with a charge *à la baïonnette,* Favian's party would be in deep trouble. They might provide a chance for the pirates to rally behind them; they might even keep the issue in dispute until the main corps of enemy, barracked on Cat Island, could be alerted and come to their aid. Plans flickered through Favian's mind. He took a deep breath and gave his orders.

"We've got to charge those men, boys! Let's hear it for the old *Macedonian*!" Screaming like wild men, Favian led them onto the old French bayonets. The Guard quietly cleared the ramrods from their weapons and stood at the ready, their ground chosen, waiting for their enemy. Favian slowed his charge, picked a tall, gray man in a bearskin cap, and launched a feint; the bayonet slid away, parrying, then came back into line and thrust. Favian parried, hearing shouts and the clatter of steel on steel on all sides; for some reason he absorbed the pointless information that his own opponent was wearing massive gold earrings. The bayonet came flickering out again; Favian parried it to his left side and came forward, his gloved left hand seizing the bayonet in a desperate grip. Pain rocketed up his arm, but he disallowed it; his own lunge was launched, but was turned away on his enemy's ribs. The bayonet came free of his hand, and he hacked desperately at his enemy's arm, feeling the shock of contact, hearing the man's grunt at the impact. There was movement to Favian's right, and he parried desperately at the bayonet that came out of the dark, aimed at his heart, then hacked at its wielder, a wild blow that connected with a thud. The first bayonet was coming at him again, swung one-handed; he blocked it with his own crippled hand, thrust at the face of his first opponent, felt contact as the keen hanger-edge tore along a cheekbone. Two more strikes, ahead and right, brought his opponents down, but he knew his party was in trouble.

There were perhaps ten of these guardsmen at the start; Favian's own party had perhaps five men in it. Now, as Favian stepped back to catch his breath, a few had fallen on each side. The Macedonians, hesitant to come to grips with such numbers, were being driven steadily back, fencing at long range. Favian considered calling his men off, pulling back beyond the huts to where Stanhope, by now, should have the rest of his column ready—but that would concede the initiative to the enemy. He had based his plan on surprise, he realized with biting anger at himself, but the Guard, old veterans who had seen it all before, were constitutionally incapable of being surprised.

There was a sickening thud nearby; a Macedonian spun to the earth, impaled, his eyes horror-struck and wide. It was time to pull back. But then there were cries of "Macedonian! Macedonian!" to the right, and Byrne's marines came lunging out of the darkness. The Guardsmen spun to fight them, but the marines were the elite of their own school and in greater numbers. The Guard fell back, step by step, bayonets clattering, but they never broke. In the end it was Stanhope's party, arriving at last, who surrounded them; they died then, in their places, fighting without complaint, silently, until overwhelmed.

"Sorry I took so long, sir," Byrne reported. He'd been in the thick of it, was nursing a long cut on his neck. "But we found a line of pirogues out there. Had to put a guard on 'em to keep the enemy from giving the alarm. Laffite's holding 'em with ten men."

"Very good," Favian said, breathless. "Send a half dozen of your men to find the magazine and guard it—we don't want anybody blowing it up. Then search those huts, confiscate any weapons. Send a messenger back to find Chapelle and tell him to bring his column up—tell him he's to guard the rampart against any attempt to retake the fort. Understood?"

"Aye, sir."

Nothing to do but clean up, Favian thought. A few pirates would be found in the morning, hiding in one out-of-the-way spot or another, and the rest would have run off onto the island; perhaps Chapelle's reserve party would have captured a few. If Laffite was guarding all the boats, then there would be no way for them to alert their comrades. And it was only a few hours until dawn in any case—by then *Malachi's Revenge, Franklin,* and the gunboat would be in a position to assist. The only question remaining involved the success of Hourigan's party, on the other side of Cat Island Pass.

"Mr. Stanhope."

"Sir."

"D'you have your lanterns?"

"Aye, sir."

"Make the signal, then."

Stanhope had been carrying two dark-lanterns in his pack; he saluted and made his way to the seaward rampart. There he would light the shuttered lanterns, direct their beams into the Gulf, and signal to the *Macedonian* that her children had successfully stormed the enemy bastion. The shuttered lanterns would not be visible to the other battery on the Isles Dernieres—nor would Hourigan's lanterns, when he made a similar signal, be visible to Favian. Only *Macedonian*'s long telescopes would see, and then the signal for mutual success would rise up its masts.

"Mr. Chapelle is within the works, sir. He's taking his position on the rampart." The messenger was Chapelle's midshipman, Killick.

"Thank you." Other messengers reported back: several prisoners had been secured in the huts; the magazine had been found and a guard placed over it; Stanhope's signal had been made. Favian gave orders for half the men to sleep while the others stood guard, and to rotate every hour.

Favian felt weariness flooding him. His injured left hand throbbed with pain. The fight had been sharp and quick; he doubted if, from start to finish, it had lasted longer than five or six minutes. An insignificant amount of time in comparison to the days it had taken to plan the assault and the hours it would take to clean up the fort, stitch up the wounded, bury the dead . . . Not so many dead, all things considered—certainly not like the bloodbaths Favian had seen in his life: the Tripolitan gunboats slippery with gore after the American seamen had cut their way through the corsairs; the well deck of *Macedonian,* when Favian had first seen it swimming in bloodred seawater, dismembered bodies floating in the brine. For good or ill, he thought, he had always been on the Navy's cutting edge, and the Navy itself was the cutting edge of the American republic. Cutting edges drew blood; that was their function—and it was Favian's function to decide where to cut. At the moment, standing amid the human rubble of the Guard's stand, the brave and capable warriors he had overwhelmed with his own New World elites, he was heartily sick of his work.

"Mr. Byrne, I'm turning in," he said, taking off his heavy helmet. "Wake me in an hour. I'll be over there, lying in the grass."

"The huts are secured, sir. You could rest in there."

"They're probably full of bugs, Mr. Byrne. I don't think they take a lot of baths out here."

There was a flash of Byrne's white teeth in the dark. "I'm sure you're right, sir. Have a good sleep."

Favian unclipped the sword from his belt and took the two unloaded pistols from his pockets; he pillowed his head on his arms; despite the pain from his injured hand he fell instantly into sleep. It seemed only a few moments before Byrne was standing over him, shaking his shoulder.

"Hourigan's men have run into a fight, sir," he said. "I think you might want to take a look."

"Yes." Favian shook his head to clear it of sleep. The chill land breeze ruffled his hair; it had increased in velocity since he'd gone to sleep. "Thank you, Mr. Byrne."

He stood up, reaching for his sword and pistols. Byrne led him to the water battery, where the long iron noses of the eighteen-pounders stood silent guard over Cat Island Pass. "Here, sir," Byrne said and handed him a night glass.

The inverted image swam slowly into focus: the breakers, the dark shadow of the island on the moving, shifting sea. And then Favian saw pinpricks of light flashing on the island, and knew it for what it was: musketry. The flashes were silent; the wind had taken the sound and swept it out to sea. There was another, bigger flash, reflecting off trees. A big gun. Hourigan was in trouble.

Favian glanced nervously into Terre Bonne Bay, wondering if the pirates had seen their battery under attack, if they were raising an alarm. The winds were strange when it came to musketry and gunshots: sometimes they shook the earth and startled bystanders a dozen miles away, while two miles from the fight men sipped tea in ignorance of a major battle being fought almost under their noses. But there was no sign that the pirates had seen anything, no rockets or false fires, no signals raised high on masts. Favian put the telescope to his eye once more.

He watched, for what seemed a long time, the lights dancing like fireflies on the distant island, straining his ears to discern the sounds of battle over the moan of wind and roar of waves. Eventually the flickering lights died away, the battle remaining mute to the end, and Favian was left with uncertainty gnawing him. If Hourigan was repulsed, he'd have to signal in the morning for the ships to keep to his side of the channel, avoiding those guns on the battery. At least the larger fort had fallen. But Hourigan had forty men with him: what of those? How many of the Macedonians had fallen to the pirate defenders?

But then there was the sound of cheering nearby, and Favian looked where a jubilant Byrne was pointing. Two miles offshore, the frigate *Macedonian* lay hove to, near-invisible on the seas. She had raised a signal up her tall mainmast, a red lantern over a yellow one, the sign that both Favian and Hourigan had reported success.

Both forts had fallen. The way to Cat Island was open.

SEVENTEEN

The eastern sky turned a pale gray just before dawn, revealing *Malachi's Revenge* tacking back and forth off the entrance to Cat Island Pass, *Franklin* and the gunboat a little farther out to sea. *Macedonian* sat in black-hulled magnificence behind the island, the ochre stripe over the gunports subdued in the faint light. Looking in the other direction with his long glass, Favian saw the pirate vessels riding to anchor, six of them, a pair of brigs, a sloop, two schooners, and a felucca. "The one with the white masts and yards, that's Mortier's ship," Laffite said, pointing out the larger of the two brigs. "*L'Aigle*." He gave a satisfied smile. "We've caught them entirely by surprise."

"It seems so, Mr. Laffite," Favian said. He turned to Stanhope. "Light the false fires, Mr. Stanhope."

"Aye aye, sir."

Two green false fires would be the signal for Gideon to take the tern schooner through the pass, heading swiftly into the bay to cut the enemy ships off from Cat Island. Fontenoy's *Franklin* and the gunboat would assist, principally to take possession of the privateer vessels—presumably there was only an anchor watch on each boat, easily enough overcome.

The false fires spurted green flame on the ramparts, and the schooner tacked, steadied onto its new course, and headed smoothly for Terre Bonne Bay, flags rising on its halliards. Favian saw the American ensign at the peak, streaming brightly in the dawn, and a giant white flag at the fore with the legend PARDON FOR DESERTERS, the same flag Patterson had flown at Barataria in September. Then Favian saw a long red streamer rising at the main, a gold rattlesnake writhing along its length, fangs bared. Favian smiled in satisfaction; he had flown that pendant himself, at *Experiment*'s forepeak during the fight with *Teaser,* and in the Narrow Seas of England when he had burned over forty British merchantmen. It was the Markham family banner, designed by Malachi Markham, Favian's hellion uncle, in 1778, flown first when Malachi's *Royal George* privateer had captured the fifty-gun ship of the line *Bristol,* the most spectacular prize of the Revolution. . . . The Markham family had flown it ever since, over every desperate combat, over every capture.

Favian turned to the flagpole his men had improvised out of two masts and a long sweep taken from the boats and pirogues drawn up on the shore and lashed together. "Raise our flag, gentlemen," he said. "Prepare to dip her in salute as the *Revenge* passes, if you please."

Stanhope had constructed a pole for his signal flags out of the mast from Favian's pinnace. The fifteen-striped American flag came slowly up the improvised pole, the mast bending dangerously in the stiff land breeze, but in the end remaining upright. *Malachi's Revenge,* propelled by her great white wings, slipped gracefully past the point only half a mile from the fort; Favian could see Gideon clearly through his glass, dressed in an old brown coat, a round beaver hat tilted back on his head, one cheek full of tobacco. His privateersmen were standing at their stations, ready to raise their port-lids and run out their guns at Gideon's command, and Favian could see the tall, broad-shouldered black man, Long Tom Tate, standing with one arm thrown around the breech of his pivot gun like a man holding his lover.

Then Gideon was waving his hat and bellowing out orders, and his men swarmed to the lee rail, facing Favian, their own hats raised. Three roaring cheers came distinctly over the water, and Favian raised his own hat. "Dip our ensign, please," he said, and the men at the halliards brought the flag down in salute.

Malachi's Revenge sped into the bay. *Franklin,* unable with her square rig to ride as near the wind, tacked several times before drawing even with the fort; Gunboat Number 5, unwieldy and slow, took even longer. The top of the sun's disk touched the dark cypress swamp to the east. It was getting light enough for *Macedonian* to be able to read signals.

"Haul our ensign down," Favian ordered. "Mr. Stanhope, throw out a signal for *Macedonian* to send us a surgeon."

There were seven wounded Macedonians, three of them hurt seriously; and two of the attackers had been killed. The losses among Favian's boat crew had been particularly severe, one killed and two hurt badly by those Guard bayonets. The pirates had suffered twelve killed and sixteen wounded, plus fifteen captured; the rest had run and were presumably scattered up and down the island. Favian expected them to surrender when they got hungry enough. There had been no casualties at all when Patterson had captured Grand Terre in September, but then there had also been no resistance—most of Laffite's men had fled into the swamp, while the leaders stayed behind and surrendered.

"*Macedonian* acknowledges our signal, sir."

"Thank you, Mr. Stanhope." Things were moving smoothly enough.

And then there was the boom of a distant gun. Favian spun around, amazed, an oath on his lips; everyone around him was frozen into place, standing stiff as statues in surprise. Another gun banged. Favian saw white splashes in the water as a roundshot skipped across the waves, two hundred yards east of *Malachi's Revenge*.

"Another battery, by God!" he burst out, fury seizing him. He stood quivering with anger for long seconds, then stalked to the northern extremity of the rampart, his subordinates, Stanhope, Byrne, and Chapelle, falling into pace behind him. There was a black-garbed shadow racing ahead: Jean Laffite, a telescope under one arm.

"Where the devil is it?" Favian fumed. From the angle of the splashes it had to be on Timbalier Island somewhere. He jumped up onto the cypress rampart of the fort, next to Laffite who already had his own telescope trained. Another gun boomed.

"There it is!" Laffite shouted. The belch of gunsmoke had given it away. Favian, furious, clapped his telescope to his eye.

The battery, three or four miles away, came into focus just as its second gun fired, producing another puff of gray smoke, and things fell into place. Apparently the pirates had been uneasy about their back door, east of Timbalier Island at Petite Passe Timbalier. Even though the water was only a few feet deep, it was deep enough to admit small boats. Perhaps they expected the Laffites to attack with pirogues, sculling in the back way. At any rate they'd put a two-gun battery on the north side of Timbalier to discourage just that attempt—they couldn't put it on the eastern end because that half of the island was all swamp. The battery had seen Gideon's schooner slipping in, flying the American flag, and had opened fire. The range was hopelessly long, but the booming guns were quite enough to alert the pirates on Cat Island.

Favian swung his telescope inland. He could see running figures and pointing arms on one of the schooners, and a startled man running spiderlike up the rigging of *l'Aigle*. He couldn't see any developments on Cat Island itself—the settlement was on the other side—but he presumed that they would be alerted shortly.

"You didn't tell me about this, Mr. Laffite," Favian said.

Laffite raised an eyebrow at Favian's angry tones. "I didn't know, Commodore," he said. "They must have set those guns up in the last week. Perhaps they heard I was trying to work against them."

"Sir," Byrne said. "I could take my leathernecks and silence that battery. March down the south shore of the island, cross through the trees, and take them from behind."

"Very well," Favian snapped. The battery had already done as much damage as it was ever likely to, simply by ending the surprise Favian had hoped for—the range was far too long to damage any of the attacking vessels—but there was nothing else for the marines to do, and the battery seemed the only target left on the island. Furthermore, Byrne's plan would work. The island was long and narrow, running east-west, a strip of beach on its northern and southern edges, with vegetation sprouting down its middle. Byrne's men could approach the battery unseen along the southern beach, then cut across the narrow island to strike the enemy from the rear.

"Thank you, sir," Byrne said, saluting. He turned to bellow orders for his marines to form in their ranks. Favian lowered his telescope, his anger ebbing. Perhaps it would work out well enough. *Malachi's Revenge* was well into the bay, and *Franklin* had just passed the fort. The pirates would have to be quick indeed to prevent their being stranded on the island. But his memory of those tall, gray veterans disturbed him—there were, according to Laffite, over five hundred men in the Guard of the Eagle who had marched in the ranks of the Middle or Old Guard in Europe. Most of those five hundred would probably be in New Orleans, but there were bound to be many on Cat Island. Favian remembered their expert bayonet work, their imposing presence, their steadfast refusal to be surprised, the stolid acceptance with which they faced their death. Those men might have more resources than the ragtag bunch of pirates with whom they'd allied themselves.

The two-gun battery spat out another pair of shot that fell far short. The dandy-rigged gunboat tacked into the bay, heading for the nearest enemy vessel, its boarders massing on its bulwarks. Byrne's marines shouldered their rifles and marched out of the fort. Gideon's black schooner swept deeper into the bay.

And then Favian saw the black swarm of boats heading past the southern tip of Cat Island, and in astonishment snapped his telescope to his eye. "*Merde!*" Laffite burst out.

There were a lot of boats: pirogues, rowboats, little sailboats, a tattered disorderly fleet heading for the two vessels nearest the island, the *l'Aigle* brig and a little sloop. Crammed with pirates, with former *Chasseurs* and *Grenadiers à Pied*, Napoleonic fanatics ready to do battle for their vessels. Favian gave vent to a blistering series of curses. The original plan was badly out of trim. Fortunately, in their daily gaming sessions in *Macedonian*'s wardroom, they had worked out possible actions in the event the enemy managed to get men aboard their vessels.

A gun boomed from *Malachi's Revenge*, and Favian saw a waterspout appear in line with the fleet of boats. Thomas Tate, no doubt, trying to get the range with his pivot gun. But the *Revenge* was still a good two miles distant from the little flotilla, and even with Tate's expert gunnery any hit at this range would be pure luck.

Favian could do nothing but watch. The swarm of boats reached the sloop first, and Favian could see men swarming up its sides, casting loose the gaskets on the sails, making the boat ready. He could see the glint of sun off bayonets, and imagined some of them had tall caps. *Malachi's Revenge* was finding the range now, dropping eighteen-pound roundshot into the mass of boats, but Gideon seemed concerned chiefly with the brig *l'Aigle*, which was big enough to put up a fight if the Guardsmen got to it first.

In the end the *Revenge* and the boats arrived at nearly the same time. Black figures were still swarming up *l'Aigle*'s bulwarks as the black tern schooner came proudly alongside; Favian saw a wall of gray smoke gushing up, followed a few seconds later by the thunderous crash of a broadside, as Gideon loosed his guns right across the enemy decks. Favian found a cheer bursting from him; he wanted to wave the telescope and caper on the ramparts. He knew the enemy could not reply: they would have to cast loose their guns, bring up cartridges and shot, light their slow matches—it was a job that took seven or eight minutes even on a well-practiced ship, and on the little schooner in this situation it would be chaos. Gideon's guns, reloaded, began to roar again. The enemy's only hope would be to board, a difficult job even at the best of times, and Gideon would know enough to be able to prevent that. Even the disciplined corps of Napoleonic veterans would be little help; this kind of warfare simply wasn't their style. Their best hope would be to jump back in their boats and run for the swamps.

Gideon's guns fired again and again, gunsmoke wrapping both vessels. Favian found himself grinning. His cousin seemed to have the situation well in hand. He turned his telescope to the sloop.

It had got clumsily under way, cutting its anchor cable and getting its mainsail up halfway before the peak outhaul jammed. The main came down again, the sloop spinning out of control, and then the sail rose properly to catch the wind, the sloop heeling, a bone building in its teeth. A staysail and jib rose up as well; the sloop's speed increased. Favian could see the its decks black with men; there seemed to be at least a hundred men crammed shoulder to shoulder on the little boat. Even so there was little hope. *Franklin* had, obeying the plan worked out on *Macedonian*'s wardroom floor days before, abandoned its task of taking possession of the other pirate vessels and was steering to intercept. The popguns that a sloop of that size would carry could not hope to match Fontenoy's broadside. It would be as one-sided a fight as *Revenge* versus *l'Aigle*.

But then, as Favian watched in surprise, *Franklin*, moving swiftly across the surface of the bay, came to a shuddering halt, slewing wildly, its sails slatting back and forth so loudly that Favian, two miles away, could hear them plainly. Aground! Favian scowled, damning the shallow waters. Fontenoy, striking the mud at that speed, would have to wait until high tide to kedge himself off, and that would be another two hours yet. It looked as if the sloop would get away—assuming, of course, it was light enough to get over the Petite Passe Timbalier to the east of the island.

Strange, Favian thought, it seemed not to be heading for the Passe. The track of the vessel was taking it westward—could it be heading for Cat Island Pass? That made no sense at all; Favian could sink the sloop easily with the fort's eighteen-pounders. One or two hits with the large-bore cannon here would shatter the sloop's fragile scantlings beyond hope of repair.

There was a series of gunshots as Cunningham's gunboat, only half a mile or so in the bay, fired its guns at long range, the round shot splashing far short of the sloop. Still the sloop continued its curve to the west. What the devil were those men doing?

Favian felt his heart sink as he realized what the enemy were up to, the revelation coming with an almost physical impact. How blind could he have been? He turned his glass on the sloop, seeing the swarming men in tall caps, the muskets and bayonets, his worst fears confirmed.

They were coming to retake the fort. They had forsaken a sea battle, knowing they were outclassed; instead they were going to land their veterans on Timbalier Island and turn the fight into the sort they understood, assaulting a fortification with picked troops at the point of the bayonet. And Favian had sent off his marines, the men who were best at defending the ramparts.

"Mr. Stanhope!" he bellowed. "Throw out a signal to Mr. Byrne! Tell the marines to return to the fort immediately! Then send Tolbert to them as a runner. I want those men back!" Byrne, marching east along the beach, had no way of seeing a signal from the fort, but *Macedonian*, lying off the island, would repeat it—and then it would be up to Byrne's memory, or the swiftness of Midshipman Tolbert's running, for the marine lieutenant had no signal book with him. "The rest of you—have the men muster by this battery! Take every captured musket, every pistol, make sure they're ready. Open the magazine, begin moving cartridges here to the land battery. They're going to try to take the fort back!"

He saw Laffite looking at him in amazement, Chapelle in horror. Stanhope sprinted for the improvised signal halliards. He still had sixty men, Favian thought; that might be enough to hold the parapet.

The next few minutes confirmed Favian's worst fears. The sloop, its sails pockmarked by some near hits from the gunboat, ran itself aground right west of the little battery, men pouring ashore carrying muskets. The old uniforms worn by many of them were clearly visible now in Favian's long glass, the old blue swallowtail coats, fur caps, a standard with a gold eagle winking from its summit. Favian began firing the fort's six-pounders as soon as he had cartridge and ball, knowing the range was impossibly long but hoping to familiarize his men with the guns. Besides, Byrne might hear the guns and march to them.

Across the bay there was now silence; *l'Aigle*'s resistance had ended, and the gunsmoke dispersed. Gideon's schooner was moving again, having left a prize crew aboard the brig; apparently he had realized the danger and was coming to the support of the fort. It was clear, Favian thought, that he would be too late; he'd have to detour around the shoal that *Franklin* had run aground on.

"Cease fire," Favian said, seeing that his six-pounder crews had familiarized themselves with the guns. He could feel hopeless anger rising in him, like bile; he knew this fight would be bitter. No one had foreseen anything like this.

"Fire on my command," Favian said. "You with the muskets—that will be as soon as they start coming across the open ground. Keep your heads and aim low." He took a deep breath, trying to calm his whirling mind. He had scented disasters before, and this was certainly beginning to smell like one. "Just keep your heads," he said, "and we'll do well." He reached into his pockets for his long duelling pistols, a gift from his father many years before, and began loading them.

Down the beach the Guard column had formed up, a narrow, deep column of men—just like the columns with which Napoleon had triumphed on the battlefields of Europe. They were carrying the standard to the front, but there was no flag—perhaps they didn't want to give themselves away flying the tricolor; perhaps they only had the eagle. They were coming on briskly. The gunboat, its sails down, moving deliberately under sweeps, had taken them under fire, but most of Cunningham's shots were high. That was the problem with those little gunboats; they rocked so much on the waves that their value as gun platforms was nearly nil, even trying to move under sweeps. But still Cunningham scored some hits, striking into the densely packed column, men flying before the impact of the ball, lying raglike on the beach as the column hastened on.

"Mr. Chapelle," Favian said. The portly fourth lieutenant was bending over the only six-pounder that could fire straight down the beach, his eyes intent. "You may fire when ready."

"Thank you, sir. I believe I'll hold fire for a minute longer."

"As you wish, Mr. Chapelle," Favian said, trying to affect a casualness he did not feel. If only Byrne's marines were present! There would be no fear then.

"Drive the quoin in a bit there, Koskey," Chapelle was saying. "Just a touch—there! Give me the slow match." His voice was dry and matter-of-fact. "There we go," he said. "Stand back, now."

Favian, concentrating on the advancing column, scarcely heard the bang, but he did see the sudden whirl of arms and legs as the six-pounder shot struck home, driving into the dense column. He felt his lips draw back from his teeth in a snarl. This was the way to punish them.

The column increased its pace. The tall men in the lead, their brows shadowed by their bearskin caps, were bent over, leaning forward as if into a high wind. Favian could hear the sound they made, a kind of low droning, ominous and terrible. Chapelle's gun banged again, striking home. The column never hesitated, though men were left behind on the sand.

"Muskets to the parapet!" Favian shouted. "Guns two, three, and four, load with grape on top of roundshot!" There was a rattle as the muskets were trained across the rampart. The column was within two hundred yards. Favian could see the eagle standard waving wildly; caps had been raised on bayonet tips; they had doubled their pace, were coming on at a run.

"Ready . . ." Favian shouted, knowing it was going to be bad. And then suddenly there was a crackling thunder from the vegetation ahead, gunsmoke bursting from the trees. The column writhed and slowed, men stumbling. Chapelle's gun roared out, striking home. The column came staggering on, but there was another volley from the flank, and the Guard broke up, some heading onward regardless, others turning to face the new enemy, yet others running. And then came the whoops and shrieks as

Byrne's forty marines came running out of the trees, striking the column in flank, destroying it.

Byrne's memory had proved providential, Favian thought, relief flooding him. He'd known what the recall signal meant. He'd pulled his men back and hit the column in flank as it advanced down the beach, an inspired tactic.

The Guard of the Eagle were running back down the beach, their last chance gone. "Three cheers for Mr. Byrne!" Favian shouted, jumping up on the parapet, waving his boarding helmet as he led his sailors in salute to the marines.

La Société de la Garde de l'Aigle was finished, their menace to New Orleans ended. Now, Favian knew, there was only the cleaning up to be done. And the counting of the dead.

EIGHTEEN

On the sand they found the body of M. le Chevalier Jean Noel Gabriel de la Tour d'Aurillac; he had fought on hopelessly until run through the body by a marine bayonet. Near him they found the eagle standard, still held by a stern gray man who had the colors of the *Premier Régiment des Chasseurs à Pied* wrapped around his waist. "This is what happens," Laffite said, looking down at the little knight in his bloodstained, elegant clothes, "when one gets carried away by causes. Here you see the results of virtue at work, Commodore, nothing else."

Mortier, their admiral, was never found, though some of the prisoners remembered him with the little squadron of boats heading for *l'Aigle*. He had made his escape into the swamps, or perhaps he'd been killed and the sea took him. Guieu's body was found on the brig. Pijon had been wounded and taken prisoner. None of the other leaders were found. About fifty prisoners were taken, many of them wounded. Another fifty bodies were found and buried in the sand.

Laffite left later in the day on a pirogue. He had shown himself to the captives, receiving their dour glances and letting the rebel pirates know that he had brought the government down on them, and that he was in favor; then he asked for two of the prisoners and a cypress dugout to take him back to New Orleans. "Aren't you worried your prisoners might escape?" Favian asked him. "Or do you some injury?"

The pirate looked at the captives with scorn. "These dogs know their master," he said. "I shall be perfectly safe." Two heavy pistols stuck in his sash, he set out across the bay.

Favian made a private trophy of the eagle and the Guard battle flag. There was no point in sending it to Washington, he decided; they would only be politically embarrassed by the idea of flying a French tricolor alongside the torn ensigns of the *Guerrière* and *Java*. It would look more interesting as a curiosity in his father's study, a place ornamented with the souvenirs of other wars.

After Laffite's departure Favian received Mr. Midshipman George Killick, who had been with Hourigan and Eastlake in the attack on the Isles Dernieres. Killick carried Hourigan's report, written in a painfully unclear hand on a piece of scrap paper, telling of the near disaster that had befallen his party. Apparently the pirates had seen their approach, for Hourigan's first attempt to storm the walls had been met with a charge of grapeshot and a volley of musketry. Lieutenant Eastlake had been killed outright, and Hourigan shot in the leg; the party was pinned down for several long moments, unable to advance or retreat.

Hourigan manfully gave the credit for the capture of the fort to Midshipman Killick and to Dr. Solomon. The martial chaplain had managed, under fire, to work a group of sailors around to the left, where they had succeeded in storming a part of the rampart less well manned than elsewhere. Then Killick had rallied the rest of the party and stormed the place frontally while Solomon hit the remaining defenders from the flank. In the end there were four Macedonians killed, including Lieutenant Eastlake, and six wounded, including Hourigan.

"Dr. Truscott says Mr. Hourigan will not lose his leg," Killick said. "But he will be unable to walk for some weeks."

Favian frowned at the report. His first lieutenant, Stone, was off with the *Carnation*, and now his second was useless and his third had been killed. It was sad to lose Eastlake, the only one of his juniors with actual combat experience; he had been a credit to the wardroom, a wealthy young man from Virginia who had shipped crates of fine Madeira north to supply cheer to the officers' mess, and who advocated the smoking of Indian hemp as a relief from bodily ills. . . . Now Favian would have to spot-promote some of the midshipmen to fill the lieutenants' places, and he didn't know the mids well enough. Stanhope would do well enough, he supposed, but Stanhope was very junior, and the senior midshipmen might resent it. Tolbert, on the other hand, was senior enough, but it would be difficult to find a more blockheaded young man within a thousand miles. He'd have to ask the advice of the surviving lieutenants.

"Mr. Hourigan was very brave, sir," Killick offered, mistaking Favian's frown for criticism of his superior. "He kept his head even though he was in a great deal of pain. It was he who ordered the move to the left, though the doctor executed it."

"I'm sure everyone did their best," Favian said. "Please give my compliments to Mr. Hourigan—he performed very well under difficult circumstances. And," he said, grudging it, "give my compliments to Dr. Solomon. You will all receive particular mention in my report."

"Thank you, Captain!" Killick said, saluting enthusiastically. For a midshipman to be mentioned in dispatches was unusual. Favian returned the salute, and Killick returned to his boat.

It took three days to clean up the debris at Cat Island. *Franklin* was kedged off the mud, but the snow proved to have sprung some planks and had to be pumped six hours out of twenty-four. It was therefore decided that *Franklin* would provide the prize crews for the captured vessels and would convoy them all back to New Orleans; it was a duty that no one envied. The prisoners were stuffed into the prize vessels' respective cable tiers, to be sorted out once they got to the Cabildo. Favian wrote his reports to Claiborne, Jackson, and the Secretary of the Navy; the names of Byrne, Hourigan, Killick, and Solomon were all duly set down.

On the second day a schooner appeared on the horizon, making signals. Favian recognized the British recognition codes that he had captured with the *Carnation*, but he wanted the British to know that Cat Island Pass was closed to them; he feigned ignorance, hoisted his own American ensign over *Macedonian*'s poop, and set out in chase. There was a brisk three-hour pursuit, but the schooner traveled quickly in light airs and made its escape to the east, as Favian had intended. It would carry the news that an

American force had possession of Cat Island, and that the strength of the pirates had been broken. Admiral Cochrane would have to find another route to New Orleans.

The huts on Cat Island were burned; the small arms, ammunition, and cannon transferred to *Macedonian*, and the forts on Timbalier Island and the Isles Dernieres were blown up by setting a match to their magazines. The smoke of destruction was still looming overhead when Dr. Solomon approached Favian on the poop.

"I would like, Captain Markham, to tender my resignation as chaplain of the *Macedonian*," Solomon said.

Favian looked him up and down and shook his head. "I shall accept it, sir, with regret," he said. "But I cannot say, Doctor, that it comes as a surprise."

The chaplain smiled. "I have looked into my heart, Captain," he said, "and I know that I am not cut out for this duty."

Favian held out his hand. "I wish you the best of success," he said. "I'm sure your next congregation will be a little more elevated than our tars."

"Sir, you mistake me," Solomon said. "I have no intention of continuing with the ministry. Indeed, I hope you will honor me with a midshipman's warrant here in the *Macedonian*."

Favian looked at Solomon with blank astonishment. Could the man be serious? "Doctor Solomon, I hope you will reconsider this," he said. "You are, ah, how old?"

"Twenty-nine, Captain."

"A year younger than I," Favian said. "Educated by the College of New Jersey, with a doctorate. You will be confined to the gunroom with boys half your age—and these boys will be your seniors in rank, Doctor—and your background will be nothing like theirs; their education is far inferior to yours; their temperament, er, will be different," Favian said hastily, by no means certain of the last point.

"We are alike, Captain, in the desire to earn glory, and to serve our country," Solomon said, his eyes looking proudly into Favian's. "I would be proud, sir, to be among their company. Besides, I understand that Captain Jacob Jones did not receive his midshipman's warrant until he was over thirty; and Captain Jones is one of the greatest stars in our naval constellation, one whose glory—"

"Captain Jones," Favian said, "is a very unusual man." He regarded the chaplain carefully, bemused by the whole incident—it was so typical of the man! Glory-struck, having had a taste of action and liking it, ready to throw away his career to embark on another that promised more excitement. Talthibius Solomon, Favian thought, was very much like Favian himself had been at the age of seventeen, cruising off Tripoli in the *Vixen*, before the war had ended and the Embargoes had wrecked his own hunger for glory. . . . But it was one thing, Favian thought, to lust for glory at the age of seventeen; quite another to throw up a comfortable life as a pastor and take a midshipman's warrant in hand at the age of twenty-nine.

"I will ask you to withdraw your request for now, Doctor Solomon," Favian said, seeing the wind go right out of the man—Solomon seemed to deflate before his amused eyes. "I want you to think some more about it. But I am short of officers on this cruise, and if you renew your request forty-eight hours from now, I will accept."

Solomon brightened again, a smile breaking out on his features. "I will do as you ask, Captain," he said. "But I will not change my mind."

"Forty-eight hours, Doctor," Favian said. "Please remember that, if you resubmit this request, I will never again call you *Doctor*. You will be *Mister* Solomon, the rawest middy on the frigate."

"That *Mister* is music to me, sir," Solomon said, and offered his salute.

Favian watched Solomon's sprightly stride as he left the quarterdeck. He suspected the man's enthusiasm for the Navy might not survive the war; Solomon's heart would be in the task only so long as there was glory to be gained. The long years of peacetime duty would wear him down; his effervescent personality would not be suited to a naval truce. Then, Favian thought, he'd throw in his warrant and commence another career.

The captured vessels were marshaled inside the bay, ready to be convoyed the next day to the Southwest Pass of the Mississippi— *Franklin*, *Revenge*, the gunboat, and the prizes would be able to get over the bar, but *Macedonian* would have to shape its course for the Southeast Pass again. Favian's little squadron would disperse, and then Favian once again would simply be the man who had taken *Macedonian* from New London without permission, putting his career at hazard, and then careened off to sea on a dubious series of adventures. Would the Navy Department see the Cat Island expedition as a necessary thing? Could they possibly credit Laffite's story of a society of Napoleonic grenadiers hiding in the Louisiana swamps? Or would they censure Favian for gullibility as well as disobedience?

That, Favian knew, would depend on the outcome. If New Orleans fell, Washington would want the heads of the men responsible, and Favian's neck was already conveniently stretched out on the block. The Navy had sought scapegoats before, and the fates of James Barron, who had lost the *Chesapeake* in peacetime, and of William Cox, the unlucky midshipman who, after the captain and all the lieutenants had been killed or wounded, had found himself in command of the same frigate when it had surrendered to the *Shannon* a year ago, and who had been drummed out of the service because Captain Lawrence had been martyred gloriously and could not be held responsible for his fatal stupidities—these dire examples showed themselves plainly before any officer who was stupid, careless, unlucky, or simply available. There were further complications—in the event of disaster, Commodore Patterson might well be able to shrug off the responsibility onto Favian. Patterson might not be such a calculating man, but he could be put into a situation in which he had no choice in order to save his own hide. Favian, looking out the stern windows of the frigate at the setting sun, stared gloomily into his cup of coffee and wondered when the British would come.

The next morning brought the answer. The convoy had barely managed to get out of Terre Bonne Bay on the land breeze when the sails of a schooner were sighted on the horizon. *Macedonian* and *Malachi's Revenge* sped to intercept, but Favian's telescope confirmed the stranger's identity long before Gideon's swift schooner discovered it officially. It was the pilot boat *Beaux Jours*, Captain Poquelin presumably bearing dispathces from New Orleans.

But that was not all Favian's telescope confirmed. As the pilot boat drew nearer, Favian saw a small figure in a white gown and straw bonnet standing by the taffrail, looking anxiously at the frigate—and with the paralyzing suddenness of a clap of thunder, Favian realized he was looking at Campaspe.

She was out of the bosun's chair and into his arms before he could utter a word. Favian's mind was in a whirl; all he could think of was New Orleans in ruins, burned by Jackson as the British advanced, the inhabitants scattered to the four winds.

"What's happened?" he asked. "Has the city been destroyed?"

She looked up at him, her eyes wide. "No," she said, plainly taken aback by the question. "But the British have come—their fleet's been seen. I wanted to be with you."

Favian looked at her in astonishment, then looked up, seeing the reception line of officers ranked by the entry port, watching their embrace with guarded amusement. "Campaspe," he said, remembering himself. "Allow me to introduce Lieutenant Chapelle. This is Lieutenant Ford, Lieutenant Swink, Lieutenant Byrne of the Marines. Mr. Seward, the master . . ." Each officer bowed, getting his first glimpse of his captain's wife; Campaspe gave a little curtsy at each introduction. "Mr. Swink," Favian finally said, "please escort Mrs. Markham to my cabin. I'll be with you soon, dearest. Captain Poquelin, please join me on the quarterdeck." For Poquelin was carrying a fistful of dispatches, some of them with heavy seals and ribbons dangling, and Favian wanted a clear head to read them; Campaspe seated opposite him at his cabin table would not give him a clear head. He took his captain's privilege on the weather quarterdeck, examined the heavy envelopes, and broke open the one from Jackson.

It was dated December eleventh, two days ago. "I expect this express will find yr. expedition gloryously succéssful," it began, and then got straight to the heart of the matter. The British, it seems, had begun, in twos and threes, appearing off Cat Island—the other Cat Island, in the Mississippi Sound—on the eighth; a large fleet, "perhaps fifty sail," according to the letter, had dropped anchor on the tenth. Favian frowned and tried to think what that said of British intentions. Perhaps nothing, but it seemed likely that their chosen anchorage indicated commitment in a certain direction. The most feasible attack on New Orleans from the Mississippi Sound would be through Lake Borgne, where Tac Jones had his five gunboats and two schooners. If he were Jones, Favian thought, he'd try to get his little squadron through Les Rigolets and into Pontchartrain very quickly. Jones could not hope to keep the British out of Borgne for very long, but he could hold Les Rigolets indefinitely—the British could not get any of their strength through there: the current was too strong and the waters too shallow. Jones's gunboats, and the guns of the fort at Petites Coquilles, could shoot them to bits as they struggled against the force of the waters.

Borgne, Favian thought. That meant the British would not be coming up the Mississippi against the guns at Fort St. Philip, the most obvious way. From Borgne they could try to get through the bayous, which would put them right near the city, probably just below it. Or they could land on the Chantilly Peninsula and march to the city, coming out above New Orleans and cutting it off from reinforcements. If they managed to defeat Jones, they could break into Lake Pontchartrain, which would also put them well north of the city, and then try to take Fort St. John, which would give them a plain road to New Orleans. From the Mississippi Sound they could even attempt Mobile once more. Where did the British intend?

Jackson was no help. "I expect this is a faint," the letter said, the backwoods spelling adding, somehow, to the grim purpose of the message. "They wish to draw my attention to that point when they mean to strike through Terre Bonne Bay. However I will look for them there and provide for their reception elsewhere. I expect hard knocks once the Fandango commences, but Coffee and his Tennessee men is within call and Father Time has now enlisted in the American camp.

"The situation with regard to martial law is growing more expedient. The time is not yet ripe, but once the citizens see a few more score of British sail they will fall in with our purpose.

"It is our earnest hope that Yr. Excellency will find some means of annoying the enemy at their anchorage. May the Eternal bless your arms and grant you success."

Well, Favian thought. He and Jackson understood one another well enough. If the British intended the move off Borgne to be a "faint," drawing attention from a real strike through Terre Bonne Bay, then they would have to change their plans in a hurry. Presumably Laffite had carried the news of the defeat of the Guard to Jackson by now: Jackson would know his rear was safe.

And then there was that piece about "annoying the enemy." One thirty-eight-gun ex-British frigate could not hope to do much to a fifty-ship armada but annoy it, and even then the odds were higher that it would be the Americans who would be far more annoyed, ending up in chains in some prison hulk. Jackson had left the thought to the last paragraph, rather teasingly, Favian thought; Jackson's words seemed to suggest that he would very much like the British to be "annoyed," but that he would leave the decision up to Favian—as if it would ever be left up to anyone else. Favian was under no obligation to obey Army orders; but Army suggestions were another thing.

Next Favian opened the dispatch from Patterson. The news concerning the British appearance off Cat Island was repeated. "Lieutenant Jones is reporting to me daily by the *Alligator* tender," Patterson wrote. "I have ordered him to Pass Christiana to keep the Enemy under observation. If pressed, he is to retreat to Les Rigolets. I hope it may be possible for you to move to his relief." Favian snorted—Tac Jones was on his own at Pass Christiana; there was no way for *Macedonian* to get into the shallow water to help him, nor any way the British would let Jones get his boats out into deeper water to help the *Macedonian*. Patterson was suggesting something else, much in the same way Jackson had made another, similar suggestion.

All along, ever since Favian had captured the British plans with the *Carnation* corvette, the battle for the Lower Mississippi had been fought, not so much against the British, as against time. Time to alert the city to its danger, time for the Louisiana troops to be called in and the city's population to be mobilized. New Orleans still needed time, time for Coffee and the Baton Rouge men to march to the city's aid, time to declare martial law, organize the Creoles, recruit the Baratarians, finish getting the forts in order, find crew for the *Louisiana*. With a raid on the enemy, *Macedonian* could provide a little time—even if that time was bought by *Macedonian*'s loss. Patterson, Jackson, and Favian all knew that the ultimate fate of *Macedonian* was a minor matter compared to the fate of New Orleans. If New Orleans could be bought a little time by sacrificing the frigate in a suicidal raid on Cochrane's fleet, then both Patterson and Jackson, their letters suggested, were willing to see the sacrifice made. But they were wise in the way of military formality and precedence, and they did not say it straight out.

Favian looked up from the letter, seeing the captured pirate craft still fighting to keep station as they headed for the Mississippi, seeing Poquelin standing politely by, seeing Lazarus, the mad preacher, looking at him with his strange, insinuant eyes. Lazarus had predicted all along that this voyage would end with disaster. Well, maybe it would. But the *Macedonian* was not a card Favian would throw away lightly.

He read on. "M. de Marigny, in General Jackson's absence, has persuaded Judge Hall to release the pirate Baratarians from prison, provided that they enlist in the service of the United States in this desperate hour. Several batteries of artillery are forming, and I have received a few men for the poor *Louisiana*, tho' not as many as I had hoped. It is intriguing to see these pirates swaggering up and down the streets of the city, protesting their devoted allegiance to a Nation whose laws they are so fond of violating."

Bernard de Marigny had repaid Jackson's slight by having released the men Jackson was so fond of denouncing, Favian thought, amused. It would work, he thought, to the city's benefit in the end, and perhaps to Jackson's—the general no longer had the dangerous burden of making the decision. Now that Marigny and Judge Hall had taken the initiative, Jackson could recruit the rest of the Baratarians, presumably including both Laffites, under the cloak of vox populi.

There was another letter from Claiborne, proclaiming the "Lion at the Gates," and calling the blessings of the Almighty and all his angels down on Favian's squadron—nothing important there; Favian knew that Claiborne's hour was over. The governor had been moved to the sidelines of history; now the fate of the city would be decided by Jackson, Patterson, and perhaps by Markham of the *Macedonian*. Plus, of course, the British.

Favian folded the letters and frowned. Poquelin would be taking the *Beaux Jours* back to New Orleans, and Favian's dispatches, already written for delivery to Claiborne, Jackson, and Patterson. Did this news require that he send acknowledgment? Perhaps so.

"Captain Poquelin, I'd be obliged if you'd carry some mail back to the city," Favian said. "I'll have to go below and dictate some letters—can you and your boat wait?"

"But of course, Commodore."

That title again. If he heard it much more often, Favian would forget to resent it. "Please hail *Beaux Jours* and tell them to follow in our wake," Favian said. "Mr. Seward, take us back to our station. I'm going below."

It was time to deal with Campaspe.

She seemed very much alone in Favian's cabin, very small, sitting nervously in her white gown, her bonnet lying before her on the table. Her eyes flickered nervously to his as he entered the room, and he hesitated before he came to sit beside her and took her hand.

"Did I do wrong?" she asked. "Captain Poquelin tried to talk me out of it, but I insisted. He was very nice to me on the trip, though."

"Campaspe, my dear," Favian began. "I can understand why you came. But it wasn't wise. I shall ask Captain Poquelin to take you back to New Orleans."

Her eyes widened for a moment, as if in fear; then he saw her lips narrow with defiance. "Favian, what if there is no New Orleans now? Jackson will burn it, you told me. I feel safer here, with you."

Should he tell her that *Macedonian* was a card that might shortly be thrown away to the enemy? That he might have to buy time with the lives of his crew, with his own life if it came to that? No: he would protect her from that knowledge. It seemed a little enough courtesy, perhaps the last he would ever offer her.

"This is a ship of war, my love," Favian said. "There isn't a place for you here. There isn't a place for any woman. Ships are dangerous for anyone who doesn't know them."

"I've been on ships before. I've been on Fontenoy's privateer."

Favian frowned: he'd forgotten her history. Even been in a battle, for heaven's sake.

"You were dressed as a boy. You're not a boy now, you're my wife."

She looked up at him nervously, her dark eyes wide. "I'm your wife," she repeated quickly, then took a breath, steeling herself. "If that's so, I should be here, not in New Orleans. If Maria-Anna hadn't been so far gone with child, she would have come with me. She's sailed with Gideon before; she was in the fight off Fort Bowyer, and with him in the Creek War. She's safer with Gideon than in New Orleans or Mobile. And I'm safer with you."

He recognized this stubbornness; he remembered, the morning he'd asked for her hand, that he'd heard the same tone in reply to Gideon's and Maria-Anna's objections. He'd admired it, then; now he knew facing it wasn't going to be easy. But this time her determined manner crumbled.

"I was so frightened for you!" Campaspe cried. "*And I missed you!*" She threw herself into his arms, pressing her face into his neck. He clasped his arms around her fiercely, hearing her gasps as she struggled for control. For everyone's sake, he thought, this madness had to end.

"Campaspe," he said gently. "You must go back with Poquelin. It's for the best, truly."

She fell back, swiping awkwardly with her fingers at the colored patches on her cheeks. "I'm not a good sailor's wife," she said. "When you're away I can't forget you, I can't forget a whole part of my life. You shouldn't have married me."

"Don't say that!" he said. "Don't ever say that!" She spoke the truth, most likely; but he didn't want her touching that truth, even by accident. He took her two hands in his own and spoke quickly. "We're sailing for the British, dear," he said. "It will be a dangerous situation. I will have to worry about this ship, all these men. I don't want to worry about you as well."

"I'll worry about *you,*" said Campaspe. "I'll die without knowing."

"Maria-Anna will take care of you," Favian went on, matter-of-factly. "She'll know what to do if the British come."

"Maria-Anna isn't there!" Campaspe cried. As Favian stared at her in surprise, she went on. "I have her letters to give to Gideon. When the British appeared, she decided to go to Mobile; she'll meet him there. She took her birthing stool and went north across Pontchartrain and then overland. She thought Mobile would be safer. She should be there in a few days."

Favian was taken aback by the news. Was New Orleans in such danger that sensible, hardheaded people like Maria-Anna were evacuating? Or was it simply that she wanted to get to her own house, her own property, before her child came?

"She wanted me to go with her," Campaspe said, a bit embarrassed. "She was angry when I said that I wouldn't."

"I'm not surprised," Favian said. He could imagine that scene, Maria-Anna firing her withering logic at the stubborn girl. But why did Maria-Anna run from the city? "Campaspe, tell me truly," he said. "Why did she leave? Did she think the British would take the city? Or did she want to visit her own property in Mobile before her time came?"

"Both, I think," Campaspe said. "Gideon wants to leave the South, take her to Portsmouth until the war is over. They were going to leave as soon as their prizes were sold. She was afraid the British would take the Head of the Passes and blockade the river. She knew the *Revenge* could get in and out of Mobile even with a blockade."

Yes, that made sense. Once Gideon had his wife's message, he would be running for Mobile—that would take him past the British fleet, but *Malachi's Revenge* could run away from any British ship in the world; there would be no danger there. New Orleans *was* a danger, he decided, if Maria-Anna had left. Campaspe would not go with Poquelin back to the city; he would give her to Gideon and let the *Revenge* take her to Mobile and then home to New England.

"I see," Favian said. "Then we're lucky. You won't have to return to New Orleans; you can go home with Gideon. Then go to stay with my family in New Hampshire. It will only be a journey of a few weeks in the *Revenge*."

Campaspe shook her head; the stubborn look was back. "If I'm going in any ship, it will be in yours," she said.

Favian realized he had to tell her what he'd hoped to spare her; there was no other way. He tried to keep his voice matter-of-fact. "There are over fifty British ships," Favian said. "Many of them are larger than mine. There's a good chance we won't win, but even if we lose it may help General Jackson." He shook his head. "I don't want to expose you to that. A beaten ship is a bad thing. And you would be taken prisoner. I don't want you a prisoner, Campaspe."

He put his arms around her, and he could feel her body steeling itself, readying the next protest. It came in a quiet, meditative voice that surprised him; this seemed no childish complaint, no girlish stubbornness, but gave rather the impression of a fully formed, mature decision. "Then I'll stay, dear," she said. Her eyes were calm. "I won't leave you. Can't. I'd go mad. Being a prisoner would be better."

"You don't know what you're saying."

She reached out to touch his cheek. "Of course I do." There was a slight, sad smile on her lips. "Don't worry about me. Just do what you must."

"I'll call Gideon, have him take you," Favian said. Through the stern cabin windows he saw *Beaux Jours* riding in the frigate's wake, ready to take his dispatches back to New Orleans. "I've got work to do now, Campaspe. Letters to write."

"I won't leave you."

"You swore to obey me," Favian said, bereft of any other argument.

"Then the Lord may strike me dead for breaking my oath, but I still won't leave you." Campaspe had a quiet, triumphant smile on her face, as if she knew the matter was settled. She turned to look around at his cabin, at the improvised cabin furniture, bought half in New London secondhand shops, half built by the ship's carpenter when the *Macedonian* hastened to leave the Thames after Favian's usurpation of command.

Favian looked at her sternly. "We will speak of this after Gideon comes." He left the cabin briefly, told Seward to heave the frigate to, and ordered Stanhope to fly the signal ordering all captains to report aboard.

In his cabin again, he wrote to Claiborne, Jackson, and Patterson, briefly acknowledging receipt of their dispatches. To Patterson he wrote that he hoped he would be able to relieve Lieutenant Jones; to Jackson he wrote that he hoped to commence annoying the British within a few days. He imagined Jackson's feral pleasure at the receipt of that message, the glow in the deep-set eyes. *War to the knife; knife to the hilt*. There was nothing, he realized now, to do but throw *Macedonian* at the foe. The frigate's appearance would surprise them, make them revise their plans, perhaps make them hesitate or blunder. All he could hope for. He looked up again at Campaspe. For a moment his mind swarmed with the images of the *Macedonian* beaten and rolling, as he'd first seen her, the frigate's decks awash with blood. He would have to get her away from this. Madness to let her stay.

He went on deck again, seeing *Malachi's Revenge* hove to off the port beam lowering a boat for Gideon. He handed his dispatches to Poquelin. "You may head back for New Orleans, sir," he said. "Good luck to you."

Poquelin looked at him carefully. "And your lady, Commodore?"

"She will take passage on the *Revenge*, yonder," Favian said.

"I see," Poquelin said. "I bid you farewell, Commodore. I wish you all possible success."

Favian saw his eyes; Poquelin knew it was hopeless. "I thank you, sir," he said, and saw the man over the rail.

Beaux Jours filled its sails and sped to the east just seconds before the *Revenge* hove alongside the frigate. "Favian," Gideon nodded in greeting as he stepped through the entry port; Favian took his arm and led him to the cabin, stopping on the way to give orders for the noon meal. As Gideon stepped into the cabin, he stopped short as he saw Campaspe and frowned.

"I brought a letter from Maria-Anna," Campaspe said, jumping up from her seat. She looked in the lining of her bonnet, brought out the envelope.

"Best read it first," Favian said. "We'll have time before Fontenoy comes. The letter will probably tell you why Campaspe is here, what the situation is. The British have arrived, Gideon."

"As the Lord wills," Gideon said, his mouth tightening. He took the letter, opened it as he walked to the stern windows, and stood alone, silhouetted darkly against the bright light as he read his wife's words. Concluding, he looked up for a long moment, still facing aft; he seemed to be at prayer.

"I think she's done a wise thing," he said finally, and turned to look at Campaspe. "You're a fool, girl," he said.

"I've heard from Jackson," Favian said. "There are at least fifty sail anchored off Cat Island in the Mississippi Sound. I'm going for them, probably tomorrow night. That will give you a chance to get into Mobile while I'm keeping the British busy."

Gideon nodded, the frown still on his face. "Fontenoy's privateer won't swim; she'll still have to go up the river. He can take the prizes with him; they'll be as safe at New Orleans as anywhere in the Gulf." He looked up at Favian, speaking earnestly. "I'll support ye, of course. When ye strike the British."

Favian felt sudden warm, gratified surprise; there was no way he could have expected a privateer to help him in this quixotic attack. "Gideon," he said."I'm grateful beyond measure. You're taking a risk for your country, beyond—" He would have said, *beyond what any Navy man could expect in a privateer*, but stopped himself in time. "I would never have—" he essayed again.

Gideon waved his hand. "The Lord may provide profit in this," he said. "If I can make prize of a few transports, the head money alone will pay for it. And if the British are so alarmed they spend all their time guarding their convoy, they won't be blockading me in Mobile."

Very well. If Gideon wanted to disguise this generosity with a profit motive, let him. Favian hoped that *Revenge*, at least, would get away: with luck it would.

There was a military tramp overhead, followed by the shrill

of pipes. "That's Fontenoy," Favian said. He waited for the knock at the door, then stood. Midshipman Lovette, his arm still bound in a sling from his encounter with Levesque, opened the door for the Mauritian to enter; like Gideon before him, Fontenoy hesitated when he saw Campaspe, then walked into the cabin; she smiled graciously as he kissed her hand. Favian wondered if she'd been practicing her gracious smiles.

"Mr. Lovette," Favian said, "would you be so kind as to take Mrs. Markham to the wardroom, give them my compliments, and ask them to offer her their hospitality for the next hour or so? My dear, I hope you will excuse us."

Campaspe rose, curtsying to Lovette's bow. "I would rather have a tour of the ship, if I may," she said. Favian found himself surprised by her accent; it was a surprisingly successful imitation of the languid, affected way the Creole women in New Orleans spoke their English. She *had* been practicing a genteel act and had also demonstrated a good ear.

"If you're not otherwise occupied, Mr. Lovette," Favian said. It was courtesy only; midshipmen had no set duties and served entirely at the pleasure of their seniors.

"Of course, sir," Lovette smiled. "I'm not much good for anything else at the moment." He bowed to Campaspe, she bobbed a curtsy, and they left the room, Campaspe still acting the gracious lady. In the company of *Macedonian*'s mids, Favian thought, he gave that ladylike act about three minutes. He was proved right: very shortly he heard a peal of feminine laughter through his skylight, mixed with the polite laughter of at least three of the midshipmen. It appeared they had made prize of his wife. He hoped they would not encourage her in her notion of staying aboard.

"The British have arrived, Captain Fontenoy," Favian said. "They're anchored off Cat Island, near Lake Borgne."

"I see," Fontenoy said, frowning. He fingered the odd weapon at his waist, his fighting iron, and then looked up, first at Gideon, then at Favian.

"You will attack them?" he asked. Favian smiled inwardly; this man knew Gideon very well, better than Favian himself.

"Aye," Gideon said briefly.

"Tomorrow night," Favian said. "We know your *Franklin* is in no condition to join us. I think it would be best if you convoyed our prizes to New Orleans. You can't get them to

Mobile or Pensacola without danger; New Orleans is by far the safest place.'' Fontenoy seemed caught by contradictory emotions, relief at the knowledge he was not expected to participate in the attack on fifty enemy, regret at missing the possible prize money. ''Once in New Orleans you can get *Franklin* repaired and then act as seems best to you,'' Favian said.

''Very well,'' Fontenoy said. ''I understand.''

''I hope,'' Favian said, ''that you may find room for Mrs. Markham on your vessel.'' He turned to Gideon. ''I was going to ask her to travel with you, Gideon, but if you're coming with us in the attack . . .''

''New Orleans is the best place for her,'' Gideon said. ''Tell her to head for Mobile after she arrives.''

''I will give Mrs. Markham my own cabin and take my rest in the chart room,'' Fontenoy said. He smiled. ''I've had her aboard once before, you know. She was a brave little powder monkey.''

There were more tramplings and whistlings: Lieutenant Cunningham, of the gunboat, coming aboard. Favian called to Crane, his steward, for charts of the area, and then for coffee. The four captains spent an hour working over the maps, working out plans for attack on the British anchorage. Cunningham was to accompany Fontenoy as far as Fort St. Philip, where he would anchor and prepare to support the fort against any British attack on the river. *Macedonian* and the *Revenge* would part from the convoy at the Southwest Pass of the Mississippi, then sail in a wide curve around the delta, the Chandeleur Islands, and into the narrow gap between the northernmost of the Chandeleurs and Ship Island on the Mississippi Sound to strike at the British anchorage. That gap worried Favian: it was only ten miles across and could be sealed off behind them once they entered. He was uncertain whether the frigate had any other way out; the Chandeleur Sound seemed too shallow for his frigate, and he didn't want to chance the Mississippi Sound without a pilot.

''Sir, I can send you a man, a master's mate named Stephens,'' Cunningham said. ''He's sailed with gunboats in the Mississippi Sound for years. He's not a regular pilot, but he knows the water.''

''Sailing in a frigate, with a pilot used to boats that draw only three feet of water,'' said Gideon, ''may be more dangerous than sailing without a pilot altogether. Ye draw eighteen feet, Favian, and that Stephens may not know the water beyond the fact that parts of the sound are deeper than a fathom."

"He's a little better than that, sir," Cunningham said, defensive.

"I'll take him," Favian said. "I hope I won't have to chance the Mississippi Sound at all, but if I do, I suppose I can always disregard his advice."

"Shall I have my boat fetch him, sir?"

"Very well."

Crane entered, while Cunningham was out, to report that dinner was ready, "dinner" being the noon meal, at present served closer to the hour of two.

"Good," Favian said. "I think we've made all the plans we can, at least until we see the enemy. Clear away the charts, Crane, and then ask Mrs. Markham to join us."

"Certainly, sir."

Campaspe entered with a streak of slime on the hem of her gown, which she tried futilely to clean with a napkin; she explained it came from the cable tier.

"The cable tier?" Favian asked. That was far below the waterline, where the anchor cables had been stored just that morning, hauled dripping from the mud. "What were you doing down there?"

"I wanted to see the ship," she said with a laughing smile that Favian had seen once before, and which made him instantly suspicious.

She was smiling and charming throughout dinner, her eyes sparkling, her cheeks bronzed a bit with the sun. There was an undertone that made Favian uneasy, but nothing clear he could point to; in the end he decided it was the sea air, the sun, and the company of midshipmen nearer her own age than the stern captains gathered in his cabin. After their meal, Lieutenant Cunningham was sent to rejoin his gunboat, and Gideon then took his leave. He took Campaspe's hand.

"Try to make for Mobile if the British haven't got above the city," he said. "We can join you there. I wish ye hadn't been separated from Maria-Anna. If there is confusion in the city, and you can't decide what to do, seek out Pastor Hobbs at the Presbyterian chapel."

"Thank you, Captain Gideon," she said. "I'll follow your advice, I'm sure."

He looked at her carefully, his eyes narrowed; clearly he was suspecting some plot as well. "Pay attention to yer husband, girl," he said, then looked at Favian. "Good luck, Favian."

"And to you." Favian turned to the French privateer. "Captain Fontenoy, I hope you will excuse Mrs. Markham and me. We'd like to say our farewells."

"Of course, Commodore. Madame Markham." He kissed her hand again, Campaspe smiling merrily at the gesture, and then made his way out of the cabin. Favian looked at his bride.

"Let me stay, Favian," she said quietly. Her eyes were full of he knew not what: hope, anxiety, some secret of her own he could not penetrate. "I want to be with you in this."

Slowly, he shook his head. "You must go with Fontenoy to New Orleans," he said. "It's for the best. Truly."

She came forward and took his hands, then leaned her head on his breast. "I'll go if I must," she said. "I spoke to Lovette and Tolbert; they told me I could not stay, there was no place for me."

"Did they indeed?" That was a surprise. Favian would have thought they would have been in love with the idea of the captain's young wife joining them on the voyage. And, though he could imagine Tolbert preaching on behalf of a discipline that he, Tolbert, had never put into practice himself, he couldn't imagine Campaspe swallowing it.

"Favian, I don't want to go in Fontenoy's boat," said Campaspe. "I'm a captain's wife, and I want to go in the captain's boat, with all your crew and cox'n. And one of those midshipmen as escort."

"If that's what you want, dearest." Her arms went around him; they held each other for a long minute, their bodies swaying gently with the scend of the sea. There was something wrong here, but Favian could not tell what it was. Why the devil was she suddenly so concerned about her status?

Favian continued to be troubled throughout the rest of the good-bye: as Fontenoy went ahead to get his cabin ready, as a boat was swung out and Campaspe's baggage put into it, as Favian kissed her farewell, there by the entry port in front of the honor guard, receiving an extra little twist of pleasure from kissing her in front of men who hadn't seen a woman for months now . . . It was Campaspe's dazzling smile, her famous smile, that troubled him most, the smile that flashed out over the boat's stern sheets as it pulled away for the *Franklin;* it suddenly occurred to him that he hadn't seen the smile all day and that there was something wrong in seeing it now, when she was leaving against her will.

He smiled and waved back. Campaspe was off the frigate and could not come back; so what could the smile mean? He stood on the quarterdeck, watching through one of the quartermasters' long glasses as Campaspe and baggage were swung aboard the *Franklin,* as Killick and Tolbert stepped aboard as her escort. Well, that was done.

He paced, irritated, until the boat began its journey back. The boat stayed an inordinately long time, until Favian was tempted to fire a gun to signal its recall—but then he thought that perhaps Campaspe was complaining about her accommodations, and that if that were the case he had best not try Fontenoy's patience any further by rudeness in signaling. Eventually the boat began its progress back to the frigate, and Favian, before going down to his cabin, gave curt orders to Seward to get *Macedonian* back to its station. He would try to get some sleep; it was clear that tomorrow night he would get none.

It was some hours later, after he'd slept for three hours, signaled farewell to Fontenoy and the convoy off the Southwest Pass, and took the frigate out into the deepening evening with *Malachi's Revenge* ranging ahead as a scout, after the hands had eaten their supper and had their evening whiskey ration, that he realized how he'd been fooled. Grim as the Angel of Death in his black coat, he rushed down the quarterdeck ladder, then went down the hatch to the gun deck. The little candle in the first battle lantern he picked up had melted in the tropical heat and fell over, snuffing itself; he hurled it aside with a curse. The next candle stayed alight, and he rushed along the guns, startled seamen stepping aside with grunts of surprise and half-sketched salutes, knowing with a single glance at his anger that the quarterdeck was in a flogging mood and it would be wise to step warily around the captain for the next few days.

Favian went down another hatch, between the swaying hammocks of the berth deck, then through a bulkhead and down another hatch. The smells of the cable tier assaulted him: bottom ooze, decaying vegetation, wet hemp.

"Campaspe," he said. "Come out. At once."

* * *

It had been quite neatly done; he had to admit it. The conspiracy had been plotted while Favian and his council of war were laying their own plans. Killick and Tolbert had been the active agents, though no doubt the entire ship knew the scheme by heart by the time the next watch was called. Campaspe had been delivered, all smiles, to her new quarters on the *Franklin*, announced that she was tired and had a headache, and asked not to be disturbed. Killick, to delay things, had asked for a tour of the snow from Fontenoy's lieutenant; while Killick was admiring the neatly worked stropping on the privateer's runner blocks, Campaspe had been dressing herself in midshipman's gear, trousers, jacket, and round hat.

And then had come the most extraordinary piece of diversion, demonstrating that whoever had come up with the plan—Killick or Stanhope, Favian thought—had a fine tactical mind and would probably go far in the Navy if he survived the stern right arm of Sailing Master Seward. Mr. Midshipman George Killick had, at a signal from Tolbert, jumped up onto *Franklin*'s capstan and began to lift his fine tenor voice to the heavens. He'd chosen the perfect song, old Charles Dibdin's "Tom Bowling," a lachrymose, sentimental, popular, and very long ballad about the death of a young sailor. While the privateers stood about in various stages of amazement, and Killick was sobbing out the chorus with hands clasped piteously to his breast and a manly tear glinting in his eye, Tolbert and Campaspe slipped quietly out of the aft scuttle and slid into the waiting boat. Killick, finishing wailing "His soul is gone aloft," bowed, thanked his audience, and jumped for the boat.

There was no trouble getting Campaspe aboard *Macedonian;* the officers and crew present were more interested in getting the pinnace aboard and the frigate put before the wind than in counting heads. Campaspe had saluted the officer of the deck carefully, keeping her hat in front of her face, which was probably unnecessary because Swink was very likely not paying any attention to the midshipmen anyway. She then nipped below to the cable tier, where the thoughtful mids had gone so far as to provide her a pair of lanterns and a picnic lunch done up in a steel box to keep the rats away.

The discovery of the captain's wife hiding in the cable tier had set in motion a number of inquiries. Chapelle, now acting as executive officer on the absence, death, or incapacity of all three of his seniors, had grilled the gunroom thoroughly. Tolbert and Killick had cheerfully confessed, and Stanhope had admitted his complicity—it was dishonorable, of course, to lie to one's superior about a matter as trivial as this. While the guilty mids were bent over one of the aft eighteen-pounders and given two dozen cuts each from Mr. Seward's cane, the master-at-arms, Martin Herzog, had been interrogating the boat's crew. Each, from Kuusikoski down, admitted knowledge of Campaspe's delivery to the *Macedonian* but affected to have been surprised by her appearance, denied participation in any conspiracy, and said they'd simply been obeying orders from their superiors, Tolbert and Killick. Favian's initial impulse to flog them till their backbones showed moderated swiftly; he remembered the way they'd stood up bravely to the Guard's bayonets on Timbalier Island, and in the end stopped their liquor ration for a week. Most likely even that would prove no hardship; no doubt the midshipmen's berth would be slipping them whiskey. Killick had also lost his acting-lieutenancy; Favian would consult with Chapelle on a substitute.

Favian had been tempted to let Campaspe watch the midshipmen's punishment but decided against it. Instead he'd invite the young men to join him at breakfast tomorrow and watch them squirm in their hard, straight-backed chairs—they'd be doing no sitting down for some days, he was certain. Perhaps the worst of it was that Favian could not get the words and music to "Tom Bowling" out of his head, and the constant mental repetition of the syrupy lyrics had him grating his teeth.

Yet shall poor Tom find pleasant weather,
When He, who all commands,
Shall give, to call life's crew together,
The word to pipe all hands.
Thus Death, who kings and tars dispatches,
In vain Tom's life has doff'd,
For, though his body's under hatches,
His soul has gone aloft.
His soul has gone aloft.

There was a silent late supper with Campaspe. She was dressed in the one gown she'd brought with her, wrapped in a sailor's bundle; her smile broke out frequently as she dawdled over her plate. "I'll have to go on deck for a few minutes," he said, pushing back his chair; and with an impulsive move she seized his hand.

"I want to be your wife always," she said, her eyes upturned, imploring. "Not just when you're on shore. Please understand."

"I'll be back in a few minutes," he repeated, and went on deck. He checked the set of the sails, the estimated position and speed chalked by the officer of the deck on the slate, and paced for a few minutes on the weather quarterdeck before being interrupted by Talthibius Solomon.

"Sir," Solomon said. "It's been two days. I would like to repeat my request, sir."

"Accepted, Doc—Mr. Solomon," Favian said. "Hand your resignation to my clerk tomorrow; he'll do the necessary paperwork."

"Very well, sir." Solomon made as if to leave, then hesitated. "I hope, Captain Markham, that you will allow me one last exercise of my chaplain's privileges—my eleemosynary duties, as you once called them."

"What, sir, is the nature of this exercise?" asked Favian, having a good idea.

"To inquire whether all is well between your lovely bride and yourself?"

"That," Favian said coldly, "should remain between myself and my bride, don't you think?"

"She's a lonely young girl, you know," Solomon said, refusing to accept his dismissal. "Only been married one night before you went away. She knows she has no rivals but the Navy, and it was the Navy she wanted to deceive. Not yourself."

"I *am* the Navy in these waters, Mr. Solomon," Favian said. "Get the hell off my quarterdeck."

"Aye aye, sir."

Favian turned and frowned at the frigate's wake. What rankled was not, he knew, the fact that Campaspe had made a fool of him—he could live with that, even laugh at it; he knew it would make a good story in wardroom messes for years to come—rather it was that she was here at all. He had hoped to busy himself with the Navy, forget the fact of his unfortunate marriage, at least for a while. Now he was confronted by his own folly and adversity, confronted by its physical presence in the form of Campaspe, and he knew he was not ready for it. He had needed a breathing space, a piece of time buried in military abstraction, and he had not got enough.

He nodded to Lieutenant Ford, who was keeping watch, and went below. Campaspe, still sitting at the table that Crane had cleared while he was out, looked up as he came in.

"Was everything ataunto?" she asked. A word she had picked up from Gideon, no doubt.

"Aye," Favian said. "We're doing eight knots. Not bad in this damn Gulf wind."

"Davis brought a pot of cocoa. I thought you might like some."

"Thank you." He sat down at the table, and she poured cups of cocoa. They sipped in silence.

"Campaspe," he said. "Don't do this again. I could laugh at it, but others won't. If the men see the captain's authority flouted successfully, they might try it themselves. And then I'd have to punish them."

"I'm sorry," she said. "Not for what I did. But for any punishments, yes."

"Don't feel too sorry over the mids; they were just caned. They knew they'd be caned when they agreed to help you. But if one of the seamen misbehaves, I may have to have him tied to a grating and flog him with a cat. That's not so delicate an operation."

"No," she said. Her voice was low, subdued.

"I can't," Favian said, "blame the midshipmen for falling a little in love with you. But it was wicked to use them."

"Yes," she said. "I've often been wicked. But it's always been for love, Favian."

"Not always. Remember M. Listeau."

She smiled. "That was a special case. Revenge. Fontenoy called me ugly last year when Gideon took me out of the *Franklin*."

"That was ungallant of him," Favian said. "And untrue."

She seemed touched by his compliment. "Thank you, Favian." She took his hand. "No matter what happens, I'm happy to be here with you." He knew a cue when he heard it.

If, he thought as he carried her to his cot, there were sweeter ways to make up a quarrel, he had yet to find them. Her eyes shone as she turned her head up to receive his kiss, and he felt her fingers eagerly plucking at his clothing as he got rid of it. Favian's bed, built by the ship's carpenter, was long enough to hold him—the first ever in his long career that didn't require him to fold up like a clasp knife when he went to sleep—but the bed was chastely narrow, and there didn't seem room enough for elbows and knees; the movement of the sea provided a few surprises until they got used to it. Campaspe was a little more venturesome than before, beginning to understand her capacity for pleasure and her power over it: a little more practice and this could be a lot of fun!

The narrow cot forced them to lie in one another's arms; it was still very warm in the close cabin, and Favian eventually found an old shirt and put it on so they wouldn't keep sticking together. She wrapped herself around him and put her head on his shoulder. He kissed her lazily.

"Aren't you glad you didn't send me off with Fontenoy?" she said with a sly smile.

"Tonight I'm glad. Tomorrow night, when we pitch into the British, I won't be glad at all."

"It's a big ship. There's room for me here."

"The Navy frowns on taking ladies into combat. There have been some bad examples."

"Really? Who?" Interested, she propped her head up on her arm and looked at him quizzically.

Favian frowned. It was not customary to discuss Navy affairs with outsiders. "There was a man named Morris, Commodore Richard Valentine Morris," he said. The story was public knowledge, anyway. "Held command off Tripoli for a time. His wife liked the society in European ports, so that's where the fleet spent most of its time. That's the story, anyway."

"Did you ever meet him?"

"Morris? Aye, and his wife, and his son, and the colored slave girl they took with them. I had two cruises in the Mediterranean under Morris, but on the first I had a mad captain who ignored all his orders and never made contact with the commodore. The second cruise, in the *Vixen*, there was a dinner in Palermo that Morris gave for the junior officers. I'm afraid we were all rather contemptuous of him by then, and it showed. He was relieved right afterward."

"A mad captain? I've met one!" Campaspe cried. "Captain Addams of the *Prinsessa*! His men mutinied. Gideon saved all our lives." She looked at him with a grin. "Addams was a drunk," she said. "But he's teetotal now, serving as a sailor on the *Revenge*. What was your mad captain like?"

"Daniel McNeil?" Favian repressed a shudder. That had been his first cruise and only the resilience and fervor of his youth had got him through it. "He may have been a drunk, but if he was it didn't show. He was just crazy. Sailed all over the Mediterranean, never made contact with the commodore. Marooned three of his officers in France, and kidnapped three French officers to take their place. They didn't suit either, so he stranded them in Algiers. He was dismissed the service at the end of the cruise. I heard he joined the Coast Guard."

"Are there any mad captains in the Navy now?"

"Nay. Not since Commodore Preble took command in the Mediterranean. After that the Navy knew what a good captain looked like."

"I've heard of Preble," Campaspe said. "Lieutenant Blake used to talk about him."

"Bull Blake? I heard he was on the New Orleans station. I served with him on the Delaware, in gunboats."

"His gunboat used to be stationed at Mobile. Gideon and him are friends."

"He and Gideon."

"He and Gideon are friends." Smiling, doing her lazy Creole dialect. The rich-planter tones faded, and she spoke rapidly. "He's jealous of you because you were with Preble and he wasn't. He says that Preble's Boys look out for one another."

"You shouldn't have told me that," Favian said.

"Isn't it true?"

"Perhaps it is. Preble ran a good school, and the graduates have been outstanding. Decatur, Jones, Lawrence, Hull, Bainbridge, Porter . . ."

"Markham," Campaspe said promptly.

He smiled. "Markham. Very well. But what Blake said to Gideon was in confidence. It shouldn't be repeated."

"I don't mind," she said, "if people are jealous of you." She looked at him, her eyes bright as a sparrow's, then went on. "Did you do well at Cat Island? I forgot to ask." She frowned, her eyes narrowing. "Your body went all stiff when I asked you that." She touched his arm. "Didn't it go well?"

"Well enough," he said. "We lost some men. Lieutenant Eastlake—he was at the wedding, remember? Some others."

"I'm sorry." She kissed him gravely. "If you don't want to talk about it . . ."

Favian tried to smile. "There are better things to talk about." There was a fatalistic lesson in Navy deaths, seen in the random spread of grapeshot or cannister. It could happen to anyone, to anyone who wore the uniform, and at any time; if the sentry in that sand fort had been a little more alert, it could have been Favian lying in a grave at the water's edge instead of Eastlake. A man with Favian's experience could reduce the risk, but could never end it altogether. Favian had been at Navy wakes. There was a secret in those insensate debauches: that the uniformed men were mourning their own deaths as well, knowing it could easily have been them on the *Intrepid* when it was blown up off Tripoli or standing on the quarterdeck of the *Chesapeake* when Broke's broadside tore it to pieces . . . The secret was brutal and somehow cherished; it was one Favian hoped to keep from Campaspe's knowledge. It was a thing the young should not share. Not knowing it, he thought, would be a mercy to her.

"All right." Campaspe smiled, a little nervously. "I didn't want to—" She tossed her head. "Never mind."

"It went well enough," Favian insisted.

Campaspe nodded, tight-lipped. There was a heavy silence. Favian fiddled self-consciously with the blanket. Campaspe put her arms around him, held him tightly. "I love you," she whispered. "I really do." Favian had the sensation she was speaking to herself rather than him. He touched her hair.

"You're scared," she said. Her voice was close to his ear. "That's all right."

He felt himself stiffen and couldn't help it. Damn this narrow cot! He had to speak. "Afraid for you, perhaps," he said. Campaspe said nothing, her cheek pressed to his neck; he added, "That's not it, fear. I've been through this kind of thing many times. It's the Navy. It's what I do. You'll understand some day."

"So cold," she said; again there was that unearthly feeling she was speaking to herself. "So cold. That's all right, my darling."

Bewildered, he let her clasp him; he could feel the moist warmth of her breath against his neck. "I've been through it, remember?" she said after a pause. "I was on the *Franklin* when we fought a British schooner. We got beat. Fontenoy managed to get alongside, and we tried to board three times, failed each time.

Fontenoy was wild, went bright red. The *Franklin* was all he had. Gideon finally saved us.'' She kissed his neck, propped her head up on her hand again. She shuddered. ''It was awful. Blood everywhere. I was carrying powder. Tried to carry a cutlass with the boarders, but I got stepped on, so I hid behind a gun till it was over. The smell was the worst. You know what I mean.''

Yes. Warm blood, torn bowel, fear. One never forgot. ''You shouldn't have been there,'' he said. ''It must have been terrible for you.''

''Same for me as for anyone. At least I didn't get hurt.'' Campaspe took his hand in both of hers. ''Favian,'' she said. ''Give me something to do tomorrow night, when you meet the British. I don't want to sit in the cable tier alone.''

''I can't, darling. There's no place.''

Her dark hair fell across her face. She tossed her head. ''I'll carry powder again. It's better than sitting in the dark and *remembering*. I don't want to think; I'd rather have something to keep me busy.''

''There's no place,'' he said.

Campaspe dropped his hand and frowned. She leaned back and pushed her hair back from her face; for a moment Favian saw her young, rounded breast, pink-nippled, not yet mature . . . there was an odd tenderness that touched his thoughts, not erotic but in a strange way fraternal. Good God, he realized, she would rather risk getting killed than sit in the dark with the guns going off, sitting with only her imagination for company. Risk her young body, her promise. Nothing, of course, he hadn't done at the same age; but the circumstances had been far different. He had worn the uniform, had taken joy in the risk, the chances for glory. Favian saw none of that midshipman eagerness in her eyes. ''I'll talk to Dr. Truscott, the surgeon,'' he said. ''Maybe there will be a place in the cockpit. With the wounded, you understand? It won't, ah . . .''

''It won't be pleasant,'' Campaspe finished. ''I know.'' She hugged him again, her arms around his neck. ''Thank you, Favian. I'll try to be brave.''

''I know you will,'' he responded; it was the sort of thing captains said. She lowered her eyes and flushed red.

''I hope you're right,'' she said. Her voice was very faint. ''I'm very frightened, you know.'' She looked up at him. ''How was it for you?'' she asked. ''What was it like, that first fight?''

"It was a duel," Favian said. The incident was famous, both in and out of the Navy, but he had never spoken of it, not of this or any of his fights. "In Spain, arranged by the *Vixen*'s lieutenant. Pistols. There was a Spanish ship there that had insulted us, so he challenged their ship on behalf of ours." He had been seventeen, on his second Mediterranean cruise. The memory was vivid: the scent of the orange grove where the fight took place, the look of the darkening bark as the combatants all voided their bladders against a tree to prevent medical complications in case they were hit in the groin, the strange intensity with which the Spanish *guardiamarina* was viewed over Favian's quaking pistol . . . Favian remembered his absolute terror, the taste of bile in his throat, the way his fear was mingled with fury, a rage that denounced the duel, the Spanish, the Navy, the officers who had arranged this without consulting him. It was the anger, he supposed, that had got him through it.

"I missed," he said. "One of our midshipmen was wounded. Our lieutenant shot his man dead. Honor," he said, wondering if the irony he felt was audible in his voice, "was satisfied."

"How do they do it? Arrange a duel, I mean." He felt her nestle against him; he stroked her flank with his scarred hand.

"It's very formal, all written in the codes," he said. "Their ship had fired its guns at our captain when he was being rowed ashore, so our lieutenant went aboard the Spanish ship and called them all cowards. Then their second lieutenant, who was acting as their second, came aboard *Vixen* to talk with our master, who was *our* second, and the terms were arranged. Next morning we marched out into an orange grove and fought."

"So you had to do what this master and the Spanish lieutenant had arranged. You had no choice?"

"No. If you refuse the second's arrangements, the second can challenge you himself. That's why you have to choose a clever second, so he doesn't give away too many advantages and force you to refuse and fight another duel. Ours was clever enough, I suppose. Arranged for pistols at twenty paces so that most of us would miss; nobody wanted a ship full of cripples. I wanted it to be swords, though."

"Why?"

"I was good with a sword, less so with a pistol. Since then I've got better with pistols." He smiled at the memory. "I was angry when I saw my opponent. He was so clumsy I knew I could have won a swordfight in a few seconds. Instead the code required that I stand up like a scarecrow and let him shoot at me. It's not something I ever intend to do again."

He felt her shudder through his hand. "Horrible," Campaspe said. "Why did your captain ever allow such a thing?"

"He knew we'd have to face fire sooner or later. Wanted to give us a taste of it, maybe. We were so eager we would have fought even if the captain had forbidden it."

"Is that why you let that man Solomon fight his duel? And Mr. Lovette?"

"I don't like duelling," Favian said. "I especially don't like the way it's practiced here, with a few bullies swaggering around provoking fights. I tried to arrange Lovette's duel so it wouldn't hurt anyone. I disapproved of Solomon's duel, but there was nothing I could do to prevent it." Campaspe's eyes were only a few inches from his, gleaming softly in the lamplight; she seemed totally absorbed in his words. Their physical intimacy allowed him to feel the play of her muscles, hear her heartbeat and the regular, gentle suspiration of her breath. The situation seemed to encourage candor. "Duelling isn't necessary, and I won't encourage it," he said. "But it's a thing that happens. It's possible to get backed into it, and then honor demands a fight. My first duel was fought because the Spanish had insulted the United States, and the Navy has to stand up for our country. My second was fought against a man who slandered the Navy, knowing I'd have to fight him."

"That Captain Brewster," Campaspe said. "I heard Gideon mention him once."

"That was the man. A bully and a drunk." If she knew the name, he thought, she knew the result: a hasty burial and a warrant out in New Jersey. He spoke on. "I don't think anyone mourned his passing."

"I don't think it's fair," Campaspe said. Her swift indignation was plain. "That you should have to fight like that—it's not like you're fighting for yourself. Why should you have to accept a fight for the Navy?"

The question struck home; his own resentments were clear enough on that point. He composed his answer carefully. "There's not much of a Navy man's life that's private," he said. "We represent the Navy in the people's minds, and the Navy's been under attack—the Republicans wanted to plain abolish us, and there are other people who resent us for other reasons. They look for weaknesses in us so they can justify an attack on the Navy."

There was anger in Campaspe's eyes. "I won't!" she said. "I won't let you be used in that way! They'll have to fight me first!"

"I'll keep you away from that," Favian said. "I'll be careful, truly."

Campaspe hit him, not lightly, in the chest with her fist. "No! Damn!" she shouted. "I won't!" He captured her hand, wondering if they could hear her through the skylight. "No more of this fighting! Let the Navy defend its own goddamn honor!"

It was what he'd said to Solomon; now the words came back to him. So did something else said to Solomon, something he'd said just that evening: "I *am* the Navy in these waters."

Campaspe was looking at him with angry eyes. "Hey," she said. "I won't go away. Goddamn, answer me."

"What must I say? That I won't fight any more duels?" Favian asked. "I can't make that promise, no one can."

She struggled to free her hand; he hung on. "Bah," she said. "I don't want a promise like that, I know how much it'd be worth. I don't want any fighting in secret, that's all. I'm your wife."

"I don't understand."

"Keep me out of it and I'll kill you myself," she said. "Understand?"

"It doesn't have to be your fight," Favian said. "I don't want you involved in that way. It could hurt you."

She shook her head. "No. Not my way," she said. "You fight the British, and I come with you. You get called out someday, and I come with you. That's my way."

He looked across the few inches at Campaspe's vehement features, and for some reason Maria-Anna came into his mind. Was Campaspe's ferocity learned from Maria-Anna? he wondered. He had admired Maria-Anna's plainspokenness, her decisive nature; he knew she formed a unique partnership with Gideon. Was this part of the compromise she had exacted?

"Very well," he said. "You'll know." He felt her relax; he let go of her fist. She hugged him again, kissed his cheek.

"I love you, Favian," she said. "I won't let you go. Not for some quarrel about the Navy."

"Campaspe. It's late."

"I think I'd like some cocoa," she said, and crawled over him to the table and filled her cup. "It's cold," she said. "Would you like some?"

"No. Thank you." Campaspe drank her cocoa, her body gleaming whitely against the dark furnishings of the room. She turned to him, reaching out with her free hand to touch a chair. "I've never been naked with a man," she said.

"I should hope not!" he said. She grinned.

"It feels strange, standing here with you looking at me," she said. She put the cocoa aside and walked to him, then crouched by the cot and took his hand, regarding him intently. "How does it feel for you?" she asked.

"I think you're very lovely," he said.

Campaspe's head came back, and she flashed her impudent smile. "I think I like it," she said. "Being here in front of you. You don't think it's forward of me, do you?"

"No."

He watched as she stood, and then began to dance around the cabin—leaping, doing dizzying, inexpert pirouettes, then collapsed giggling onto the thwartship settee. Favian, following an impulse he could not quite trace to its source, got out of bed and walked to her, then crouched and kissed her laughing face.

"I think I like it, too," he said. She hugged him, arms around his neck.

"I don't want you to regret me," Campaspe said.

"I don't," he said; it was strange that he didn't feel it to be an insincerity. Favian kissed her suddenly, with an ardency that surprised him. She tasted sweetly of cocoa.

"Oh," she said. "Are you—?" She laughed. "Can we do this more than once each night?"

"It's impolite to count," he said, "but we can if you like."

Her laugh came close to his ear. He would regret it tomorrow, he supposed, but for the present he was more than content that Campaspe should be here.

NINETEEN

The changing watch woke Favian the next morning, before dawn. *Macedonian* had a different watch schedule than other Navy ships, one of the innovations Captain Jacob Jones had made before he'd been reassigned to the Great Lakes and given Favian the chance to steal the frigate. Most changed watches every four hours, giving the men breakfast at eight, dinner at noon, and supper at four. Jones's innovation had been to break the day into two six-hour watches, from six to noon, noon to six, then keep the rest of the day on four-hour watches. This not only alleviated the problem of the hands going twelve hours at a stretch without a meal, but allowed the watches to rotate daily in a normal manner, and made certain that the off-duty watch, in the daytime, could get six hours uninterrupted sleep at need.

Thus it was just before six, rather than at eight, that Favian was awakened by the quartermasters calling up the midshipmen, mates, and lieutenant of the other watch. Accustomed to being shaken awake at odd hours, Favian was alert instantly; he was aware of Campaspe's warmth against him, the scent of her hair, the way she had absently clasped his hand to her breast—her back was to him; they were cuddled like spoons on their sides—he glanced at the telltale compass over his head, mentally gauged, through the motion of the ship, its heading and probable speed. The stern windows showed it was still dark, though the beginnings of dawn could not be far away. As there were standing orders to call him at first light, Favian knew there was no point in going back to sleep.

"Campaspe. Darling," he whispered. He stroked her gently.

"Mm." She turned to him, stretching lazily, her arm going around his neck. He kissed her.

"I've got to get up. You should get dressed because I'm going to call the ship to quarters before dawn. You can go back to sleep after breakfast if you like." He was going to have every gun manned, every man standing to his station before the eastern sky lightened. The sun might rise to show them in the middle of a British convoy, and he wanted to be ready. Calling the hands to quarters would also mean breaking down the screen between his cabin and the frigate's gun deck and moving all his furniture below; the thought of leering tars breaking in on the captain and his naked wife lolling about in their cot was a little hard to contemplate this early in the morning.

"All right." She kissed him again, then opened her eyes.

"When I call quarters, I'll send a midshipman to escort you to the cockpit," Favian said. "Take one of my heavy coats from the locker; it'll be cold down there. Or you can come on deck with me. It'll be colder on deck, though."

"I'll come with you," Campaspe said.

They dressed. Favian could hear the men being mustered and sent to breakfast; he called to Crane for coffee and shaving water. A cup of coffee in hand, Favian kissed Campaspe good-bye and came up on deck, shrugging deeply into his pea jacket as the cold wind began to cut into him. He glanced at the set of the sails, received the salute of Ford, the officer of the watch, and took his stance on the weather quarterdeck. *Macedonian* was on a beam reach, heading to the northeast, the Mississippi Delta somewhere on the larboard beam. Except for the lookouts, Ford, and the quartermasters, the frigate's deck was deserted; the rest of the crew were having breakfast.

Campaspe, dwarfed by an old green coat she'd found in Favian's locker and wearing one of his undress round hats, came on the quarterdeck just as the men were finishing breakfast. When Ford saluted her she replied with a curtsy and almost went flying into the monkey rail when the frigate was caught by a crosswave and gave an unexpected lunge. Campaspe laughed, declined Ford's offer of an arm, and joined Favian at the rail. She looked aloft at the great spread of stars, her eyes softening at the awesome sight, holding the hat on her head with a free hand. "You'll have to teach me navigation," she said, "so I can learn the names of the stars in English. I only know them in Spanish."

"Very well. D'you know how to find Polaris?" She shook her head. Favian turned to Ford and told him to send the men to quarters. While the drum beat out, the men ran to their stations, the lookouts mounted into the rigging, and the eastern sky began to pale, Favian went on with his astronomy lesson. By that time the stars were beginning to fade, so Favian bade Campaspe farewell and went on a tour of the frigate, inspecting each station, seeing the men standing by their guns, ready to lift the port-lids and haul the iron beasts out to do battle with the enemy.

There was no enemy revealed by the dawn, only *Malachi's Revenge* cruising off *Macedonian*'s starboard bow and the flat mass of the delta a long distance to weather. The frigate secured from quarters. Favian, reflecting that Campaspe might be aboard for some time, and that she might not appreciate being ogled by Crane every morning when Favian got his shaving water and coffee, gave orders to bring up the screen that separated his sleeping cabin from his day cabin—in order to give himself more room, he'd had it consigned to the hold when he'd first taken command. The captain's table would be a little more cramped, but Favian assumed that a few leaves could be taken out of the table and that the cabin servants would have to take more care when passing the wine.

After breakfast and the furniture-moving, Campaspe set herself to making another gown from purser's slops, while Favian rolled half-clothed into his cot for a long sleep. He was awakened for dinner, and shortly after rolling out of bed was interrupted by an agitated Midshipman Killick.

"Signal from the *Revenge*, sir! Strange sail in sight!"

"Very well," Favian said, filling his pockets with biscuit. "Tell Mr. Seward I'll be on deck directly." He gave Campaspe a kiss on the cheek. "Most likely we'll have to go to quarters again. I'll send Mr. Killick to show you to the cockpit."

She looked up at him with a frown. "I hope I'll at least get a look at the enemy," she said.

"Very well. One look, then below to Dr. Truscott."

The strange sail proved to be His Britannic Majesty's armed transport *Emma*, and was captured by Gideon's *Revenge* without firing a shot before *Macedonian* even got within five miles. Lulled into a sense of security by Gideon's use of his copy of the British signal book Favian had captured with the *Carnation*, the *Emma* found itself with no choice but surrender once *Revenge* came alongside, lowered the British ensign, hoisted the American one, and ran out its overwhelming broadside.

Favian sent his men to quarters anyway, running out the guns in order to prevent *Emma* from reconsidering her decision;

he let Campaspe stay on the quarterdeck, however, considering there was no danger. He and Campaspe watched the transport through long glasses as they approached, seeing the men massed on her decks, cursing fortune and contemplating their captivity. There were a number of tall, sunbrowned men in red coats, black feather bonnets, and tartan trousers—Favian seemed to remember that *trews* might be the appropriate word for Highland pantaloons—there were also about a hundred men in blue coats and black leather helmets with a plume running fore and aft like a furry caterpillar. Gideon and Finch Martin had their muster-list in hand before they had themselves rowed to *Macedonian* to share the news.

"May we offer you dinner, gentlemen?" Campaspe asked with a mischievous smile as Favian brought Gideon and his first officer into the day cabin.

Gideon contemplated her with a sour expression. "I thought ye were up to mischief," he said. He raised an admonishing finger. " 'Tis obedience ye must learn, girl!"

Finch Martin seemed perfectly delighted by the sight of Campaspe; he broke at once into a twisted, broken-toothed smile. "I take it ye ain't supposed to be here? Good for thee! A girl with spirit is worth any dozen of them unlovely, languishin' manatees that call themselves sailors' wives!"

She laughed, adroitly evaded his clutches as he hobbled in for a pinch or two, and offered to take his cane. " 'Presented to Mr. Finch Martin, Sailing Master, from ye Officers and Men of the Privateer *Cossack*, upon his leaving ye Vessel. August 1778,' " Campaspe said, reading from an inscription engraved in silver on the cane. She looked up at the white-haired old sailor. "It's nice of you to carry your father's cane," she said.

"My father's cane!" Martin howled. "By Saint Mary's tits!" He looked at Favian, leering more than usual, ignoring Gideon's black frown. "I truly wish I'd boarded her first, young Favian! She'd have put her fingers on a cane warmer than that one." He slapped his knee. "King George swimming in shit!"

"Enough, Mr. Martin," Gideon said, his tired expression showing he'd been through this many times before. "We have business to settle." He took a seat.

Favian seated himself across from Martin. The man was an antique from an older, bawdier age, Favian thought, the lamented, astonishing eighteenth century. As perhaps Favian was himself, in quite another way. Certainly he did not find his tastes, his style, quite matching those of his contemporaries, the romantic and dashing young men like Decatur, Lawrence, and that de la Tour d'Aurillac whose body lay in the sand on Timbalier Island; he'd learned to imitate their style without quite believing in it. In a strange way he'd never understood, he'd always felt older around such as they; perhaps, at the age of thirty, he was as obsolete as Martin.

Campaspe ordered dinner. Martin threw out *Emma*'s manifests and other official papers. "Eighty-three officers and men of the Ninety-third Highlanders," he said. "Late in arriving at the rendezvous at Negril Bay, or left behind as sick when the rest of the fleet left."

"The rest of the Ninety-third are at Cat Island, then?" Favian asked.

Martin shrugged. "Maybe," Gideon said. "This *Emma* seems to be a latecomer; that's why it's without escort."

"They're big buggers, them Highlanders," Martin said. "All over six feet, even without their bonnets. I remember we had trouble with 'em in the last war; they wouldn't just surrender like the other redcoats. Kept retakin' the prizes and tryin' to sail 'em home."

"A pair of *Emma*'s six-pounders trained down the main hatch and loaded with cannister should discourage that kind of conduct," Gideon said.

"Th' rest of the prisoners is a few quartermaster sergeants of the Seventh Royal Fusiliers with their supplies, and then the rest are Royal Artillery, the ones in the blue coats. Two batteries of field guns, with limbers." He looked up significantly. "There ain't no limber horses. I guess they're goin' to try to find horses in the countryside."

"Good luck to them," said Favian, remembering New Orleans' scarcity of carriages, and presumably the carriage horses to go with them. He suspected that the sailors of Cochrane's fleet were going to end up acting as horses for these artillerists—assuming, of course, they managed to get any guns across the swamps in the first place.

"Here are some British newspapers from Jamaica," Martin said, separating them from *Emma*'s manifests. "They're recent. We haven't had time to read them all."

"Thank you, Mr. Martin."

Crane brought in dinner; they ate while discussing what to do with the *Emma*. In the end they decided the prize crew would have to come from Gideon's schooner: Favian couldn't spare the officers to send off with the *Emma*, and the faster *Revenge* could also spend the afternoon escorting the prize in the direction of Mobile, and then double back to strike the British off Cat Island.

"There are British ships that know the *Revenge*," Gideon said. "That squadron that was off Mobile in September, and others. There aren't any other Yankee-built tern schooners in these waters, especially with the kind of rake I've got in the mizzen. If I'm seen in company with ye, it may make the British suspicious. We're best acting alone, Favian."

Favian reluctantly agreed. "We should try to coordinate our actions, though," he said. "If one of us attacks the British before the other, the second vessel in the attack may run into a hornet's nest stirred up by the first."

"Guile, Favian," Gideon said. "We can try to arrange an hour for the attack, but ye know that winds and tide cannot be counted on; that sort of plan is likely to go awry. But we can both get in under false signals after dark, even the *Revenge*, and try to cut out as many enemy as possible. If an alarm is given, we'll have to run and find our own way out."

"Aye," Favian said. The uncertainty nagged at him; he remembered all too well the confusions of the Cat Island night attack. Night signals weren't very useful; they were still at a primitive stage, hoists of various colored lanterns, false fires, and the firing of guns, mainly used to help ships keep station at night, letting them know when to tack and in what order, and to identify friend from enemy. Complicated tactical instructions and detailed identification of friendly ships, complete with personal messages from one captain's wife to another's, all common enough using flag hoists in daylight, were impossible at night. All this, Favian finally decided, would probably work more to his benefit than to the enemy's: though he wouldn't be able to communicate with Gideon, the enemy's own communication would be equally hampered, and they had an entire fleet to coordinate. But still there were so many things that could go wrong. He wished he had some way of communicating with Gideon.

"Aye," Favian said again. "But we must have a private signal between ourselves, and between our prizes. I don't want you firing into my prizes by mistake, or *Macedonian* firing into yours. Two white lanterns from the main chains—make certain all your prize masters know it."

"Aye," Gideon nodded. "I'll tell them."

They finished their meal, raising their glasses to success, Favian feeling doubt touching his heart, knowing himself and *Macedonian* to be a card cast away in a game played between Jackson and Sir Edward Pakenham, a sacrifice to buy time. At least he was not alone, he thought; Gideon had stood by him, and would probably achieve the escape that *Macedonian* would not. "Lord bless you both," Gideon said as he stood at the entry port clasping Favian's hand, looking at Favian and Campaspe. Campaspe hugged him, kissing his neck, and then surprised everyone present by hugging Finch Martin as well, the old man blushing scarlet, so surprised he forgot his earthy blasphemies entirely. Favian watched as Gideon's boat made its way over the sea to the low, black schooner, and as *Revenge* and its prize shaped their course to the northeast, heading for Mobile.

They were in sight for many hours, as their courses were only diverging slightly from the frigate's, but Favian did not stay on deck to watch. Instead he went to his cabin to glance at the British newspapers captured with the *Emma*—there was a news item in one that enraged him, but there was nothing he could do about it, so he went to his cot and tried to sleep again, and he passed the word among the officers and men for any individuals currently off duty to do the same. At some point in the afternoon Campaspe joined him, resting her head on his shoulder as he dozed. His body was used to his keeping irregular hours; it made the most of the time available for rest.

The Chandeleur Islands passed slowly by off to larboard throughout the afternoon, and *Malachi's Revenge* and *Emma* faded into the eastern horizon. Favian found half a dozen tactical plans spinning through his mind in succession, even in his half sleep—they were useless; this was a situation impossible to anticipate until he saw how the enemy were drawn up. The battle plans were replaced by details of battle, visual memories of cannons recoiling in their confined spaces on the gun deck, smoke billowing from the whitened stone walls of Tripoli, James Decatur lying dead in *Constitution*'s cockpit, his mourning brother Stephen standing over the body with anguish on his face, *Macedonian* as he'd first seen her, the blood spouting from her scuppers . . .

At that Favian awoke with a start, seeing at once the brown eyes of Campaspe.

"Your heart is beating fast," she said, her voice low in his ear. "Did you dream?"

"What time is it?"

"I don't know. It's getting dark."

Favian glanced at his watch: five forty-three. The hands would be given their supper at six. He wished he could brew some coffee for them at the same time, so he could serve the refreshing drink cold later that night, but there was no coffee aside from his small private supply: the British blockade had kept all the coffee from reaching the United States, and the dark beans were worth their weight in gold. The frigate's crewmen would have to keep themselves awake in other ways.

"Is there going to be a battle tonight?" Campaspe asked.

"I don't know. I hope not," Favian said. How could he tell her that *Macedonian* was a sacrifice? That the frigate would be of little use in the shallow bays and lakes that guarded New Orleans, and so would be thrown away in hopes that it would delay the British long enough for Jackson to ready his defenses?

"Campaspe," he said. "There are a great many British out there. Their fleet is bigger than the one they had at Trafalgar—it's very powerful. They may take us tonight."

"Yes," Campaspe said. "I know that. I've been on a beaten ship; I know what it's like."

"I know, but—" How to say it? There had been so many dead captains in this war on both sides; it was no longer just an American trick to shoot at officers. "If anything should happen to me, darling," Favian said, "my will is in the upper drawer of my desk—" She put her fingers over his lips, but he took them away.

"Don't talk about it."

"It has to be said. Gideon has another copy, and another copy has been sent to the county courthouse in New Orleans to be filed there."

Campaspe shook her head. "I don't want to know. I don't care about your money."

"I care," Favian said. "I care what will happen to you."

Her eyes were bright with tears. "Damn your money!" she said. "I wish you were poor!"

"Whatever happens," he said, "I want you to know this.

You have made me happy. The happiest I've ever been." Oddly enough it seemed to be the truth; he found himself speaking with perfect sincerity. He was amazed at the total unlikeliness of it all.

Campaspe's eyes brimmed over, and she hugged him. They kissed and then, just like in a novel, there was a knock on the partition door. "It's nearing the second dogwatch, Captain," came the voice of Favian's steward. "Will you be wanting your supper now?"

"Aye," Favian said. "Set the table for two."

At six thirty Favian heard the ship's drums begin to beat out "Drops of Brandy," and he knew the crewmen were gobbling whatever remained of their supper and lining up at the whiskey tub for their liquor ration. Outside it was fully dark; the frigate was cruising alone in the blackness. "I've got to go on deck now," Favian said.

"Do what you must," Campaspe said. "Can I come with you?"

He nodded. He took his Portsmouth hanger from the rack and put it on the table, then brought his long duelling pistols out of their case and loaded them carefully. They were motions he'd performed many times before; his hands did their duty without instruction from his conscious mind, handling the familiar, deadly weapons that he'd used in fights so many times before. The ritual calmed him; it was a meditation, a gathering of strength before the battle. He became aware of Campaspe's eyes on him.

"I was on the *Intrepid* when we burned the *Philadelphia*," Favian said, wondering to himself whence had come this compulsion to speak. "It was a very dangerous mission, trying to take a little ketch into an enemy harbor in order to board a frigate. I was very junior, just a midshipman, but Decatur liked the look of me and he accepted me when I volunteered." He rolled a lead bullet in his palm, making certain it was round before he dropped it down the barrel of his pistol, and then rammed a wad down on top of it.

"The night before we were scheduled to board the ketch," Favian said, "my right arm suddenly ceased to function. It was completely paralyzed, just hung limp." He looked up, surprised at his own candor. "I've never told anyone about this," he said. "Not ever."

"What happened?" she asked.

"I put my hand in my pocket and went anyway," he said.

"Things were so busy that morning that I don't think anyone noticed, and as soon as we were out of sight of the fleet the paralysis went away. But that night I was so afraid that someone would find out and think I was shirking . . . and yet I hoped that someone would find out, because if I had a paralyzed arm I couldn't go. I was afraid to go, but also afraid of being thought a coward." Campaspe reached out to touch his right arm as it held the pistol; the muscles were taut, hard as iron with the memory. Favian smiled.

"The paralysis never came back," he said. He put the loaded pistols in his belt, then slipped his keen-edged hanger from its scabbard, inspecting the blade with care, then nodded, sheathed the sword, and clipped it to his belt. "It won't come tonight. But those fears are still there, the fear of fear most of all." Fear could paralyze in other ways, could numb the mind and sap the spirit. "Now's the worst time," Favian said. "I'll be all right when the shooting starts, when I'm busy. It's best to keep active."

"That's why I wanted you to give me work," Campaspe said. "Carrying powder, anything."

"Dr. Truscott can use you," Favian said. "Just tell him you want to keep busy." He took his boarding helmet from the rack and held it under his arm, then as an afterthought took one of the Jamaica newspapers from the table and put it in his pocket. He was ready.

She wrapped herself in one of his old coats again and held his hand as they mounted to the poop deck. Favian ordered a new calculation of their position, and after confirming Sailing Master Seward's calculations, ordered a change in course to the northwest. Forward in the well deck and on the fo'c'sle the crew stood in small groups, sipping their ration of spirits. Normally the time was a merry one, the hands laughing and talking loudly among themselves, but now they seemed subdued; Favian saw heads turning involuntarily ahead, looking for the enemy in the darkness. Favian turned to Seward.

"Pipe all hands. I'll speak to them," he said. As soon as Seward turned forward to bellow the order, the relative stillness was broken by the shrill of bosun's pipes echoed by the ship's trumpet, then the tramp of feet on the companions, the fife and drum of the marines as they marched double time to their stations on the quarterdeck. Then Favian was standing on the break of the quarterdeck, looking over the barricade at the nearly four hundred men below him on the well deck, crowded on the gangways and the fo'c'sle. It was a black, expectant mass, one man indistinguishable from another, their eyes glinting starlight. Favian felt Campaspe standing near him at the barricade, a slight figure wrapped in a big coat.

"Bring me a light from below, there," Favian said. "Pass up a battle lantern. I want to read something to these men."

There was a murmur among the crew as someone went down a hatch, then came up with a battle lantern. It was passed from hand to hand and came up the poop ladder. "Mr. Killick, will you hold the lantern for me?" Favian asked. Killick stepped out from the line of other midshipmen and took the lantern, holding it over Favian's shoulder as he took the Jamaican paper from his pocket.

"This is an advertisement in a Jamaican newspaper that we captured with the *Emma,*" Favian said. For the moment he spoke in a low voice, avoiding the use of a speaking trumpet, forcing his audience to listen carefully to his words; his volume would go up later on, when he had their attention. He looked down at the newspaper in his hand, letting his voice rise a bit so it wouldn't be muffled by the paper in his hand.

" 'Masters of vessels about to proceed to England under convoy,' " he read, " 'are informed they may be supplied with a limited number of American seamen (prisoners of war) to assist in navigating their vessels, on the usual terms, by applying to George Maude, agent.' "

He paused and put the newspaper down, then nodded to Killick, who stepped back to his place. Favian frowned for a few deliberate seconds—those lessons in debate his father had given him, years ago before he'd joined the Navy, were coming in handy; he knew how to build suspense—and then he looked up at the dark mass of men before him.

"That advertisement," Favian said, "tells us what we Americans may expect from the British. Should we fall into their hands, we may expect to be shipped out aboard British convoys, for the benefit of George Maude, Esquire! *They are using American prisoners as slaves!*"

Favian involuntarily took a step backward as the hands responded; the growl of anger rising from the well deck struck him with an almost physical impact. Favian smiled grimly; his shot had struck home.

"We know the British list of outrages," Favian shouted. "We know of the prisoners honorably surrendered to the British on the frontier, only to be murdered by Indian hatchets. We know of their pressing American seamen and forcing them to fight against their countrymen. We know of their bribing the Barbary pirates to attack American merchant ships. And now we know this!" He brandished the newspaper, then tore it in half and scattered the shreds to the wind, the leaves flickering whitely over the rail into the frigate's lee. "Slavery!" Favian said. His voice was rising in pitch now, the three-reef quarterdeck voice he used to fling orders aloft in a gale. "Thirty years ago we fought a war to throw off such slavery, and now we fight again, to prove once again to the British that we are determined to stay free of their Crown, their governors, and their press-gangs!"

There was a roar of agreement from Favian's audience. Favian lowered his voice, forcing them to strain to catch his words. "The British fleet has come to enslave Louisiana. We know where they are. *And tonight we will strike them!*" The last sentence was shouted out again, the three-reef voice. They shouted, stamped, waved their hats; Favian had the impression of a miniature storm in the well deck, stirring the seamen like water. If only, Favian thought, the men of the Hartford Convention could see these men, could see that there were Americans prepared to sacrifice their lives in a war in which the convention men were afraid to sacrifice their pocketbooks.

"The British fleet is under Cochrane," Favian told them. "Cochrane, who burned Washington. He transports the same army that set alight the Capitol!" The voice shrieked out again. *"Will we seek vengeance for Washington tonight?"*

"*Aye!*" the men howled. The storm on the well deck had become a hurricane, stirring the sailors into foaming madness. Favian stepped back, an intent smile on his face. He knew full well what he had just done: he had deliberately and coldly readied these men to throw away their lives on the most fantastic kind of gamble, and to do it willingly; it was one of the little tricks of the officer's trade, and Favian knew he had learned it well. He had earned their trust, and later tonight he would abuse it.

"One more thing," he said, his voice quiet again, when the hurricane had blown itself out. "It may be that some of you may be detailed as prize crews tonight, and that the prizes may be retaken by the British." He gave a deliberate, snarling leer, though he doubted any of the men could see it. "You may even meet Admiral Cochrane," he said. "If you do, you may tell him—nay, you may *boast,* that *Macedonian* is not the only American man-of-war in these waters!"

He had their attention now; the only sounds were the wind keening through the rigging and the sound of the keel cutting the sea. "We are the vanguard of a squadron, boys!" Favian proclaimed. "The *Independence* seventy-four has broken out of Portsmouth, with the *Congress* frigate! *President* has got out of New York and joined with the *Constitution* and *Hornet* out of Boston. They're all under Commodore Decatur, and they're all in the Gulf! Admiral Cochrane had better guard his backside!"

The men laughed even as they looked at one another, trying to discover from their neighbors whether this news was true. It wasn't, of course; Favian was lying through his teeth, and doing so with quite deliberate intent. It was very likely that the British would capture *Macedonian* in the next twenty-four hours, or at least one of its prizes, and if so, every American prisoner would give the British the same story, of an American squadron of unprecedented size ready to strike at Cochrane's fleet. With luck the news would make Cochrane hesitate as he sent out his frigates and sloops of war to find the Americans; if he was busy guarding his back, he would think twice before sending out any small expeditions; he'd have to use the whole fleet in any attack, without any diversions. And he'd have less time to plan his attack on New Orleans.

"That's all I have to tell you, boys," Favian said. "When the shooting starts, mind your officers and remember your drill. I'll give you some time to finish your bob smith and to chew a little tobacco, and then I'll send you to quarters. Bless you all. You're the finest gang of shellbacks I've ever commanded."

That was meant to serve as a cue to his officers: one of them should now step forward, wave his hat, and call for three cheers for the old *Macedonian,* but before that could happen Favian was aware of Campaspe at his elbow. She'd taken a speaking trumpet from the rack, and now she leaned forward over the poop barricade, her magnified voice echoing from the rigging.

"You men, there!" she cried. "If you don't fight for my husband, I'll cut your thumbs off!"

That thoroughly Spanish threat raised a gale of laughter that was better than any cheers, so Favian waved off Swink when he stepped forward to lead the cheers, told Tucker to pipe the men down, and gave Campaspe a hug as she lowered the speaking trumpet. She looked up at him, her face flushed with triumph.

"A better speech than mine," Favian said. "Brief and to the point."

They walked the quarterdeck arm in arm for a few minutes, enjoying the stars, and then Favian set the drums beating to quarters. The frigate was cleared for action in six minutes, and then Favian made a tour of the ship, slapping backs, telling stories, making sure everything was in readiness, the decks sanded to provide traction through the spilled blood, the iron shot lying nestled in their garlands, the frigate's grindstone putting a fresh edge on cutlasses and boarding pikes. His last stop was the cockpit, where the surgeon, Truscott, was in his leather apron setting out his knives. There was a book set out as well—a surgical text, Favian thought, until he saw the gold-embossed title: *Paradise Lost*.

"I'll be sending Mrs. Markham here when we sight the enemy," Favian said.

"Very good, sir. I'll take proper care of her."

"Give her something to do. Have her rolling bandages, warming your knives, anything. If she doesn't have anything to do, she'll grow anxious."

Truscott frowned at Favian from beneath his heavy brows. "This isn't work for a lass, you know," he said. "My mates and loblolly boys have to have strong stomachs."

"I think Mrs. Markham will be all right," Favian said. "She's been in sea fights before." He didn't want to tell Truscott that it was very likely he'd have more wounded than he'd know what to do with and need every hand he could muster to care for them.

"Has she?" The surgeon was surprised. "I'll think of something for her, I'm sure."

"Very well, Dr. Truscott," Favian said. "I'll say farewell now—I trust I'll not be seeing *you* tonight."

Truscott smiled. "I hope not, sir," he said. "Good luck to you."

On deck the night had turned suddenly cold; the breeze had backed to the north, and the frigate fought close-hauled through the water on the starboard tack. As Favian mounted to the poop, he saw Lazarus standing by the ladder.

"Captain Markham," Lazarus said, saluting by raising his old leather cap. "My powers tell me thou wilt do well tonight."

"Aye?" Favian said with suspicion, looking into the madman's strange eyes. "Is the voyage no longer doomed?"

"It is tomorrow thou must beware, Captain," Lazarus intoned. "Then shall our Dr. Truscott's knives taste warm flesh. Thine, perhaps. I cannot say."

"I see," Favian said. "Thank you, Lazarus, for your warning." He stepped onto the poop deck. Lazarus touched his arm.

"Captain," he said urgently. "Remember your promise!"

"I remember," Favian said. The promise to bury him sewn head-downward in canvas and without Christian rites, an inverted burial to match his inverted faith, had been extracted from Favian when Lazarus had predicted his own death. That particular prediction had failed, and Lazarus had continued as a robust, healthy menace to the *Macedonian*'s sanity—prophecy seemed to be a hit-or-miss sort of affair, even for those who alleged themselves to commune with spirits—but every so often, at moments like these, he reminded Favian of his promise.

"Thank'ee, Captain," Lazarus said, drawing back. Favian joined Campaspe at the taffrail.

"Who is that old man?" she asked with a shudder. "He's like some kind of evil spirit, standing there by the mast. Watching us all."

"He's a madman, does more harm to himself than anyone," Favian said, his voice carefully pitched low. "I'll tell you the rest some time, when he's not here to listen."

Macedonian, heeled far over as the land breeze from the north freshened, continued on its new course, the men standing at their guns, murmuring in low voices. Favian passed the word that any who were not on lookout, and who wished to sleep, could stretch out on the deck, but most were too excited to take advantage of it. Favian stood with Campaspe by the weather taffrail; they spoke of whatever came into their heads: the behavior of whales, the composition of stars, the mode of fashion in Japan.

A little after nine o'clock the lookouts sang out that they could see the riding lights of the British fleet dead ahead, and Favian felt, rather than elation or despair, a strange sort of weariness. He had been doing this sort of thing too long, he thought, making speeches, leading men into battle, imitating a public type of nautical *beau sabreur* in a blue coat. He wanted the war over, he was tired of it all.

I'm finished, he thought, surprised. *I'm no good for this anymore.* Well. Another twenty-four hours and it would be over, one way or another. He stood straight, took a breath, and called aloft to the lookouts.

"Masthead, there! How many?"

"Dozens, sir! Fifty, maybe!"

No doubt they would see more anon. Jackson had reported only fifty, but Favian's captured documents had given him an indication of the scope of the British armada: a hundred fifty at least. Jackson's news was days old; it was very likely a hundred additional British ships had dropped anchor off Cat Island since he'd written. Favian looked down at Campaspe.

"Time for you to go below, my dear," he said.

She accepted her fate with a nod. He took her arm and led her to the cockpit. Truscott, his feet propped up on one of the sea chests he would use as an operating table, was quietly reading *Paradise Lost* by the light of his candles. He jumped to his feet and bowed.

"Dr. Truscott, I am entrusting Mrs. Markham to you."

"My pleasure, I'm sure. Ma'am, I'd be much obliged if you'd step over this way and look to these little bandages. . . ." The surgeon moved expertly in the dark, low room, painted dark red so it wouldn't show the blood. Campaspe gave Favian a swift embrace, then surrendered herself to the doctor. Favian quietly turned and walked up the companion.

It was another three quarters of an hour before he could see the riding lights from the deck. They were lying between Ship Island and the northernmost of the Chandeleur Islands: Favian could detect no particular order. The lookout could see another, larger group of lights farther in, beyond this first squadron—those would be the ones off Cat Island.

Favian thought he could detect a pattern to the British dispositions. This first group south of Ship Island would be the larger warships, sail of the line and heavy frigates, unable to get into the more restricted waters near Cat Island and so stationed out here as a guard for the others. The rest would be the lighter, more vulnerable vessels, the transports and their escorts, anchored further inland both so the heavier ships could protect them and so as to be nearer their ultimate goal, New Orleans, when the time came for moving troops to shore.

Macedonian would have to penetrate the screen of heavier vessels, then strike swiftly at the transports, hoping to cause as much chaos as possible and then escape in the confusion. The raid could never be repeated: afterward the British would change their signals and would be on the alert. *Macedonian* would have to cruise out of sight in the Gulf and hope to pick up British strays like *Emma*.

The lookouts were already doubled, Stanhope was standing by with his lanterns ready to return a British challenge, and the men were at quarters: nothing to do but keep on course and wait. So much of war was waiting. Favian found impatience twitching at him as he stood on the quarterdeck and forced himself to be still. Another twenty-four hours, he thought, and it's over. Dead or a prisoner, or at liberty on the wide oceans with the freedom to pick off the occasional British prize, living off them as he went, perhaps even return to his original goal of striking at the British East Indies; the war would be over for him.

The white riding lights came closer. Favian took a night glass from the rack and stepped out to the mizzen shrouds, standing on the ratlines twenty feet above deck, one elbow hooked through a shroud, peering at the enemy. The image in the glass was inverted, the ships riding in the sky, but still he could make out his enemy. Giant ships, sail of the line, their great masts hung with a web of sturdy cordage that cut the stars. Any one of them could have blown *Macedonian* out of the water with a few well-aimed broadsides. That leviathan to starboard was surely a three-decker, a hundred guns or more, probably with an admiral's flag. He called down orders to alter course a little to larboard to avoid it; if there was an admiral aboard, he might wonder what a strange frigate was doing running under topgallants through his fleet at night without his orders.

The huge ships grew larger, and the night glass was no longer necessary. Favian returned to the quarterdeck and put the glass in the rack, then stood quietly and watched the massive ships swing at their cables. He chose a gap between two of the line-of-battle ships and told Seward to steer for it. A snatch of music was heard on the wind, a massed, male chorus: one of the ships was putting on an entertainment.

He had never seen anything like it in his life, this armada of giants come to seize the Mississippi. Even at night, the details indistinct, it was breathtaking. He could sense the men near him standing speechless with awe as they came within a cable's length of a great ship's stern windows, looking in at the tiny figures in bright uniforms, blue and green and red, all atwinkle with gold and lace, men of power and privilege whose word was life and death, all rollicking at their late-night supper. But then a gun boomed, and Favian's heart leaped into his throat.

A white false fire was burning from the liner's foredeck. There was another cannon shot, the loud thump echoing from the other ships. Several of the tiny figures in the great cabin were trying to peer out of the stern windows.

"That's this week's challenge, sir," Stanhope reported. "White false fire from the fo'c'sle, two guns. The correct reply is two red lanterns displayed from the maintop and three guns."

"Very well, Mr. Stanhope," Favian said, trying to calm his thundering heart. "Hoist your lanterns. Mr. Tucker, three guns!"

The red lanterns rose swiftly up the signal halliards; the guns banged out from the fo'c'sle. The little figures in the great cabin returned to their table. None of the other ships seemed to be taking an interest.

Favian found a grin spreading across his features. This might succeed after all! "Two points to starboard, Mr. Seward," he said, unable to keep the glee entirely from his voice. "But keep her full."

"Aye aye."

Macedonian sped on through the night, sailing through the screen of warships for the bright lights on the western horizon—the transports that carried Pakenham's troops, lying snug and vulnerable off Cat Island.

There was another challenge from a little corvette patrolling between the two bodies of ships, but once again the captured signal books proved their worth, and the frigate was allowed to continue unhindered. Shortening sail to topsails alone, *Macedonian* crept carefully into the midst of the pack of ships; Favian picked his target, a small ship-rigged vessel, a little at a distance from the others, that seemed, in silhouette at least, a sister ship to *Emma*. The boarders, black, plumed shadows in their bearskin-covered helmets, crouched by the bulwarks, armed with glinting cutlasses and pikes, and *Macedonian* slipped down on her prey. There was an exclamatory chorus from the enemy ship, half a hundred voices crying out to watch your damned course, there, and then the frigate smashed right alongside, grinding its way along the enemy bulwarks as Favian stood in the mizzen chains and demanded surrender to the United States frigate *Constitution*—he'd decided the *Constitution* was better known among the British; it was also a larger ship than the *Macedonian*, and hence more to be feared. The babble on the enemy decks rose to a greater volume—there seemed to be a lot of troops on board—and then Favian called for his boarders. The enemy chorus took on a panicked tone, and they stampeded for the hatches. The official surrender was forthcoming in a few minutes, as soon as their officers had time to consult and realized there was nothing to be done. The prize proved to be the troopship *Otter*, with nearly two hundred men in the dark green coat of the 95th Rifles. Favian's heart lifted as he realized he had captured, without a shot, a telling number of what was almost certainly the most elite regiment of light troops in the world. Favian had the officers transfer to *Macedonian* and clapped in the cable tier under guard so they would not foment insurrection among their men, then watched reluctantly as the captured stands of arms, Baker rifles accurate to two hundred yards, perhaps better even than the Tennessee long rifles of Jackson's men, were thrown in the drink. Jackson could have used them, Favian knew, but the likelihood of Jackson getting them in time were slim and the chances of their being used in a rising of the prisoners was all too great.

Favian stepped aboard the prize for a hasty, whispered conference with those who led the prize crew, in this case Midshipman George Killick and a master's mate named Allen; then the two ships parted. The *Otter* simply cut its cable and began to drift downwind, setting just enough sail to make certain it would accomplish its mission; Favian watched as it fouled another transport and swiftly sent its boarders over the rail. Two prizes: Favian would shortly make it three.

He had already picked his target, a little brig swinging at the weather end of a long straggling line of transports, but the brig was to windward, he had to tack to get to it, and that would take a while. He stood in the cool air, listening with half an ear as Seward gave the orders for tacking. "Ease the helm down . . . Aft the spanker sheets. Helm's alee! Keep fast the foretack! Rise tacks and sheets! Mains'l haul!"

Favian heard the braces roaring through the sheaves, the snap of lifting canvas. The two prizes had got under way, heading for the open sea, but suddenly his attention was caught by *Macedonian*'s uneasy motion beneath his feet. He looked forward sharply. The ship was hanging in the wind, refusing to fall on its new tack. In another few moments they'd be gaining sternway, slipping backward through the water.

"Put the helm hard over! Brail up the spanker! Flatten the head sheets, board the fore tack!" Favian's voice joined Seward's as he jumped to cope with the emergency. He could feel water gurgling beneath the frigate's transom as she began to slip backwards. "Haul taut!" he roared. "Square away the after yards!" *Macedonian* shuddered, falling off on its new tack; Favian sensed the main topsail beginning to fill. "Rise fore tack and sheet! Haul taut, brace around the foreyards! Flow head sheets . . . Brace up!"

Macedonian slowed, wallowing, then began to gather way, the sea hissing beneath its stem. There was a brief cheer from the hands. "Silence fore and aft!" Favian shouted. Cheers could carry for miles at night.

The brig approached, showing no sign it was aware of being stalked. Cat Island was a black shadow half a mile to the north, its beach dotted with the British army's campfires. Favian looked at his watch: a little after two. Sunrise would be around six thirty, but it would be light for some time before that. In spite of the cold December wind he felt perspiration collecting under his helmet; he wiped his brows with his sleeve and calculated bow lines. "Back the main tops'l, Mr. Seward," he said. "Steady . . . there you go."

Favian had achieved another surprise, the frigate coming to a halt with backed fore and main topsails, the boarders tumbling over the bulwark like a black wave. There was not so much as a hail from the brig until the shudder that meant contact; then there was a confused cry from a couple of lookouts that had been sleeping under the break in the poop, followed by the stamping of the boarders' feet. Favian grinned; he could work his way up the line of enemy vessels, picking them off one by one. Then there was a pair of shots—Favian's grin vanished, and he peered into the enemy ship—and then an outraged growl from the boarders. There were shouts, more stampings, then a flood of men and a babble of American voices from the hatchways.

"Prisoners, sir!" Byrne called from the enemy quarterdeck. "American sailors! They had prisoners battened down below!"

"Navy men? Or merchant sailors?" Favian asked. Damnation! He'd wanted more of those green riflemen.

"We've got a man wounded, sir," Byrne said. "They had guards over the hatch. They seem to be Navy men."

Some business for Truscott, down in his dark cockpit. But where did these Navy men come from? Had Cochrane's fleet encountered some American warship on the high seas, just escaped from New York or Boston, or were they from a lot closer to New Orleans—say Lieutenant Jones's gunboat flotilla on Lake Borgne?

"Who's in charge of the prisoners, there?" Favian asked. "Send him up."

"I believe I'm in charge, sir," called a strong, southern voice from the quarterdeck. "I am Lieutenant Archibald Bulloch Blake, of Gunboat Number 163—whom do I have the honor of addressing?"

The voice brought back a flood of memories: two gunboat lieutenants stuck in the Delaware during the Embargo five years ago, cursing their luck and watching American commerce starve. Archibald Bulloch Blake of Augusta, a gentle, genial man named after the first president of revolutionary Georgia, a penniless cousin-german to half the aristocracy of the South, seemingly doomed to rot half his life away in the gunboat service. There was another, more recent memory: Campaspe had said that Blake was jealous of his success. But *Macedonian* was short of officers—perhaps this was a stroke of luck after all.

"It's Favian, Bull!" he called. "Come aboard!"

"Favian Markham, by thunder!" Blake called, jumping for the frigate's mizzen chains. "Is Gideon with you?"

"The *Revenge* is out here somewhere," Favian said. Blake swung aboard, dropping to the quarterdeck. "We came in separately."

Blake raised a hand to a battered round hat, uncovering in salute. Favian returned it.

"I was in Tac Jones's squadron on the lake," Blake said breathlessly. "We've all been taken, sir. Yesterday—two days ago, now. All five gunboats, plus the tender and the schooner."

Overhead the sails roared as a contrary gust of wind tore at them. Favian paid no attention, concentrating on Blake's disastrous news. With the gunboats gone, the lakes were unguarded—Borgne was a British possession, and they stood a good chance of taking Pontchartrain.

"Is Lieutenant Jones here?" Favian asked.

"He was badly wounded, Captain," Blake said. The informality caused by Blake's unexpected release and the meeting of two old friends had disappeared beneath the reestablishment of instinctive military protocol; the *sirs, captains,* and *misters* were second nature. "The British put him ashore on Cat Island with the other wounded. I'm in charge of the rest—ninety-three men here on this brig."

"Can you detail some to take the prize to Mobile? I'm short of hands here."

"Certainly, sir."

"I'll want you to stay, Mr. Blake. Do you have a man you can leave in charge of the prize?"

"Aye, sir. My midshipman knows these waters well."

"Very well. Detail twenty-five of your men to take weapons to guard the prisoners and get the prize under way." Favian looked at the line of enemy craft, then at his watch. Almost three. Perhaps there was time for another prize, perhaps not.

"Pardon me, Captain Markham," Blake said, "but what ship is this? *Congress?*"

"*Macedonian,* Mr. Blake. May I present Lieutenant Chapelle, the acting first officer? Mr. Seward, the master."

"Honored, gentlemen." Blake grinned. "And mighty relieved, too."

The wounded seaman, moaning and clutching his wounded thigh, was brought aboard the frigate in a bosun's chair, then bundled below to the surgeon. A thigh wound was always tricky; Truscott couldn't amputate that high. Blake dropped down to the prize to sort out the liberated prisoners, sending most of them aboard the frigate, then coming aboard himself. There was the sound of an axe hewing at the cable, then the prize swung free and *Macedonian* filled her sails. The frigate shaped its course for the next enemy in line, and then all hell broke loose.

It started with a rocket going up from a ship farther down the line, exploding redly over the anchored ships; the first rocket was followed within half a minute by a second from the ship Favian intended to be his next prize. Favian felt frustration rising in him.

That second rocket had been *ready*, blast it. Perhaps they'd heard those shots.

Soon there were rockets going up everywhere, bursting overhead like a fireworks display, red reflecting from *Macedonian*'s great topsails. Signal guns began booming. The warships would be getting under way soon; no time to take any more prizes. But even so, Favian thought grimly, that line of ships would suffer punishment for being so alert.

"Starboard broadside, out tompions!" Favian roared. "Load with round shot and grape, then run out!"

The seamen cheered at the order, the idiots; they were only too happy to make a flash and a noise and call attention to themselves. Another rocket burst as Favian scanned the escape route to seaward, and for an instant he saw masts and shrouds flashing scarlet, the unmistakable silhouette of *Malachi's Revenge* racing along on a beam reach. So Gideon had got among the British as well—it has been his distinctive tern schooner, rather than the frigate, that had set off the enemy alarms. He hoped Gideon had cut out some prizes before he had been discovered.

The anchored enemy ship was getting nearer; it seemed to show the typical tubby lines of a military transport. Drums beat from its quarterdeck; Favian thought he could hear the clatter of weapons being readied. The British decks would be packed with soldiers, meat for Favian's grapeshot.

"Ready, starboard guns!" he called. "Fire as you bear! Mr. Seward, put your helm down—a spoke at a time, there."

There were a few cracks as muskets were fired from the enemy decks; Favian didn't even hear the bullets whizzing overhead: those men must have panicked. *Macedonian* commenced a lazy turn to larboard just fifty yards from the British bows, slowly bringing the transport into the arc of the frigate's guns.

The first fo'c'sle gun went off with a roar, a sheet of blinding flame lapping at the water. Favian turned away to save his night vision as the other guns began to speak, the main deck eighteen-pounders, the fo'c'sle and quarterdeck thirty-two-pound carronades, each flinging a mass of metal into the helpless target. In the sudden silence that followed the broadside, he could hear screams from the enemy torn by grapeshot; and then there was a tearing crash as the transport's mizzenmast went by the board. She might well be sinking; few transports could take that kind of metal and live.

"Helm up, Mr. Seward," Favian said. "Set a course for that next ship." His voice seemed unnaturally faint to his ears; he had been slightly deafened by the roaring guns.

Rockets were flying aloft with a vengeance as *Macedonian* came up on its next target. A voice from the enemy reached Favian as the frigate came near, the clear, bewildered tones of the enemy captain, hopelessly misreading the situation.

"Don't shoot!" he shouted. "We're *British*! We're the transport *Irene*, with men from the Royal Scots Fusiliers. Don't shoot! We're *British*! Don't you understand?"

Irene, Favian thought irrelevantly, pitying the poor captain who thought *Macedonian* was a friend. *Irene* was peace, in Greek. He wondered if the man who named the transport had realized the irony of his choice.

Macedonian's broadside put an end to the captain's voice, the guns and carronades tearing into his fragile transport at point-blank range. After that there were only the moaning of the injured and the sound of water pouring through the shot holes. The third enemy ship sent more voices over the water.

"We strike!" they screamed, a chorus of crying men. "We surrender! For God's sake don't shoot! *We surrender!*"

Too late, Favian thought. They knew as well as he that if he stopped to take a prize now the enemy warships would have time to collect their wits and take *Macedonian* prize in turn. "Ready, starboard broadside!" he called. "Fire as you bear!"

At the fifth or sixth gun the enemy ship blew up, the fo'c'sle leaping into the air, lifting the foremast like a giant hurling a sapling, the bay turning bright as day. Favian saw the first burst of fire and turned to shout a warning, but was flung to the planking before he could get the words out. The impact knocked the wind from him, pain rocketing through his ribs, but even through his pain he knew what had happened. A powder ship, he thought. No wonder they were so eager to surrender.

Macedonian staggered with the blast, Favian picking himself up to scream orders to the helm, trying to get the frigate away from the flaming powder vessel. He might have saved his breath; the helm was already down, the helmsmen knowing as well as he how terrible would be their fate if the frigate caught fire, or had its hull caved in by a nearby explosion. "Bucket brigades!" Favian shouted, seeing a cinder glowing in the spanker, but the buckets were already in hand. There were men moving slowly on the decks, victims of splinter wounds, but the rest were standing by their guns, their eyes white in the reflected flames, or racing with buckets to danger spots.

The frigate put another cable between it and the powder vessel by the time the second explosion came, the whole ship going this time, the hull torn to pieces and the mainmast rising whole into the sky, illuminated from below like a painting of the True Cross rising to heaven. "Down!" Favian shouted, and threw himself to the deck. There was a storm of wreckage, splinters and burning shreds of canvas and little twisted bits of brass and iron, but *Macedonian* was spared what Favian had most feared: a great iron gun thrown into the air to drop through *Macedonian*'s decks and straight through her bottom.

Favian jumped to his feet, looking wildly in all directions while the light lasted, trusting his men to put out any fires. The British flotilla was all around him, the anchored vessels standing on the shocked yellow-white water, their masts and hulls illuminated perfectly by the blast. Many near the explosion had cut their cables and were drifting, trying to get sail up and run away from the fire, but most seemed content to lie at anchor and wait for the Royal Navy to appear in force. There were no warships obviously under way, at least not nearby; Favian wondered if they yet realized there was an enemy frigate among them, or if they assumed it was a boat attack from the mainland. *Macedonian* had fired three broadsides, but as far as any ships but the targets were concerned, those guns could have been fired at invisible Americans in whaleboats.

The light lasted a very long time as the remains of the powder vessel burned, providing a good look at the enemy anchorage. Favian set Stanhope and the other mids to counting ships and taking bearings; then he heard canvas snapping over his head and looked up to find the mizzen topsail torn asunder from the blast, reduced to tattered bits of flax flogging themselves against the yards. "Secure that canvas," Favian said. "Hands aloft to set t'gallants." He would need a little more speed to get out of here.

Favian got another glimpse of *Malachi's Revenge* in the light of the burning powder vessel, seeing the fleet, low schooner at least a mile ahead and increasing the distance rapidly. There was another ship under way near the schooner, probably someone's prize. Favian didn't dare fire again, not for fear of igniting another powder vessel but because the other ships would see him and know him for an enemy.

The mast captains called out their orders: "Stand by—let fall!" The canvas came tumbling down off the topgallant yards with a rush. "Lay in! Down from aloft, there! Sheet home the t'gallants!"

The frigate heeled over as the topgallants caught the wind, the sound of water rushing past the hull increasing. That light astern was dying out, the remains of the powder vessel coming apart in the midst of its still pool of wreckage—but then fire suddenly burst out again, from another ship: an entire mainmast had gone up, the flames towering fully two hundred feet. The first fire had spread during the explosions; the fire fighters on the other ship had just lost the fight. Favian watched in somber awe as the mizzen caught alight, then the foremast; it was the sailor's worst nightmare come true, the tar- and resin-soaked wooden ship going up in flames. Any seaman could picture it, the planking smoking beneath his feet, hot tar raining down from aloft, the panic as everyone ran for the boats . . . There would not be enough boats, not on a troopship. Favian wondered if it was the *Irene* on fire out there, with the Royal Scots Fusiliers aboard; somehow it would seem consistent with that captain's luck. Whoever it was, Favian wished him well. He had not come into the midst of the enemy fleet to burn people alive.

The sails began to roar as the wind veered; Favian had the yards braced around, then had the royals and courses set. The frigate was leaving the pool of light cast by the burning ship. Favian wondered whether to have the spare mizzen topsail set, decided at least to take the first step, and ordered men aloft to get the old one down. Then the lookouts were shouting about a British corvette on their larboard bow, and Favian had the mizzen topmen hurry their work and get to the deck as quickly as they could.

"Larboard broadside!" he shouted. "Out tompions! Load with roundshot, but don't run 'em out!" He still had the signal book; perhaps he could bluff his way out of this. He'd challenge *them* first this time. "Mr. Tucker, light a white false fire from the fo'c'sle, and fire two guns!" In the moment before the flare went off he had one last thought. "Mr. Stanhope, raise the Red Ensign." That would show *Macedonian* to be a member of the fleet of Sir Alexander Forester Inglis Cochrane, K.B., Vice-

Admiral of the Red Squadron—at least so Favian hoped. He hadn't bothered with raising British flags so far, since they couldn't be seen; but perhaps the bright flare forward, and the burning light astern, would help their imposture.

The false fire illuminated the deck with its harsh white light, blinding Favian to the corvette in the darkness outside; he shaded his eyes with his hand and peered desperately into the blackness to windward. Two guns boomed from the fo'c'sle. The corvette, he knew, was no match for the *Macedonian:* the frigate could tear the corvette apart with just a few of her heavy broadsides. But the battle would take time, it would be fought right under the noses of the overwhelming enemy heavy squadron, and the corvette might get lucky and knock away a spar, preventing *Macedonian*'s escape. Favian felt his heart in his throat as the false fire burned out, and he blinked frantically to get his night vision back. The corvette was a comfortable half mile to windward, coming down fast—but then three guns thumped out while two red lanterns rose to the other ship's maintop, and he knew he might be able to escape without a fight right under the noses of the enemy battleships.

"The corvette's answering the signal, sir," Stanhope reported, satisfaction in his voice.

"Bend on the American ensign, Mr. Stanhope," Favian said. "We may have to fire into her yet." Warships were allowed to be as duplicitous as they liked about using false signals and raising false flags, so long as they raised their own flag when the shooting actually started—to act otherwise was, technically, piracy.

"Larboard broadside, ready to run out," he cautioned. "Wait for my signal."

The British captain's voice came clearly on the wind, sounding disembodied, ghostly, shouted through a speaking trumpet. "Ship ahoy, there! This is Captain Hamshere! What ship are you?"

Favian would avoid that question if he could. He picked up his own speaking trumpet, trying to keep his voice moderate as he faced into the wind. His countrymen had always accused him of sounding English, not unexpectedly since his father had been educated in England and his mother was the daughter of a baronet—but now he'd see whether the British, too, thought he sounded like one of them. "Yankee boat attack!" he shouted. "They're in shallow water—can't get to 'em. Urgent message for the admiral!"

"What was that?" The voice was clearer now; the corvette was only two cables away. As Favian had intended, the British captain hadn't heard Favian's reply, shouted upwind.

"What did you say?" Favian demanded. "Can't hear you!"

"*What ship is that? What did you say?*" Captain Hamshere was clearly losing patience. Favian grinned behind the mouthpiece of the speaking trumpet.

"Yankee boat attack!" he bellowed, trying to sound as if he was himself losing his temper. "They're in shoal water and we can't get near them! Urgent message for the admiral! And I'll thank you, Captain Hamshere, to keep your tone civil!" He heard a stifled laugh near him on the quarterdeck: Lieutenant Blake trying to restrain himself.

The corvette swept past within biscuit's throw, close enough for Favian to see the men standing by their guns, their slow-matches glowing in the dark. A voice came from their quarterdeck, a little more measured this time, as if Hamshere was trying to restrain his temper in the face of a superior.

"What ship are you?"

"That powder vessel—what's the name?—it blew up!" Favian said. "I think that's the *Irene* on fire, with the Royal Scots Fusiliers!" Favian realized, his blood chilling, that he'd pronounced *Irene* in the American way, Eye-reen, rather than the proper British Eye-ree-nee. But the corvette surged past without firing, and it seemed Hamshere didn't notice Favian's mistake.

"Damn those Yankees!" Hamshere exclaimed. "My compliments, there, whoever you are."

And the corvette was gone. Favian numbly returned the speaking trumpet to the rack, hearing the congratulations of Blake, Chapelle, and the others on the quarterdeck. He looked ahead; there was nothing but two miles of open water between *Macedonian* and the giants of the British battle line. Time to take a breath, to walk about the quarterdeck and try to work loose his tension-tautened limbs. He took the boarding helmet off his head and felt the ache in his neck recede.

He looked at his watch: a little after five. It would be getting light soon; he'd have to try to work his way through all those line-of-battle ships and heavy frigates before the dawn made them give *Macedonian* more than a cursory glance.

There were ships moving among the British, frigates and sloops of war slipping their moorings, setting sail, and heading toward the disturbance. Favian tried to ease *Macedonian* away from them. The battleships' lookouts were more alert this time: the frigate was challenged a mile off the line. The proper reply seemed to ease their suspicions, however: *Macedonian* slipped into the midst of them, cutting the water between the giants.

The wind veered again, and the frigate was close-hauled on the larboard tack, hugging the wind, her speed slowed. Favian was growing anxious: all the other frigates were heading inland, toward Cat Island. Would the British begin to wonder why there was one frigate running the other way under topgallants and royals, dashing for the open sea as fast as it could go?

Another battleship challenged and accepted the reply, then a third. The eastern sky was growing pale, and Favian could see *Malachi's Revenge* five miles off, following a pair of prizes: Gideon had made a successful escape. In another twenty minutes flag hoists would be visible, and then the pattern of signals would get more complicated.

Favian slipped to windward of a big three-decker and was able to alter his course to starboard, putting the wind a little more abeam, increasing his speed.

And then Favian saw a shadow to leeward—no, a pair of shadows, two frigates slipping out of the pack on the larboard tack, steering to cut *Macedonian* off from the open sea. British suspicions had been raised at last; some alert frigate captain had wondered why a heavy frigate would run into the Gulf as if it had good reason to run. Favian, heart sinking, glanced hopelessly to windward, confirming the hopelessness of the situation. He had passed through the last of the heavy British battleships, but he still needed to head more to starboard to reach the open waters of the Gulf, and it looked as if these frigates meant to cut off his retreat. He had no other choice: he had to run for the sea or be pinned against the land. "Knock the wedges out of the masts," he ordered. "Crew to stand by the larboard rail." That would give the masts more play and trim the ship a little better, letting the frigate pick up a little more speed.

The two enemy frigates were a little nearer the wind, steering a course that would intersect *Macedonian*'s. It seemed the lead enemy frigate was smaller than the other—Favian could hope for a twenty-eight-gun jackass frigate, but it was probably larger. The frigate astern seemed more heavily sparred, but Favian would have to wait for dawn to confirm any details. It would be half an hour before the frigates' courses came together. Plenty of time to prepare. Favian ordered the spare mizzen topsail roused up from the sail locker forward, then bent to the yard. He also sent bucket brigades aloft to wet the sails and had the fire pumps play on the courses: wet sails held more air than dry sails, and the trick had worked for Favian twice before.

It didn't work this time: by the time the sun touched the edge of the sea, it was clear that both enemy frigates were faster than *Macedonian*. Even if Favian managed to get ahead of them into the open sea, they would soon overtake him. Favian had a Union Jack raised to the jack staff and a St. George commission pendant from the main, but he doubted that the British would be fooled. If they were out here at all, it meant they were suspicious.

Carefully he studied them through his long glass. The lead British frigate was clearly a lightly built small frigate, rated at thirty-two guns or so. It wouldn't stand twenty minutes in combat with *Macedonian*, but it wouldn't have to: its consort was overhauling her and might well engage first.

The other frigate was, as Favian had suspected, a heavy thirty-eight, *Macedonian*'s equal in size and firepower, but unfortunately faster. He would have a chance with it alone, but not with its lighter playmate, and in any case *Macedonian*'s gun crews had been standing at quarters for nearly twelve hours, hadn't had any sleep, and were exhausted. Favian sent below for a cup of cold coffee—the galley fires were out—and leaned against the weather shrouds while he considered the problem.

Macedonian was an old-fashioned British frigate; it was fast with the wind behind it and a slug heading to weather. These other two seemed to be better at working to windward. If he could sail off the wind, he could spread his studding sails and perhaps give them a run for their money, but it simply wasn't possible. Somehow he'd have to fight them.

His ship had lost men to prizes, thirty to the *Carnation*, which was balanced by twelve volunteers they'd got from the British ship; they'd lost fifty the night before, but got fifty-odd of Blake's men in exchange. Favian ordered Chapelle to assign battle stations for the new men, and Chapelle and Blake put their heads together over the watch and quarter bills.

"Signal from the second British ship, sir," Stanhope reported. The young midshipman looked exhausted, his eyes shadowed by dark circles, but he still smiled gamely as he reported. "It's today's challenge, sir."

"Hoist the reply, Mr. Stanhope," Favian said. Play the game out, he thought; perhaps that British captain is a moron and will believe us.

"Another signal, sir," Stanhope said a few moments later. "What ship are you?"

"Tell them we're *Endymion*, Mr. Stanhope." *Endymion* was a forty-gun British frigate Favian had often seen blockading New York; *Macedonian* had barely escaped *Endymion* and two other British ships a few days after they'd got out of New London, back in October. Even if the enemy didn't quite believe the signal, they might hesitate a bit before engaging a proclaimed forty-gunner.

"They're identifying themselves, Captain," Stanhope reported. "That first ship is the *Thames*." He pronounced it with a theta and long *a*, like the river in Connecticut. He flipped through the British signal book. "That would be Captain the Honourable C.L. Irby. Thirty-two guns. The other is the *Trave,* thirty-eight, Captain Money. One moment, sir—another signal from the *Trave*." Favian, idly wondering whether *Endymion*'s captain, Henry Hope, was senior to Captain Money and could perhaps venture to give him some orders, could see a series of flags breaking out at the larger frigate's peak. " 'What are your orders?' " Stanhope read.

"Tell them, 'Am carrying dispatches. Am under Admiralty orders,' " Favian said. "Then add, '*Thames, Trave* chase enemy privateer to windward.' Perhaps they'll obey my orders." He had no fear for *Malachi's Revenge:* the tern schooner would outrun the British frigates without trouble.

The next British signal was followed by a gun, meant to give it emphasis. " 'Heave to and await my orders,' " Stanhope reported.

"No reply, Mr. Stanhope. Is the American ensign bent on? Very well." So much for the impersonation, he thought. He could still hope for a lucky shot that might dismast one or another of the frigates and leave him to fight the other.

The exchange of signals had absorbed a quarter hour; the frigates would be within range of one another soon, though they would have to alter course to fire, and Favian suspected that neither would. He studied them: *Thames* was a couple of cables ahead of *Trave,* but the heavier frigate, its larger spread of sail catching the brisk wind and propelling it with greater speed, was overhauling fast and would pass a little to leeward of the thirty-two.

"Deck, thar!" It was a lookout. "Another frigate's chasing astern!" Favian looked aft with his glass: there was indeed another frigate making sail in pursuit, a heavy ship with beautiful lines, gold winking from the figurehead on its stem, but it was six or seven miles back and no immediate threat. It was a reminder not to dawdle with these first two frigates, but to try to end it fast if he could.

His brain swimming with weariness, Favian returned to contemplation of the first two frigates. There were two possibilities, assuming everyone kept on their current course. The British frigates might win the race, in which case they would get upwind of *Macedonian*, seizing the weather gage: they would then be able to engage whenever it suited them. If *Macedonian* won the race, the British would pass astern of the American frigate, perhaps firing a couple of raking broadsides while they were at it—since they were faster, they would take the weather gage that way, too, though it would take them longer.

Either way would work to the ultimate satisfaction of the British. Captain the Honourable C.L. Irby and Captain Money would have *Macedonian* between hammer and anvil. Frowning, Favian looked astern, seeing the American fifteen-striped battle ensign bent to the halliards, ready to raise aloft. Within another half hour or so, he might have to bring it down in surrender.

There were too many irregularities; he was in command of *Macedonian* without permission from the secretary of the Navy—in fact he was in opposition to his latest set of orders, which had directed him to ready the *Shark* sloop of war currently building in New London. There was only one thing that could clear him in the eyes of a court-martial board. The Fourth Article was very clear: "If any person in the navy shall treacherously yield, or pusillanimously cry for quarters, he shall suffer death, on conviction thereof, by a general court martial." In order to be found innocent by a court-martial, Favian would have to prove his surrender was not treacherous or pusillanimous—in other words, he would have to resist to the last.

Such resistance would make a slaughterhouse of *Macedonian*. Butcher the crew, tear the ship asunder, topple the masts. The Navy Department would probably be happiest if Favian fought *Macedonian* until she sank out from under him, leaving the

British only floating wreckage, and then conveniently drowned to spare the expense of a trial.

Well, he'd do what the Navy Department wanted; he'd fight until he could fight no more, and then haul the flag down. He would give the Navy what it desired just this one more time, and then let the fates judge him as they wished. He looked forward, seeing the men standing at their stations, their eyes moving from the two British frigates to Favian and back again, trusting him, it seemed, to get them out of this. The trust was what the Navy counted on; if the Navy was lucky, *Macedonian*'s entire complement would go on trusting Favian until they died at their guns. Favian saw mad Lazarus standing at his station by the barricade, his pale eyes resting on Favian, confident in their knowledge of disaster.

No, Favian thought. I'm not giving in to your prophecy yet. There's little I can do, but I'm going to do it.

He put the heavy boarding helmet on his head, tying the shaggy bearskin chinpiece under his chin. "Starboard broadside, out tompions!" he called. "Load with roundshot. Stand ready to run out!"

There was a brief, weary cheer from the exhausted men, as if his decision to fight had confirmed some private opinion. Favian looked up at the two British frigates, seeing light winking from the enemy telescopes on the quarterdeck, seeing the larboard gunports on the *Thames* suddenly open, the iron muzzles moving deliberately out the ports.

What to do? It seemed as if *Macedonian* would win the race, passing ahead of the two British frigates; maybe he'd be able to bow-rake one or both with his guns, firing his shot the length of their decks and perhaps knocking out a mast. It was unlikely they'd allow it, though; no doubt they had a counterstrategy prepared.

He'd fought a running fight before, just last October when he'd run from the real *Endymion* and its two consorts, one of which, the *Tenedos*, had overtaken him. That had been a mad action, both frigates racing along under full canvas, their broadsides bellowing. Eventually Favian had managed to knock away a mast and left *Tenedos* behind.

Favian could hope for that sort of success here, but the hope was a slender one. There were two frigates overtaking him now, not one; the odds were just that much more against him. But, so far as his weary mind could discern, it was the only hope he had. If only he'd had a few hours sleep.

For the next few moments he had the weather gage, which gave him the option to start the fight, or to wait until the British took the weather gage and started it for him. The initiative was his, and he thought he would probably use it when the time came. Try to knock out *Thames* first, then concentrate on *Trave*.

The masts of the larger frigate were beginning to be obscured by those of the *Thames: Trave* was overtaking about a half cable to leeward of its cohort. In another few seconds the thirty-eight would be entirely obscured and shortly thereafter would emerge from behind *Thames* to take the lead. A minute or so after that Favian would haul his wind and order the first broadside at two hundred yards range, but for the moment he watched *Trave*'s masts slowly moving behind the thirty-two's—and then inspiration struck him so suddenly he slapped his helmeted forehead with anger at his own idiocy.

"Helm up!" he shouted. "Raise the American ensign! Starboard broadside, run out—prepare to fire at two hundred yards! Wait for my signal!"

The helmsmen, caught by surprise, took an extra second or two to react, and then *Macedonian* was turning ponderously to starboard, heading on what seemed a direct collision course with *Thames*. Favian could hear the gridiron flag snapping over his head as the wind caught it, as well as the grinding roar of the starboard broadside being hauled out the ports by men straining at the side-tackles. "Hands to clew up the royals!" Favian shouted, the deck heeling beneath his feet.

He could imagine the reaction of the *Thames*'s captain—*Macedonian*, now identified fully as an enemy warship heavier than his own, was suddenly altering course and bearing down on him, obviously with the intention of bow-raking him at very close range. The Honourable C.L. Irby would be horrified by the prospect: eighteen-pound iron shot from *Macedonian*'s cannon and thirty-two-pound shot from her carronades would tear straight across her decks, wrecking her from stem to stern, without a single one of his own guns being able to reply. The only way to prevent such a calamity was by fast action, throwing up the helm—at once!—to round downwind and present his own broadside to *Macedonian*'s, resulting in a running fight in which his own ship would still be outgunned, but without such a horrendous tactical disadvantage.

Favian caught a glimpse of scarlet forward, a snakelike tongue of red ascending the mainmast. It was the Markham viper pendant that Gideon had flown at Cat Island, the badge of his family designed by his uncle Malachi back in 1778. Favian grinned: Malachi, he thought, would approve of his tactics.

Favian saw figures rushing about on *Thames*'s poop as the frigate began to make its abrupt turn, just as he'd anticipated—but what happened next was totally unforeseen. Favian had intended his sudden aggressive move to take advantage of the fact that *Thames* was sandwiched between *Macedonian* and *Trave*. The heavier *Trave* would not be able to fire at Favian without hitting the unfortunate *Thames*, and with luck and skill Favian would be able to keep the British in that situation for some time. *Trave* would have to give way to avoid collision with *Thames*, turning downwind inside the thirty-two—which would keep *Thames* between itself and the American.

What Favian had intended to gain was the chance to pound *Thames* for five or ten minutes without *Trave* being able to fire a shot, possibly knocking the lighter frigate out of the fight. What happened instead was astonishing and—Favian realized afterward—perfectly logical.

Thames made its hurried turn downwind, presenting its larboard broadside. The British frigate's black-painted side was suddenly enveloped in smoke, *Macedonian* shuddering as shot came home. There was a cry of pain from forward as a twelve-pound solid smashed into the hammock nettings among the sail-trimmers standing on the gangway, but Favian, intent on his prey, ignored it. The British, he thought abstractly, had delivered an accurate broadside under trying circumstances—these men were well drilled. Damn it.

"Starboard broadside, ready!" Favian shouted. "At two hundred yards—wait for my signal!" His own broadside was ready. "Clew up the royals!" That would reduce *Macedonian*'s heel a bit and make her a more stable gun platform. "Remember to fire low, boys!" he bellowed. "Give her a hulling!"

And then there was a grinding crash from the *Thames*, an agonized, tearing sound of rending wood, and suddenly *Trave*'s bowsprit was thrusting its massive way through *Thames*'s forecourse, and *Thames*'s mizzen topmast was pitching forward into the mainmast from the impact of the collision. Favian goggled, completely surprised—but not surprised enough to take advantage of it.

"Helm down a bit, Mr. Seward. Starboard battery, fire as you bear!"

The guns began their thunder, spitting their iron at the tangled British frigates. They had collided, Favian realized. *Thames* had turned suddenly to avoid being raked, without having time to inform *Trave* of its maneuver. *Trave* probably hadn't seen *Macedonian*'s turn because *Thames* was in the way, and so hadn't realized there was a threat. *Thames*'s turn had caught *Trave* completely by surprise, just as the larger frigate was trying to overhaul her from leeward. *Trave* had not given way in time, and had rammed *Thames* on her starboard bow.

Favian watched as *Macedonian*'s broadside went home, tearing into the stricken enemy, the quarterdeck carronades leaping in on their slides. There was a crack and *Trave*'s fore-topmast tumbled in ruin upon *Trave*'s foredeck, locking the ships together. "Reload!" Favian roared. "Double shot, with grape for good measure! Mr. Seward, up with the helm, if you please! Hands to clew up the t'gallants!"

Its progress slowed as the canvas spilled wind and came up to the yards, *Macedonian* came in close to the enemy and raked them twice at point-blank range, the British unable to get off a single shot in return—just a little musketry that made *Macedonian*'s quarterdeck unpleasant for a few minutes, with all the officers walking about rapidly to discourage the sharpshooters from drawing a bead on them. Favian was tempted to continue the battle until he forced the enemy to surrender, but he knew there was no way he could get the crippled British frigates away even if he did take them, so he ordered the helm put down and the guns housed.

The crewmen cheered madly as *Macedonian* left the enemy bobbing astern, tangled in wreckage. Favian acknowledged the cheers with a weary wave—now he could get some rest. His war, he thought, was over.

"Order the galley fires lit," he said. "Let's give the men their breakfast."

And then he looked aft, beyond the tangled frigates. The heavy frigate he'd seen earlier was still in pursuit, its beautifully cut sails drawing perfectly. It was, he thought, a little nearer than when he'd last seen it.

Perhaps the war was not over, after all.

TWENTY

"That would be the *Forte*, of course," said Captain Nichols of the 95th. "An ex-Frenchy, you know, captured in '99 by the *Sibylle*. Very famous action, of course; I remember the church bells ringing when I was a lad."

"Aye," Favian said politely. "I seem to remember hearing about it." He was lying, of course, in truth the action was famous. The thirty-eight-gun *Sibylle* had captured the forty-four-gun *Forte* in four hours fight, at the cost of its captain's life. A classic action, a brilliant example of a smaller ship prevailing over a larger. Favian's lies were principally to extract from the genial Captain Nichols as much information as possible.

"Captain Corbett of the *Forte* had an entertainment for us three nights ago," Nicholas said. "A bawdy play put on by the sailors. Some hornpipes, then a tour of the ship. *Forte* was rebuilt a year ago, you know, after this war with you Americans broke out. Rebuilt with Roberts's iron-plate knees, whatever those may be, and Snodgrass diagonal braces, specially to match your big frigates." Nichols smiled and accepted the offer of some Madeira from Campaspe. "Thirty twenty-four-pound guns, sixteen thirty-two-pound carronades on the upper decks, plus a forty-two-pound carronade on a pivot forward. Captain Corbett had his marines equipped with rifled carbines, like Broke of the *Shannon*. Not as accurate as the Baker, of course, but quite nice for close work; and they'll take a bayonet, too. Corbett's quite an admirer of Broke, I gather. Oh, aye, the *Forte* is quite a splendid frigate—wish I'd taken my passage on her instead of that blasted *Otter*." He brightened. "Of course, I might take my passage in her yet, eh? Later this afternoon."

"We'll see," Favian said.

Earlier that morning he'd piled on every sail that could draw, left the *Macedonian* in Seward's hands, and dropped dreamlessly into his cot after going below to the cockpit and kissing Campaspe good morning, listening with only part of his attention to Dr. Truscott's earnest compliments; it seemed Campaspe had made herself useful during an exceptionally tricky amputation. He'd awakened about noon and gone on deck to find the large pursuing frigate a good four miles nearer than she'd been at dawn, sailing beautifully on a bowline astern and slightly to starboard. *Malachi's Revenge* lay about two miles to weather, apparently keeping the frigates under observation. Favian had gone below to have half *Macedonian*'s water casks stove in, then sent men to the pumps to get the water out of the bilges and lighten the ship. The on-duty watch had had its hammocks piped down and two roundshot placed in each; then Favian had shifted this mobile ballast over his ship, trying to get her in better trim. *Macedonian* had gained a knot and a half, but it wasn't enough. The heavy frigate astern—the *Forte*, as they'd now learned—was still gaining, and would probably catch them around sunset.

There was a certain deadly inevitability in a chase to windward. The pursuer would stay on the same tack as its prey until the chase was right abeam; then the pursuer would tack to make up distance to windward, then tack again until the enemy was abeam. The procedure would repeat itself over and over, the distance between the ships steadily narrowing no matter what maneuvers the prey tried. *Forte* had been tacking back and forth all morning, the distance narrowing. Favian knew very well that unless he could somehow outspeed the enemy, battle would be inevitable, and that in battle intelligence regarding the enemy could prove decisive. The only source of intelligence was the prisoners he'd taken the night before.

He'd been reminded of that fact just after he'd come on deck, when a marine had approached Favian with the information that the British officers in the cable tier were asking permission to exercise on deck. Favian had given permission, provided they gave their paroles; he'd then introduced himself to them as they came blinking into the sunlight, trying to wipe slime from the cable tier off their clothing. After Captain Nichols had proven an amiable, talkative gold mine of information, he and Captain Innis of the *Otter*—actually a very junior Royal Navy lieutenant from Scotland; dour and frowning in his captivity—had been invited to dinner with Favian, while the junior officers were invited to the wardroom, also in the hopes of extracting information. Lieutenant Blake, their liberated prisoner, was also invited to Favian's cabin, both because he was an old friend, but also because he was a good conversationalist, and perhaps had information of his own to convey.

Favian had known the pursuing frigate was larger than *Macedonian:* he'd been hoping she'd be a forty like *Endymion*—that could have been coped with, perhaps—but the news that she was *Forte*, a forty-four, was terrifying. Assuming, of course, that Nichols was telling the truth, and not simply a glib liar trying to mislead his enemies, much as Favian had when he'd told his men of the fictitious American squadron in the Gulf.

"But your British ships, Captain Nichols, are notoriously short of men—that's why you people have to resort to press gangs," Favian said, priming the pump once again. "Our American ships usually have so many volunteers that we're well over complement. You may have the heavy guns aboard the *Forte*, but if you don't have the men to man 'em the guns aren't going to do your Captain Corbett any good, are they?"

Nichols frowned. He tugged uncomfortably at his worn green uniform coat, stained with the slime of the cable tier. "There seemed a goodly number of men aboard, Captain Markham," he said, "but I don't know how many. Corbett didn't complain about his lack of sailors."

"Ah, well," Favian said. "No doubt he's used to being shorthanded."

He'd drawn a blank, there. Perhaps it was time to change the subject before even the cheerful Nichols grew suspicious.

"Lieutenant Blake," he said. "I wonder if you could tell us about how you came to be in a British prison ship?"

Blake, having had enough Madeira to be comfortable in the cabin of a superior officer, leaned back in his chair as if stretching out his long legs beneath the table. "Bad luck, mostly," he said. "May I borrow one of your cigarillos? I thank you, sir." He lit the cigarillo from a candle on the table, then went on.

"We were observing the British from the moment they first dropped anchor," he said. "We kept in the Gulf as long as possible, retreating to Bay St. Louis at night—we had a little fort there, and a supply cache. On the thirteenth—that would be three days ago—we saw a fleet of barges heading for Pass Christiana, north of Cat Island. Turned out there were forty-eight of them, each with a heavy carronade in the bow, under my old acquaintance Captain Nicholas Lockyer." He smiled with considerable irony. "I shot up his *Hermes* last September, you see, when the British tried to take Mobile—set his sloop of war on fire and his men had to run for the boats or be blown up. I expect he was eager for revenge. He certainly got it."

He blew smoke into the air. "Tac thought they were trying to land troops, but they kept on past Pass Christiana, and we knew they were heading for us. We pulled back into Lake Borgne after sending the *Sea Horse* schooner to Bay St. Louis to bring off the stores. Sailing Master Johnson of the *Sea Horse* put up a nice little fight, by the way, later that afternoon. The British managed to cut him off from us, you see, so he retreated back into the bay and tried to defend the fort. Held off an attack of seven barges, drove 'em off, then scuttled the schooner and blew up the fort when he saw he couldn't hold any longer. That's what Lockyer told me afterward, anyway. Johnson and his men should be on their way to New Orleans by now, I suppose—I'm sure they got away.

"Our five gunboats ran like the devil—beg pardon, ma'am—into Lake Borgne, but the current was against us and so was the wind. We were trying to get through Les Rigolets into Pontchartrain, but the wind died after dark, and we couldn't row against the current. By morning the level of water in the lake had ebbed, and most of us were aground. The British had been rowing all night, and we could see 'em nine miles to the east of us, still pulling at their oars. We tried to lighten our boats, but it was still dead calm, so we used warps to get us into line between Malheureux Island and the mainland.

"Lockyer's men had been rowing for twenty-four hours straight, so once he saw we were ready to fight, he anchored his boats and gave them breakfast. Around ten thirty he gave the signal to attack, and his men came forward."

He scowled and sipped at his Madeira. "Even then luck was against us," he said. "The current was so strong it dragged two of us out of line. Jones's 156 boat got drug a couple hundred yards down from the rest of us, and my own 163 was pulled down halfway between Jones and the rest. We couldn't support each other, and the British knew it.

"We hurt 'em badly as they approached. They were in three divisions, each under a different captain, with Lockyer's division pulling for the 156 boat, all alone where it couldn't be supported.

Our guns sank two of the barges and spread grape through some others, but we couldn't stop them all. Number 156 was attacked by over ten barges. Poor Jones got a musket ball behind the eye and had to crawl below. Lockyer was wounded twice but his men kept fighting, and eventually the gunboat was taken.

"Then it was my turn. The British turned Jones's guns on my boat while all three divisions attacked. It was the same story—I fought until they got over the rail and had me surrounded, and then I struck. Never really had a hope. Four of my men were killed, and fifteen wounded. It was the same for the rest: the British used the captured gunboats to fire on their next poor victim, and then the barges would attack one gunboat at a time and overwhelm it. We had the damnedest bad luck." He stubbed out his cigarillo. "Poor Lieutenant Spedden of Number 162 had both arms shattered, but kept his men fighting," he said. "When the British boarded, they refused to strike at him even though he couldn't defend himself. Well. Diamond cut diamond, as Dacres said. If we could have maneuvered, it might have been different."

"The luck may swing the other way yet," Favian said. It would have to if he was going to be able to do anything about the *Forte*. He found himself frowning into his wine, then realized that Blake's gentlemanly gloom was beginning to infect him. He raised his cup and assumed a cheerful smile. "I should like to offer a toast that we may all drink to, gentlemen," he said. "To peaceful amity between our two countries!"

"Amity!" they echoed, and drank. There were a few more toasts: Nichols offered one to thank the officers of *Macedonian* for their hospitality, and Innis roused himself from his scowling isolation to raise his glass in a surprisingly eloquent toast to the American commodore's lady. It soon became clear that Nichols was not able to provide any more relevant information about *Forte* and its crew, and Favian, citing duty, called an end to the dinner.

He turned aft to see the big frigate, by now only three miles or so astern, its tall masts gracefully cutting the sky. Campaspe joined him by the window, and Favian, thinking of what those enemy twenty-four-pounders could do to him, absently put his arm around her.

"Was Nichols telling the truth?" she asked, looking up at his frown. "Is the enemy so much bigger?"

"Aye," Favian said. "Will you get me some coffee, darling? I've got to think. Clear my head of wine."

"Is it so much a difference, between thirty-eight guns and forty-four?" Campaspe asked. "Only six guns between you?"

Favian shook his head. "It's worse than that," he said. "For one thing, every ship carries more guns than its rate. We've got twenty-eight long eighteens on the gun deck, sixteen thirty-two-pound carronades, and two pair of twelve-pound chase guns. That's forty-eight guns right there, ten more than our official rating. If that is *Forte* out there, with thirty twenty-four-pound long guns, sixteen thirty-two-pound chase guns, that forty-two-pound pivot smasher, and probably four chase guns, that'll be fifty-one guns—a difference of three guns only, but it's the weight of broadside that counts.

"They've got twenty-four-pounders on their gun deck, but we've only got eighteens," Favian explained. "They throw a much heavier weight of shot, and they can throw it farther and more accurately. They can chop us up at long range. That's how *Macedonian* was first captured from the British, by the way, with one of our twenty-four-pound frigates, the *United States*. I was aboard her as first lieutenant; I directed the gunfire. They didn't stand a chance."

He spared her the statistics. Thus far in the war there had been three engagements between twenty-four-pounder forty-fours and thirty-eights: *Constitution* vs. *Guerrière*, *United States* vs. *Macedonian*, and *Constitution* vs. *Java*. In each case the heavier frigate had won, and in the second case, when Stephen Decatur had used brilliant, unusual tactics to keep the range long, the victory had been particularly lopsided.

Campaspe handed him his cup of coffee; he continued to gaze aft while he drank. "And there's the difference in construction," Favian went on. "A twenty-four-pound frigate has to be built more stoutly in order to hold all that heavy ordnance. It's a much tougher ship; it'll stand more punishment than we will. I might have hoped it would have been neglected since it was captured in '99, but Nichols tells me it was rebuilt just last year. Probably tougher than ever." The vision of *Macedonian*'s well deck came again, the bloody seawater with the limbs of the dead slopping from side to side with the roll of the ship. With an effort of will he banished it.

"The British captured *Forte* with a thirty-eight, Captain Nichols said," Campaspe said. "Can't you do the same?"

"The British captured it from the *French*, you see," Favian said. "The French can build beautiful ships, but they can't sail 'em or fight 'em—haven't had the practice the British and Americans have had, and they haven't had Nelson or Preble either. With Americans and British it's diamond cut diamond, like Blake said. The crews and captains are more evenly matched, and that means that any difference in ordnance will matter that much more.

"We do have one advantage, though," Favian said. "Our Navy uses sheet-lead cartridges for its guns. The old-fashioned cartridges were made out of linen. . . ."

"I know," Campaspe said. "That's what we used on the *Franklin*."

"Well, then you know that the guns had to be wormed and sponged after each shot, to remove bits of burning linen that might ignite the next cartridge prematurely. The sheet-lead cartridges don't catch on fire like that, and the guns don't need to be wormed at all, and don't have to be sponged except for every five shots or so. Our rate of fire will be higher; we can count on that."

"You must think, Favian," Campaspe said. She put her arms around him, resting her head on his chest. "There must be some way."

"There are two, perhaps," Favian said. "I can try to stay at long range and hope to knock away a spar or two with good gun practice. But the British will be firing as well, with those twenty-four-pounders. I think at long bowls we'll lose, just like *Macedonian* lost to *United States* two years ago."

"What is the second plan?"

"To get close, as close as we can," Favian said. "At very close range an eighteen-pound ball has about as much power as a twenty-four. I think that's our best chance, but it may not work. Captain Corbett may not want us to get close, and since he's the faster ship, he can enforce his decisions." He sipped his coffee, wishing for some lightning stroke of inspiration. "Nichols said he was a disciple of Captain Broke, though—Broke seems to believe in close action, in fact he took *Chesapeake* by boarding. It usually isn't British practice to fight at long range. So I think we've got to get close if we can."

He spared her the implications of that strategy. Men would die in heaps, torn apart by grape and cannister. *Forte*'s marines had rifled carbines, just like Broke's marines on the *Shannon* when they took the *Chesapeake:* and all of *Chesapeake*'s officers but one had been killed or wounded. Perhaps not all by those deadly carbines, but their accuracy was a factor a professional officer could not afford to ignore, particularly since Favian's own marines were armed with rifles and he'd seen their practice on an enemy before. If he came within range of those enemy carbines, he might be signing his own death warrant.

He sipped his coffee again. Campaspe said nothing. There was a brief knock on the cabin door.

"Beg pardon, sir." It was Ford's voice. "*Malachi's Revenge* is coming within hail."

"In a moment." For a few seconds Favian luxuriated in the feeling of Campaspe's arms around him, the scent of her hair, the feel of her warm body against his own . . . all over in a few hours, perhaps. If only the war were over, he thought. It was strange; just a few days ago he'd been wondering if the best thing he could have done for Campaspe would have been to get himself killed. But now he didn't want to lose this.

He *was* finished, he knew. The minute he began to have thoughts like that, it was over: the Navy demanded that the service come first in the lives of all its officers; and Favian knew too well what happened to those who let others get in the way.

He turned Campaspe's face up to his and kissed her. "Let's go talk to Gideon," he said.

Revenge was hove to ahead and to leeward, waiting for the frigate to catch up. As *Macedonian* sped past—Favian wasn't about to stop for a conversation and watch *Forte* close the distance—Gideon filled his sails and rode twenty yards to leeward of where Favian stood on the quarterdeck. Gideon was plain to see on *Revenge*'s deck, standing by the weather rail with his speaking trumpet.

"We kept our prizes in sight all morning," he shouted. "We took four last night, and I think they all got to Mobile!"

"Very good!" Favian shouted back. "Did you see any of our prizes? We took three!"

"I saw at least two make their way out."

"We blew up one powder vessel," Favian said, "and put some broadsides into two others. We saw one ship on fire afterward. And we damaged two frigates this morning." This was not boasting: Favian wanted word to get back to Jackson and Patterson of what he'd done. If he were killed or captured later in the day, at least Gideon would be able to give an accurate report. Gideon nodded at the news, then got to the matter that had brought him here.

"Ye boys won't be able to outrun that frigate, there," he said. "I'll support ye, when the time comes."

"One of our prisoners says that's the *Forte*," Favian told him. "She's a twenty-four-pound ship, so beware of her."

Gideon was silent for a moment, absorbing the news. Favian could sense a stir among his sailors at the information. Well, they'd find out sooner or later anyway, after those twenty-four-pound roundshot began tearing up their frigate.

"I think we're nimble enough to stay out of their way," Gideon said. It was meant to be comforting, but Favian knew how little Gideon's promise meant. The nineteen-gun *Revenge* was a big schooner, but it had been built for speed, not for taking punishment. A single broadside from *Forte*, at effective range, could leave her a shambles, perhaps even sink her; whereas *Forte* could shrug off any number of *Revenge*'s twelve-pounder broadsides as mere nuisances. *Revenge* had no carronades; only her chase gun, the eighteen-pound pivot captained by Long Tom Tate, was big enough to cause *Forte* anxiety, and it was the only gun of its size aboard the privateer.

Yet *Revenge* looked big enough; it was almost as long as *Macedonian*, though narrower and a great deal lower. She might serve to intimidate Captain Corbett a little, and any assistance was welcome—if General McIntosh of the White Stick Creeks were to appear with fifty painted warriors riding a fleet of canoes, Favian would welcome him with open arms.

"I don't think the enemy will be up with us till dusk," Favian said. "We'll wait till then; we might have some luck if one of her spars carries away."

That sort of luck never came: *Forte* continued closing the gap between it and the American, its sturdy spars showing no sign of strain, its great white wings braced precisely to the wind. At five, with the enemy only a mile astern, he gave the men supper an hour early, then, after they'd finished their whiskey ration, had the trumpeter call them to quarters. The British prisoners were sent below to the cable tier, and a marine guard placed on them.

"You'll have to join Dr. Truscott, darling," Favian said to Campaspe as he stood in his cabin—it was being rapidly torn down around him, the screens and furnishings carted below by *Macedonian*'s crewmen. Favian clipped on his sword, checked the priming of his pistols, and thrust the pistols into his waistband.

She gave a little frown. "I'd rather be with you than down there with the doctor."

"The wounded may need you."

She nodded resignedly, gave him a hug, and then made her way—a strange, small figure, still wrapped in a coat many times too large for her—out of the cabin. She paused at the doorway to give him a smile, her dazzling, impudent, wholehearted smile. Favian felt a leap of reckless optimism in her radiance, but then she was gone, her place taken by a burly bosun's mate who rushed in with a gang of men to move Favian's wardrobe. The optimism faded with the smile's afterglow. It was time to sacrifice his ship and his men to the gods in the Navy Department.

The sun was low in the sky, hanging red-orange off *Forte*'s larboard quarter, gilding the enemy frigate's spars, turning her sails a pale gold. *I'll see if I can knock some of that gilt off,* Favian thought sourly, viewing the frigate over the taffrail as he stood on the quarterdeck. He had just finished his inspection of the *Macedonian,* going among the hands, his usual round of joking familiarity. He hadn't made a speech this time, sensing that the hands wouldn't take it well; instead he'd talked quietly among them, telling them that their enemy was a twenty-four-pound frigate and that they must expect to be hit hard. But, he said, the *Forte* was probably under complement. *Macedonian* still had its sheet-lead cartridges, which meant a faster rate of fire. They'd been up against bad odds before, just this morning in fact, and they'd come through. Besides, *Forte* had been taken by a thirty-eight fifteen years ago and could be taken again the same way. The sailors had nodded calmly, listening to his words, and no doubt made their own judgments.

On the quarterdeck he'd turned to the afterguard, and his eyes had met the pale eyes of Lazarus the prophet. Lararus, oddly, had turned away, a strange expression on his face. It seemed surprisingly like guilt. Favian thought. Was the madman blaming himself for this, the approach of the doom he had preached for so long? Or was it some other form of remorse, that he had lived so long in the night of his derangement and was now seeing its consequence?

Troubled, Favian turned aft and gazed at the enemy. *Forte* was three quarters of a mile astern and to leeward. There was no hope of escaping after darkness: the enemy could easily keep them in sight at this range. Nothing to do but fight.

"A signal to *Malachi's Revenge*, Mr. Stanhope," Favian said, his eyes still on that sun-burnished frigate, hoping to spot some weakness, some flaw that would let him escape the hammering that would tear *Macedonian* to bits. "Throw out Number 120, 'A signal for battle.' "

"Aye aye, sir."

"Hands to furl the royals! Hands to furl t'gallants and main course! Douse the outer and flying jibs!" He glanced aloft: the big American ensign raised that morning was still flying from the peak, and the long Markham serpent was still writhing from the main. More flags, he thought, we might lose a few soon. "Mr. Chapelle, I'll thank you to raise our jack to the fore and a battle flag to the mizzen."

The frigate resounded to the tramp of feet, the shouting of the mast captains, and the roar of canvas as the yards were lowered, the sails clewed up, then furled. Favian stood apart from the noise and bustle on the weather quarterdeck, watching *Forte* through narrowed eyes. It would be clear to the enemy that *Macedonian* was shortening sail for battle—what would be their reaction? What Favian most feared was that the enemy would tack, coming about to seize the weather gage, but he didn't think it was likely. If the British took the weather gage, *Macedonian* would have a chance to run downwind; perhaps off the wind *Macedonian* might prove faster and make its escape.

Forte's answer came swiftly: royals and topgallants began to be clewed up to the yards, battle ensigns, bright spots of color, rising to the mastheads. Captain Corbett was willing to let Favian have the weather gage, then; and Favian was perfectly happy to keep it. From windward he could control the early stages of the battle, perhaps be able to narrow the range without exposing himself to the consequences of deadly enemy fire.

"Up with the helm, Mr. Seward!" Favian called, before the last of the sail-furlers had come tumbling down the shrouds. "Steer us about eight points to starboard . . . there! Amidships!"

Macedonian rocked on the waves as she steadied on her new

course, the gilded figurehead of Alexander the Great turning sternly to the British frigate. Now would come the first major clue concerning enemy intentions. Favian had taken *Macedonian* downwind on an intercepting course, carefully avoiding the arc of *Forte*'s broadside guns. If Corbett hoped to get the most out of his heavier guns, he would fall off the wind a bit and open fire, chewing *Macedonian* up as she approached. If Corbett were intent on opening the contest at close range, he would keep on his present course.

Across the water came the booming of canvas as *Forte*'s main course was hauled up to the yard. She was shortened down for battle now, under topsails only, the reduced canvas reducing her angle of heel and making her a better firing platform. If Corbett were to make his move, he'd do it now. Favian could feel his jaw muscles clenching, the hand that had been paralyzed off Tripoli closing into a white-knuckled fist, anticipating that first enemy broadside. If he saw the enemy turn, he'd tell everyone to lie down, to minimize casualties.

Forte kept smoothly on its present track, its guns housed within its blank ports. Favian felt a wild surge of optimism—Corbett was a hackum after all! A true lay-alongside thunderer! —but he knew his hope was totally unjustified. Perhaps he was sailing *Macedonian* into Corbett's trap: there was no way of knowing until after the battle was over. *Forte*'s broadside would be bad enough at close range.

Favian moved to the lee side of the quarterdeck to keep *Forte* in sight as the range narrowed and the enemy frigate began to disappear behind *Macedonian*'s giant forecourse. Should he furl it or not? He'd left it set to help *Macedonian* narrow the range, but once battle began it might get in the way. The big sail was hard to control, it limited Favian's visibility, and it was a fire hazard hanging so low over the firing guns, but it also might give Favian an extra burst of speed if he needed it. He decided to keep the sail set and drawing. He could always clew it up at need; and the chance of fire was reduced because he'd been keeping the sails wet all day trying to run away from the enemy. Besides, a plan was beginning to form in his mind. . . .

"All guns, out tompions! Starboard guns load with roundshot and grape! Larboard guns load with roundshot!" He had no intention of using the larboard guns at present, but perhaps there would be need later. In the meantime it would give the men something to do other than contemplate the possibilities of death and mutilation. Favian peered out around the forecourse. Five hundred yards from the enemy, four hundred fifty . . . Would they let him close the range so easily?

And then Favian saw the curve in *Forte*'s wake, the port-lids rising to wink their red-painted interiors at him, the gun muzzles sliding out. "Down!" Favian roared. "Everyone lie down!" He threw himself full-length to the deck amid the clatter of the quarterdeck gun crews, sail-trimmers, and officers doing the same, and then there was the thunder of the enemy broadside. Favian felt *Macedonian*'s planks shudder beneath him as enemy iron smashed home, hearing the crashes as iron punched through the oaken bulwarks or wailed overhead with the shrieks of the damned. Then there was a sudden silence, and Favian jumped to his feet, seeing the British frigate shrouded in a pall of its gunsmoke.

A damned good broadside, he knew. Corbett had his men trained well: far too many of those twenty-four-pound solids had struck home. There were a few tears in the forecourse and a gap in the fo'c'sle bulwark, but most seemed to have struck low on the gun deck or waterline. To reply or not? If he bore up to fire, he would delay his approach, but if he didn't, he'd have to take another two or three broadsides before being able to fire a shot. No, he thought, he'd have to take it. He'd made his decision to fight at close range, and he'd stick to it.

There was the report of a single gunshot to windward, and Favian turned his head in surprise at the sound. *Malachi's Revenge*, ahead of *Macedonian* and to windward, had fired a round from its chaser. The privateer made a brave sight with its ranked masts and long, low hull, the Markham pendant whipping from its mainmast, another homemade flag flying from its fore, a plain white banner with FREE TRADE AND SAILORS' RIGHTS inscribed on it in black letters. He had forgotten about the schooner altogether, but Gideon was bravely taking it into battle. It couldn't do much to affect the outcome, Favian knew, but perhaps it would give Corbett a little extra to worry about.

Forte's guns were beginning to come out of its ports again, slowly as the British gunners struggled to roll their iron uphill against the frigate's heel. Favian saw anxious eyes directed at him, Chapelle, Blake, Kuusikoski at his station on a quarterdeck carronade, the other gunners of the quarterdeck battery, all wondering when he'd luff and return the enemy fire.

"Down!" Favian said. "Everyone lie down!"

They obeyed swiftly; perhaps they still trusted him to have a plan. And perhaps he did: it was one he'd used before, when he'd taken the *Teaser,* and with luck it would work here.

The enemy guns fired one at a time, or in clusters of two or three: Corbett was allowing them to fire at will, as soon as they could be loaded and hauled out the ports. The British fire was deadly accurate: Favian felt the deck shuddering and knew *Macedonian* couldn't stand much more of this; he looked up to see the sails drawing and prayed for a gust of wind that would bring him nearer the enemy. There was another shot, a crash, and a scream; Favian jumped up to see one of the fo'c'sle carronades lying on its side, two of its crew lying near it in their own blood, a third with his leg under the carronade, pleading with his mates to get it off him. Meat for the surgeon's saw, Favian thought. It was going to get worse.

The infernal barrage continued, Favian jumping up from time to time to gauge the enemy's rage, watching it narrow. The British carronades joined in as the range narrowed, the intensity of their fire hellish. It was impossible to anticipate the enemy fire, and that made it nerve-wracking; if they'd been firing regular broadsides it would have been much easier. Favian saw the giant American battle flag he'd raised to the mizzen masthead drifting slowly in the wind toward the enemy; the flag halliards had been shot away. The flag was trailed by little squares of color that fluttered in the breeze, his signal Number 120 that he'd forgot to have hauled down. He hoped no one regarded it as an omen.

At last it was time. "Mr. Seward, put down the helm!" Favian shouted. "Starboard battery, on your feet and run 'em out. Range a hundred fifty yards! Let's give the British three Yankee cheers!"

Eager for blood after their long punishment, the cheers came spilling from *Macedonian*'s gun deck as the beams echoed the sounds of the guns running out. Now we'll see who's the better disciple of Broke, Favian thought. It wasn't only the British who could learn from the captain of the *Shannon*. Favian himself had adopted Broke's trick of nailing light wooden laths behind each gun and carronade, each lath calculated, when lined with the barrel of the gun, to send the shot on a precise intersecting line with the shot of every other gun. Used properly, every gun would be aimed at the exact same spot of the enemy ship; as the ships changed their relative positions during the fight, the guns would tear up each section of enemy decks in turn.

"Remember to fire low! Hull her, hull her!" Favian roared. "Ready, boys! *Fire!*"

Macedonian trembled as the guns lashed out at the enemy, leaping in on their tackles, Favian clearly hearing the crashes from the *Forte* as the guns struck home. Rifle shots snapped out from *Macedonian*'s fighting tops as sharpshooters took their aim. "Fire by section, boys!" Favian shouted, smelling powder, his heart racing. "Roundshot and grape! A hundred fifty yards! Mr. Seward, I need those sails well trimmed! Keep narrowing the range, here!" He looked at the quarterdeck carronades, seeing their crews madly working to reload. A thought struck him. "Mr. Chapelle!" he snapped. "I want you to supervise the quarterdeck guns, here! Roundshot only, not grape. Keep 'em aimed for the enemy mainmast—I want her mainmast down! Mr. Blake, give 'em some help." The number two starboard section fired, its guns spitting flame. Favian bent down himself over the first gun to finish loading, the one manned by his boat's crew under Kuusikoski's direction, giving brief commands to the men with the side-tackles, keeping the carronade slide trained on the *Forte*'s mainmast.

"Fire!" he shouted, and Kuusikoski tugged at the lanyard, the carronade jolting back on its slide as it spat out its roundshot. Favian heard a bang from the enemy frigate and knew he'd hit something, though perhaps not the mainmast.

And then there was a horrible wooden shrieking overhead, and Favian looked up to see the mizzen-topgallant mast toppling over to leeward. *Macedonian* lurched as the mast stopped short in its fall, hanging by its shrouds, and then snapped or tore free its few remaining supports and came down, Favian leaping like a madman for the weather quarterdeck, the carronade crews jumping with him. The heavy mast came smashing down into the rail, knocking a carronade over onto its side, and then, with a rending moan, tore itself free and disappeared over the side, dragging along in the frigate's wake, held still by a few remaining backstays. "Clear away that wreckage!" Favian snapped. "Get those guns back in operation! Axemen to cut that mast free!"

He seized a handspike and helped to lever the fallen carronade upright: its lashings seemed to be undamaged. Bits of smashed rail were flung overboard; the mast was cut free by a dozen sail-trimmers with boarding axes, and there was a perceptible jerk as the deadweight was left astern and the frigate moved more swiftly through the water.

A musket ball spanged off the carronade as Favian helped to aim it: the enemy marines had spotted him as someone in authority. He was wearing an old pea jacket and a plain beaver hat, not a uniform—his height made him conspicuous enough, he thought, without wearing a uniform and all his medals like Lord Nelson, to attract enemy musketeers—but he found himself mentally counting off the seconds it would take that marine to reload, and then, after the carronade was aimed and fired, jumping back and beginning a brisk pacing to discourage his marksmanship.

The range had narrowed; Seward had kept the frigate edging down toward the enemy. "Range one hundred yards!" Favian shouted. "Odd guns load with cannister on top of roundshot!" For a moment he considered triple-shotting the guns, then decided against it—triple shot wouldn't do much more damage than double shot, since all the shot ended up hitting the same place on the enemy ship anyway, and it increased loading time. His sense of the battle was that *Macedonian*'s guns were firing much quicker than *Forte*'s; it was his only advantage, and he needed to keep it.

There was the sound of a broadside, then the noise of shot striking the enemy. Favian's head jerked up and he saw *Malachi's Revenge*, its side wreathed in smoke, luffing up into the wind off *Forte*'s starboard bow. Gideon could keep that position forever, firing his broadsides into the enemy bows without the British being able to hit him with a single gun. Good for Gideon, Favian thought; he'd managed to find a place to harass the enemy and avoid retaliation.

A bullet twittered past his head. Favian clenched his fist and kept pacing: wouldn't one of his own marines take care of that man? *Macedonian* had seven men in each fighting top, six men all reloading for the best marksman, who fired himself as fast as he could aim and pull the trigger; the rest of the marines were lined on the gangways and quarterdeck, taking what shots they could.

Favian glared at the enemy, seeing her masts through the smoke, trying to sort out the meaningful information from the random, noisy chaos of battle, the roar of guns and wail of grapeshot, the screams of dying men and the boom of canvas. *Forte,* it seemed, was falling astern. With the mizzen-topgallant mast finally cut free, *Macedonian* seemed to be moving more swiftly, aided by that big forecourse, the fact that she was to windward of *Forte* and stealing her wind, and perhaps more intangible factors—it was possible that *Forte* was simply slow when sailing under topsails alone, but a witch with all canvas set. Favian paused for a moment, his fist clenching and unclenching by his side as he gauged the movements of the two ships. It was time, he thought, to try his plan.

"Helm up, Mr. Seward!" he called. "We'll try to cross her bows!"

It had worked when he'd taken the *Teaser* with his old *Experiment* brig, in just this situation, though he'd been aided by a lucky shot that had knocked away *Teaser*'s jib tie and kept her from turning away from him. He was a little ahead of *Forte* now; he'd try to turn across her bows and hope for a collision that would allow him to rake her.

The deck surged as the rudder bit, *Macedonian*'s bluff bows turning downwind toward the enemy, her canvas bellying out full. An enemy roundshot widened the aftmost carronade port, sending its crew flying before a sheaf of oak splinters: Favian knit his brows and watched *Forte* through the shroud of gunsmoke, watching her for a clue as to her intentions.

"Damn!" he bellowed, smashing his fist into the rail. "Damn the man!" Corbett had seen it coming; there was a widening gap of darkening blue between *Forte*'s upper masts. She was turning downwind, curving easily inside *Macedonian*'s own turn. But that in itself might present an opportunity, if only Favian could judge the moment . . . Their change of tacks had brought them out of the shrouding gunsmoke, and Favian could see *Forte* clearly now, her black-painted bulwarks showing white scars where *Macedonian* had struck her, red-coated marines lining her quarterdeck and gangway. She was turning nimbly, drawing a little ahead with the advantage of the inside track. *Malachi's Revenge* was darting nimbly off the British bows, still managing to keep itself out of *Forte*'s broadside arc.

Now. "Mr. Seward, helm hard aweather! Larboard broadside, load doubleshot and grape! Hands to the braces!" He would spin onto the larboard tack and cross her track, firing a triple-shotted broadside through her Frenchified gingerbread stern. If he had judged the moment aright, he could pull it off, perhaps the telling blow . . .

The starboard broadside fired their last few shots as *Macedonian* spun neatly on its heel, their extra hands running to the larboard broadside to help them run out their guns. There was a sudden silence as both frigates ceased fire, and Favian forced himself to walk calmly to the larboard side, his view of the *Forte* suddenly blanketed by the big forecourse. Then the silence was broken as the larboard guns began to growl out of their ports and the sails began to luff, adding a crackling canvas roar to Favian's perceptions, the spanker gybing over with a crash. *Macedonian*'s sails were braced on the larboard tack, and the sudden move to the starboard tack had the wind catching them edge-on, making them useless. Sail-trimmers were already casting off the tacks and braces, hauling hard, almost vertical with the deck as they struggled to get the yards around. And Favian, as the canvas boomed, caught a perfect, tantalizing glimpse of the enemy's stern as *Forte* continued its turn. He had to fire in the next few seconds or the opportunity would be lost.

But *Macedonian*, its sails flapping uselessly, wallowed in the swell, the gunners madly training their weapons all the way forward while their officers screamed livid curses. No help. *Forte* completed its turn, moving neatly to the starboard tack, a black line of guns coming out of their ports to meet *Macedonian*'s broadside. *Macedonian* staggered as the newly braced sails filled with wind, then began to surge forward. Too late. Favian felt his heart sink. Too late.

Macedonian and *Forte* had simply about-faced without changing positions, like dancers at a ball. The American frigate still had the weather gage; all that had changed was the fact both ships were on the starboard tack instead of the larboard. Far to leeward Favian heard the sound of cannon: *Malachi's Revenge* was firing over the enemy's larboard quarter. The thought of *Malachi's Revenge* brought an interesting thought to Favian's mind, and he wondered at its significance. As *Forte* had made its turn, the British larboard broadside had been in a perfect position to fire a broadside into the *Revenge*, but the broadside hadn't been fired. Either Corbett didn't consider the tern schooner worth bothering about or he'd had a reason for not firing. Perhaps he only had enough men to man one broadside at a time, and in order to fight the more deadly American threat—*Macedonian*—he'd had to shift all his men to the starboard guns and pass up the chance to hit out at Gideon. Favian filed the thought away; it was too early to know if it had any significance.

Macedonian was slightly astern of *Forte* now, both ships rounding up into the wind, *Macedonian* overhauling. The sun was below the horizon, and Favian had to strain to see *Forte* through the smoke. There were a few shots from the American fighting tops as the marines chanced their luck, but no other firing. *Macedonian*'s jibboom slowly drew even with *Forte*'s taffrail. Soon the fresh, unused broadsides would open up. Who would fire first? Neither side would want to fire piddling little individual shots; both would want to delay long enough to fire a full broadside if possible. But the first broadside fired would be the most devastating, tempting both sides to fire early. Fire discipline, Favian thought; it was critical.

"First, second, and third larboard sections ready!" Favian called down. It was a compromise, firing the first ten guns and the fo'c'sle carronades earlier than the rest, but he desperately needed to get that first shot in. "Fire when the aftermost gun of the third battery crosses the enemy mizzen! Range one hundred fifty yards! Fourth and fifth sections, fire as your guns bear!" He glanced up at *Forte,* wondering what orders Corbett had given. There was a tiny blossom of smoke from the enemy taffrail, and a musket ball gouged white wood from the fife rail next to Favian. Damn those rifles; it was time to move again.

He ran below, heading down to the gun deck where he could supervise the guns properly. Fire discipline was critical; the orders he'd given were unusual; and perhaps the Macedonians weren't used to his system yet. The gun deck was black with night and smoke: in the ghostly light provided by the battle lanterns, Favian caught a hurried impression of overturned guns, blood on the planking, the second and third gunports on the starboard side beaten into one, a giant chip taken out of the mainmast where an enemy roundshot had struck it a glancing blow. Horrible, a defeat in the making. But the men were standing to their guns, their bared teeth and eyes standing out white against their powder-streaked faces: they still trusted him, the fools; they didn't know he'd pulled his one trick and failed. Ford and Swink, assisted by Midshipmen Solomon and Tolbert, were patrolling the deck, swords bared to run through anyone who tried to flee below, giving out a litany of orders: "Remember to aim low, there . . . hold your fire, wait for the order. Keep your fire low, boys. Cock your piece, there, Clisby, you've forgotten. That's better."

"Fine work, boys!" Favian shouted, knowing he had little to add to the orders already given. "Just a little lower on that number three gun; knock that quoin in a little more." There was crackling musketry overhead as the sharpshooters began their work. He peered at *Forte* through the narrow number ten gunport, seeing the French-built frigate's gingerbread quarter galleries rolling closer. "Ready, lads?" He clapped the number ten gun captain on the shoulder, seeing his fierce grin. "Ready to give it to 'em, there?" Would the moment never come? He bent over the gun. "Ready, man? I see her mizzen. Wait for the moment, wait for the wave . . ." The swell rolled *Macedonian*'s guns low as it caught the frigate, then lifted it; for a moment *Macedonian* hung poised on the edge of the wave, a perfect, still gun platform. Preble's old drill, bless the man's memory. "Fire!" Favian called, and the gun deck filled with flame and thunder.

Each gun fired at least once more before Corbett deigned to reply: Perhaps the British hadn't been ready, or perhaps they were waiting for the chance to fire full broadsides. But when *Forte* did fire, it stunned Favian with its power; suddenly *Macedonian*'s gun deck was a chaos of tearing shot, flying splinters, and screaming wounded. This couldn't go on. "Hot work, eh?" he said, trying to grin. He must have pounded that fellow's shoulder raw; he pulled his hand back. "You're doing well, lads, we're smashing 'em up! Fire at will, now, when you bear!" Ford was lying against the mainmast, looking in slow surprise at his severed forearm sitting in his lap. Tolbert's round hat had a ten-inch oak splinter stuck right through it; there was an expression of fierce, uncomprehending stubbornness on the boy's face. Somewhere in the smoke Favian could hear the sounds of vomiting. Hopeless.

He ran back up to the quarterdeck, shouting wild orders to aim the carronades for the mainmast again. It was the only hope, he knew; he'd have to cripple *Forte* somehow and then run for it. Favian saw Blake bending over a carronade, and seized him by the collar, shouting into his ear over the crash of guns. "Go below to the gun deck and see what you can do! Ford's been wounded!"

"Aye," Blake nodded calmly; there was a splinter wound on his cheek that oozed blood into his side-whiskers. He looked at Favian and clasped his shoulder. "Good luck, Favian." Blake knew it was pointless, Favian saw, but he'd do his best. As they all would.

Favian bent over one of the carronades, shouting instructions for it to be trained at the enemy mainmast. They were almost abeam by now, *Macedonian* narrowing the range and overhauling as it had before. Favian recognized the leather cap and broad shoulders of one of the men at the carronade, and saw the wild look in his mad eyes: Lazarus, his face smeared by powder, taking the place of one of the fallen. What was he thinking, Favian wondered, now that the doom he'd preached so often was actually on them?

"Fire!" Favian shouted, and the carronade banged. In the same instant blackness seemed to strike him between the eyes. He blinked, his hands groping, feeling the planks, the warm tar oozing up between them. Light gradually returned to his vision, and he saw Chapelle's round, horrified face just a few inches away.

"Are you hurt, Captain?" Chapelle was demanding.

"I don't know," Favian said numbly. He looked down, seeing his body sprawled on the planking, Stanhope, Chapelle, and a handful of seamen clustered around him. Somewhere a familiar voice was shrieking curses, cadenced measured curses, infamous. There seemed to be blood on his coat. Stanhope tore at the coat, getting it open, and Favian felt the first burst of pain. Stanhope ripped his shirt away.

There was a line of angry red across his chest, blood oozing slowly from the wound. A glancing musket shot, Favian thought with stunned relief. That voice was still crying curses to the wind. "Can you move your arm?" Chapelle was asking. What did the arm have to do with anything? Favian wondered, and then he looked. There was more blood on his upper left arm; apparently the musket ball had pierced his arm after it scored his chest.

"Get me on my feet," Favian said. "We'll see." He was picked up by half a dozen hands and set gingerly on his feet; for a moment his ankles failed to support him, but then balance returned with a ferocious act of will, and a lightning-bolt of pain struck his upper arm. He tried to move his fingers and succeeded;

perhaps it wasn't broken, then. "Help me get my coat off," he said.

The wound was a lucky one: it hadn't struck the bone, and seemed not to have cut the artery. Blood oozed slowly from the entrance wound, and Favian could feel the lump that was the musket ball on the other side. Truscott could cut it out later; for the present it would do well enough if Stanhope would tie it up with his handkerchief. Chapelle seemed quite relieved, perhaps for Favian's sake, perhaps, remembering Acting Lieutenant William Cox, because he didn't want to be in command of the stricken frigate. That ranting voice continued unabated. Favian muzzily looked up as Stanhope dextrously wound his handkerchief around Favian's arm, and to his astonishment saw Lazarus standing in the mizzen chains, waving his fist at the enemy and screaming curses in his harsh voice.

"My the hosts of Satan smite thee and thine!" Lazarus was shrieking. "May the spirits of the sea devour thy heart! May Leviathan rise to tear thee asunder, and may Davey Jones rend thy planks!"

"What the devil?" Favian wondered. "Lazarus, get down there!" The man's mind had snapped.

"The spirits of the air break thy masts like twigs!" Lazarus roared, and then a flight of grapeshot blew him to the deck. Favian looked down at the madman, seeing most of the left shoulder gone, arterial blood pumping out of the wound, the left leg broken in at least two places. No hope, he knew, but he seized his pea jacket as Stanhope was trying to slip it back on his arm, knelt by the old preacher, and pressed the jacket to the shoulder wound, trying to stop the jet of blood. "Stretcher, here!" he shouted, and he heard the order echoed. Lazarus's pale eyes opened, seeming to see nothing, and then they turned to Favian.

"My life for thine, Captain," the man whispered. "I have arranged it. Remember thy promise!"

"I remember," Favian said. Was that what the madman had attempted, calling up the spirits of the deep to defend a vessel he had always claimed was doomed? Some strange act of devotion to Favian, whom he had followed unbidden for two years? Even Lazarus, Favian thought, had trusted him: look how the man was paid.

Lazarus tried to say something else, but his strength was gone;

the spark behind the pale eyes faded. The stretcher-bearers came to take him away, and Favian stood. He would probably die before he reached the orlop.

There was a crash, and Favian looked up in alarm, knowledge of the battle swimming into his mind. What was happening here? Only a little more than a minute had passed since he'd been struck; there couldn't be that much difference. There was a cheer from the American gunners, and Favian gasped relief: *Forte*'s main-topgallant mast had gone by the board, falling like a great tree to leeward. It was dragging in the water, slowing the British frigate; and then Favian was shouting orders to the helm.

"Helm to weather, Mr. Seward! Hands to the braces!"

The situation had duplicated itself: *Macedonian* had gradually overhauled the enemy and closed the range. Favian would try his trick again, hoping to rake *Forte* one way or another while the British were slowed by the drag of the mast. If it didn't work, Favian thought numbly, he'd strike his colors. He was all out of tricks; he could sense *Macedonian*'s fire slowing, fading as the enemy fire had its effect.

Like a fever-nightmare the battle repeated itself. *Forte* saw the move early and turned inside *Macedonian*'s track. Favian threw the helm all the way over, hoping to catch the enemy's vulnerable stern in a rake, but the drag of the mast actually helped the British: it lay in the water off their larboard side, helping to act as a sea anchor to swing their ship around while *Macedonian* lost way, rolling in the swell while her sails were braced around. Then the mast was cut free, liberating the British from the wreckage, the mast lying like a log in *Macedonian*'s path. The frigate ground over the piece of floating rubbish, Favian staring hollow-eyed to leeward, hypnotized by his brief vision of the enemy stern, vulnerable and fleeting, forever unreachable.

But there was a difference this time, Favian realized as the gun crews made ready the battered old starboard broadside, running the guns out the ports, training them on the enemy. *Forte*, seen dimly through dark and smoke, its hull-stripe reflecting the flashes of *Macedonian*'s cannon, was farther off the wind than before, not rounding up close-hauled as *Macedonian* had. Corbett was letting *Macedonian* fire into *Forte*'s quarter, the British unable to answer. Favian felt glee surge through him: perhaps the British were crippled. Perhaps they were even running!

"Starboard broadside, ready!" he shouted. Strange, he thought, how shouting seemed to make pain shoot through his arm. "Roundshot only! Range three hundred yards! *Fire!*"

The guns leaped inboard to the limits of their tackles, *Macedonian* shuddering to the full broadside. "Helm up, Mr. Seward. Starboard broadside reload with roundshot!" He'd follow *Forte* downwind for the present, luffing to fire his broadsides, in case Corbett had some scheme in mind. He saw the black sky widening between *Forte*'s masts; she was luffing, presenting her broadside. Favian tried to fight off the feeling of hopelessness. *Forte* wasn't out of the fight after all.

"Mr. Seward!" he called. "Helm down. Starboard broadside, fire as you bear!"

"Mr. Seward's dead, sir." It was Midshipman Lovette, his arm still bound to his side, his face plainly reflecting his shock at seeing Favian with bloody shirt and bandaged arm.

"Helm down!" Favian repeated, shouting. "Did'ee hear me, there!"

"Aye aye, Captain!" The firm voice came from below the poop overhang, and the frigate was already beginning to luff up. One of the quartermasters, at least, had survived whatever shot had killed the master.

"Stand by the helm, Mr. Lovette," Favian said to the midshipman. "Make sure they hear my instructions."

Lovette swallowed hard. "Aye aye, sir," he said; and then the British let loose their broadside, a ripple of brightness in this peaceless night. Favian stood frozen as shot wailed overhead, smacking through the sails, and as there was a crash somewhere forward where a roundshot struck home. It was a ragged broadside, he thought, and fired too high. He felt a slight encouragement. It was the first sign the enemy, too, was weakening.

Lovette ran for the poop ladder. *Macedonian*'s own guns were going off as they bore, spitting out the American reply. Favian peered at the enemy, seeing the dark, starry gap between their masts disappearing. Odd, he thought, what was Corbett doing? And then he knew.

My God, Favian thought, the man's tacking. He'd headed downwind to give himself some room, and now he was going about. Anger burst into Favian's mind. Haven't I hit him at all? he demanded. Haven't I cut away a single blasted brace?

"She's *tacking*!" Chapelle shrieked, his astonishment equaling Favian's.

Forte was swinging its bow through the wind's eye, coming to the larboard tack. To tack thus in battle was very unusual, particularly after heavy gunfire might have cut away the lines controlling the sails. There was danger of the tacking vessel going into irons, caught with all sails flat aback with her bow into the wind, drifting slowly backwards out of control.

But Corbett seemed to be tacking his frigate with perfect confidence despite the dangers, and furthermore he was doing it successfully. *Forte* hesitated slightly in the wind's eye, but Favian saw the jib backed, the bow swinging over, and the yards hauled around. The enemy maneuver had worked.

It was plain what Corbett had in mind. On his new tack he would pass astern of *Macedonian*, perhaps delivering a raking broadside if Favian was careless enough to let him. Whether he achieved his rake or not, he would seize the weather gage, Favian's only tactical advantage, and be able to control the battle. There seemed nothing whatever Favian could do to prevent it.

Favian continued to gaze to leeward, his mind swimming with astonishment, seeing *Forte*'s sails filling through the murk of gunsmoke. *Macedonian* was headed the wrong way; she needed to be on the starboard tack to prevent Corbett's getting to weather. There wasn't room to wear her, and Favian doubted very much whether any attempt at tacking his own ship would succeed: *Macedonian* hadn't demonstrated herself as nimble at working to leeward as *Forte*, and in fact had, just the night before, shown a tendency to sail backwards when the maneuver was attempted. . . .

And then Favian was shouting out his orders, the officers staring at him in dumb astonishment. "Man the clew garnets and buntlines! Man the braces!" he shrieked. "Put the helm down! Ease off the head sheets! Haul in the spanker sheet! You there, haul taut! Up foresail! Haul taut—brace aback, fore and aft! Brace aback, all!"

"That'll put us aback," Chapelle's shocked voice mumbled wonderingly. Favian spared no thought for his enlightenment.

Macedonian rocked on the waves as she lost way, as the forecourse was clewed reluctantly up to the mast with a protesting boom of canvas, and then the topsails, crashing as if lightning had struck the masts, were hauled aback by main strength. The wind was now hitting the front of the sails, stopping the frigate dead as if the hand of a giant had halted her. Favian ran to the taffrail, hanging over *Macedonian*'s stern, gazing at the water as it lapped up around the frigate. Slowly he saw the water rippling beneath her stern, a clumsy wake forming—*Macedonian* was sailing backwards, stern-first through the water!

The starboard guns blasted out as Favian ran forward, trying to ignore the pain that was throbbing through his arm, the trickle of warm blood he felt on his wrist. Coughing in the gunsmoke, he jumped for the poop ladder, hanging by his good arm from the rope safety line as he peered at the helmsmen standing by the wheel and demanded: "*Does she answer?*"

The quartermasters stared at the gangling, powder-blackened figure, dressed in a bloodstained shirt and hanging like a monkey from the safety line. "*Does she answer, damn you?*" Favian shrieked.

Midshipman Lovette, standing by the binnacle, leaped to the double wheel and hauled it to port. Favian looked aloft, the topsails pressing against the masts from the front, and tried to gauge *Macedonian*'s motion through the water.

"Rudder's biting, sir," Lovette reported. "She's biting—by God, sir, she answers! The helm answers!"

Favian threw his head back and laughed, feeling madness overwhelming him. He had it, by the Eternal! He leaped back up to the quarterdeck. "Fire, starboard battery!" he babbled. "Fire at will—whether ye bear or not! Keep firing—fire, fire, fire! It's smoke we want, the smoke!"

Macedonian was gaining speed as she moved stern-first through the water, the sea chuckling under her stern as she gained way. *Forte*'s masts were dimly seen astern and to leeward, rising above the gunsmoke. The wind was blowing the smoke into Corbett's face, he knew, blinding him. Favian was counting on his blindness. If it weren't dark this probably would never work, but as long as the *Macedonian* made its move under cover of night as well as gunsmoke there was a chance.

Macedonian's guns lit the blackness, reflecting off the banks of smoke drifting downwind, briefly illuminating *Forte*'s topsails and spars. Favian strained his perceptions, trying to make certain of the enemy's movements. "Put your helm to, ah, to port there," Favian called to Lovette. Sailing backwards the helm was reversed; he had to be careful in giving instructions.

"Aye aye, sir."

"Amidships."

"Aye aye."

Forte was quite near now, looming darkly through the smoke off the starboard quarter; Favian gave the order to add grapeshot to the guns' charges. He wondered when Corbett would see his danger; the British could avert Favian's trap simply by putting their helm up, if they saw it early enough: but Favian was counting on surprise, and on their not believing *Macedonian*'s maneuver when they saw it. When was the last time a warship had backed down in combat like this? He thought 1704, when the British had taken Gibraltar. Clowdisley Shovell and his entire squadron sailing backwards through the water to the rescue of his admiral. Gunfire lit the night, revealing *Forte*'s massive hull only thirty yards away, the black, disbelieving silence of its ports. *She's done,* Favian thought, and bellowed his orders.

"Hard to port, Mr. Lovette! Grapnels ready to starboard!"

Corbett saw at the last minute and tried to get his helm up, but *Macedonian* was moving too fast by then and came backing down across his bows, a little bone bubbling from her stern. *Forte*'s jibboom suddenly loomed like a great spear across *Macedonian*'s decks, thrusting just forward of the mainmast, and then came the crash. "Grapnels away!" Favian roared, trying to keep his feet as the frigates ground together, as *Macedonian* was shoved sideways and then upwind, her sails roaring again. "Grapnels away!" It was *Forte*'s sails that were aback now, booming against the masts.

Forte was bows-on, stuck right amidships, held by tangled rigging and half a dozen grapnels. Every single remaining broadside gun bore on her; they could fire right down the length of her decks, a rake that would tear the life from the ship. The British hadn't a broadside gun that could reply, just that forty-two-pound carronade on the foredeck pivot and perhaps her chasers. "Odd guns load with double shot, even guns with roundshot and grape!" he shouted. "Range point-blank! Fire at will!" Favian felt the energy drain from him; suddenly he felt cold and tired. All that was needed was more shooting, and he wasn't needed for that. He walked to a carronade on the unused larboard side and sat down on it. Everyone would know what to do.

The British didn't give up easily. They made half a dozen sallies to try to cut the ships free, running out on the bowsprit into the rifle fire of *Macedonian*'s marines. Their bodies dropped from the sprit to hang in the bowsprit rigging, or to fall to the

American frigate's deck. One of the bodies was Captain Corbett, shot through both lungs, but Favian didn't know it. *Malachi's Revenge* swept in close, its full broadside going at point-blank range into *Forte*'s stern, then Gideon tacked, ranged up off *Forte*'s starboard quarter, and stayed there forever, backing and filling, hammering away where the British couldn't reach him, and where none of *Macedonian*'s guns might accidentally hit him by mistake.

The American frigate took some damage: that forty-two-pounder was deadly at such close range and did considerable execution on *Macedonian*'s quarterdeck, upending two carronades, killing a dozen men outright with grapeshot, and bringing Chapelle down with a splinter wound in the thigh, before Kuusikoski trained his own carronade around carefully and blew the forty-two-pounder clean off its pivot. Chapelle, who refused to go below, sat on the carronade next to Favian, smiled encouragingly, and let Stanhope bind up his wound with his own handkerchief. "I wish I had some tobacco," he said, the smile still on his plump face, and then he passed out. The stretcher-bearers carried him to the surgeon.

After half an hour, perhaps, the frigates came apart. The grapnels had been cut by the British or by *Macedonian*'s own shot, and then the wind pushed the British slowly downwind, *Forte* gaining sternway as *Macedonian* fired its few last raking shots. *Forte* paid off on the larboard tack, managing at last to get a few shots at *Malachi's Revenge* before the schooner could fill its sails and dance out of the way. Favian stood, limb-weary: it was time to give orders again. He wished he had some coffee.

"Man the lee braces, tacks and sheets! Put the helm up, flatten in the head sheets, ease off the spanker." *Macedonian* and *Forte* were lying like logs in the water, parallel to one another, neither having way on yet. Flame blossomed from the British flank, and a shot crashed home. Favian wasn't worried about the British fire anymore: after all that raking half her broadside must be dismounted.

"Haul taut! Brace up!" It was a miracle, come to think of it, that *Forte* hadn't lost any lower masts—surely they must be chewed up. *Macedonian*'s topsails filled with a crack; Favian felt the frigate jerk. "Clear away the rigging—haul aboard! Draw the jib!" Slowly, clumsily, a bit reluctantly, the frigate began to move. "Put the helm up!" He'd head down on *Forte* and try to finish her. As long as his own masts stood, he had a good chance to take her.

Forte, gaining way, began to turn downwind, *Macedonian*'s shot pursuing her. Favian looked at her with interest: was she running away, or somehow out of control? She was showing a light off her stern, hanging down near her transom, and Favian, an odd excitement moving through him as he began to draw a conclusion the facts could not yet justify, snatched up a glass and trained it on the enemy stern. Aye, there was someone hanging off the stern with a lantern, surveying the damage, and in the winking, bobbing light Favian saw what it was. *Forte*'s rudder was hanging only from its lower gudgeon, torn away entirely from its post. *Forte* was no longer under control, could not forge upwind. Gideon had done that with his persistent rakes from astern.

"Set the forecourse!" Favian shouted. He'd need speed, now, to catch her.

They were heading downwind, now, *Macedonian*'s fastest point of sailing. *Forte* did not, perhaps dared not, set any more sail: Favian concluded triumphantly that they knew their masts would go if they did.

Gideon's schooner, suddenly, was doing brilliant work, taking incredible risks: she rocketed up under *Forte*'s bows to fire a raking broadside, then gybed around and fired another while Favian watched speechless with astonishment, terrified the heavy frigate would run the reckless schooner down and turn her into matchwood, or somehow turn to bring her broadside to bear. But *Malachi's Revenge* danced away, gybing again, firing another bow-rake just as Favian put his own helm down, crossing *Forte*'s stern to fire his triple-shotted larboard broadside into those gaping, shattered, pockmarked stern windows. Favian gybed himself, coming across *Forte*'s stern again to fire his starboard broadside just a few seconds after *Revenge* tore across *Forte*'s bow again, sandwiching the British between two raking fires.

It was then that Favian saw white flags going up in the darkness, and began to hear voices, heard dimly through his ringing ears, announcing surrender. The American cheers were faint: they'd been too heavily battered, and fought too long, to have much breath left for celebration. Favian looked at his watch: a little after nine o'clock. He told Blake to go aboard and take possession.

While Blake was assembling the boarders, *Malachi's Revenge* came surging up, heaving to under *Macedonian*'s lee. "Cap'n Favian! Cap'n Favian!" Finch Martin's voice, strangely choked; perhaps he'd lost his voice shouting orders and obscenities.

Favian felt light-headed as he stood with his speaking trumpet; the deck seemed to reel under him. He'd have to go below to the surgeon soon, he knew. Couldn't stay on his feet much longer.

"Aye, Mr. Martin! My congratulations to your captain!" Favian said.

"My captain!" It was a half-laughing, half-choking exclamation. There was something in Martin's tone that chilled Favian to the heart.

"It's Cap'n Gideon, sir!" Martin cried. "He's dead! The British killed him, sir!"

TWENTY-ONE

It was the last, Favian hoped, of many funerals. The little Presbyterian churchyard in Mobile, overgrown with vines and Spanish moss. Maria-Anna, hugely pregnant, standing in her black dress, looking blankly at the flag-draped coffin while Campaspe held her arm. Finch Martin, red-faced, with the tears falling down his cheeks—he, too, Favian knew, was done with war; he'd buried too many Markhams, and his spirit was gone. *Macedonian*'s officers, Hourigan on his feet again, Chapelle standing with his cane, Ford with his sleeve pinned up, bright-eyed and sweating with the fever he hadn't yet got rid of, Swink and Blake somehow unharmed, Stanhope and Solomon and Killick and all the rest—all with mourning bands on their arms, standing in full rig while the frigate's trumpeter played taps. It should, Favian thought, have been me. I took the mad risks; it was Gideon who played carefully, and only to help me.

He owed Gideon a debt of service; and he knew he could never pay it back.

It had been those few shots *Forte* had fired at the *Revenge* just before the end that had killed Gideon. He'd been standing on the quarterdeck, watching the fight with his cunning brown eyes, his mouth charged with tobacco, when he'd been clipped by a twenty-four-pound shot and died in an instant. All acknowledged that Martin had gone crazy then, bringing *Revenge* in absurdly, recklessly close, bow-raking the enemy four times in revenge for the captain he'd so strangely loved.

It took a long time to get *Macedonian* and its prize in order, and it wasn't until near dawn that Favian was able to go below and see the surgeon. The cockpit had overflowed with wounded; men lay in rows up on the berth deck, waiting their turn beneath the saw. Campaspe, who had been working all night as Truscott's assistant, held his hand and tried to smile bravely as the *Macedonian*'s physician and surgeon cut the ball from his arm and probed the wound to remove any stray pieces of cloth that might cause infection.

It took five days to get the prize to Mobile. *Forte*'s lower masts, as Favian had suspected, were wounded; Favian sent *Macedonian*'s carpenter and a gang of workmen to strengthen them while he took the enemy frigate under tow and worked his way northward, anxious to get out of the area while it was still dark. Two days later they'd reached Pensacola and anchored for two more days of hasty repairs. Favian hadn't liked Pensacola—it was occupied by Jackson's men, true, but the British had blown up one of the defending forts when they'd evacuated the place, and it was too open. On the fifth day Favian had got his ships into Mobile and found all seven of his and Gideon's prizes floating at anchor in the bay.

By that time there'd been half a dozen funerals. The first was massive: *Macedonian* had suffered thirty-seven men killed and over fifty wounded, the most horrible victory Favian could imagine. *Forte*'s casualties had been worse, over forty percent. There had been massive structural damage inflicted on both ships; they'd both need a haul-out in a dockyard before any more fighting was done.

Favian could think of nothing to say at the first funeral; he'd delegated the task to Midshipman Dr. Solomon, who read the service for the dead in a cheerful voice, unable to summon the proper solemnity after surviving his first battle. Lazarus, a victim of his last act of loyalty, was buried at the same time, quietly, head-downwards as he'd wanted, over the other side of the ship, sewn up in canvas with his fiddle. Solomon had objected to the man going without rites, but Favian had been firm; Lazarus had renounced his earlier faith and died true to his new one, and Favian would keep his promise.

"Thank you," Favian said in a hoarse voice, after thirty-seven men were tipped over the side. "Thank you for trusting me." Another Markham triumph, another set of congratulations from Congress and the President; another medal struck for the survivors. Favian would get three-twentieths of *Macedonian*'s share of the prize money; it would make a wealthy man a good deal wealthier. A lifetime of banquets, speeches, testimonial dinners. More requests by portrait painters, biographers, politicians. Nothing for those thirty-seven men but the dark sea bottom and oblivion, no reward for trust.

There were more funerals as the wounded took ill and died; *Macedonian* left behind it a trail of corpses and satisfied sharks. Captain Corbett, strangely, had survived: even Dr. Truscott, who hadn't been able to think of anything to do with the man but sew up his wounds and hope he wouldn't linger too long, could think of no rational explanation. He hung on the edge of death for a week, then suddenly woke up lucid and asked for pea soup and a cup of tea. Apparently he thought he'd won the battle; it was several days before Truscott dared to disillusion him. It was clear, afterward, that he wished he'd been killed, but he perversely continued to thrive, and in another week was walking. Favian visited him daily, but they seemed to find little to say to one another.

Corbett's first lieutenant had been killed early in the fighting by an American marksman, and his second, wounded lightly, had cleverly gone below to the surgeon at the last minute and left the actual surrender to the third officer. It would be an interesting court-martial, Favian thought; the Royal Navy would be looking for a scapegoat somewhere. Would it find it in Corbett or in the third lieutenant? It was clear where Corbett felt the blame to lay; he simply refused to talk to his third officer when the man came to visit him in the Mobile hospital. Favian was certain the second lieutenant would escape censure; he hadn't actually hauled the flag down.

And so it came to the last funeral, the closed casket in the Presbyterian churchyard. There was the flag lying on the coffin, with Gideon's diamond-hilted presentation sword, the sword he'd taken from an enemy last year, lying on the flag; the trumpet played taps, and *Macedonian*'s marines fired their rifles in the air. The rifles were echoed by slow mourning gunfire from *Malachi's Revenge* and the two frigates lying off the town. Then the guard took the sword from the coffin, folded the flag, and handed both items to Maria-Anna, who watched expressionlessly as the box was lowered into the earth.

Favian looked at her standing across the grave and wondered if it could have turned out otherwise. Maria-Anna was free now, and if Favian hadn't married Campaspe, he would have been free as well. And then he looked at Campaspe, standing in her own black gown, and knew he wouldn't change things if he could.

Favian took Maria-Anna's other arm and walked home with her. Her second widowhood, he thought; unfair for someone so young, but not unusual, he supposed, in this climate where the yellow fever thrived. At Maria-Anna's home they drank brandy and set the diamond-hilted sword over the mantel. One of *Forte*'s Red Ensigns—Favian would send another to his father—already stood on a pole in the corner of the parlor. Maria-Anna looked at Favian for a moment of silence, then spoke.

"Would you mind terribly," she asked, "if we played a few rounds of *poque*? I think it might do me good."

So they played *poque* for the rest of the afternoon, the new version Favian and Maria-Anna had invented in long-ago New Orleans. Favian lost several hundred dollars. When tears began to spatter the baize tablecloth, he pretended not to notice.

"She told me," Campaspe said, early the next morning, "that she wants to name the baby after you, if it's a boy."

"She should give it Gideon's name," Favian said. He and Campaspe had been given a bed in Maria-Anna's house. Favian was happy to sleep away from the frigate, away from the reminders of duty and war.

Campaspe shook her head. "She wants to thank you," she said, "for what you've done."

What have I done? Favian wondered. What have I done but get her husband killed?

Maria-Anna went into labor on the day the news came from New Orleans; the boy, delivered on the birthing stool, came quickly and easily to the sound of celebrations, gunfire, and bell ringing, from the town. Young Favian seemed a thriving youngster.

Favian the Elder found himself uninterested in the news, as if it concerned a long-ago matter in a far-off land. It was, of course, all he had worked for during his time in New Orleans—he knew he should be pleased—but somehow he couldn't celebrate it.

The story was told over and over. How General Keane and the British army had come out of the swamp on the twenty-third of December, one week after Favian's raid on their fleet and eight days after General Jackson had finally declared martial law in New Orleans. Keane had brought sixteen hundred men to within eight miles of New Orleans via Bayous Bienvenue and Mazant, but the work hadn't been accomplished secretly, and Jackson, using the Louisiana troops, the regulars, and General Coffee's Tennessee men who had just arrived that afternoon, determined to strike them that night. Commodore Patterson opened the battle with the *Carolina*, dropping silently down the river and opening a bombardment that had the British hugging the safety of the levee. Then Jackson's men came charging in, guided by Pierre Laffite; the melee continued for hours before Jackson withdrew. Keane, astonished by the fury of the attack, decided to wait for reinforcements and Pakenham before he made any further moves.

Carolina was burned by hot shot fired by a British masked battery, but by then *Louisiana* had been crewed fully by martial law decree and was ready to take the smaller vessel's place. The British made three assaults on Jackson's lines behind the Rodriguez Canal, the first on the twenty-eighth of December, a bombardment on the eighth of the new year, the third on the fifteenth. In each case the British marched across the plains of Chalmette, the narrow gap between the levee and swamp that had been Favian's first glimpse of New Orleans from the *Beaux Jours*. Each attack was a failure, none more so than the grand assault of the fifteenth, where Pakenham himself died before the American bulwarks. The defending guns, manned by Laffite's pirates, a few regulars, and city militia, and by Patterson's naval crews, did massive execution; many of the defending infantry never even got to fire their muskets because the artillery had wiped the enemy from the ground in front of them before they got a chance to shoot. If he were vain enough, Favian thought, he could take credit for convincing Jackson of the worth of artillery on that trip downriver.

The campaign cost the British over three thousand casualties, a third of their army. Jackson lost a few dozen. The British withdrew secretly on the eighteenth; the Americans did not contest their departure.

In the meantime Fort St. Philip, on the lower Mississippi, had been under bombardment from British vessels since the ninth. The British attempted to advance on the eighteenth but failed under the concentrated fire of the fort's batteries. Another laurel for Favian, should he choose to claim it.

Presently, he thought, he would feel the proper elation, but for the moment he wanted only to hold Campaspe in his arms, watch young Favian II in his cradle, and play *poque* with Maria-Anna. His life seemed full enough without the Navy. It was most unfair, he thought, when the war came again to Mobile, and he realized his retirement had been premature.

News came on the eighth of February. The British fleet had appeared off Fort Bowyer, guarding the entrance to Mobile Bay, and were putting troops ashore. Major William Lawrence, the fort's commander who had driven off the British assault in September, was requesting immediate aid. General James Winchester, Jackson's deputy in Mobile, requested urgent consultation. The end result was that *Macedonian* was hastily got ready the next morning to go to the fort's relief. *Malachi's Revenge,* under Finch Martin—blazing with eagerness to avenge his captain—was volunteered for the expedition by Maria-Anna, the schooner's new owner. It was obvious that if the fort fell she would lose the schooner in any case.

Favian was fairly certain the case was hopeless. *Macedonian* was too weakened to stand up for long to any cannonade, let alone the vast number of guns the British fleet could mount, and his crew losses had not been replaced. He was inclined to think the British could sail their fleet into Mobile Bay anytime they wished. But perhaps they weren't interested in such conquests anymore; perhaps they simply wanted to take Fort Bowyer in order to have a victory to flaunt in the face of their loss on the plains of Chalmette. In that case, Favian supposed, he was ready to do his part. He kissed Campaspe farewell, hoping too many men would not be sacrificed in this silly historical postscript.

The morning of the tenth he was off Mobile Point with the frigate and the tern schooner. The British had envisioned a conventional assault on the fort, with batteries of siege guns, parallels, trenches, and saps, all with the intent of producing a bloodless conquest. Favian positioned himself off the flank of the British approaches and blew such trenches as his guns could find into ruins. The British spent the rest of the day reconsidering their position, then the next morning decided to go ahead with their saps and approaches on the other side of the point, under cover of the guns of their own fleet where *Macedonian* couldn't reach them.

Major Lawrence knew the end had been reached. "They've got heavy siege guns out there, Captain Markham," he said. "They can knock my parapets down in two hours." Favian had gone ashore to survey the fort and was inclined to agree with him.

"How long before the British will complete their preparations, d'you think?" Favian asked.

"Another twenty-four hours."

"Hold on for today and tomorrow, then," Favian said. "Then I'll evacuate your garrison, and you can blow up the fort. We can fall back to Mobile." To Mobile, he thought, where I'll try to hold off the whole British fleet with two battered frigates, one of which doesn't even have crew, and a schooner.

But the British completed their preparations sooner than Lawrence had anticipated. By noon the next day their guns were emplaced where *Macedonian* couldn't reach them. Lawrence sent his noncombatants and dependents to the British under a flag of truce and grimly prepared to defend his ramparts to the end.

It was then that the flag of truce came out from the British lines. Word had just arrived: a treaty of peace, it seemed, had been signed in Ghent on Christmas Eve. Hostilities were over. A British band marched out from their lines and began to play "Yankee Doodle" and "God Save the King." The fort's garrison climbed out of its trenches to meet the British and swap tobacco for coffee.

Favian, the next day, met Admiral Cochrane. Favian found him a vigorous, active man of fifty-six, a courtly old-fashioned gentleman, gracious and soft-spoken. Favian rather liked him. "To tell you the truth," said the man who had burned Washington, "I have hated this war from the beginning."

The British brought other news. Stephen Decatur, the young meteor who was regarded, with a great deal of truth, as Favian's patron, had in January surrendered the USS *President* to an enemy squadron off New York, the *Majestic*, *Endymion*, *Pomone*, and *Tenedos,* the same squadron *Macedonian* had escaped in a running fight back in October. *President* was the fastest frigate in the American list, and Favian was amazed that any Briton had managed to catch her.

"That part was bad luck for Decatur," Cochrane confided. "He ran aground on Sandy Hook during a storm and was beaten on the bar for hours. Couldn't get away from the *Endymion*. Of course Captain Hope's conduct in the battle itself was quite brilliant—can't take that away from him."

The very thought of Decatur surrendering to any enemy was astonishing. His career had been nothing but a resounding string of successes, marked by gallantry and high style. Favian knew him well and wondered how Decatur's high-strung, reckless temperament would take the idea of defeat. Not well, he thought: Decatur would be half-mad to accomplish some feat of daring to erase the blot on his record. And with the war over, feats of daring might be difficult to come across.

"So it was all for nothing, then," Maria-Anna said later. "All the battles were fought after peace was signed. It was all pointless."

"No," Favian said firmly. "Peace was signed in Ghent, but the treaty has to be ratified by the Senate and by the prince regent in England. Do you think that idle drunkard will ever sign the document until he's heard from the New Orleans expedition? If the British had seized Louisiana, there would be no peace. The battles for New Orleans not only saved Louisiana, but saved the peace."

One peace, perhaps. When Favian's orders finally came from the Secretary of the Navy, later in February, he was astonished to discover that while he and Patterson, Cochrane and Jackson and Pakenham had been grappling over the fate of New Orleans, Algiers had declared war on the United States. An American squadron was being prepared to go to the Mediterranean, and Favian was ordered to sail *Macedonian* to Boston to return her to her original captain, Jacob Jones, and then proceed to New London to resume command of the sloop of war *Shark*, his original command, now ready for its trials. The language of the orders were terse, formal: the Secretary was reserving his judgment on Favian's abduction of the frigate until apprised of the results.

"It won't be much of a war, I expect," he told Campaspe. "It won't be like the war with Tripoli; we have a real Navy now. And we can have a honeymoon, at least until we get to Boston." Secretary of the Navy be damned; he was going to have his wife on shipboard as long as he could.

The British abandoned their entrenchments when word came of the ratification of the treaty, taking with them Captain Corbett and his survivors, and Favian split his crew between *Macedonian* and *Forte*. The British frigate, he thought, would make a fine sight sailing into Boston Bay, an unexpected addition to the fleet making ready to surprise the Dey of Algiers.

Maria-Anna, though offered a space on the *Macedonian*, declined. She would stay in the South with her property, with her own and Gideon's money. "I don't know those kin of yours in New Hampshire, Favian," she said. "Here I know people and can make a go of things. Maybe get married again." She smiled. "Though if any man tries to take Gideon's sword down from my mantel, he's going to get an unpleasant surprise."

Just before he left, Favian received two unexpected volunteers: Long Tom Tate, Gideon's gunner, and Wallace Grimes, Gideon's former steward and perhaps his cousin. Favian was glad to have them, particularly since Grimes, who could cook, could replace Crane, who couldn't, but he wondered at the reason. "We liked Gideon, sah," Tate said. "A fine captain and a Christian gentleman. But we don't want to work for Miz Markham. We're just another pair of niggers to her."

There was one last piece of news from New Orleans. The state legislature, led by Bernard de Marigny, had voted to deny Andrew Jackson a silver sword in thanks for his victory of January 15. Favian smiled when he heard. It appeared that Louisiana politics had returned to normal.

Favian stepped on deck one morning in March, ready to order the anchor hove short prior to launching, and found to his surprise the ship's company mustered formally before the quarterdeck, his officers in full dress drawn up in a reception line. Hourigan stepped forward to read a proclamation. The men of the United States Navy in Mobile begged Commodore Favian Markham to accept this scroll of honor, this set of silver goblets with decanter, and this pair of silver commodore's stars, in appreciation for his kind treatment of them, and in thanks for his brilliant successes in the defense of New Orleans.

Favian looked at the men assembled, at the officers, and at Campaspe, who was watching him with glowing eyes. He couldn't turn it down, of course.

He took the scroll and stars, and then the commodore's forked pendant went up the main truck while *Forte*'s guns boomed out a slow salute. It seemed he was a damned commodore after all.

The war with Algiers lasted scarcely more than a day once the American fleet appeared in Algerine waters. Favian found the *Shark* to be as fast and powerful as he'd expected—it was a brilliant piece of design—and only regretted that the Secretary of the Navy had declined him permission to take Campaspe along.

His intuition, earlier that year, concerning Stephen Decatur's reaction to his capture was disturbingly fulfilled. Decatur had, through ruthless exercise of service politics, obtained command of the advance frigate squadron sent to the Mediterranean, when command of the entire expedition ought rightfully to have gone to William Bainbridge. Later, in the war's only battle, with the Algerian flagship the forty-four-gun *Mashouda* surrounded by the entire American squadron, Favian watched from *Shark*'s quarter-deck as Decatur ran his flagship *Guerrière* between *Constellation* and the enemy, determined to have the glory for himself. Even though his officers were babbling their praises for Decatur's dash, Favian found himself saddened by the sight.

It didn't surprise him, a few years later, to hear that Decatur had died in a duel with a brother officer over an old quarrel that should have been settled years before. Favian was living in New York by then: Campaspe had shocked so many of the New Hampshire ladies by her scandalous conduct that she and Favian spent most of their time in genteel, happy exile, while Favian gradually creeped up the seniority list and waited for a squadron to command. "I'll go to the funeral, of course," Favian said. "The poor man. I was afraid he wouldn't survive the peace."

"Poor man indeed," said Campaspe. "And his poor wife—she didn't know until he was carried bleeding into the house." She and Susan Decatur had met, and got along quite well; it was unusual for service wives to like Campaspe. "Poor Susan," she said again. "I like her, but she's such a thoroughbred. Stephen should have married someone unsuitable, you know. Like me. I'd have given him something to live for."

And that, truly, seemed to sum it up.

Clarence's son-in-law said to me

but seldom in his bed. Because of his asthma. Born in his house; right where the TV set is now. The one he sleeps upright in the very same chair he slept upright in when he was a boy. Then he had asthma.

If the house was added on to [illegible]

Last piece

Clarence is in bed at 11:30 each night, up at 4AM, or he sleeps sometimes 12-2.

"Have my urine right here beside me. Gets up 2 or 3 times a night until I'm pissed out." The [illegible] when he's most lonely or has to get so much [illegible] is he rides up and down the hills around the county — Beyond Halfmile(?) Stella he pointed out where a woman died just last month, then where a man has four retarded kids, before going to a [illegible] to have tubes tied. Clarence drives 30 MPH when he can. There are five widows right around here including my sis. Stomach trouble [illegible] passing to a white funeral, drinking trouble one man, heart trouble. My sis's husband had heart trouble. The last ... he just went away and left her. [illegible] Now what we have are all these ice cream socials. Big piles of women, now that the men are all gone.

His grandfather [illegible] was a [illegible]; his father wanted to go west and came in 1900 to Nebraska.

I received a letter from him [illegible] told me to gather up all those pregnant widows + bring them to a [illegible] for [illegible]

It's his house to Wheel of Fortune Clarence says turning his old truck around ~~just a~~ 1/4 mile before the turn south to ~~[illegible]~~ his homestead; we pass a ruined farmhouse the corrugated [illegible] that was shining with ice last winter and now appears to have grown ~~soft and [illegible]~~ in the heat.

~~It's his house to Wheel of Fortune~~ [illegible] as we turn about we approach [illegible] between the [illegible] of earth [illegible] like [illegible]. The air's [illegible] around the ~~[illegible]~~

"Going down to dirt is the way" Arlene describes it. Speed ~~[illegible]~~ alert, is one of the [illegible] ~~half [illegible]~~ ~~[illegible]~~ machinery as these are: a one-row cultivator, that would have been used from the late 1800s on; a corn planter that would have been drawn by a horse, a horse or mule pulled mower (with a bee now going through it) all cast iron, brittle but don't rust. You plowed it, disced it, harrowed it, cultivated corn that was knee high by July. Now the [illegible] pass of [illegible] machine + all chemicals. But you can't [illegible]

the fat baby

stories by Eugene Richards

a flower in the desert

KSI 170

Wade Rankins keeps watch out the front window of the apartment, pressing his face against the glass whenever he sees a car slow down or someone plodding along the street. Every ten minutes or so he crosses back into the kitchen for another nip. Holding the bottle away from his body, he observes how the sweet red wine ripples and seems to give off sparks. Then, fast as he can, he's back at the window on the lookout for his wife.

Outside it's grown a bit brighter. Wade's eyes flutter, close, suddenly jerk open again when his fourteen-year-old, Junior, runs past dribbling a basketball. "What'd you say?" he mutters, straightening up. There's a smile on his face now that's no smile. A couple of hours ago, his wife, Shirley, had run out to the store with her daughter, Yvonne, and Adrian, who Wade's been calling "the writer girl." Shirley had promised him she'd be right back.

So while Wade's standing there, pissed, having a dialogue with himself, counting off the minutes, I'm nosing around the apartment for some sign of the terrible things that have gone on. Some evidence of them, I guess. But a couch is just a couch. There's the round formica-topped kitchen table the wine's sitting on, linoleum floors, a small-screen TV. Then there's a tiny basketball hoop, the kind you'd find at a Wal-Mart, hanging high up on a wall. But what's there to make of that?

I hear laughter coming from a bedroom, someone running up and down the hall, the basketball being bounced off a wall. Kids are playing, and it sounds so normal. You know, like one day there's some problems, a child is murdered, another is in jail, and the next day the neighborhood children are playing so well together. Wade turns to face me. "Got something on your mind?" he asks. "No," I reply, looking down so that he won't see that I'm lying.

I have to admit I'm not in a good mood. I've been sitting around on my ass all afternoon, waiting for Adrian. I'm having to act cool hanging out with a guy I'm actually a bit afraid of. And I still don't have the slightest idea why the parents of a child who killed another child would ever let reporters into their home unless they're certain it's going to benefit them. And if all this isn't enough, moments after Wade let me in here and sat me down, he launched into a kind of apology for himself and his son. "Hey, you've got to know I've done some things, but I'm no bad man," he said, his voice rising and falling like that of an evangelical preacher, "and I can't explain, no I can't explain what happened, 'cause Gregory wasn't any kind of bad child."

The sky is darkening when Shirley, Yvonne, and Adrian stroll in. I expect Wade to explode; instead, he acts as if nothing at all has happened. He flutters about, grabs a McDonald's burger out of one of the bags the women are carrying, slips an arm around Shirley. Though he still looks a bit squirrely to me, he offers up a few jokes, mostly tits-and-ass jokes at Yvonne's expense. I go down the hall to the bathroom. When I return, twenty-one-year-old Yvonne is buzzing and scraping, pleading for Adrian to drive her out somewhere to pick up something she'd forgotten when they were last out. Like crack, I'm thinking, for if nothing else, I'm habitually cynical. But I know that's not what Adrian's thinking. Deaf to me, needing to keep on the best side of the family to do her job, she leaves on the mysterious errand.

I should have known. Since following Adrian out here a few days ago, it hasn't been easy. First off, I had to photograph the murdered boy's aunt and grandmother. The two women were sitting pressed together, leaning on one another. Four months after the killing, they still seemed to be in shock. Afterwards I drove with the aunt and a friend of hers out to the Homestead Cemetery in the suburbs. But there was no gravestone, no name, no flowers. During a televised speech President Clinton had referred to five-year-old Eric Morse as "a flower in the desert," whereupon Chicago civic groups pledged that the dead child would have a decent funeral and a cared-for grave site. Yet all that was out there was a patch of sunken ground crisscrossed with truck-tire tracks.

Yesterday I did as the editors at *Esquire* magazine suggested and took a walk through a section of the sixty-nine-acre Ida B. Wells housing project, across the dismal cement courtyards, past boarded-up buildings, around the garbage-filled dumpsters gangbangers employ to close off interior roads to other gangs. The cold wind off Lake Michigan whipped at my pants and coat, and I found myself kicking at stones and bits of crumbling cement the way I imagined a young boy like Eric Morse would have done.

I asked my old friend Les Clark to meet me outside 3833 South Langley Street. We took the graffiti-scarred elevator up to the thirteenth floor, then climbed the last flight, past a gang of five or six teenage boys who cursed us under their breath. Apartment 1405 was closed with a plywood plank. Yanking it away, we felt our way into the dark room, found the window, and pulled down the board covering it. I climbed up, leaned out. With Les holding my legs, I took pictures, trying to draw on what I had learned of the crime. The killing was allegedly done by two boys, one of them Wade's son. Gregory was ten years old at the time; Tony, eleven. I'd read that both of the boys' fathers had spent time in prison (Wade got locked up for drug possession) and that both of the boys had a history of getting into serious trouble. Gregory's rap sheet, I was told, included gun possession, drug possession, and robbery. Late in September 1994, Eric Morse and his eight-year-old brother, Derrick, had been detained for shoplifting. They had blamed Gregory and Tony for putting them up to it.

On the evening of October 13, 1994, Gregory and Tony lured Eric and his protective older brother up to the deserted fourteenth-floor apartment local kids called "the clubhouse." Playing around, trying to intimidate the boys, or in a premeditated act of murder (no one is wholly sure why they did this), Gregory and Tony dangled three-and-a-half-foot-tall Eric from the window. Derrick fought to hang onto him. Then Tony bit Derrick's hand.

So now, if anything, it's better to be sitting here in this apartment than standing up in that window. Adrian's gone, but so are Wade and Junior. A few minutes ago, father and son pulled on their coats and wool caps, and ran out the back door, yelling something about a neighbor being "a bitch." Wade's voice was so loud that when the door slammed shut behind him, it seemed for a moment that the world had fallen silent.

Shirley pours me a cup of coffee. She's shrugging, apologizing in a whisper for having taken up so much of Adrian's time and for having come home so late, when Wade bursts back into the room. A woman living one floor below was complaining that Junior was bouncing his ball on her door. "So let's just say, we told her...," Wade guffaws. Then he sees me loading a camera. Quick as that, he pulls Shirley up and towards him so that I can take a picture. But Shirley pulls gently away; the two of them circle each other. "Do you hear me?" Wade says, "I need a picture." Still Shirley hesitates, wary of being pulled into her husband's arms. She's an attractive woman, maybe thirty-eight years old, large, deep brown eyes, and a full mouth. Through the camera lens Shirley looks girlish, coquettish. Wade reaches around and puts a hand on her breast. Now Shirley looks disappointed. Wade purposely grazes her cheek with his teeth. When she begins staggering forward and backward to get out of his grip, he squeezes her face until it hurts.

The first few frames of this roll will show Wade staring at me with a smile on his face. Junior is on his right; Shirley, attempting a smile, is on his left. Junior is sticking out his tongue at me. When six-year-old Emmanuel, Yvonne's son, Wade's grandson, walks in, Wade tries to pull him into the photographs. In an odd, cruel mimicry of the photo I took minutes ago of Wade and Shirley, he says to the little boy, "Come on, give me a kiss," before biting his cheek.

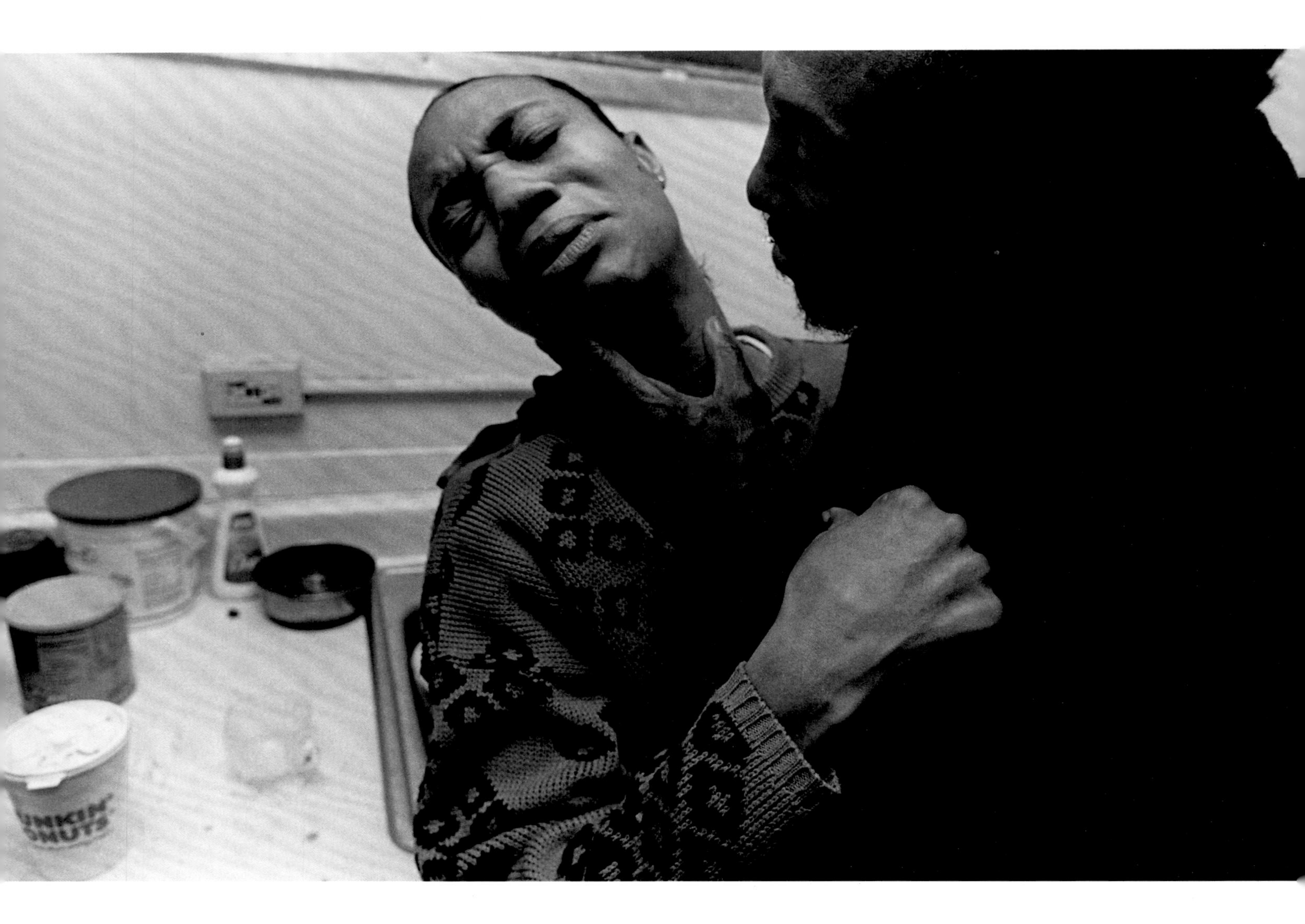

Wade's grandson hides in a closet down the hall, covering himself with boots, until his grandfather calls him back to the table. Then he comes into the kitchen with his eyes half shut, a little weepy. He opens them wide for a mouthful of McDonald's. I have no idea what Shirley's thinking at this time. The only thing I'm certain of is that no matter what Wade says, she appears to agree with him. Right now, she's just sitting there, slumped in the chair.

Wade begins chasing Emmanuel around the table—both of them laughing—in and out of the bedroom, into the bathroom where he throws the boy down. His hands are upon him, teasing, tickling him under his arms and in the ribs, then punching him, hurting him, as if he doesn't give a damn about anything, even that I'm taking pictures.

"You hurt him, man!" I yell at Wade from the corner of the living room. He pays no attention. When things start up again, I follow right behind, like some kind of war photographer: you know, rather than think about it, take the picture, then if you have to, think about it later. I rub my eyes. I'm sweating, cool as it is in the apartment, but Wade never takes his cap or pea coat off. Shirley is annoying me now. She sure as hell is aware of how agitated Wade's getting, has to hear Emmanuel crying, has to notice me using my camera. I see little Emmanuel running down the hall into the bathroom, and think of the time I slapped my five-year-old son, Sam, on his ass so hard that he didn't cry. He just looked at me, chewing on his bottom lip. I could see the future in his look if I kept doing things like that.

Now I'm the war photographer again. Junior and a neighbor kid who's been hanging out with him join in with Wade yelling, "Come on out, come on out, come on out." Hesitantly, Emmanuel unlocks the bathroom door. Right then I consider walking away, going back to the hotel, to stay clean, like the writer is staying clean having gone out shopping somewhere. I ought to leave so that I can tell myself later that I wasn't in any way responsible for what's happening. Out of sight, out of mind.

I hear laughter in the bathroom, then a yelp of pain. Wade just hurt his hand. While grabbing Emmanuel, he whacked the sink. He's beginning to curse. No street profanity, just some unintelligible muttering from inside his head. Emmanuel struggles to stand up. Seeing this, Junior's pal joins in the fun, jumping on Wade's back. Wade flips the boy over onto the floor and bends the fingers of his hand back. This gives Emmanuel a chance to escape.

"And behold, this is the land of your inheritance, and the Father hath given it unto you."

—*The Book of Mormon, Nephi 15:13*

the wore-out farm

I'm on the road when there are still a million stars in the sky. To return to Virgin, I take 9 East, which climbs high above the one-stoplight town of Hurricane before dropping into a long, wide valley. From one or two miles away, Virgin, Utah is a few dots of yellow light against some purple mountains.

I pull the car off into a field to sip coffee snatched from the motel and watch the night become morning, something I've been doing regularly since coming out here. The desert, pitch black and bereft at night, is now full of color and looming shapes. To the north the sand and red clay erupt into steep, flat-topped hills; to the south's a vast, undulating expanse of boulders, sink holes, and stunted trees that I imagine to be a kind of ancient burial ground with bones strewn about all the way to the horizon.

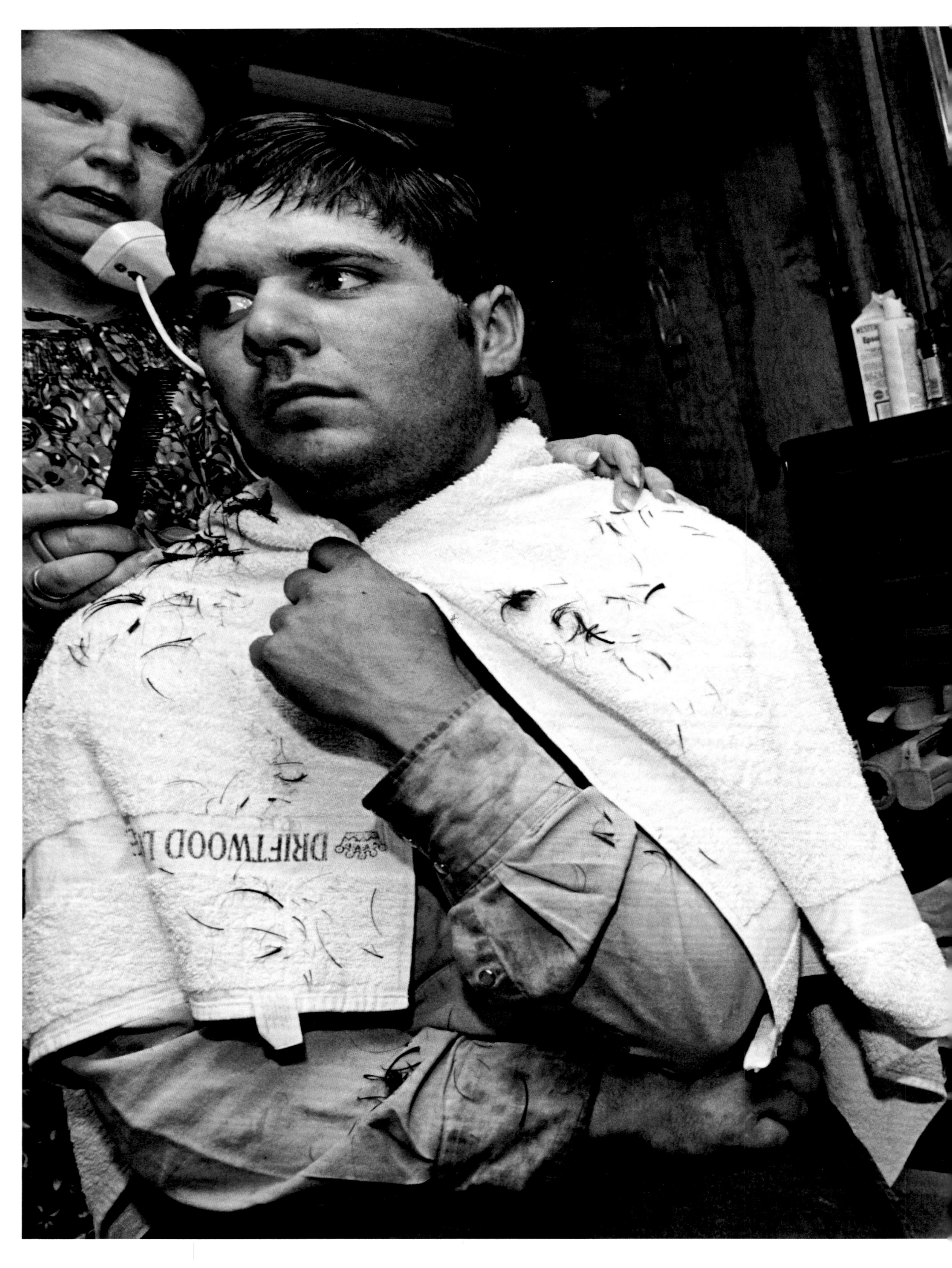
DRIFTWOOD

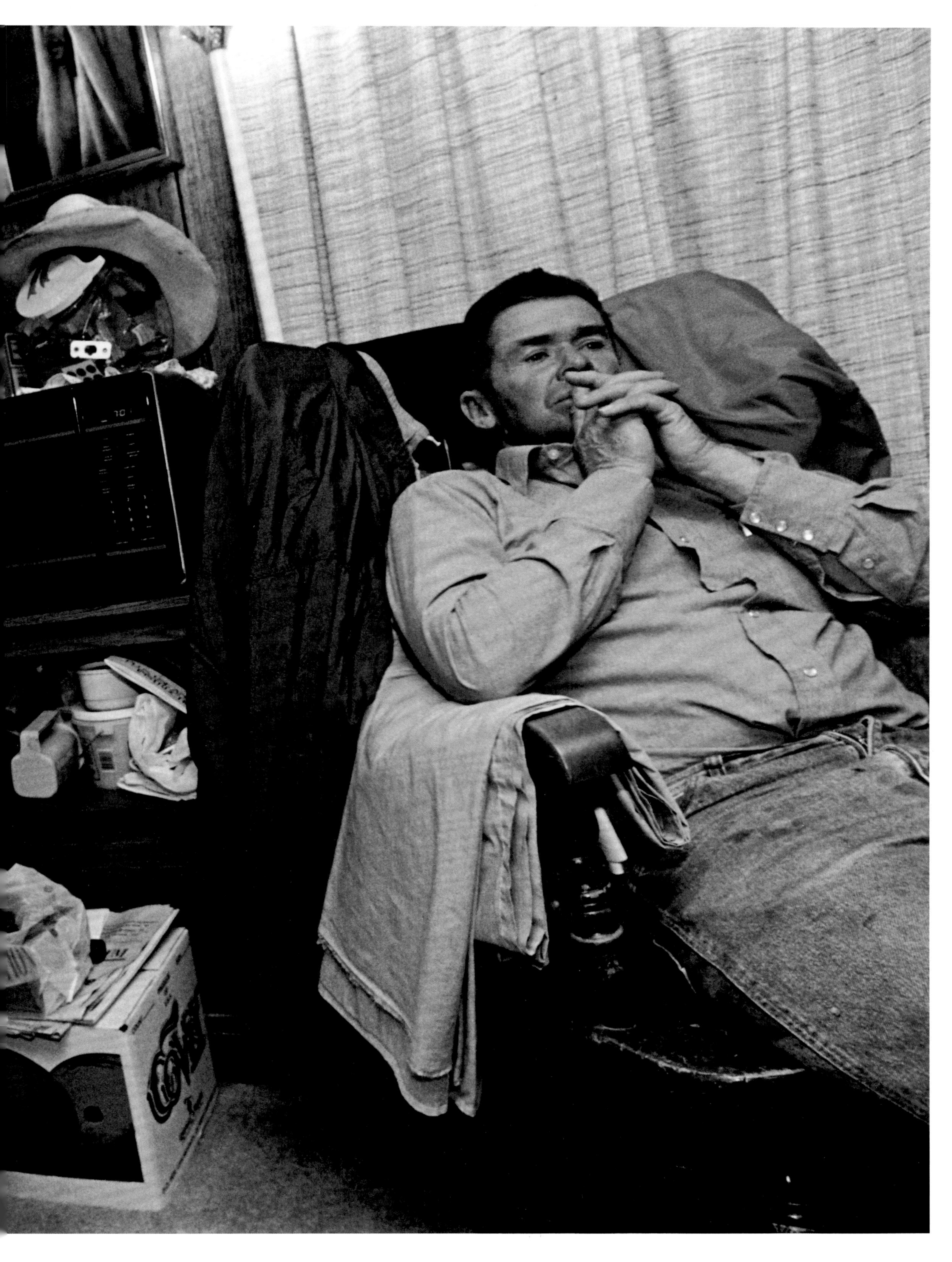

10
ustom
deluxe

a little war

There was an ominous, three-foot-high FH, for the Fremont Hustlers, spray-painted on the wall of the house, across from where the gang members hid their guns. Because of the high weeds, unless you'd been searching, you wouldn't have seen it from the street. There were punctures and gashes in the front door, bullet holes from drive-by shootings. But you had to get close to see them. From a distance there was really nothing particularly dangerous or rebellious-looking about the place.

The Kansas City cops turned onto Fremont Street once or twice a day looking to charge someone with loitering or possession. Lori and Sarah would wave, sometimes stick their tongues out at them, while the guys who were on probation or carrying would push past each other to get inside. Most of the rest of the afternoon the house was quiet. I'd only see Lori's mother when she'd venture out of her seclusion looking for a match to light her crack pipe. When I'd run into Thomas, Lori's younger brother, often as not he'd also be high. Thomas and his ten- and twelve-year-old pals would be sitting cross-legged on the floor in the dimly lit parlor shooting craps and smoking pot.

All I knew about the short, skinny kid with the hint of a mustache was that, unlike other members of the gang, he was sure I wasn't a cop. As everyone out the back of the house looked on, the kid took a hit from a dank stick, an oversize joint soaked in a mixture of PCP and formaldehyde. His eyes rolled back, he started shaking. Just when I thought he might fall, he snatched the swollen, smelly thing from his mouth and pushed it in mine. As a dare, I suppose, a kind of test.

Whenever Lori and Sarah had the money, they'd shut themselves up in the bedroom on the second floor and smoke pot. Huffing on a large glass pipe, inhaling in a frightening rush, they'd feel less angry, they'd tell me, a little less depressed, for a few minutes, anyway.

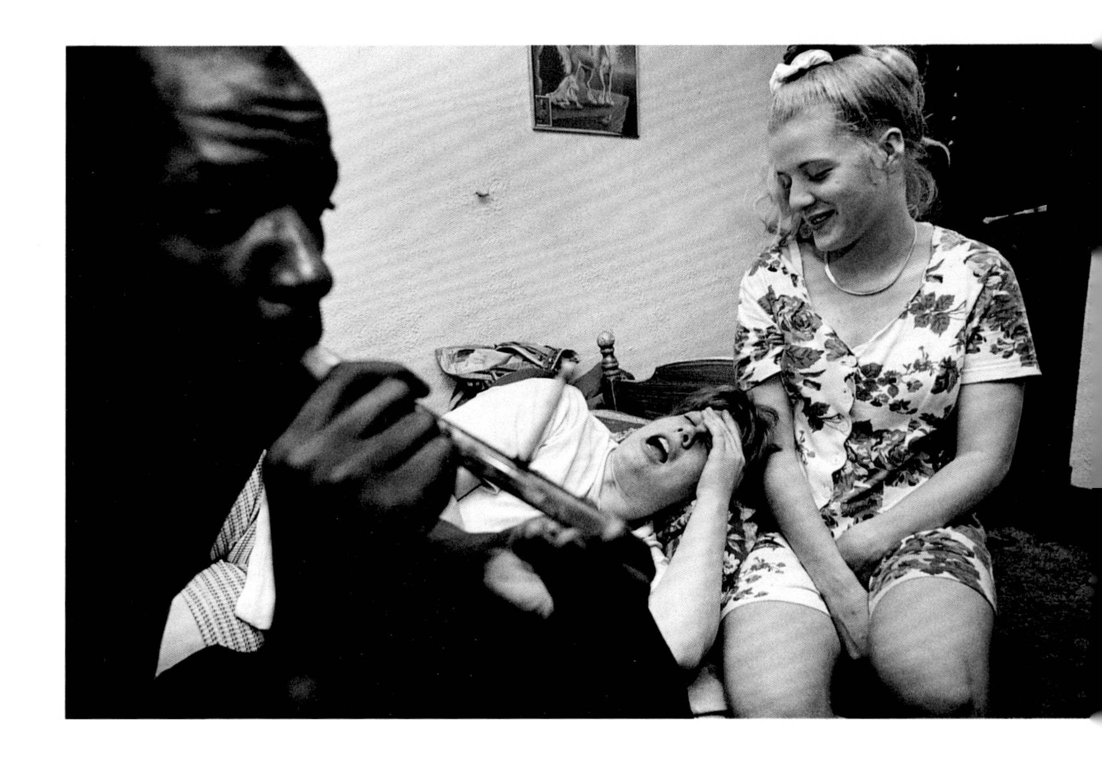

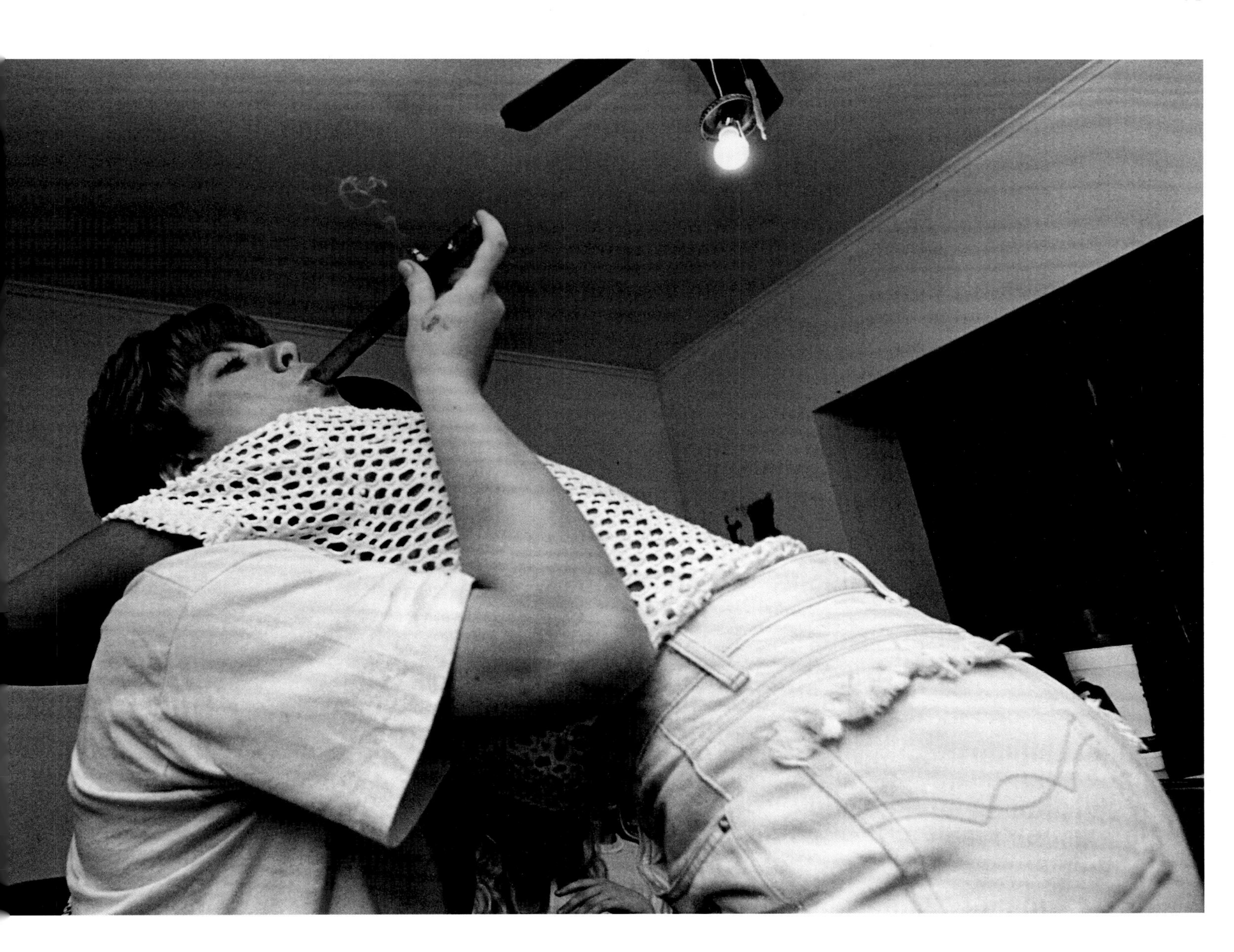

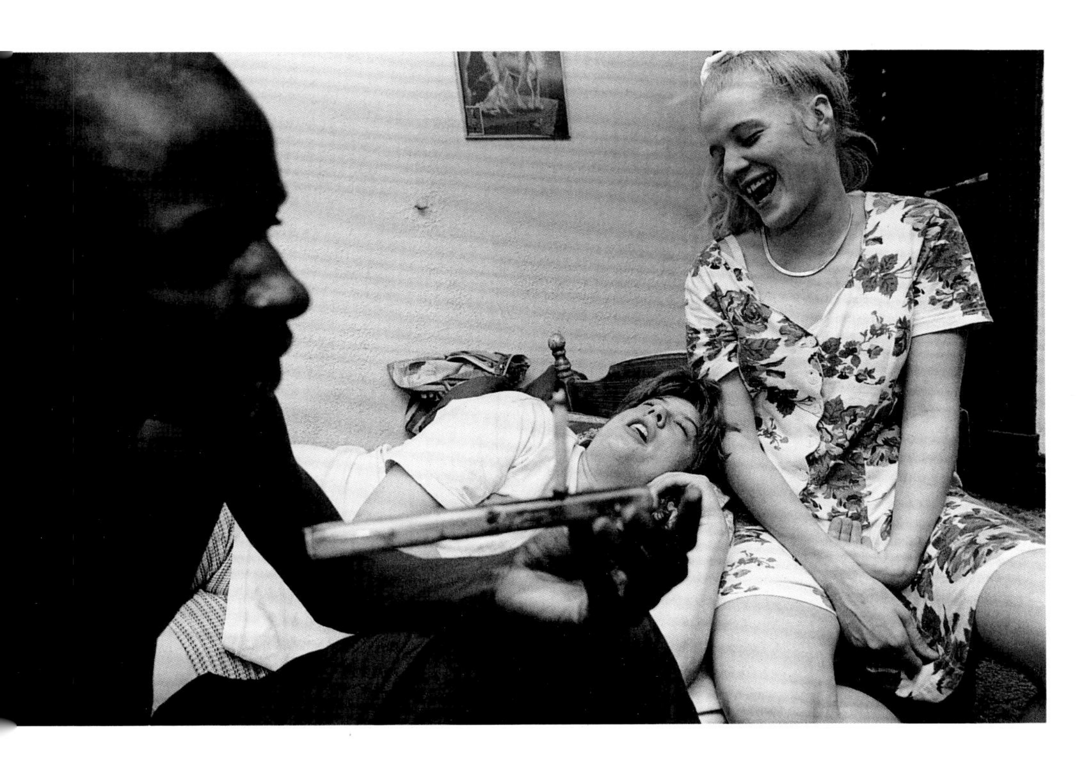

QT
VINYL
WEIGHT
SET

The guys would be chilling, listening to music, playing video games; the girls would be stoned, half-asleep upstairs. The summer days would be rolling uneventfully and monotonously along when it would happen. A car would slow down, stop at the corner revving its engine, then tear past the house, spawning a little war. There would be no more small talk. Cursing that "the bitches are coming," boasting that they were going to "bust someone," the homeys would run for their shotguns and rifles. They'd pull shiny, ugly little pistols from down inside their pants. You'd hear a shot, then some yelling over the hill beyond the trees.

I don't know why I was so focused on Sarah. Maybe because she always talked to me when some of the others wouldn't. Maybe it was the way she looked. Sarah had the palest blue eyes, which, no matter what, always looked worried, and dead white skin, meaning it had a grayish hue and no shine. It was her skin that betrayed how tired, medicated, and depressed she was. It wasn't hard to imagine her dying. Dead white skin, red blotches like half-healed blisters, long wispy bleach-blonde hair, wearing a little girl's plain, above-the-knee cotton dress, she'd blow into a room larger than a sickly, nowhere-to-turn gang girl ought to.

Sarah could be loud, and if someone didn't like it, so what. She'd tell no matter who it was that she wasn't talking to them anyway. She could be so much in people's faces--cops' faces, rival gang members' faces, lovers' faces--that I'd become afraid for her, more afraid for her than for the other girls. Then, almost in the next breath she would soften, become warm and flirtatious, so that almost everyone in the house was swayed.

Sarah would sit alone in front of the mirror up in Lori's room for half an hour, brushing her hair and touching her face. But there was nothing vain about this. She was thinking about "bad things," she'd tell me. About her stepdad, who used to beat her mom and her; about her real father and her very first boyfriend, both being in prison for murder; about all the time she'd spent in "psych-hospitals" and detention centers; about how afraid she was that her best friends would get killed; about the day when she and Lori were shot at while sitting out in a car and very nearly died. She'd look at herself in the mirror, turn away, press closer to her reflection, let her mouth drop open, bite her lips, close her eyes.

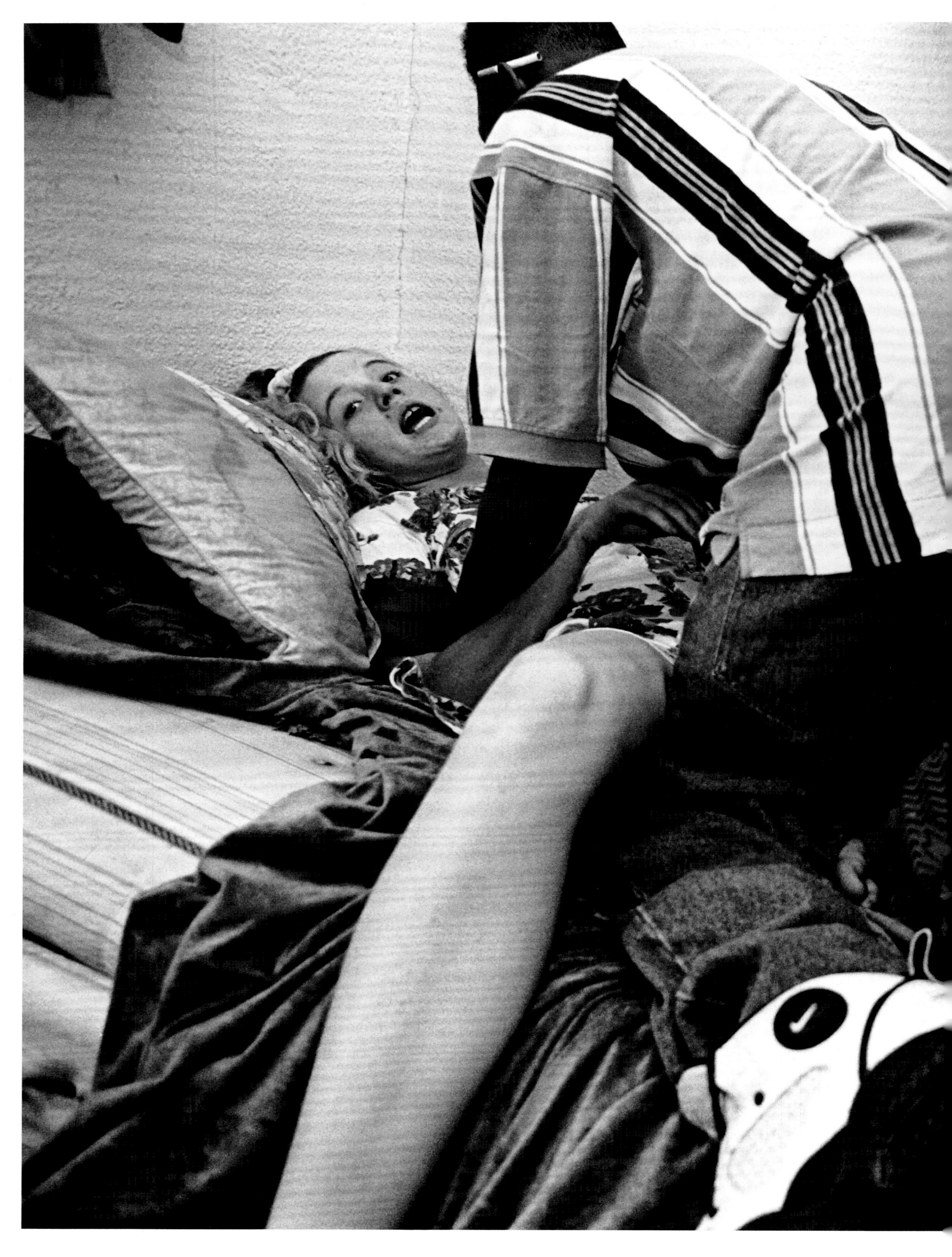

On what turned out to be my last day there, I drove with Lori and Sarah and a few of the other homeys out to the Forest Hills Cemetery to visit the grave of a gang member who had been shot to death the year before. The five of them stood in front of the tiny marker with their heads lowered, trying to think of something to say, then sat down on the grass. Lori pulled out a joint and lit it. Looking numb, exhausted, she passed it around.

PROVIDED BY
FOREST HILL &

the fat baby

This morning, the sky over Niger is clouded over and foreboding. The moon and the stars, an astonishing web of diamonds, appear to have dropped to earth. "It's going to rain," Leslie whispers, feeling the first breaths of wind; before this, for days the air was utterly still. In our car's headlights, we watch straw and feathers and scraps of toilet paper being blown up and down the street. Halos of dust form above the tiny bumps of lantern light which mark where whole families are sleeping.

We drive cautiously leaving Maradi, a city of twenty thousand, dodging naked babies who have crawled onto the road, piles of trash, and the goats that wander everywhere. We are out on the brushy flatlands a few miles from our destination when the air abruptly turns hotter, the sky brighter. Yesterday, when we were in Safo, the home of 3,500 Hausa, traditional healers performed a dance for rain around a sacred baobab tree. The women danced to the beating of drums until they couldn't anymore. Yet here it is again, the sun, sickly white, streaming upward, draining what color, moisture, and relief the nighttime lent this parched place.

As we continue east, the soil is less orange, paler, sandier, the landscape even more desolate. A few minutes after jouncing across the wide, dried-up riverbed, we pass two boys plowing with oxen, then climb a hill into the clay-walled village. We'd come here to do a report on the area's health conditions. Now time is up, this is our last day in Safo before heading home.

The village chief resides in a high-ceilinged complex of rooms just inside the village wall. We say our thank-yous and good-byes to him, then continue along the rutted, dusty road to Hassanna's home. Hassanna had been Leslie's friend and mentor the years she worked here as a Peace Corps nurse. The kind village matriarch has been an enormous help to us on this trip.

The United Nations magazine I'm working for has asked me to ask a person living here, in what has to be one of the most impoverished places on earth, what it means to him or her to be poor. But I'm not sure whether it's appropriate to do this. And as if she's reading my mind, Leslie can't recall the Hausa word for poverty, nor find it in her Hausa dictionary. There are Hausa expressions for possessing things, for having food and clothing, but apparently few ways to express being without. Rahamou catches me staring down at my hands. As a way to begin, I ask her age.

"Eighty years," she answers with a polite nod.

"How long have you lived in Safo?"

"Since the day I came out of my mother."

"Was Safo different when you were a child?"

"Yes, very different," she answers, lifting her head and speaking louder. "There were many trees and the river was here all year and it rained a lot. People were able to eat more food and were able to eat bush meat. Elephants. And we would also kill those animals that eat people—lions—and we would eat those too. There were fish in the river that we would eat."

The growing crowd around Rahamou is now joining in, calling out answers: "Yes, yes..."; "Now the rain never comes...."; "Now, the millet doesn't grow...."; "Our stomachs are never full."

"So why do you think you have lived for so many years?"

"Allah," Rahamou replies, without hesitating.

"How many times did you give birth?"

"Eleven times, but only three are alive."

"Why did some of them die?"

"Because of Allah."

"Were they sick or malnourished or did they have accidents?"

"Don't you remember the baby who was very sick?" Rahamou asks. She looks away, bites her lip, obviously thinking that I might have forgotten her great-grandson Bilia. "I'll never forget him," I tell her. "Well," she adds, "my children died like that."

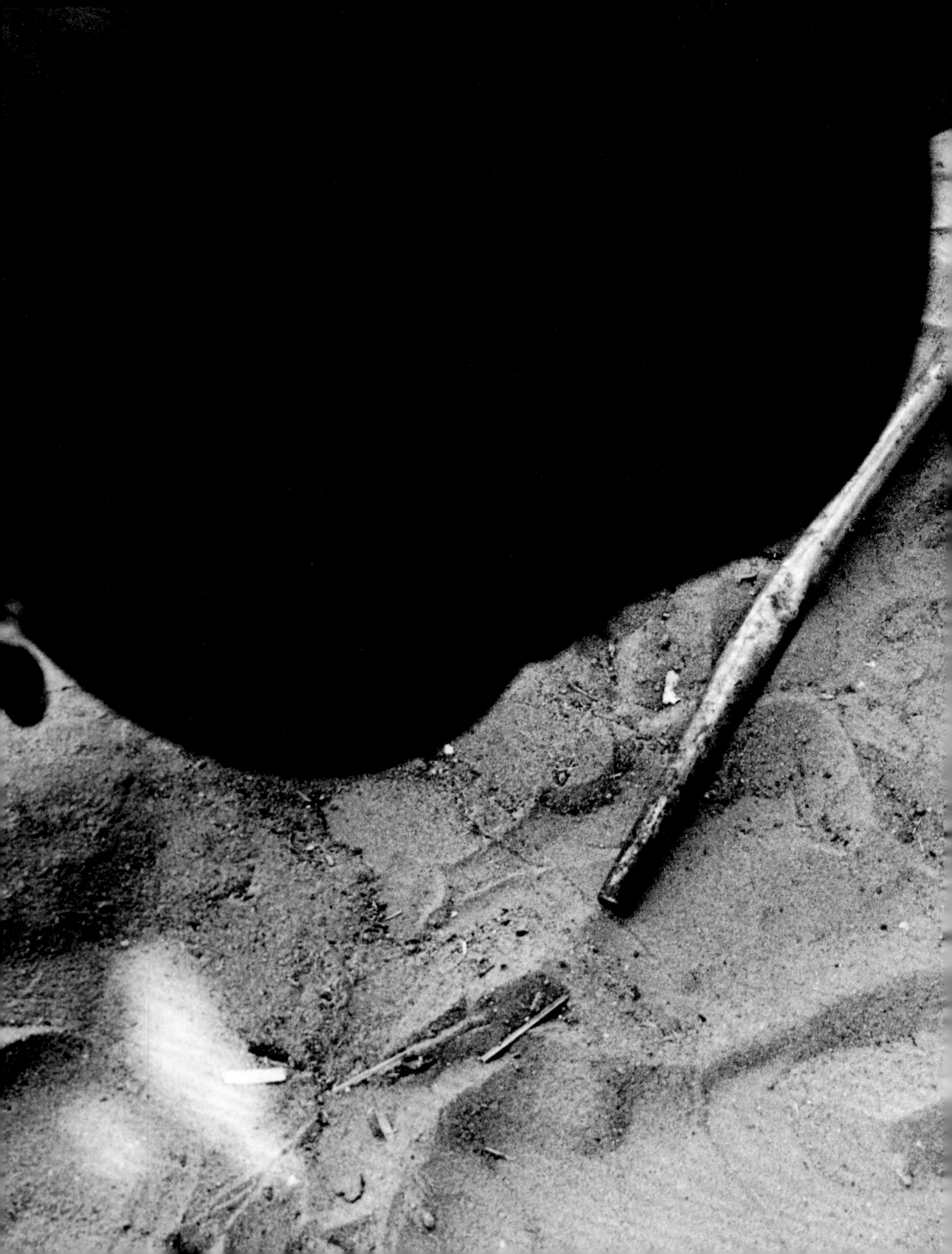

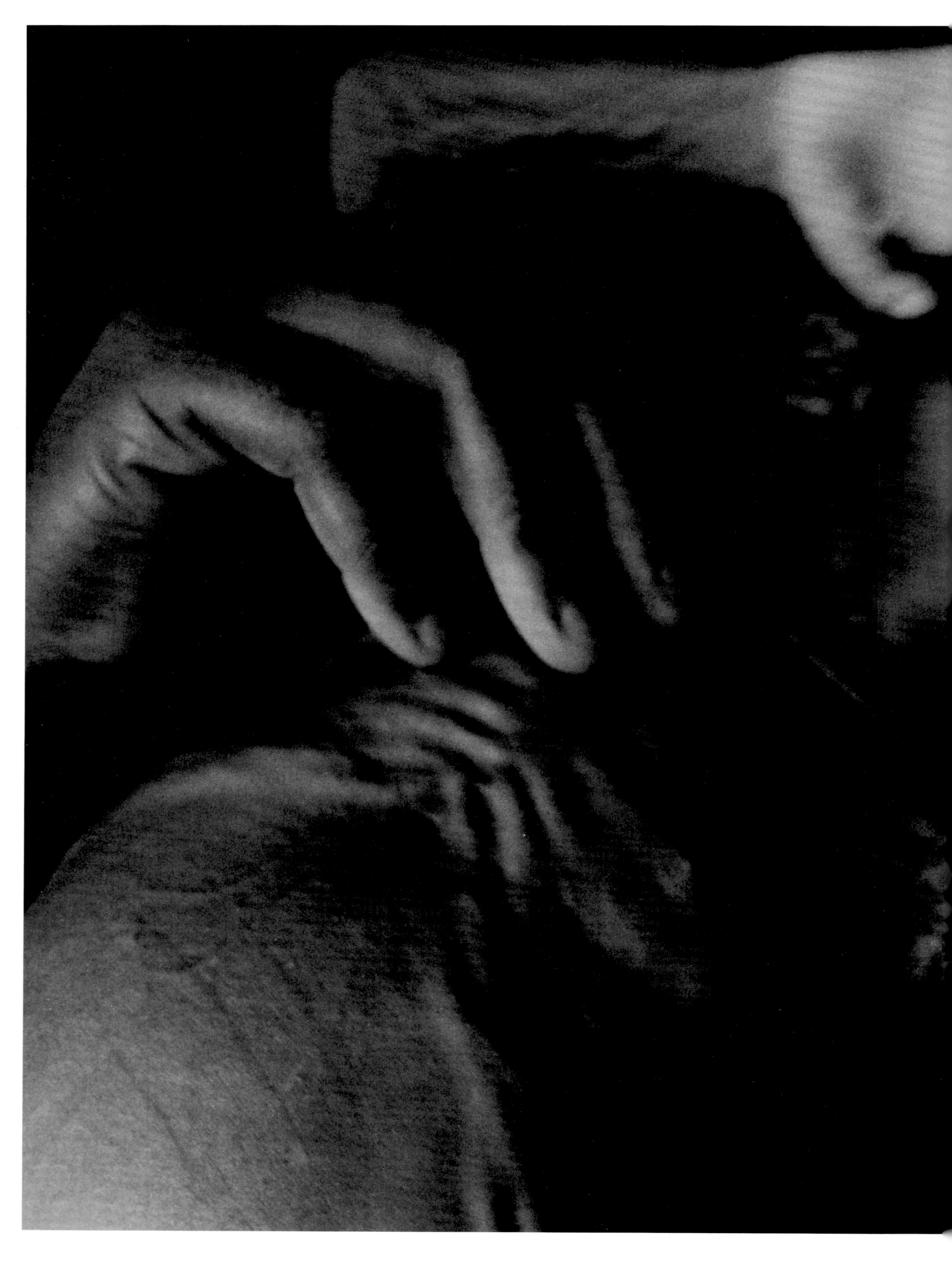

The very first child the village midwives wanted us to see when we arrived was a tiny, skeletal-looking ten-month-old. Born to a sixteen-year-old girl and her truck-driver husband, the baby's lymph nodes were swollen, her liver enlarged. The baby—Leslie is certain she has AIDS—had been given a penicillin injection at the local clinic. The malum, *the village's spiritual healer, sewed together tiny leather amulets for the child to wear, believing they might encourage her to eat.*

The second child brought to us was Bilia. He was being carried on the sinewy back of Rahamou. The boy's mother, Rahamou's granddaughter, had died two years earlier of diarrhea and fever, of what could have been cholera, and now Bilia was refusing water as well as food. We immediately offered to transport the boy to the hospital. But whether Rahamou didn't understand how critically ill the three-year-old was, or whether, like other villagers, she was afraid of the hospital, she declined. Leslie helped Rahamou prepare an oral rehydration solution with water, salt, and sugar. Then, after asking the old woman's permission, I took a photograph, inches from her and the boy, who cried in pain as he slipped in and out of sleep.

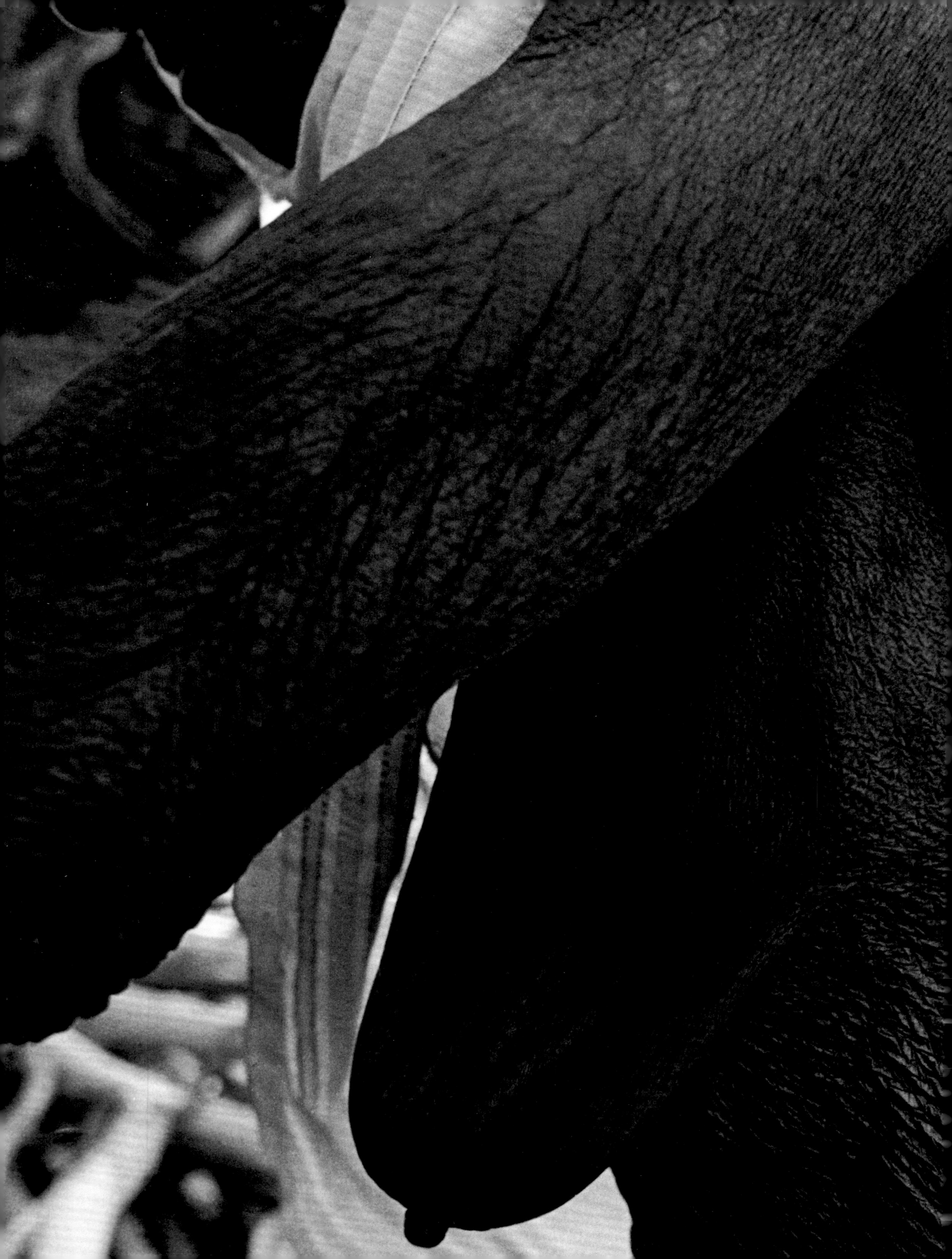

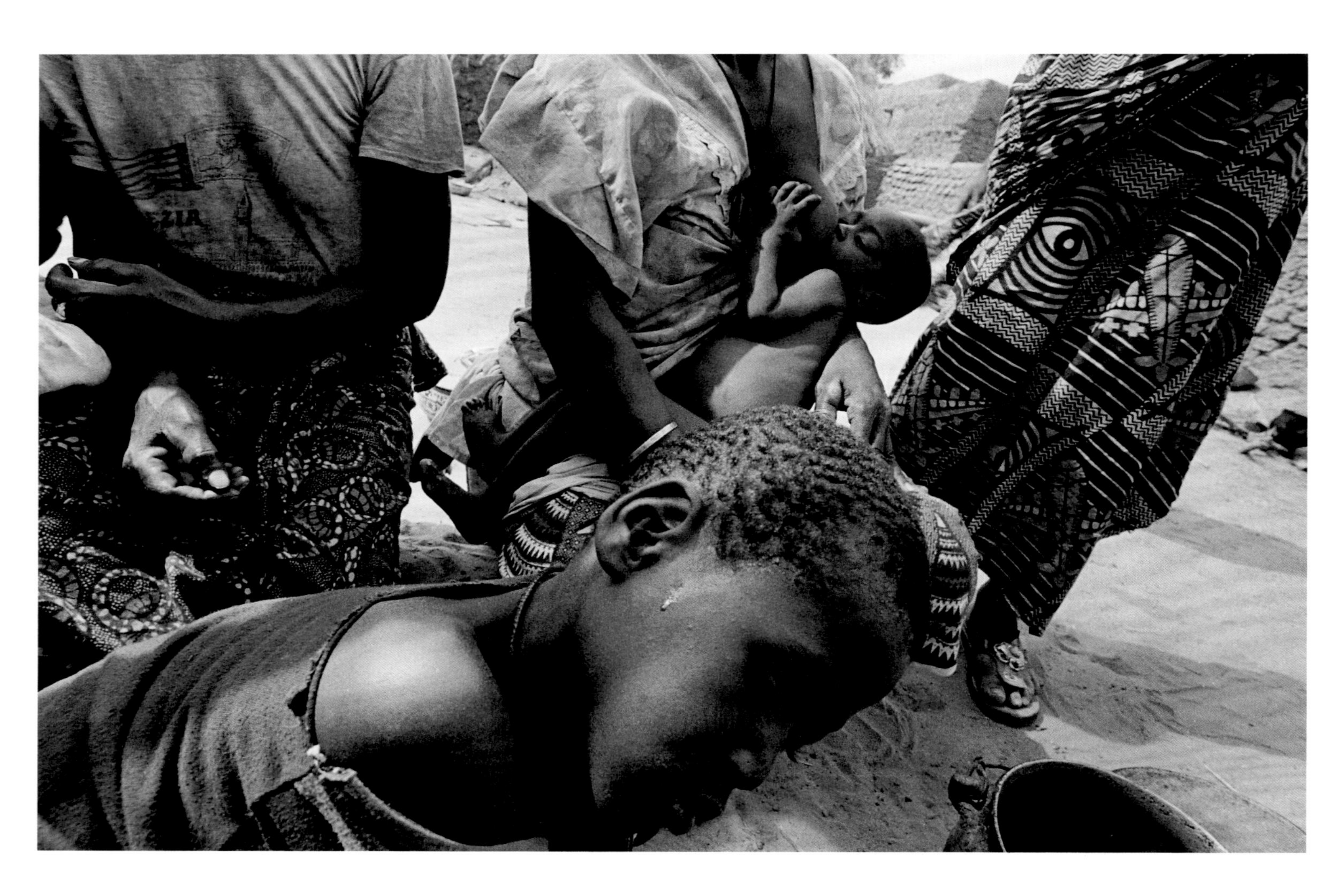

This morning, Leslie and I awoke early, both having slept badly. At Rahamou's compound, a great crowd of villagers is gathering to express their sympathy.

"I heard the news about Bilia," Leslie says.

"Ba shi," *Rahamou softly replies.* "Ba shi *(he's no longer here, he's not anywhere)."*

"When did it happen?" Leslie asks.

"Yesterday, when the sun was straight overhead."

From the day we arrived in Safo, Leslie did her job as a reporter while also helping people: lancing pustular sores, cleaning cuts and burns, handing out precious aspirin to villagers who were running fevers. All I could do was hold an occasional hand and take pictures. Now it isn't appropriate to take any more pictures. I stand in the very back of the crowd. It grows quiet. Suddenly Rahamou motions for me to step forward with my camera. Recalling that the photographs I took earlier in the week were of her and the emaciated, dying Bilia, she asks if I will please make a different picture of her, one that speaks of the future of her village, of a happier time. "One with a fat baby," she says.

Rahamou carefully adjusts her head cloth and her dress and lifts what has to be the plumpest infant in the compound onto her lap. The baby squirms and gurgles. The old woman looks straight at me. I take the picture.

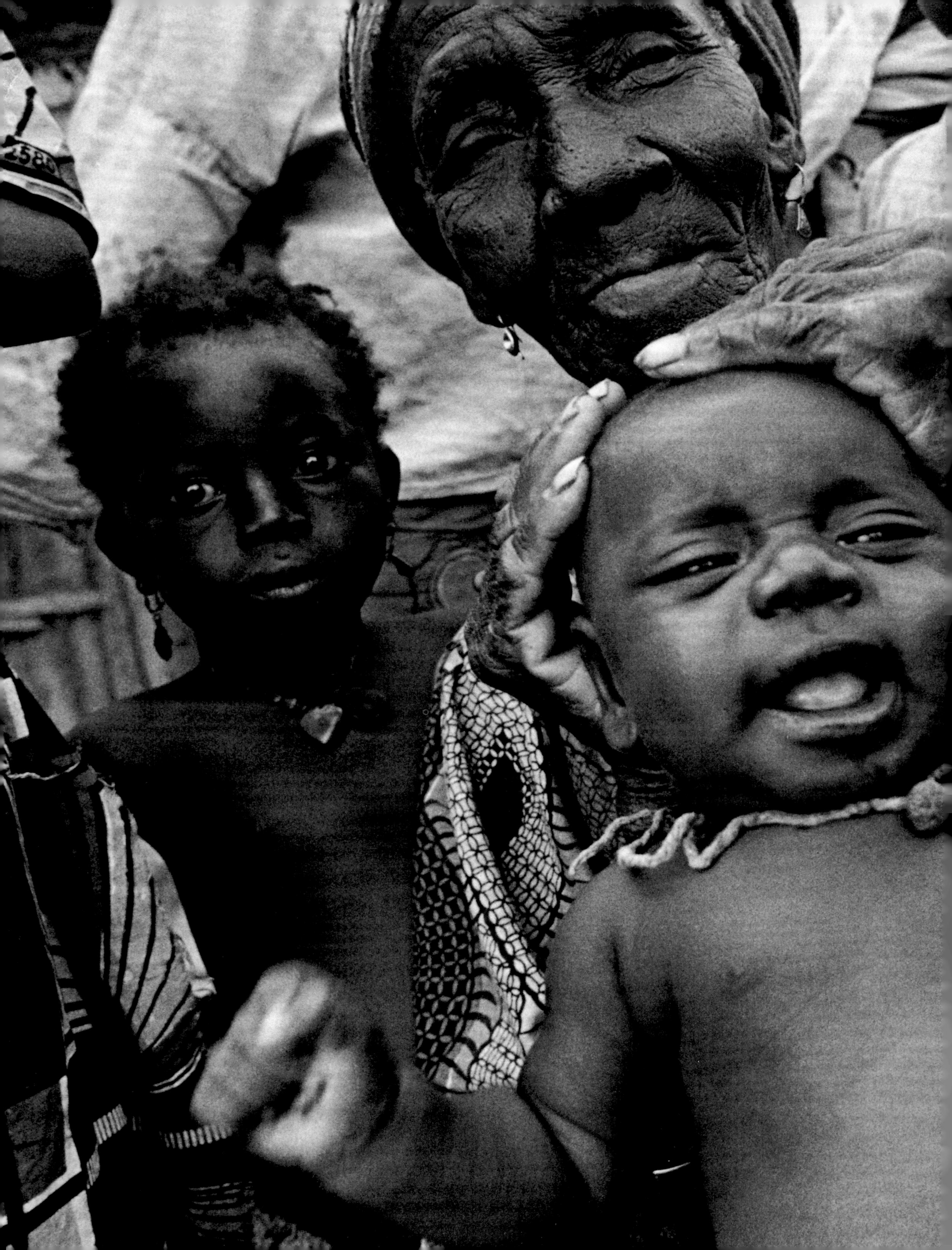

tommy clarke

ChuCho

POLICE

2206

August

I wait for Tommy Clarke on Front Street outside North Philadelphia's 25th Precinct—"number one in robbery, murder, rape, and guns"—then ride with him into "The Badlands." Neither of us remembers exactly when it was that we last saw each other, except that it has been nearly a year, which is probably why he doesn't put me off again when I ask him to show me where he was born and raised.

As we turn down Indiana, Tommy pulls his off-duty pistol from the waistband of his jeans, near his spine, and rests it in his lap. As if on cue, someone in the darkness yells, "Ready rock, ready rock"; someone else, "Boombah," slang for police. I peer out at the passing street corners where dozens of young pushers stand with their hands jammed into their pockets, strolling out to the curb whenever a potential buyer comes close, then backing up into the shadows.

When we slide to a stop, I glance over at Tommy, who's swiveling in his seat, assessing what's on our left, our right, behind us, his whole body on alert. He stares at the men huddled together in the street a hundred feet away until they step around the corner, then focuses his gaze on a row of flat-roofed houses. Except for the graffiti scrawled on them, they look pretty much alike in the flickering streetlight. "Mom's house," he says, leaning his forehead against the side window. "The bricks are gone; the aluminum siding's ripped off. My buddy Jojo's house is gone. Frank Dixon, five houses up from me, became a cop. Me, Frankie, Jimmy Gillespie, all of us took the test together. All scored good enough. Frankie's still a cop. Look at his house. Boarded up."

A few cars are parked this end of Orleans Street, but lights are on in only one of the houses, making the others around it look even more abandoned. Obviously shaken, Tommy hisses, "We shouldn't be here." He slams the car into motion. "Used to sit outside at night with the neighbors. Big family of eight kids. We'd bring a TV out, watch the Phillies. Now," he mutters, "you'd get fuckin' shot sitting out at night."

We drive for ten minutes, not talking, through a maze of one-way streets, and pull up in front of Mick's Inn, Tommy's old haunt in West Philly. Entering off Clearfield, which has little traffic this late, we stand in the church-like glow at the back of the bar. Tommy still seems upset, but it's hard to know. At forty-eight, he has a lean, reddened Celtic face that is stern in repose. When I ask him if he's okay, he just shrugs. So I tease him about being so totally, stereotypically Irish, then, seeing the beginning of a smile, imitate how crazy he gets on the job: "'Clarkie,' the sergeant would yell out, 'can you get up on that goddamn roof?' 'Sure, I can get up on that roof.' So you shinnied up the drainpipe. 'Sarge, I just fell through the fuckin' roof. And the drugs are falling down all around me.'"

"*Moi?*" Tommy guffaws, pointing at himself. He rises to his full height, six-foot-one, and pantomimes disbelief for the drinking men around us.

"You've had some real shit happen."

"Run over by a car, thrown out a window, stabbed, bitten, lost part of my finger, been shot at. My wife, Kathy, says we've been in every hospital in Philadelphia. Hit by a car, to Temple. Lost my finger, Episcopal Emergency. Through the roof, to Northeast. But I'm still here.... Thank you God and Saint Patrick."

Tommy buys another round. We move closer together as he chatters in his sped-up, stream-of-consciousness way about Kathy, his stepsons, John and Joel, his love for everything Irish, his dislike of the "fascist Brits," his desire to retire. He interrupts his musing about growing old in Ireland to introduce me to the bartender. "This here is Gene. He's—can you goddamn believe it—a reporter." Then he bellows, "But, he's *pro cop*," loud enough for all the customers to hear.

2863

Nasdaq
Bonds for the Week
Amex for the Week

KIWI
HONOR GUARD
HIGH GLOSS
INSTANT SPIT SHINE
Consumer-Loan Rates
should you keep records? Three years.
Sept. 1, 1995 $56
Sept. 20: AT&T says it will split into three separate companies and lay off 8,500 workers
Jan. 2: Company announces 40,000 job cuts
1655
1655

tommy clarke Philadelphia, Pennsylvania

January

"You come see us anytime, buddy." That's what Tommy will say when he picks up the phone. If it's Kathy who answers, she'll tease me: "You're coming back to visit us? When? End of the week? Heard that before." Cradling the phone, I lean across my desk and watch the snow fall through the wires and the bare tree behind our house. After a couple more rings, I get their answering machine.

When Tommy doesn't call back by one o'clock, I leave another message. Feeling a little put off, I telephone again at three. Even if he had been in church all morning, then had run over to see his mother, Tommy would be home by now. Sure enough, someone lifts the receiver. Silence. One of the kids, I'm thinking. Finally I hear a man trying to clear his throat. Tommy begins talking, haltingly, very, very slowly for him. "A... cop... from the 25th... she's... been shot. The funeral... come with us. It'll be in the morning."

I pack a bag and hurry out into what forecasters are calling the first major nor'easter of the year. The subway out of Brooklyn is stalled for two hours after the signals freeze at an aboveground station, so it's six o'clock when I arrive at Penn Station. I wait there with the other stranded travelers for the Philadelphia local. Vaird, that's what Tommy said the police officer's name was. Lauretha Vaird. Did I meet her when I was photographing at the 25th? The delays, the waiting, not being able to remember the fallen cop... I pace up and down, cursing to myself. Three hours later, my train, along with all other rail service, is canceled.

Tommy calls early in the morning to say that, because of the twenty-seven inches of snow that Philadelphia has received, the funeral's been postponed. Still, I'm upset that I didn't make it down there and can't think about anything else. I close the doors to my office and sift through the cardboard boxes of photos I made of the so-called War on Drugs. The great photographer Robert Frank has referred to his pictures of 1950s America as "stored-up memories." But mine mirror the particular rot of our times: a black man pushed to his knees at the side of a police car; bloated corpses; a young mother smoking crack, her baby flopped a few feet from her on the same bed, waving her arms and screaming. In the photograph I made of Donna, a young prostitute, she was still plump, childlike, with unlined skin and enormous eyes that would become unfocused, would flutter when the cocaine was lifting her up.

The funeral has been rescheduled. I arrive at the Clarkes' house late the night before the service and sit in the parlor until Kathy cages Irish, the more vociferous of their two huge rottweilers. Then I move into the kitchen beside her. "Tommy said I could spend the night here," I explain. "He told me it's the only way. But I wasn't sure if you knew." "What's one more," Kathy says, patting my shoulder so I'll be sure to know she's teasing. She asks how my wife and son are, but afterward we drink our tea in silence. Kathy, age thirty-nine, is a community affairs cop stationed, like Tommy, in North Philadelphia. I don't ask her if she knew Officer Vaird.

When Tommy comes home, he doesn't say much either. He directs me to what had been his oldest son's bedroom on the second floor, where I try to, but can't, fall asleep. Around two or two-thirty, I hear noises and feel my way down the stairs, past three young boys who have fallen asleep watching TV, and into the kitchen. Tommy's sitting at the table beneath the too-bright lights, polishing his shoes, his gun belt, his badges, and each silvery round of his pistol. "The proper way for a cop to remember a cop," he says, when he sees me.

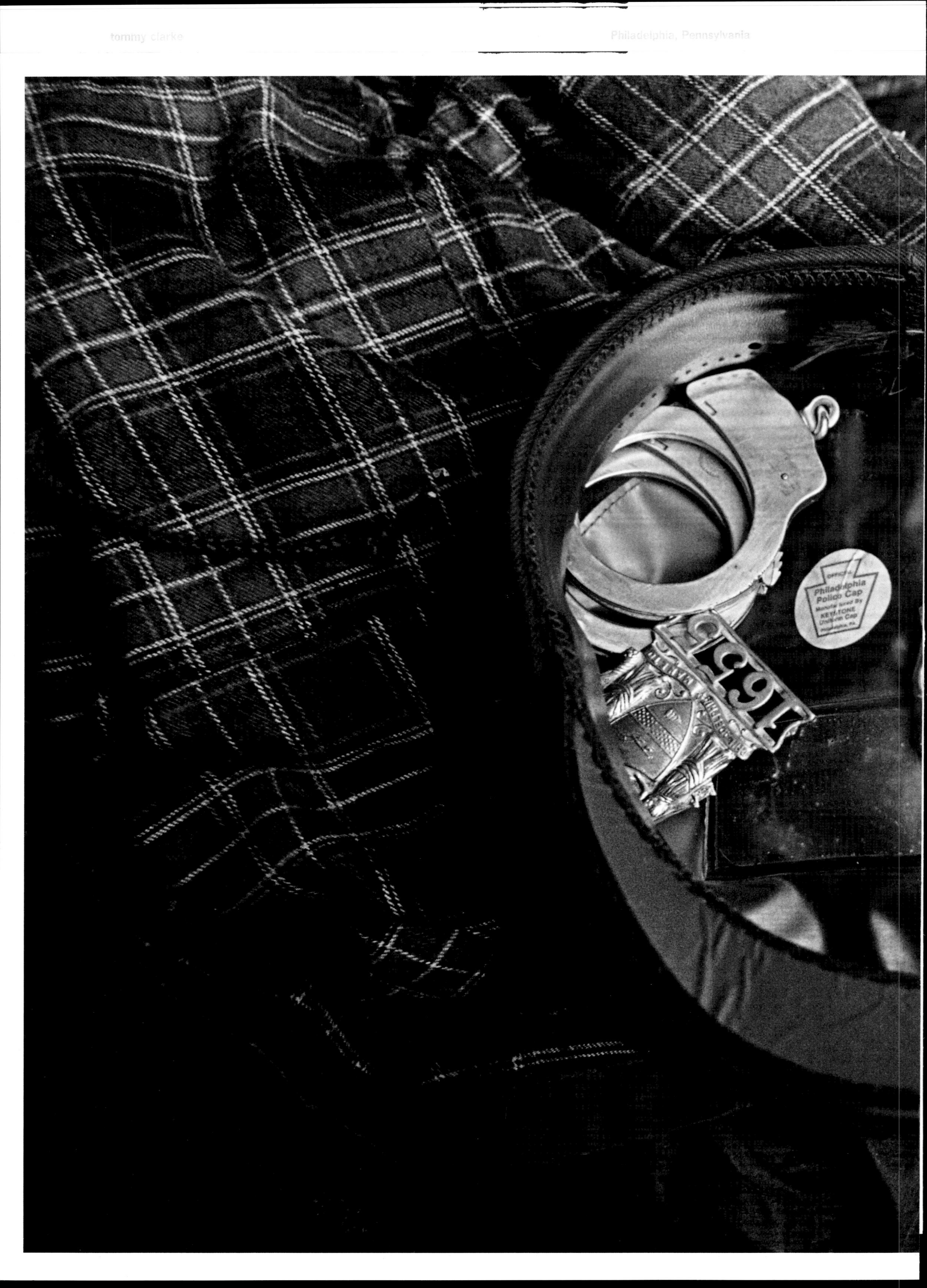
OFFICIAL
Philadelphia
Police Cap
KEYSTONE
Uniform Cap

PHILADELPHIA
1655

Mitre

PUSH
Thanks
for

June

Back on the force, Tommy's usual shift these days is eight-to-four. Tommy Jr., who lives nearby with his girlfriend and their two kids, works split shifts: sometimes eight-to-four, sometimes four-to-midnight, sometimes midnight-to-eight. And Kathy, who has transferred to traffic, is on eight-to-four or four-to-midnight. Late for work, Kathy is trying to convince twelve-year-old Joel to finish his breakfast. Failing that, she pries open his mouth to check his braces. "They're costing us three thousand dollars," she groans. Tommy comes downstairs and swings fake punches at John, who's thirteen. "Tommy, don't," Kathy yells at him, as if he, too, is a child. He apologizes, then kisses her good-bye as she rushes out the door.

Tommy lets their two rottweilers into the kitchen and yells for the boys to go back up and finish getting dressed. Tommy's both happy and a little pissed to be working overtime today. His testimony against a drug pusher he busted won't be needed before nine, but he has to be in court by eight. He's in the mood to complain. "The cops, they're not liberal," he grumbles. "But the media is liberal, the courts are liberal, the newspapers are liberal. So no one cares about the cops. The stereotype is cops hanging around Dunkin' Donuts, cops being brutal, being corrupt. Pardon me for saying so, but they can kiss my Irish ass."

"Boys," Tommy calls out again. John and Joel bound down the stairs. Joel is chewing on a handkerchief, his nose showing the irritation of a cold. John is swinging his belt like a whip. Both are outfitted in parochial-school uniforms: pale blue dress shirts, black neckties, and navy blue pants. If you squint your eyes, they look like miniature cops.

"Future police officers?" I ask Tommy, once the kids are out the door. "*Noooo!*" he bellows, "No." His last no is more like a sigh. "John and Joel, their mother won't let them be cops. With three cops around this house, no way. 'You ain't being a cop, you ain't being a cop,' she harps at them."

Tommy reaches up to retrieve his on-duty pistol, his old six-shot, from the top of the china closet. "Now Tommy Jr., God bless him, he's already a veteran. After only a couple of weeks on, he busted shoplifters and auto thieves. But bad guys have no conscience. Tommy Jr. nearly had his finger chopped off chasing a drug dealer. Crazy! The exact same finger I lost part of. And just before Christmas, coming off his shift, his car was struck by a drunk driver. He's lucky to be alive." Tommy's eyes grow teary. "Oh, I worry about my son now. Every time he goes to work, I tell him that I love him. 'Be careful. Be careful. I love you.' Every day."

Tommy grabs his coat from the back of a chair. "You never want to think about burying your kids.... Jesus, I'd be in the nuthouse.... And I don't want to die, either. I don't want to die on the streets of Philadelphia. I want to die in Ireland, singing of the glory of the Irish." He's laughing now. "Then I'd go to heaven, because Ireland is heaven. God, it's so green."

a procession of them

Everyone in the van stopped talking and held their breath. All the planning and pondering about the ethics, legality, and consequences of what we were doing had come down to whether or not the gate at the end of the road leading into Ocaranza was unlocked.

"Hurry, hurry!" There were nine people sneaking into the mental hospital that November morning: human-rights lawyers, a psychiatrist, a medical doctor, social workers, reporters, and the activists from Mexico City who'd brought us there. The group split up. Three of us were hurried through an archway down a gloomy corridor to the men's ward, where the attendant, talked into believing that ours was an official tour, unlatched the door.

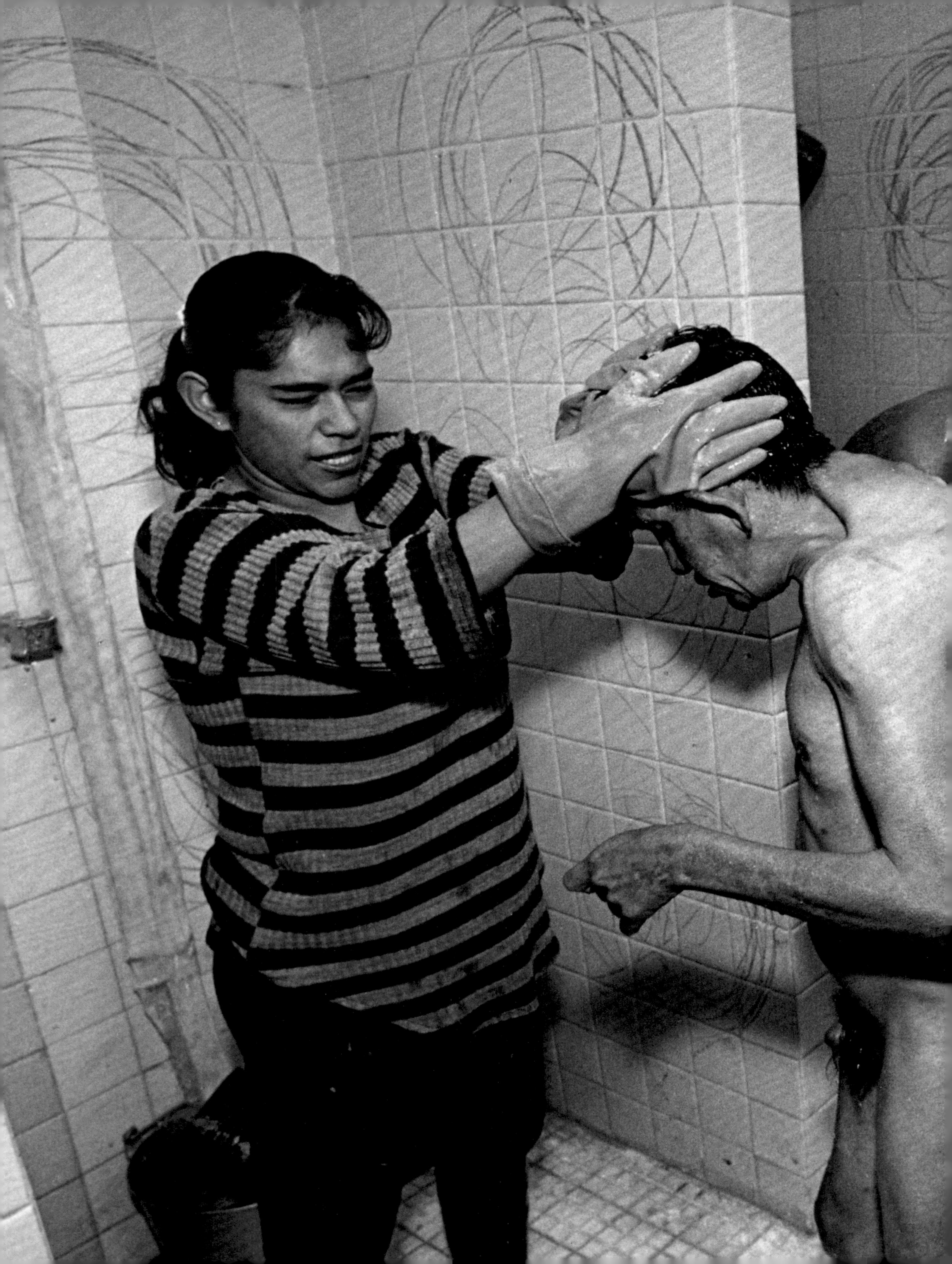

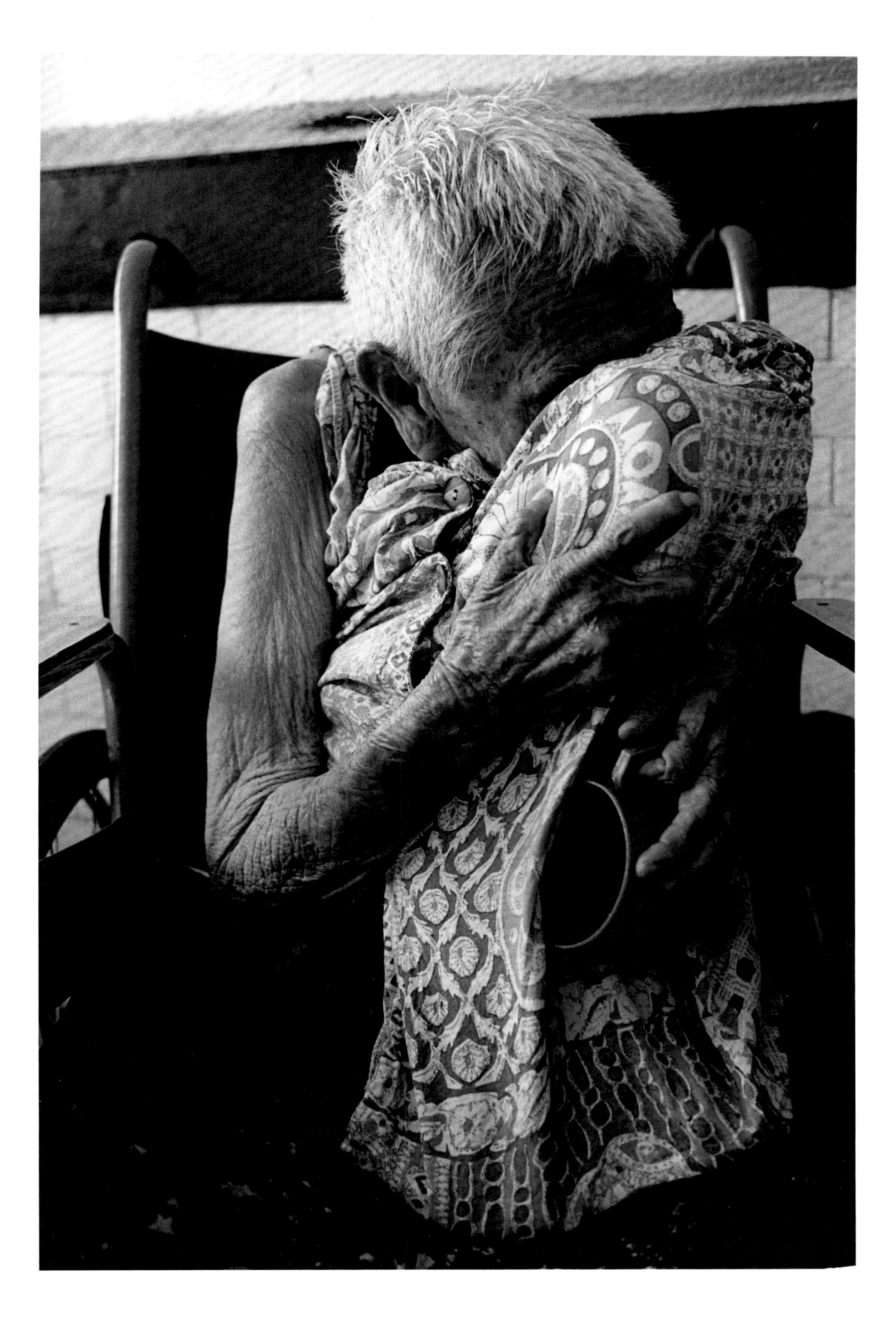

Hidalgo, Mexico

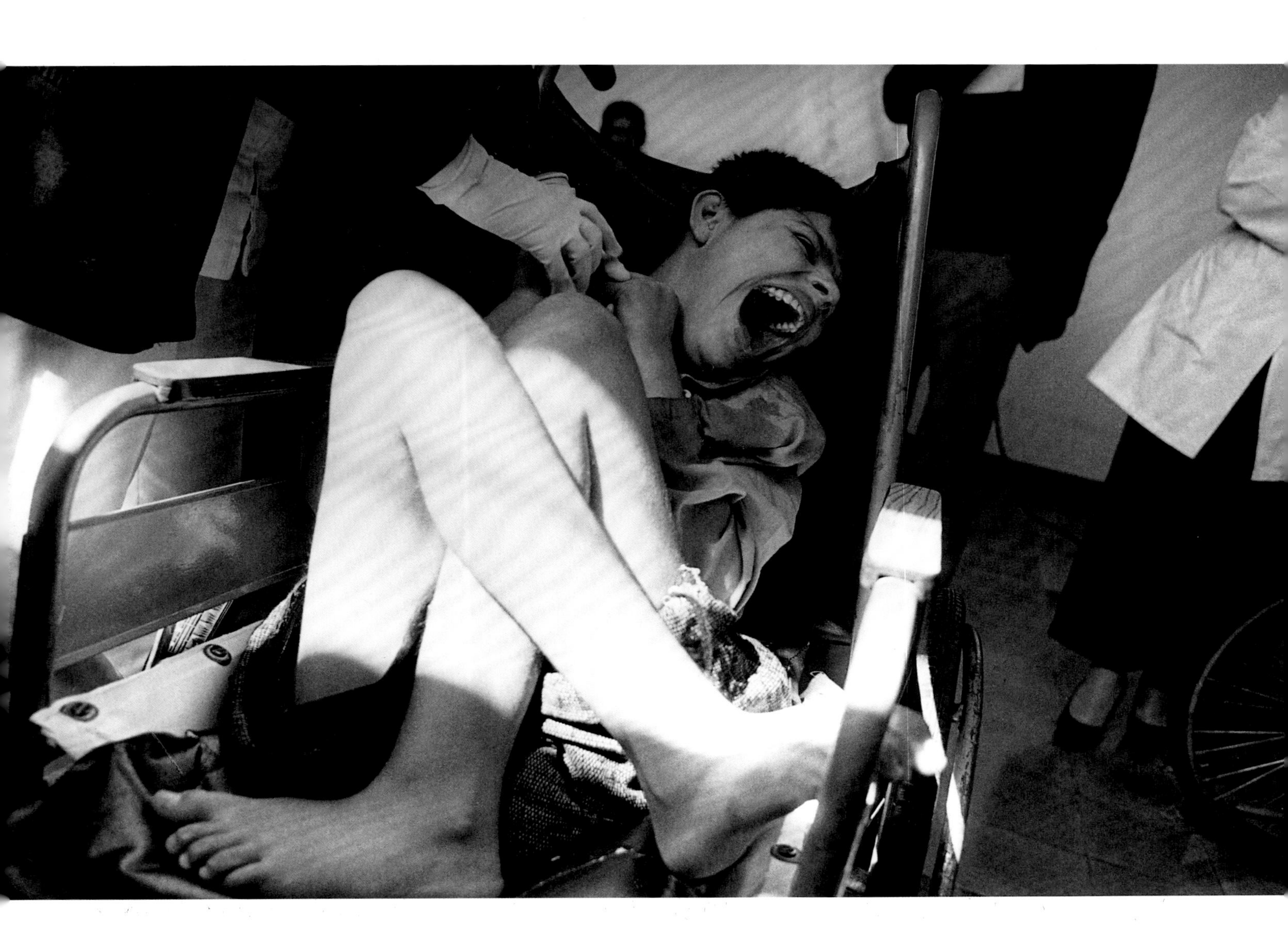

the next step

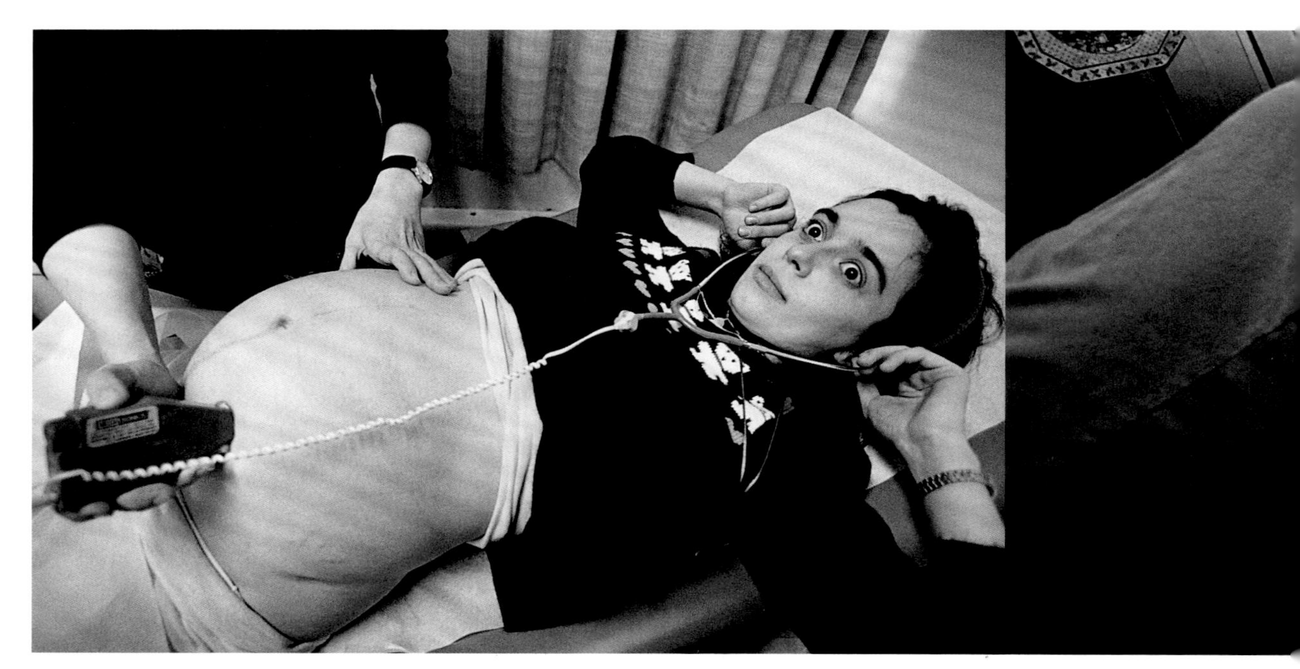

Around the fourth or fifth month there were times...

there was something wrong between Jim and me and I was thinking, "Oh my God, we're having a child!"

Once I came home from work and he was on the phone with an ex-girlfriend of his that I had never met. I'm Italian. So I thought, "God, here I am carrying a child. My body's changing, I feel tired. Oh God, he forgot me." I thought Jim didn't care, didn't understand what it means that I'm having a child. His life doesn't change, but mine does.

I was jealous too much. Jim's not as jealous as me. In the beginning, he wasn't at all, and that would drive me crazy, because I was thinking he didn't care about me. He'd say, "Oh, I saw a man looking at you." But then after a second, I knew he wasn't thinking about that. It was my insecurity. When we met in Paris, it was a physical attraction. He was beautiful. By the time we got to Italy, I felt like maybe he'd made a mistake. Yeah, look at me. Would he appreciate me once I had a child? Or would he look at me always like I was a mother? In Italy, that kind of happens. After they get married and have children, the woman takes care of everything, while the man, if he's like my father, goes out to work. Other men go out to the bar.

In the first months birth seemed far away. Even when it was like six weeks
I wanted to see what was inside me. The doctor said, "You are a very
syndrome or a birth defect. I started thinking, what would I do!

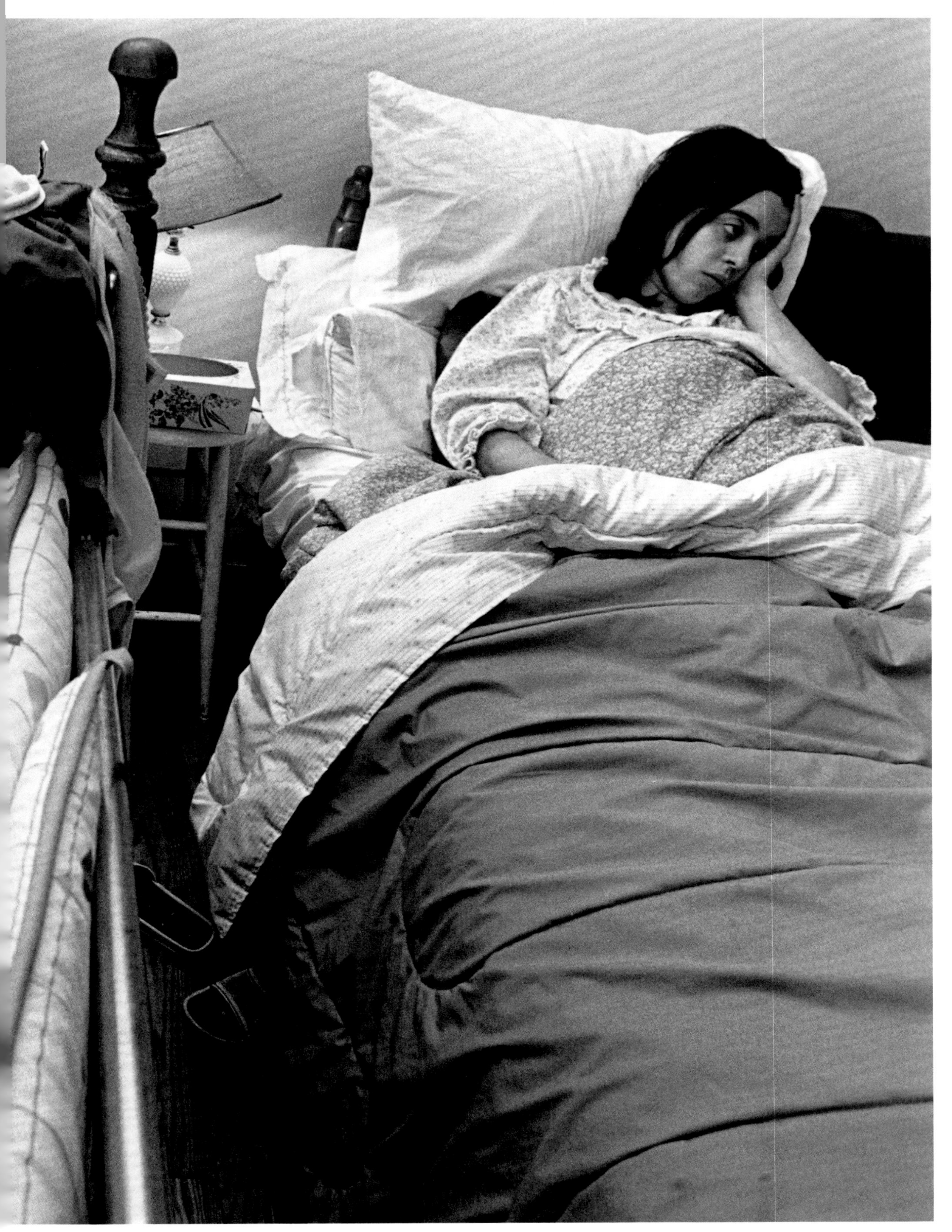

away, it seemed a long time. But then the weeks became days. I lost patience.
young, healthy person." But I worried anyway. I worried about Down's
He'll still be my child.

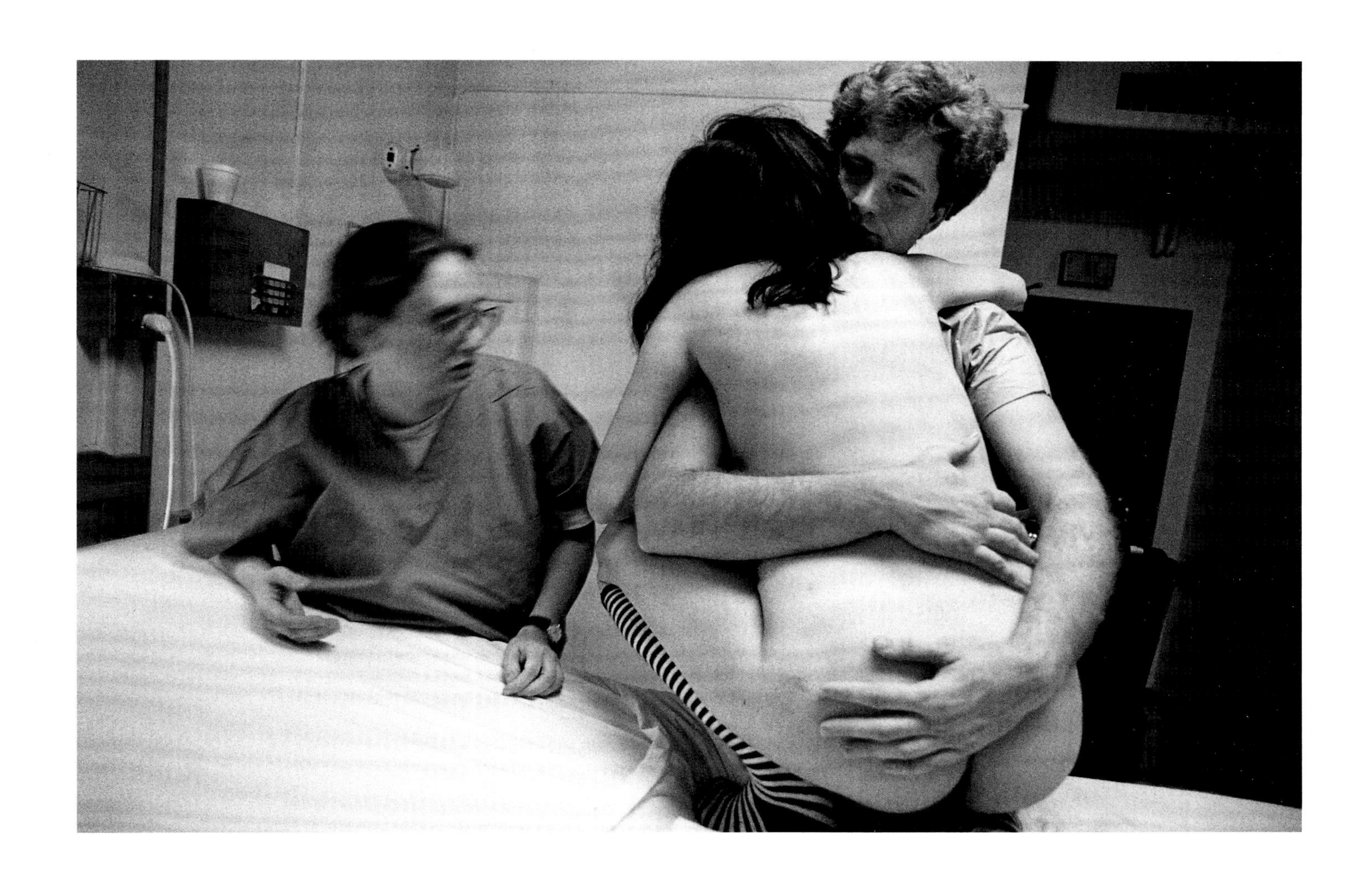

I was going to the hospital in a big hurry in the back of the car. I wanted to be with midwives; still, I wanted Jim there with me in the birthing room because I love him. It was a two-way feeling. I wanted him close, because I felt I wanted his help, but at the same time not too much help. I was tired. I wanted to be a mother. I was ready for the next step.

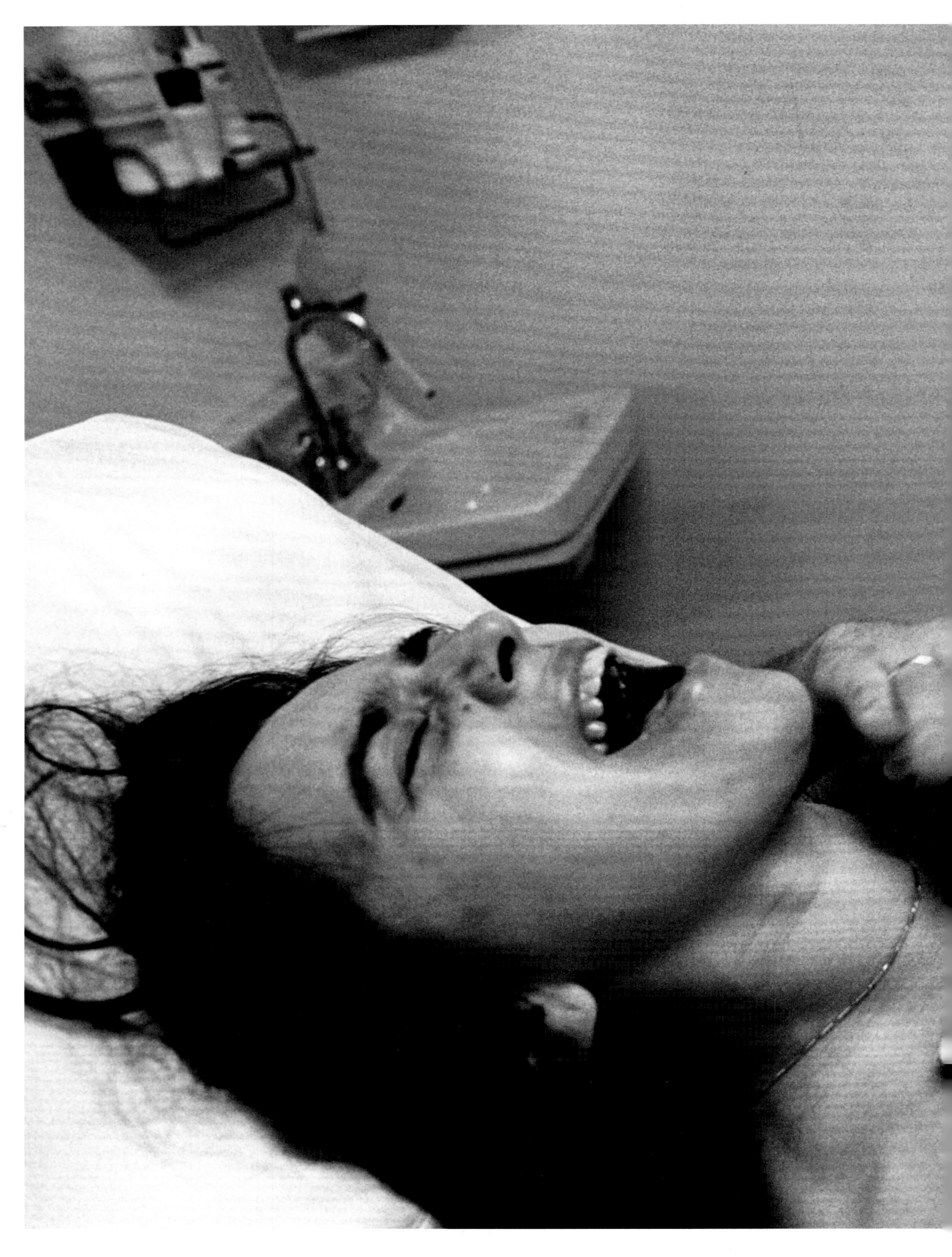

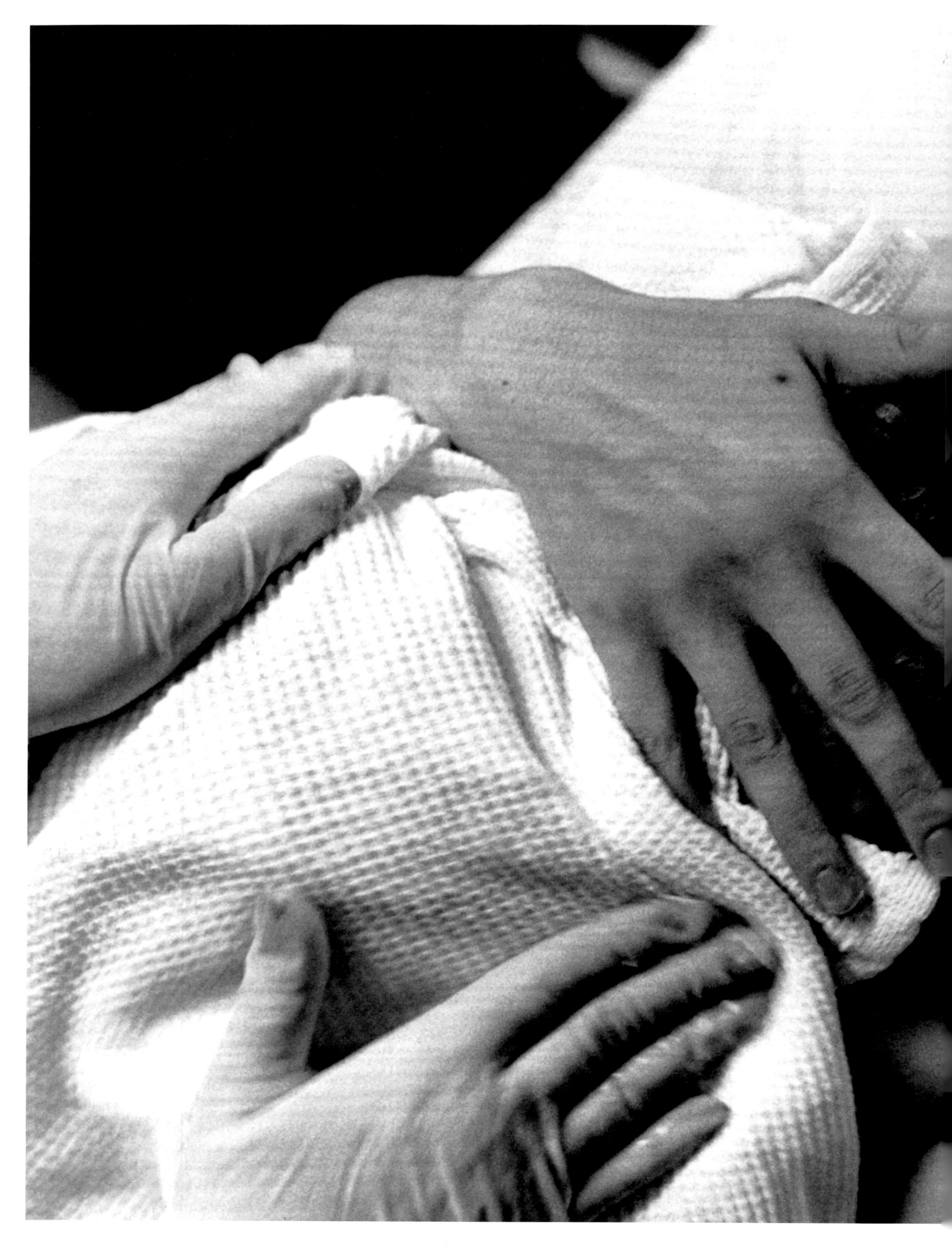

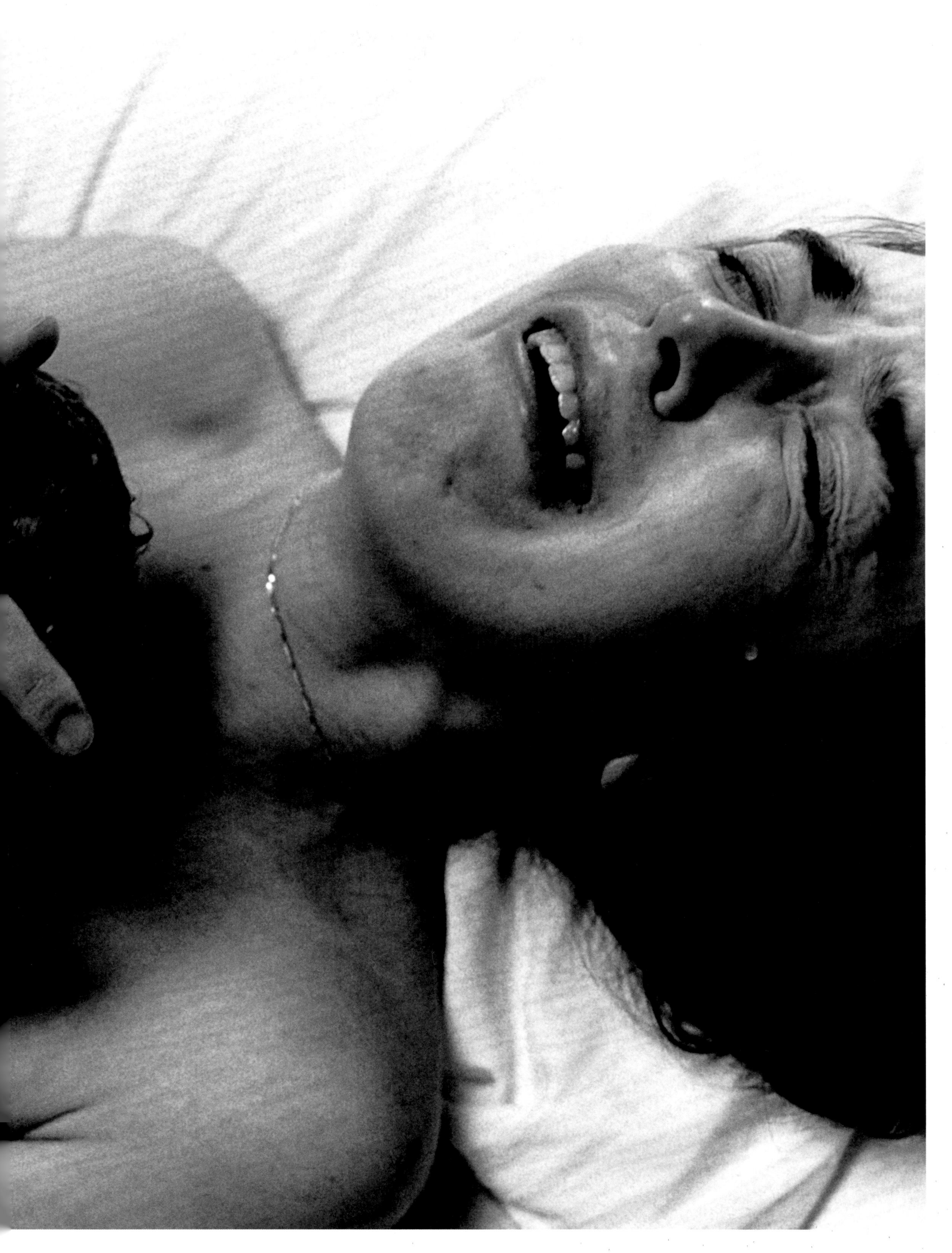

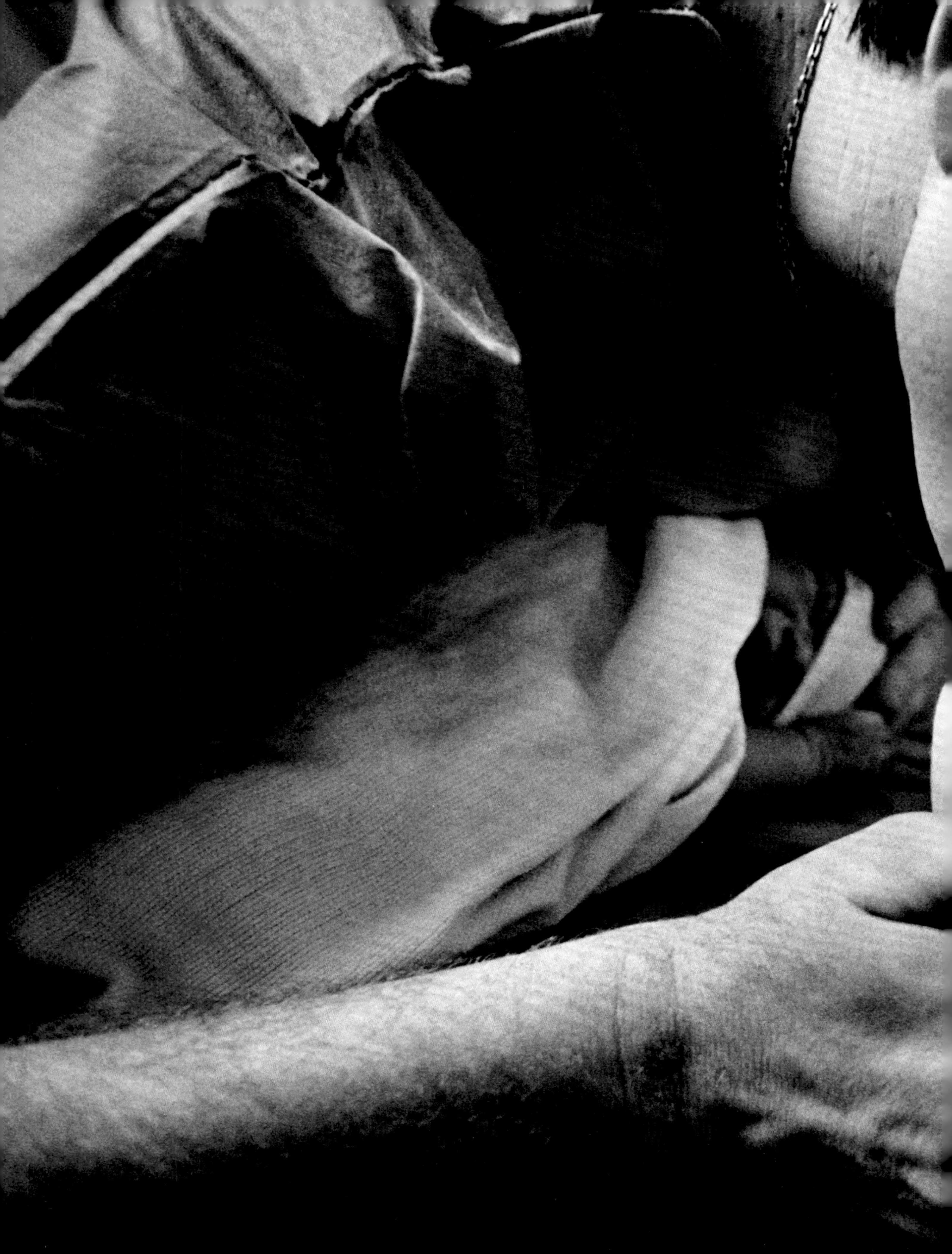

from cradle to grave

Where the road south was lined with woods and dark like a tunnel, I could only catch glimpses of things—the roof of a farmhouse, the sky, a deer running away, clumps of gravestones. Surrounding me now are low grassy hills veined with purple where there are still brakes of trees. When I wave at an old couple sitting out on a porch, they wave back, their pinched brown faces becoming smaller and smaller in the rearview mirror.

TOWN OF FARMVILLE
Gen.

yses S. Grant
GEN. STONEWALL JACKSON
M T. SHERMAN
Gen. Robert E. L
ROBERT E. LEE

$/pharmacy
MOTH
FATHER
MOTHER
MOTHER

Wary, thinking someone is watching, I walk around the small school and try the doors. The place is locked tight. I'm about to leave when I notice the cast-iron marker at the edge of the front lawn. ON THIS SITE, 4-22-51, THE STUDENTS STAGED A STRIKE PROTESTING INADEQUATE SCHOOL FACILITIES.... I read, reread the raised letters, then crossing Griffin Boulevard into the shopping center, ask the first person I meet, a middle-aged pharmacy clerk, what she knows about the school. Alberta White—it's printed on her badge—tilts her head, glares at me out of the corner of her eye.

"Honey, you want me to tell you what? That I went there?"

"During the student walkout?" I blurt out.

"Honey, the only thing I was wanting then was a recess," she shoots back, covering her mouth, trying to stop herself from laughing.

When I return to the pharmacy at noon, I find Mrs. White sitting alone at the back of the store, slumped at a makeshift table, worried that I might have taken to heart things that she said but didn't really mean. "The time of the school walkout, I wasn't goofing off. I was worn out. I was in the eighth grade; still, every day after school and on weekends, till the sun went down, I worked alongside my dad in the fields. There were seven kids. We ate, but we were p-o-ooor... p-o-ooor."

After graduating from Moton, in 1955, Mrs. White married and moved away to New Jersey, only to return to Farmville with two young children. Her second husband is a custodian at Longwood, the local teachers' college. "I work lots harder than he does," she jokes. But her laughter fades when I ask her about job opportunities for other black people in town. "If you really got to, talk to the president of our women's group. Ms. Allen's kind of our historian." Then, leaning closer, she answers my question. "There are a few little black-run grocery stores, a beauty shop, two black dentists in town. And three black funeral homes. Still, if you want a white person to bury you, they'll do it. I went out to this funeral home some years ago, and there lay this dark-complexioned lady, with one little flower in her hand. She didn't have anybody left, so she left her house to this white undertaker, willed it to him, so her dying wouldn't be any trouble to anyone, and he buried her the cheapest way he wanted. With just one little flower in her hand."

The following morning, Vera Allen is waiting for me, a lone, slight figure at the entrance to the school. Rushing up the stairs, I explain that I was waylaid outside the Chamber of Commerce office. Seeing me take pictures, one of the town councilmen took it upon himself to advise me to focus on what's happening today in Farmville, rather than on the past. Ms. Allen shrugs. "Consider what people say and follow your conscience," she advises me without drama, then unlocks the doors.

I peer inside. Thousands of pinholes pit and scar the bulletin boards in the entryway; in a corner hangs a faded American flag. We cross the dark auditorium into a hallway patched with rectangles of dusty light. The empty rooms creak and echo with our footsteps and voices, with what, Ms. Allen remarks, could be the sounds of children. Noticeably weary when she walked in, having just come from a funeral, the seventy-four-year-old woman seems to stand straighter. When Moton opened in 1939, she explains, there were eight classrooms for the 180 students; a dozen years later, about three times as many children were crammed into the so-called separate-but-equal facility, the overflow attending classes in tarpaper shacks and in an old bus driven onto the lawn.

I lie awake most of the night, worried, feeling shut out, and am up early walking in Farmville. I peek into backyards, photograph the warehouses along the river and, as the fog is clearing, the Confederate cemetery. Ms. Allen and her women's group apparently aren't the only ones in Farmville striving to preserve what you'd think people living here might want to forget. There are announcements posted in all the store windows downtown. The annual reenactment of Sayler's Creek—the last major battle of the Civil War in Virginia—is scheduled to begin today at 1:30 four miles east of here.

On the way out to the battlefield, I stop to say good morning to Ms. Allen, who's gathering up her things for church. When I mention where I'm going today, she responds with a weak smile and what's almost a whisper. "They still think they won that war." I follow her into the dining room where she gets her prayer book, and out onto the porch. She pauses at the screen door and says, "There is so much else in the world that should concern us," before pulling it closed.

Bright yellow tape, the kind the police use to cordon off crime scenes, has been stretched the length of a meadow. Behind it, the two thousand or so spectators jockey for the best view of the action, then stand and wait, as the already brutal sun grows even hotter. Bugles are blowing, and there are flurries of gunshots, but soon the younger children have had enough; they're moaning, tugging, and kicking at their parents when General Robert E. Lee suddenly appears. The general, I'd read, wasn't actually at the battle, though this historical error doesn't seem to bother anyone. The squat, bearded man playing the part rides past on a potbellied old mare, waving to the spectators as if blessing them and the war that once raged here.

"Yea, Virginia! Go, Virginia!" the crowds holler as the battle opens with blasts from Confederate cannons. Reenactors swarm from the woods, raise their battle flags, level their muskets, fire, fall back, regroup. The volleys come faster and faster until the men, gulping for air, are swallowed up in clouds of acrid smoke. Like zombies, the soldiers who fall dead or wounded in one skirmish show up in others as the fighting moves up the hill toward us. Finally, the Federal troops crash into the last stand of rebels, mock clubbing, shooting, bayoneting them, and it's over. A few of the reenactors pose for pictures; everyone else is hurrying to their cars. As the road fills with dust, I look at my watch. The reenactment has lasted a little over an hour; the actual battle, in which there had been a mass surrender of Confederates, had slogged on for two pitiless days.

blue snow

ОПЕРАЦИОНИ Б

СТРОГО

ЗАБРАЊЕН УЛАЗАК

МОЛИМО ЗА ТИШИНУ

Rushed home on Sunday from a Florida assignment to repack my bags for a 7 p.m. flight to Zurich which ended up departing at 1 a.m., causing me to miss my connection to Budapest. I was relayed onto a later flight, but without any of my luggage. At 10 p.m. Monday, having missed the arranged truck ride, wired, still not having slept, I boarded a half-packed JAR bus for Belgrade and journeyed for seven hours through a heavy snowfall. At some point during the long ride I fell asleep.

In fits and starts I dreamt of the war in Beirut. Shivering, scared, I was huddled down in a boat approaching that once besieged city. In the distance artillery shells were exploding, the dull thuds carrying over the water. Other memories of the bus ride in the near-total darkness: the blue snow, drinking apricot juice supplied by a flight attendant look-alike, clumsiness, nervousness, removing my passport for inspection, then a failed attempt at the Hungarian-Yugoslav border to exchange dollars for local currency so that I could eat and use the pay toilet. The woman in the dusty, glass-walled bank refused my business. "American?" she asked, sneering. Maybe it was just as well because the roadside cafeteria, a stop for truck drivers, was a gray, fluorescent-lit, wholly depressing place, with people slumped over coffees. I pissed on their wall before climbing back aboard, fell back to sleep as the bus pulled into Belgrade, and awoke to see people exiting into the blankets of snow.

The following morning, fidgeting with excitement, I walked into the offices of Médecins Sans Frontières. Because I'd traveled a considerable distance and volunteered to work for the aid organization, I figured someone might want to talk to me. No one did, unless you count the project manager, a French woman who reminded me at least four times how unfortunate it was that I couldn't speak French. Most of the relief workers were out in the field, so I wandered aimlessly around the offices, glancing at magazines, eavesdropping on conversations, studying maps of the region, until it suddenly dawned on me that, except for what I was wearing, I had no clothes. A kindly MSF driver named Muriel (there's always someone) rushed me through the Belgrade streets, from outdoor market to outdoor market, to replace some of what I'd lost. The only underwear in my size for sale had stitched-together panels of green, yellow, and red—the colors of a Yugoslav flag—with bright yellow at the crotch. Then I was back at the MSF office in time to be introduced to Dr. Davidovic, the director of the hospital I'd be photographing in. Before the tall, curt, white-haired neurosurgeon hurried out to catch a plane, he explained that while the facility in Milici was striving to meet the local population's medical and surgical needs, the priority was the Serbian war wounded.

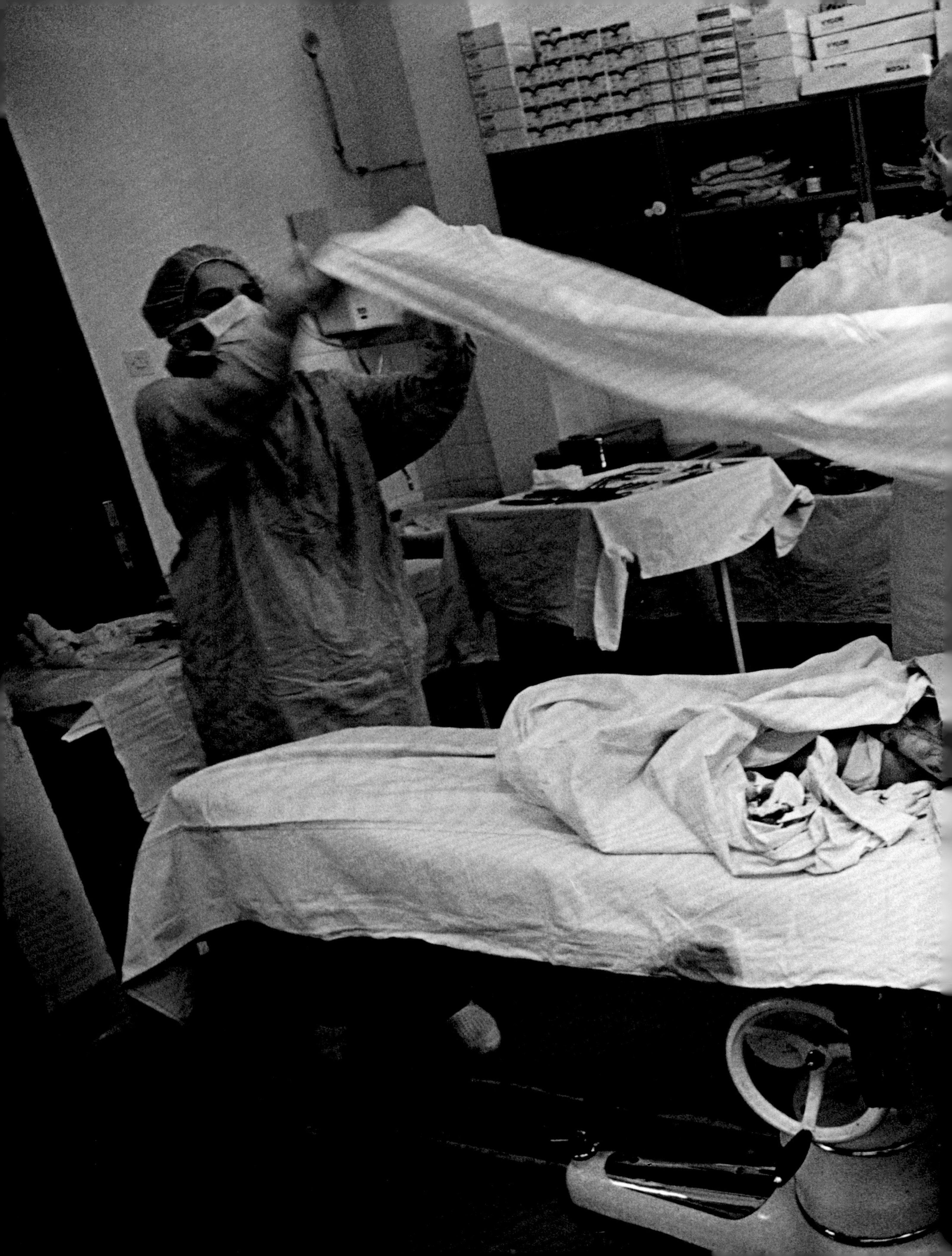

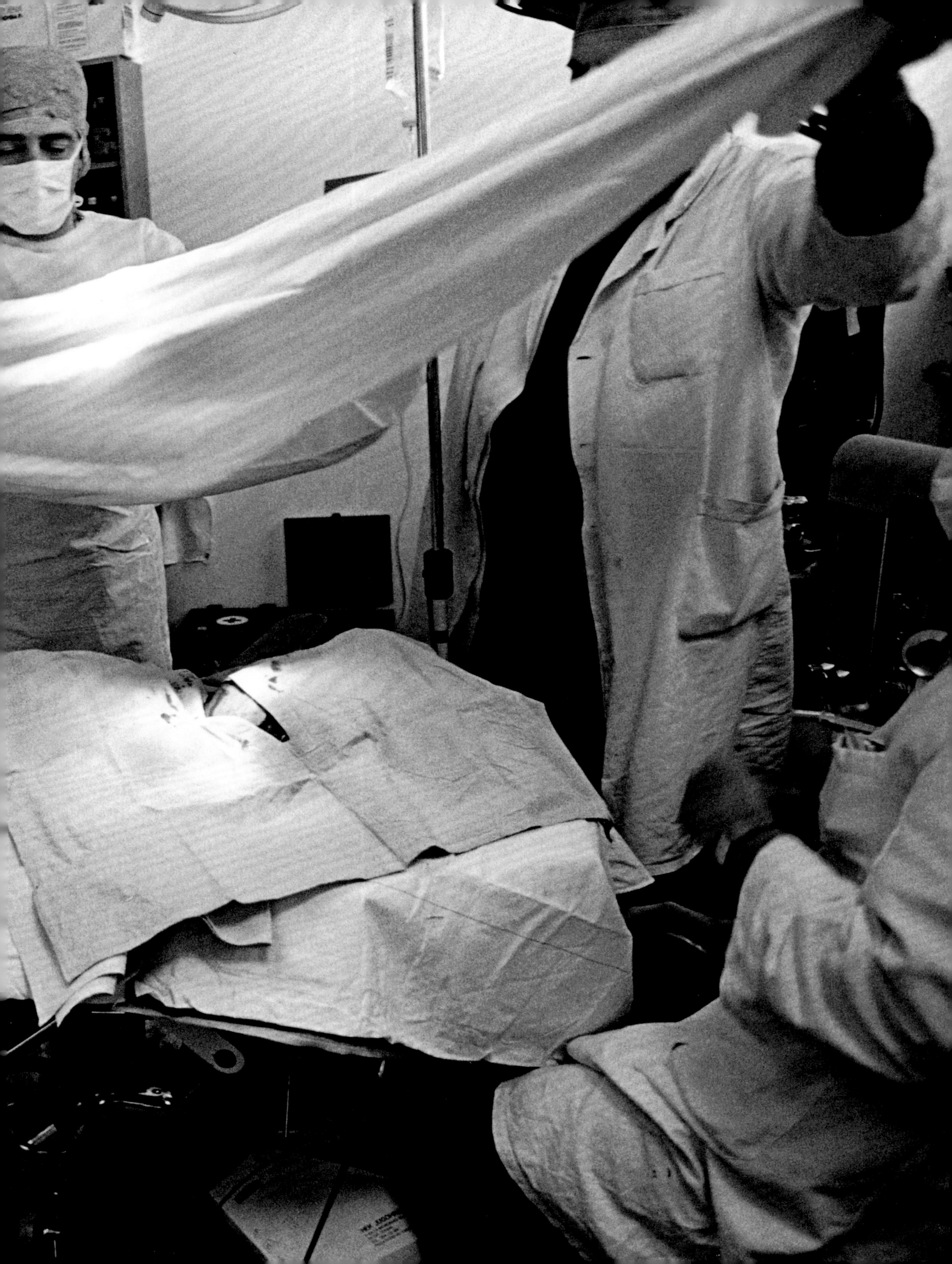

I understood from the doctor that Milici was south of Zvornik in Bosnia and Herzegovina, east of Sarajevo, less than ten kilometers from the front. The soldier who arrived to drive us there was straight out of a Hollywood war movie—square-jawed and handsome, wearing a form-fitting uniform, driving not a military vehicle but a silver Mercedes sedan. Crammed into the backseat beside me was a short, bald general surgeon from Italy named Giuseppe (also an MSF volunteer) and a Serbian anesthesiologist who almost never spoke. The driver ran the doctors to a warehouse to pick up medical supplies, then stopped for coffee at a government office, putting us on the road at 3 p.m., disastrously late, because Bosnia was no place to be after dark.

The roads were icy, winding, empty. Convinced that there were snipers hiding in the mountains around us, the driver drove very fast. An hour out of Belgrade, the car hit a patch of black ice and began a slow-motion, cinematic kind of slide down a steep slope to the edge of a cliff. The Mercedes hung there, engine racing, releasing a white exhaust, while we scrambled out and up the snowy hill. Before we got the least bit cold, another official car arrived.

An hour later we came to a sudden stop in a high mountain pass. Peering through his binoculars, the driver pointed out the vultures circling round a corpse. "Sniper," he whispered. With the killing so close and the sky blackening, we sought lodging for the night across the Yugoslavian border near Zvornik. The proprietor at the first village hotel demanded three hundred dollars from Giuseppe because he was a foreigner, five hundred dollars from me because I was an American. The inn where we finally spent the night had a pretty good restaurant downstairs where we ate, drank, and felt safe. The driver, like the hero of every bad war movie, knew the pretty blonde waitress. When the bar closed, he left to spend the night with her.

A little after noon on Wednesday, we dropped down into a wooded valley, then into the town of Milici. As we drove along what appeared to be the main street, Giuseppe asked the driver to tell us a little something about the place and the people who lived there. The driver would not answer him. Through the windshield, Milici appeared peaceful, a ski village with chalet-style houses. The hospital, a two-story, gray-brick building with white trim, looked more like a contemporary American high school than an embattled trauma center.

Parked out front was a red Mercedes ambulance and a much smaller white station wagon marked with a red cross. Grabbing our bags, we walked up the ramp through the double-doors. The hospital immediately offered up a view of war in the terrible abstract. Lying on a gurney next to a glassy-eyed soldier with an "inoperable bullet in his brain" was a four-year-old boy who had shot himself in the mouth with his father's gun.

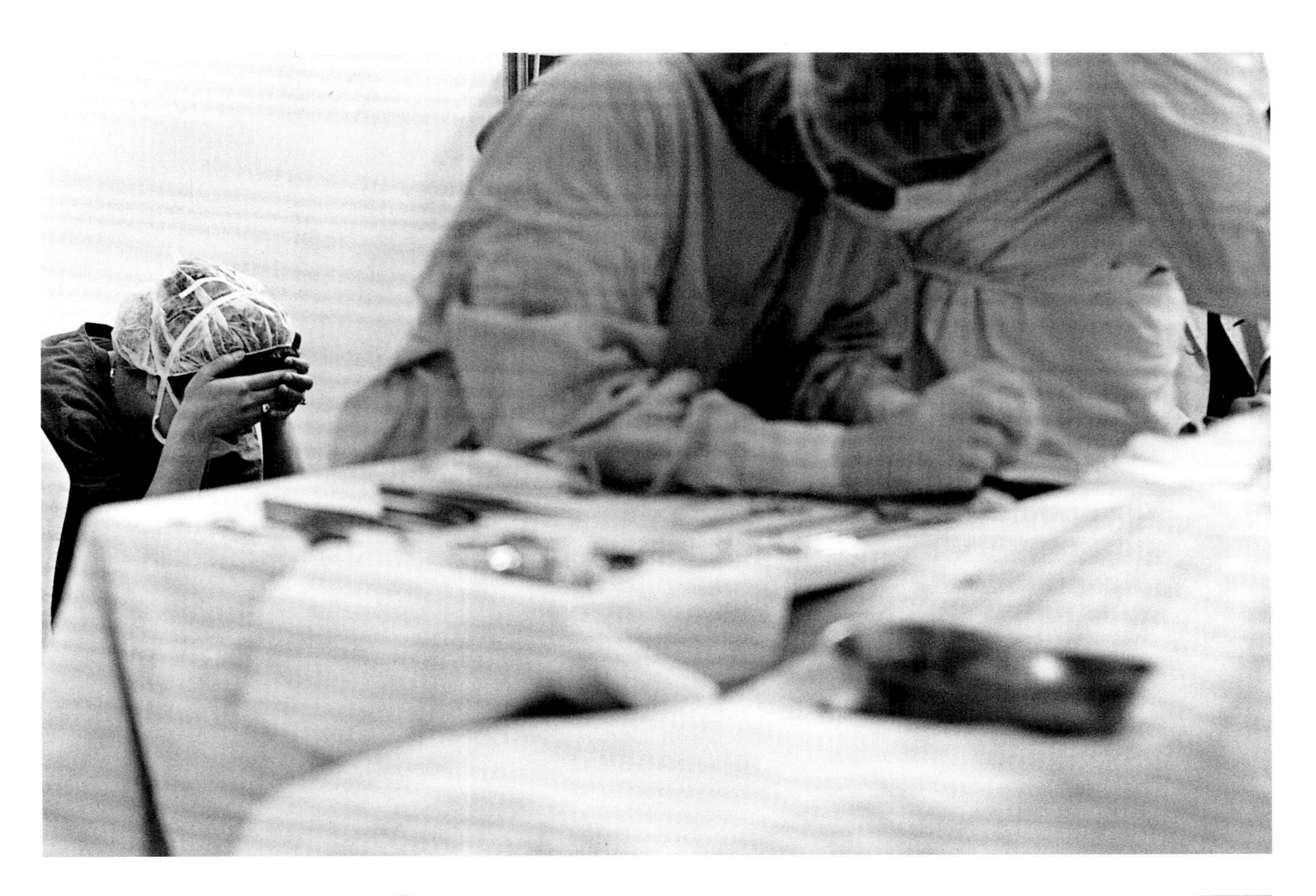

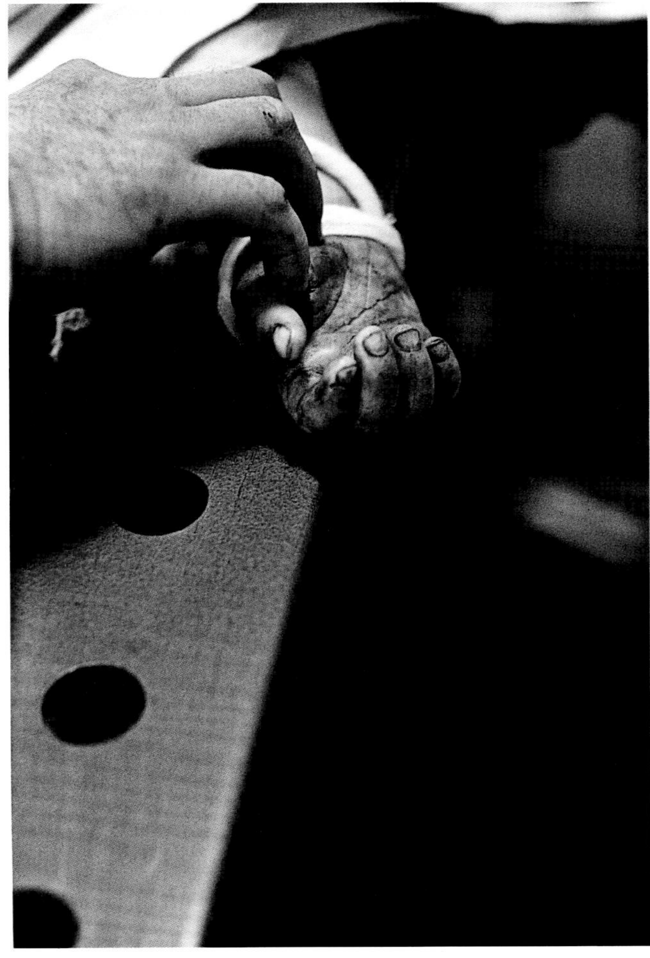

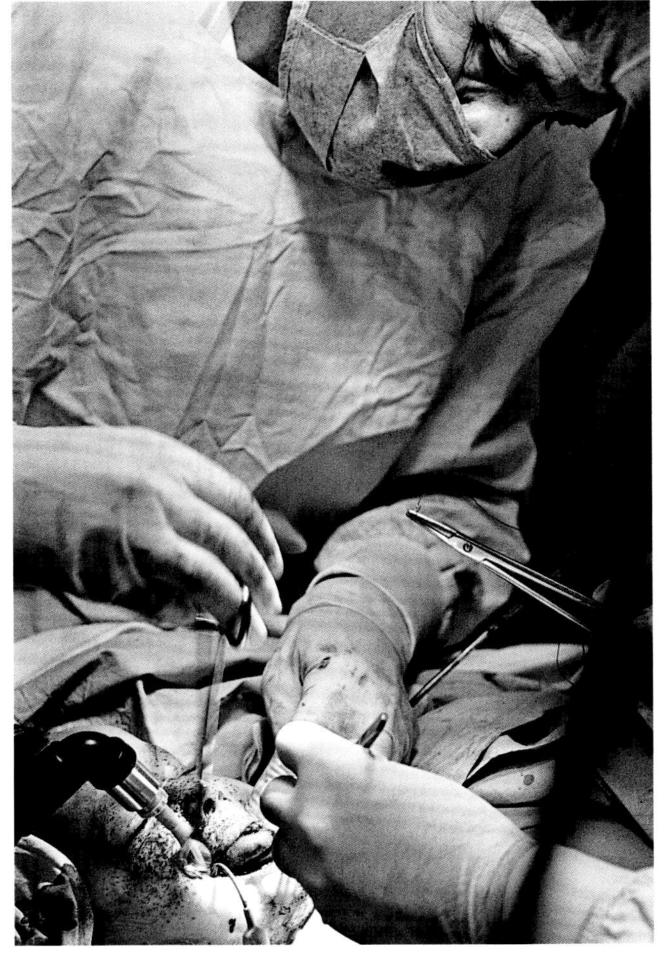

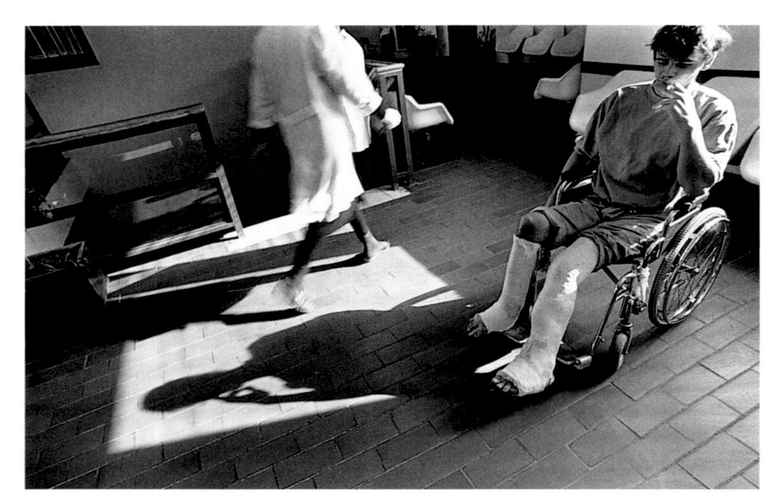

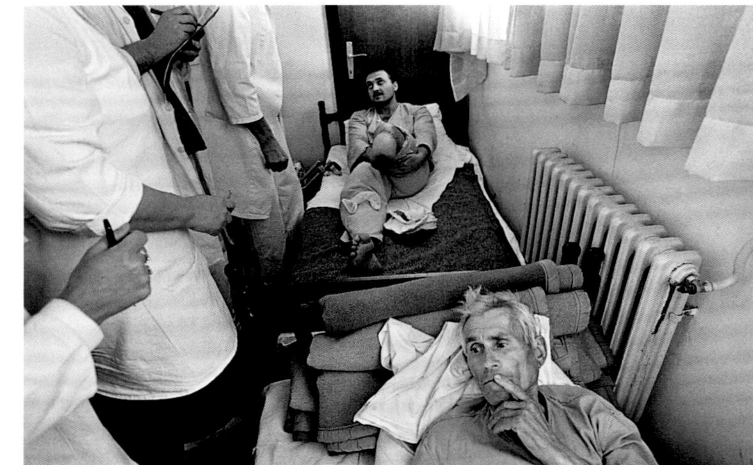

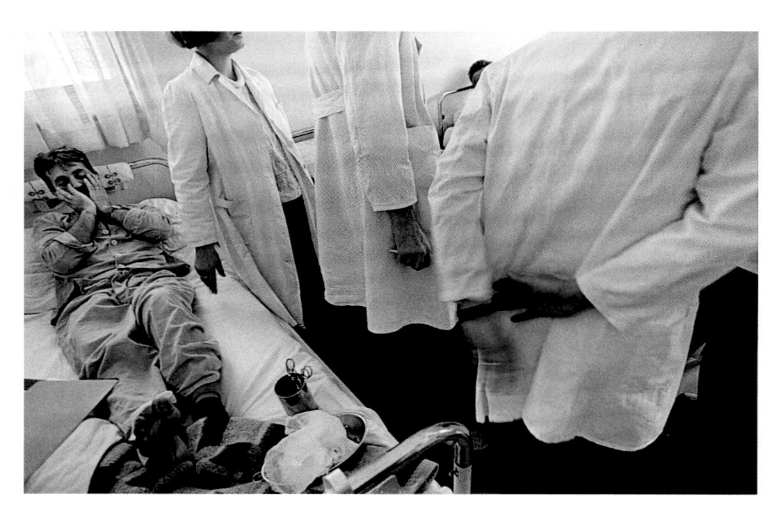

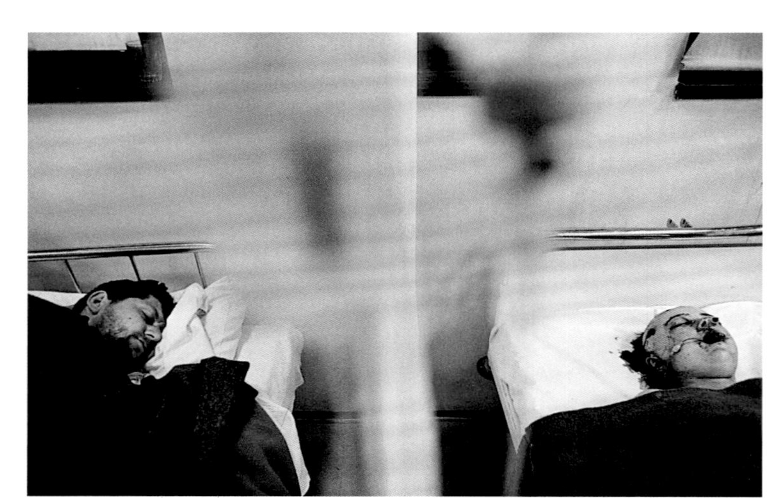

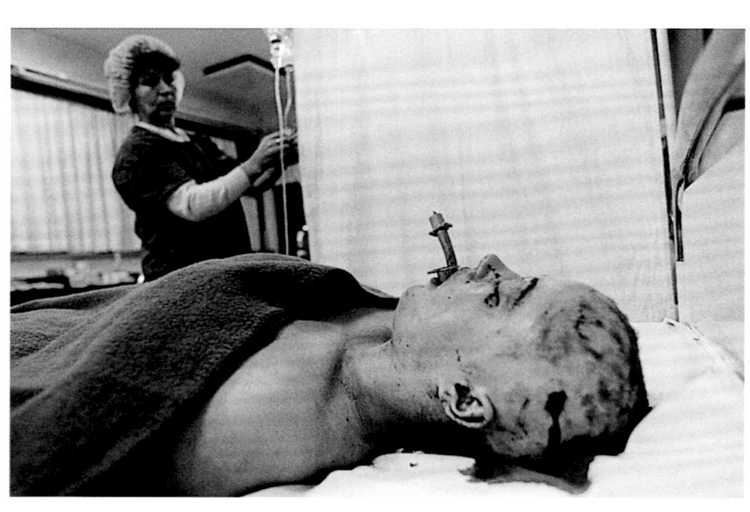

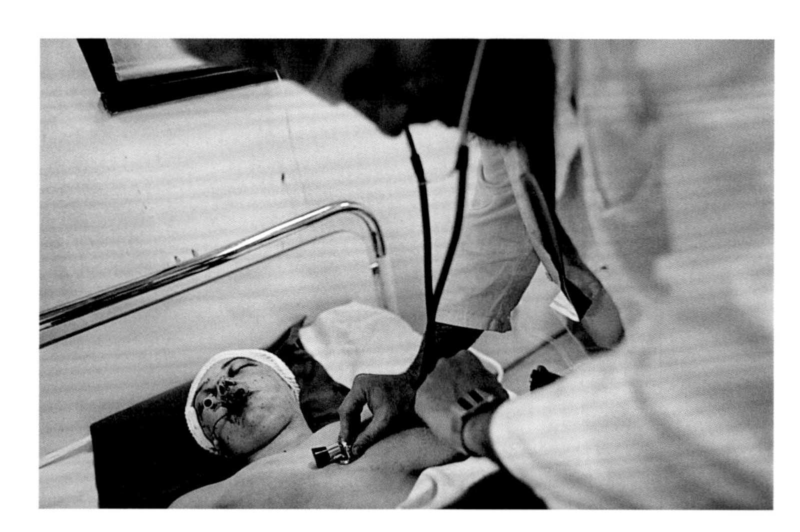

Pulling us along, a big, brusque, English-speaking nurse named Mira explained that the hospital had fifty beds. With the war such a bloody mess, she said, they could use lots more. She showed us the small, cramped operating room, then the intensive care unit. Thinking we heard someone weeping, we peeked inside. Except for the hiss of the respirators and some of the patients' labored breathing, the ICU was quiet. The birthing room was at the end of the general medicine corridor. It had one gynecological couch, one cast-iron birthing table, and padded benches for women to rest on after giving birth. Next to what would be Giuseppe's and my bedroom was a tiny office where children were inoculated. This was also where families could inquire about patients' progress. The wards for the patients with war-related wounds were on the second floor.

The first ward we entered was filled with what we initially thought were crippled old men, but these were actually young men who only weeks or days earlier had been on the front lines. Almost everyone who wasn't in terrible pain nodded hello. A man with a military haircut and a beard immediately began calling to us to shake his hands, though he had none. Another soldier, spotting my camera, asked me if I'd take pictures of his feet, "to bring back to America," he said. Then, laughing, he pulled the sheet up to his knees, revealing that he had only one foot.

The first man we approached in the second ward lay looking up at the ceiling, the stub of an unlit cigarette in his mouth. In his mid-twenties, he was running his hand from his mouth up across his eyes, through his fair hair, again and again, as if he were having difficulty recognizing himself. Directly across from him was a fellow with a bandage on his torn-apart hand who didn't stop grinning for as long as we were there.

After eating dinner in the cafeteria and spending a bit more time on the wards, Giuseppe and I wandered back to our room at the rear of the hospital, where we unpacked our bags and spoke to each other for what was really the first time. Dr. Giuseppe Valenti was fifty years old. His home was Venice. He had three children, ages twenty-four, twenty, and sixteen. And this, he explained, was his second MSF mission in a year. When he had left home this time, his wife, Miranda, became very upset. "Why do you go there?" she asked him. "Why do you leave your children?"

Giuseppe slept like a baby that night, while I sat up staring out the window at the mountains, hearing bursts of gunfire, one after another like Fourth of July fireworks. "Of course, of course," Giuseppe snapped at me in the morning when I began to complain that the shooting (the *boom-boom*, he called it) had kept me awake. I suppose I was hoping for a little sympathy from him, but he didn't have the time. Having slept later than he had intended, Giuseppe yanked on his surgeon's scrubs and rushed out the door.

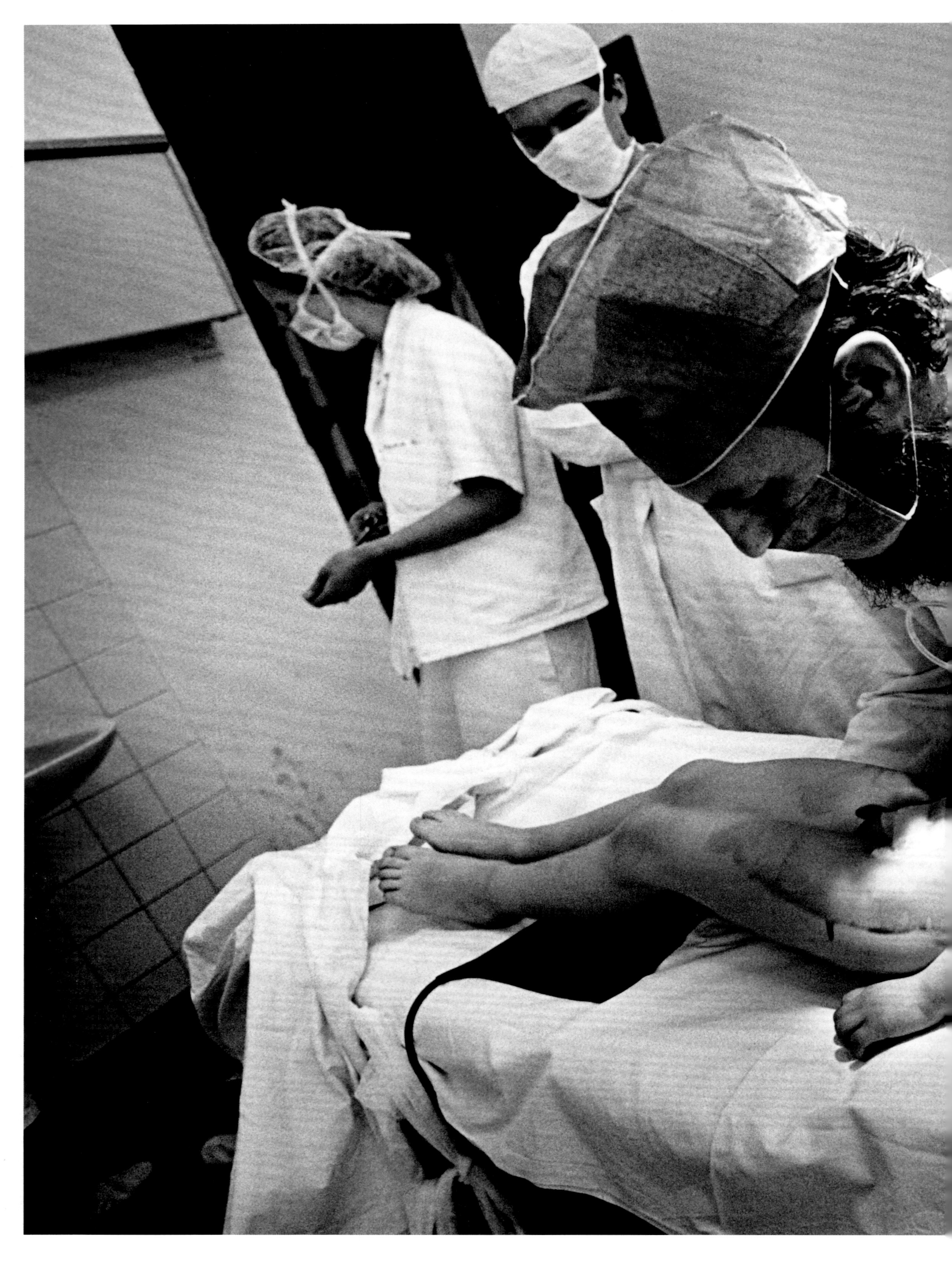

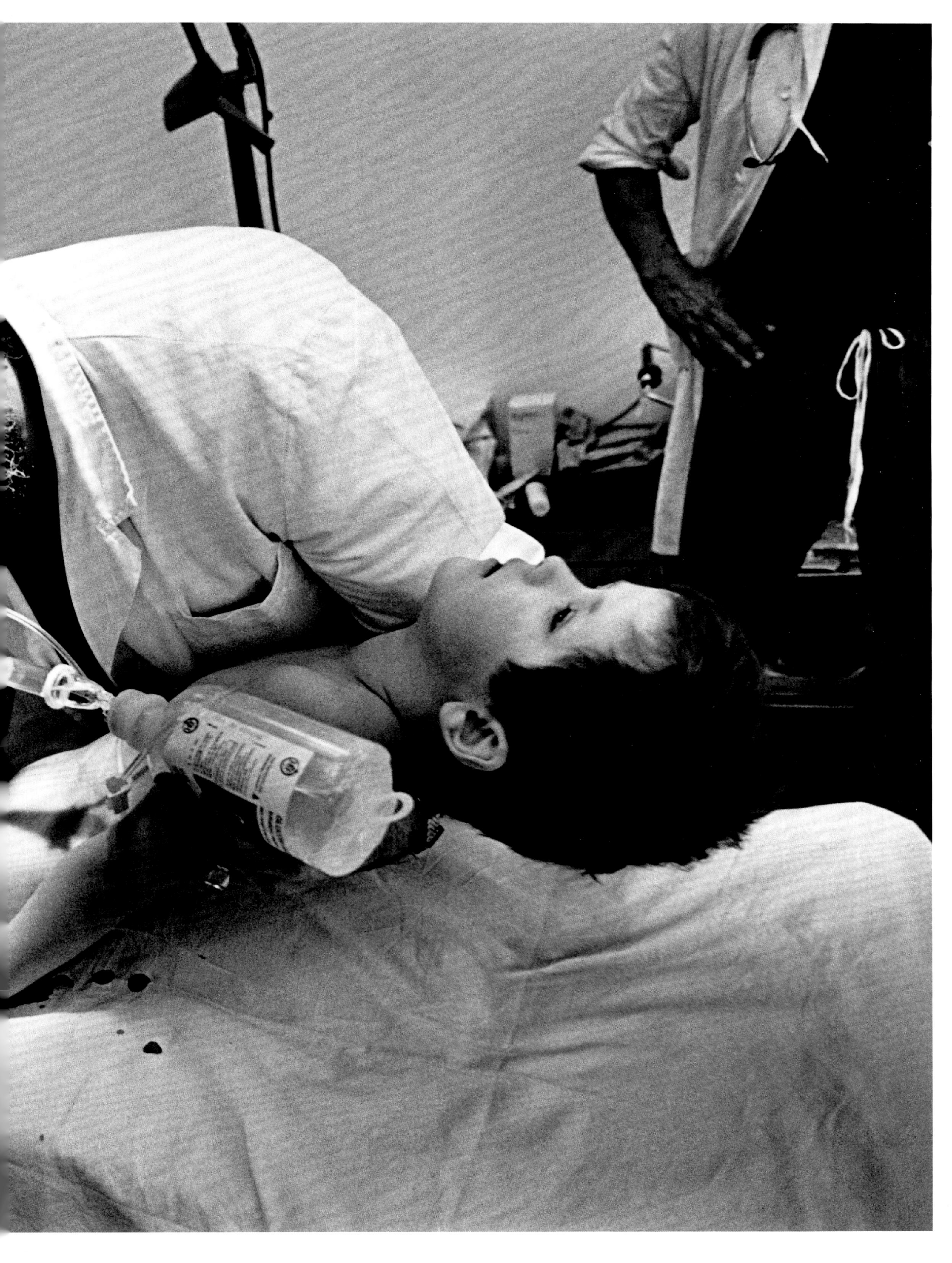

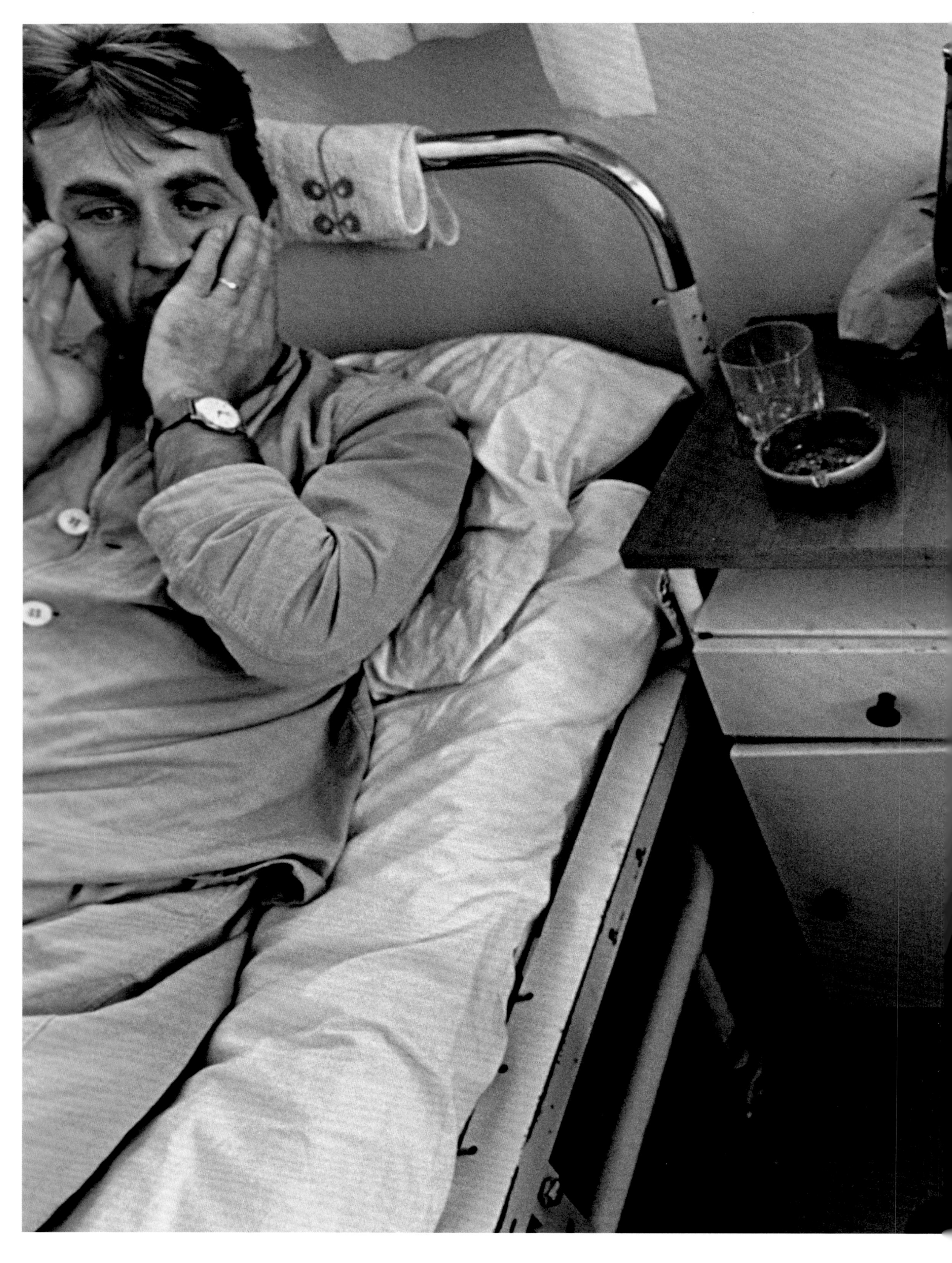

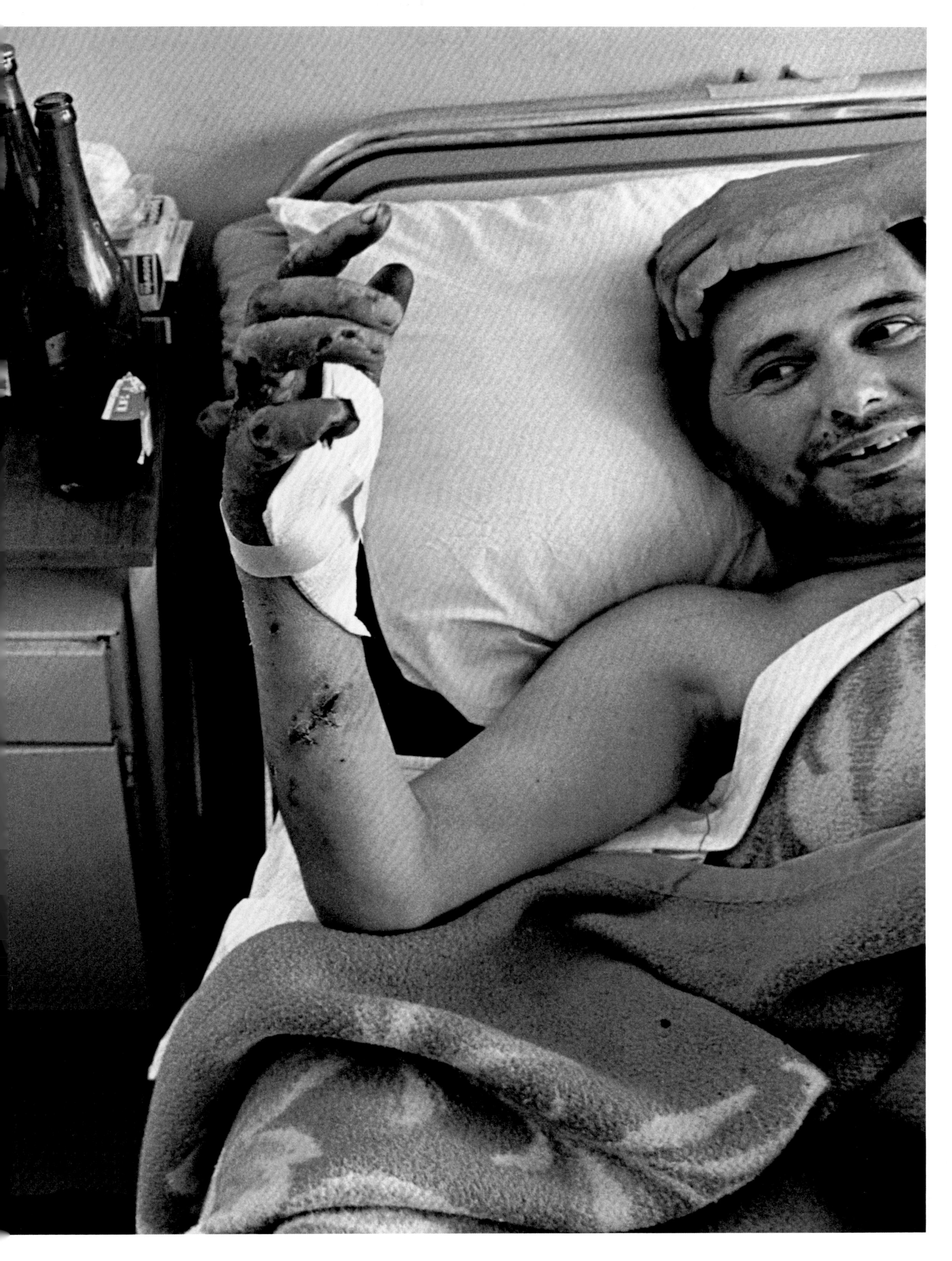

The first patient we encountered on Thursday morning was a beautiful four-year-old boy who'd suffered a hernia. He seemed otherworldly, a vision, lying there in the OR with only a small surgical cut in his abdomen, while there were gunshots to the head upstairs.

When we peered into the intensive care ward we discovered that one of the beds was empty. The woman who had shot herself had died, we were told. I'd sat at her bedside before going to our room last night, while Giuseppe talked technique with the other surgeons. She was young, no more than twenty years old, with a young woman's body; you could see that when the doctor examining her pulled the covers back. But she also had this shaved, gouged, woefully damaged head that you wanted to believe was some kind of prosthesis or mask that could some day come off.

It was still early when I grabbed a camera and followed Giuseppe into the operating room. The OR was crowded with people preparing for what would be the third surgery of the morning. Floors were being scrubbed, the stickiness washed away, fresh instruments and towels laid out. The blood-splattered patient being wheeled in was what they called a "lucky one." Having shrapnel embedded in only the fleshy parts of his arms and legs, he was "lots luckier" than the previous one, whose spine had been severed by a bullet.

While a nurse tried to keep him calm, the soldier was strapped down, stuck with needles, draped, and put under. I knew enough to stay out of the way, but from the moment the chief surgeon returned from having a smoke, he made it clear that he was less than thrilled that I was there. Tall, bony, with jet-black hair and a deeply lined Slavic face, he was a fearsome presence. Whenever he stepped away from the operating table to examine an X-ray or change gloves, he would wave his long arms at me, yelling, "Out of the way, out of the way," and I would press back against the wall. The chief anesthesiologist soon chimed in, making things even more difficult. He started joking around about how Muslims, with three, five, six wives, were having so many children they were taking over the world. Then he began questioning me, offhandedly at first, then with increasing ferocity, about what I was choosing to photograph. Did I or did I not agree "that the news coverage of the Balkan war was biased? All that stuff about rapes and atrocities committed by Serbians. Only by Serbians?" he bellowed from his work station. My morning in the OR ended abruptly when the chief surgeon accused me of brushing against the sheets draped over the unconscious patient, compromising the sterile field. He ordered me out.

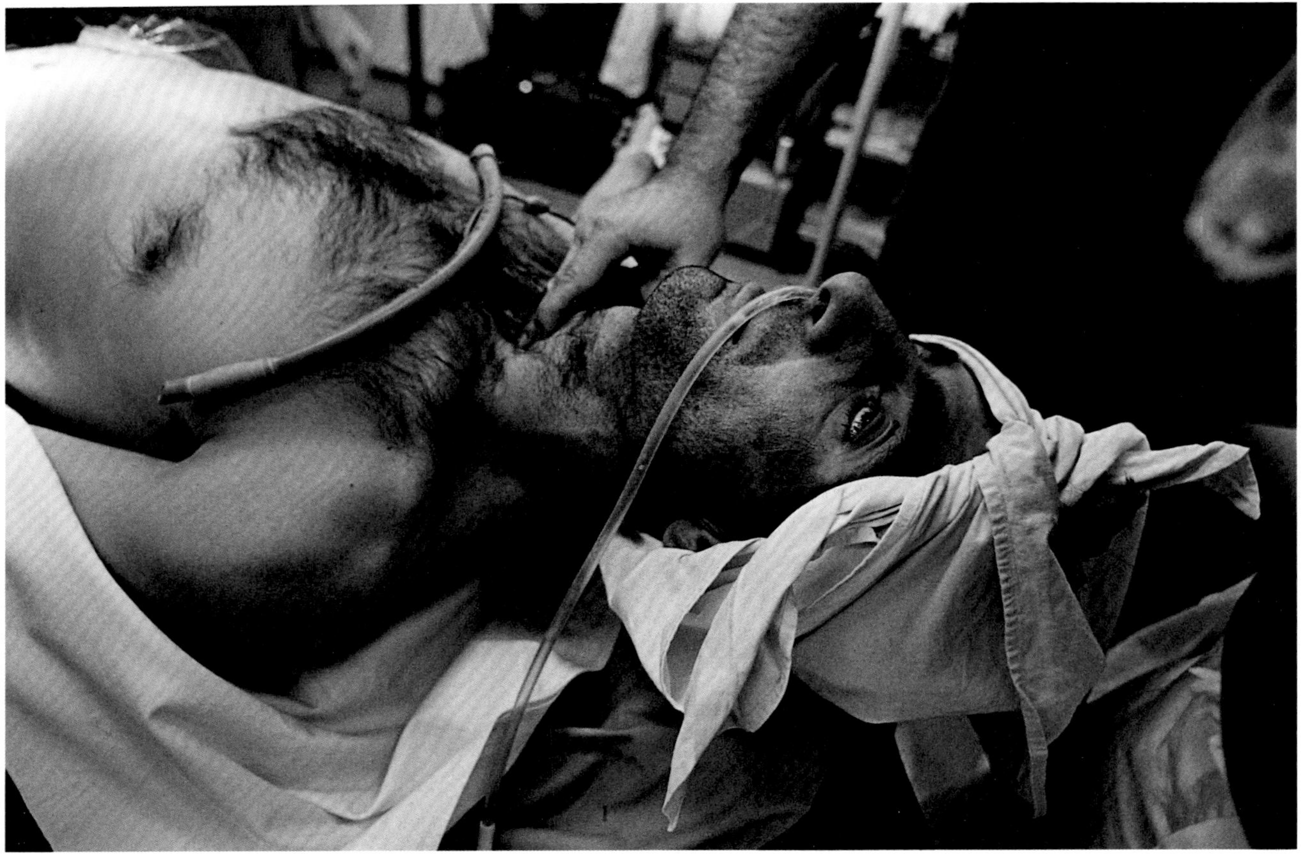

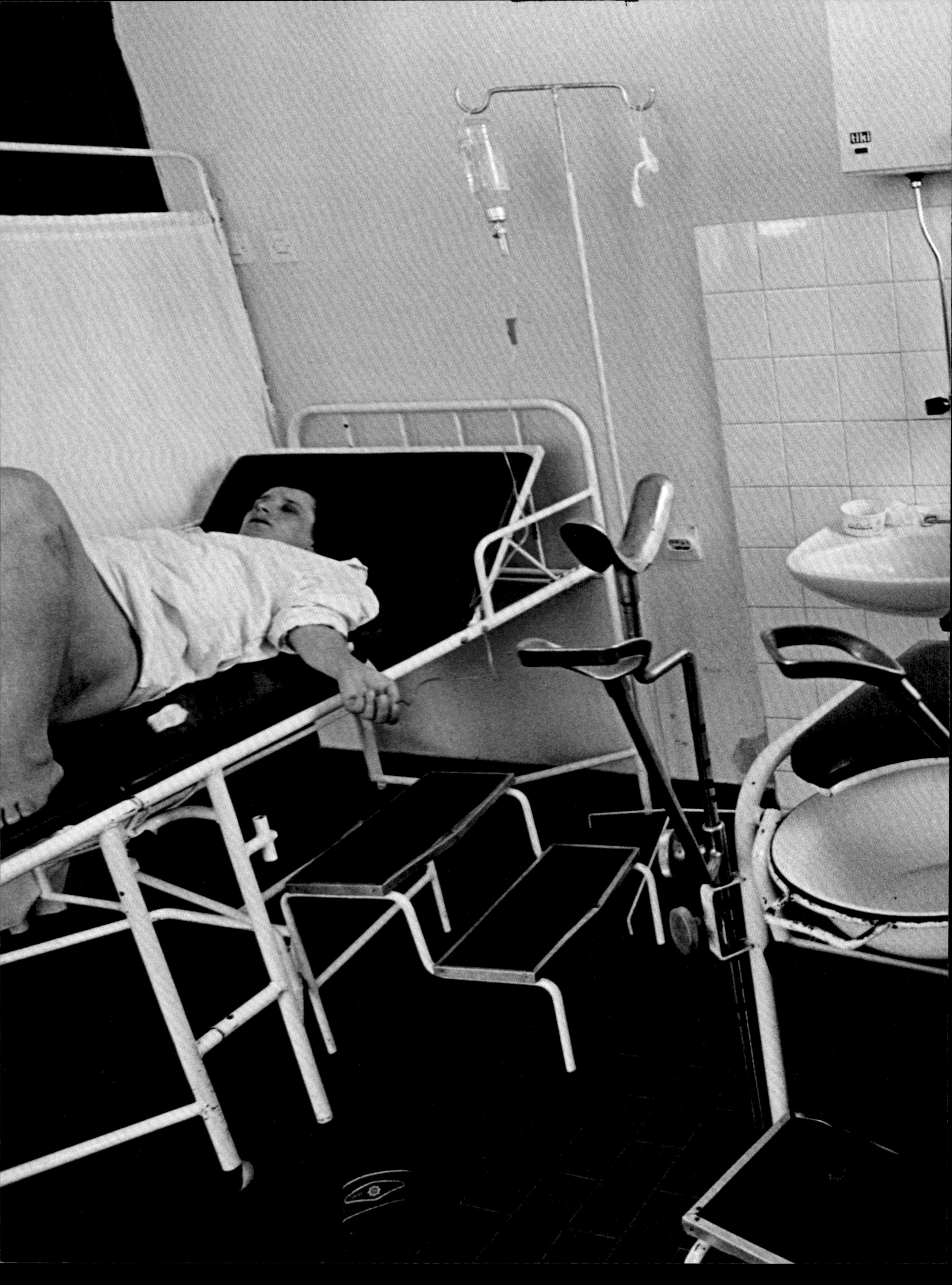

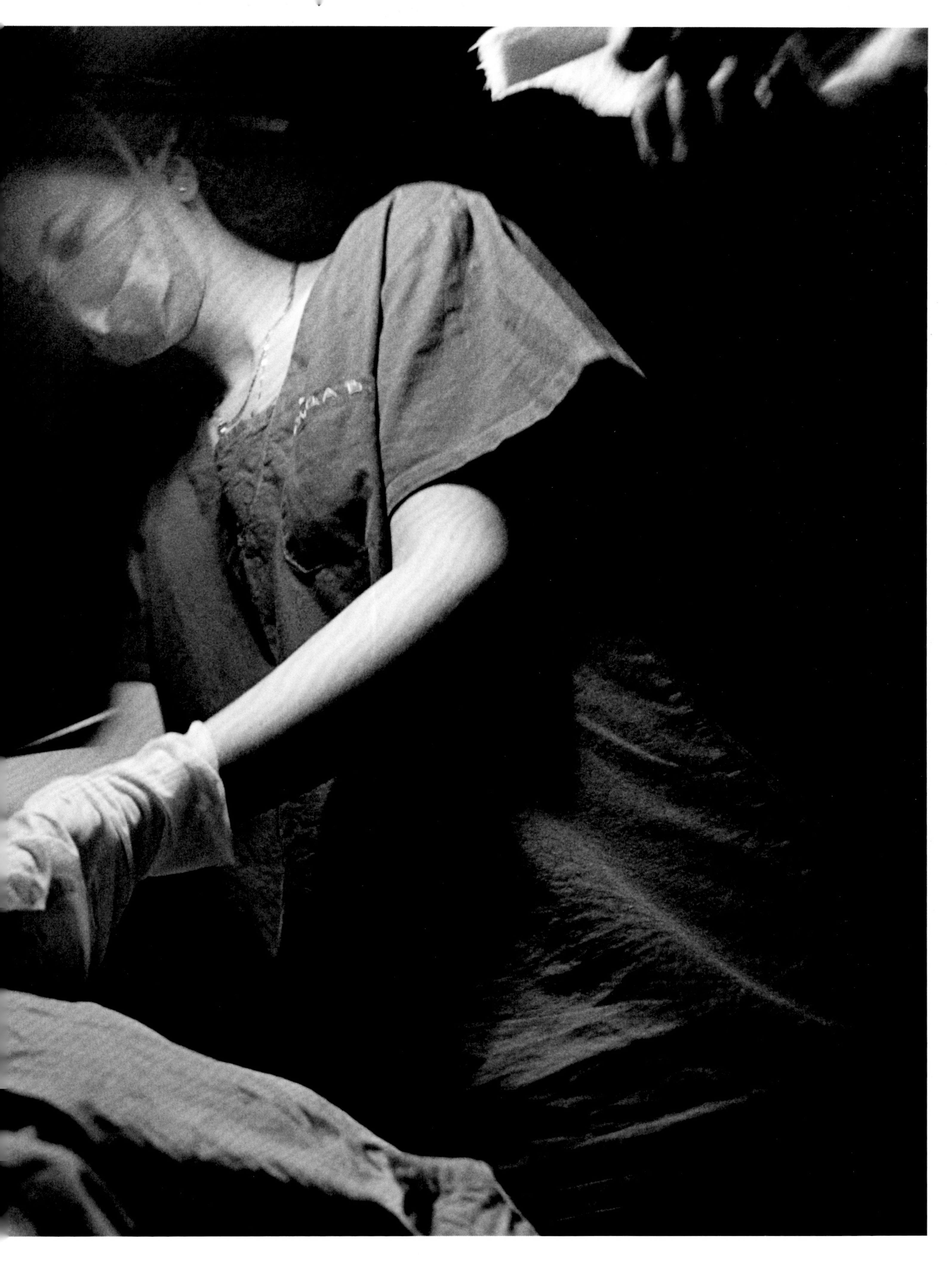

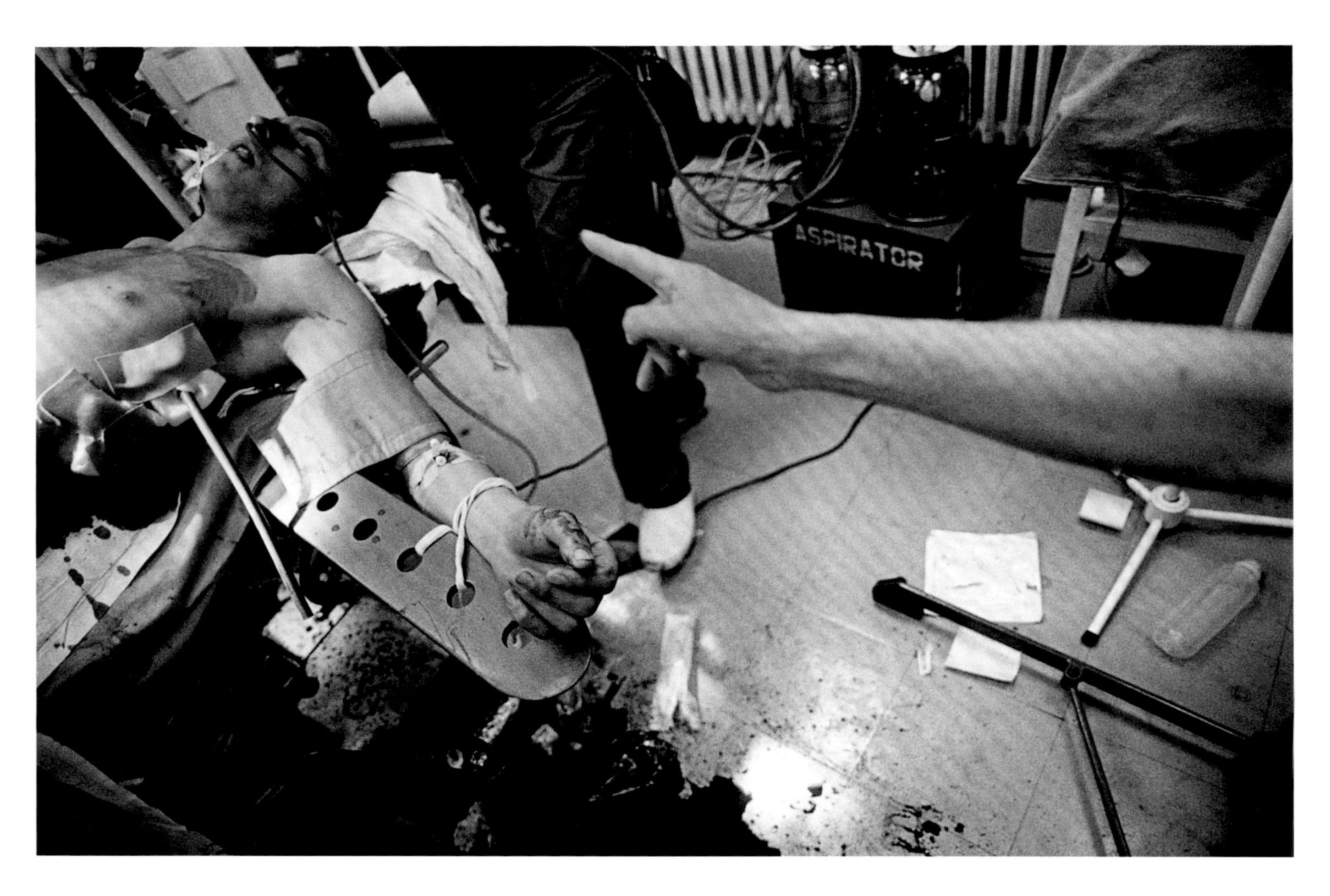
ASPIRATOR

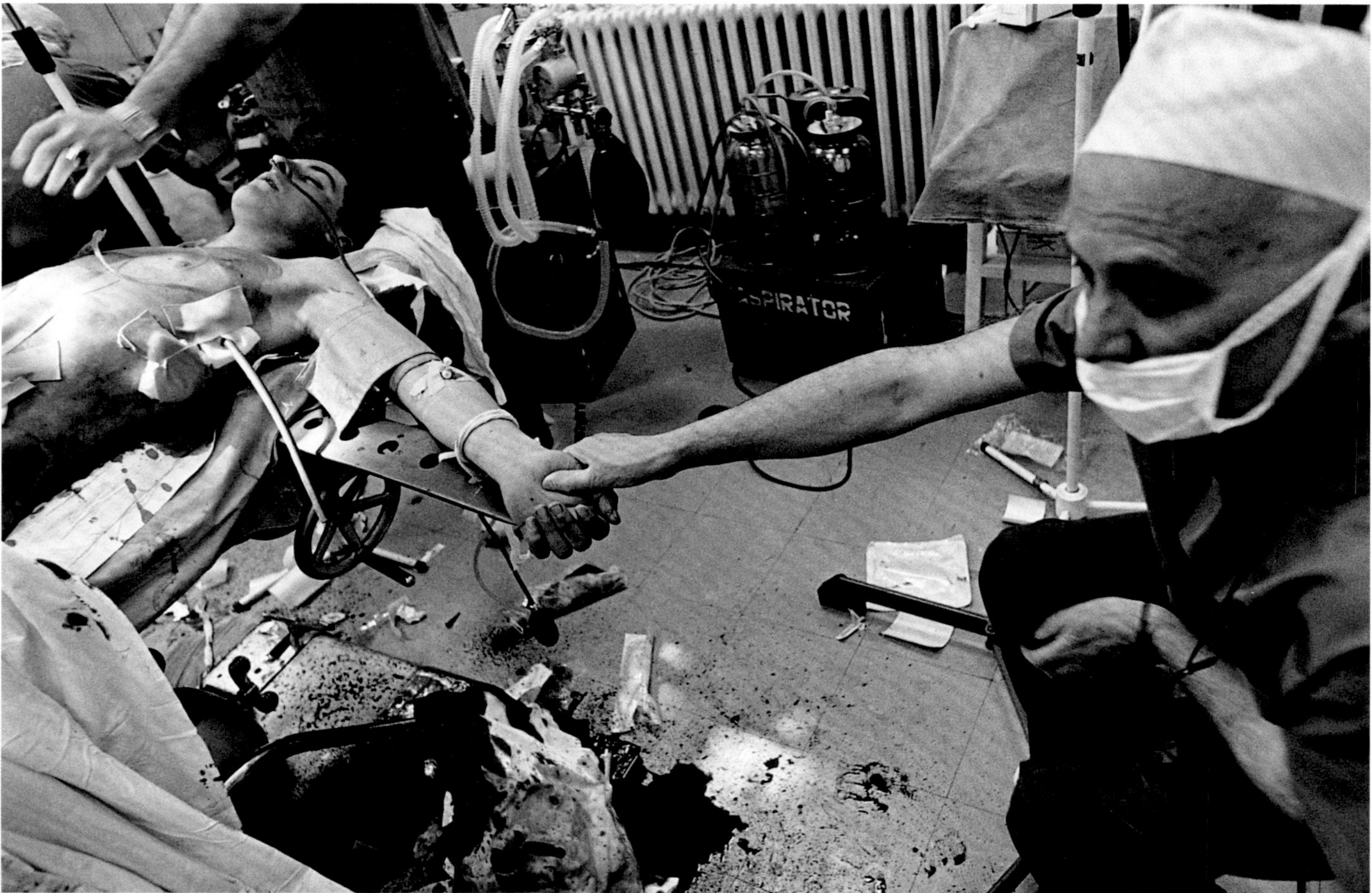
ASPIRATOR

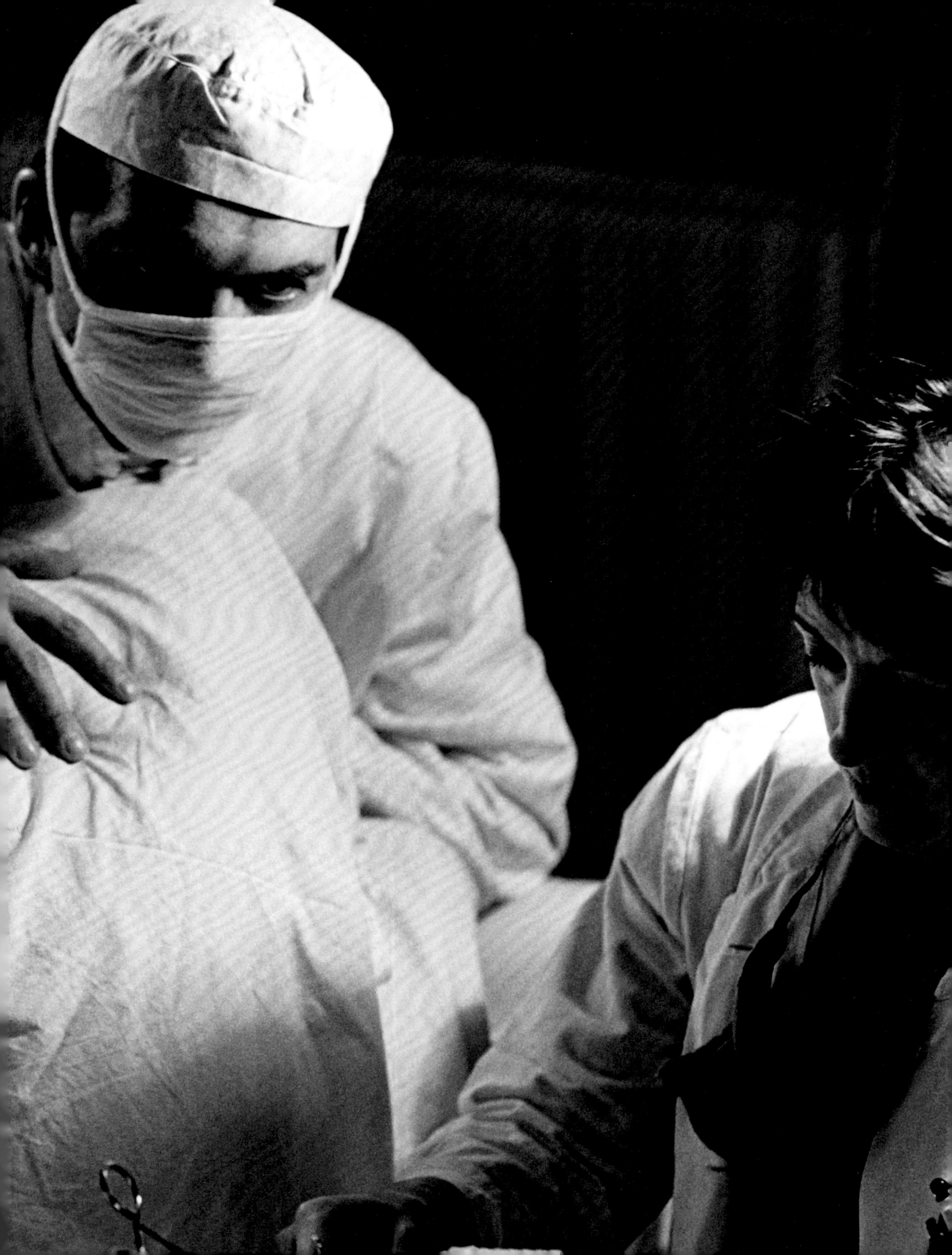

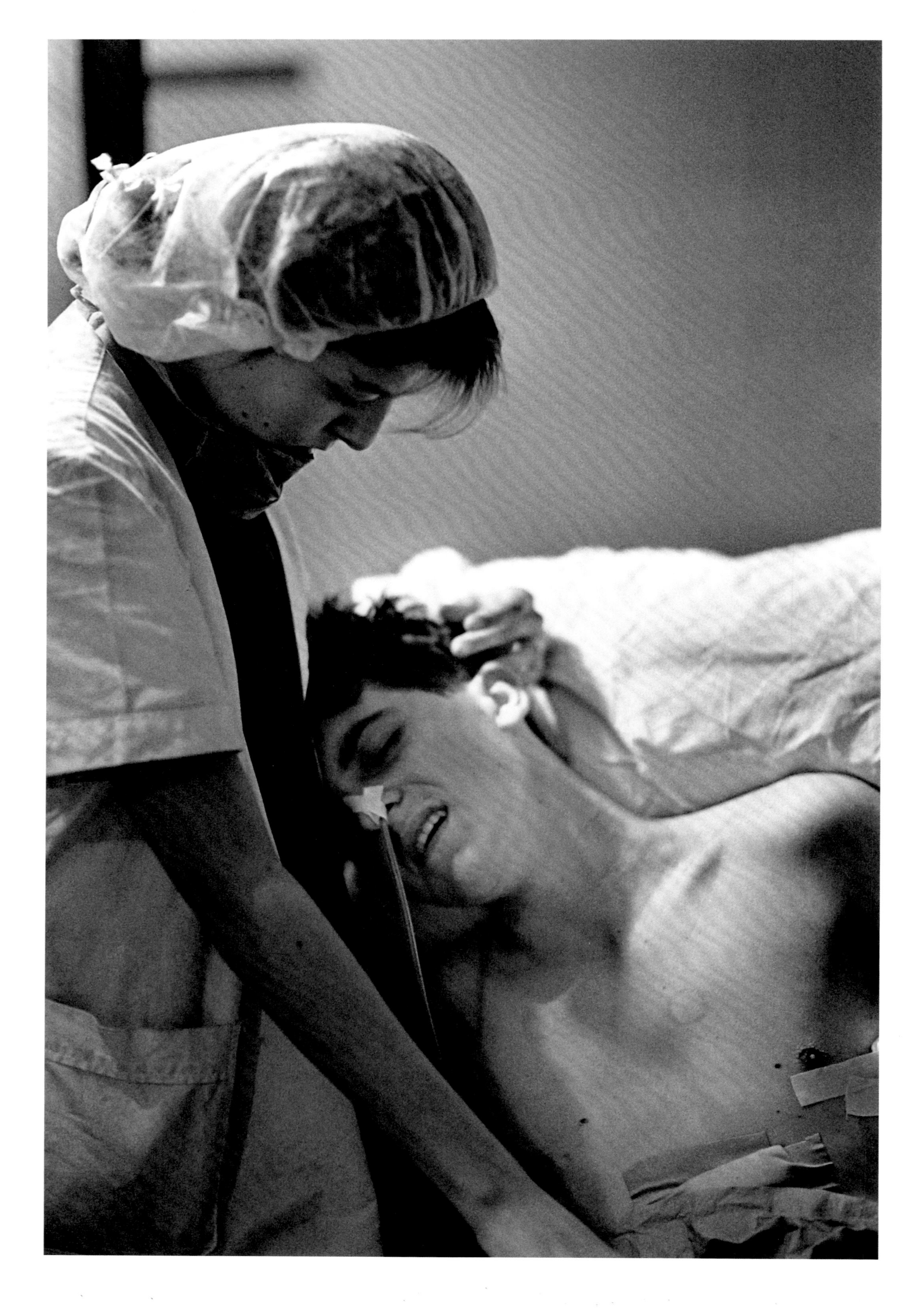

Grand rounds began at 8 a.m. All fifty beds were full. There'd been two more births while the morgue was overflowing down below. I was especially nervous returning to the operating room, though I knew that both Giuseppe and Dr. B. would be there. Dr. B. had always seemed out of place in this sullen, guarded institution. After a surgery, when the other doctors would break for a cup of sweet, thick, black coffee and a cigarette, the thirty-three-year-old internist would want to find a place where we could talk about the progress of the war, about his most grievously wounded patients, about our families. It was during one of those chats—after I'd shown him a picture of my wife and son—that he revealed, in strictest confidence, that he, a Serbian Christian, was married to a Muslim woman.

The emergencies had been streaming into the OR all morning; the place was noisy, slippery with water and blood. I photographed Giuseppe clutching the hand of a young soldier who'd been shot twice in the side (he'll be a cripple, a nurse whispered), then turned to take pictures of the care being given another wounded man. There were nurses and doctors surrounding the first soldier. Moaning "Jesus help me," his face flushed, his eyes rolling back in his head, he was being forced to sit up. The tube into his lung was repositioned to allow the fluids collecting there to drain.

Sunday morning I awoke just as it was becoming light and lay in bed staring out the window at the mountains. There was no fighting going on, none that I could see or hear anyway. I fell back to sleep. A little later a nurse knocked on my door to say that my car was waiting. Grabbing my camera bag and sack of clothing, I went looking for Giuseppe and found him in the OR. I barely had time to hug him good-bye or wave to the nurses before the so-called "official," who was to drive me to Belgrade, directed me out the door.

Unshaven, wearing a long, tattered leather coat a size too large for him, the driver wasn't, from the looks of him, a soldier or policeman, at least not the usual kind. But he had a gun, one that he meant to hide. I could see it, the black, ugly butt of it sticking out from under a blanket on the front seat of the car. Opponents of the war were disappearing, journalists had been murdered, people were being killed and maimed at that very moment all over the region. So if I was paranoid, there were reasons. I had my hand on the door latch and was ready to leap from the car when Dr. B. began banging on the windshield.

"Something terrible happened," he shouted. "My wife just telephoned. One of our children is missing.... You're going to Belgrade. I must get home to Belgrade," he shouted in a mix of English and Slavic dialect. Before the driver could respond, the doctor trotted around to the side of the car, yanked open the door and jumped in. The three of us then rode all the way to Belgrade in silence.

prospects

PMC
PMC
PMC

CAUTION
CAUTION

the run-on of time

Part 1
Going to Good Sam

The way I remember it, there was such heat and humidity rising off Auburn that first morning that the low jumble of a small eastern Nebraska town could have been a mirage. More tired than I ought to have been from the drive from Missouri, I stopped for breakfast at the Korner Kitchen and was halfway through a short stack of pancakes when some old men—I call them old men because they referred to themselves as old men—invited me over to their table. There were ten of them. And all of them had the sunburnt faces and the bulk around their shoulders that identified them as farmers, except for the retired mortician sitting next to me and Dr. Scott, who introduced himself, with just a hint of a smile, as "every undertaker's best friend."

In his early eighties, Paul Scott was bony, with silver hair, pale blue eyes, a veiny nose, and what one of his patients at the nursing home would teasingly describe as "a miserly mouth." He was tapping his long delicate surgeon's fingers on the table nonstop, which made me think he'd be rushing out at any minute. "What do you say, young fella?" he called from the head of the table when he caught me staring, "Tell us old guys what you know."

Feeling a bit nervous, I stood up and explained that I was a photographer from Brooklyn who'd been traveling around the country doing stories. I told the men about my wife, my son, my eighty-year-old mother, and my dad, who was eighty-six. But I couldn't tell them what I was thinking when I looked out at them. These were seventy- and eighty-year-old men; I had recently turned fifty-one, but not very gracefully. Meaning I was having kind of a bad time with the idea that I was now, somehow, closer to being their age than young.

ANTIQUES

Mustard

The next morning, awakening early, I wandered out into the country. What I recall of that drive is poking in and out of abandoned farmhouses along the dirt roads and hearing train whistles echoing in the distance. It had to have been around eight when I met up with Dr. Scott. A bit frazzled, he explained that he was due to work at the Good Samaritan Center, the local nursing home, but first he had a house call to make. I followed behind him along Central Avenue, up the hill past the high school to the assisted-living facility. Vera Young was expecting him. Having fallen several times, no longer able to see to do her paintings, the seventy-six-year-old woman had been feeling increasingly frightened living alone. The time had come. As she looked on, dabbing her eyes with a handkerchief, Doc Scott phoned the nursing home to confirm that a room would be available.

By the time we arrived at Good Samaritan, it was ten o'clock. When we stepped inside, a couple of the residents in wheelchairs waved hello. "What do you know?" Dr. Scott called out to them. From then on, "What do you know?" was pretty much the way he greeted every resident. "How are you feeling today? You hurting anywhere?" he'd ask, reaching for a hand to hold, a shoulder to grasp. A plump, large-boned woman was moving up the hall toward the chapel, powering her wheelchair with her sneakered feet rather than her hands. As she passed, she said hi to Doc Scott, who broke into a smile, then called hello to me. When I didn't immediately respond, she bellowed out, "Cat got your tongue?" I apologized, told her my name, asked hers. "Donna Goings," she replied. She raised her arms, fluttered her fingers so they looked like birds. "Goings." She was grinning now. "Like in goings, going, gone."

In the front parlor of Good Sam were maybe a dozen residents, groupings of them, staring at the glass cage full of songbirds, chatting, trying to be neighborly. Walking along, glancing into their rooms, you could see that each of them was only slightly different from the others. Satin pillows on one bed, crocheted afghans on another, family pictures all over the walls, a single framed picture by the bed. The rooms were meticulously clean, smelled fresh, had two beds, two bureaus, two windows, and were rectangular and hard-edged, fundamentally unchanging in their basic configuration regardless of who was living there.

Darlene Grotrian, sixty-six, had been stricken with Alzheimer's five years earlier. She'd been at the home twenty days, whereas her more elderly roommate Charlotte was brand-new to the facility. The eighty-three-year-old was watching a television show on house construction when we entered. "You're not really interested in rebuilding?" Dr. Scott asked her, attempting a joke. "Well, yes I am," Charlotte shot back, staring up at him. "Can't you see I don't have a home anymore?"

Kate Fike, in the room next door, made it immediately clear that she needed to tell someone, anyone who'd listen, her life story. She grabbed my hand. "I'm always trying to tell my story," she said, "but because of the headaches, it doesn't always come out. I was married in Alaska... well, then he died. Got remarried, *he* died. So I gave the marriage business up, didn't even think about it. My last husband, I can't tell you... forgot his name...."

Just before noon, rounds over, I trailed after Dr. Scott down to the end of the hallway into a room where the lights were turned down and the curtains were drawn. A man he'd known for forty-nine years was close to dying. After tucking in the edges of the blanket and readjusting the oxygen tube, Dr. Scott, in an instinctive, futile gesture, bent down to check his friend's pulse.

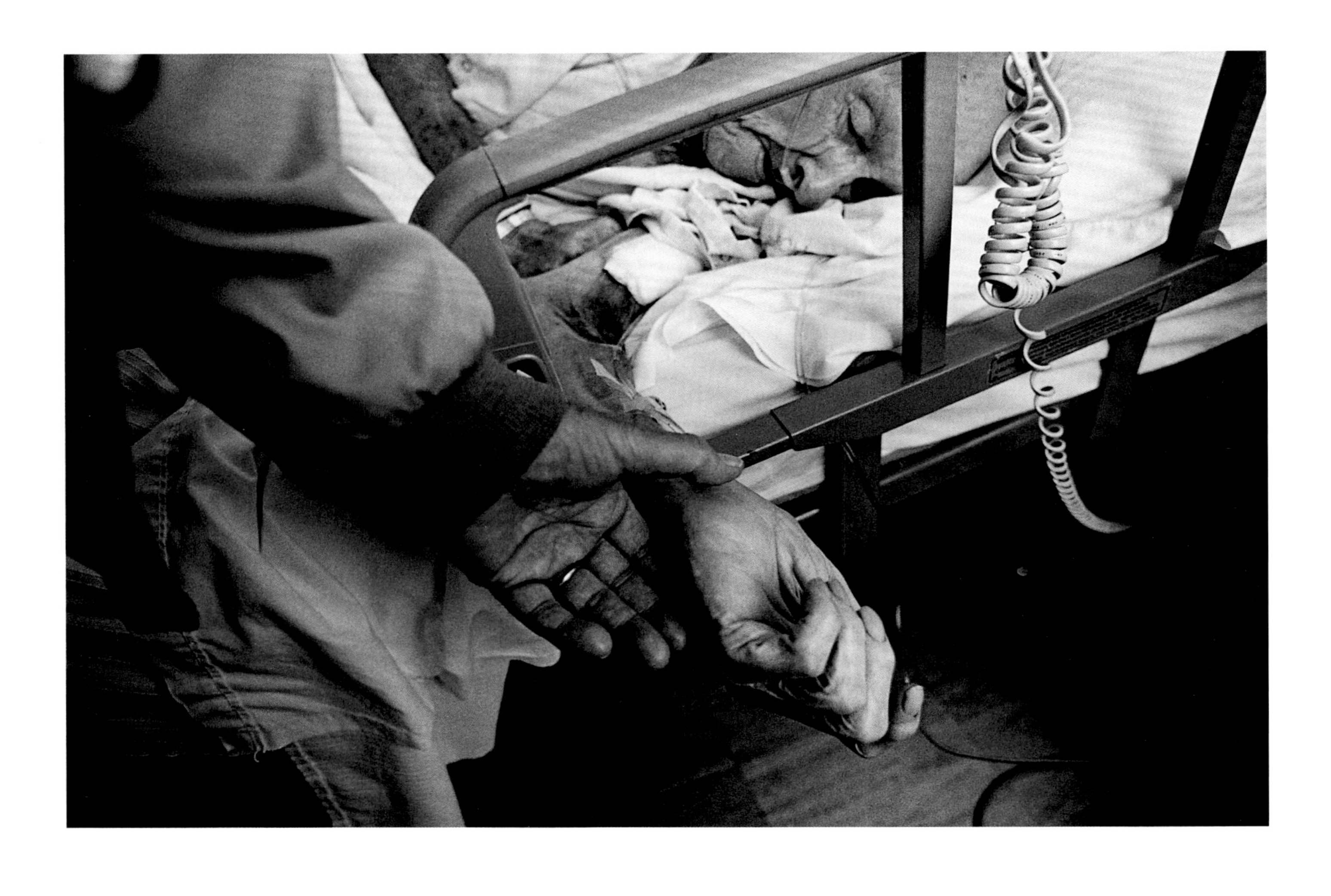

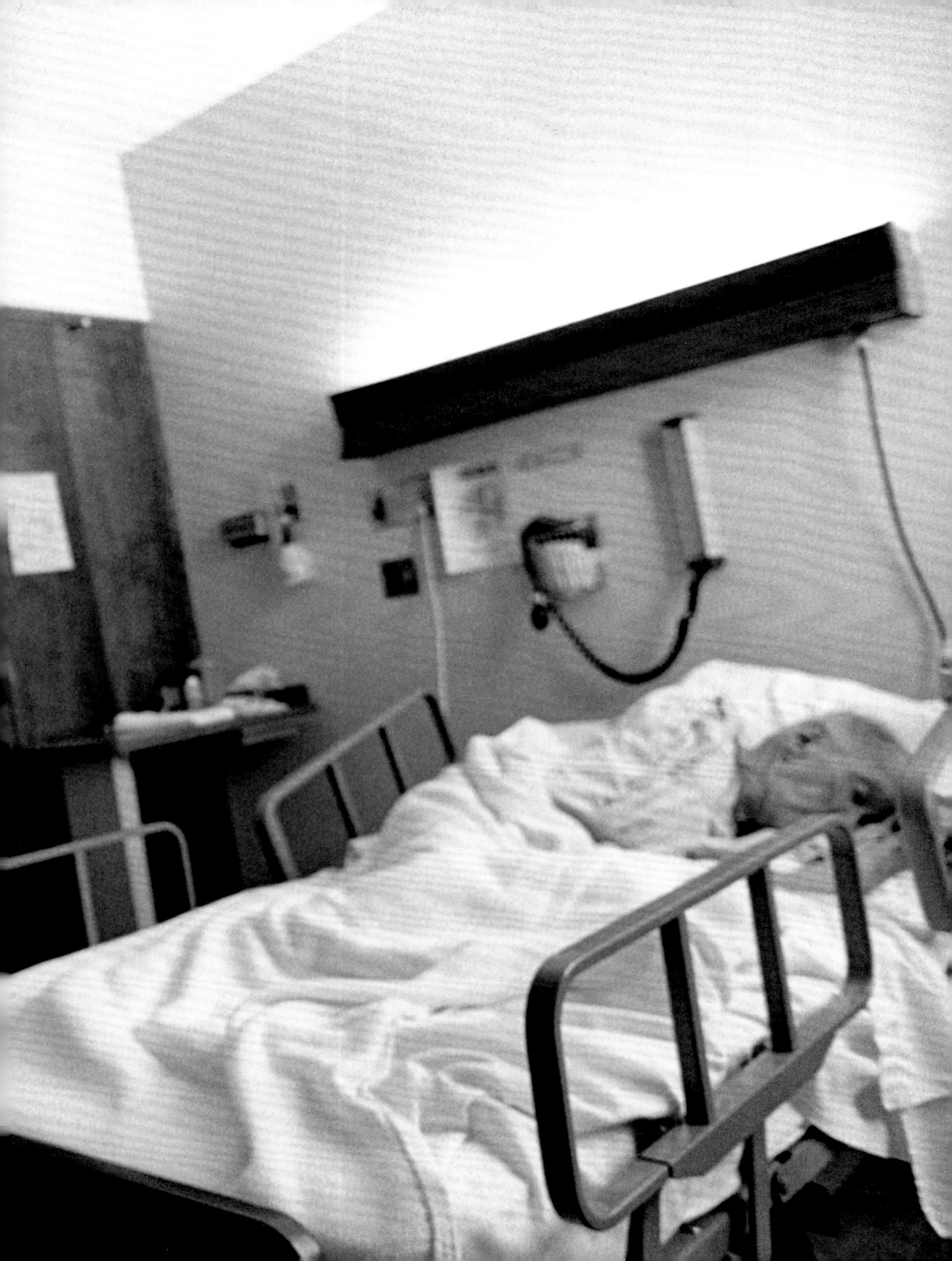

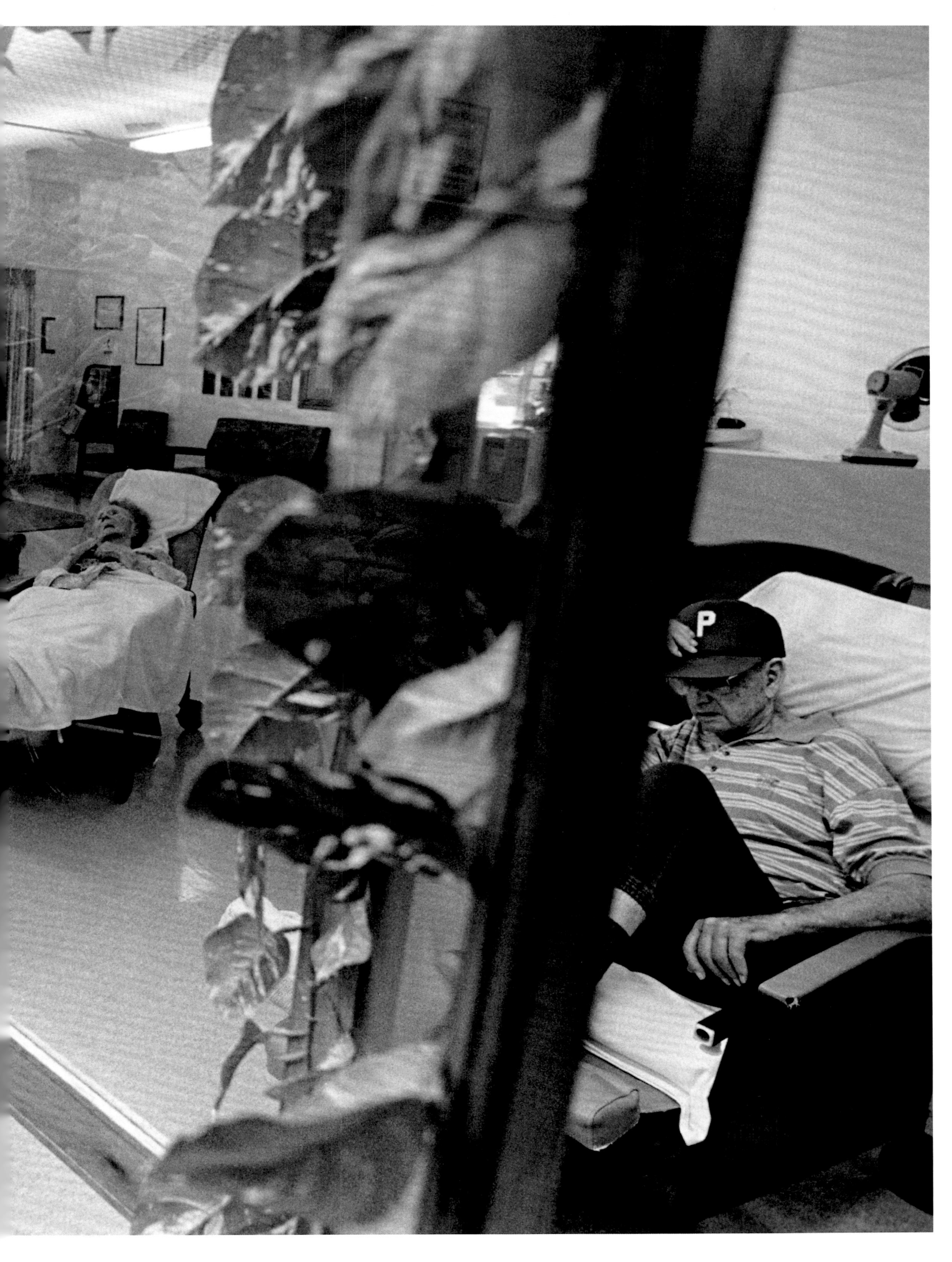

KOHLER

JOHN
60

The bedroom Arlene keeps clean and orderly for him is just a few feet off the parlor but, afraid he'll fall getting there, Clarence sleeps most nights slumped over in his old armchair. He dozes off at about 11:30 p.m., gets up two or three times during the night to use "the bucket" until he's "all pissed out," and is awake by 4 a.m., "the damnedest hour," he says.

The mornings he can get to his feet, Clarence drives five miles south of his farm to the grain elevator in Stella. If he starts out late for the farmer's get-together, anytime after 7:15 a.m., he drives a bit fast on the gravel roads for a ninety-one-year-old, and has been known to blow right past the bright red stop signs along the way. This morning, though Clarence did leave a bit late, he arrives earlier than he needs to. Slowing the pickup, he gazes around the tiny village, still crisscrossed with shadows, and upward through the cracked windshield at the grain elevator standing above the houses. One hundred and forty feet tall, perfectly cylindrical, painted bright white, it's beautiful and haunting. Overflowing with wheat or corn, the lofty, totemic structure speaks to the local farmers of "the good life"—empty of indebtedness, exhaustion, ice storms, grasshoppers, and drought.

Clarence pulls alongside a trailer-like office building a hundred yards from the elevator, stretches for the railing and hauls himself up the steep stairs with his left hand, his right hand grasping his cane. When he turns to tell me who we'll be visiting with—men he's known since they were infants—he stumbles. His crabbed, blocky body pitches dangerously forward and back, like a rowboat on a wave. "Can't walk too damn far," he mutters angrily. Since his second stroke, and with osteoarthritis crippling both shoulders, Clarence has been unable to do much more than oversee the 118 acres he inherited from his mother and father. He can't scramble over the plowed fields and sloping pastureland to check on the cows and crops the way he used to. He can only drive around the edges of the property.

"What good am I now?" Clarence asked me the first time I was alone with him. We were sitting in his living room, both gazing out the window; the trees were a shimmery green. "I wouldn't want to do it again the way I did it. Lost Ida, my first wife, to breast cancer. My second, Vern... she died of Alzheimer's four years ago." Clarence turned toward me when I touched his arm, "Truth is," he said, "I've got it made. Got to piss all the time, but I've still got my memory. I can think back. I'm not crazy, like so many old people."

There are a couple more steps up onto the landing. Clarence is wheezing, coughing. He bites his lip, attempts to straighten up. The farmers, who've come together to study market and weather reports, gab and sip coffee, turn to look at him when he shuffles in. For a moment or two they don't say anything, shaken, it seems, by the increasing frailty of the man they've known all their lives. When Clarence sees them, he grins, breathes out, "Mornin'."

WILL HAVE TO PICK
AFTER YOURSELF
Black Angus Bull
1780 lbs.
Interested?

Play it Safe

Part 4
Crossing Over, Letting Go

—*"Inez, you gotta know I can't cook your lunch this morning, 'cause I'm dead. That stupid woman, your cousin from way around the family tree, called to find out when it was that I passed."*
—*"It is upsetting to get a call like that early in the day.... How do you want your potatoes today, dear?"*
—*"Mashed, of course. Who's the boss here?"*
—*"You do plenty of bossing. Kleenex. I put 'em one place, you put 'em another. I like carrots just boiled."*
—*"I like them creamed."*
—*"Do you feel like fighting today?"*
—*"I always get the last word when we argue."*
—*"Yes, dear."*

When Rex Colerick died last summer as a consequence of his wife's dying, I grieved for him. My thoughts would wander and he'd be there—big and gruff-looking in farmer's overalls—a chewed toothpick hanging from his mouth, watching over tiny Inez. Or else he'd be leading her outdoors for a walk, urging her to take just one more step. As for Inez, she was what Rex was always bragging she was, "a tough little gulp of a woman." Though she'd been suffering from heart disease for fifty of her eighty years and was thin to the point of vanishing, she was almost always smiling.

Today, angry at myself for not having done so earlier, I'm returning to Auburn. On the flight from New York, I listen to a tape recording I made of them at home, not long after Dr. Scott had introduced us. Inez's voice is thin and screechy, as if she'd just inhaled helium; Rex's loud and twangy. They're having one of their mock arguments; she lets out chirps of laughter. They're speaking to each other, not as longtime marrieds, not as nurse and patient, but in the teasing and sweet-nothings way lovers do. I hold the recorder to my ear until the plane lands, then lay it beside me on the car seat, running the old tape over and over again on the drive into Nebraska.

"It's impossible," I brood, stepping out of the car. Everywhere I look, everything's the way it was before—scrubbed streets, trimmed shrubs, and lawns. Even the trees along 15th Street are the same powdery green color that I remember. Number 78 is a small white bungalow. All the window shades are pulled down. Inez had had her cataracts removed years before corneal transplants were possible. Her pale blue eyes, triple their size through her thick glasses, were extraordinarily sensitive to light. And right now, the glaring late-morning sun is beginning to chase the last of the shadows back under the house.

Crouching down, I search for cracks between the sills and shades through which to glimpse anything that was theirs: the armchair Rex sat in watching Inez watch television; the framed photo of Tony, Inez's son from her first marriage; *The Last Supper* on velvet; lamps, tables, medicine bottles, even an edge of the worn brown carpet. I try the door to the side porch, then walk down the grassy incline past the garden. Rex would grow his rosebushes as tall as possible so that Inez could smell the fragrant yellow blooms without having to bend down. There were always fresh flowers on top of her birthday cakes. Now the garden has been picked clean and the garage, which usually stood open, is padlocked shut.

906

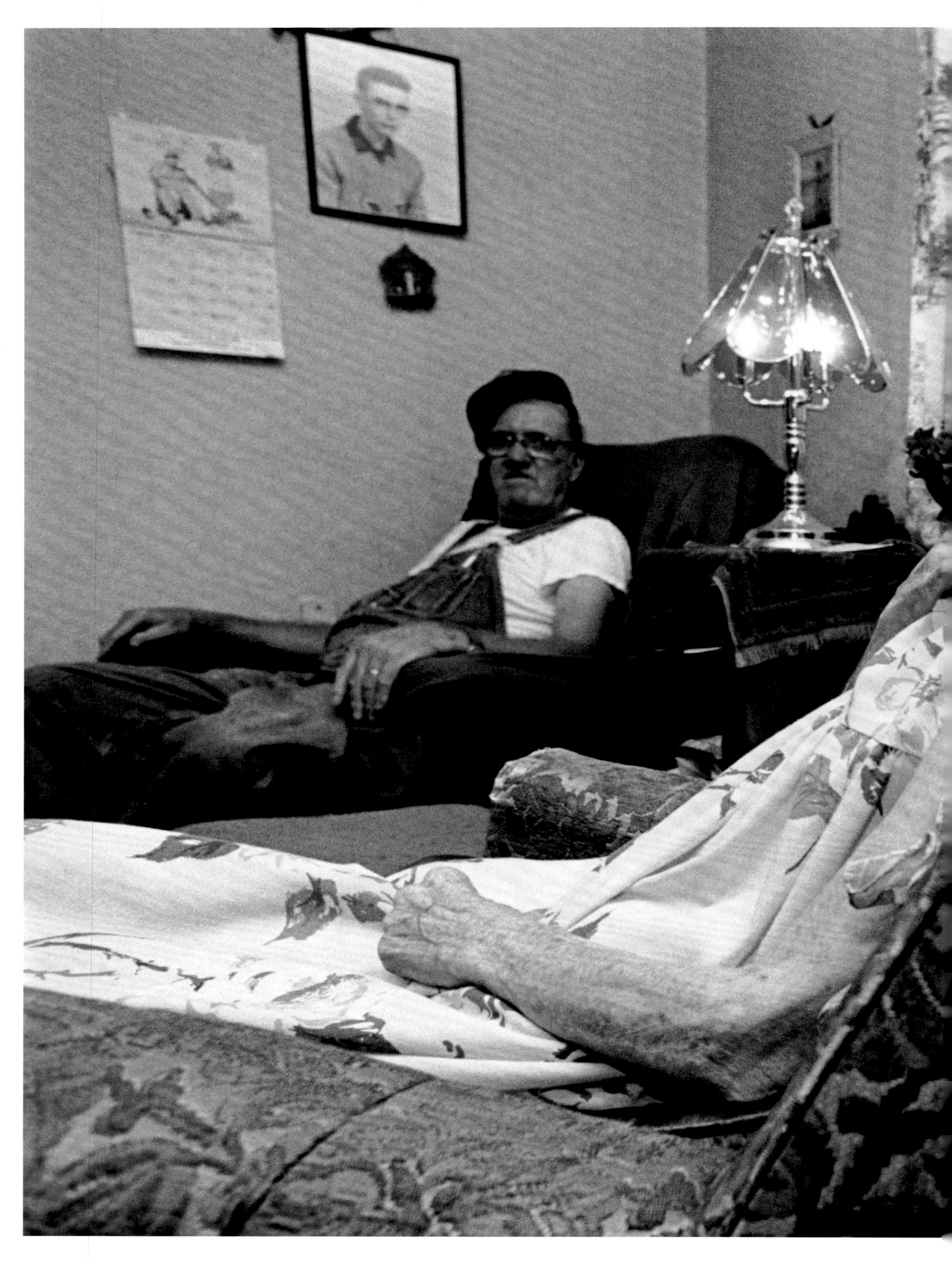

The next morning I stop by the house on 15th Street again, and, finding it as lonely as I left it, search for some of the people that Rex and Inez had been closest to. Dr. Scott is at Good Samaritan, sitting drooped and pensive, having just come off rounds. There are elderly residents hovering near him and pacing up and down the hallways; they remind me of the stunted songbirds in the cage against the wall. "Inez was bedfast at the end, tired of it all," he says, wanting to console me when I tell him where I've been. "She couldn't have gotten better. She had her burial dress all wrapped up in plastic at the back of the closet. She wanted to go. Except," he adds, "she knew Rex would be all alone. And he was, for one and a half years, when he used to be with her twenty-four hours a day. Got her baths, did laundry, made good noodles, baked pies. He was the best nurse, though I used to tell him he'd never look good in one of those little white uniforms."

Dr. Scott draws his chair closer. "A cancer specialist had been coming down from Omaha. Rex took the chemotherapy and it made him sick. It was in his bones, you know. He stopped working in the garden and gave away his vegetables to his neighbors. But he left no note. There was no cry for help, no great to-do, no great commotion."

"Rex's birthday was June 13, 1926," his sister Mable says. She looks up at the ceiling of her house, as if she sees her brother, then back at me. "On June 15, 1997, he killed himself. The funeral, Rex had it prepaid, including a spray of flowers. He had a suit all cleaned," she smiles faintly saying this, "though those who knew him felt he should have been in his overalls. This one lady at church, she did say it was his fault what he done. That it wasn't God's will. But that woman couldn't know about suffering the way he did. The other day, a minister told a friend of mine that Rex could get into heaven easy as anyone else."

Near dusk, Dr. Scott and I talk to Rex's neighbors, the retired dentist and his wife, who found Rex's body hanging in his garage. "He had used a nylon cord... threw it over a high beam," they tell me. Then trying to forget all that, I drive alone out to the cemetery. It's on the outskirts of Nemaha, the tiny town where Rex and Inez were married.

I've come out here, I suppose, to say my final good-bye. But I'm tired of remembering and questioning, and drop down beside the graves. The mound of earth holding Inez's body has become cracked and flattened by the rain, snow, and high winds that bedevil Nebraska. The mound right next to it that holds Rex's body is still some five inches high. It's graced by a plastic rose. I lie back. When I shut my eyes, I can hear Rex and Inez whispering to each other in the drowsy noises the insects make.

COLERICK
INEZ M.
1916 – 1996

REX R.
1926

here's to love

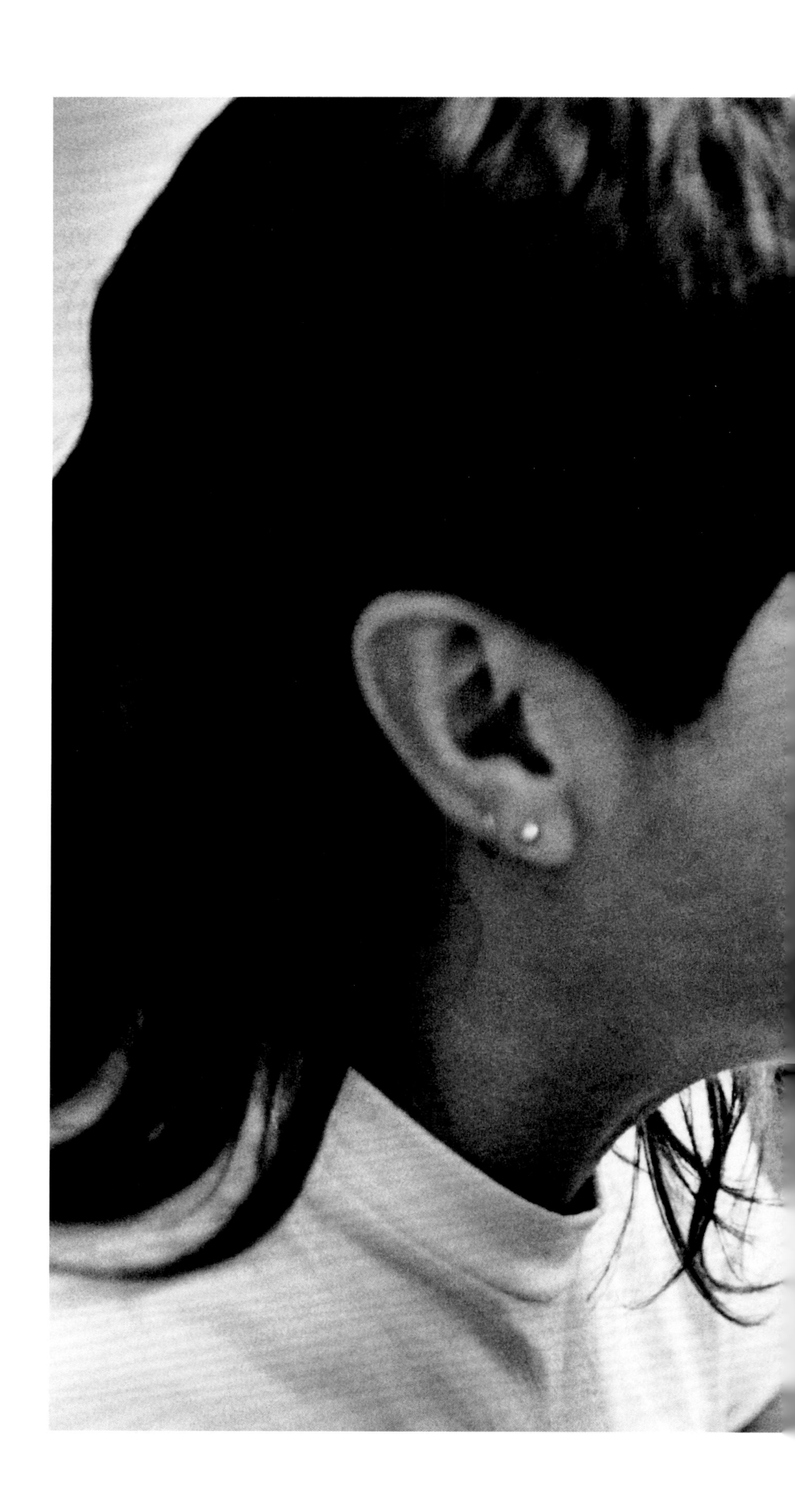

Renée I was very independent from a very early age. I tried to be separate from my family. My parents were drunk a lot, and there was a lot of arguing and fighting. When I was sixteen I ran away. I took two checks from my parents and forged them. One was for $50, the other was for $25. I bought a one-way ticket to Omaha, Nebraska, because I had an older sister and brother who lived there. The bus was $74.50, and it was a three-day trip. When I got to Salt Lake City, Utah, the police were waiting for me. But they let me go. My father, who they contacted by phone, said, "If that's really what you want, then leave." So I got back on the bus. When I got to Omaha, my uncle was waiting there for me. I lived with him and my cousins for three weeks, but I really missed my friends. So I called my dad, told him I wanted to come home, asked him to send me a plane ticket. I went home, stayed for four weeks, then ran away again.

I always knew I was gay, but I didn't know how to act upon it. I didn't know anybody who was gay. Turns out, I did. When I finished high school, I moved away, came back, and went to some gay bars in San Jose where I saw many of my high school buddies. I didn't date guys, but there were a few girls that I experimented with. Wendy, a high-school friend, was my first real sexual partner, although she had a boyfriend. She was not willing to say that we were a couple. That was very confusing to me, because she used to come on to me all the time. It was hurtful. She ended up getting married.

I didn't actually come out until I was twenty-two years old. I was twenty-five when I met Anne at a potluck for lesbian parents that summer evening. We were both cautious at first. A few times during our friendship Anne would call and say, "I need to talk to you." Then we'd get together and she'd say, "No, this isn't the time." It was never the right time. Finally, in December, I baby-sat for her daughter, Karen, so she could go out. It was about 2 a.m. and she'd been to a bar and I waited up. There was absolutely no way that she could tell me that this was not the right time. Then she told me that she had feelings for me and she was interested in pursuing them. At that point we became lovers. We had a ceremony a year ago last April, as a committed married couple. We are partners, we are spouses, all those things. For a long time, Anne would never use the word "marriage"; she called it the M-word. But when we had our commitment ceremony to each other, it was forever.

Scott I was born in Wichita, Kansas. We moved all around. My dad was in the air force. He went to Vietnam twice. He was a pilot and a project engineer working on electronic systems. He's very intelligent and really perceptive, but I think he had a pretty strict definition of what it meant to be a man. A cut-and-dried, all-American version of manhood. I'm the baby in my family, the fourth child, and my dad didn't want me. It took him probably about thirteen, fourteen years to resolve that. I didn't hear it all the time—he didn't talk to me about it—but he was angry with me all the time. So I sure got the message.

I felt I was probably gay as far back as when I was ten, but I didn't talk about it until years later. For one thing, talking about it to someone would have been admitting it to myself. And then I didn't have any friends that I developed enough trust in to do that with. I dated a little in high school, went to two proms. I had wanted to be an astronomer, so I went to college for two and a half years. Still, nothing was working in my life. I came to a crisis point. I had a relationship with a woman that was serious and lasted almost a year, but there was very poor communication between us. How can you have good communication when you're so much in denial? I remember taking a shower one morning and realizing that I couldn't go on this way. So I called a crisis line, asked for referral to a counselor who would deal with gay issues. There was a real mixture of issues in the group. Some people were dealing with divorce, others were dealing with different childhood abuse situations. I was the only gay.

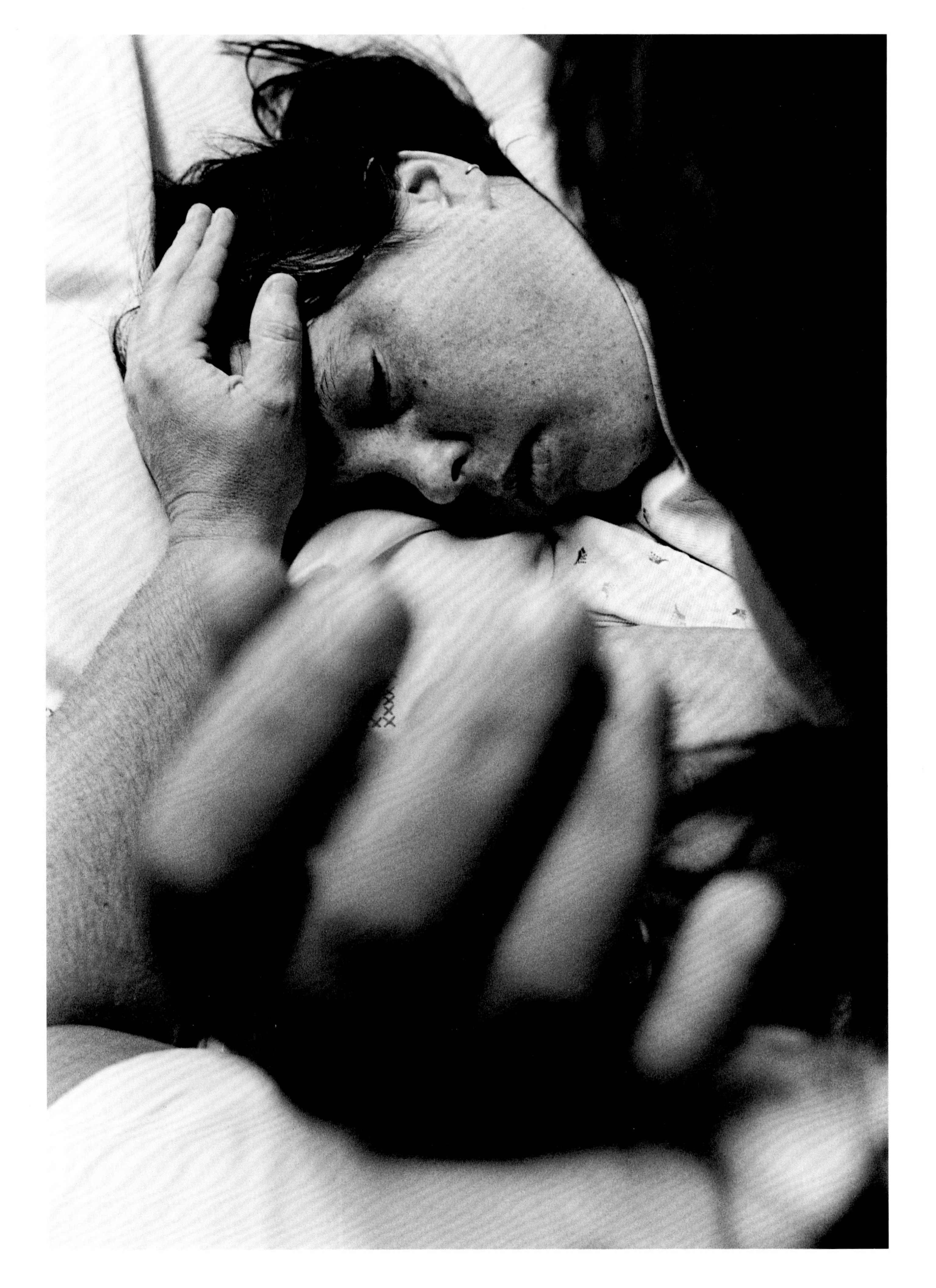

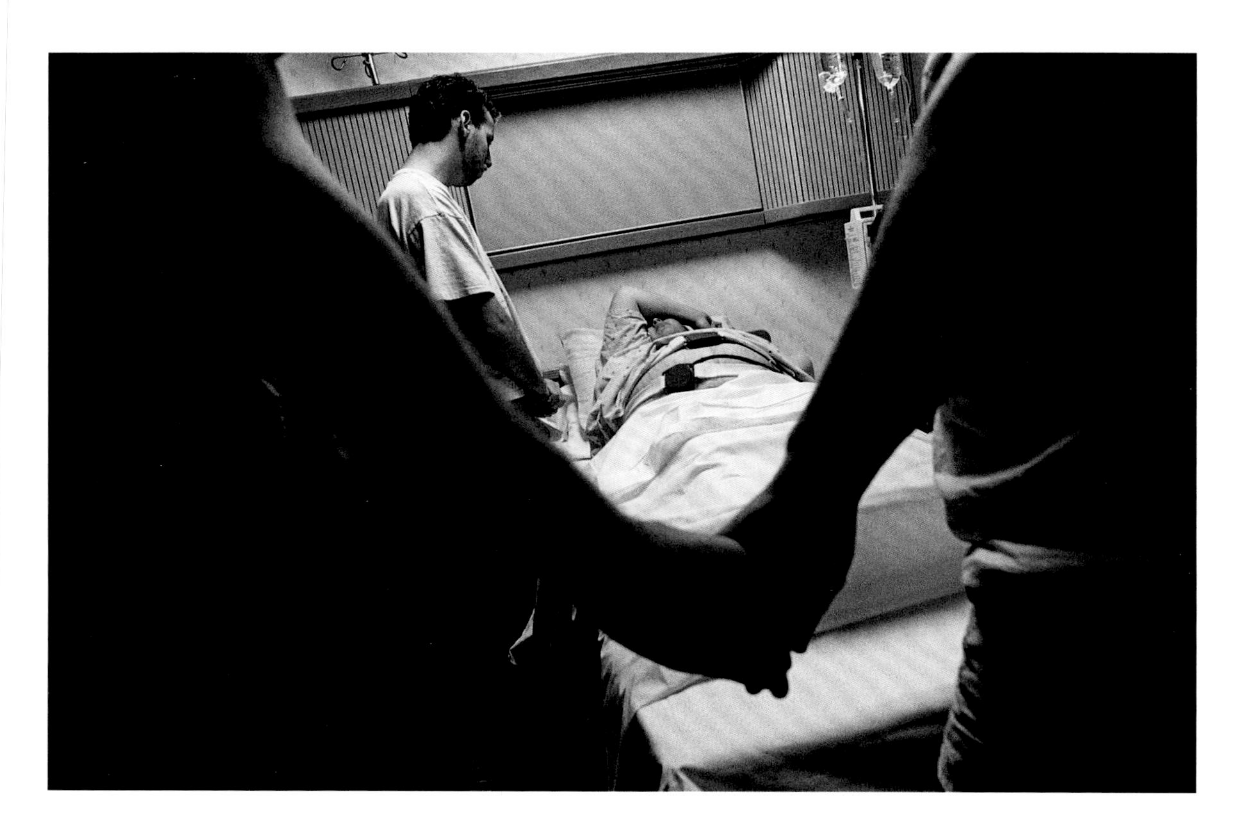

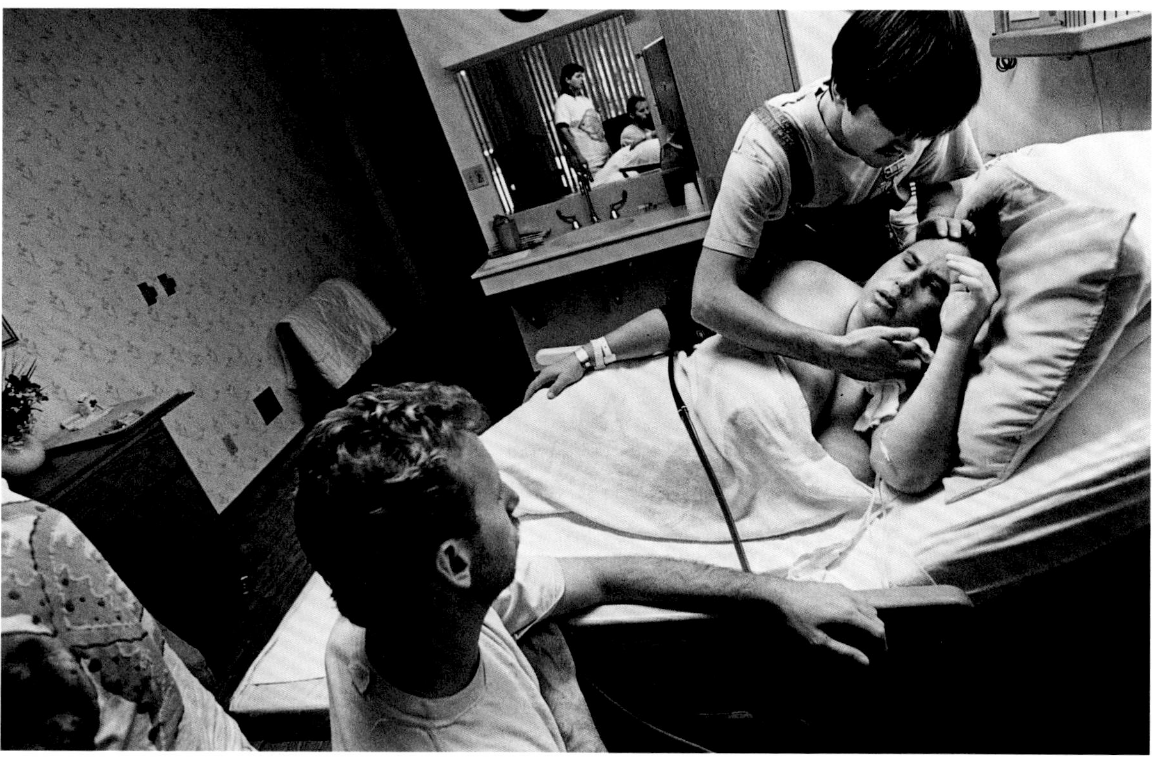

I went to my first gay bar on a Tuesday, had a drink, looked around. Nobody tried to pick me up, but going to that bar alone was really my first step into the gay world. Then I met a man who was a friend of my counselor. He was the first guy I had sex with. It was nice, not a lot of pressure. There wasn't love or romance there. It was more friendly, at least for me.

Friends played matchmaker and introduced me to Gregg. He asked me out on a date. I thought he was cute. We went to the Blue Willow to eat and saw a movie, then he took me home and, uh... we kissed goodnight, made another date. We had a quick and intense courtship. We were gonna go up to the mountains to make love for the first time... that was the plan. But I couldn't wait. I jumped in the night before we were supposed to go. We made love everywhere, lots of times. Not long after that Gregg wanted a commitment from me. He was pressing for it kind of quick. And I got freaked out by that. Gregg and I made an agreement not to see each other for a week or so, but I came back in three days. I wanted to be with him. We had a ceremony after we were together about a year. It was real simple. We played some music, read some poems, and exchanged rings. Gregg invited only his sister, but she was out of town. And I invited my parents and my youngest sister, but they didn't come. I don't know if they were ready to accept it emotionally. They sent some flowers and a telegram.

Gregg Anne, Renée, Scott, and I first met in our theater group. We became friends. So, at first, it was really easy. We talked about this whole concept of having a child together. Renée had noticed my interest in Asia, an infant girl that she and Anne were taking care of at the time, and said, "If you ever want to have one of your own, let me know." I had always wanted a child of my own. So a few days later we got together and talked about co-parenting, about our child spending time here, spending time there. And it seemed like we were all in agreement. We talked about discipline; we talked about medical backgrounds, emotional backgrounds. We'd all had AIDS tests. But the fact that we never discussed an initial period of time that the baby would stay with Anne and Renée is amazing to me. Then, after the pregnancy started, Renée's concept seemed to change. We were all sitting in a restaurant one night when Renée suggested that the baby should stay exclusively with them for the first two years. Anne, Scott, and I were floored. We asked her why, and she said that it wouldn't be feasible to have the baby going back and forth. We agreed that there was a certain period of time that it would be nice to breast-feed the baby, but perhaps he only needed to live exclusively with them for about two months.

After that night, Scott and I sat and talked and realized that we needed to write some kind of contract. So we wrote it as it is now and presented it to Renée two or three days later. After reading it, she said that she was pretty much in agreement with it, which was very strange. I told her I was shocked, surprised. She didn't understand why. So I reminded her about the request in the restaurant, and she blamed it on her hormones at the time. She asked to change the two months to three, but since I was so surprised that she had no problems with the rest of it, I said "Okay, three months." Renée has told me that if it weren't for me, she would probably have continued to go into bars and pick up men and try to get pregnant. In fact, when she first asked me if I'd be interested in fathering a child, she had already posted advertisements looking for a donor. I just don't know how much importance she really places on fathers.

Anne We started talking about it in October and started inseminating the following February. We actually know someone who used a turkey baster, but we ended up using a spinal tap syringe, a big one, without the needle, of course. Some friends of ours who already had a baby had given it to us as a joke. Initially Gregg was the donor. One month he had to go out of town on business. We were all sitting around talking about how unfortunate it was that we had to skip a month when Renée said, "What's Scott, chopped liver? Why can't we use him?" Gregg was initially threatened by that because he wanted real bad to be a dad. But I guess they talked it over and decided why not. So every month they would mix their sperm together and give it to us, and I would inseminate Renée with the spinal syringe. She would have to keep her hips up in the air for a half hour, which she hated doing. It was very uncomfortable, but she did it.

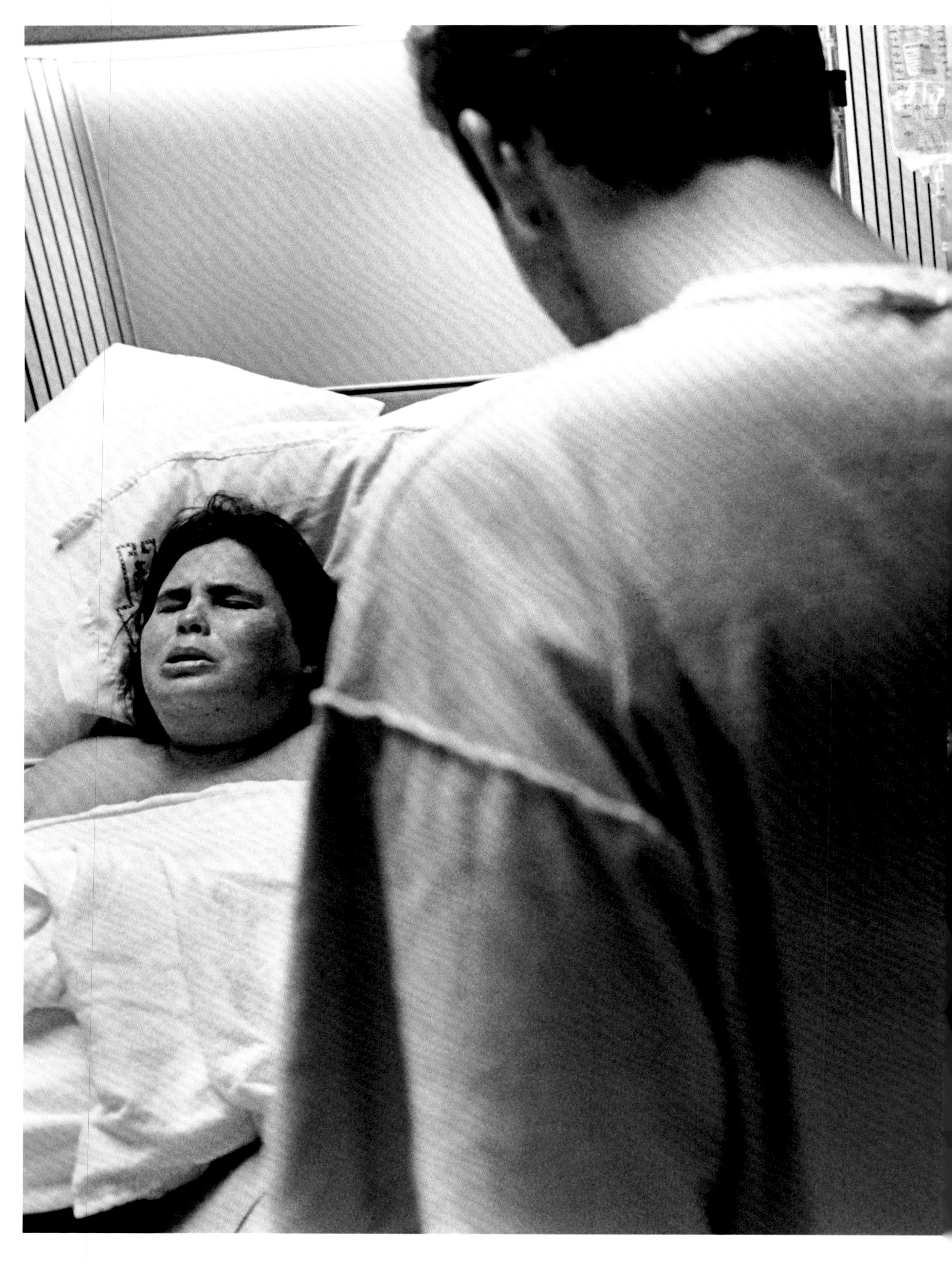

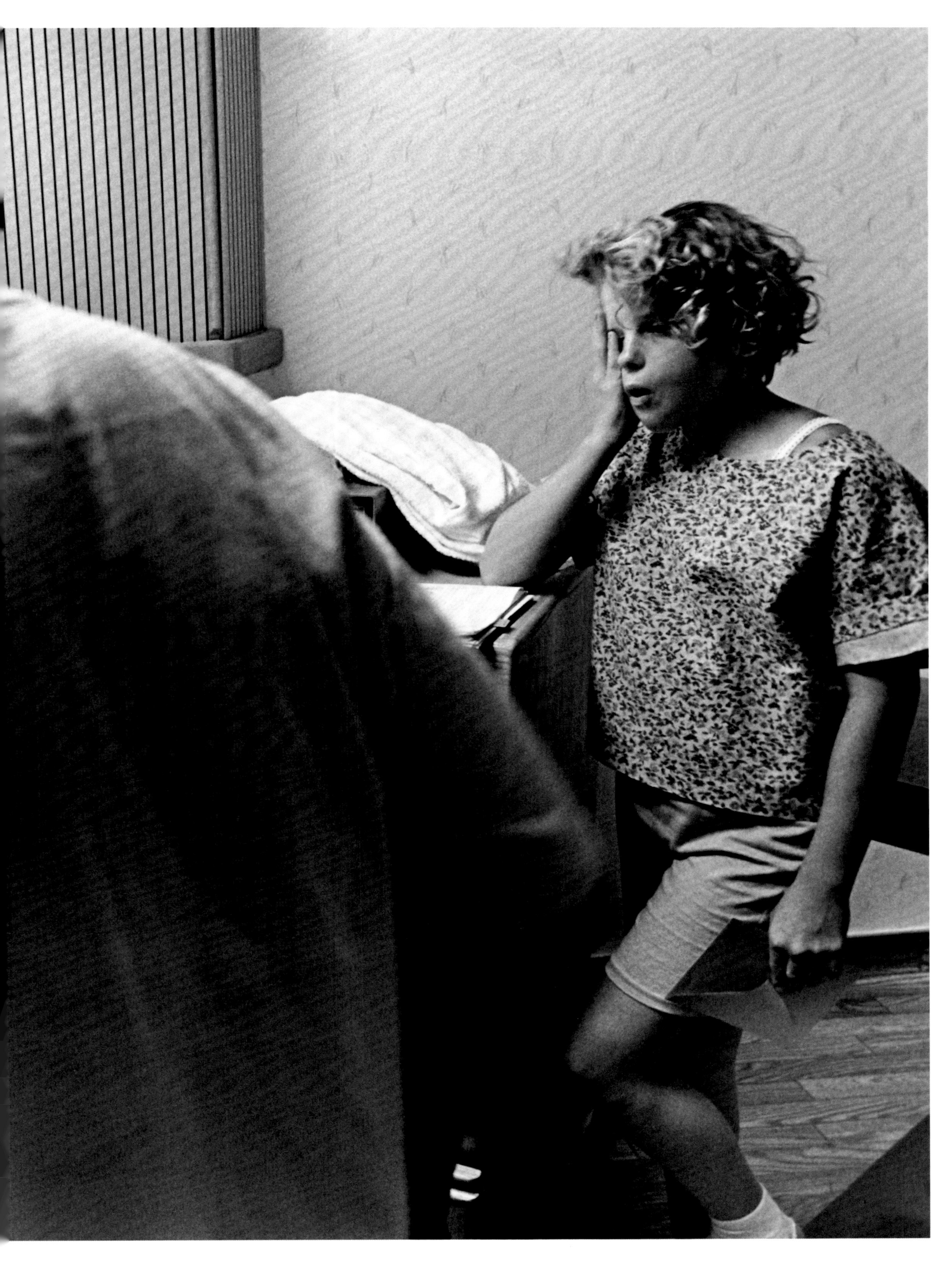

The very first time we did it, we had a little bottle of champagne and we all toasted. They said silly things like, "Here's to babies" and "Here's to little spermatozoids" and "Here's to love" and "Here's to new families." I don't know if we loved the guys then. I think we had developed enough of a relationship with them that we trusted them. But I love them now. The first few times they came over here, they would disappear in the spare bedroom and we'd go into our bedroom and wait for them. A majority of the time, we'd make love while they made love. They'd bring it out in a cup, and I'd put it in the syringe and plug away. Scott or Gregg would run out into the living room and grab our earth rattle and shake it over Renée's womb and shake it over their penises and shake it over my head. And they'd say, "Come on, baby, come on." It was a lot of fun. We'd just be so silly, and Gregg would be saying, "Shove that thing in there. Make sure that sperm doesn't come out." We'd make jokes all the time. As the months passed and it got to be more of a chore, we all agreed to make it more casual. They'd stay home and I'd go over and pick it up. Instead of calling the sperm "it," Karen suggested that we give it a name. Scott said, "How about Grover?" The night Renée got pregnant, we had to go out for a while, so we picked up little Grover. We talked to him as we drove along, saying, "Now we're going past the university." We thought he'd be okay in the car for a few minutes, so we found a little spot to put him on so he wouldn't spill.

Renée When I learned I was pregnant I didn't know what to do. I had a meeting scheduled with Gregg, but I knew it would be hard to keep it from him. I wanted to tell Anne first. I went home, and Karen was on the phone with Anne, who was on a break from school. Taking up the phone, I finally told her I was pregnant. She told me to come and we sat on the steps of the Desert Institute, where she was studying massage therapy, and cried. At this point we were having some problems in our relationship, so it was... I mean, I was very glad to be pregnant.

Anne I was on a break from class. I told Renée, "Well, come on over now. Come see me now." So she drove over real quick. We sat on the steps outside the school and hugged and kissed. She was all glowing, of course. I felt very misty-eyed, very sentimental, and excited. But part of me was numb. It was so hard to believe. We had been waiting so long for it to happen it felt unreal.

Renée stopped over at Gregg and Scott's house before I came home. She made sure they were both there. She went into the other room, put a pillow under her shirt, came out, and said, "Guess what?" They just looked at her. Gregg said, "What are you doing?" All of a sudden, he realized the symbolism of it all.

Scott When Renée became pregnant, we had mixed feelings. There was joy, certainly, but then reality set in, and there was fear. Like, "Oh shit, this is real." There were fears of being responsible for another life and fears of tying our lives with Anne and Renée. Renée was very moody and emotional. I think lots of it was hormone changes from her pregnancy, but some of it was all the emotions coming up from doing this.

Renée I was a bitch on wheels during the first three months. The second trimester was much easier, much better. By the third trimester, I just felt uncomfortable, but our sexual life disintegrated to nothing. Anne knows intellectually it's not uncommon; still, she had a hard time with it emotionally.

The morning of the birth, while I was in the shower, I felt real nervous, full of anxiety. I knew I would experience the most excruciating pain I'd ever felt in my life. But I also felt real sad. I thought that if I could do it all over again, I wouldn't have had the guys involved. It had nothing to do with it being Gregg and Scott. I didn't want the baby to come out because I would have to share him. And I didn't want to share him; I wanted to keep him to myself. Once he came out, he'd be detached from me and my whole life would be spent slowly letting go. When it happened, I had only about four hours of labor. They induced at 7:30 a.m., I didn't go into labor until about 11 a.m., and Connor was born at 3:02 p.m.

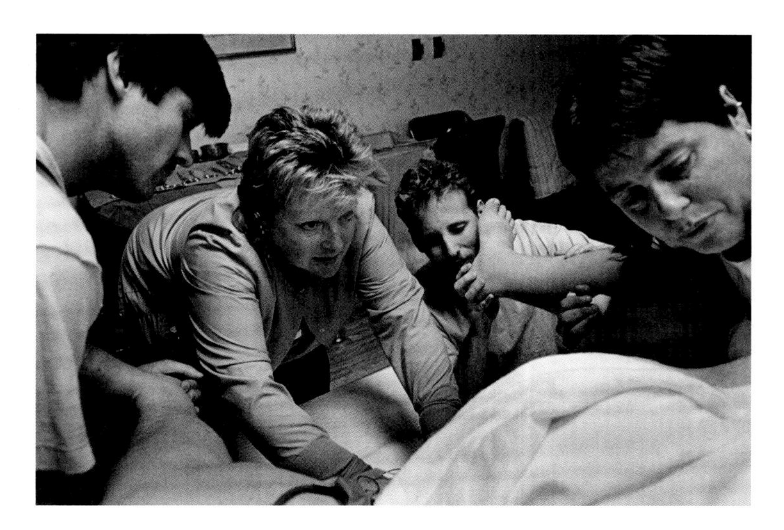

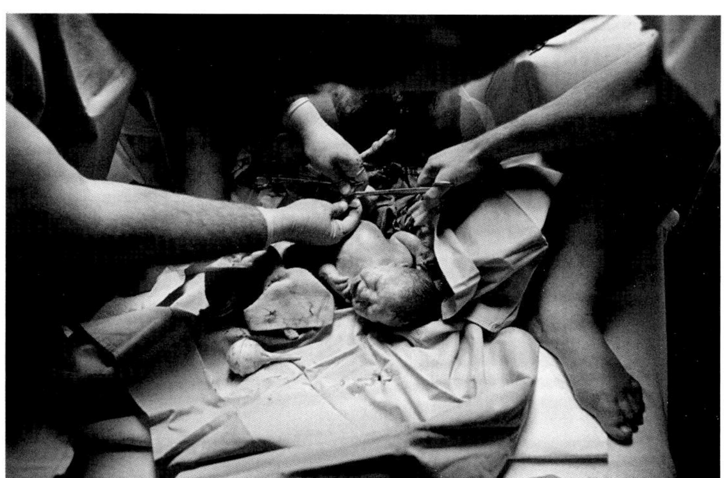

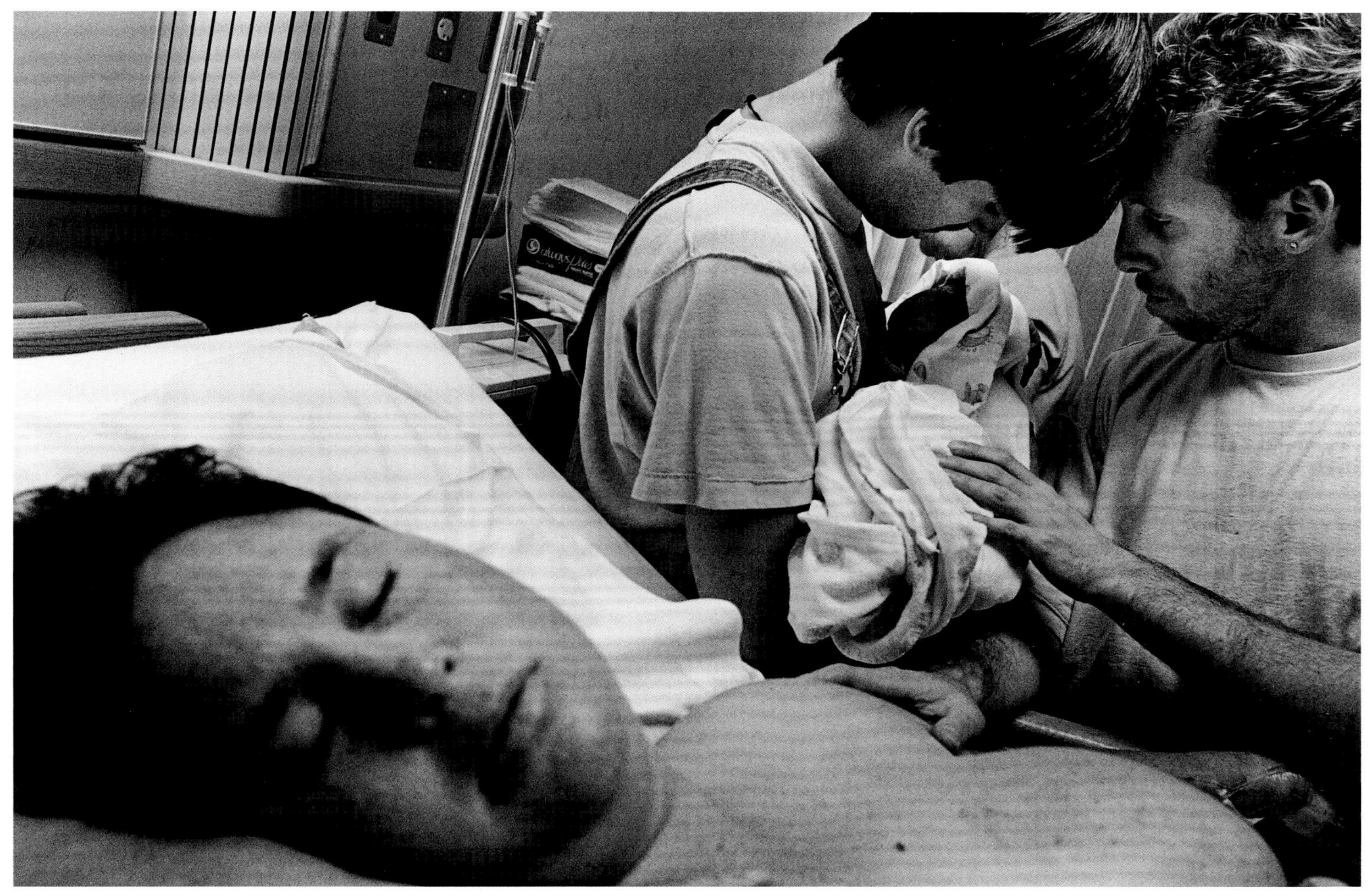

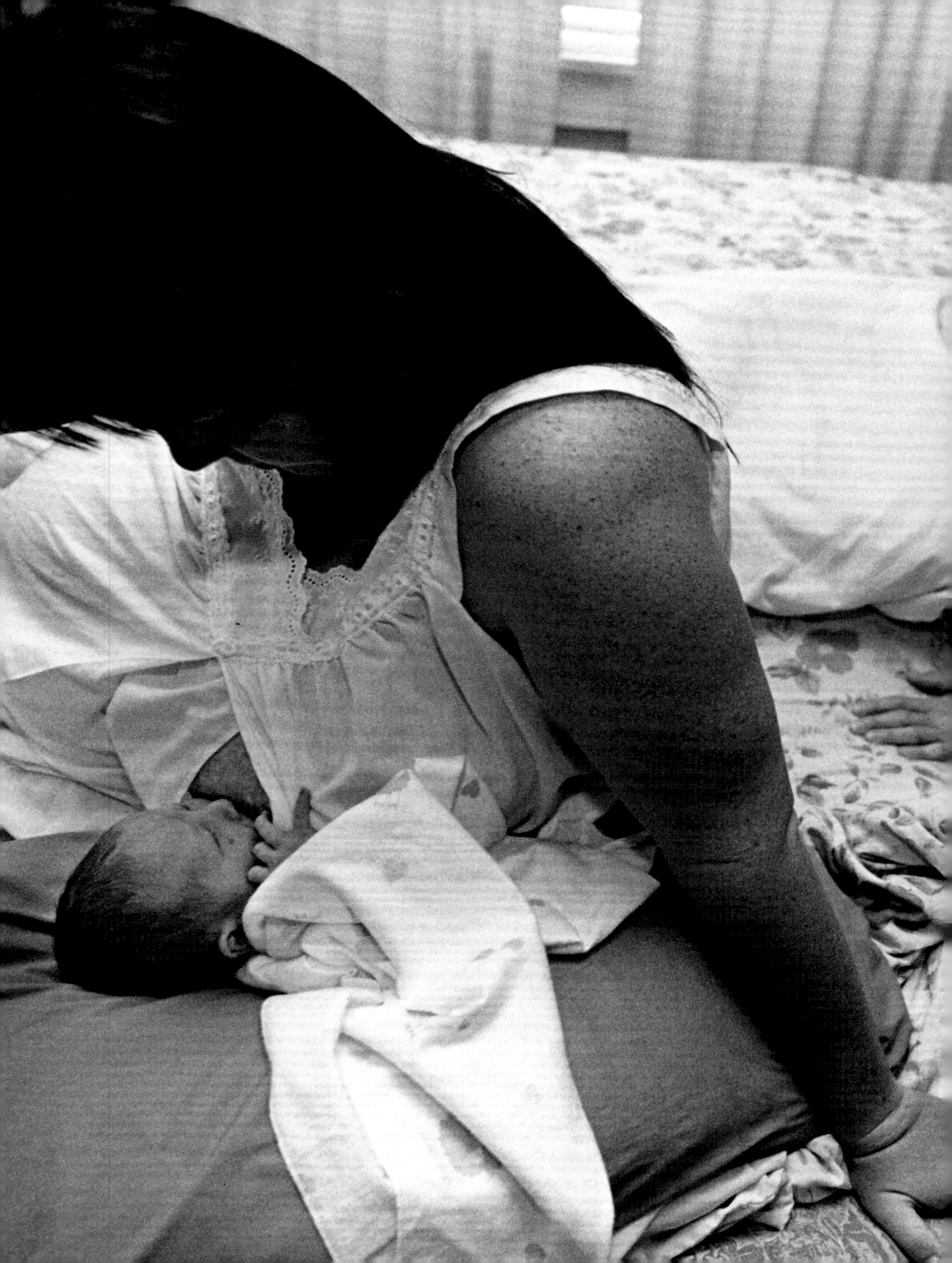

Anne I was the seventh of thirteen children and was very close to my mom. Very. She used to sing lullabies to us when we were tiny. We would all line up at night. We each had a turn to get up on her lap, and she'd hold us and sing us each a different lullaby. Mine was "I See the Moon." It goes: "I see the moon / The moon sees me / That's where my heart is longing to be...." My mom committed suicide when I was twenty-one. We had this grotto that my dad built. It had a statue of the Virgin Mary in it. My mother's name was Mary. Ironically, that's what she hit when she jumped out the window.

I had one semi-serious dating relationship in high school. After that I met the man who would be Karen's father. We dated for a year and got married. When I was married, I was not a happy person because I knew that there was that part of me that didn't feel like it could come out. I was almost twenty-six. Karen was already a year and a half old. It was scary. I had a child, I was married, I had this Catholic upbringing. Karen's father and I had a discussion because he found some notes from a woman friend of mine, whom I had started getting involved with. He had no business getting a hold of them, but he did somehow. So he questioned me, and I was willing to admit that there was a possibility I was gay or bisexual, but I wasn't sure. When I finally went through with the separation and started filing for the divorce, he was so bitter. He told lots of people, including my father.

So it didn't give me the opportunity to make the choice as to who I wanted to have know and who I didn't. But he was also emotionally and physically abusive. He threw me up against a wall a few times and he choked me one time to the point where I thought I was going to die. Of course, he didn't stop there. But I got smart: I got help, I got support, I got out. I did all those things I needed to do.

My daughter and I never really talk about my sexuality. Karen never really asks a lot of questions. I mean, she kind of has the gist about how it's different from having sex with a man. And she has druthers about whether or not she might want to be with women herself. She's thought about it, and that's not through any prompting on my part. I think ultimately she is going to be very straight. I just have a feeling.

Gregg Up until a few years ago, I would see my parents on the side. I'd have dinner with them, or have lunch, but I would see them alone; I wouldn't bring Scott. Sometimes we would do a lot together. We were a family. But once, before we moved back here, Scott and I called my parents and asked them if we could come by. And they said, "We're sorry, but we just don't want that in our house." I guess they were afraid that the two of us were going to have sex in the living room or that we might touch each other, or maybe it was just knowing that the two of us were in a relationship.

So I said, "Well, if you don't want the two of us in the house, why don't we just meet somewhere for dinner?" My mom said, "I don't think so." I answered back, "You always have to have it your way. Let's compromise. You never want to compromise." She said, "That's not true at all. I compromise. I love you even though you're gay." The last thing I said was, "Don't bother."

When Connor was born, I thought about my parents and our relationship and felt that they should be there for his birth. They know about it. I sent them an announcement and some pictures, and now I write them about what Scott and I have been doing over the past few years. I just send these things to them. There's a part of me that thinks that if they see these things, they'll realize what they're missing.

Scott We have to determine who the biological father is. Gregg and I need to do that to get one of us on the birth certificate. In this state, when a woman who is unmarried gives birth, the father's name is not placed on the birth certificate. The mother has complete custody of the child. So in order to have joint custody, we have to prove paternity. One of us is going to be the biological father. I guess I'm being naive, but I really won't know how to feel if I'm the biological father until I experience it. Something will change probably. I don't particularly want to know right now, so maybe I'm afraid of the change. But it's not like I have this gut-wrenching fear.

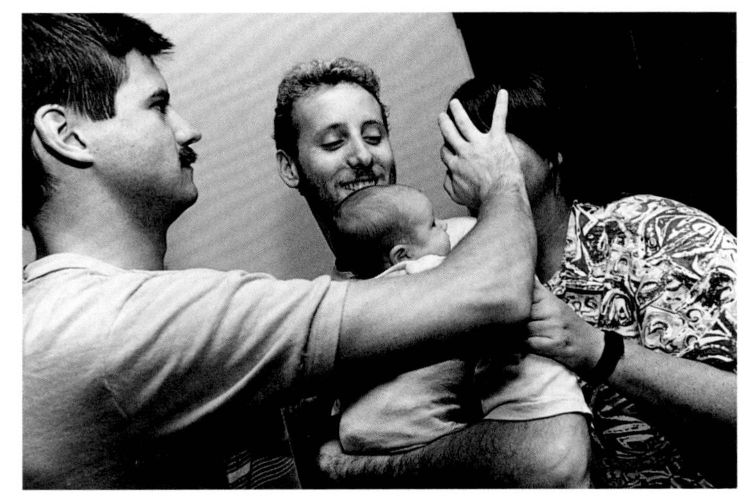

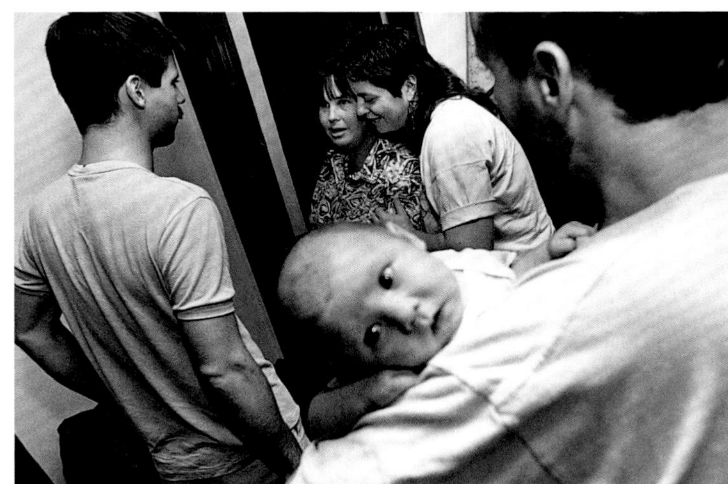

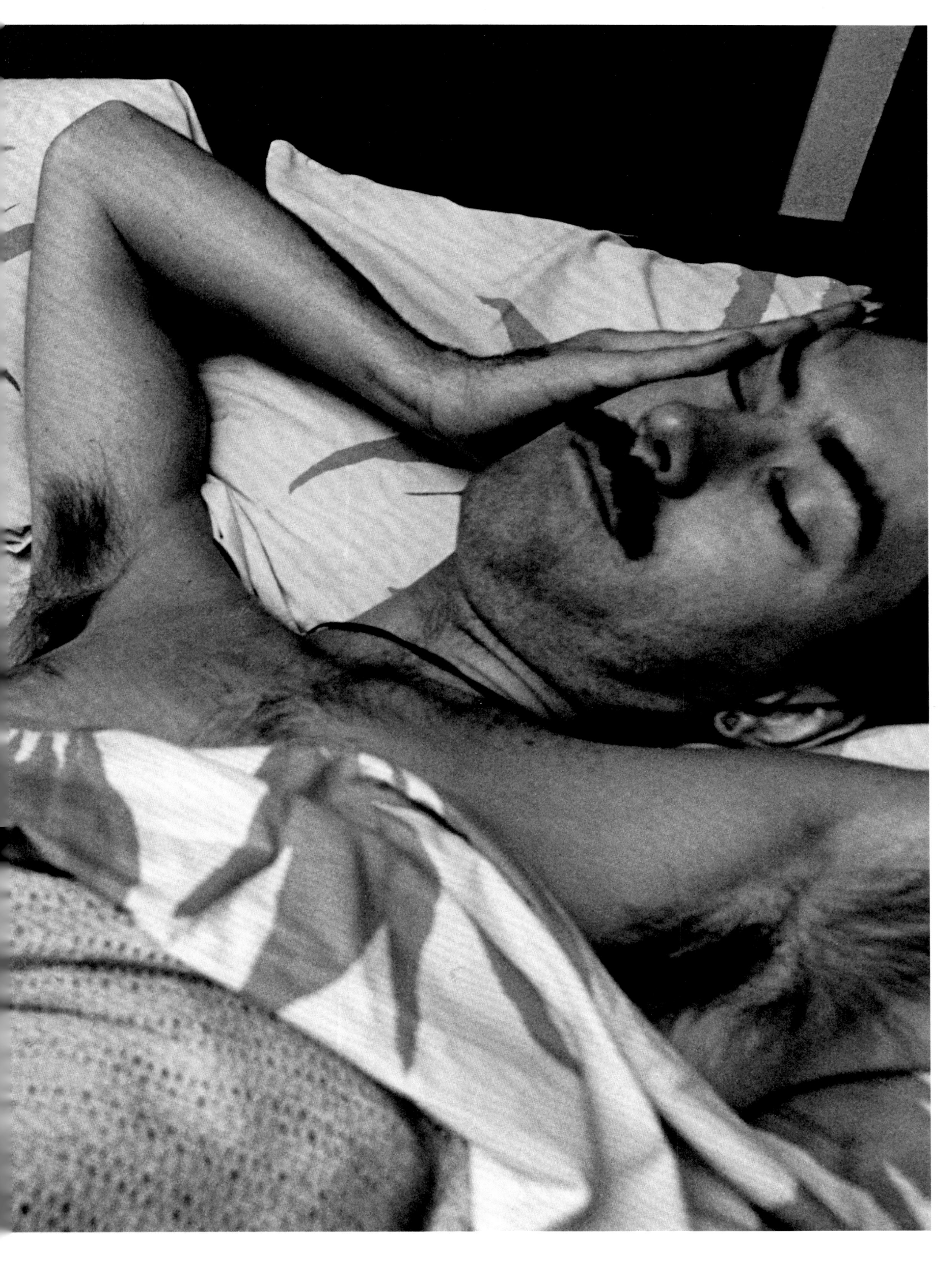

System Map
Legend

JULY 17 @1:30Am
2686 Valentine Ave
7 gunshot wounds on dea
~~Lt. Stephenson~~, Crime Sce
Sgt (Dr. Death)

(photos w/ #s)

guy. One guy in Hospital Unit

It was so dark and confined in the back of the moving police car that I dozed off. Then, quick as that, as if I'd stuck my finger in a light socket, I jerked awake. One man was down, one was dead; either I heard that on the police radio or someone said it. Hard to say. But after you've fallen asleep, even for a few seconds, it's difficult to get going again, to clear your head. What was I thinking when we turned onto Valentine Avenue? That the sergeant I was riding with (Dr. Death is what he called himself) was an actor, and that this going-to-hell neighborhood was a Hollywood set.

The sky above the city was purple, but everything else—the tenements, sidewalks, parked cars, even the clouds (wispy, soiled-looking ones)—was the same warmish, dyspeptic yellow of the streetlights. Stumbling from the cruiser, I heard the mournful wail of a siren not far off. One of the young guys who'd been shot was being run to a hospital, paralyzed, dying, no one was sure. The other one... there was lots of blood on the sheet thrown over him and more blood, wettish, snaky, running down the sidewalk toward the street. Watching where I was stepping, I made pictures of the oversize plastic numbers set around the body; the detectives on their hands and knees searching for shell casings; and lastly, the medical examiner. Stooping down, he lowered his face two or three inches from the murdered man's, then abruptly turned away.

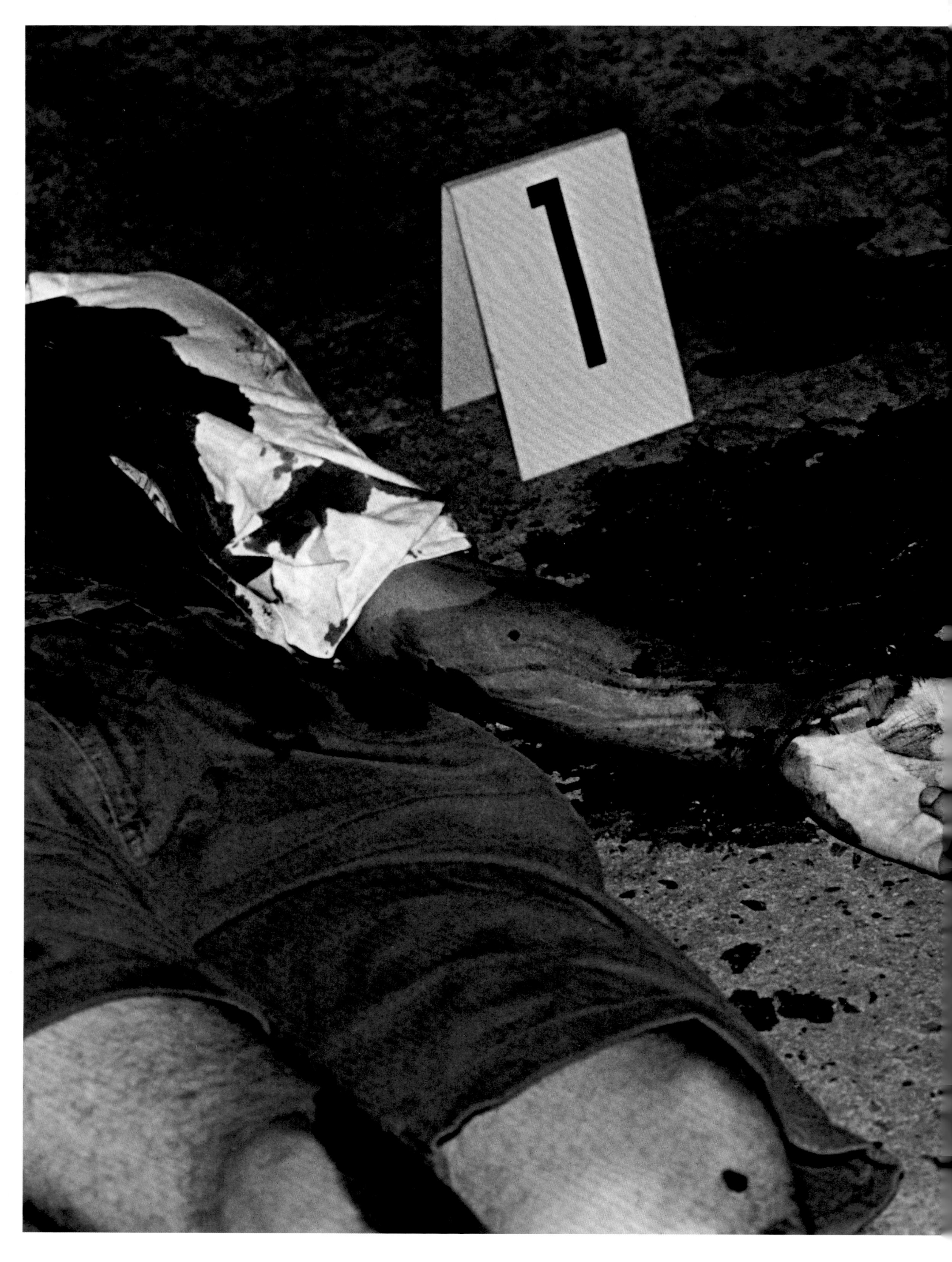
1

July 17
178th St. & Aud
Fatal gunshot
Dr. Dea

I guess you could say that I wasn't feeling much for the dead man sprawled out on the sidewalk. I didn't bother to ask the cops who he was or who they thought the murderer was. Maybe if this hadn't been killing number five of the night...

The very first time I took pictures of a dead person was in the embalming room at Logan the mortician's establishment in West Memphis, Arkansas. Down in the delta in the early 1970s, the death of an elderly sharecropper was often viewed by family and clergy alike as a gift from God, an end to barely endurable hardship. Still, the very nakedness of the old man lying there that morning shocked me, as did the pumps, the hoses, and the blood, brain, and intestinal-tract fluids billowing out. I started out using my camera the way a frightened child uses his hands, holding it up in front of my face for protection. Then, in order to keep looking without really looking, I began to abstract things. I photographed the dead man's scarred torso, his gnarly fingers, then the slit of a wound under his arm, filling the whole frame with it, making it enormous.

2:30am

son Ave

to chin

am i a poor man?

"I was also made aware of being poor in other ways. When I was a small boy, and for a very long time afterward, I felt very afraid when I saw people riding in cars. The only transportation we had then, the same that we have now, is eleven. We go places by eleven." Holding up two fingers, he walks them puppet-like down his leg. "And, we're Lenca, pure Lenca, true Hondurans, native people, first and foremost. We had our own language. I didn't know how to talk to the people who were inside the cars, didn't even know how to say hello to them, and they could never know our customs, passing us by like that. And so at an early age I became certain that all the pain of the world is on us." Ricardo looks over at Reina, who has the baby in her arms. "Anyway, that was then," he says, clearing his throat.

Less than three weeks after Ricardo and young Reina were married, Ricardo was drafted into the Honduran army. Trained as a combat infantryman, he spent most of the next five years on patrol in the jungles and along the embattled borders of his country. For this he was paid four dollars a month, out of which the military took money for taxes, food, clothes, and medicine, leaving him twenty-five cents a month to send home. His parents helped support Reina, and, when he finally did return, deeded him a quarter of their two hectares of land. Ricardo now works six months of each year for the large landowners and six months on his own farm growing corn, bananas, plantains, and chilies for his family to eat, with coffee as a cash crop.

Together, Ricardo and his father own eight thousand coffee trees, which, weather permitting, could produce twenty thousand pounds of berries this season. Still, growing coffee is a desperate gamble. Each tree costs more than two dollars in labor and materials before it bears fruit, and there is no fruit for the first two to three years. Then they must contend with low prices. American consumers, shopping at places like Starbucks, pay seven to twelve dollars a pound for premium mountain-grown coffee beans, but the buyers, known as coyotes, pay Honduran farmers twenty cents per pound for their coffee berries. And this is an improvement over what the farmers once received. The first coyotes in the La Sierra Mountains claimed that since they had to pay for transportation, communication with the outside world, and interest on loans, they were doing the growers a favor by offering them seventy-five cents per quintal (about 220 pounds) of coffee. Desperate and often hungry, the farmers accepted.

As the shadows begin to lengthen, Ricardo lifts the children one by one off his lap and asks to be excused. This morning he mended fences, cleared weeds, spread fertilizer, dug holes, and picked his own coffee. He needs to run those coffee berries through the de-pulping machine before night falls. When I approach him to say good-bye, he clutches my hands and beseeches me to visit other campesinos living in the mountains. "You won't know the truth," he says, "until you meet those who live farther up, farthest away. The ones we call the forgotten ones."

The Cabreras' farm sits at 3,900 feet. Farther up the mountain, as the road grows steeper, are patches of virgin forest being cleared to grow coffee, and fields of broken, shredded corn stalks. These stand like bleached bones in the dusty earth. Augusto Hernandez, who'd promised yesterday that he'd be our guide, isn't home when we arrive. It's the season of coughs, his young son tells me. He has gone on ahead to try to assist a family that has fallen ill.

A former medical corpsman, Augusto was elected three years ago to be his community's guardian, or medicine man. Drawing on training he received in the army, he sets his neighbors' fractured knees, arms, and ankles, and treats as best he can their chronic diarrhea, depression, parasites, and flu. He does this for no pay. He prescribes indigenous herbs and plants for many ailments—eucalyptus for coughs, *sacate* tea for parasites. Two years ago, when there was cholera, all he could do was advise people to purify their water. Two died.

Augusto's son leads me, stumbling up the boulder-strewn trail his father has taken, to the Lopez's home, a mortar-and-stick shed at the edge of a cliff. Benito Lopez moved onto this unwanted isolated tract of land long before the road was built. The forty-nine-year-old subsistence farmer with nine children struggles to grow the food his family needs, then works whenever he can as a day laborer.

There's a small square of sunlight falling through the half-open door; otherwise, the interior of their house is gloomy and damp, bare but for the bundles of Indian corn hanging like stalactites from the roof beams. The older children, their eyes red and watery, sit pressed against each other along the wall, the younger ones on the dirt floor. Mrs. Lopez, who's closest to the fire, seems oblivious to the clouds of yellowish smoke it throws off. Although it's obvious she's very ill, with what Augusto believes is pneumonia, she refuses to let anyone else hold her baby.

The baby's temperature has risen to 103 degrees. Augusto swabs her tiny arm with alcohol and injects her with penicillin. After pausing to look around the room at each of the other family members, he injects Mrs. Lopez, then the next youngest child. Having had no work, Mr. Lopez could only afford three doses of the antibiotic. Augusto tries to comfort the dispirited man, who's standing with his hands over his face. He hands him the little bit of money we've collected and gently pats his sagging shoulders.

When we step back outside into the sunshine, fresh air, and blue sky, it feels, for a moment, as if an evil spell has been broken and we've returned from the netherworld. On the way back down the mountain we pause at Augusto's house, where I photograph the medicine man sitting with his wife and eight children. The golden rays filtering in through the openings in the roof cause their faces to glow like candles. Then, with dusk approaching, the driver and I continue down, past thousands of birds settling on the trees, past field workers wearily trudging home, past a fading landscape of cornfields, apple orchards, and coffee groves.

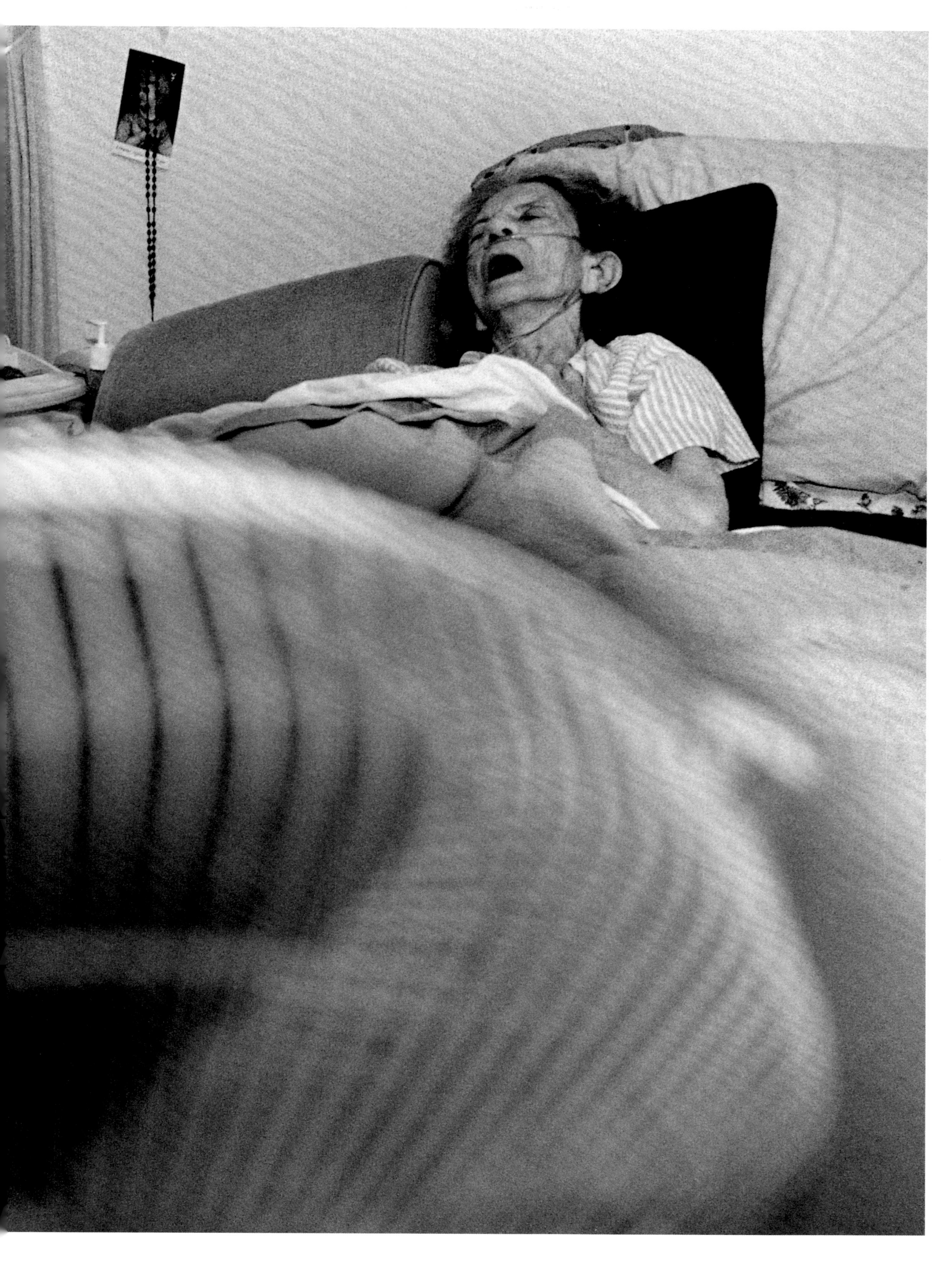

The sun was shining and I could smell the ocean on the morning I arrived to move my dad to Florida. I knew to call from the corner store and let the phone ring until he answered. The last time I drove up from New York I'd also arrived at a prearranged time, but I hadn't telephoned and found the house locked up tight. It was nighttime, chilly, and Janine was with me. I rang the bell for what had to be fifteen minutes, knocked on both the front and the back door and on the windows that I could reach. "Goddamnit, this is stupid," I yelled at no one in particular. Then, admittedly more angry than worried, I punched my fist through a pane of glass. Why so angry, I don't know. The bottled-up past, I suppose.

Getting out of the car, I looked around. The garage in back was leaning a little bit more than it had been. Except for that, the old place looked pretty much the same—a two-story with a screened-in front porch. Tan with white trim. Pleasant. Ordinary. There was a realtor's sign on the front lawn; the house was sold, was already somebody else's. But I didn't want to think too much about it, to risk getting emotional, when I was there to facilitate things. My sister and brother-in-law would be looking after my dad once he reached Florida, but I had to get him and his belongings there.

As I'd hoped, the doors were unlocked. I stepped over a vacuum cleaner and some smelly old clothes into what had once been the parlor (with wall-to-wall carpeting, a couch, his-and-hers armchairs and a TV) and was now, I couldn't help thinking, a kind of tomb. Rising up out of the dark, halfway to the ceiling, was a stack of cardboard boxes filled with family pictures, lamps, dishes, books, bedclothes, cooking utensils—the things we had decided, when I was last here, that my dad could take with him. Because the shades in the dining room were drawn, the first I saw of my father was his white hair—wispy, incandescent in the low light, encircling his round, pink skull. Since his head was hanging down, what I noticed next were his hands. There was dirt under his fingernails; nothing new there. There always has been, always will be. His knuckles were scraped, discolored. No surprise there either. I was aware that my father had taken a tumble on the front stairs. When I had phoned him the week before—it wasn't at all like him—he confessed that he had.

"You're early," was pretty much all he had said when Janine and I walked in on him one morning a few years ago and found him standing on top of the kitchen stove. My mom had just passed away, he'd turned ninety, and there he was, stretching his arms way up over his head to patch a hole in the ceiling caused by a leak. Not only that, he'd laid a skinny piece of plywood across the burners and was standing on it in order to reach a little higher. Did he understand why Janine and I got a little peeved catching him up there? No! Once I helped him down from the stove he reminded me that he was accustomed to heights, that for more years than he wanted to remember he'd supported our family working at the shipyard and painting houses. "Or have you forgotten?" he asked. "And what about the money it would cost to get someone in here who wouldn't soak the hell out of me?"

SOLD
For Sale
It's CityView!

5 CONVENIENT LOCATIONS
self service storage
the STORAGE DEPOT
WALTHAM
781·890·7867
www.thestoragedepot.com
781·329·8833

FRAGILE
FRAGILE
KAHLUA
FRAGILE
FRAGILE
W215

Anyway, that was then. Since then my father has gone downhill: his prostate cancer, his arthritis, his hearing, his eyesight. Even if he had the urge to climb up on that damn stove again to save a buck on repairs, or prove to himself that he could still do it, he couldn't. Getting on my knees, I began to push the papers that had fallen off his lap into a pile. There had to have been a thousand canceled checks, almost as many bank statements, receipts for trips to doctors, purchases of clothes, furniture, secondhand cars, my sister's wedding gown, some going back sixty years. I'd asked him, the realtor had probably begged him, to try to clean things up a bit. In his own way, I suppose, he'd begun to, legal and business correspondence first. But now I felt kind of uneasy looking at the stuff. It's not as if I was peeking into his personal diary, but considering that he'd never let my mom, my sister, or me anywhere near his financial papers, I might as well have been.

After I tossed most of those papers, I washed out a couple of cups (he enjoyed hot tea and toast in the morning), then emptied the bowl he had been peeing in. It was a blue enamel salad bowl. He kept it in a corner of the kitchen beside the washing machine for the times he couldn't get upstairs. When I returned to the dining room he was still asleep. His mouth was hanging open, but he was breathing softly, easily. So I sat there. With his bony shoulders, the cold sore on his lip and all the fat gone from his face, he looked terribly old. And everything around him—the rugs, the couch, his clothes, the air—smelled musty, sickly, old. That's what I was thinking when my father kind of snorted and got this pained look on his face. I was leaning in to kiss his forehead when his eyes popped open.

"Helen?" He raised his head, squinted, stared.

"How are you Dad?"

"Eddie"—Edward is my middle name—"I knew it was you."

"Dad, would you like me to get you some tea?" I had just put the kettle on when the neighbors began phoning, most of them people who'd known my mother as the always friendly, if a bit thin-skinned Irish-looking lady who kept a beautiful garden. The neighbors who knew my father, if they felt something emotion-wise for him, it was respect. You know, "You've got to respect the way Gene keeps on at his age, keeps his house up as best he can, flies the flag, keeps his wife's memory alive now that she's gone." Or else they felt a certain empathy for him: "What's happening to him, that arthritic, losing-your-loved-one thing is going to happen to all of us." Straight-out expressions of affection toward him—there weren't many. Not because my father was in any way a bad person. "He's a shy man"—that's what my sister says—"an insecure man." And it's true that for a whole lot of his life—he's ninety-three now—he's been wary of a lot of people.

Born in a Malden, Massachusetts tenement, my father had the kind of deprived, pathos-ridden childhood dramatized in the popular five-cent novels of his time. Except that his was no rags-to-riches story. His mother was unschooled, illiterate, from Nova Scotia, a waitress when she could find work, his father a gun-carrying insurance broker/detective/con man who didn't often bother to support his family. There were seven children. Dad's two youngest sisters quite probably died from neglect and malnutrition; his youngest brother drowned. My father was an eighth grader who'd already been held back a year for tardiness when his mother pulled him out of school. He was twelve years old when his father took off for good.

Possessed of street smarts but no education to speak of, my father's first real job was to lead a blind man around Boston for a dollar a week. In the years to follow, the Depression years, he hawked newspapers, worked as a messenger boy, and cleaned the machines in a soup-cracker factory. His job at the Watertown arsenal was to pour dirt on the red-hot barrels of newly forged cannons. He was thirty years old and holding down a job as a janitor the night he went to the Hibernian dance hall and met the woman who would be my mom. Helen Louise Hyland wasn't from the city. She was born in the tree-lined town of Manchester-by-the-Sea, into a large close-knit family with its own share of money problems. My mother wouldn't talk about that period of her life, but from what I've been told, right after high school, she was sent away to work, setting tables and cleaning rooms in a mansion on Boston's Beacon Hill. Permitted to go home only on weekends, ordered about by oftentimes abusive employers, nearly married off (by her own family) to a much older man she didn't care for, she suffered bouts of serious depression.

My father once told me with a grin on his face that at the time he met my mother, he was "a godsend" to her. Still, the two of them had so little money when they married that they honeymooned in his mom's apartment, while his mother and two sisters were there. Dad was scraping and painting walls at the American Can Company when he moved with my mom (and his by then very aged mother) to the three-decker house he purchased in Dorchester, Massachusetts. He was doing more or less the same dirty, lung-clogging work, but in a shipyard, on scaffoldings a hundred feet up, when he took out a mortgage on the house in suburban Quincy.

We were three blocks from Wollaston Beach. My mother finally had a sunny yard in which to grow roses, my father had a cellar to putter around in, Eileen and I each had our own room. Life was better. Still it was no magical escape to a whole new world. My parents fought. Even way back when my sister and I were babies, the two of them would go at each other, blaming, accusing, yelling nonstop for hours, sometimes days, mostly about money. Despite what he had gone through as a child and young man, my father came to revere those with money and power, while my mother resented them. Whenever my father wouldn't give my mother as much of the "moola" as she was asking for, for shopping or whatever, she'd snarl, "Gene, money isn't everything." She'd say this, knowing it would get a rise out of him. And inevitably he'd shoot back a look of disbelief, plus a few overworked phrases like "So tell me the Depression never happened!" or "What do you think makes the world go 'round?"

They also went at each other about my mother's cigarette habit, my father's reluctance to bathe, my father's mother, my mother's father, about real and imagined slights to one another, going back to before they were married. When my sister and I would plead with them to stop fighting, my father would tell us that the things being "discussed" weren't any concern of ours, while my mother would sit there with her eyes squeezed shut. If we cried, my parents would, in turn, blame each other for causing this to happen. If my sister and I yelled at them, "We can't sleep.... You're driving us crazy.... Why don't you get a divorce?" or something hurtful like that, my father's eyes would narrow. A very real potential for violence would show in them. Once Eileen and I grew old enough to realize there was nothing we could do to stop the arguing, we'd run up to our rooms, close the doors, cover our heads with our pillows. Sometimes I'd hang my head out the window. The nights they fought were as long as nights could get.

MASSACHUSETTS
617·CSS

SOLD
CityView
Real Estate

NANTA KET ,

SERVICE
SINCE 1916
WEST PALM
SOLD

notes

blue snow

Working as a volunteer journalist for Médecins Sans Frontières, I arrived in Milici in February 1993, hoping to spend time in the front line hospital before reporting on how local families were surviving the war. Unfortunately, I wasn't allowed to venture outside.

When I returned home, I carried my pictures around to magazines, though I knew in advance what the editors would say. The pictures were made during a very terrible war but not on the front lines, and depicted people few in the United States had sympathy for. Most of the editors immediately handed them back to me. "Serbs," they sighed before turning away.

prospects

On April 29, 1992, despite videotaped evidence, four white Los Angeles police officers were acquitted of the assault of black motorist Rodney King. People took to the streets. In six days of rioting, fifty-four people were killed, 2,383 injured. There was an estimated $700 million in property damage.

I'd been assigned by a German magazine to photograph the aftermath of the riots. My five-day assignment grew to seven days after my film was ruined. The resulting photographs were published in the June 1992 issue of *Tempo*.

the run-on of time

Undertaken in 1995 for *Life*'s "Looking for America" series, this story never ran in the magazine.

It's true what they say that when you look at pictures, you see people as they once were. The 103-year-old woman at the Good Samaritan Center, the one with the piercing, sightless eye, has died, as has Audrey Pullman and her husband, Floyd.

When we spoke in July 2003, Donna Goings told me that she's happier than she has been for years, having finally been given her very own room. Later the eighty-three year old blurted out that she'd recently received a marriage proposal from a fellow resident, a former bulldozer operator. "I was speechless, turned a bright red, because everyone heard us. Then a couple of days later... maybe it's his diabetes or because he likes all the women, but he forgot that he had ever asked me."

According to his friends, Clarence Keyser loved women, smoked cigars while plowing, had a walk like John Wayne and a valve in his heart that leaked oxygen. In May 1998, after his second stroke, with arthritis crippling his back, legs, and both shoulders, Clarence was carried up to Good Sam, where he died one month later. "His heart gave out," is how Doc Scott explained it, though Clarence's sister believes that once he was taken from his farm, he "just quit living."

here's to love

Not long after I completed the photographs on gay parenting for "The American Family" series, *Life* magazine decided not to publish them. Repeatedly turned down in the U.S., a version of this photo essay, complete with my interviews, ran in the U.K. in the June 27, 1993 issue of *The Independent on Sunday*.

In April 1993, Gregg and Scott took part in a gay march in Washington, D.C., where they were lauded by gay couples who were themselves hoping and planning to have children. When I spoke with Scott in August 2003, he explained that Connor, now twelve years old, was spending the summer months with him and Gregg and the school year with his mother, Renée. As for Anne, her commitment with Renée had ended years before.